Evnis felt a trickle of sweat slide down his forehead. "What do you want in return? What is your price?"

"My price is you," the swirling figure said, eyes pinning him. "I want you." The lips of the ancient face in the steam twitched, a glimmer of a smile.

"So be it," said Evnis.

"Seal it in blood," the ancient face snarled.

Rhin held her knife out.

See it through, see it through, see it through, Evnis repeated silently, like a mantra. He clenched his teeth tightly together, gripped the knife, his palm clammy with sweat and drew it quickly across his other hand. Curling his fingers into a fist, he stepped forward, thrusting it into the steam above the iron pot. Blood dripped from his hand into the cauldron, where it immediately began to bubble. A force like a physical blow slammed into his chest, seemed to pass through him. He gasped and sank to his knees, gulping in great, ragged breaths.

The voice exploded in his head, pain shooting through his body.

He screamed.

"It is done," the voice said.

BOOKS BY JOHN GWYNNE

Malice

Malice

The Faithful and the Fallen Series
Book 1

JOHN GWYNNE

www.orbitbooks.net

Orbit
Hachette Book Group
237 Park Avenue, New York, NY 10017
HachetteBookGroup.com

First U.S. Edition: December 2013
Originally published in Great Britain in 2012 by Tor, an imprint of
Pan Macmillan, a division of Macmillan Publishers Limited,
20 New Wharf Road, London N1 9RR

Orbit is an imprint of Hachette Book Group, Inc.
The Orbit name and logo are trademarks of Little, Brown Book Group Limited.

The Hachette Speakers Bureau provides a wide range of authors for speaking events.
To find out more, go to www.hachettespeakersbureau.com or call (866) 376-6591.

The publisher is not responsible for websites (or their content)
that are not owned by the publisher.

The characters and events in this book are fictitious. Any similarity to real persons,
living or dead, is coincidental and not intended by the author.

Library of Congress Control Number: 2013913826
ISBN: 978-0-316-39973-9

10 9 8 7 6 5 4 3 2

RRD-C

Printed in the United States of America

For my children,
Harriett, James, Edward and William.

And of course my wife, Caroline,
without whom it would all mean nothing.

THE
BAHISHED
LAHDS

THE BONE FELLS
JOTUNHEIM
Kavala mountains
ARCONA
Drassil
FORN FOREST
Haldis
Brihan
Halstat
Bairg mountains
HELVETH
Taur
Agullas Mountains
Jerolin
TENEBRAL
Balara
Ripa
Tethys Sea
TARBESH
Telassar
PELSET
NERIN

'For whence
But from the author of all ill could spring
So deep a malice.'

John Milton, *Paradise Lost*

EVNIS

The Year 1122 of the Age of Exiles, Wolf Moon

Forest litter crunched under Evnis' feet, his breath misting as he whispered a curse. He swallowed, his mouth dry.

He was scared, he had to admit, but who would not be? What he was doing this night would make him traitor to his king. And worse.

He paused and looked back. Beyond the forest's edge he could still see the stone circle, behind it the walls of Badun, his home, its outline silvered in the moonlight. It would be so easy to turn back, to go home and choose another path for his life. He felt a moment of vertigo, as if standing on the edge of a great chasm, and the world seemed to slow, waiting on the outcome of his decision. *I have come this far, I will see it through.* He looked up at the forest, a wall of impenetrable shadow; he pulled his cloak tighter and walked into the darkness.

He followed the giantsway for a while, the stone-flagged road that connected the kingdoms of Ardan and Narvon. It was long neglected, the giant clan that built it vanquished over a thousand years ago, great clumps of moss and mushroom growing between crumbling flagstone.

Even in the darkness he felt too vulnerable on this wide road, and soon slithered down its steep bank and slipped amongst the trees. Branches scratched overhead, wind hissing in the canopy above as he sweated his way up and down slope and dell. He knew where he was going, had walked the path many times before, though never at night. Nineteen summers old, yet he knew this part of the Darkwood as well as any woodsman twice his age.

Soon he saw a flicker amongst the trees: firelight. He crept closer, stopping before the light touched him, scared to leave the anonymity of the shadows. *Turn around, go home, a voice whispered in his head. You are nothing, will never equal your brother*. His mother's words, cold and sharp as the day she had died. He ground his teeth and stepped into the firelight.

An iron cauldron hung on a spit over a fire, water bubbling. Beside it a figure, cloaked and hooded.

'Greetings.' A female voice. She pushed the hood back, firelight making the silver in her hair glow copper.

'My lady,' Evnis said to Rhin, Queen of Cambren. Her beauty made him catch his breath.

She smiled at him, wrinkles creasing around her eyes and held out her hand.

Evnis stepped forward hesitantly and kissed the ring on her finger, the stone cold on his lips. She smelled sweet, heady, like over-ripe fruit.

'It is not too late, you may still turn back,' she said, tilting his head with a finger under his chin. They stood so close he could feel her breath. Warm, laced with wine.

He sucked in a breath. 'No. There is nothing for me if I turn back. This is my chance to . . .'

His brother's face filled his mind, smiling, controlling, *ruling* him. Then his mother, her lips twisted, judging, *discounting*.

'. . . matter. Gethin has arranged a marriage for me, to the daughter of the poorest baron in Ardan, I think.'

'Is she pretty?' Rhin said, still smiling, but with an edge in her voice.

'I have only met her once. No, I cannot even remember what she looks like.' He looked at the cauldron on its spit. 'I must do this. Please.'

'And in return, what would you give me?'

'The whole realm of Ardan. I shall govern it, and bow to you, my High Queen.'

She smiled, teeth glinting. 'I like the sound of that. But there is more to this than Ardan. So much more. This is about the God-War. About Asroth made flesh.'

'I know,' he whispered, the fear of it almost a solid thing, dripping from his tongue, choking him. But exciting him, too.

'Are you scared?' Rhin said, her eyes holding him.

'Yes. But I will see it through. I have counted the cost.'

'Good. Come then.' She raised a hand and clicked her fingers.

A hulking shadow emerged from the trees and stepped into the firelight. A giant. He stood a man-and-a-half tall, his face pale, all sharp angles and ridged bone, small black eyes glittering under a thick-boned brow. A long black moustache hung to his chest, knotted with leather. Tattoos swirled up one arm, a creeping, thorn-thick vine disappearing under a chainmail sleeve, the rest of him wrapped in leather and fur. He carried a man in his arms, bound at wrist and ankle, as effortlessly as if it were a child.

'This is Uthas of the Benothi,' Rhin said with a wave of her hand, 'he shares our allegiances, has helped me in the past.'

The giant drew near to the cauldron and dropped the man in his arms to the ground, a groan rising from the figure as it writhed feebly on the forest floor.

'Help him stand, Uthas.'

The giant bent over, grabbed a handful of the man's hair and heaved him from the ground. The captive's face was bruised and swollen, dried blood crusting his cheeks and lips. His clothes were ragged and torn, but Evnis could still make out the wolf crest of Ardan on his battered leather cuirass.

The man tried to say something through broken lips, spittle dribbling from one corner of his mouth. Rhin said nothing, drew a knife from her belt and cut the captive's throat. Dark blood spurted and the man sagged in his captor's grip. The giant held him forward, angling him so that his blood poured into the cauldron.

Evnis fought the urge to step back, to turn and run. Rhin was muttering, a low, guttural chanting, then a wisp of steam curled up from the cauldron. Evnis leaned forward, staring. A great gust of wind swept the glade. A figure took form in the vapour, twisting, turning. The smell of things long dead, rotting, hit the back of Evnis' throat. He gagged, but could not tear his eyes away from where two pinpricks glowed: eyes, a worn, ancient face forming about them. It appeared noble, wise, sad, then lined, proud, stern. Evnis blinked and for a moment the face became reptilian, the eddying steam giving the appearance of wings unfurling, stretched, leathery. He shivered.

'Asroth,' whispered Rhin, falling to her knees.

'What do you desire?' a sibilant voice asked.

Evnis swallowed, his mouth dry. *I must take what is owed me, step out from my brother's shadow. See it through.*

'Power,' he rasped. Then, louder, taking a deep breath. 'Power. I would rule. My brother, all of Ardan.'

Laughter, low at first, but growing until it filled the glade. Then silence, thick and heavy as the cobwebs that draped the trees.

'It shall be yours,' the figure said.

Evnis felt a trickle of sweat slide down his forehead. 'What do you want in return? What is your price?'

'My price is you,' the swirling figure said, eyes pinning him. 'I want you.' The lips of the ancient face in the steam twitched, a glimmer of a smile.

'So be it,' said Evnis.

'Seal it in blood,' the ancient face snarled.

Rhin held her knife out.

See it through, see it through, see it through, Evnis repeated silently, like a mantra. He clenched his teeth tightly together, gripped the knife, his palm clammy with sweat and drew it quickly across his other hand. Curling his fingers into a fist, he stepped forward, thrusting it into the steam above the iron pot. Blood dripped from his hand into the cauldron, where it immediately began to bubble. A force like a physical blow slammed into his chest, seemed to pass through him. He gasped and sank to his knees, gulping in great, ragged breaths.

The voice exploded in his head, pain shooting through his body.

He screamed.

'It is done,' the voice said.

The Writings of Halvor

Discovered in 1138 of the Age of Exiles, beneath the ruined fortress of Drassil. Over two thousand years after it was written

The world is broken.

The God-War has changed all things, Asroth's scheming, Elyon's wrath, corrupted and destroyed so much. Mankind has vanished, annihilated or fled these shores, and we are so few, now. We giants, Sundered, the one clan split beyond all reconciliation.

A thousand years I, Halvor, have lived, Voice of the King. Now great Skald is dead, his kin scattered. I shall not live a thousand more. I lament the past, I remember and weep.

I am still the Voice, though I do not know who will listen. But if I do not speak, do not write, then there will be nothing for those who follow. All that has happened would be forgotten. And so I shall write a record . . .

When the starstone fell we should have listened to mankind and turned our faces from it, but its power sang to us, called us. Just as Asroth planned.

Asroth was first-created, Elyon's beloved, captain of the Ben-Elim, the Sons of the Mighty. But that was not enough for him, the great deceiver. He spread his deep malice and his lies amongst the Ben-Elim, until a host grew about him. The Kadoshim they became: the Separate Ones.

Elyon saw, but could not bear to raise his fist against his beloved, and so war raged between the Kadoshim and the Ben-Elim, there in the Otherworld, the place of Spirit. Asroth was defeated and banished to a solitary portion of the Otherworld.

Then Elyon continued his plan of creation, making the worlds of flesh, of which earth was first. Giants and men were created as lords of this earth, immortal overseers of all else that roamed or grew, and they lived in harmony with their creator and all that he had created.

And Asroth hated us.

Asroth's starstone fell to earth, vast and filled with power. Somehow it carved a link between the world of flesh and spirit, between the earth and the Otherworld. Men were fearful of this strange object, but the giants forged from it, made items of wonder and power, great Treasures. First was the cauldron, its power used to heal. Then a torc, given to Skald, the giant's king, and a necklace for Nemain, his queen.

Asroth used the starstone to spread his influence on earth, whispering, corrupting. Skald was slain, the first murder, his torc stolen, and death entered the world, immortality stripped from all things as Elyon's punishment and warning. Then came the Sundering. War erupted, giant fighting against giant, and the one clan became many. More Treasures were carved from the starstone, this time things of war: spear, axe, dagger. And finally a cup, said to bring strength and long life to all who drank from it.

The mantle of death fell upon the world as war spread. Mankind was caught in it, giving their oaths to the giant clans in the hope of capturing the Treasures and restoring their immortality. Blood was spilt in rivers, and Asroth rejoiced.

Finally, Elyon's wrath was stirred. He visited his judgment upon the earth, which we named the Scourging. The Ben-Elim were let loose, spreading his judgement in fire and water and blood. Seas boiled, mountains spewed fire and the earth was broken as Elyon set about destroying all that he had created.

When his judgement was almost complete Elyon heard something, echoing in the Otherworld. The laughter of Asroth.

Elyon realized the extent of his foe's deception, saw that all had been done to bring him to this point. In horror he ceased the Scourging, leaving a remnant alive. Elyon's grief was beyond all comprehension. He turned from us, from all creation, and retreated to a place of mourning, cut off from all things. He is there still.

The Ben-Elim and Kadoshim abide in the Otherworld, their war eternal. Asroth and his fallen angels seeking to destroy us, the Ben-Elim striving to protect us, a token of their abiding love for Elyon.

And here in the world of flesh the breath of life goes on. Some strive to rebuild what was lost in this place of ash and decay. As for me, I look upon the world and mourn, here in Drassil, once-great city, heart of the world. Now broken, failing, like all else. Even my kin are leaving: Forn is too wild, too dangerous, now, they say, and we are too few. North they are going, abandoning all. Abandoning me. I shall not leave.

I dream now, and in those dreams are glimpses, perhaps, of what may come to be, a voice whispering. Of Asroth's return, the deceiver made flesh, of the Ben-Elim's last great stand, and of the avatars waging the God-War once more . . .

I shall stay and tell my tale, hope that it may serve some purpose, that eyes shall see it and learn, that the future will not repeat the mistakes of the past. That is my prayer, but what use is prayer to a god that has abandoned all things . . .

CHAPTER ONE

CORBAN

The Year 1140 of the Age of Exiles, Birth Moon

Corban watched the spider spinning its web in the grass between his feet, legs working tirelessly as it wove its thread between a small rock and a clump of grass. Dewdrops suddenly sparkled. Corban looked up and blinked as sunlight spilt across the meadow.

The morning had been a colourless grey when his attention first wandered. His mother was deep in conversation with a friend, and so he'd judged it safe for a while to crouch down and study the spider at his feet. He considered it far more interesting than the couple preparing to say their vows in front of him, even if one of them was blood kin to Queen Alona, wife of King Brenin. *I'll stand when I hear old Heb start the handbinding, or when Mam sees me*, he thought.

'Hello, Ban,' a voice said, as something solid collided with his shoulder. Crouched and balancing on the balls of his feet as he was, he could do little other than fall on his side in the wet grass.

'Corban, what are you doing down there?' his mam cried, reaching down and hoisting him to his feet. He glimpsed a grinning face behind her as he was roughly brushed down.

'*How long*, I asked myself this morning,' his mam muttered as she vigorously swatted at him. '*How long before he gets his new cloak dirty?* Well, here's my answer: before sun-up.'

'It's past sun-up, Mam,' Corban corrected, pointing at the sun on the horizon.

'None of your cheek,' she replied, swiping harder at his cloak. 'Nearly fourteen summers old and you still can't stop yourself rolling in the mud. Now, pay attention, the ceremony is about to start.'

'Gwenith,' her friend said, leaning over and whispering in his mam's ear. She released Corban and looked over her shoulder.

'Thanks a lot, Dath,' Corban muttered to the grinning face shuffling closer to him.

'Don't mention it,' said Dath, his smile vanishing when Corban punched his arm.

His mam was still looking over her shoulder, up at Dun Carreg. The ancient fortress sat high above the bay, perched on its hulking outcrop of rock. He could hear the dull roar of the sea as waves crashed against sheer cliffs, curtains of sea-spray leaping up the crag's pitted surface. A column of riders wound their way down the twisting road from the fortress' gates and cantered into the meadow. Their horses' hooves drummed on the turf, rumbling like distant thunder.

At the head of the column rode Brenin, Lord of Dun Carreg and King of all Ardan, his royal torc and chainmail coat glowing red in the first rays of morning. On one side of him rode Alona, his wife, on the other Edana, their daughter. Close behind them cantered Brenin's grey-cloaked shieldmen.

The column of riders skirted the crowd, hooves spraying clods of turf as they pulled to a halt. Gar, stablemaster of Dun Carreg, along with a dozen stablehands, took their mounts towards huge paddocks in the meadow. Corban saw his sister Cywen amongst them, dark hair blowing in the breeze. She was smiling as if it was her nameday, and he smiled too as he watched her.

Brenin and his queen walked to the front of the crowd, followed closely by Edana. Their shieldmen's spear-tips glinted like flame in the rising sun.

Heb the loremaster raised his arms.

'Fionn ap Torin, Marrock ben Rhagor, why do you come here on this first day of the Birth Moon. Before your kin, before sea and land, before your king?'

Marrock looked at the silent crowd. Corban caught a glimpse of the scars that raked one side of the young man's face, testament of his fight to the death with a wolven from the Darkwood, the forest that marked the northern border of Ardan. He smiled at the woman beside him, his scarred skin wrinkling, and raised his voice.

'To declare for all what has long been in our hearts. To pledge and bind ourselves, one to the other.'

'Then make your pledge,' Heb cried.

The couple joined hands, turned to face the crowd and sang the traditional vows in loud clear voices.

When they were finished, Heb clasped their hands in his. He pulled out a piece of embroidered cloth from his robe, then wrapped and tied it around the couple's joined hands.

'So be it,' he cried, 'and may Elyon look kindly on you both.'

Strange, thought Corban, *that we still pray to the All-Father, when he has abandoned us.*

'Why do we pray to Elyon?' he asked his mam.

'Because the loremasters tell us he will return, one day. Those that stay faithful will be rewarded. And the Ben-Elim may be listening.' She lowered her voice. 'Better safe than sorry,' she added with a wink.

The crowd broke out in cheers as the couple raised their bound hands in the air.

'Let's see if you're both still smiling tonight,' said Heb, laughter rippling amongst the crowd.

Queen Alona strode forward and embraced the couple, King Brenin just behind, giving Marrock such a slap on the back that he nearly sent his nephew over the bay's edge.

Dath nudged Corban in the ribs. 'Let's go,' he whispered. They edged into the crowd, Gwenith calling them just before they disappeared.

'Where are you two off to?'

'Just going to have a look round, Mam,' Corban replied. Traders had gathered from far and wide for the spring festival, along with many of Brenin's barons come to witness Marrock's handbinding. The meadow was dotted with scores of tents, cattle-pens and roped-off areas for various contests and games, and *people*: hundreds, it must be, more than Corban had ever seen gathered in one place before. Corban and Dath's excitement had been growing daily, to the point where time had seemed to crawl by, and now finally the day was here.

'All right,' Gwenith said. 'You both be careful.' She reached into her shawl and pressed something into Corban's hand: a silver piece.

'Go and have a good time,' she said, cupping his cheek in her hand. 'Be back before sunset. I'll be here with your da, if he's still standing.'

''Course he will be, Mam,' Corban said. His da, Thannon, would be competing in the pugil-ring today. He had been fist champion for as long as Corban could remember.

Corban leaned over and kissed her on the cheek. 'Thank you, Mam,' he grinned, then turned and bolted into the crowd, Dath close behind him.

'Look after your new cloak,' she called out, smiling.

The two boys soon stopped running and walked along the meadow's edge that skirted the beach and the bay, seals sunning themselves on the shore. Gulls circled and called above them, lured by the smell of food wafting from the fires and tents in the meadow.

'A silver coin,' said Dath. 'Let me see it.'

Corban opened his palm, the coin damp now with sweat where he had been clutching it so tightly.

'Your mam's soft on you, eh, Ban?'

'I know,' replied Corban, feeling awkward. He knew Dath only had a couple of coppers, and it had taken him moons to earn that, working for his father on their fishing boat. 'Here,' he said, delving into a leather pouch hanging at his belt, 'have these.' He held out three coppers that he had earned from his da, sweating in his forge.

'No thanks,' Dath said with a frown. 'You're my friend, not my master.'

'I didn't mean it like that, Dath. I just thought – I've got plenty now, and friends share, don't they?'

The frown hovered a moment, then passed. 'I know, Ban.' Dath looked away, out to the boats bobbing on the swell of the bay. 'Just wish my mam was still here to go soft on me.'

Corban grimaced, not knowing what to say. The silence grew. 'Maybe your da's got more coin for you, Dath,' he said, to break the silence as much as anything.

'No chance of that,' Dath snorted. 'I was surprised to see this coin – most of it fills his cups these days. Come on, let's go and find something to spend it on.'

The sun had risen high above the horizon now, bathing the meadow in warmth, banishing the last remnants of the dawn cold as the boys made their way amongst the crowd and traders' tents.

'I didn't think there were this many people in all the village and

Dun Carreg put together,' said Dath, grunting as someone jostled past him.

'People have come much further than the village and fortress, Dath,' murmured Corban. They strolled on for a while, just enjoying the sun and the atmosphere. Soon they found themselves near the centre of the meadow, where men were beginning to gather around an area of roped-off grass. The sword-crossing ring.

'Shall we stay, get a good spot?' Corban said.

'Nah, they won't be starting for an age. Besides, everyone knows Tull is going to win.'

'Think so?'

''Course,' Dath sniffed. 'He's not the King's first-sword for nothing. I've heard he cut a man in two with one blow.'

'I've heard that too,' said Corban. 'But he's not as young as he was. Some say he's slowing down.'

Dath shrugged. 'Maybe. We can come back later and see how long it takes him to crack someone's head, but let's wait till the competition's warmed up a bit, eh?'

'All right,' said Corban, then cuffed his friend across the back of the head and ran, Dath shouting as he gave chase. Corban dodged this way and that around people. He looked over his shoulder to check where Dath was, then suddenly tripped and sprawled forwards, landing on a large skin that had been spread on the floor. It was covered with torcs, bone combs, arm-bands, brooches, all manner of items. Corban heard a low rumbling growl as he scrambled back to his feet, Dath skidding to a halt behind him.

Corban looked around at the scattered merchandise and began gathering up all that he could see, but in his urgency he fumbled and dropped most of it again.

'Whoa, boy, less haste, more speed.'

Corban looked up and saw a tall wiry man staring down at him. He had long dark hair tied tight at his neck. Behind the man were all sorts of goods spread about an open-fronted tent: hides, swords, daggers, horns, jugs, tankards, horse harness, all hanging from the framework of the tent or laid out neatly on tables and skins.

'You have nothing to worry about from me, boy, there's no harm done,' the trader said as he gathered up his merchandise. 'Talar, however, is a different matter.' He gestured to an enormous, grey-streaked hound that had risen to its feet behind Corban. It growled. 'He doesn't take kindly to being trodden on or tripped over; he may well want some recompense.'

'Recompense?'

'Aye. Blood, flesh, bone. Maybe your arm, something like that.'

Corban swallowed and the trader laughed, bending over, one hand braced on his knee. Dath sniggered behind him.

'I am Ventos,' the trader offered when he recovered, 'and this is my faithful, though sometimes grumpy friend, Talar.' Ventos clicked his fingers and the large hound padded over to his side, nuzzling the trader's palm.

'Never fear, he's already eaten this morning, so you are both quite safe.'

'I'm Dath,' blurted the fisherman's son, 'and this is Ban – I mean, Corban. I've never seen a hound so big,' he continued breathlessly, 'not even your da's, eh, Ban?'

Corban nodded, eyes still fixed on the mountain of fur at the trader's side. He was used to hounds, had grown up with them, but this beast before him was considerably bigger. As he looked at it the hound growled again, a low rumble deep in its belly.

'Don't look so worried, boy.'

'I don't think he likes me,' Corban said. 'He doesn't sound happy.'

'If you heard him when he's not happy you'd know the difference. I've heard it enough on my travels between here and Helveth.'

'Isn't Helveth where Gar's from, Ban?' asked Dath.

'Aye,' Corban muttered.

'Who's Gar?' the trader asked.

'Friend of my mam and da,' Corban said.

'He's a long way from home, too, then,' Ventos said. 'Whereabouts in Helveth is he from?'

Corban shrugged. 'Don't know.'

'A man should always know where he's from,' the trader said, 'we all need our roots.'

'Uhh,' grunted Corban. He usually *asked* a lot of questions – too many, so his mam told him – but he didn't like being on the receiving end so much.

A shadow fell across Corban, a firm hand gripping his shoulder.

'Hello, Ban,' said Gar, the stablemaster.

'We were just talking about you,' Dath said. 'About where you're from.'

'What?' said the stablemaster, frowning.

'This man is from Helveth,' Corban said, gesturing at Ventos. Gar blinked.

'I'm Ventos,' said the trader. 'Where in Helveth?'

Gar looked at the merchandise hung about the tent. 'I'm looking for harness and a saddle. Fifteen-span mare, wide back.' He ignored the trader's question.

'Fifteen spans? Aye, I'm sure I've got something for you back here,' replied Ventos. 'I have some harness I traded with the Sirak. There's none finer.'

'I'd like to see that.' Gar followed Ventos into the tent, limping slightly as always.

With that the boys began browsing through Ventos' tent. In no time Corban had an armful of things. He picked out a wide iron-studded collar for his da's hound, Buddai, a brooch of pewter with a galloping horse embossed on it for his sister, a dress-pin of silver with a red enamel inset for his mother and two sturdy practice swords for Dath and himself. Dath had picked out two clay tankards, waves of blue coral decorating them.

Corban raised an eyebrow.

'Might as well get something my da'll actually use.'

'Why two?' asked Corban.

'If you cannot vanquish a foe,' he said sagely, 'then ally yourself to him.' He winked.

'No tankard for Bethan, then?' said Corban.

'My sister does not approve of drinking,' replied Dath.

Just then Gar emerged from the inner tent with a bundle of leather slung over his back, iron buckles clinking as he walked. The stablemaster grunted at Corban and walked into the crowd.

'Looks like you've picked up a fine collection for yourselves,' the trader said to them.

'Why are these wooden swords so heavy?' asked Dath.

'Because they are practice swords. They have been hollowed out and filled with lead, good for building up the strength of your sword arm, get you used to the weight and balance of a real blade, and they don't kill you when you lose or slip.'

'How much for all of these,' Corban asked.

Ventos whistled. 'Two and a half silvers.'

'Would you take this if we leave the two swords?' Corban showed the trader his silver piece and three coppers.

'And these?' said Dath, quickly adding his two coppers.

'Deal.'

Corban gave him their coin, put the items into a leather bag that Dath had been keeping a slab of dry cheese and a skin of water in.

'Maybe I'll see you lads tonight, at the feast.'

'We'll be there,' said Corban. As they reached the crowd beyond the tent Ventos called out to them and threw the practice swords. Instinctively Corban caught one, hearing Dath yelp in pain. Ventos raised a finger to his lips and winked. Corban grinned in return. *A practice sword, a proper one, not fashioned out of a stick from his back garden. Just a step away from a real sword.* He almost shivered at the excitement of that thought.

They wandered aimlessly for a while, Corban marvelling at the sheer numbers of the crowd, at the entertainments clamouring for his attention: tale-tellers, puppet-masters, fire-breathers, sword-jugglers, many, many more. He squeezed through a growing crowd, Dath in his wake, and watched as a piglet was released squealing from its cage, a score or more of men chasing it, falling over each other as the piglet dodged this way and that. They laughed as a tall gangly warrior from the fortress finally managed to throw himself onto the animal and raise it squeaking over his head. The crowd roared and laughed as he was awarded a skin of mead for his efforts.

Moving on again, Corban led them back to the roped-off ring where the sword-crossing was to take place. There was quite a crowd gathered now, all watching Tull, first-sword of the King.

The boys climbed a boulder at the back of the crowd to see better, made short work of Dath's slab of cheese and watched as Tull, stripped to the waist, his upper body thick and corded as an old oak, effortlessly swatted his assailant to the ground with a wooden sword. Tull laughed, arms spread wide as his opponent jumped to his feet and ran at him again. Their practice swords *clacked* as Tull's attacker rained rapid blows on the King's champion, causing him to step backwards.

'See,' said Corban, elbowing his friend and spitting crumbs of cheese, 'he's in trouble now.' But, as they watched, Tull quickly side-stepped, belying his size, and struck his off-balance opponent across the back of the knees, sending him sprawling on his face in the churned ground. Tull put a foot on the man's back and punched the air. The crowd clapped and cheered as the fallen warrior writhed in the mud, pinned by Tull's heavy boot.

After a few moments the old warrior stepped away, offered the fallen man his hand, only to have it slapped away as the warrior tried to rise on his own and slipped in the mud.

Tull shrugged and smiled, walking towards the rope boundary. The beaten warrior fixed his eyes on Tull's back and suddenly ran at the old warrior. Something must have warned Tull, for he turned and blocked an overhead blow that would have cracked his skull. He set his legs and dipped his head as the attacking warrior's momentum carried him forwards. There was a crunch as his face collided with Tull's head, blood spurting from the man's nose. Tull's knee crashed into the man's stomach and he collapsed to the ground.

Tull stood over him a moment, nostrils flaring, then he pushed his hand through long, grey-streaked hair, wiping the other man's blood from his forehead. The crowd erupted in cheers.

'He's new here,' said Corban, pointing at the warrior lying sense-less in the mud. 'I saw him arrive only a few nights ago.'

'Not off to a good start, is he?' chuckled Dath.

'He's lucky the swords were made of wood, there's others have challenged Tull that haven't got back up.'

'Doesn't look like he's getting up any time soon,' pointed out Dath, waving his hand at the warrior lying in the mud.

'But he will.'

Dath glanced at Corban and suddenly lunged at him, knocking him off the rock they were sitting on. He snatched up his new practice sword and stood over Corban, imitating the scene they had just witnessed. Corban rolled away and climbed to his feet, edging slowly around Dath until he reached his own wooden sword.

'So, you wish to challenge the mighty Tull,' said Dath, pointing his sword at his friend. Corban laughed and ran at him, swinging a wild blow. For a while they hammered back and forth, taunting each other between frenzied bursts of energy.

Passers-by smiled at the two boys.

After a particularly furious flurry of blows Dath ended up on his back, Corban's sword hovering over his chest.

'Do – you – yield?' asked Corban between ragged breaths.

'Never,' cried Dath and kicked at Corban's ankles, knocking him onto his back.

They both lay there, gazing at the clear blue sky above, too weak with their exertions and laughter to rise, when suddenly, startling them, a voice spoke.

'Well, what have we here, two hogs rutting in the mud?'

CHAPTER TWO

VERADIS

Veradis shifted in his saddle, trying to ease his aching muscles. He prided himself on being a good rider, smiled as he remembered his sixteenth nameday and his warrior trial, where he had become a man. He had executed a near-perfect running mount in front of his father's gathered warband, all those days of youth and practice summed up in one moment, and although over two years had passed, he could still recall every detail: how he had clicked the grey stallion into a trot when his turn had arrived, run alongside it, his shield gripped in his left hand. The sound of hooves thudding on the ground, merging with the beating of his heart. Time had seemed to stand still as he grasped a handful of mane and launched himself from the ground, landing perfectly in the saddle in one fluid move. He remembered tears streaming from his eyes, the soaring sense of elation as dimly he heard the roaring of his father's warband shouting their approval, clashing spears on shields. Even his father, Lamar, Baron of Ripa, had risen to his feet and cheered him.

He leaned forward and scratched his knee, the worn leather strips of his kilt plastered to his leg. Absently he patted the neck of the grey he was riding, a gift from his brother Krelis after his Long Night. Then he grimaced, shifting his weight again. Twelve nights straight in the saddle would test anyone, no matter how accomplished a horseman they were.

'Sore arse, little brother?' he heard a voice say behind him.

'Aye. A little.'

Krelis urged his horse forward so that they rode side by side. 'You'll get used to it,' he said, his black beard splitting in a smile. 'Anyway, I'd wager your pains are nothing compared to his.' He gestured with his thumb over his shoulder. 'The only thing *he's* ever ridden before is a ship's deck.'

Veradis twisted in his saddle to look at the prisoner they were escorting to Jerolin. Iron rings in the man's beard clinked gently with the rhythm of their pace as he looked straight ahead, blue eyes like chips of ice in his weathered face. He was covered in a lattice of scars, Veradis' eyes drawn to the man's nose, or what was left of it, its tip missing. Although his hands were bound behind his back, half a dozen warriors from Krelis' warband still encircled the prisoner.

'Do you really think he's going to tell the King anything?' asked Veradis.

His brother shrugged. 'Father thinks so. And so does our precious brother, although he was too unwell to make this journey.'

'Ektor is always unwell.'

Krelis smiled again. 'Aye, little brother, he is a sickly thing. But his mind is sharp, as Father always reminds me. He will be my counsellor one day, when I am Baron of Ripa.'

Veradis looked up at his older brother, towering above him on his great black warhorse. *You will make a good lord*, he thought. Krelis, Lamar's firstborn, had always been larger than life, leading men with an unconscious ease.

'And you,' said Krelis with a grin. 'You will become my battle-chief, no doubt. Why, if you were a few handspans taller and wider I might be scared of you myself.' He clapped Veradis across the shoulder, nearly knocking him from his horse.

Veradis smiled. 'You don't have to resemble a mountain to wield a sword, you know.'

'Maybe not that little pin *you* like to call a sword,' Krelis laughed, 'but anyway, battlechief of Ripa is for another day. Let us see what our King Aquilus makes of you first, and what he turns you into.'

Veradis walked into the great hall of Jerolin, huge black stone columns rising up and disappearing into the shadowed darkness of the vaulted ceiling. Great tapestries hung along the walls of the chamber, sunlight pouring through narrow windows dissecting the hall. Warriors lined either side of the room, wearing gleaming silver helms, hooked nose-bars giving them a raptor-like appearance. Silver eagles were embossed on black leather breastplates; even the leather strips of their kilts shone, polished and gleaming. They gripped tall spears, longswords hanging at their hips.

His steps faltered and the warrior behind trod on his heel. He balanced himself and quickened his pace to keep up with Krelis, who was striding purposefully towards the far end of the hall, his iron-shod sandals cracking out a quick rhythm on the stone floor. People were gathered in clumps about the hall, waiting on their king – servants tending to those in the court, barons come to petition Aquilus on border disputes, no doubt, crofters, all manner of people seeking the King's justice on a host of matters.

People parted before Krelis and the warrior leading them. 'Armatus,' Krelis had whispered to him, a grizzled, knobbly-armed man, his skin looking like the bark of an ancient tree. He was weapons-master of Jerolin, King Aquilus' first-sword, a man whose reputation with a blade was known to all.

They made their way quickly through the hall, a handful of Aquilus' eagle-guard striding behind Veradis, the Vin Thalun prisoner somewhere amongst them. Veradis passed through an open doorway, a spiral staircase before him. Without pause, Armatus led them down wide stone steps, then the floor levelled and they were marching along a narrow corridor.

Armatus turned off the corridor and stepped through a doorway into a large, bare room: no furniture, no windows, flickering torches the only light. Iron rings were sunk into the stone of the walls and floor, rusted chains and manacles hanging from them.

Three figures stood at the far end of the room, a man and woman standing in the light, the vague form of someone else shrouded in the shadows behind them.

Aquilus and Fidele, King and Queen of Tenebral. Veradis recognized them vaguely from the last time they had visited Ripa, half a dozen years gone, attending the barons' council. Fidele looked much the same, pale and perfectly beautiful, though Aquilus looked older, more creases around his eyes and mouth, more silver in his close-cropped hair and stubbly beard.

'Krelis,' King Aquilus said with a nod. 'Where is this man?'

Krelis had been ushered into Aquilus and Fidele's presence as soon as they had arrived at the black-stoned fortress, leaving Veradis and their warriors to guard the prisoner. Krelis had not been gone long, though, returning with orders to present the prisoner immediately.

'Here, my King,' Krelis said, stepping aside so that the eagle-guard could herd the captive forward. He stood before Aquilus with head bowed, hands shackled. In the flickering torchlight his many battle-scars stood out like dark tattoos. One of the eagle-guards grabbed a chain fixed to the floor and locked it to the man's bonds.

'I have not seen your kind for many a year,' the King said. 'How is it that a Vin Thalun raider is in my realm, in my keep?'

'He was part of a raiding galley, lord, looking for plunder. They burned more than one village along the coast, but they sailed too close to Ripa . . .'

Aquilus nodded, starring thoughtfully at the man, whose head was still lowered, eyes fixed on the iron ring sunk into the floor that he was chained to.

'And I am told that you have information for me. Is this so?'

The man did not respond, stayed perfectly still.

With a snort, Krelis leaned over and cuffed the prisoner, bringing his head up with a snap, eyes flashing, teeth bared for an instant. The iron rings woven into braids in his beard chinked together, one for each life he had taken.

'Let us start with something easier,' Aquilus said. 'What is your name?'

'Deinon,' the Vin Thalun muttered.

'Where did you come by so many scars, Deinon?'

'The Pits,' said the warrior with a shrug.

'The Pits?'

'The fighting pits. There's one on each of the islands,' Deinon said, glancing at the scars on his arms. 'Long time ago,' he said dismissively.

Veradis shuddered. When the Vin Thalun raided they took people for plunder as well as food and wealth. Veradis had heard tales that the boys and men taken were forced to fight for the Vin Thalun's pleasure, the fiercest being given a chance to earn their way out of the pits, and a spot pulling an oar on a Vin Thalun ship. This man had done well to graduate to warrior.

'And is what Krelis says true? That you were part of a corsair galley, raiding my lands?'

'Aye.'

'I see. But you raided too close to Ripa, and Krelis caught you. And now here you are.'

'Huh,' grunted the corsair.

'And you know the sentence for what you have done is death? But you have some information that I may wish to hear?'

'Aye,' the man muttered.

'Well?'

'My information in return for my life. That is what *he* told me.' The Vin Thalun nodded at Krelis.

'That would depend on the information. And if it is truth.'

The prisoner dipped his head, licking his lips. 'Lykos has a meeting planned, here in Tenebral.'

'Lykos,' Aquilus said, frowning.

Years ago, when Veradis was a child, the Vin Thalun had been a scourge along the coasts of Tenebral, even raiding deep into the realm, travelling up the rivers that flowed like arteries through the land, striking at Tenebral's heartland, stealing, burning. But something had happened. There had been a great raid on Jerolin itself, beaten off with many casualties on both sides. After that things had gone quiet, the inland raids stopping, even the coastal ones becoming rarer. Around the same time the name of a man amongst the Vin Thalun had begun to be heard: Lykos, a young warlord. Over the years he had risen high in their ranks, one by one subduing the three islands, Panos, Nerin and Pelset, defeating their warlords, uniting the Vin Thalun for the first time in their history. The last great sea-battle amongst them had been less than a year ago. Since then the raiding had begun to grow again, although mostly still along the coast.

'Tell me of this Lykos,' Aquilus said.

'He is our king,' the corsair shrugged. 'A great man.'

'And he is the sole leader of the Vin Thalun, now?' Aquilus pressed.

'Our *king*; he is more than a leader. Much more.'

Aquilus frowned, mouth a tight line. 'So, why is he planning to set foot on my land.'

'A meeting with one of your barons. I know not who, but the meeting is south of here, close to Navus.'

Veradis heard gasps around the room.

'How do you know this?' Aquilus snapped.

Deinon shrugged. 'I hear things. My brother, he's Lykos' shield-man. His tongue flaps after a jug of wine.'

'When?'

'Soon. The last night of the Wolf Moon. If I saw a map I could show you where.'

Aquilus stared long moments at the prisoner. 'How can I trust you, a corsair who would turn on his own?'

'Loyalty doesn't seem so important, when you're faced with that walk across the bridge of swords,' the corsair muttered.

'Aye, mayhaps,' Aquilus said quietly. 'And if you lie, you would only have delayed your journey. Your head would soon be parted from your shoulders.'

'I know it,' Deinon mumbled.

'We must send a warband, Father,' a voice said from the shadows behind Aquilus and Fidele; a figure stepping forward. It was a man, young, little older than Veradis. He was tall, weathered by the sun, a shock of dark curly hair framing a handsome face. Veradis had seen him once before. Nathair, the Prince of Tenebral.

'Aye. I know,' Aquilus muttered.

'Send me,' Nathair said.

'No,' snapped Fidele, taking a step closer to her son. 'We do not know the risk,' she said, more softly.

Nathair scowled, moving away from her. 'Send me, Father,' he said again.

'Perhaps,' the King muttered.

'You cannot allow this meeting to take place,' Nathair said, 'and Peritus is off chasing giants in the Agullas Mountains. The last night of the Wolf Moon is less than a ten-night away: barely time enough to get to Navus if I left on the morrow.' Nathair glanced at his mother, who was frowning. 'And this Lykos will hardly be riding at the head of a great warband. Not to a secret meeting in his enemy's land.'

Aquilus rubbed his stubbly chin, skin rasping. 'Perhaps,' he said again, with more conviction this time, though his eyes flickered to his wife. 'I will think on this, make my decision later. First, though, I shall send for someone to question our guest a little more thoroughly.' He looked at Armatus, his first-sword. The grizzled warrior nodded and left the room.

'I tell no lies,' the prisoner said, a hint of panic in his voice.

'We shall see. Krelis, I am indebted to you, and to your father.'

'We are glad to serve you, my lord,' Krelis said, dipping his head. 'We cannot guarantee the truth of what he says, but we thought it too important to ignore.'

'Aye, right enough. I will have rooms prepared for you and your men. You must have ridden hard to reach us.'

'That we have,' Krelis said. 'But my father has bid me return as soon as my task is done.'

Aquilus nodded. 'We must all obey our fathers. Give Lamar my thanks. I shall make sure your packs and water skins are full, at least.'

'There was one other matter,' Krelis said, glancing at Veradis. 'A request.'

'If it is in my power.'

'My father asks that you take my little brother, here, Veradis, into your warband for a time. To teach him, as you did me.'

For the first time Aquilus' eyes rested fully on Veradis. He bowed low to the King, a little clumsily.

'Of course,' the King said with a smile. 'It did you little harm. But perhaps not *my* warband. Peritus is away, and if I remember rightly, he was needed to keep you out of trouble on more than one occasion.'

Krelis grinned.

'My son is gathering his own warriors. You have need of good men, do you not, Nathair?'

'Aye, Father.'

'It is settled then,' said Aquilus. 'Good. Welcome, Veradis ben Lamar, to my home. You are now the Prince's man.'

'Well met,' Nathair said, stepping closer, gripping Veradis' arm. Intelligent, bright blue eyes looked into his, and Veradis had the sense of being *measured*.

'It will be an honour to ride with you, my lord,' Veradis said, inclining his head.

'Yes, it will,' said Nathair with a grin. 'But none of this "*my lord*" talk. If you are to fight beside me, for me, risk your life for me, then I am just Nathair. Now go and clean the dust of the road from you.

I will send for you and we shall talk more, over some meat and wine.'

Krelis and Veradis bowed once more to Aquilus and Fidele, then turned and left the damp room.

'Farewell, little brother,' said Krelis as he grabbed Veradis and pulled him into an embrace. Veradis scowled as they parted.

'I still don't understand why I have to be here,' he said as Krelis climbed into the saddle of his stallion.

'Yes you do. Father wishes you to become a leader of men.' Krelis smiled.

'I know, but can't I do that at Ripa?'

'No,' replied Krelis, his smile fading. 'Here you will not be treated as the Baron's son. It will be better in the end, you'll see.'

'He just wishes to be rid of me,' Veradis muttered.

'Probably,' Krelis grinned. 'That is what I would do. You cannot blame him.'

Veradis pulled a sour face, scuffed a toe on the stone floor.

'Come,' Krelis said, frowning, black bushy eyebrows knitting together. He leaned over in his saddle, speaking quieter. 'There is value in this. It will make you a better man.' He straightened, stretching his arms out wide. 'Look what it did for me.'

'Huh,' Veradis grunted, not able to keep a smile twitching the corners of his mouth.

'Good, that's better,' Krelis grinned. Behind them Krelis' warriors were mounting up. The sun was high in the sky, now, a little past midday, the stables buzzing with activity. Krelis' horse danced restlessly.

'I would stay longer, see what this warband you are joining is like, but I must get back to Father. As it is, it will be over a ten-night before I reach the bay.' He winked at Veradis. 'We'll meet again soon enough. Until then, make the most of your time here.'

Veradis stepped back as Krelis pulled his horse in a tight circle and cantered away, his warriors following close behind. The sound of hooves ringing on cobblestones hung in the air.

The young warrior stood there awhile, then turned and entered the large stable block, walking down a row of stalls until he found his grey. His horse whickered and nuzzled him as he entered the stall. Veradis found a brush and iron-toothed comb, began grooming his horse, though a quick glance told him the stablehands had already seen to him. He carried on regardless, finding a peace, a reassurance in the process, losing track of time.

'Are you all right, lad?' said a voice behind him. He turned to see a man looking over the partition door at him, the stablemaster who had organized the settling of their horses when they had arrived.

'Aye. I'm well,' he answered. 'Just . . .' he shrugged, unsure what to say.

'Never fear, lad, your grey's in good hands here. I am Valyn.'

'Veradis.'

'I saw your brother leave. A good man.'

'That he is,' Veradis replied, not trusting his voice to say any more.

'I remember well his stay with us. He was missed when he left, by more than one lass, if I remember right.' He grinned. 'I hear you're to join Nathair's warband.'

'Huh,' Veradis grunted. 'I am honoured,' he added, feeling that he should, although right now he just felt very alone.

The stablemaster looked at him for a long moment. 'I am about to take my evening meal. I often sit on the outer wall. It's quite a view – care to join me?'

'Evening meal?' Veradis said, 'but . . .' His stomach suddenly growled.

'Sundown is not far off, lad. You've been in here a fair while.'

Veradis raised an eyebrow, his belly rumbling again. 'I'd be happy to join you,' he said.

Valyn led him to the feast-hall, where they quickly filled plates with bread and cheese and slices of hot meat, Valyn grabbing a jug of wine as well. Climbing a stairwell of wide, black steps, they found a spot on the battlement wall.

Jerolin sat upon a gentle hill overlooking a wide plain and lake, fisher-boats dotting its shimmering surface. Veradis looked to the east, following the line of the river as it curled into the distance, searching for a glimpse of Krelis, but he was long gone. To the north and west the peaks of the Agullas jutted, jagged and white-tipped, glowing bright in the light of the sinking sun.

They sat there in silence awhile, watching the sun dip behind the mountains, and then Valyn began to speak, telling tales of Aquilus and the fortress. In return, Veradis told of his home, his father and brothers, and of life in Ripa, the fortress on the bay.

'Do you have a wife, children?' Veradis asked suddenly. Valyn was silent a long time.

'I had a wife and son, once,' he eventually said. 'It feels like another lifetime now. They died. The Vin Thalun raided the fortress, many years ago. You have probably heard the tale, though you would have been clinging to your mother's skirts at the time.'

Veradis coughed. He had never clung to his mother's skirts; she had died birthing him. He blinked, putting the thought quickly away. 'I have heard tell of that,' he said. 'They were bolder in those days.'

Valyn suddenly jumped to his feet and stared out over the plain below.

'What's wrong?' asked Veradis, coming to stand beside him, following the stablemaster's gaze out over the battlements. Approaching the fortress was a lone horseman, riding a large dapple-grey horse. Veradis could make little out from this distance, other than that the rider's mount moved with a rare elegance.

Valyn passed a hand over his eyes. He stood there in silence a while, watching the rider draw nearer to the fortress.

'Do you know him?' Veradis asked.

'Aye,' Valyn muttered. 'His name is Meical. He is counsellor to our King, and the last time I saw him was the night my wife and son died.'

CHAPTER THREE

CORBAN

'Oh no,' muttered Dath as the two boys scrambled to their feet.

A group of lads were watching them. Vonn stood at their head. He was son of Evnis, who was counsellor to the King, and so considered himself of some importance in and around Dun Carreg. He was a few years older than Corban, had recently passed his warrior trial and sat the Long Night, so had passed from boy to man. By all accounts he was an exceptional swordsman.

Another lad stepped forward, tall and blond haired. 'Well?' he repeated. 'What are you doing?'

Not Rafe, thought Corban. Rafe was part of Evnis' hold, a year or so older than Corban, son of Helfach the huntsman. He was cruel, boastful and someone that Corban made a point of avoiding.

'Nothing, Rafe,' said Corban.

'Didn't look like nothing to me.' Rafe took another step closer. 'Looked like you two were having a good time, rolling in the mud together.' Some of his companions sniggered. 'What have you got there?'

'Practice swords,' answered Dath. 'We just saw Tull fight, did you see him . . .?'

Rafe held up his hand. 'I see him every day in the Rowan Field,' he said, 'where *real* warriors use *real* swords, not sticks.'

'We'll be there soon,' blurted Corban. 'My fourteenth nameday is this Eagle Moon, and Dath's is not long after. Besides, you *do* use practice swords in the Rowan Field, my da told me . . .' he trailed off, realizing that all eyes were on him.

'Tull won't let you two take the warrior trial,' Rafe said. 'Not once he knows you were rutting in the mud together like hogs.'

'We weren't *"rutting"*, we were practising our sword skills,' said Corban slowly, as if explaining to a child. There was a moment of silence, then the group of lads erupted in laughter.

'Come on, Rafe,' said Vonn when they had all recovered, 'the stone-throwing starts at high-sun and I want to see it.'

Rafe looked at Corban and Dath. 'I'm not finished with these two yet.'

'They're just bairns, I'd rather spend my time in other company,' Vonn said, pulling Rafe's arm.

'C'mon, Dath,' Corban whispered, turning and walking quickly away. 'Come *on*,' he repeated with a hiss. Dath stood there a moment, then snatched up his leather bag and followed.

They walked in a straight line, their route taking them out of the meadow towards the village, trying to put as much distance between themselves and Rafe as possible.

'Are they following?' muttered Corban.

'Don't think so,' replied Dath, but moments later they heard the thud of running feet. Rafe sped past them and pulled up in front of Corban.

'You didn't ask permission to leave,' he said, jabbing a finger in Corban's chest.

Corban took a deep breath, his heart beginning to pulse in his ears. He looked up at Rafe, who was a head taller and considerably broader than him. 'Leave us alone Rafe. Please. It's the Spring Fair.'

'Don't you have anything better to do?' added Dath.

'*Leave us alone*,' mimicked Crain, who accompanied Rafe. Vonn and the others were nowhere to be seen. 'Listen to him. Don't let him talk to you like that, Rafe.'

'Shut up, Crain,' said Rafe. 'I think these bairns need a lesson in courtesy.' He grabbed Corban's arm and half steered, half pulled him towards the first buildings of the village. Frantically Corban looked around, but they were quite a distance from the crowds now, and he saw Dath had been grabbed by Crain and was being herded along after him.

Within seconds the two boys were bustled behind a building, Corban thrown against a wall, knocking the wind out of him. His fingers went limp and he dropped his wooden practice sword.

Rafe slammed a fist into Corban's stomach, doubling him over. Slowly he straightened.

'Come on, blacksmith's boy,' snarled Rafe, fists raised. Corban just looked at him. He wanted to answer, wanted to raise his fists, but just – didn't. His guts churned with a cold weightlessness. When he tried to speak, only a croak came out. He retched, feeling sick, and shook his head.

Rafe hit him again and he staggered, blood spurting from his lip. *Fight back!* a voice screamed in his head, but he only reached out an arm, steadied himself against the wall, feeling weak, scared. He looked at Dath, saw his friend launch himself forwards, punching and kicking, but Crain was older, stronger and Dath was small-framed even for his age. Crain clubbed him to the ground.

'Nothing like your da, are you,' spat Rafe.

Corban wiped blood from his lip. 'What?' he mumbled.

'Your da would put up a fight, make it more interesting. You're just a coward.'

For the briefest moment Corban felt something hot flicker within him, a spark of fire deep in the pit of his stomach, like when his da opened the door to his forge and the flames flared. He felt his fists clench and arms begin to rise, but then Rafe's fist slammed into his jaw and the sensation disappeared as quickly as it had appeared. Then he was falling, crashing to the ground with a thud.

'Get up,' jeered Rafe, but Corban just lay there, hoping it would all end soon, the metallic taste of blood filling his mouth.

Rafe kicked Corban in the ribs, then a voice shouted. A figure rounded the building and was moving quickly towards them.

'I think I'll have this,' said Rafe, grinning fiercely as he bent and picked up Corban's practice sword. Then he was running, his companion following quickly down an alley.

Dath knelt by Corban, trying to help him rise as the man who had shouted reached them. It was Gar.

'What happened here?' the stablemaster demanded as Corban pushed himself to his knees. He spat blood and stood, swaying slightly.

Dath reached out to steady his friend but Corban pushed his arm away. 'Leave me alone,' he whispered, tears spilling down his cheeks, smearing dust and blood. 'Leave me alone,' he said again, louder this time, turning away and rubbing furiously at his eyes, shame and anger filling him in equal measure.

'Walk with me, boy,' said Gar, and turned to Dath. 'Best leave us for a while, lad.'

'But he's my friend,' protested Dath.

'Aye, but I would speak to Corban. Alone.' He gave a look that sent Dath walking hesitantly away, though he looked back over his shoulder.

Corban turned quickly and strode in the other direction, not wanting anyone's company, but in moments the stablemaster was walking beside him. For a while they walked in silence, Corban feeling too ashamed to talk, so he concentrated on controlling his rapid breathing. Slowly the sound of his blood pounding in his head quietened.

'What happened back there?' asked Gar eventually. Corban did not answer, not trusting his voice to remain steady. After another long silence Gar pulled him to a halt and turned him so that they were facing each other.

'What happened?' Gar repeated.

'You trying to shame me even more, making me say it?' snapped Corban. 'You saw what happened. Rafe hit me and I – I did nothing.'

Gar pursed his lips. 'He's older, and bigger than you. You were intimidated.'

Corban snorted. 'Even Dath fought. Would *you* have let someone hit you like that?' When Gar did not answer, he tried to walk away, but the stablemaster gripped Corban's shoulder, holding him still.

'What caused the argument?'

Corban shrugged. 'He needs little reason to hit people younger or smaller than he is.'

'Huh,' Gar grunted. 'Did you *want* to hit him back?'

'Of course,' snorted Corban.

'So why didn't you?'

Corban looked at the ground. 'Because I was scared. I *wanted* to fight back, but I couldn't. I couldn't move. I tried; it was as if my arms had turned to stone, my feet stuck in one of Baglun's bogs.'

Gar nodded slowly. 'We all fear, Ban. Even Tull. It's what we do about it – that's the important thing. That's what'll make you the man you grow into. You must learn to control your emotions, boy. Those that don't do that often end up dead: anger, fear, pride, whatever. If your emotions control you, sooner or later you're a dead man.'

Corban looked up at him, his throbbing lip fading for a moment. He had never heard Gar say so many words strung together.

The stablemaster leaned forward and poked Corban in the chest. 'Learn to control them and they can be a tool that makes you stronger.'

'Easy for you to say,' Corban mumbled. '*How?*'

Gar looked at Corban a long while. 'I will teach you if you wish,' he said quietly.

Corban raised an eyebrow. Gar never trained in the Rowan Field or rode with a warband on account of an old leg wound – he'd walked with a limp as long as Corban could remember – so what the stable-master could teach him, he didn't know.

'What?' said Gar. 'A wounded leg does not mean I've forgotten what it's like to wield a sword, or to face a man in battle.'

Wield a sword. 'All right,' Corban shrugged. 'Though Da is teaching me my weapons until I'm old enough for the Field.'

Gar snorted. 'There is much Thannon can teach you, but how to hold your temper is not one of them.'

Corban smiled. His da was not well known for his patience.

'We'll keep it between us, for now,' Gar said.

'What, can't I tell Cywen?'

'Especially not Cywen.' A rare smile touched the edges of Gar's mouth. 'She would not leave me alone. *Gar, teach me this, Gar, teach me that,*' he mimicked. 'No, she keeps me busy enough with the horses.'

Corban chuckled. Gar held out his arm and Corban gripped it. 'Good. So,' said Gar, 'are you going to come back to the fair?'

'Not yet.' He looked past Gar at the milling crowds.

'You'll have to face them sooner or later, and the longer you leave it the harder it will be, like falling off a horse. And your friend will be worried.'

'I know. I'll come back after, just not right now. I think I'll go and see Dylan.'

Gar nodded. 'It's a long walk to Darol's hold. Let's get you cleaned up and Willow saddled, that way you'll be back by sunset for the end of the handbinding.'

Corban fell in silently and they made their way into the streets of Havan. Everywhere was deserted, the lure of the fair having emptied the village. Corban looked up, saw Dun Carreg high above, but even the fortress seemed still and empty. No one moved on the walls or around the great arch of Stonegate, looming above the only entrance into Dun Carreg.

They reached the stable and soon Corban was sitting on top of a solid bay pony, his face stinging after washing in the water barrel.

'Hold one moment,' said Gar and disappeared inside the stable. He soon returned with a leather saddlebag. 'Just a few bits: some bread, cheese, a blanket, some rope. Always be prepared,' he added in response to Corban's quizzical look. 'You never know what's going to happen.'

Corban smiled ruefully, touching his cut lip. 'That you don't.'

'Remember, back by sunset. Look after Willow and he'll look after you. And stay away from the Baglun. There's been talk of wolven being seen.'

'Huh,' grunted Corban. He didn't believe that. The only time wolven had ventured to the forest's fringes was in winter, tempted by the smell of horseflesh in Dun Carreg's paddocks. And that was only rare, when the Tempest Moon had come and snow was drifting deep. They preferred deep forest to open spaces.

Soon Corban was clear of Havan and riding on the road that led to the Baglun Forest. The giantsway, all called it, as the vanquished Benothi had made it, the giant clan that had ruled here long ago, before men had taken the land from them. It cut a line through Ardan and Narvon, though there was less traffic between the two realms than there had once been. So now the road was overgrown with grass and moss, its raised banks crumbling. In the distance Corban could see the small hill that Dylan's home was built upon, the river Tarin glistening behind it in the midday sun, and further in the distance the dark smear of Baglun Forest filled the horizon.

The day had grown hot, the breeze off the sea only a faint caress. Tentatively, Corban touched his lip, which was throbbing painfully. His head hurt and his ribs were aching where Rafe had kicked him. He sighed: where had the day gone so wrong?

Rafe's face came back unbidden, his smirk as he had taken the practice sword and run from Gar. Corban's neck flushed as he felt the shame of it all over again. *Maybe I am a coward. I wish I was like my da, strong and fearless.* What had Gar meant about controlling his emotions? How could you be taught to do that? Whatever it was, if it helped him teach Rafe a lesson, then he was willing to give it a try. As far back as Corban could remember, Gar had always been around, was a close friend of his mam and da's. In truth he was a little scared of the man; he always seemed to be so stern, so serious. But he *was* intrigued by Gar's offer of help.

Slowly a noise filtered through his thoughts and he looked up. In the distance he saw a large wain coming towards him, two figures driving, others walking and running beside it.

'Dylan.' Willow's steady pace had eaten up much of the journey, the rocky grassland around Havan giving way to fertile meadows as he drew nearer to the river. Yellow gorse had been replaced by juniper and hawthorn, and Darol's hold loomed large before him.

Darol, Dylan's da, was sitting in the front of a heavy-laden wain, driving a dun pony, his wife next to him. Dylan was walking one side of the wain and his sister and her husband striding along behind, their son Frith running circles around them. Corban smiled at the sight. He had seen too little of them over the winter; his mam hadn't let him travel much past Havan during the season of storms, her fears fuelled by tales of hungry wolven. But the summer before he had spent more of his time out here, mostly in the company of Dylan. They had argued the first time they had met, Corban defending his sister over something she had said. Somehow it had ended in laughter, and soon after Corban and Dylan had become firm friends, even though Dylan was a few years older.

Dylan worked hard for his da, but when Corban visited, Dylan more often than not made time for him, quickly showing him the tasks of the farm, digging holes for fence posts, planting and reaping their crops, catching salmon, a host of other things. More interesting to Corban, though, had been being shown how to use a sling, how to recognize different animal tracks, and how to hunt, skin and cook hare. Most exciting of all were the short forays into the fringes of the Baglun Forest. The forest seemed to be a different world, sometimes unnerving, but always alluring. He looked at the Baglun now, its vast sweep disappearing into the distance. A larger forest he could not imagine, not even the fabled forest of Forn, far to the east, said to be bigger than half the realms of the Banished Lands put together. He snorted, remembering his trips with Dylan into the Baglun. Towards the end of last summer, when Dylan had been busy from dusk till dawn with harvest, Corban had taken to entering the forest alone, had felt proud when he had confided in Dath and invited his friend to join him. Dath made the sign against evil, turned pale and told him he was either very brave or more likely mad. Truth be told, it was nothing to do with bravery, which he was distinctly lacking if his encounter with Rafe was anything to go by. He just *liked* it in the forest, although the thought of his mam finding out made him shiver even in the warmth of the sun.

Dylan was only a hundred or so paces away, now. Corban pulled Willow to a halt and waited. Darol nodded as he drove the wain past Corban, Dylan peeling away from the cart and strolling over to him.

'Hello, Ban,' he said, then frowned as he saw Corban's bruised face. 'What happened to you?'

'I fell,' said Corban. 'I was coming to see you, maybe help with the salmon. Looks like I'm too late.'

'Da had it all sacked up by sunrise. And we've got to get the food to Havan in time to prepare it for the feast. Another time, eh?'

Just then Frith ran up behind Dylan and, with a loud crack, kicked him in the ankle. He giggled and turned to run but Dylan, hopping on one leg, grabbed the youngster and hoisted him into the air, legs pumping as if he were still running. When he realized escape was futile he went limp and grinned. Dylan swung him higher to sit upon his shoulders.

'You're getting too old for this – it's your ninth nameday soon.'

'But I like it up here,' Frith protested.

'Very well, if it keeps you out of trouble.' Dylan turned back to Corban. 'Come with us? I can't wait to have a look round the fair.'

'No thanks. I've just come from there.'

'All right, Ban, but you'll be back for the handbinding, won't you?' Corban nodded.

'Good, then you can tell me all about this fall.'

'*Argh*,' Dylan yelled as Frith gripped his ears and gave them a mighty tug. 'What are you *doing*?'

'You're my horse. Charge!' Frith shouted, pulling Dylan's ears again. Dylan grabbed his nephew's hands in his and trotted after the wain, calling goodbyes to Corban over his shoulder.

Frith grinned at Corban, who raised his fist and shook it, trying not to laugh.

For a while he just sat on Willow, watching the wain dwindle into the distance as he wondered what to do. Then his eyes turned back to the Baglun and with a click of his tongue he urged Willow on down the road.

CHAPTER FOUR

EVNIS

Evnis took the skin of mead from Helfach, his huntsman. He unstoppered it and drank, the taste of honey sweet, the alcohol warming his gut.

'It's good, eh?' Helfach said.

'Huh,' grunted Evnis. He had more important things on his mind than the quality of the mead he was drinking. So many years had passed since he'd sworn his oath to Asroth and become accomplice to Rhin, Queen of Cambren. And now he had risen far, was counsellor to Brenin, King of all Ardan. That night in the Darkwood Forest seemed like another life. It had been terrifying, but intoxicating as well. He felt some of that now: fear and excitement mixed as the consequences of that oath were emerging from the past.

They were sitting in a dell on the southern fringe of the Baglun Forest, almost half a day's ride from Dun Carreg. Further south a great herd of auroch trampled the moorland, the ground vibrating at their passing. A dust cloud hovered above the herd, marking them like some enormous predator.

'Where is he?' Evnis murmured.

Helfach looked up, shading his eyes. 'You said highsun, so should be any time now.'

'I hate waiting,' Evnis growled. He wanted to get back to Fain, his wife. She was unwell, needed him. The worry of it chewed at him.

Helfach grinned. They sat in silence, passing the skin between them. Then Evnis' horse lifted its head, ears twitching.

'There,' said Helfach, pointing.

A figure slipped between trees and made its way towards them.

'Hood up,' Evnis said, pulling his own to cover his face.

The figure drew closer and Evnis rose, strode towards the new-comer. He was tall, an unstrung bow in his hand, a face full of lines and creases. And cold eyes. Evnis thought he was younger than he looked.

'This is for you.' The man held out a leather cylinder.

Evnis pulled the parchment out, cracked the wax seal and read in silence. After long moments he grimaced, rolled the parchment and slipped it into his cloak.

'Your mark is a hold to the north-east of the Baglun,' he said, 'on a hill just beyond the river. Stockaded wall.'

'That sounds close to Dun Carreg.'

'It is.'

The man grunted. 'How many.'

'A family of six.'

'How many able to hold a blade?'

'Two men, one boy that's started in the Rowan Field. The rest are women and a bairn.'

'I'll not be killing women or bairns.'

Evnis squinted. 'Has Braith picked the right man for this job?'

'He's not complained so far.'

Evnis shrugged. 'Do it tonight. There's a wedding feast at the fortress, so if you need corpses to make your point you will have to wait for them to return home. Make sure their hall burns bright.'

'Aye,' the man grunted and strode back into the trees.

'We done here?' Helfach asked.

Evnis pulled the parchment out from his cloak and read it again:

Greetings, faithful one. Braith is well placed, now, his position strong. Use his men well. Stir Brenin from his lair, as quickly as you can. The time approaches. On the matter that you contacted me, if your wife's ailment is beyond the healers, you must use the earth power. Find the book. You know where it is. Find the door and you shall find the book. Uthas says it will help you, though nothing will save her except the cauldron. Take her to it if you can.

Remember the cause, remember your oath.

He hawked and spat, then lit a taper and burned the message.

'We'd best get back,' he said, swinging into his saddle. 'If I do not make it to the handbinding Alona will curse me for a traitor and petition Brenin for my head on the block.' *Traitor. If only she knew the depth of my treason.*

Helfach snorted. 'Let the bitch try: you have Brenin's ear.'

'Aye, but so does she, and more. And she hates me, will always blame me for her brother Rhagor's death.' *And rightly so, he thought.*

In silence they rode their mounts out of the dell, through a thin scattering of trees and back onto the road for Dun Carreg. With the wind in his face, Evnis' thoughts returned to the letter. *'The time approaches . . . remember your oath.'* How could he forget? *To make Rhin high queen, to bring about the God-War, and Asroth made flesh.* He grimaced. Had it really been eighteen years since that night in the Darkwood? Sometimes it felt like a dream, sometimes he wished it *had* been a dream. Things had seemed much simpler then.

See it through, he told himself. *No other choice now.* His thoughts drifted to Fain, as they were always wont to do, given enough time. *One thing for sure, I must find that book.*

CHAPTER FIVE

CORBAN

As Corban drew closer to the river the ground began to level out. To his right he saw the salmon weir.

He looked at the trees that dotted the far bank; they quickly became dense and thick, marking the boundary of the forest. The same tingle of excitement that he always felt whenever he was near the Baglun rippled through him.

He rode his pony across the ford, hooves splashing and cracking on stones, up the other bank and into the embrace of the forest.

The giantsway continued into the Baglun, its stones slick with moss. Latticed branches above cast the world in twilight. Somehow the shadows eased his mood, soothed him.

He allowed the pony to walk at its own pace, imagining himself a great huntsman like Marrock, tracking a band of lawless men come raiding from the Darkwood on the northern border. He had heard as much from his da. Thannon liked to talk as he worked, and had told many a tale of the Banished Lands, the continent upon which they lived. He had also spoken of their realm of Ardan, as it was *now*, of the growing distance between King Brenin and Owain, King of neighbouring Narvon, and the sudden increase of lawless men roaming the Darkwood that separated their realms. Thannon had told of a band of these men raiding into Ardan, burning crofters' homesteads and robbing travellers along the way. He said they might even be heading for the Baglun.

Corban felt his stomach clench and his eyes grow wider as he looked about, imagining outlaws lurking behind bushes, ready to waylay him. But who would be fool enough to set up camp within sight of Brenin's own fortress?

Nothing to fear.

The forest grew much closer here, thickets of thorn bushes dense between the trees. Just ahead, the giantsway spilled into an open glade, sunlight dappling the ground as the canopy above grew thinner. Corban trotted into the glade, bluebells carpeting the ground, rolling up to the oathstone.

It towered over the clearing: a single slab of dark rock scribed with runes in a language long forgotten, another remnant of the giants that had dwelt here once. The stone was still used for the solemnizing of some occasions, but it had not been visited officially since Brenin had taken up his father's sword and become King of Ardan, over fifteen years ago. It felt old, solitary. Corban liked it here.

He dismounted and strode closer to the stone. It looked different: somehow *wet*, dark streaks staining the rock, trickling from the deep-carved runes. He reached out and touched the stone. Suddenly the glade darkened, clouds rolling across the sun, and he shivered. He pulled his hand away, his fingertips stained red. Was that *blood*?

He realized his heart was pounding, the noise filling his ears. Then his vision blurred and he was falling.

Corban blinked into consciousness and looked around.

He was in the glade of the oathstone, leaning against the great slab, but something was different. Wrong. Everything was pale, as if all colour had been leached from the world. He looked up. Dark clouds boiled above him, bunching and flowing like an angry sea. And it was so quiet. *Too* quiet. No birdsong or insects, no sounds of the forest; just the hiss of wind amongst branches.

Then suddenly, footsteps, the crunch of forest litter, so loud in the silence. A figure emerged from the thickets about the glade, a man with a sword at his hip, his cloak travel-stained. Seeing Corban, he paused, bowed his head, then marched towards him.

'I've been looking for you,' the man said, squatting in front of Corban.

Corban could not place his age. There were creases about his eyes, his mouth, though a close-cropped beard hid most of those. His hair was dark, dusted with grey. Then Corban looked into his eyes, yellow like a wolf's, and old. No, more than old. *Ancient.* And wise.

'Why?' Corban asked.

The man smiled, warm and welcoming, and Corban felt himself smile in return.

'I need help. I have a task to complete, and I cannot do it alone.' He pulled an apple from a pocket in his cloak, startlingly red in this bleached world, and took a bite, juice dripping. The man's nails were cracked, broken, dirt caked in their grain.

'Why me?' Corban muttered.

'A direct mind,' the man observed, smiling again. He shrugged. 'It is a difficult task, dangerous. Not all are able, capable of helping me.' He inhaled, long and deep, closing his eyes. 'But there is something about you. Something of value. I feel it.'

Corban grunted. He had never felt particularly special, never been told it, except by his mam, of course.

'What is the task?'

'I must find something. Let me show it to you,' the man said, placing a hand over Corban's eyes.

Then Corban was standing in a stone room, arched windows black against torchlight, the darkness outside seeming to suck the light into nothingness.

In the centre of the room sat a great cauldron, a squat mass of black iron, taller and wider than a man. A scream burst from the cauldron's mouth, echoing around the room. It rose in pitch, containing an anguish that had Corban covering his ears, then suddenly silence fell, broken only by the soft crackle of the torches. Pale fingers reached out from within the cauldron, grasping the black rim. A body heaved itself upwards and spilled out onto the stone floor. Slowly it stood: a man dressed only in loose woollen breeches, long dark hair unbound except for the warrior braid falling across broad shoulders. His skin was a pale grey, thin and stretched, and *things* seemed to be moving beneath it, as if trying to find a way out. Veins stood proud, bulging and purple against the pallid tissue, forming an intricate spider web on the man's body.

Then he turned and looked at Corban.

Eyes as black as night, no pupil, no iris, stared at him. The mouth creased in a grisly smile, a thin line of blood trickling from its corner. A droplet gathered, dripped to the floor.

Corban took a step backwards. The figure mirrored him, taking a step forwards. Corban was about to turn and run but froze abruptly, sensing a presence behind him. He told himself to turn but his body would not obey, the hairs on the back of his neck standing on end.

The thing before the cauldron paused as well, face contorting as the black eyes stared past Corban. There was movement from behind. Out of the corners of his eyes he saw two great, white-feathered wings sweep about him. The figure in front grimaced, raising its arms as if to ward off a blow. It hissed at him, threw back its head and howled, a high, piercing cry. Corban looked at the wings, felt his panic and fear draining away and a sense of peace taking its place, even though the creature was still howling its ululating cry. Slowly the room faded and all was darkness again.

With a gasp his eyes snapped open. His back was wet with sweat. He shook his head, still hearing the inhuman howling from his quick-fading dream. Willow was stamping the ground, hoof gouging the earth. As Corban came fully awake the howling did not fade but grew clearer, taking on a different tone from his dream, and suddenly he realized that Willow could hear it too.

He leaped to his feet and tried to soothe the animal. Willow snorted, slowly quietened, even though the howling continued to ring through the forest. Corban stood for a moment, listening.

'Whatever that is,' he murmured, 'it sounds *scared*.' He patted the pony's neck a while longer, then made a decision and led the pony in the direction of the howling.

Within heartbeats the forest became a twilight world. The branches were too low for him to mount Willow, but he moved easily enough between the trees, although he had to pay attention to where he put his feet, the forest floor thick with vines that snared his boots.

Small shallow streams crossed his path and the ground became spongier, Willow's hooves making sucking noises as they sank into and pulled free of the damp earth.

I should turn back, he thought. Dylan had warned him of the deadly bogs within the Baglun, appearing as firm ground at first, which would suck you down and smother the life from you. He stopped. The howling began again, and it sounded so close.

Just a little longer. He stepped forward and the howling suddenly stopped.

Corban walked around a dense stand of trees, elbowing red ferns aside and pulled abruptly to a halt.

Not more than twenty paces in front of him was the head and shoulders of a wolven, jutting from the ground. Its canines gleamed, as long as his forearm and sharp as a dagger. Corban could not believe it. They were fearsome pack hunters, bred by the giant clans during the War of Treasures, if the tales were true. They were wolf-like but bigger, stronger, and with a sharp intelligence. But they were rarely seen here, preferring the south of Ardan, regions of deep forest and sweeping moors, where the auroch herds roamed. For a moment boy and beast stared at each other, then the wolven's jaws snapped, froth bubbling around its mouth. One of its paws scrabbled feebly at the ground. It looked close to death, weak and thin. There was a squelching sound and the animal sank a little deeper into the earth, as if someone was tugging on its hind legs. The ground around it looked firm enough, covered in the same vine, but Corban knew the wolven was caught in one of the Baglun's treacherous bogs.

He stood in silence a while, not knowing what to do. Crouching, he stared at the creature's head, grey flecked with white, spattered with black mud.

'What am I going to do?' he whispered. 'You'd eat me, even if I could get you out.' The beast stared back with its copper eyes.

He looked about, picked up a long branch, thrust it at the ground before his feet and began tentatively to edge his way forwards, Willow watching disapprovingly. Suddenly the branch disappeared into the ground, his left leg sinking up to the knee before he could stop. He knew a moment of panic, tried to pull out and felt the mud firm up around his leg, gripping him in an airless embrace. He shifted his weight and leaned back, slowly freeing his leg, which was covered in viscous black mud. He fell backwards.

Slick with sweat, he just lay there a moment. There was a gurgling sound and he looked up, saw the wolven sink deeper. He stood up and strode back to Willow, suddenly knowing what he must do, at the same time knowing it was foolish. He patted Willow, the pony's eyes rolling white. She was close to flight. When she had calmed a little he pulled Gar's rope out of the saddlebag and tied one end to his saddle, slowly coaxing the pony to walk closer to the sinking mud. He looped the other end of the rope as Cywen had taught him and cast it towards the beast. His second attempt fell across the animal's head and shoulder. Gently he lifted the rope and slowly, ever so slowly, he began to pull. The rope tightened and held fast. Corban led the pony away from the bog. The rope creaked, shuddering under the strain as Willow took up the slack. The wolven whined, snapping at the air as the rope bit into its skin, then with a great sucking sound it began to pull free of the mud. Willow took a step forward, then another . . . and within moments the creature was lying on its side at the edge of the bog, panting and slick with mud. It staggered to its feet, head bowed.

Corban could not help but marvel at it, even in its bedraggled state. It stood not much shorter than Willow, its coat a dull grey, streaked with bone white stripes. Slowly it raised its head, its jaws snapping as it sliced through the rope about it. Then it howled. Willow neighed, reared and bolted. Corban wanted to move but could not, his eyes fixed on the wolven's long, curved canines.

Then Corban was aware of movement, a presence around him, of deeper shadows pacing. Eyes gleamed out of the darkness, many eyes.

Its pack has come. I'm dead, he thought. Before him, slow and deliberate, the wolven he had saved padded towards him, thick muscles bunching about its neck and shoulders. Its belly swayed from side to side, full and heavy.

'You're in pup,' he whispered.

It circled him, stopped in front of him, copper eyes locking with his, then took in a great sniff and pressed its muzzle into his groin, snuffling. He resisted the urge to leap back, knew his life hung on a thread. The beast lifted its head, still sniffing, tracing his abdomen, his neck, his jaw. Hot breath washed over him, the scent of damp fur heavy in his throat. The wolven's muzzle pushed against his skin, its teeth cold, hard. Corban felt his bladder loosen. Then the beast took a step back, turned and bounded away, disappearing into the darkness of the forest.

The eyes in the shadows faded and Corban let out a huge breath, slumping to the ground.

What have I just done?

He lay upon the damp ground awhile, waiting for his racing heart to calm, then he rose and walked away from the bog. The forest looked different now, darker. It was difficult going, constantly having to focus on the ground in front of him to avoid tripping in the dense vines that carpeted the forest floor. Some time had passed before he realized he had not seen any of the small streams that he had crossed earlier. He stamped his foot on the ground, which was no longer spongy, but hard under the forest litter.

'Oh no.' Frantically he looked around, searching for some familiar sign, but recognized nothing. Diffuse sunlight filtered through the treetops, giving no glimpse of where the sun lay in the sky. With a deep breath he began walking again. *Just have to keep going*, he thought. *Look for a stream that will take me back*. He shuddered, trying to control the panic starting to bubble inside him. He knew full well that he stood little chance of surviving a night in the forest, and to find his way out he had to think clearly. *Just keep walking*, he told himself, *and hope I'm not travelling deeper into the forest*. He quickened his pace, glancing constantly back and forth between the floor at his feet and his chosen path.

His feet were sore, toes numb when he finally stopped. It seemed that he had been walking for an age, and still no sign of a stream. Looking around, he selected a tall elm, then began to climb. The higher he got, the thinner and wider apart the branches became. He reached a point where even balancing on the tips of his toes he could not reach the next branch above. If I can just reach the top I should be able to see Dun Carreg. Then at least I'll know if I'm walking in the right direction. Desperation fuelling him, he crouched slightly and jumped. Both hands gripped the branch he was aiming for and he hung there a moment, suspended, swinging slightly as the tree's limb flexed. Then one of his hands slipped. He windmilled wildly, desperately clinging on, then he was falling. After colliding with a number of branches, he blacked out, to find himself in a heap on the forest floor. He sat up, groaning and then heard a faint sound. It was distant, but the forest was mostly silent, not even a breeze rustling the trees. He strained, almost certain he could hear a voice, someone calling. He jumped up, forgetting his exhaustion and ran. When he stopped there was silence for a moment, then he heard the voice again, much closer now. It was calling his name.

'*HELLO!*' he called back, cupping his hands to his mouth. He set off again, calling. Soon he saw a tall figure step from behind a tree, leading two horses, a large piebald and a pony. The figure limped.

'Gar,' cried Corban, running wildly now, tears streaming down his face as he threw himself onto the stablemaster. At first the dark-haired man stood there, still as a statue. Then, stiffly, he put his arms about the boy and patted his back.

'What are you doing here?' Corban asked shakily.

'Looking for you, of course, you idiot. Willow knows his way home, even if you don't,' replied Gar, stepping back to look at Corban. 'What has happened to you? You looked bad enough when I saw you last, but now . . .'

Corban looked down at himself, covered in mud and leaves, with scrapes on his skin and holes in his cloak and breeches.

'I was . . .' Corban paused, knowing how stupid he was about to sound. 'I just wanted some quiet, to be alone . . .' he said sheepishly, looking at the floor. 'I got lost.' The look on Gar's face convinced him that this would not be a wise time to mention the wolven.

The stablemaster looked at the bedraggled boy in front of him, took a sniff, and sighed deeply.

'You can thank your sister. She insisted I come and find you when Dath told her about Rafe.'

'Oh. She knows,' said Corban, shoulders sinking.

'Aye, lad, but never mind that now, let's get you home. If you can keep up with me we should still be able to get back for the hand-binding. At least that way I won't have saved you just for your mam to kill you.'

'I think she's going to kill me anyway,' Corban said, looking at his torn and tattered cloak.

'Well, let's go and find out,' said Gar, turning his horse and walking away.

CHAPTER SIX

VERADIS

Veradis flexed his shoulders, trying to readjust his chainmail shirt. His skin was chafed raw even through the linen tunic underneath, made worse by the rhythm of his horse as he rode a dozen paces behind Nathair.

Should have worn it more often, he thought, but he had felt uncomfortable. Only a handful of warriors had owned chainmail shirts in Ripa: his brother Krelis of course, as well as his father. Also Alben, the fortress' weapons-master, and two or three of the local barons' sons. The few times he *had* worn it in public he had felt different, set apart, and he'd had more than enough of that feeling already, without adding to it. So the chainmail shirt had remained boxed in his room for the most part.

Nevertheless, he treasured it. Mostly because Krelis had given it to him after his Long Night, the final seal on his warrior trial, when he had passed from boy to man, but also because of the truth in what his brother had told him. *Leather may turn a weak or glancing blow, but this will turn a strong one. Treat it like a good friend.* And he had, taking it out every night from a wooden chest, oiling it, scouring it, then folding and putting it away again.

Aquilus had granted Nathair's request, allowing him to lead the warband sent to interrupt Lykos' meeting, the self-proclaimed king of the corsairs. So Veradis had only slept two nights in Jerolin before climbing back into his saddle again.

He glanced over his shoulder. He was riding near the head of a short column, three abreast, around four score of them, though only half of that number were Nathair's own recruits in his fledgling warband. The others were picked from Aquilus' eagle-guard, insisted upon by Fidele, Nathair's mother.

Either side of him rode Nathair's followers: Rauca on his left, the third son of a local baron, likeable, easy natured and quick in the weapons court; on the other side Bos, son of one of Aquilus' eagle-guard. He was thick necked, broad shouldered, with arms like knotted oak.

They had made good time travelling south of Jerolin, passing through leagues of undulating meadow splashed with patches of open woodland, and now, three nights out, Veradis spied the mountains that roughly marked the halfway point of their journey, rearing out of the land like the curved spine of a withered, crippled old man.

'Veradis,' Nathair called from up ahead.

Veradis touched his heels to his stallion's ribs and drew alongside Nathair.

'We have not yet had the conversation that I promised you,' Nathair said, glancing at Veradis with an easy smile.

'You have been busy, my lord,' Veradis said.

'Ah ah, none of that "*my lord*" talk. Remember what I told you?'

'Apologies, my lo—' Veradis began, then closed his mouth.

Nathair chuckled. 'I am glad to have you in my warband. There are not many of us yet, but it shall grow.'

'Aye.'

'And you, I hear, are the most skilled swordsman ever to come out of Ripa. A most welcome member to my warband.'

Veradis snorted. 'Who . . .?'

'Your brother. I spoke with him briefly, before he left. He spoke very highly of you, and of your skills.'

'Oh,' Veradis breathed, a smile touching his mouth.

'Your father must be very proud.' Nathair said.

'Huh,' Veradis grunted. He opened his mouth but could think of nothing to say. 'Aye,' he eventually mumbled.

'Krelis. He is well liked. Has it been *difficult*, growing up in his shadow?'

Veradis frowned, but said nothing.

'Forgive me if I pry,' Nathair said, 'only, it is a subject of interest to me.'

Veradis shrugged. In truth it had been, especially as his father only ever seemed to have eyes, praise, for Krelis. His other brother Ektor had never seemed to care, being content with his books, but Veradis had felt it like a thin sliver of iron working its way deeper and deeper into his flesh. But he loved Krelis, rarely resented him for it, and then only for a passing moment. If anyone were at fault, it was his father. He shrugged again. 'Sometimes,' he said.

'I know something of what it is like, growing up in another's shadow,' Nathair said quietly.

Looking at the Prince, Veradis noticed his eyes were bloodshot, dark circles beneath them. 'Are you well?' he asked.

'What? Oh, it's nothing,' Nathair said. 'I did not sleep well, that's all. Bad dreams.'

They rode together in silence for a while, winding their way through open woods, white campion dotting the ground about them. A handful of woodlarks burst from branches ahead and above, startled by their passing.

'Did you see the riders that left Jerolin before us?' the Prince suddenly asked.

'Aye. I did.' Over a score of warriors had left the fortress on the day Veradis had been preparing for this journey, all with extra horses, well-provisioned for long journeys. 'I thought perhaps it was something to do with the return of Meical – he is your father's counsellor, isn't he?'

'Yes, he did play a part.' The Prince scowled a moment, then carried on. 'The riders are messengers. My father is calling a council, summoning all of the kings throughout the Banished Lands.'

'*All* of them?'

'Aye. A messenger has been sent to the king of every realm.'

'Why?'

'Ah. Of that I should not speak, not yet. It is for my father to tell, at the council.'

'Will they come, the kings of every realm?'

'They should, my father is high king,' Nathair said.

'Perhaps,' Veradis pulled a face. Aquilus *was* high king, though more in name than deed. Generations gone, when the Exiles had washed ashore and begun their war against the giant clans, there had been but one king, Sokar, and after the giants had been thrown down and the Banished Lands populated by men, all had bowed to him.

But that had been a long time ago; new realms had grown, and now there were many kings in the Banished Lands, though they all still recognized the sovereignty of Tenebral's master, descended from their first king. In theory, at least.

'Father says they will come,' Nathair said with a shrug. 'Between you and me, I do not really think it matters.' He leaned closer, spoke more quietly. 'Did you know that the giant-stones are *bleeding*?' He smiled, looking excited. 'We are living in exceptional times, Veradis, times when we shall have much need of your famed sword-arm, I think. We are on the edge of something new. So this is a good time to be raising a warband. As I said, I am glad that you are a part of it.'

The Prince glanced back at the column behind them. 'They are good men – brave, loyal, every one of them. But you are a baron's son. We are more alike. You understand me?'

'Aye, my lo—' Veradis said. 'Yes, I understand. And I am glad to be part of this.' He felt his curiosity rising, his blood stirring at Nathair's words. Some part of the Prince's enthusiasm was infectious. And for the first time in an age he felt a glimmer of something stir deep inside. He felt of value.

The days rolled past as Veradis and the warband headed steadily southwards. For a time they hugged the mountains Veradis had seen in the distance, crossing fast-flowing, white-foamed rivers that tumbled out of the high places. As the mountains faded behind them, the land began to change: the woods and forests of sycamore and elm disappearing, replaced by leagues of rolling grassland, which in turn grew steadily thinner, paler, the colour and moisture leached from everything by the ever-increasing heat of the sun.

In time they struck the banks of the Nox. The warband crossed the river by an ancient stone bridge, built by the giants generations before. From here they followed the river south, carving a line through the ever-rockier land, until one morning, well before high-sun, Veradis tasted salt on the air and heard the call of gulls in the distance.

The column of riders rippled to a stop as their captain, Orcus, held his hand up. Nathair gestured to summon Veradis and Rauca to join him.

The Prince and his eagle-guard were huddled over a scrolled

map. Veradis leaned closer, frowning. He had always struggled with understanding maps, and certainly did not love them as his brother Ektor did, who would spend days in the library at Ripa, poring over the many parchments they had stored there. Some even outlined the boundaries of the giant realms that had ruled the Banished Lands before the Exiles had been washed up onto these shores.

'We are here,' Orcus said, finger jabbing at a spot on the map near a coastline.

'Aye,' Nathair said. 'And that would appear to be the mark that the Vin Thalun prisoner spoke of.' The Prince pointed at a tall cedar, its trunk split and charred by lightning. 'If he spoke true, this meeting is supposed to take place about a league east of that tree.'

'We shall see.' Orcus rolled the map up with a snap and slid it back into a leather case.

'Let the men know we are near,' Nathair said to Veradis and Rauca.

The two warriors rode back along the length of the warband, spreading the word. With a wave of his arm, Nathair led them onwards, turning east with the stream.

They soon found themselves in a barren land of low hills, sharp crags and sun-baked, twisting valleys. Nathair halted them a while after midday, the sun a white, merciless thing glaring down at them.

'We walk from here,' Nathair called, and with a rattle of harness and iron the four score men dismounted. A dozen stayed behind with the horses, the rest picking a path into a string of low hills.

Veradis wiped sweat from his eyes and took a sip from his water skin. He was more used than most to this heat. His home, Ripa, was much further east along the coast, and almost as far south as they were now, so the climate was similar. The only thing missing was the constant breeze off the bay that seemed always present in Ripa, and here, without it, the heat felt so much worse, suffocating, burning his nose and throat with each breath.

They were climbing a hill, spread out in a long line behind Nathair and Orcus, the hobnails in the leather soles of Veradis' sandals scratching on the rock-littered ground. The two leaders stopped, heads close together. Orcus signalled for the small warband to spread out into a loose arc before carrying on up the hill.

Veradis used his spear as a staff, shrugged the shield slung across his back into a more comfortable position and laboured up the hill behind Nathair. Before the Prince reached the top of the slope he ducked down onto his belly and crawled the rest of the way. The warband followed, and soon they were ringed about a long ridge, Veradis one side of Nathair, Rauca the other. Cautiously, Veradis peered over the ridge.

The ground dropped steeply away for forty or fifty paces before it levelled out, a stream cutting a gully through a flat-bottomed bowl of stony ground. A small stand of scraggy laurels clustered along the stream's edge.

Before the trees, in the shade of a huge boulder, was a man. An old man, judging by his silvery hair, pulled back and tied neatly with a leather cord at his nape. He was squatting beside a fire, prodding sparks from it with a stick, something spitted across the flames. He was humming. Behind him, to the left of the laurels, was a brightly coloured tent.

Veradis glanced at Nathair's frowning face, then back to the old man.

He seemed alone, though it was impossible to be certain. There could be men hiding behind many of the scattered boulders, perhaps hidden in the stand of laurels, and the tent could have concealed at least a dozen more.

'What do we do?' Veradis whispered to Nathair.

The Prince shrugged. 'Wait,' he muttered.

So they did, the sun beating down on the warband spread along the ridge, Veradis feeling as if he was slowly roasting inside his shirt of mail. The old man in the dell continued to cook and eat whatever it was that he had spitted over the fire. He licked his fingers contentedly when he had finished, cuffed a neatly cropped silver beard and washed his hands in the shallow stream before staring up at the ridge, to where Nathair was crouched.

'You might as well come down,' the old man called. 'I'd rather not have to climb all the way up to you.'

Veradis froze, appalled. He looked at Nathair, who appeared as shocked as he was. The old man repeated his invitation, shrugged, then sat with his back against the boulder.

'I am going down,' Nathair whispered. 'Veradis, Rauca, with me. All else will wait here. He may only have spied one of us moving.'

The Prince stood and slithered down the slope, Veradis and Rauca behind him. Veradis scanned the dell for lurking enemies.

The old man smiled as he rose, waiting for Nathair to draw closer. There was a scuffing sound behind them; Veradis then saw Orcus sliding down the ridge to join them.

'Welcome, Nathair ben Aquilus,' the old man said, bowing low.

Veradis scanned the old man for weapons, but could see none. There was a strength, a sense of energy about him, his bare arms wiry with lean muscle. His face was deeply lined, a hint of good humour dancing in his eyes, which looked *strange*. Were they tinged with yellow?

'King Lykos?' Nathair said, stopping half a dozen paces before the man, Veradis, Rauca and Orcus spreading either side of him, a pace behind.

'Me? Lykos?' the man said, still smiling. 'Sadly, no. I wish it were true, I envy his youth and vigour. I am but a servant of Lykos. He bid me apologize for his absence.'

'Where is he?' Nathair asked, eyes flitting amongst the boulders.

'He has been unavoidably detained,' the old man replied. 'So he sent me, instead.'

'And you are?'

'I am the counsellor of the Vin Thalun, adviser to Lykos, King of the Three Islands and the Tethys Sea,' the old man said, bowing again. Orcus snorted.

Veradis noted that the man had not actually given his name.

'And the baron that you are to meet?' Nathair said.

'Ah, yes.' The old man tugged at his short beard. 'You must understand, Lykos and I were very eager to meet you. The rendezvous with a baron was an . . . elaboration. It seemed the best way to ensure your presence.'

'What? But, how did you know I would come?'

The counsellor smiled. 'Well, it is common knowledge that Peritus your father's first-sword is leading a campaign against the giants, dragging the bulk of Jerolin's warband around the Agullas Mountains, so that rules him out. Then, as suspicion has been cast on one of your father's other barons, Aquilus would be most unlikely – in fact, foolish – to send one of *them* on this task. Who else was left

55

that your father could trust? And it is no secret that you are, uh, *over-due*, in leading a campaign.'

Nathair scowled, flushing red. 'So all of this,' he said, waving a hand around the dell, 'it was just a *ruse*?'

'Aye, although that would not be my word of choice. As I said, I was very eager to meet you.'

'Why?'

'Now *that* is a very good question. Right to the heart of the matter,' the old man said. 'A question that requires a detailed answer. Perhaps you would care to step into my tent? There are chairs, wine, fruit. A more fitting environment for a long conversation.'

Nathair frowned, eyes narrowing.

'Not quite ready for that yet,' the counsellor shrugged. 'I can detect a distinct lack of trust in you, Prince.'

'Understandable, I think, under the circumstances,' Nathair said.

'Indeed, indeed. Well, for now perhaps the short version, then. Lykos wishes there to be an understanding between us.'

'Us?' Orcus snapped.

'The mainland of Tenebral and the Islands. A truce, an alliance, even.'

'Pfah,' spat Orcus, but Nathair just stared at Lykos' counsellor.

'Father would never agree. He hates the Vin Thalun islanders.'

'Yes, we are aware of Aquilus' disposition,' the counsellor said. 'That is, in part, why I am speaking to you, Nathair. But, more than that, you are the future of Tenebral, and of any treaty between us. You.'

'My father is king, not I.'

'At present, true. But that will not always be so.' The old man smiled, as if talking with an old friend. 'The older you get, the more likely you are to become fixed in your ways, in your opinions. Sometimes fresh blood is needed to guide the way. These are exciting times, as I would think your father has discussed with you. Perhaps *your* opinion, *your* guidance, is of worth.' He looked intently at the Prince.

Nathair snorted, but did not look away from the counsellor's gaze. 'Even if I were to agree that there may be some value in an alliance between us, how would *I* ever trust you?' the Prince said. 'A people that have preyed upon those weaker than themselves, that burn and steal, that, until now, have not even been able to maintain a truce amongst themselves?'

'Back to that again,' the counsellor frowned. 'Trust. A most important foundation to any relationship. I could smother you with words, promises, but they are easily spoken. I do not think you would be swayed by them. The old man took a step towards his cooking fire. 'Perhaps a more *practical* demonstration of trust is required here.'

'Demonstration of what?' Orcus said suspiciously.

'Alcyon, join us,' the counsellor called out, and out of the laurels strode a huge form, black braided hair and a drooping moustache framing a weathered, deep-lined face. Swirling blue tattoos coiled up massive arms and disappeared under a coat of chainmail. The hilt of a great broadsword jutted over one shoulder.

'Giant,' Rauca spat like a curse, and, as one, Nathair's three companions drew their swords.

At the same time the counsellor dipped his head and muttered something. The flames of the cook-fire suddenly sprang up, higher than a man and leaped forwards, cutting a line between Nathair and his companions, leaving the Prince on the wrong side, alone with the giant and counsellor.

Orcus took a step towards the flames and staggered back as they flared in his face, the heat searing.

Veradis heard the scuffling of feet as the rest of their warband poured over the ridge behind him. On the far side of the flames he could see the blurred figures of the giant, Nathair and the counsellor. The giant had drawn his huge sword and was levelling its tip at Nathair.

Veradis sucked in a deep breath, ducked his head behind his shield and ran at the flames.

CHAPTER SEVEN

CYWEN

Where are they? thought Cywen as she ran her hand down the fore-leg of a large roan colt – Gar had asked her to check over a number of horses while he was gone. She grunted as her fingers found a small lump on the underside of the horse's hoof.

'What's wrong?' asked the horse trader who owned the colt.

'He's lame,' she said with a shrug, absently pushing back a strand of dark hair fallen from her pin.

'What?' said the trader, eyes narrowing, staring at Cywen down a long, thin nose.

'He's lame,' Cywen repeated.

They were standing in a roped-off section of the meadow amongst rows of horses brought for the Spring Fair. Cywen was having the time of her life. First Gar had asked her to help him choose and haggle for the new stock that Brenin wanted bought in, and on top of that he had asked her to aid him with the King's horses. It had been as close to a perfect day as she had ever known. That was, until she had seen Dath with a face as long as one of the horses she was tending. He had told her everything, but only after she'd threatened him with a fist in the eye. *Poor Corban,* she thought, swinging between worry about him and anger at Rafe. She felt a swell of rage, imagined punching Rafe's arrogant face. *No, Mam'll skin me if I'm caught fighting again.* And now Gar had been gone for so long, saying that he must go and find Corban. Now she was beginning to worry about *him* as well. With an effort she focused back on the horse trader in front of her.

'Where is Gar?' the thin-faced trader asked.

'Not here,' she shrugged. 'He said he had urgent business, could be gone all day. Like I said, the horse is lame. I'm sure Gar would still be interested, but not at the price you're asking. Come back next spring, if you'd rather barter with him.'

The trader scowled, moaned a little more but still accepted the coins that Cywen offered her, then walked away stiffly, muttering under her breath. Cywen smiled to herself and patted the roan's neck.

'That was well done,' a voice said from behind, startling her. She turned to see a tall, willowy girl, long golden hair framing a pretty, serious face.

'Thank you,' she replied. Then she recognized her. 'You're . . .'

'Edana, and you are?' the young princess said.

'Cywen. I help, at the stables. Thannon the smith is my da.'

'I've seen you before, mostly with Gar, around the stables. I just didn't know your name, that's all. You handled that trader very well.'

Cywen smiled. 'The horse *is* lame, but not for long. Look.' Cywen lifted the roan's foreleg, resting the upturned hoof above her knee, Edana looking over her shoulder.

'See here,' Cywen ran a finger over a lump on the tender part of the hoof. 'Watch.' She pressed the tip of the knife to the lump and gently sliced the skin. 'This has been here a while, the skin has grown thick,' she explained. Grunting in concentration she continued to cut carefully away at the tough skin. Placing her thumb behind the lump she pressed, and, with a pop, the skin burst, yellow and green pus leaking out. The horse's muscles twitched. Cywen murmured soothingly, still applying pressure with her thumb until the cut stopped weeping.

'That's disgusting,' said Edana.

'We're not finished yet.' Cywen dipped a cloth into the water trough next to her and began cleaning the wound. She pressed the knife's tip firmly into the cut, pushing hard on the other side with her thumb.

'There it is,' she whispered, pulling a sliver of wood from the cut. She held a long thorn up for Edana to see. 'He'll be fine now.' She grinned, slapping the horse's neck.

'How did you know that was there?' said Edana.

She shrugged. 'Gar has taught me a lot.'

'He has indeed.'

Something caught Cywen's attention over Edana's shoulder, a

flash of blond hair, a familiar swagger. Rafe. 'Watch the colt for me,' she blurted as she broke into a run, ducking under the rope that ringed the paddock. She sped through the crowds and with a loud thump threw herself into Rafe's back. They both fell to the floor with a crash, limbs tangled.

'How do *you* like it?' she shouted, jumping clear of Rafe as he rolled over. She aimed a kick at his stomach and leaped upon him again, raining down a furious barrage of blows. They rolled on the ground, Rafe trying to protect himself, then Cywen was grabbed and hauled off.

'Get off me!' she screamed, squirming in the grip of Vonn and Crain, aiming a last vicious kick at the prostrate Rafe.

'Calm down, wildcat,' Vonn said.

She struggled a moment longer, before realizing that the two holding her were not about to let go any time soon. Rafe groaned, holding his stomach as he rolled onto his side and rose unsteadily. He was covered in grass stains and mud, his fair hair sticking out wildly in all directions. A thin trickle of blood ran from his nose.

A crowd had gathered around them, and someone laughed. Rafe's cheeks coloured.

'Are you *mad*, girl?' he said, wiping blood from his face with the back of his hand. He glanced at the crowd. 'You should be more careful, you're lucky I didn't hurt you.'

'*You're* the lucky one,' she snapped. 'Lucky you've got two *bodyguards* to protect you.'

'What illness do you have,' Rafe said, 'that causes you to attack innocent people? From behind, like a coward.'

Cywen renewed her struggling; Rafe began to laugh. It spread round the crowd as Cywen tried more and more frantically to break the hold on her wrists, spitting and snarling at Rafe.

'Please, stop,' Vonn said, 'or I'll have to ask Rafe to fetch a bucket of water to cool you down.'

'He's – the – coward,' Cywen grunted, but stopped struggling. 'Rafe. He's been doing his warrior training for over a year, picking on someone who hasn't even set foot in the Rowan Field.' She spat at Rafe. 'Have you got round to learning the code yet? Or are you too slow-witted to understand it?'

Vonn's face creased in a smile. 'Got some spirit, hasn't she?'

Rafe's eyes narrowed. 'Your brother needed to be taught a lesson, as do you,' he hissed, a fist bunching as he took a step towards her.

'*Stop*,' cried a voice from within the crowd. Rafe paused, fist still balled as a slim figure stepped out of the mass. It was Edana, mouth set in a stern line, her back straight as she strode into the circle that the crowd had formed.

'Let her go,' she snapped, shooting a withering glance at Crain and Vonn.

'We would not have harmed her,' Vonn said, releasing Cywen. 'Just didn't want her harming Rafe.'

'She attacked me,' Rafe said, licking his lips. 'She should be taught a lesson.'

'A lesson?' said Edana. 'Well, maybe, but not by you, Rafe ben Helfach. I've heard what your father's *lessons* are like, and I would not wish that on anyone. Even you.' Rafe coloured.

'Come on,' Vonn said to his friends. 'Best to make a retreat. I feel we're outnumbered.' He winked at Edana.

'It's a shame,' Rafe called over his shoulder, 'that Corban doesn't have some of his sister's courage, then maybe he wouldn't need her to fight his battles for him.' He pointed a finger at Cywen. 'And you should remember that the King's daughter may not be around to get you out of trouble next time.' Then he strode into the crowd.

Cywen made to follow him but Edana touched her arm and she stopped.

'Come on,' Edana said, steering Cywen gently towards the paddocks. They walked in silence.

'Thank you,' said Cywen, stroking the colt. 'Sometimes I do things before I think. Actually, a bit more than *sometimes*.' She blushed at the thought of what she'd just done, and in front of Edana, daughter of the King. 'Sorry,' she said.

'Are you going to tell me what that was all about?'

Edana listened intently as Cywen told of what had happened between Rafe and her brother, the sun dipping slowly towards the western horizon, turning the bay into an undulating sea of bronze. Around them the paddock gradually emptied of people, a crowd gathering towards the northern edge of the meadow as sunset approached.

'. . . and now I'm starting to worry about Gar as well, because neither of them has returned, and look how late it is,' Cywen finished.

Edana looked past Cywen towards the giantsway. 'I can see two riders. Look.'

'I think it *is* them,' Cywen said.

The girls marched across the meadow, Cywen half running and Edana walking beside her, her long strides keeping pace easily. They reached the road and followed it until the point where it forked east and west. The riders were closer now, one on a horse, the other a pony.

Cywen ran forward, hugging Gar's leg as he pulled his piebald to a halt. 'Where have you been?' she cried. 'You've been gone so long.'

'Best ask your brother,' said Gar, his face its usual stony expression.

Cywen looked at Corban as he trotted up on his pony. 'Oh, Ban,' she said, seeing his cut and bruised face.

'Cywen,' he mustered a smile. Then Edana walked up behind his sister. Corban flushed a shade of red.

Gar nodded to the blonde-haired girl.

'I've been watching Cywen working with the horses,' Edana said. 'I am most impressed with her skills. She told me she has a good teacher.'

'She learns quickly, when she stops talking long enough to listen,' said the stablemaster.

'Where have you been, Ban?' Cywen asked.

'In the Baglun.'

'What? Why?' gasped Cywen.

'Never you mind. But don't tell Mam,' he added quickly.

'We'll talk about the *other* thing later,' Corban whispered, glancing at Edana.

'The other thing? Do you mean Rafe?' Cywen followed Corban's gaze. 'Don't worry about Edana, she knows all about it.'

'Oh,' said Corban, shoulders slumping.

'Your sister has had words with Rafe,' said Edana.

'What?' Corban said with a squeak. 'What do you mean?'

'I was so angry, Ban, when Dath told me what happened to you. Well, I saw him walking in the crowd, Rafe, that is, and . . .'

'What did you do?' said Gar sternly, a sick expression settling upon Corban.

'Well, I don't remember it very clearly, but I did knock him over, and punch him a bit. And kick him.'

'His nose was bleeding when I arrived,' added Edana.

Gar just stared at her, so Cywen looked to her brother for support. His face was set like stone.

'My thanks,' said Corban eventually, coldly, sounding as if he was having trouble breathing.

Cywen just looked at him, a weightless sensation growing in her stomach.

'The next time I have a fight to conduct, I shall call for you to fight it for me.'

'Rafe said something like that,' Cywen said, then closed her mouth quickly and clasped a hand over it.

Corban grimaced.

'Ban, don't be silly,' Cywen said. 'Nobody will even remember it tomorrow. And stop screwing up your face like that, it makes you look like old Eluned, and that's not a good thing, you know.'

Corban took a deep breath.

'Anyway, better get you cleaned up and see what we can do about your cloak before Mam sees you. She's likely to skin you if you turn up at the handbinding like that.'

'I know,' he said dejectedly.

'Speaking of mothers,' said Edana, 'I think I'd better go, otherwise my mam will be wanting to do something terrible to *me*.'

The stablemaster dipped his head. 'My lady.'

'Gar,' Edana said with a smile, then she turned and walked quickly back towards the crowds in the meadow.

'What an *idiot*,' said Corban, scowling.

'No she's not,' snapped Cywen.

'Not her, *me*.'

Cywen stopped herself from agreeing with him. *I'll remind him some other time*, she thought, *when he's not quite so distraught.*

'And I'm not talking to you,' said Corban, pointing a finger at his sister.

'Come on, you two,' said Gar. Suddenly he stood in his saddle, peering eastwards down the giantsway.

'What is it,' asked Cywen.

'Two riders,' Gar murmured. With a shrug he sat back and together they headed on towards the village.

'What were you doing in the Baglun?' Cywen asked. Corban ignored her. 'Come on, Ban, I know it's not nice, what happened with Rafe. Your poor face.' She rested a hand on his leg. With a jerk of his wrist Corban steered Willow away.

'Why are you punishing *me*?' she said, tears blooming. 'If you want to get angry with someone, why don't you try Rafe?'

Corban scowled at her and kicked Willow into a trot. Cywen began to jog after him, but when she drew level with Gar, the stable-master called her.

'Leave the lad a while,' he said.

'But . . .'

'Leave him be,' he said sternly. 'You're not helping.'

'Not you too,' she muttered, kicking at the road.

'I know you meant well, but sometimes, *this time*, it would have been better if you had thought before you acted. Do you not see, in Corban's eyes your bravery has made him a coward twice over.'

'He's not a coward,' she snapped.

'It doesn't matter what you or I think. He thinks it.'

'Is it really such a big thing?' she asked. 'He's only got a cut lip. I've had worse falling off a horse.'

'It's not about the cut. He will be entering the Rowan Field soon to begin his walk to manhood. This will rest heavy on him.'

'What can I do?' she asked.

'Do? Nothing else, Elyon forbid. This is something he must come through by himself. Teach yourself to think before you act, that is something you *could* do.' He looked at her bowed head. 'Give him time.'

She nodded.

Dath came running down the road to meet them. Corban pulled to a halt, Dath reaching him just before Cywen and Gar.

'How are you, Ban?' said Dath, looking intently at his friend.

'I'm well, Dath,' he replied curtly. Then he sighed. 'My chin's a bit sore, to tell you the truth, so is my lip. And my ribs.'

'I've got your gifts,' said Dath.

'Oh, I'd forgotten,' said Corban, rooting around in Dath's bag.

'I heard what you did,' Dath grinned at Cywen, 'people are talking about it all around the fair.' She pulled a face, causing his smile to flee.

'This is for you,' Corban muttered and threw something to Cywen.

'It's beautiful,' she said, running her fingers over the horse carved on the brooch. 'Thank you, Ban.' More tears sprang to her eyes.

The sound of hooves grew behind them: the two riders Gar had seen cantering along at a ground-eating pace. They drew alongside the group. Both had large round shields strapped to their horses' saddles, and longswords at their hips, their cloaks travel-stained. Gar nodded a greeting. One – the younger, Cywen thought – bright blue eyes sparking in a boyishly handsome face, flashed back a grin.

'Greetings,' he said. 'Judging by that great pile of stone perched over there we have reached Dun Carreg.'

'Aye,' answered Gar. 'You have.'

The blue-eyed man smiled at his companion and clapped him on the back. 'You hear that, brother.'

The other sat silently on his horse, staring at the fortress. 'We would speak with King Brenin,' he said, black hair framing a stern, weathered face.

'You will find him in the meadow,' Gar said. 'His nephew is hand-bound today.'

'My thanks,' the stern warrior said, and the two men urged their horses off the road towards the meadow.

Gar watched them go, a frown creasing his face, then he turned to Corban. 'Come, the sun has almost set. Cywen, try and work some kind of glamour on your brother's cloak while I introduce him to a bucket of water.'

CHAPTER EIGHT

KASTELL

Kastell stretched in his saddle, filling his lungs with a deep breath. The air was crisp, laced with the scent of pine from the mountain slopes they were riding towards. As his home faded behind him, the fortress Mikil, he began to feel his spirits lift. Life in the fortress had become almost unbearable of late, so when his uncle Romar, who was also King of all Isiltir, had suggested he ride in the guard of this merchant train he had accepted without hesitation.

Maquin, his shieldman, rode at his side, a tall spear cradled easily in the crook of his arm. Kastell had known Maquin longer than any other, the last remnant of his father's hold. They were all dead ten long years, slain by the giants as they raided out of Forn Forest.

Kastell reined in his horse and looked back, brushing his red hair from his eyes. To the east was Forn Forest, oldest and most dreaded in all of the Banished Lands. Kastell looked at the brooding darkness only a few leagues away and shivered, though the sun was hot on his face. The giant trees rose like a murky bulwark, a dark undulating ocean that travelled endlessly into the northern horizon. Although Mikil lay only a few nights' journey from the great forest, this was the first time he had really looked upon it in years. Since the slaughter of his family. Many of Isiltir's warriors rode patrol along its borders, protecting against the beasts that would stray from within Forn's depths: the savage Hunen giants, bent on revenge for grievances long past, packs of wolven and swarms of great bats that would drain a man of every last drop of blood.

'I hate that forest,' he whispered.

'Aye. Bad memories,' Maquin grunted beside him.

To the west he could spy Mikil, its grey walls clear in the flat plains around it. He was glad to be away from it, and his kin that lived there. One of them, at least. Jael, his cousin, whose father had been killed in a similar attack to the one that had claimed his own mam and da's lives.

He and Jael were close enough in age to be brothers, but there was no love between them. Jael took great pleasure in humiliating Kastell. When they had been younger it had been unpleasant, almost a game, although not one that Kastell could ever remember winning or enjoying. Now, though, well past a year since they had both turned sixteen, come through their warrior trials and Long Night, and changed from boys to men, the baiting had become something deeper, something more *real*, and a rage was building within Kastell, simmering and bubbling, closer to exploding each time that Jael goaded him.

It's better to be away from Mikil.

Kastell focused on the path they were following, a wide stony track that wound its way into the mountains. He kicked his horse on.

He and Maquin were at the rear of a long column, the merchant train they rode guard to twenty wains long, all heavily laden with goods bought from Mikil: rods of silver from the fortress' famed mines, as well as vats of mead, rolls of cloth and barrels of apples. They were heading for Halstat, a mining town in Helveth. Two score warriors rode guard about the wains, a mix of mercenaries from Helveth that served the merchants in Halstat and more warriors hired from his uncle Romar, who was always quick to see profit in any situation; the giant raids were the perfect incentive for more protection, especially as the only path through the mountains to Helveth wound so close to Forn Forest.

'How long till we reach Halstat?' Kastell asked as they caught up with the column.

'Twelve, fourteen nights, maybe longer at this pace,' Maquin said. 'Who'd have thought salt could buy so much.'

Halstat was a town grown fat on its salt mines, supplying most of Helveth and the countries around it, Isiltir included.

'I'd like to lighten the load by a jar of mead or three,' he added.

'If it helps the wains move faster.' The slow pace was chaffing at Kastell already. *Better than Mikil and Jael*, he reminded himself.

The rest of the day passed uneventfully. They continued along the path that climbed the mountains until the sun dipped low, sending their shadows stretching out far in front. A halt was called and the travellers quickly set about making camp.

Kastell sat a little apart from the warriors and merchant crew, methodically sliding his whetstone down one side of his sword, then the other. He was lost in the rasp and rhythm of his nightly routine and his own thoughts when a pair of boots appeared on the grass before him. Looking up, he saw Maquin looming above him, carrying two cups, a skin of mead gripped under his arm. Maquin grinned.

'Here, lad,' the old warrior said, thrusting a cup at Kastell.

The mead was sour and strong, going some way to balance the night's chill.

'We could always go and sit by the fire,' Maquin said as Kastell shivered.

'I'm fine here,' Kastell said. Around the fire sat warriors of Mikil, mixing with the mercenaries and merchants. *Most likely poisoned against me by cousin Jael's lies*, he thought irritably.

Maquin gave him a long, measured look, but he said nothing.

A warrior appeared from amongst the wains, Aguila, captain of the mercenary guard. He wandered over and squatted in front of Maquin, offering a skin of something to the grizzled warrior. Maquin took it and drank deeply, dark liquid spilling into his beard. He coughed.

'Better'n that horse piss you're drinking,' Aguila said, smiling. 'It'll warm you quicker, as well.'

'I believe that,' Maquin said, taking another gulp from the skin and then passing it back.

Aguila offered it to Kastell. He sniffed at the skin.

'Won't kill you, lad,' the guard captain said.

Kastell took a long gulp, swallowed, then coughed violently. His throat and belly felt as if they were on fire. 'What is it?' he wheezed when he'd caught his breath.

'Best not to ask,' Aguila grinned. 'It gets easier, and better.'

Kastell didn't believe him, but took another, smaller swig, nevertheless. This time the fire didn't burn quite so strong.

'Good lad,' the captain said, slapping his shoulder. 'Glad to have you both with us.' He eyed Kastell's sword and whetstone.

'It's good to be out of Mikil for a while,' Maquin said.

'Aye. It's different from the last time I was there, for sure. This time I couldn't visit an inn for Romar's swords getting in your face.'

'That's my uncle you're talking about,' Kastell said, his voice not as steady as he'd wish.

'I know that,' Aguila shrugged. 'It's not an insult. More an observation. Something's different, that's all.'

'You're not wrong,' Maquin said. 'Strange things have been happening, in and around Mikil.'

'What things?' Aguila asked.

The giant-stone, marking Isiltir's border. We had word in Mikil that it was *bleeding*.'

'I have heard whispers of such things,' Aguila said. 'There's a circle of giant-stones in Helveth, south of Halstat. Same thing is said to have happened.'

'And there's more – worse as far as Romar is concerned. The starstone axe has been stolen.'

'Ah. That'd do it,' Aguila nodded.

The starstone axe was a relic straight out of legend, from a time before the Exiles had set foot in the Banished Lands, from before Elyon's Scourging, even. Legend told of a star falling from the sky, when giants and men lived in peace and harmony. Kastell did not believe there had ever been a time like that. According to the tales, Treasures had been forged from the starstone, seven Treasures – cauldron, torc, necklace, spear, dagger, axe and cup. Wars had been fought over them, culminating in Elyon's wrath being stirred and dished out: the Scourging. The axe at Mikil was said to be one of those Treasures, and people travelled from far and wide to visit it, believing it had magical qualities, that somehow it could bridge the gap between this world of flesh and the Otherworld, where the gods Elyon and Asroth dwelt.

Kastell did not know anything about that, doubted all of it. But what he did know was that the axe had made Mikil rich, that the constant trail of pilgrims visiting the relic brought with them a steady stream of silver and gold. Romar knew this too, and so his rage had been great indeed when the axe had been stolen. All the more reason for Kastell to get out of Mikil for a while. Between Jael's taunting and Romar's rages it had not been a pleasant place to be.

'When did this happen?' Aguila asked.

'A ten-night gone,' Maquin said.

'Who took it? The Hunen, it must be,' the mercenary muttered.

'The Hunen,' said Kastell. 'They want it, sure enough, and they are the only giant clan within a hundred leagues. But I think they would be noticed walking into Mikil – anyone that stands fifteen handspans tall would be.' He took another drink from the skin, the warmth feeling almost pleasant this time.

'Aye, but still. They are Elementals – maybe they used a glamour,' Aguila said.

'Maybe,' agreed Maquin, reaching for the skin in Kastell's hand.

'They are sly and fierce, the Hunen,' Aguila said.

'I know it,' muttered Kastell.

'You've had dealings with them, then?' Aguila asked.

'The Hunen slew his kin, the man I was oathsworn to,' Maquin said darkly.

Kastell closed his eyes, remembering the hulking shapes striding through the broken gates of his hold, swinging their great-hammers and war-axes, outlined by flames. He shuddered. He had been six years old. He wished Aguila would stop talking about it. Silently he took the skin back from Maquin and drank some more.

'Did they ransom you?' Aguila asked.

'The Hunen do not take prisoners,' Kastell said. 'Maquin saved me, carried me away.'

'The Hunen are raiders, murderers, nothing more,' Maquin growled.

Kastell wiggled his fingers, making the sign against evil.

Aguila saw the movement and smiled. 'You need not worry about giants now, lad. We are forty blades strong, and besides I'd wager you know how to use that sword of yours. Elyon above knows it's sharp enough.' He glanced at the whetstone, and winked at Maquin.

'Are you mocking me?' Kastell asked, feeling his temper stir. 'Been talking to Jael, have you?' he growled. He felt blood rushing to his face and his hand moved to hover over his sword hilt. Aguila's easy smile vanished, his expression hardening.

'Have a care,' the warrior said as he rose. 'Romar's kin or no, it won't protect you always.'

Kastell glared at Aguila's back as he walked away.

'See how I am mocked,' Kastell muttered, 'because Jael does, all others think me fair game, think I can be scorned.' He ground his teeth.

Maquin took a long deep breath. 'Sometimes, Kas, you see enemies where there are none.' Maquin shook his head. 'Aguila meant nothing by it. Surely you understand that?'

Kastell snorted.

'I did not want to have this conversation with you,' Maquin said, 'have stopped myself many times, hoping you would see it for yourself. When you passed your trials and Long Night, became a man, I thought it would end.' He shook his head. 'It is about time you heard some truths, I think. Jael has not turned all against you, even if he tries to. You are not considered by all as a figure to be scorned. But many do think you haughty, arrogant. Too proud to mix with the rest of us. There is much good in you, Kas, but take care lest it is buried beneath a cairn of self-pity. Your da would be disappointed, to hear you speak so.' With that he rose and walked away, leaving Kastell sitting wide-eyed in the grass.

He sat alone the rest of the night, listening to the quiet talk and murmured songs that rose from the other travellers. As most of the camp descended into sleep, Maquin told Kastell he was on the next watch. Silently he walked out of the ring of wains and took himself to the rim of the camp. *Self-pity*, he thought, scowling in the dark, wavering between anger and shame.

He pulled his cloak tighter, a chill wind blowing through the mountains, the moonlight fleeting as clouds scudded across the sky. He was still shocked at Maquin's words to him and spent his watch mulling over them. Grudgingly he reached the conclusion that Maquin was right, leaving him embarrassed, angry, mostly at himself for behaving the way he had, but also at others: Maquin, Aguila, many, faceless others for misunderstanding him. He had acted like a child, a sulky, spoilt child. Alongside those feelings, though, was a faint glimmer of hope. The thought that most of the fortress was not in league with Jael, in a pact to goad and bait him, was a good one. He made a decision then, in the dead of night. *In the morning*, he told himself. When his watch candle guttered and went out, he lit a new one from the dying embers of the fire, then woke the next warrior whose turn it was to stand guard. Soon after he was asleep.

*

The sky was grey with the approaching dawn when Kastell opened his eyes. He rose quickly and went about the morning's duties, saddling his horse, helping to harness the draught horses to wains, load his pack. When all was done and most were breaking their fast, Kastell saw Aguila walk alone to his horse, a big dun animal. Kastell trotted to catch the warrior and tapped him on the arm.

'I-I am sorry, for my words to you, yestereve.' There was a slight tremor in his voice. 'I misunderstood your meaning.'

Aguila looked at him, then his easy smile returned. 'It is forgotten, lad,' he said. Kastell nodded and then, not knowing what else to do, turned and walked away, a smile starting on his own face. Out of the corner of his eye he saw Maquin watching him.

CHAPTER NINE

CORBAN

Heb raised his hands into the air, his frame outlined by the fading sun.

'Fionn ap Torin, Marrock ben Rhagor,' he cried in a loud voice that did not seem to match his spindly frame. 'Your day is done. You have been bound, hand and heart, and lived the day as one. Now is your time of Choosing. Will you bind yourselves forever, or shall the cord be cut?'

Marrock and Fionn looked at each other and raised their bound hands into the air. 'We will be bound, one to the other, and live this life as one.'

A murmur rippled through the crowd and Heb stepped forward, taking their bound hands in his.

'Make your covenant,' cried the loremaster.

'Fionn ap Torin,' Marrock began, 'I vow to you the first cut of my meat, the first sip of my mead . . .'

Corban shifted restlessly. *I'm half starved*, he thought, looking at the long benches that stood in rows near the firepits, bowed with steaming food. His mam was gazing at the couple in front of them, moisture shining in her eyes. Thannon, his da, stood beside her, a bear of a man beside Gwenith. His hound Buddai lay curled at his feet. A bruise was purpling around one of Thannon's eyes and he had a split lip, but it didn't seem to bother him – he was pugil champion for another year.

Things have worked out much better than they could have, Corban thought as he stroked his own cut lip. His mam had asked where his cloak was, but seemed satisfied, although nettled, when he told her that he had left it on Willow in his haste to make it back for the handbinding ceremony. The questions about his cuts and bruises had been explained as an accident involving Dath, himself and a tree, which was close enough to the truth. His mother's raised eyebrow and his da's silent stare had given him some cause for concern, but he had handed out his gifts at that point and managed to avert any further interrogation.

He sighed. *Why are these ceremonies so boring?* Fortunately Heb was now singing the closing benediction . . . *peace surround you both, and contentment latch your door.*

He held up a wide cup, the couple gripping it with their bound hands. They drank together, then the loremaster cast the cup to the ground and stamped on it.

'It is done,' he cried and the crowd erupted in cheering.

'Come on,' Dath said, nudging Corban in the ribs. 'Let's eat.'

Corban nodded, steering Dath towards the food bench where he had seen Dylan earlier.

Dylan smiled at him. 'You made it back then.'

'Aye.'

'So what happened to your face?' Dylan asked.

Corban shrugged, anger flickering inside as he thought of Rafe. 'I went to the Baglun after I saw you,' he said, wanting to change the subject.

'Alone?' Dylan said.

'Aye. Alone.'

'You shouldn't have done that, Ban, you could have got yourself into real trouble.'

Corban snorted. *I did get into real trouble.* 'I'm not a bairn,' he snapped instead, not quite sure why. He instantly regretted his words, knew he was angry with Rafe, not Dylan. A call from Darol summoned Dylan away. Corban and Dath piled wooden trenchers high with meats and warm bread, Dath balancing a jug of gravy under his arm. Suddenly Dath froze.

Standing in front of him was a woman, filling her own trencher, silver hair spilling down her back. It was Brina, the healer.

'What's wrong, Dath?' Corban muttered.

'Her,' hissed Dath. Brina had a reputation amongst those that lived around Dun Carreg. 'She's a witch.'

Brina must have heard something, for she looked straight at Dath and twisted her mouth at him.

Dath looked as if his eyes were about to burst from his skull. Turning quickly, he crashed into a solid wall of leather and iron, dropping both his plate and the jug over the warrior he collided with.

The Queen's brother, Pendathran, loomed over the boys, scowling as gravy dripped down his tunic and onto his boots. With good reason he was often called the Bear.

'I'm s-sorry,' stuttered Dath as he attempted to wipe the mess off the warrior, but only succeeded in smearing it around a wider area. Pendathran gripped Dath by the wrist and growled. For a moment Corban thought his friend might actually collapse from fear, then Pendathran's scowl cracked and he chuckled.

'Don't worry, boy,' the warrior said. 'My nephew has wed today, so I will forgive you, even though you *are* a blundering idiot.'

Dath smiled, mostly from relief, then Pendathran glanced over the boy's shoulder and his good humour vanished, the scowl returning.

'Pendathran,' said a slightly built man, shadowed by a broader and taller young lad. Pendathran glowered at him for a moment, then turned and strode away. The slim man watched Pendathran's back, shook his head and walked on.

'Who was that?' Dath asked Corban as they refilled the spilt trencher and jug.

'You don't know? That was Anwarth and his son, Farrell. Rumour says that Anwarth's a coward, that he played dead when Queen Alona and Pendathran's brother, Rhagor, was killed by brigands in the Darkwood.'

'I thought the counsellor Evnis was blamed for that.'

'By Alona he was, but King Brenin wouldn't punish Evnis or Anwarth. Said he didn't have the evidence.'

Dath puffed his cheeks out. 'Lot of bad blood, there, then.'

'Aye.'

Dath nodded. 'So how did Farrell get so big? His da's so small.'

'Have you seen his mother? She's a big lady. And he's the same age as us – a bit younger, even. He is *sensitive*, though, or so I've heard. About his da's reputation.'

'What do you mean?' Dath said.

'He hits people that mention it.'

'Oh. Remind me not to bring the subject up in earshot of him then. He looks as if he could be as big as your da soon.'

Corban chuckled. 'His mam must feed him well.'

'I wish I lived in the fortress,' said Dath, 'you get to hear all the exciting stuff.'

'Oh, I don't know, there's plenty to get excited about living in the village. All those different types of fish that you get to find out about.'

Dath kicked his friend in the shins.

They found Gwenith and Thannon sitting on a cloak, picking at half-empty trenchers, sharing a jug of mead. Cywen was there as well, but Corban looked past her as he sat down.

'I found your cloak, Ban,' she said, passing it to him. Cywen had stitched it as she had promised. Relief was quickly replaced by annoyance, though; he did not want to feel indebted to her after what she had done.

'Thank you,' he managed.

'Where's your da?' Corban asked Dath.

His friend pulled a sour face. 'I'm not sure where he is, now . . .'

Corban knew what that meant. Dath didn't *want* to know where his da was. He had taken the loss of his wife hard, had turned to drinking earlier and earlier.

'Come, eat with us,' said Gwenith, patting the ground beside her. Dath smiled gratefully.

It was dark now, many small fires lit all across the meadow. As he looked around, Corban spotted Brenin and Alona, laughing with Marrock and Fionn. Beside Brenin, Edana appeared. She was smiling and waving at him, Corban . . .

A giddy smile stole across his face and he raised his hand, self-consciously giving a little wave back. Edana beckoned, motioning for him to join her. Shocked, he began to rise, then Cywen spoke behind him.

'Mam, Edana's calling me to go see her. I'll be back later,' she said and ran over to the King's daughter.

Corban threw himself to the ground, his cheeks burning. When he eventually found the courage to look up again he was staring straight into the eyes of Ventos, a smile on the trader's face, a jug of mead in his hand. His hound Talar stood beside him.

'I've been looking for you,' he said to Corban.

'Hello, Ventos.' Corban introduced the trader to his mam and da, who insisted he join them.

Thannon held his hand out for Talar to sniff. The hound growled. Buddai sat up and gave a rumbling growl of his own.

'My Buddai is not one to start a fight,' Thannon said, 'but he will finish it if one comes his way.'

'Talar,' the trader snapped and the hound's growling stopped.

'Ventos is from Helveth,' said Dath.

'That's where Gar is from, isn't it, Mam?' Corban asked.

'That's right,' his mam said, sharing a glance with Thannon.

Just then Gar limped out of the darkness. He patted Thannon on the shoulder, and sat down awkwardly, stretching one leg out in front of him. He frowned when he saw Ventos.

'How's the saddle?' Ventos asked Gar.

'A good fit.'

'Hear you're from Helveth,' Ventos said.

'Aye. What of it?'

'Nothing. So am I, that's all. This is a long way from Helveth. How did you end up here?'

Gar closed his eyes, and for a moment Corban thought the stablemaster was going to ignore the question again. Then he looked up and began to speak.

'I lived in a village close to Forn Forest. One day the giants came raiding, burned out the whole village, killed almost everyone. I escaped, just, along with a handful. All my kin were dead,' he shrugged, 'there was nothing left to stay for, so I just kept walking. Ended up here, somehow. Brenin took me in, has been good to me.'

Thannon passed him a cup of mead. He took a long draught of it.

'Giants, eh,' Ventos said. 'The Hunen are still a curse on Helveth's arse, and getting braver of late, striking further out of Forn Forest. There is rumour of Braster, King of Helveth, raising a force to lead into the forest, to crush them once and for all.'

'Good,' Gar said and sipped from his cup of mead.

Corban saw Darol leading his pony harnessed up to the wain. Dylan was sitting in the back. Jumping to his feet, Corban ran over.

'Why are you leaving so early?' he asked Dylan, walking beside the wain.

'Da's tired,' Dylan grimaced. 'I wish we *were* staying, I hear Heb's going to tell one of his tales tonight.' He sighed. 'Da's in a foul mood. He won't stay. And you still haven't told me why you look as if you ran into a tree.'

'I'll come see you tomorrow,' Corban said as the wain picked up speed. He waved as Dylan and his family faded into the darkness.

Others were leaving the field, now, drifting away into the night. Corban made his way back to the small circle of his family and sat beside his mam. Cywen had returned. He was still annoyed with her, but his mood lightened as he sat listening and laughing with the small group. He lay back, hands folded behind his head, looking up at the stars and moon in the dark blanket above, listening to the rhythmic lapping of the sea. Absently his mam reached out a hand and stroked his hair.

Some time later he heard clapping and sat up. Heb had climbed onto a table near the firepit. Groups around the meadow began to draw in closer, eager to hear one of the loremaster's famous tales, and Corban and his family joined them.

'What would you hear tonight?' cried Heb.

Voices called out from amongst the crowd, but before Heb could respond, Queen Alona stepped into the light of the firepit.

'It is tradition that Marrock should choose,' she said, beckoning to her nephew and his bride. Heb looked enquiringly at Marrock, who gazed into the fire a while, then smiled to himself.

'Tell us the tale of Cambros,' he said.

'A tale so tragic on so happy a night?' said Heb with a raised eyebrow.

'Any tale that tells how I came to be born in this land and so meet my bride is not a sad tale,' he replied, looking at his wife.

'He's drunk already,' a faceless voice called from the darkness, followed by a ripple of laughter.

Heb held up a hand. 'The tale of Cambros,' he cried, then he bowed his head and a hush fell over the meadow.

'Our ancestors came to this land in a great fleet; the Exiles, they called themselves, banished from the Isle of Summer after a long and bloody war. They were washed ashore far south and east of here, and called this new world the Banished Lands. Sokar was our king.

'It was not long before our ancestors discovered they were not alone, that the land was filled with giants, survivors of Elyon's Scourging. Old hatreds run deep, and the enmity between mankind and giants had not lessened, for all the generations that had passed since the Scourging, when Elyon's wrath had brought both men and giants close to extinction. And so the Giant Wars began, of which the tales of victory and of sadness are too great and too many to tell this night.

'During this great war Sokar sent out his warlords. To the west he sent Cambros, the Bull, with his sons Cadlas and Ard, to fight the Benothi, those giants that dwelt even here, that built Dun Carreg.' Heb paused, pointing at the fortress high above them. 'The giants were defeated, pushed back, Cadlas and his warriors following them . . .'

Corban closed his eyes, picturing the tale. This story was known to him, as his mam and da were often teaching him the histories. As Corban listened, Heb spoke of the campaign that defeated the Benothi giants, forcing them to retreat ever northwards.

'Then the giants rallied for one last battle, on the slopes of Dun Vaner,' Heb said. 'The Benothi, in their pride – which was ever the giants' downfall – marched out of their stronghold of stone to meet Cambros the Bull and his warband. The battle raged for two days. The battlefield was stained black with blood, the sky darkened with the gathering crows come to glut on the dead.

'At the end of the second day,' Heb said, 'as the sky grew red with the fading sun, Cambros and his shieldmen broke the lines of the Benothi and he came face to face with Ruad, their king. Alone they faced each other, their shieldmen dead and strewn on the ground around them, and alone they fought. Ruad smote Cambros with his great war-axe and rent his shield. Three times Cambros drew the blood of Ruad, but eventually his blade was shattered and he was beaten down.'

Corban heard people groan around the meadow, saw his mam wiping away tears.

'In desperation, Cambros grabbed a branch fallen from a tree. As Ruad raised his axe Cambros gave his last strength and hammered the giant's knee a mighty blow, smashing bone and sinew. Roaring, Ruad fell. Cambros crawled upon the giant's chest and drove his broken sword deep into Ruad's heart. Seeing their king's death, the will went out of the Benothi, and the battle ended.

'And so it was that the Benothi were broken, and fled to the north, where they dwell still. And Cambros divided the conquered lands between himself and his two sons, Ard and Cadlas, and lived in peace.' Looking at Marrock and Fionn, Heb continued. 'And that, Marrock ben Rhagor, is how you came to be standing in this meadow in the realm of Ardan, with Fionn handbound to you.'

Marrock bowed his head in thanks, Brenin calling for a toast, the crowd standing, roaring their approval.

Corban sat in silence a long while, thinking on the story. The conversation between his companions lasted long into the night, families around them slowly drifting back to the village or to their nearby farms and holds. Fires withered and the stars grew brighter.

A murmur of voices grew behind Corban. People were staring into the distance, west, towards Baglun Forest. Corban rose and moved closer for a better look.

A red and orange light flickered far away, rising and falling, like the flame of a candle blown in the breeze.

Gar came to stand next to him.

'What is that?' he asked the stablemaster.

Gar was silent a moment, then cried in a loud voice, 'To horse, to horse!' and broke into his limping run towards the village.

'What is it?' Corban called after him.

'Darol's stockade, boy,' Gar shouted over his shoulder, 'it burns!'

CHAPTER TEN

KASTELL

Kastell's days passed pleasantly as they wound their way towards Halstat. Often Aguila would drop back down the column and ride with him and Maquin awhile, and after the first night Kastell and Maquin sat with the rest of the travellers around a warm fire. Kastell spoke little, but nevertheless enjoyed the sense of belonging, something he had forgotten in the politicking of Mikil. On their fourth day of travel, just after dawn, a rider appeared on the track ahead, riding hard towards them. It was a lone warrior dressed in the insignia of Tenebral, a realm far to the south. He refused to stop and eat with them, saying he carried an urgent message for Romar.

Early on the sixth day, one of the mercenary guards cantered back down the column, to Kastell and Maquin's customary position.

'Chief wants you to ride up front with him,' the warrior said.

'What will you both do, once we reach Halstat and this job is done?' Aguila asked them when Kastell and Maquin joined him.

'Head back to Mikil, I suppose,' Kastell said. 'Why do you ask?'

'If you are not ready to go back, then I could always find work for you, riding with my band.'

'I don't know,' Kastell said, surprised. He had not really thought past Halstat, but the thought of returning to Mikil did not fill him with joy. Life on the road, life without Jael's presence, was good. 'Maybe we will take you up on that offer,' he said, glancing at Maquin.

'I'm in no rush to go back to Mikil,' his shieldman shrugged at him.

Their path had run parallel to Forn Forest for some days. Now it curved back, forced by a sharp-sloped spur that cut a groove towards the forest. Kastell gazed up at the mountains looking like jagged, chipped teeth against the rising sun. Legend told that this range had been formed in the ruin of Elyon's Scourging, when the land was broken and remade. Far to the north, beyond the borders of Forn, it was said that there was league upon league of devastation, fields of ash and great rents in the land itself, chasms that had no end.

The wains followed the path as it inched closer to Forn, until Kastell could make out individual branches swaying in the wind.

Aguila pointed. 'Once we pass that spur, the path turns away from the forest, heads straight into the mountains. We will follow the Danvius from there, as it cuts a road right through to the gates of Halstat.'

'Good,' Kastell said with some feeling, and both Maquin and Aguila chuckled.

As they drew closer to the mountain spur, rising sharp and jagged into the clouds high above, the road dipped into a dell skirting its base. 'This is likely as close to Forn as we'll ever get,' said Maquin as the caravan began the descent into the dell. 'Unless you join those that guard the Dal Gadrai.'

'This is close enough for me,' said Kastell. The Dal Gadrai was a valley cut by a river through Forn Forest, on the eastern borders of their homeland. A group of warriors, all volunteers – as none was ever *sent* there – patrolled the river's edge as it wound through Forn, mostly to guard merchant ships that used the river, but also to act as a bulwark against any forest-dwellers tempted to wander into Isiltir. Only those that had killed one of the Hunen, the giant clan that dwelt still within Forn Forest, were allowed to join the Gadrai, as their troop came to be called. Warriors of the Gadrai often went on to serve as shieldmen of Romar, King of Isiltir.

The road dropped steeply, mist rolling up to meet them, swirling around their horses' hooves. Kastell turned in his saddle, saw it creeping up the wheels of the wains behind. He shivered, suddenly cold.

They rode in silence for a while, the ground levelling beneath them, engulfed by the mist, sound muted. Kastell could only hear the jangle of his own horse's harness, the creak of a wheel behind him, and, more faintly, the trickle of the stream somewhere up ahead.

'I don't like this,' he muttered to himself. Maquin and Aguila were dim forms either side of him.

'Aye, lad,' Maquin grumbled. 'Neither do I.' He dug his heels into his horse's side.

Suddenly there was a hissing sound all about them and, with a wet *thunk* and a blur of motion, Aguila disappeared from his saddle. Screams erupted all around, Maquin and Kastell spinning on their mounts, ducking low, searching for Aguila.

They found him, a spear shaft as thick as Kastell's wrist jutting from his chest. His eyes stared sightlessly, dark blood pooling around his back, running from his mouth. Kastell fell to his knees beside the fallen warrior.

'Quickly, lad!' Maquin shouted. 'You can't help him now.' He spurred his horse towards a cluster of shadows behind them.

Kastell followed, the thought of being left alone in this cursed mist setting a fire beneath his feet.

He burst upon a scene from a nightmare. A horse harnessed to a wain was pinned by a spear to the ground, screaming, eyes rolling white, blood frothing from its mouth. More dead bodies were strewn on the floor, merchants and warriors caught in the rain of spears. Then, out of the dense whiteness came huge shadowy figures. The Hunen. Kastell saw a giant, at least half a man taller than him. Black braided hair framed a snarling, angular face, eyes sunken to dark pits. Kastell gasped as he realized it was a woman, breasts wrapped tight in strips of leather. She came howling into their midst, an axe whirling above her head. Blood sprayed and another man fell to the floor, head and body rolling in different directions. Maquin pulled his arm back and threw, his spear piercing black leather armour, sinking into the giant's shoulder, spinning her. She straightened, plucked it out, looking more angry than injured.

Maquin rode at the giant, slashing with his sword. There was a crash of iron as the Hunen blocked Maquin's strike and lunged forwards with the head of her axe, hurling Maquin from his saddle. Kastell hefted his spear, thought better of it, dug his heels into his horse's flanks instead and charged straight at the massive warrior as she raised her axe above Maquin. Too late she heard the thud of hooves. Kastell held tight to the reins as his horse reared, hooves lashing out, catching the giant in the face, turning it to bloody ruin, sending her crashing to the floor like a felled tree. Kastell stabbed down hard with his spear and Maquin scrabbled on the prone figure, sword rising and falling in a red arc.

Kastell caught Maquin's horse, shook the reins at him. The old warrior was standing over the giant's corpse, nostrils flaring, matted blood making his grey hair dark and slick. He blinked as Kastell thrust the reins into his hand, then shook his head and climbed into his saddle. They were alone again, the sounds of battle still all around, but could see nothing.

'We must find higher ground,' Maquin muttered. Kastell nodded and they struck out together, hoping that they were moving in the right direction. Very soon the land steepened and in a few more moments they burst into sunlight, turning to look back into the dell.

The entire hollow was filled with the treacherous mist, dim figures moving here and there within it. Looking beyond it there was an open space of sunlit meadow before the forest. A handful of men burst from the dell into this space, heading for the treeline, but giants lumbered out of the gloom and fell howling upon them, hacking until none was left standing.

'We must leave,' Maquin said quietly. 'And quickly, before we are seen. Our horses can outrun the Hunen in a sprint, but they are like hounds. If they spot us and decide to chase they could follow us for nights without end.'

'But . . .' Kastell began. Every sense within him screamed to run, to turn his horse and gallop as fast as he could from this place of madness and blood, but something kept him from doing it. 'But we were supposed to protect them.'

'Aye, lad,' Maquin growled, 'but there is no one left *to* protect down there. Listen.'

He was right, the sounds of battle were gone. Kastell heard the whinny of a dying horse, the squawking of crows that circled greedily above, smelling blood even if they could not see it, but nothing else. The silence was almost as frightening as the earlier sounds of battle. He nodded and they wheeled their horses, kicking them towards the track they had ridden in on.

A fierce baying caused Kastell to rein his horse in and stare back down into the dell.

The mist was evaporating now, the bodies of horses and men

scattered about the wains in bloody ruin, the stream flowing a sickly pink. Giants were clustered about a wain, hacking at the crates piled upon it. Suddenly a great cry rose up from them, one reaching into the crate, pulling something out and brandishing it in the air. It glinted in the sunlight.

Maquin hissed. 'The starstone axe.'

'What? How?' Kastell gasped.

'Damned if I know,' Maquin said.

A strange-sounding horn blast rose from the dell, and a cold shaft of fear spiked into Kastell's gut. They had been seen: at least a score of the Hunen breaking into a loping run up the mountain track after them.

Kastell exchanged a glance with Maquin and they wheeled their horses and spurred them up the path.

'Careful!' Maquin shouted over the drum of their horses' hooves. 'If we press for the gallop our mounts will be blowing before high-sun. This pace is faster than the Hunen can manage, so stick to it, put some distance between us and them, hope they give up the chase.'

'But, you said . . .'

'I know what I said, boy,' Maquin growled back.

Kastell breathed deep, holding the panic at bay and focused on the track in front of him.

They rode in silence, the only sound the drumming of hooves and the blasts of air blowing from the horses' nostrils. As the sun passed its highest point they splashed into a stream that ran across their path. They reined in their horses and climbed out of their saddles, filling their water skins, giving the horses a chance to drink and rest.

Maquin drank deeply. He stood staring at the road behind them, then suddenly sprang towards his horse.

'On your feet, the Hunen are coming.'

The old warrior was not someone to be argued with, particularly as he appeared now, with giant's blood drying black on his hair and face. Kastell looked towards the horizon and saw a mass of lumbering shapes come into view. Quickly he mounted up, sweat drying salt-white in his horse's coat and set off again.

Their horses settled into a steady canter on the wide track. Occasionally Kastell glanced over his shoulder, sometimes catching a flicker of movement at the edge of his vision. As the sun sank into the horizon before them, their shadows stretching far behind, Maquin called another halt.

'How was the axe on that wain?' Kastell said.

'Stolen by Aguila's employer, is my guess,' Maquin shrugged.

'But the Hunen – how did they know it was there?'

'I don't know, lad. Foul magic?' He shrugged.

'How did we ever beat them?' Kastell asked.

'We?'

'Mankind. How did we ever beat the giants?' The black-haired giant that had almost killed Maquin stood clear in his mind's eye.

'Hard to believe, eh,' Maquin said. 'Truth be told, although the old tales tell of great deeds of valour, I suspect it came down to numbers. There were more of us than them. That and the pride of the giants. They looked down on us, never considering us a real danger. There's a lesson there. Even if you're as strong and fierce as a giant, never underestimate a foe.' He hawked and spat. 'So, lad, you going to join the Gadrai now?'

Kastell looked at him, confused.

'You killed a giant. I'll speak as witness. I saw you do it with my own eyes.'

Kastell snorted. 'Giantess,' he corrected. 'And if they give a place to anyone in the Gadrai, it should probably go to my horse.' He patted its trembling flank. 'It was him that killed the giant, though you made sure of it.'

'Just didn't want her getting back up,' Maquin said with a quick smile. 'Took grit, what you did, lad. And you saved my life. I won't be forgetting that.'

Kastell looked away, embarrassed. 'What do you think our chances are?'

Maquin was silent a long while. 'I do not think they'll follow us much past the Rhenus. If we can cross the river into Isiltir, they will likely give up the chase. As they have followed us this far I doubt they will stop before then.'

'But we have travelled five days since the Rhenus,' Kastell said, trying to keep the fear from his voice.

'Aye, true enough; but that was at a different speed, with wains setting the pace. Already we have crossed ground that it took almost two days to cover with the wains.' He pulled a face. 'But the horses are tiring; we have ridden them too hard. We must travel through the night if there is to be a chance of living till the morrow, but it will be slower going. My guess is that, if the Hunen have not caught us by highsun tomorrow, we will be in sight of the river. *If* we travel through the night *and* if the horses have not died beneath us.'

'What good is sleep if it means a spear up your arse?' said Kastell. Maquin nodded grimly.

They ate some salted meat, washing it down with water.

'Mount up. Let's see if we can live to see the sun rise.'

The night passed in a daze for Kastell, the horses slowing to an exhausted walk for most of it. He dozed fitfully many times, only to jerk awake as he started to slip from the saddle, and more than once he put out a hand to stop the same happening to Maquin. He thanked Elyon in mumbled prayers through the night for keeping the sky clear, so that the moon and stars shone bright, giving light enough to see the mountain track. Dawn came unnoticed, the sky greying, turning a deep blue before they realized the night was over. Maquin would not let them stop yet, though. A thick mist covered the meadows below, forming a grey mantle up to the feet of the forest. Maquin eyed it suspiciously and kept his mount moving doggedly forward.

The sun was hot on their backs, the mist below burned away when they eventually did stop, almost falling from their saddles. Kastell tried to check for followers, but the sun was low in the sky, and blinded him as he squinted back along the mountain path.

'Drink,' Maquin muttered, pouring some water into a cupped hand and giving it to his horse.

Kastell checked behind him again. Black forms materialized out of the bright sun, closer, much closer than he had thought possible. He grabbed Maquin's arm, squawking a warning.

'Ride!' Maquin yelled and shoved Kastell towards his horse.

They kicked their mounts mercilessly, urging them into full gallop, all thoughts of pacing lost as death closed in behind them. Panic rose bubbling in Kastell and he shouted at his mount, urging it on. They crested a ridge and he saw a flash in the distance, the Rhenus curling away from the mountains, then the track fell into a shallow dip before another ridge and the river disappeared.

Something screamed behind him, followed by a crash. He twisted in his saddle, saw Maquin lying on the ground, his horse behind him, its foreleg twisted impossibly beneath it. He turned his mount, rode back to Maquin, who was scrambling to his feet, dirt and blood caking one side of his face. One look at his mount showed it would not be getting up.

'His leg's broken,' said Maquin. Kastell offered his hand and Maquin grabbed it, swinging into the saddle behind Kastell. His horse danced on the spot, its legs trembling. Kastell cursed and kicked and the horse began to move, but not much faster than a walk. They travelled only a few paces, then Maquin swore and slipped to the ground.

'Ride, boy,' he said to Kastell. 'If one of us makes it, it will be something.' Kastell stared silently back at him. 'Ride on, lad,' Maquin grunted as he calmly strapped his helmet on. 'Go *now*,' Maquin urged, ''fore it's too late for you as well. Did you see the river?' Kastell nodded. 'With the time I buy you here, there is still hope. There is no shame in this, lad. *Live*.'

For a moment Kastell sat there, thoughts swirling through his mind in an exhausted jumble, then he shook his head and climbed off his horse. 'Can't get rid of me that easily,' he mumbled.

Maquin smiled grimly. 'Then give me your spear at least. I left mine in a giant, and you could'na hit the broadside of a ship at ten paces.'

Kastell grinned. He passed his spear to Maquin, unstrapped his shield. His horse was exhausted, certainly no use in the fight to come. He slapped it hard on the flank, sending it trotting up the incline and disappearing over the ridge.

The men stood shoulder to shoulder as the Hunen crested the ridge they had just crossed. Kastell felt a stab of fear in his belly, his bowels turning to water as the giants saw them and began howling strange, ululating cries. Then they fell silent, their iron-shod feet thudding on the ground. Kastell tried to count them. At least a score, maybe more, it was hard to tell; the women amongst them only discernible by the lack of moustaches and beards. Sunshine glinted on iron as they pulled axes and hammers from straps on their backs.

He heard a whisper beside him, saw Maquin, eyes closed, lips moving. Then his eyes snapped open, arm drawing back, whipping forwards, Kastell's spear flying into the air. It rose and fell in a fluid arc. A giant stumbled, fell and did not rise again.

Kastell's sword hissed from its scabbard. With a blade in his hand he felt a different person, no longer clumsy. He vowed to take at least one of these monsters with him across the bridge of swords. In the distance behind him he heard a rumble, as of thunder, and glanced up at the sky, but it was a clear blue. The giants were close enough to make out individual features. Black leather armour covered them, wrapped about them in strange patterns. Tattoos spiralled their arms, dark eyes glowered in pale faces, all framed with braided black hair, the males with long drooping moustaches.

The giants swept around Maquin's fallen horse. Kastell muttered a last prayer to Elyon and raised his sword. Thunder sounded again, louder. This time, instead of fading, it grew, and suddenly Maquin was shoving him out of the track. He fell and rolled in the gravel, cursing a protest. The rumbling grew until the ground shook, and Kastell realized it was not coming from the sky, but from beyond the ridge behind them. Horses suddenly crested it, sweeping down like a great wave, and riding at their head, in a coat of gleaming mail, was his uncle. Like an avenging angel from the time before the Scourging, Romar had come.

CHAPTER ELEVEN

CORBAN

Corban clung to Gar as they rode down the giantsway. He could hear more than he could see, as his face was filled with the stablemaster's billowing cloak. An orange glow flickered about them, light from the torches that many had lit on the way to Darol's hold, but nevertheless the journey in the dark was slow and tedious and he had no way of knowing how much longer it would take them to reach the stockade, for the company rode in grim silence. All he could hear was the thud of hooves on the ancient road. *Still, at least I'm here*, he thought, remembering how he had pleaded with Gar to take him.

'How far?' he said into Gar's back, not for the first time, but the stablemaster was silent. He repeated himself, a little louder.

'Not long,' Gar grunted, 'and I swear, if you ask me that question again, I shall throw you from my horse.'

Corban pulled a sour face but chose to say nothing. Dylan's face flashed into his mind again, where it had been almost permanently since he had seen the hold burning. Many had run to the stables at Gar's call, and Corban was riding in a party at least two score strong, including Brenin the King. He sighed and clung tighter to Gar.

After what seemed an eternity he felt Gar's piebald, Hammer, turn and begin to climb a slope. They had arrived. The sky around him grew lighter, and at first he thought that dawn had crept up unannounced, but then he heard the crackling of flames, smelt the smoke and realized that the light was from Darol's hold, burning.

The riders pulled to a halt and Corban slipped off, gasping as he looked around. Tongues of flame licked the stockade walls, curling into the dark sky above. A dark hole gaped amidst the flames, billows of black smoke issuing from the open gateway.

Brenin marched up the remainder of the hill, shieldmen rushing to form a half-circle before him.

'Try not to call attention to yourself, you're not supposed to be here,' Gar whispered. Corban nodded, knowing that only those who had come through their warrior trials and the Long Night should have ridden with the King. Not even the likes of Rafe, who now trained in the Rowan Field, had been permitted to join them.

Clouds of smoke enveloped him as he stepped through the open gateway. Mingled with the smell of burning wood was a sweeter, sicklier scent that stuck at the back of his throat. Buildings within the stockade were not burning as fiercely, little left of them but charred beams where the feast-hall and stables had once been.

Brenin knelt in the middle of the yard, a handful of warriors about him. Then the King stood and strode on. Corban sidled forward to see what had held Brenin's attention.

A figure lay on the floor. It was Darol. A dark stain spread around his stomach. His fingers, bloody and twisted, were fixed in the earth, grasping, gouging.

There was a call from up ahead. A warrior was standing next to a black mound in what had been the feast-hall, prising it apart with the butt end of his spear. Someone else went to help, one of the brothers that had ridden into the village the night before, then others were crowding round, obscuring Corban's view. He forgot about not calling attention to himself, and shoved his way through the massed warriors until he stood starring at the dissected mound, his boots blackened with soft ash.

On the ground before him were figures, black and twisted from the fire. The smell hit Corban like a blow and snatched his breath away, stomach lurching. He counted five, all of them burned beyond recognition, one much smaller than the rest: Frith. He couldn't tell which one was Dylan, but he knew his friend was there. His stomach lurched again and tears sprang to his eyes. He rubbed them away, dimly aware he was standing amidst the pride of Dun Carreg's warriors. He turned and stumbled away, falling to his knees, and vomited onto the ash-covered yard.

A hand rested on his shoulder. He blinked away stinging tears and saw Thannon. His da lifted him effortlessly from the ground. 'You shouldn't be here, Ban,' he growled.

'Dylan . . .' Corban mumbled, then Thannon pulled him close. He couldn't seem to stop his shoulders shaking. They stood like that a while, warriors moving about the enclosure, sifting through the ash. Eventually Corban pulled away. Gar joined them as Corban rubbed his eyes, smearing ash across his face.

'Brenin has just sent people to scout around the hill, see if they can find any clues as to what happened here.'

'What do *you* think happened?' Corban asked.

'Blood-feud or thievery, what else?' growled Thannon.

'My guess is lawless men,' said Gar. 'There have been rumours that some of Braith's outlaw band from the Darkwood have travelled east, burning and thieving on their way. The Baglun is not as large as the Darkwood, but it is still a tempting place for them to dwell.'

'Apart from the wolven, and being so close to Brenin,' said Thannon.

Gar shrugged. 'There are wolven in the Darkwood too. Do you think this is the result of a blood-feud? Do you think Darol had enemies that would do this?'

Thannon sighed, shaking his head. 'Just don't like the thought of it: lawless men so close to home.'

Noise drifted up from beyond the gates. A string of wains had arrived, filled with people from the village and fortress. Many were carrying tools of some description, from buckets to shovels. Corban spotted his mam and sister hurrying up the hill towards them. Gwenith ran to him and took his hand.

'Dylan's dead . . .' he mumbled, feeling a lump swell in his throat, fresh tears forming. Gwenith tried to pull him into an embrace as villagers passed them by, but he stepped away.

The newly arrived villagers set to work, pilling up charred timber, shovelling ash, sifting through the debris. The rest of the morning passed quickly. Corban climbed onto the back of Gar's piebald again and went with the stablemaster to the river, where many were already hard at work, including Brenin. They tore down Darol's salmon traps and piled wains high with rocks from the riverbed to build a cairn.

Back at the stockade the stones were unloaded from the wains, a large stone cairn built around the bodies of Darol and his family on the brow of the hill. The final stones were laid in place as the sinking sun began to melt into the horizon. Then Brenin stepped forward.

'Most here knew Darol and his family. They were good people, they and their children. Lawless men struck here last night.' He beckoned to Marrock.

'We found two sets of tracks,' the huntsman said, 'one set coming from the forest, one set returning, about a dozen horses strong. Some climbed the wall and opened the gate for the others, I believe. Darol heard and came out and was slain. The others were killed inside the feast-hall. We followed their trail a way into the Baglun before it disappeared.' He grimaced and beckoned to the crowd. One of the brothers that Corban had met on the road the night before, the older, sterner one, stepped forward.

'Halion found this.' Marrock nodded to the man, who held his arm out, showing them a pearl necklace that Corban had seen worn by Elin, Dylan's sister.

Brenin drew his sword. 'A dark thing has been done here,' he growled. 'This I pledge: I will not allow thieves and murderers to do as they please in Ardan, let alone on my very doorstep. Darol and his family will have justice. Blood will be shed by the guilty; I swear it on my father's sword, and seal it with my blood.' He clenched his fist around the blade, a thin red line running down its edge, then slammed the sword back into its scabbard.

The next morning, Corban woke and for a moment felt normal, then the weight of memory fell upon him. Dylan. The fire. Tears formed in his eyes and he would have turned over and tried to sleep again but Gwenith must have heard him moving, for she bustled into his room and pulled his blanket off. She sat beside him, running her fingers through his hair, leaned over and gently kissed his cheek. 'Come and break your fast.'

Corban picked at a honey-cake and a mug of milk for a while. 'Where's Cywen?' he asked.

'At the stables with Gar.' His mam looked at him out of the corner of her eye. 'Your da said he needs you in the forge today.'

Corban stood with a sigh. 'I'll go and find him.'

Thannon told him that he was not needed until highsun. Corban made for Dath's home. Bethan answered when he knocked.

'Dath's out with Da,' she said.

'Huh,' he muttered, shuffling his feet.

'They sailed with the tide, just after sun-up,' Bethan offered.

'Oh,' said Corban, and began to walk away.

'Corban,' she called after him, 'you were close, to Darol's family, weren't you?'

'I was.'

She took a step closer and squeezed his hand. 'Brenin will catch them,' she said.

With a sigh he walked away.

The meadow that had been so full of people and noise two days before was almost empty. Corban saw a tall figure with a large hound on the far side of the meadow, loading up a wain.

Talar's ears pricked forward as Corban ran over to Ventos, who was hefting a large sheepskin bundle.

'You're going, then,' Corban said.

'Aye, lad, I have goods to sell. I hope to have travelled most of Ardan before midsummer. A sad business yesterday. You knew the family well?'

'Aye. Especially Dylan. Darol's son.' His eyes misted. 'Thank you for helping.'

'This is a good place,' Ventos grunted. 'Good people. It's not everywhere in the Banished Lands that you would see so many help as they did yesterday.'

'Murder does not happen, here,' Corban mumbled. He had heard of the crimes of lawless men, knew that holds had been torched closer to the Darkwood, but living at the fortress, things like that were always a tale, something never seen.

Ventos nodded. 'You have a good king, keeping such things at bay. Much worse happens elsewhere. I do not doubt he will catch and judge those that committed this crime. Come, help me finish loading.' He wiped sweat from his face.

After they had piled up the wain, the trader climbed into the bench seat at the front. A sturdy-looking pony was harnessed to the wain, and another, heavily loaded, was roped to the tailgate.

'Stay clear of the Baglun,' Corban said as the trader picked up his driving reins.

'Don't fear for me, lad; I have Talar to look after me.' He cracked the reins and the pony pulled away, Ventos flashing a wide smile and waving as he rode towards the giantsway, Talar trotting steadily alongside. Corban stood watching as the trader disappeared into the horizon. Then he looked up at the sun and cursed, breaking into a run towards the fortress.

Buddai raised his head to look at Corban as he ran up, jumped over the hound and through the forge's doorway. He leaned against the timber frame and drank great gulps of air, chest rising and falling much like the bellows being pumped by Thannon's hand.

'You're late,' his da said, the glow of the furnace illuminating him in a stark contrast of shadow and light. He was stripped to the waist, an auroch-hide apron covering his bull chest and stomach. The smell of burning hair lingered in the air, where sparks had leaped from his hammer and singed either his beard or thick forearms.

'Sorry, Da,' Corban managed in between ragged breaths.

'No matter. Although a man should do as he says,' Thannon said with a stern look. 'I need you to strike for me. Torin has asked for half a dozen scythes.' He looked at Corban, who was still leaning against the doorframe. '*Now*, lad. We have to draw this iron out before it cools.'

Corban slipped his pitted leather apron on and took the hammer that Thannon was waving at him. A thick length of iron was held in long tongs on the anvil, glowing white hot, a dark honeycomb running through it. Corban knew what to do, and the hammer began to ring as he beat the metal, incandescent sparks flying as impurities were slowly coaxed and beaten from the iron.

The rest of the afternoon passed in a blur of heat and ringing noise, and occasionally frozen moments of the previous day would form in his mind. It was a shock when he found his raised arm enveloped by Thannon's huge paw of a hand.

'Ban, we're finished for the day,' his da was saying, looking at him with a worried expression. Corban blinked, hung the hammer with the other tools and began to rake out the furnace, banking the day's half-burned charcoal around the edges.

As the two of them left the forge, the cool air of early evening making Corban's sweaty skin tingle, a horse and rider clattered up the cobbled path that led towards the fortress' stables. On the rider's shield was an emblem Corban had never seen before.

A white eagle on a black field.

CHAPTER TWELVE

VERADIS

Searing heat flashed all about Veradis as he leaped through the wall of flames and rolled into the shallow stream, smelling burned hair, leather, flesh. He was dripping, steam smoking from patches all over him. He did not pause to assess the damage done by the flames, just hurled his spear straight at the chest of the giant that was still holding a sword to Nathair.

Somehow, moving faster than Veradis could track, the giant swung his great blade. There was a crack, and two parts of his shattered spear spun away in different directions.

The giant made no move towards him, just stared with emotionless, black eyes. Veradis scowled and drew his sword with a hiss.

'No, Veradis!' Nathair shouted, but Veradis was already moving. He circled to his right, tucking behind his shield, moving in quickly. The giant swung two-handed at him, but Veradis ducked low, felt the blade whistle over his head, then lunged forwards. The tip of his sword slid off the giant's mail shirt, no power in the blow as the giant stepped backwards. Instead of retreating out of range, Veradis carried on moving forwards, trying to stay too close for that broadsword to be used against him. He rammed his shield into the giant's gut, chopped his sword at an ankle.

The giant grunted as his blade bit, though not deeply, and Veradis felt a moment of elation before his shield rim was grabbed by a huge hand and ripped from his arm, the leather straps snapping. There was an explosion in his chest, a blinding pain and then he was flying through the air, crunching into the ground, rolling, then his face smashed into something solid. White lights burst in his head.

'You fight well, little man,' the giant said as it took great strides towards him, the traces of a smile twitching its drooping moustache, voice sounding like an iron hinge rusted from lack of use.

Veradis tried to push himself up, groping blindly with his other hand for his sword hilt, which had somehow disappeared. A black fog was pushing at the edges of his vision, drawing in. He tried to focus, concentrate, knew death was a stride, a heartbeat away.

Then Nathair was there, standing over him, sword drawn.

'Hold!' a voice cried, somewhere beyond the giant. Veradis pushed against the ground but the pain in his head exploded with the effort, then he was falling, sinking, and he knew no more.

Pain. Rhythmic, throbbing pain. Tentatively Veradis opened his eyes, sharp knives jabbing into his skull, sending waves of nausea pulsing from his stomach.

Where am I? Nathair.

He moved, too fast, pain spiking behind his eyes. He took a deep breath, blew it out slowly and waited for the world to steady.

'You live, then.' It was Rauca, looming over him. The warrior put a hand under his arm and helped him semi-upright, leaning against the trunk of a laurel.

'Nathair?' Veradis muttered.

'In that tent,' Rauca nodded over his shoulder.

They were still in the dell, Veradis in the shade of laurels beside the stream. He saw warriors scattered around about, some silhouetted on the ridge-line, standing guard. The dark-haired giant stood in front of the entrance to the bright-coloured tent.

'What happened?'

'You mean after you tried to set yourself on fire?' Rauca said, squatting next to him, grinning.

'Huh,' grunted Veradis.

'Well, as far as I could see, you chopped away at that giant for a while, then he clumped you, sent you flying into these trees . . .'

'I remember that,' Veradis muttered, lifting a hand to his face, his nose, which was throbbing, sticky with blood.

'Then it looked like the giant was going to stick you with his sword, but Nathair put himself between you both.' Rauca grinned again. 'Weren't *you* supposed to be protecting *him*?'

Veradis flushed red. 'Things didn't go according to plan. What happened next?'

'Well, the old man got involved then, calmed the giant down. It seems the whole thing – the flames, the giant, the sword – were about making a point.'

'A point?'

'Aye. That Nathair was in their power, and that if they'd *wished* to harm him, they could have.'

'Oh. But they didn't.'

'No. As I said, that was their point. Nathair seemed convinced by it, anyway, because after he saw you were still breathing, he has spent the entire time in that tent, with the counsellor.'

Veradis looked at the tent, at the giant guarding the entrance, and grimaced. 'What of the fire?' He remembered it leaping up from the small cook-fire, becoming a searing wall.

'I don't know,' Rauca shrugged. 'I've heard tales of those that can do such things. Elementals?' he whispered.

'So have I,' Veradis muttered, shivering.

Rauca helped him upright, supported him over to the stream and assisted him, with much groaning and bursts of pain, in removing his chainmail shirt. He hurt in a score of places: where he had fallen, where he had hit the tree, patches of raw skin that the flames had singed, but two spots hurt the most. There was a dense purple bruise blooming where the giant had punched him in his chest, though his mail shirt seemed to have protected him from broken bones, and his nose still throbbed where he had connected with a tree.

'It's broken,' Rauca proclaimed, with too much pleasure for Veradis' liking. 'Shall I set it for you, or would you rather stay look-ing like one of Asroth's Kadoshim?'

'Set it,' Veradis grunted, unclasping his leather belt and biting down on it.

Rauca placed both hands either side of the bridge of Veradis' nose, then twisted them suddenly. There was a muffled crack. Veradis gasped and bit down hard. He cupped a handful of water from the stream and washed away the fresh blood that gushed from his nose.

'My thanks,' he grunted as Rauca crouched beside him.

'You're welcome,' his friend grinned, patting his shoulder.

They made camp in the dell that night, Nathair not emerging as the sun dipped below the horizon and the sky slowly turned to black velvet, with stars like shards of ice.

Orcus maintained a guard on the ridge, and set another group to watch over the tent and giant all through the night.

Veradis woke stiff and sore.

Quietly the warband broke their fast, waiting for their prince. Soon after, the giant, still standing guard, lifted the tent's entrance, Nathair and the silver-haired man emerging into the daylight.

Nathair sought out Orcus, then the warband were making ready to leave. As they did so the giant dismantled the tent, the old man standing with arms folded, eyes fixed on Nathair.

As they went about the business of breaking camp Nathair saw Veradis and marched over to him, grinning broadly.

'I am glad you are well,' the Prince said, gripping Veradis' shoulder. 'I shall never forget what you did.'

'It was you that saved *me*, from what I hear,' Veradis said.

'That's true,' Nathair grinned. 'Nevertheless, you jumped through flames for me, Veradis, did what no other even attempted . . .' The Prince shook his head. 'It won't be forgotten.'

In a short while all was ready. Nathair spoke with the counsellor again, taking a leather scroll-case from the silver-haired man. Veradis stood at the Prince's shoulder, his eyes drawn to the giant, who towered half a man over them all, glowering. He was clothed in dark leather and chainmail, a tattoo of vine and thorns swirling up his left arm and part-way down his right, the hilt of his broadsword jutting over his shoulder. His face was human enough, though all sharp planes and ridges. A drooping moustache was tied with leather strips. Suddenly its black eyes fixed on Veradis. He looked away.

'Safe journey,' the old man said and gripped Nathair's forearm in the warrior fashion.

'Until we meet again.'

'Until we meet again,' the counsellor echoed, and then they parted, Nathair leading his warband up the steep slope and down the other side.

Soon they were mounted and riding north along the banks of the Nox, Orcus taking the lead, along with a handful of the eagle-guard. Nathair rode with his own men, Veradis and Rauca either side of him.

Nathair had not spoken since leaving the dell. 'I have negotiated a peace,' he said suddenly, startling Veradis.

Rauca frowned at the Prince.

'I know it will be a shock for most, but its impact will be significant, I think.'

'Shock. Many will struggle, Nathair.' Veradis had grown up along the coast, and although the Vin Thalun had been quiet for over a decade, their reputation remained. And recently the raiding had begun again.

'Nevertheless, it is for the greater good,' Nathair said.

'But how can you trust them?' Rauca muttered.

'I don't. But they did prove their point,' the Prince said. 'They could have slain me, if they wished. They clearly *want* me to trust them. Why, we shall find out. And a great deal of what they said is true – an alliance would be useful. There is much that could be accomplished with their aid. I will use them as they seek to use me.'

'Just be careful,' Veradis said, glancing at Rauca.

'Of course,' Nathair grinned. 'Friends close and enemies closer, eh.'

'Did he tell you his name?' Veradis asked.

'Aye. Calidus,' Nathair said quietly, almost a whisper. 'It is not to be mentioned. Apparently he and my father had some kind of disagreement, many years ago. I would not have my father reject all I have achieved because of a name.' He looked at Rauca and Veradis. 'I will have your oaths on this.'

'Of course,' Rauca said. Veradis nodded.

Nathair smiled suddenly, nodding to himself. 'As I said, it is for the greater good.'

The black walls of Jerolin glinted in the bright sun as Veradis crested a low rise, saw the fortress and lake before him, on the horizon the Agullas Mountains a serrated line separating land from sky.

The journey back had been uneventful, the warband making good time, and all were relieved to escape the heat of the south. It was still hot here, in the north of Tenebral, but it was tempered by a breeze that blew down from the mountains.

Fisher-boats and larger merchant rigs bobbed on the lake as the warband rode past the palisaded walls of the village by the lake and up a slope to the fortress. The eagle-banner of Tenebral snapped in the wind, and with a clatter on stone they were through the wide-arched gates and dismounting at the stables.

All was chaos, stablehands and warriors and horses crushed together. Veradis saw Valyn trying to bring some semblance of order to the situation, his voice raised over a cacophony of sounds. Then King Aquilus and Queen Fidele were there, flanked by warriors, and the stables noticeably calmed.

Fidele ran to Nathair and hugged him tight, the Prince looking stiff in her embrace, eyes searching for his father. Aquilus stood further back and greeted his son more soberly. The King called Orcus, and the four of them left, heading towards the feast-hall and tower beyond.

A good while later Veradis followed Rauca and Bos into the feast-hall. Bos slammed a jug of wine on the table. He poured three cups and drained his in one motion.

'I can see how you got so big,' Rauca said, looking at Bos' overflowing trencher. Bos shrugged and continued eating.

Veradis tucked in to his food, sitting back when he was finished and pushing his empty plate away. He sipped on his cup of wine and looked around the half-empty hall.

'Is that Peritus?' he asked quietly, looking at a group of warriors on the far side of the hall. Sitting in their centre was a slim-built older man, of average height, his close-cropped hair and single warrior braid not hiding his thinning hair.

'Aye,' Bos grunted.

'I thought so,' Veradis said. He had seen Aquilus' battlechief once before, but that had been at least eight summers gone, and he had only been ten years old at the time. Peritus had led a warband to his home town and helped his father deal with a band of lawless men that had taken root in Tenebral's greatest forest.

'He arrived this morning,' Rauca said, 'not long before us. With only half the warband he set out with.'

'What happened?' Veradis asked.

'Giants. They've been raiding south of the mountains. Local barons prodded at Marcellin; he prodded Aquilus; Aquilus sent Peritus.'

'Only half came back? I didn't know there were enough of the giant clan left to do that,' Veradis said, thinking of Balara, the ruined fortress that sat crumbling near his home. Tenebral was full of reminders of the giants, but the giant clan had been broken, scattered generations before; or so he had thought.

'Don't need to be too many of them to do a lot of damage,' Bos said. 'My da served under Marcellin before he took up the eagle here, said you need at least four handy warriors to be sure of taking one giant down.'

'Not if your name's Veradis,' Rauca said. 'He'll take them on one on one.' The warrior grinned and cracked his cup of wine into Veradis', spilling red liquid on the table. Veradis scowled.

Just then a small group of warriors entered the hall, Armatus, the weapons-master, at their head. He saw Peritus and strode over to the battlechief. They embraced, thumping each other on the back.

'They grew up in the same village,' Rauca said. 'Came to Jerolin together to join the warband, back when Aquilus was the Prince.'

Soft footsteps sounded behind them and stopped next to Veradis. He looked around, saw Fidele standing above him. The Queen's face was pale, highlighting her red-painted lips; touches of silver showed in her jet hair.

The three warriors made to rise but she held a hand out and rested it on Veradis' shoulder.

'I heard what you did for my son.'

Veradis felt he should say something and opened his mouth, but nothing came out.

'I wanted to thank you,' Fidele continued. 'He needs good men around him. Men like you.'

'Thank you,' Veradis mumbled, feeling heat in his face.

Fidele smiled, squeezed his shoulder and walked away.

'Brave you might be,' Rauca said, 'but eloquent you certainly are not.'

Bos chuckled and Veradis blushed redder.

The next ten-night passed quickly for Veradis, life falling into a routine, most of his time spent in training with Nathair's fledgling warband. The Prince was rarely with them, though. Upon his return Nathair had outlined their journey and the meeting with Lykos' counsellor to Aquilus, detailing the treaty proposed by the

Vin Thalun. Aquilus had not been as enthusiastic as Nathair had hoped, though, taking days to deliberate over the proposal. So when Veradis had last seen Nathair the Prince had been tense and short tempered.

The warband, though small, continued to grow: any that came to the fortress hoping to serve as a warrior for the King of Tenebral being offered the choice of joining Nathair's band instead. On the eighth morning since their return from the south, Veradis was in the weapons court, sweating heavily after sparing with Bos, his knuckles red and stinging from a glancing blow. He had won the bout, though, and was quickly getting a reputation amongst Jerolin's warriors. On more than one occasion he had noticed weapons-master Armatus watching him approvingly.

As he sat watching others train, letting the sun dry his sweat, footsteps sounded behind him. He turned and saw Nathair striding towards him, grinning broadly.

'It is done, Father has agreed,' the Prince said, clapping Veradis' shoulder.

'That is good,' Veradis said, though years of mistrust where the Vin Thalun were concerned dampened his enthusiasm.

'Our prisoner Deinon will take the answer to Lykos.'

'Aquilus not separating his head from his shoulders, then?' Veradis said.

'Of course not. That would not be the best way to begin a new alliance,' Nathair grinned.

Voices and footsteps rang behind them. King Aquilus strode past the court, Deinon and two eagle-guards behind him.

Nathair watched them for a moment, then followed, signalling for Veradis to accompany him. They caught up at the stables, where Deinon was mounting a horse, as were the two eagle-guards. With a brief farewell the Vin Thalun rode away, the scroll-case strapped safely inside a saddlebag. The eagle-guards fell in behind the corsair and rode with him from the fortress.

'Walk with me,' Aquilus said to his son. He strode away, Nathair and Veradis following.

They walked in silence a while, Aquilus leading them until they stood upon the battlements, looking out across the lake and plains beyond. Deinon and his escort were pinpricks in the distance, now.

'Why the warrior escort, Father?' Nathair asked. 'It is a simple enough journey to the coast.'

'They are to make sure he *reaches* the coast, Nathair, that he does not linger, or take any detours. I do not trust him. I do not trust *them*.

'For generations the Vin Thalun have raided our coasts, along with the coasts of our neighbours. And now, suddenly, they want to make peace, form an *alliance*, and with us only. Why not Tarbesh, or Carnutan? Why Tenebral? Meical thinks the timing of this is more than coincidence. I agree with him.'

Nathair's face clouded. 'Counsellor Meical.' He snorted. 'I don't trust the Vin Thalun either, Father. But they are useful, that is beyond doubt. We must be wary, that is all.'

'Aye, son. You must bait a trap well to catch your prey. I would know *what* the Vin Thalun seek to achieve. This seems the best way to do that.' He pinched the bridge of his nose. 'You have done well, but these are dangerous times. War is coming, and we must be vigilant . . .'

War, Veradis thought. He was still tracking the departing Vin Thalun when he saw a large group of horsemen on the road, riding towards the fortress. 'Who are they?' he said.

The three of them stared in silence until the approaching horsemen were almost at the gates. They were a party of forty or fifty warriors, carrying a banner that Veradis had never seen before, a sickle moon in a star-filled sky.

'So it begins,' Aquilus said quietly. 'They carry the banner of Tarbesh. I believe it is Rahim, Tarbesh's King. The first to answer my call to council.'

CHAPTER THIRTEEN

CORBAN

'Where do you think he's from, Mam?' Cywen asked. Corban was picking at a bowl of porridge, stirring a spoonful of honey into swirling shapes. Gwenith frowned at Thannon absently as she sat in front of the hearth, toasting bread on a long fork.

Gwenith sighed. 'I don't know, though doubtless you don't believe me, because if you've asked me once you've asked me five score times.'

'Someone must know,' said Cywen despairingly. 'Da?'

'Sorry,' mumbled Thannon over a mouthful of honey-cake.

'A white eagle on the shield. That's what you said, Ban, wasn't it.'

'Aye.'

'Who's sign is that?'

'We'll eat in the feast-hall tonight. Maybe Brenin will announce who his visitor is over the evening meal,' said Gwenith, sliding another thick piece of toasted bread onto a plate in front of everybody. Belying his size, Thannon snatched it first, and smiled to himself as he spread a thick scoop of butter on it. Cywen was silent, her nose crinkling in that familiar way when she was thinking.

'You're probably right, but that's *ages* away.'

'Patience, lass,' said Thannon, leaning contentedly back in his chair, rubbing his belly. Corban frowned. That was one phrase that he really found objectionable, as it usually meant *shut up*, or *let's change the subject*. By the look on Cywen's face she was thinking something similar.

'C'mon, lad, let's get the fire lit. More scythes to make today.'

Corban grimaced. His shoulder was aching from yesterday's

hard work, and a particularly painful blister was throbbing in the crease where his thumb met his hand.

'Oh, I forgot,' Cywen said, 'Gar told me he needs to speak to you today, Ban. I'm going straight to his stables – walk with me, eh, go to the forge after? If that is all right with you, Da.'

'Aye, that'd be fine. I'll see you after, Ban,' said Thannon, standing and brushing crumbs from his tunic. He strode from the kitchen, his hound Buddai following. Corban and Cywen left soon after, leaving their mother still sitting by the fire, staring into the crackling flames in the hearth.

'What does Gar want?' Corban asked Cywen. He was back on speaking terms with her now. The horror of Dylan's death had at least caused him to reassess the gravity of Cywen's impulsive crime.

'I don't know. I did ask, but he wouldn't tell me. He can be very close-mouthed sometimes.'

'Huh,' Corban grunted in agreement.

The stables were a massive building of wood and thatch. The giant Benothi had of course not ridden horses, and so had not built stables, thus Ard had had to build his own amongst the stone buildings of the old fortress.

They found stablemaster Gar in the paddocks near the stables with the roan colt that Cywen had bought at the Spring Fair. He had the colt's foreleg balanced across his knee and was applying some kind of salve, digging it out of a pot with his fingertips, plastering it liberally on the cut where Cywen had removed the thorn. Corban and Cywen stood quietly by while he finished bandaging the hoof, Corban wrinkling his nose at the smell of the salve.

'He's doing well,' Gar said, patting the roan's neck.

'Cywen said you wanted to see me.' Corban said.

'That's right.' Gar looked pointedly at Cywen. She frowned and didn't look up, picking instead at a burr in the colt's mane. The silence stretched for long, uncomfortable moments, then a voice called Cywen's name.

Edana was walking quickly towards them, a smile on her face, a warrior striding close behind her.

'Hello, Cywen, Gar, Corban.' The Princess smiled in turn at them. 'I was hoping to find you here,' she said to Cywen. 'If you have the time, I was wondering if you might like to join me on a ride.'

Cywen grinned. 'I'd like to very much, but Gar has not told me what my morning chores are yet.' She looked at her feet.

The stablemaster gave a rare smile of his own. 'Ride with the Princess,' he said. 'Please.'

Cywen wrapped her arms around Gar, planting a kiss on his cheek, then she and Edana set off towards the stables, the warrior with Edana taking long strides to keep up with them.

'How are you, Ban?' said Gar.

'Well enough,' Corban said with a shrug, feeling suddenly uncomfortable, looking at the turf.

There was a long silence. Corban eventually raised his eyes, meeting Gar's gaze. 'How am I *supposed* to be? My friend is dead. Dylan was murdered.' He sighed. 'I am many things, Gar: angry, sad. Sometimes I even forget about what has happened and feel happy, for a time. That is the worst.'

'Have you seen that young bully Rafe since the Spring Fair?'

'Only from a distance. It doesn't seem as important now.'

Gar grunted. 'That is good. But it will not go away. My offer still stands – do you remember?'

'Yes.'

Cywen, Edana and the warrior rode out of the stable doors.

'Do you still wish to meet?' the stablemaster asked, quietly.

In truth Corban had all but forgotten Gar's offer of teaching him, but memories of Rafe came vividly back.

'Aye, I do.'

'Then meet me here, tomorrow morning. If you are not here when the sun touches the peaks of the cliffs I will know you've changed your mind. We'll not speak of it again.'

Without another word Gar limped towards the stables.

Corban had never seen the feast-hall so full. All were welcome at the King's table, but in reality most of the smaller holds within the fortress, such as Thannon's, took their evening meals in their own homes. Not tonight, though. Conversation thrummed around the room as Corban sat on a bench, squashed between his da and his sister.

A door at the rear of the chamber opened; the murmur of voices in the hall faltered. Brenin swept in, Ardan's King stern-faced, accompanied by the eagle-messenger.

Brenin made his way to the firepit and cut the first slice of meat to begin the meal.

All became noise again as the rest of the hall set about eating.

Corban washed his food down with a mug of ale, scowling when he saw Rafe standing behind Evnis.

Brenin pushed his half-filled trencher back and stood, all eyes turning to him.

'On the morrow I must leave Ardan, for a time,' he said.

Silence.

'A messenger has come from Tenebral,' he continued, gesturing to the man sitting at his side.

'Aquilus, King of Tenebral, High King of the Banished Lands, has called a kings' council.'

Gasps around the hall now.

'This is the first time this has happened since the Exiles were washed up on the shores of these Banished Lands, over a thousand years ago. I must be there. I leave Alona in my stead. She will rule in my place until I return.'

'What about Darol and his slaughtered family?' a voice cried out, faceless in the crowd. Brenin nodded slowly. 'I have not forgotten my oath. Pendathran will take a warband into the Baglun Forest. He will not return until he has caught those responsible. Alive, I hope, so that they may face my judgement when I return.'

Pendathran thumped the table with his fist, trenchers and cups leaping into the air.

'May the Ben-Elim protect you while I am away,' Brenin said, then he turned and left the chamber.

Noise erupted around the room as the door closed, everyone in the hall talking at once.

Corban lay in his bed, fingers laced behind his head as he stared at the roof, watching shadows flicker across it cast by torchlight from the hall. The muted sound of conversation drifted into his room, his mam and da talking in the kitchen. He snorted. They had been annoyingly silent when he and Cywen had wanted to talk about

Brenin's announcement, but since he and his sister had been bustled off to their beds the two had not seemed to *stop* talking.

His mam paid special attention to teaching him and Cywen their histories, as far back as the Scourging, and he had recognized the name of Tenebral as soon as Brenin had mentioned it, a hot country far to the south and east, where men wore sandals and skirts, not boots and breeches. He snorted at the thought of it. *Tenebral.* Just the sound of it had him excited, somehow. He sighed. He could not sleep, although he had been lying here a long while.

A soft tapping filtered into his room, the latch of the kitchen door turning, a draught suddenly blowing around him. Footsteps and then the door clicked shut. He held his breath to hear better, but there was only silence, then the clinking of mugs and the scrape of chairs. Silence again.

Sleep completely banished by curiosity now, he carefully pulled back his woollen blanket and inched himself out of bed. He tiptoed to his open doorway, crept a few paces down the corridor to the kitchen, stopping when he dared go no further, and held his breath again, straining to hear who the visitor was. More silence, then Gar's distinctive voice drifted from the kitchen.

'It is coming then. We must be more vigilant than ever.'

'Aye,' his mother sighed. Then chair legs scraped and Corban fled back to his bed.

CHAPTER FOURTEEN

EVNIS

Evnis stood by his wife's bedside. And for now, his duties as King Brenin's counsellor were far from his mind. She was sleeping, her chest rising in shallow, bird-like breaths. He felt the frustration in him like a weight, a raw anger at his uselessness. Her fingers twitched and he reached out, stroking the back of her hand.

There was a time when all he had felt was hatred; for his brother, Gethin, for his mother, with her mocking condescension. Then he had been handbound to Fain. Strange that his brother's most spiteful deed had resulted in Evnis' greatest happiness. Gethin thought that wedding Evnis into such a minor family would be a source of immense pain to his younger brother, and at first he had been right. But Evnis had fallen in love with Fain. Not instantly, like a thunderbolt, but gradually, incrementally, day by day. It was her kindness that had won him in the end, her ability to see only good. And somehow his love for her dulled his hatred of others, never completely removed it, but made it feel less *important*, somehow.

But, seeing her like this, he could feel it all bubbling back to the surface, fuelled by his great fear of losing her. He wanted to lash out and kill something. Or someone.

He thought back to Rhin and that long-past night in the forest, when he had learned of the book beneath the fortress that contained the secrets of the earth power. He had to find the giants' book.

Uthas had told him of it on that night in the forest long ago, and in a handful of whispered meetings since. Told him that Uthas' giant clan had dug a labyrinth of tunnels beneath Dun Carreg, and that in those tunnels were treasures, one of them a book teaching the secrets of the earth power. When Evnis first came to Dun Carreg and worked his way into Brenin's good graces, he had searched long and hard, but to no avail. He was in the right tower, was looking in the right region, he was sure, but *nothing*. Over time he had given up. But now, looking at Fain, he had to find the book. He had been told it could prolong Fain's life long enough to take her to the cauldron, hidden far to the north in Uthas' homeland. Since he had received the message from Rhin on the day of the Spring Fair, reminding him of the power of the book, he had renewed his efforts. Day and night he had set men of his hold to digging out the basements of this tower. But the rock was hard, the basements deep and wide, and so far nothing had been found.

And now King Brenin was leaving, had announced in the feast-hall that on the morrow he was going to Tenebral, at his fellow king's summons. *The time approaches*. Events were escalating, all that he had waited for, planned for, was coming to a head. He felt his pulse quicken: *fear, excitement? Probably both*.

There was a soft knock on the door. His chief huntsman, Helfach. 'We've found something.'

Evnis almost ran to the basement, down spiral stairs and through a series of low-ceilinged rooms. A handful of warriors were in the corner of a room, most of the stone floor torn up, only dark earth or rock beneath. Bricks had been levered from the wall, revealing a door, thick oak, iron-banded.

'It won't open,' one of the warriors muttered.

'Of course not,' Evnis said, 'it will be locked. Axes.'

In short time the door was splintering, two men hacking at the old oak. When it was wide enough for a man to walk through, Evnis called for torches. Helfach had fetched one of his hounds, a tall grey beast. It whined as the huntsman led it through the doorway into the darkness. Evnis followed, two spearmen behind him.

They were in a tunnel, high and wide, the walls slick and damp. Helfach led them on, the path sloping gently down, turning. Smaller openings dotted the tunnel wall, passages burrowing into the darkness. Suddenly they were in a cavern, walls arching high and wide, veins of blue spiralling through grey rock, glistening. Two archways led out of the cavern, one going up, one down.

Helfach called out. His hound was sniffing at the wall, ears flat. Helfach held his torch out, burned away cobweb as thick as tapestry to reveal another doorway.

It led to a smaller room, round, two rows of giant axes and war-hammers edging it, all thick with dust and web, meeting at a tomb. Larger than any man would need.

'Elyon save us,' whispered one of the spearmen.

He won't even listen, let alone save you, Evnis thought.

With great effort they heaved the flat stone lid off the tomb.

Inside was the corpse of a giant, its hands clasped at its chest, holding a casket.

Evnis pulled out the casket, his fingers clumsy, sweaty as he fumbled with the clasp. Within it was a book, leather-bound, pages of dry parchment. Reverently he lifted it. Beneath the book was a stone, dull, black, yet leaking light. It almost seemed to pulse, like a heartbeat. It was mounted in silver, wrapped within a chain. Evnis touched it and recoiled.

He closed the lid with a snap. 'We must go,' he whispered. His guards were peering at the casket.

Suddenly Helfach's hound growled at the boulders at the foot of the tomb. There was a loud *crack* as one of them split, a mucous-like substance oozing out of it.

Helfach held his torch closer.

The crack in the boulder lengthened, pieces of it breaking away. The hound barked, jumped forwards, snarling, then backed away from the boulder.

'That is no boulder,' Helfach hissed, 'it's an egg.'

As he spoke, thick plates of shell broke away, a flat, scaly muzzle poking out, a long reptilian tongue flickering. Then the egg exploded, shell and slime splattering them all.

Helfach's hound leaped forwards, snarling, then a blur of something, white and sinuous surged about it. There was a hissing, a high-pitched whine, cut short.

Evnis took a step back, eyes fixed in sick fascination on the scene before him.

It was a great, milky-white snake, longer than two men, as wide as a barrel. And it was *eating* Helfach's hound, already half of it swallowed. The snake's body pulsed, rippled and the hound slipped a little further into the snake's dislocated jaws. One of his spearmen vomited.

'A white wyrm,' Evnis whispered. A creature from faery tales, supposedly bred by the giant clans and used as weapons in the War of Treasures. He tore his eyes away, saw more boulders at the foot of the tomb – *eggs*.

Helfach lunged forwards, stabbing the wyrm with his knife, thrusting his torch into the beast's head.

The snake convulsed, regurgitating the dead hound. Its tail lashed at Helfach, knocking the huntsman through the door.

One of the spearmen lunged in, raking at the wyrm's torso. Dark blood welled. The beast sank long fangs into the spearman's neck and shoulder. He screamed, jerked, but the snake held fast, its coils seething about him.

'Back!' Evnis yelled as he staggered for the doorway, clutching the casket tight to his chest.

He helped Helfach slam the door shut, the remaining warrior pointing his spear at the door. There was an impact, door hinges tearing free. Evnis and Helfach braced themselves against it. Another impact sent them staggering, a third and the door splintered apart, the two men flying backwards. The remaining spearman lunged forwards, stabbing blindly into the doorway. His spear sank into something; he fell back as a sound between roar and hiss escaped the snake. It burst through the doorway, tail lashing into the doorframe, cracking it, shards of rock spinning. Then the wall came down, blocking the doorway, a cloud of dust rolling out.

Evnis clambered to his feet, still clutching the casket. He'd dropped his torch, its flame flaring, sending shadows dancing wildly about the cavern. He drew his sword and approached the writhing snake, a spear lodged in its throat. Helfach circled it, still gripping his long knife in one hand, torch in the other.

The beast was wounded, perhaps fatally, clearly in agony. It saw Evnis, and lunged at him, but he danced back, slashed with his sword, leaving a black line on the creature's muzzle. Helfach darted in, stabbed, then jumped away.

The wyrm weakened quickly, blood and energy leaking away. The other warrior joined them and together they hacked, slashed and stabbed until the creature was dead.

They stood in silence long moments, breathing deep, ragged breaths.

'Take its head,' Evnis said.

*

'I must see the King,' Evnis said to one of the two guards standing before Brenin's chamber. 'It is urgent.'

He had returned to his hold from the tunnels, ordering the doorway bricked up, in case any more eggs hatched, and then quieted himself away to study his find. The book was magnificent, a gateway to the earth power, and he was brimming with excitement over it. The jewel was more troubling. It was obviously giant-made, and possessed power of some sort, but it *scared* him. He locked it away for a time when he could give it more consideration.

He had decided that he must see Brenin, before the King rode out for Tenebral. It would be moons before he was back in Ardan.

Evnis' son, Vonn, had heard the commotion in the basement and seen the wyrm's head, and had begged to accompany Evnis to Brenin. He had denied him, of course. He loved his son, but he was still too young, still saw the world as black and white, when life in reality was all differing shades of grey. He could not bring Vonn with him to see Brenin, because he had lies to tell, and Vonn would not yet understand.

'It is before dawn,' the warrior guarding Brenin's chamber said, frowning. 'He will be asleep.'

'He will wake for this,' Evnis said, opening the hemp sack he was carrying the wyrm's head in. The guard slipped into Brenin's rooms.

Evnis was ushered into an anteroom, and soon Brenin emerged from his bedchamber, bleary-eyed and bare-chested. 'This better be good,' he muttered.

Evnis emptied his sack onto a table and Brenin recoiled.

'It is a white wyrm,' Evnis said.

Brenin rubbed his eyes and leaned in close.

'Where did you find it?'

'Helfach came upon it, hunting in the Baglun,' Evnis said. It would not do for Brenin to know about the tunnels beneath the fortress. 'It killed a hound and one of my warriors.'

'This is strange timing,' Brenin muttered. 'Aquilus' message spoke of strange beasts roaming the land . . .' He scratched his beard and frowned. 'I will take this with me to the council. My thanks, Evnis. Helfach, is he well?'

'Yes my King.'

'Were there more of them?'

'He only came across the one, but who can say.'

'What days are we living in?' Brenin murmured, 'the oathstone weeping blood, white wyrms roaming the land again, after two thousand years . . .'

'Strange times indeed,' said Evnis. *If only you knew, my King, you would be quaking with fear.* 'My King, there is another matter I wished to speak of with you. As you are leaving . . .'

'Go on.'

'Fain. She is a little better, suddenly. She has asked me to take her home, while she is well enough to do so. I would have your permission to leave Dun Carreg for a while, to take her to Badun. And there is a healer there that I know from childhood. It may do her good.'

'When?'

'Soon, my King, within the next ten-night.'

Brenin grimaced. 'I am sorry, Evnis, I must say no. I am taking Heb to Tenebral with me – he is my loremaster, and, from what I can understand, knowledge of the histories will play a large part in Aquilus' council. So you must be here, to help Alona in her rule. When I return, of course you may go.'

'But it is important, vital, that I go soon . . .' Evnis trailed off. 'Please, is there no way?'

'No. If you are not here Alona will only have Pendathran to advise her. Between her and her younger brother I would be returning to half my barons' heads on spikes. I am sorry, Evnis. Send for this healer – I will send an escort to speed them here.'

Evnis bowed his head, squeezing his eyes shut.

'There must be a way,' he said.

'No. I am sorry for your situation, but these are dark times. More is at stake than a pleasure trip to Badun.'

Pleasure trip. I must get her to the cauldron, somehow. 'As my King commands,' Evnis said. As he left the room he brushed a tear from his cheek.

CHAPTER FIFTEEN

CORBAN

Corban wandered in a grey, lifeless world. Visions swam before him, wraiths in the mist, made *of* the mist. He saw the oathstone weeping fat tears of blood, startlingly red; he saw snakes, coiling, writhing, surging, feeding on flesh. Up above, warriors with great feathered wings were fighting with sword and spear against a horde of others, their wings dark, leathery. He saw a tree, its trunk thicker than the keep at Dun Carreg, its roots burrowing deep beneath a never-ending forest.

Then he was sitting by a pool, trailing his fingers in the water. A figure was walking towards him, sword at hip. A man with a close-cropped beard and yellow eyes. He smiled at Corban, sparking a memory.

'I know you,' Corban said.

'Yes. We will be friends, you and I,' the man said with a smile. He sat beside Corban and threw a stone in the pool, waves rippling out.

'Such is your life. Impacting many things, people, realms, events.'

'I don't understand?' Corban said.

'Help me. I need your help. Find the cauldron, bring it to me.'

'Why?'

'To avert disaster, more terrible than you can imagine.' The man fixed Corban with his yellow eyes. 'The God-War is coming. All will fight, it is only a matter of choosing what side you will fight for.'

'Are you the All-Father, Elyon?' Corban breathed, feeling his blood stir at this strange man's words, his pulse quickening.

'He is gone from us,' the man said, shaking his head. Sadness swept his face, infecting Corban with the emotion. 'But the war goes on. There is a hole in your heart, an empty space. You must fill it with *meaning*. You need a cause to live for, to fight for, perhaps to die for.'

'Where am I?' Corban whispered.

'Choose me,' the man said.

'Who are you?'

'You know, in here.' The man poked Corban in his chest, over his heart. Something rippled through him, a shock of power. 'Time stands still for no one. Make your choice, before it is too late.'

Corban gasped, lurching awake in his bed. It was still dark outside, though he could hear the call of gulls. *It will be dawn soon*. His dream flitted on the edge of memory. Something about it made him shiver. He dressed quickly and slipped quietly out of the house. The sky was greying with the approaching dawn now, the familiar smell of the stables reaching him. He ran around them, pulling to a halt and leaning against the wooden rail that ringed the paddock behind.

A footfall sounded inside the paddock. He thought he had been alone, but Gar was standing in the deeper shadows behind the stables. His face was slick with sweat, long black hair plastered to his temples and neck.

'Well, here I am,' said Corban.

'So I see.'

'So, um, what should I do?'

'Run.'

'Run?'

'Aye. Start running around the paddock.'

Corban took a breath to protest, then thought better of it and set off slowly. He did one lap and came to stand by Gar, who was performing some strange movements, almost like a dance, but much slower.

'What?' said Gar.

'I've run around the paddock, as you asked.'

'Again,' Gar grunted.

'Again?'

'Yes, again. I will tell you when to stop.'

Corban sighed, bit his lip and set off. A while later, Corban was unsure how long, Gar raised a hand and called him as he reached the stables. Thankful, he leaned against the paddock rail, sweat dripping from him.

'How – does – this – stop – me – from – being – scared?' he asked between ragged breaths.

'To train the mind you must train the body. Follow me.' Corban did as he was told, scowling.

Inside the stable, Gar jumped up, caught hold of one of the roof beams and began pulling his chin to the beam, then lowering himself. He did this something between two- and three score times – Corban lost count – then dropped back to the ground.

'Your turn,' he said to Corban, who looked dubiously at the beam, jumped up and grabbed it. With a groan he pulled himself up, the muscles in his back stretching and contracting, feeling as if his skin was about to tear. When he lowered himself his grip slipped and he fell to the floor. He stood, dusting himself off.

'Again,' said Gar.

'But I can't. You saw.'

'I will help you. Again.'

So Corban tried again, straining to raise himself with very little effort. Just as he was about to give up he felt Gar's hands grip his ankles, lifting him. He strained again and reached the beam. With Gar's help he lowered himself in a more controlled fashion, then repeated the process eight or nine more times before Gar allowed him to drop back to the floor, where he stuck his palm in his mouth and tried to pull a splinter with his teeth. Immediately Gar set Corban to another equally painful exercise, and then another. Eventually the stablemaster called a halt.

'Why am I doing this?' wheezed Corban, none too happily.

'As I said, to train the mind you must train the body. Right now this may seem pointless to you, but your body is only a tool, a weapon. One that you must learn to master. Fear is no different from your other emotions – anger, distress, joy, desire – they can all overwhelm you. You must learn to recognize and control them. A strong, disciplined body will help. It is not the whole answer, and today is only the first step. Depending on your progress, we may try putting a blade in your hand, at some point.'

'When?' said Corban, brightening.

'That'll depend on you. Now, to finish, copy me. This is an

exercise about control. Most battles are not won by brute force, no matter what your da tells you.' Then he set about showing the intricate set of movements that Corban had glimpsed as he had been running around the paddock. It was much harder than it appeared, having to hold still in unusual positions until his muscles trembled.

'You see, lad, this is about control as well. Your body *will* do as you tell it,' Gar said to him with a rare grin. Corban grunted, concentrating too hard to be able to answer.

'My thanks,' Corban muttered when Gar declared the session over. 'Your leg,' he added with a nod, 'it did not seem to pain you as much. Is it getting better?'

'My leg? No. Some days it is a little better than others. Now, be on your way, before these stables get busy. I'll see you here at sunrise on the morrow.'

Corban walked home, the fortress beginning to come to life around him. His limbs felt heavy, and the morning air felt cool on his body as his sweat dried.

The courtyard that spread wide before Dun Carreg's great gates thrummed with activity and noise. Four score warriors sat upon horses, Tull, the King's champion standing before them, holding his horse's reins. He was clothed in wool and boiled leather, greystreaked hair pulled back and tied at the nape of his neck, his longsword strapped to his saddle. Pendathran stood next to him, holding the reins of King Brenin's roan stallion.

A cheer went up as Brenin strode into their midst, his Queen Alona beside him. The King swung into his saddle and looked around the gathered crowd.

'I shall return before Midsummer's Day,' he cried, raised his hand in salute and nudged his horse into a trot towards the arch of Stonegate. Behind him rode the messenger from Tenebral and Heb the loremaster, whom Corban thought looked decidedly illtempered, a frown knitting his bushy eyebrows. Then the warriors lurched into motion. They rode across the bridge to the mainland, the sea crashing against rocks far below. Corban and Cywen stood, watching the column of riders shrink into the distance.

Princess Edana was standing with Queen Alona and Pendathran.

She saw Corban with Cywen and called them over. Queen Alona smiled warmly, her eyes lingering on Corban.

'Cywen works with Gar, mother,' Edana said. 'She has a way with horses – you should see her ride.'

'Anyone who learns from Gar is likely to have a way with horses. Gar has a gift from Elyon, I think,' said Alona, smiling at Edana. 'I remember when he first came here. You had only just seen your first nameday.'

As they walked into the fortress, a figure stepped into view. Evnis, his son Vonn still with him.

'There is a matter I would discuss with you. A private matter,' Evnis said to Alona.

Alona frowned.

'It's all right,' her daughter said. 'I'll wait here.'

Alona nodded and walked on briskly, Evnis falling in beside her. Pendathran kept pace with them.

Vonn turned and winked at Edana, as he followed his father.

Edana scowled. 'Look at him: he thinks he's Elyon's gift.'

'Well, he *is* fine looking,' said Cywen.

'What makes it worse,' Edana continued, choosing to ignore Cywen's remark, 'is that he's got it into his head that he and I will be wed.'

'Why does he think that?' asked Cywen.

'Evnis has been hinting at it for years. Father has never given him a definite answer, but I think they just take it for granted now.'

'So you don't *want* to be bound to him,' said Corban.

Edana glared at him. 'No. I am not some slab of meat to be sold at market.'

The group in front of them stopped, Pendathran's voice raised.

'No, Evnis. You cannot go,' they heard the battlechief say.

'I was under the impression that it's the Queen of Ardan who makes the decisions whilst the King is away,' Evnis responded coldly.

'I am sorry,' Alona said. 'Under other circumstances of course, but Pendathran will be leaving on the morrow, and my King has made it most clear to me that he wishes your counsel to be at hand during this time.' Her face softened. 'I really am sorry. Tell Fain I shall visit her tonight.'

'Visit,' Evnis repeated, a tremor in his voice. 'This is because of

Rhagor, is it not? You still blame me for your brother's death. Petty vengeance.'

'What?' Alona said. 'No . . .'

'Do not mention his name,' Pendathran growled. 'Not ever.'

Evnis stood a moment, trembling. He inclined his head, turned swiftly and strode away, Vonn almost running to keep up with him.

A ten-night later, Corban was making his way down to the village, thinking to find Dath, when he saw a rider in the distance, galloping up the giantsway.

It was Marrock, whom he'd last seen at his handfasting. He had ridden out to the Baglun Forest with Pendathran's warband, the day after King Brenin had left. Corban ran as fast as he could to the keep, his target the feast-hall as Marrock's most likely destination.

Marrock was standing before the Queen, who was sitting in an ornately carved oak chair, Evnis at her shoulder.

'What have I missed?' Corban whispered to his sister.

'They have picked up a trail in the forest, found a corpse of a man, half-eaten by wolves or wolven, and they think he was one of the brigands. Marrock has come back for more warriors. Pendathran wants them to patrol the western border of the forest in case he and his warband flush the brigands out and they attempt to flee.'

'I will see to it at once, my lady,' Evnis said and hurried from the hall.

CHAPTER SIXTEEN

CAMLIN

Camlin's feet ached. He had been walking all day, trying to force a way through this cursed forest. Blood trickled in thin lines down his arms and cheeks where thorns had snagged at him, the cuts stinging as sweat mingled with them.

It was Braith, Lord of the Darkwood that had put him in charge of this crew. *Braith, Lord of the Darkwood. Lord of a rabble of cut-throats, more like.* Still, Camlin had been happy enough about his promotion, back in the Darkwood. Fourteen men had followed him into Ardan, into the Baglun Forest; only nine walked behind him now. They were entering a dense part of the forest, as thick with thorns and foliage as any he had ever seen. He did not like the Baglun. Although the Darkwood was so much bigger, it had been his home for more years than he could count. He was the wrong side of thirty, and more than half of those years had been spent living in woodland, but a sense of unease had been growing in him ever since he had arrived here. He sighed. They had left the Darkwood and Braith full of pride and excitement: the first chosen to found a new lair deep in the heart of Ardan. How had they come to this? And so quickly: discovered and hunted by a warband, and worse, one led by Pendathran, who bore a personal grudge against Braith and all who rode with him.

Still, they must have lost them now, or at least put more distance between them. They had entered a part of the forest so dense it could only be travelled through on foot, and that with great difficulty, and the warband hunting them had been mounted.

Camlin and his crew trudged on in silence, the only sound their laboured breathing, the occasional *snap* of a twig or the flick of a branch. In time Camlin heard the sound of running water. The ground began to slope downward, became spongier under foot, and suddenly they walked into a shadowy dell, the trees and foliage opening a little around them. At its far edge was a sharp drop to a stream. It was almost dark now.

'We'll stop here for the night,' he declared. His crew unslung their packs and began making camp. Camlin drank deeply from his water skin and pulled his boots off.

'Hey, Cam,' called Goran, a bull of a man that had been with Braith almost as long as he had, 'put your boots back on. Your stinking feet are making my guts churn.' Laughter rippled. Camlin forced himself to smile good-naturedly. A few nights back he'd come close to putting a knife in Goran's gut, *should* have. He hadn't done it, had allowed Goran to break his order and done nothing about it. Now, the lads were low, on edge and, worse, unsure of him. He could feel it unspoken between them – mutiny. Gutting Goran now would most likely tip them over that edge.

'At least I can wash my feet,' he said. 'Besides, they cover the stench of your breath. What did you break your fast with? Dung?'

More laughter.

Goran scowled at him, then winced as his skin creased an angry-looking cut running from his left eye down to his lip.

They ate a poor meal as Camlin would allow no fire, but they all knew the sense of it. Then Camlin sent a couple of the lads back up the path to watch their backs.

'Covered a lot of ground today,' he grunted. 'Don't think Brenin's lot'd leave their horses, march in here after us. And even if they did, they'd do it a lot slower than us.'

'An' louder. We'd hear 'em coming half a league away,' threw in Goran.

Camlin tried to grin, to look confident for the lads, but he was not so easily cheered. All in their small band were woodsmen, had spent years living in the Darkwood. That was one of the reasons why they had been chosen for this task. And he was not the only one in the small circle that did not smile. He knew some must blame him for the situation they were in. Things had started well enough. They'd burned out a dozen holds and reached the Baglun Forest without any problems, then he'd made contact with Braith's man from Dun Carreg and been given his first job. Personally, he thought the hold had been too close to the fortress for the first strike – but the contact had insisted, and he knew the idea was to stir things up with Brenin quickly, lure him out of his stone walls. Why, he didn't know, but over the years he'd become used to following orders and keeping his head down, so he'd just shrugged and got on with it.

That was when things had started to go wrong. He'd climbed the hold's wall, opened the gates for the lads and put a sword in the belly of the first man to hear them. A couple more had put up a fight, but two against fifteen was never good odds. They'd rounded up the women and a young lad, but Goran had knocked the lad around and, the next thing, one of the women had a knife out, had cut Goran from eye to mouth. 'Course Goran hadn't taken that well, all hell had broken loose, and before Camlin could do anything about it the two women and the lad were dead. He'd not been happy about that. The whole crew knew he wouldn't have the killing of women and bairns. Not that he had the morals of the sainted Ben-Elim, far from it: he'd lied, cheated and murdered as much as any lawless man, but he drew the line at women and bairns. He had his reasons. It had never been a problem before, in many ways it had been better. Braith wanted word to spread of who was doing the burning and killing, and survivors told a better tale than the dead.

He'd wanted so badly to kill Goran for that, had felt the blood-rush, even had his knife out before he'd realized what he was doing. Maybe he *should* have killed him. Braith had warned him not to give an order he wasn't prepared to gut a man for. He sighed; no point worrying about *should haves*. He'd hoped that'd be the end of the bad luck, but it was only the beginning. A couple of nights later he'd lost a man on watch to one of the Baglun's bogs, and the next day lost four men to wolven. And then they'd heard about Pendathran's warband hunting them, so had fled deeper into this cursed forest.

And now here they were, sitting on a cold, hard shelf of rock, no fire, an angry warband close behind.

'So, what next, chief?' Goran asked him, a sour twist to his mouth.

'We lie low. Either they will miss us or they won't.' Camlin picked at a blister on his foot. 'If the worst does happen, then we'll break east, head for the marshes. They'd never find us in there.' He looked around at the dark expressions.

'We've been in tight spots before and come through. This'll be no different.'

'That was with Braith as chief,' he heard Goran whisper.

Camlin stared at the big woodsman, fingers twitching for his knife. *Half the warriors of Ardan wouldn't be hunting us if you hadn't started killing children.* The boy's face appeared in his mind, screaming over the corpse of a woman – his sister, his mam? It reminded him of another child, crying over another woman. He blinked. More than twenty years, yet still he could remember his brother Col and his mam as if it were yesterday.

It was the year after the wasting disease had taken his da. He had been fifteen summers old, and was repairing one of the walls on their farm, piling stone upon stone. Then he had heard his mam scream, high and shrill.

He had run, seeing smoke bloom around their hold, crept to the edge of their barn, peering around to see his mam lying still on the hard-packed ground before his home. A blond-haired warrior sitting on a roan stallion towered over her body, other riders holding spears or drawn swords milling about the yard. Then Col had burst into the yard, his older brother by two years, waving a spear. The raiders had spurred their mounts at Col and cut him down.

Camlin had been too scared to move, huddled shaking while the raiders emptied their house and barn of everything of value and rode back to the Darkwood in a cloud of dust.

Eventually he crept out into the yard, knelt beside his mam and brother and shed uncounted tears. A terrible rage consumed him, fed brighter by his shame at hiding. He fetched a pony from the pasture and rode after the raiders.

He was not a warrior, not being of age yet, but his da had taught him much about the ways of wood and earth. It had taken him half a day to catch up with the raiders, who were riding carelessly through the Darkwood. He followed them two more days, out of the Darkwood and into Ardan, saw his mam and brother's killers pass through the gates of Badun.

After that he had made his way back to his burned-out home, then taken his news to the lord of the nearest village, but the man had not been interested. Camlin was not of age to hold a spear or come from a family of high blood. The next day warriors had ridden from the village to see if there was anything left worth taking from his home. When Camlin had shouted at them and cursed them as cowards they had laughed, then chased him. He fled into the Darkwood, wandering there days until he was found by the brigands that lived there.

They took Camlin in, taught him the way of the wood, and slowly but surely he had risen through their ranks.

And so here he was. He snorted. *Done well for myself.*

He awoke with a start, had to blink repeatedly to remove the picture of his mam's dead eyes from his mind.

Dawn's shadow-light was seeping into the forest. He leaned up on one elbow, rubbed his eyes, saw movement in the shadows. He squinted and stared. Something glinted.

'Awake!' cried Camlin, his voice hoarse with sleep. He leaped to his feet, dragging his sword from its scabbard.

The forest came to life around him. He kicked Goran to speed him to his feet, heard footfalls to his left. Stepping backwards, he wobbled on the edge of the rock face, saw a blade pass through the space that his head had just occupied. He rammed his sword into the chest of an onrushing warrior, pulling it free with a spray of blood, stepped over a body slumped at Goran's feet.

There were enemies everywhere, all a chaos of tangled limbs, battle-cries and screams. Couldn't be sure, but it looked as if his lads were doing badly. Another warrior lunged at him and he blocked the sword blow, punched the man in the mouth, sending him tripping over a corpse.

Suddenly a high keening filled the air, more warriors rushing out of the mist, bare iron in their fists.

'Time to leave,' Camlin grunted to Goran, who was fighting beside him. Camlin ran for the edge of the rock face, leaping off the ledge. With a splash he fell into the stream and dropped to his knees, gashing them on slick stones in the stream bed. *No time for pain*, he told himself, lurching forwards into the stream's shallows. Behind him he heard another splash and hoped it was Goran.

He followed the stream's edge for a long time, until he could not force his legs to pump forwards any longer. He heard splashing, growing louder. He gripped his sword hilt, then the hulking figure of Goran came into view.

The two men set off quickly, shadowing the stream, the forest growing lighter around them. Before long the foliage began to thin. 'What are we going to do?' Goran whispered as they approached the fringes of the forest. An open plain lay before them, with occasional stands of trees breaking up the horizon.

'Follow this stream all the way to the marshes is my bet,' said Camlin. 'If they tracked us this far they're not going to just let us get away now. The only place we can hope to lose them is the marshes.'

'If we get there.'

'Aye, if we get there. But that's not going to happen standing here. Come on.'

They checked the plain once more and then burst from the forest, running for a stand of alders in the distance. When they were halfway to the trees, Camlin heard rumbling somewhere behind. Three warriors were riding towards them. The trees ahead were too far. He glanced at Goran and they both nodded. Stopping, they drew their swords and spun to face the approaching warriors. The middle horseman dismounted, his nose swollen and red, looking as if it had recently been broken.

'You are safe,' the man said. 'Quickly now, let's get out of the open. We will take you to safety.'

Camlin's shoulders slumped as he sheathed his sword, relief flooding him. Goran did the same. The other two riders slid to the ground. Then suddenly branches crashed from the forest. Camlin and Goran turned to see men pour from the trees. He heard the whisper of a blade being drawn behind him – surely Goran preparing for a last stand. Then his comrade crashed lifeless to the grass beside him.

'Don't kill them,' a voice cried faintly from the warriors running out of the forest. As he began to turn, a searing pain lanced into his side. His legs were suddenly weak, his vision blurring as he slumped to the ground.

CHAPTER SEVENTEEN

CORBAN

It was still dark when Corban rose. He dressed quickly and made his way to the paddocks.

Gar was waiting as usual, sweat drying on him from whatever he had been doing. Corban nodded a greeting and began his routine, running around the paddock. Soon they moved inside the stables, Corban working at the exercises Gar had introduced him to.

For almost two ten-nights now this had been his morning routine, and he was starting to feel stronger, more flexible. Finally they moved into the intricate slow dance that Gar had taught him, progressing fluidly from one position to the next, holding a stance until his muscles trembled, burned, then moving to another. When they had finished, Corban wiping sweat from his forehead, Gar called him. He turned quickly, saw the stablemaster throw something to him. He flinched but instinctively held his hand out to catch it.

It was a practice sword.

Finally, he thought, breath catching in his throat.

A shadow of a smile flitted across the stablemaster's face. 'Come,' he said, 'let's see what you can do.'

'Are you ready?' Corban asked, squaring up to Gar. The stablemaster just nodded, not even raising his weapon.

'Don't worry, I won't hurt you,' Corban said, grateful for the opportunity to show how good he was with a blade.

Weapon raised high and resisting the urge to shout a battlecry, Corban threw himself at Gar. A flurry of motion followed and Corban found himself on the ground, straw poking up his nose and in his eyes, his knuckles stinging.

'I must have tripped,' he muttered as he rolled over, letting the stablemaster help him to his feet.

'Clearly. Come now, let us try again,' said Gar. 'And please, go easy on me. I am not as young as I was, and my wound slows me.'

'Of course,' said Corban.

Three more times in quick succession Corban found himself face down in the straw, unable to figure out how he had arrived there. Gar leaned on his practice sword, chuckling. Corban felt a flash of anger and rose, scowling, but as he looked at Gar something inside him softened. The stablemaster seemed different. He realized he had never seen Gar laugh properly. It changed his face, taking away the sternness that was such a part of him.

'So, my young swordsmaster. There may be a few things an old, broken warrior like me can still show?'

'I think so,' muttered Corban, 'like how to stay on my feet.'

The glimmer of a smile, just a brief twitching at the corners of Gar's mouth.

'All right then. You remember the slow dance, as you call it. Its correct title is the *sword dance*. Each position is the first stance of a sword technique. Let us begin with the first one.' The mask was back on, all signs of humour gone.

Corban listened avidly, soaking up all that Gar told him. They went through a series of moves based on the first stance of the dance, but this time with the sword in his hand. Then Corban hurried home to break his fast.

Only his da was home, and he would not say where Cywen and his mam were. Instead, he put Corban's food on the table and told him to hurry, as there was something that he wanted Corban to see. Soon they were marching across Stonegate's bridge, Buddai following at Thannon's heels.

'Where are we going?' asked Corban, not really expecting an answer.

Thannon smiled at him. 'Gar's stallion has sired a foal, it was born this morning. A skewbald colt. He's yours, if you want him.'

His da set a fast pace, and soon they were descending the winding road to Havan. White-tipped waves crashed against the shore beneath them. Corban could taste salt in the air, the wind snapping around him, bringing with it a taste of the sea far below. In the distance a line of riders moved along the giantsway, the smudge of Baglun Forest behind them.

'The warband,' Thannon said.

Corban felt a rush of excitement. *So many. Something must have happened.* He stood with his da and waited for the warband.

Marrock rode behind Pendathran, then the newcomers, Halion and Conall, and behind them a column of warriors. Near the centre of the procession walked a number of riderless horses, Corban counted a half-dozen, and then a wain pulled by two shaggy-haired ponies. Something was piled high inside the wain, covered with a sheet of ox-hides stitched together. A wheel hit a stone and a hand and arm slipped out from beneath the hide, skin pale, the nails black with dirt.

CHAPTER EIGHTEEN

VERADIS

Banners rippled on the plain before Jerolin's black walls, all answering the call to High King Aquilus' council. Many had come to join the sickle moon and stars that Veradis had seen arrive the day he had stood on the battlements with Prince Nathair, watching the Vin Thalun prisoner leave: the black hammer of Helveth, the bull of Narvon and the burning torch of Carnutan, as well as others that he did not recognize. A snarling wolf, a rearing horse, a red hand, a lone mountain, a broken branch. All stood rippling in the breeze amidst groups of tents erected to hold the shieldmen and entourages of these foreign kings, all come at the call of Aquilus. Veradis felt a swell of pride.

He turned and made his way to the practice court. The fortress was crowded now, full with the Banished Land's warriors, most looking to prove themselves on the weapons court, to earn a reputation beyond their own realms.

Veradis was still surprised at how different so many of them looked. The local warriors were all easy to pick out, in their hobnailed sandals, tunics, leather kilts and close-cropped hair. Most of the newcomers wore boots and breeches, coming from colder lands most likely, many with long hair and beards to match. Others were dressed in loose-fitting clothes. There were variations in the colour of their skin, some as pale as morning sky, others weathered as old teak, and all the tones in between. No matter how different they appeared, though, there was one thing that bound them. Whether their hair was close-cropped like Veradis', or long and wild, or neatly groomed and bound, all wore the warrior braid.

Rauca was sparring, showing off the strength of Prince Nathair's band. His opponent, stripped to the waist, wearing checked breeches, was taller and broader, thick-corded muscles rippling as he fought, but Veradis was not concerned for his friend; the person he was facing had grey-streaked hair. Big *and* old meant slow.

They'd obviously been sparring for a while, both covered in a sheen of sweat. Rauca circled, forcing the older man to pivot to protect his shield side, then Rauca darted in, lunging at his opponent's chest. At the last moment, as his opponent's weapon was whistling to block the blow, Rauca shifted his weight, spinning around to bring his sword arcing at his now off-balance opponent's neck. It was a perfect manoeuvre, feint and strike, except that his opponent was no longer where he was supposed to be. Somehow he had read the feint, and instead of trying to right himself he used his momentum to step forwards, avoiding the intended blow and regaining his balance at the same time. Now it was Rauca on unsteady feet, and a moment later his adversary's sword swatted his wrist, making him drop his weapon.

His opponent laughed, deep and loud, and slapped Rauca on the back. With a rueful smile the younger man picked up his weapon and the two left the court together, allowing two more warriors waiting on the courtyard edge to take their place.

Veradis met his friend as the older warrior whispered in Rauca's ear, then wrapped a grey cloak around his shoulders and strode off, the crowd parting for him.

Veradis smiled at his friend. 'You should have won.'

'That's what I thought,' Rauca muttered with a shrug.

'What did he say to you?' Veradis asked.

Rauca pulled a sour face. 'He said *"There's no point getting old if you don't get cunning."*'

Veradis chuckled. 'He's right enough. Who was he?'

'Said his name was Tull. He came here with the shieldmen of Ardan.'

'Where's that?'

'You really need to start looking at maps, Veradis. You won't make a very good battlechief if you don't know where you're marching your warband to.'

'That's what you are for,' Veradis said and chuckled.

Laughter called their attention back to the practice court, where a tall, dark-haired man was standing over another figure.

The one on the ground tried to rise but the dark-haired man lashed out with his practice sword and knocked an arm away, sent him tumbling back to the floor. An older warrior made to enter the practice square, more grey streaking his hair than black, but he was restrained by other warriors.

The man on the floor rolled away and rose to his feet. Veradis saw he was a thickset youth, wide shouldered but also wide at the waist. He pushed a hand through a shock of unruly red hair as he bent and retrieved his practice sword.

The dark-haired warrior raised his sword, smiling. The red-haired man suddenly lunged forwards, surprisingly fast. He rained a flurry of blows against his opponent, causing the warrior to step backwards, although he blocked every blow easily, the smile never leaving his lips.

They fight well, Veradis thought. Then the dark warrior blocked another lunge, twisting his wrist so that his opponent's weapon was sent spinning, raised his sword for an overhead strike.

It never landed.

The red-haired warrior stepped forwards, bringing his knee up hard into the other's groin. With a groan he sank to the ground and lay there in a curled ball. The red-haired man stood over him a moment, then stomped out of the practice court. A handful of warriors ran over to the felled man and helped him to his feet.

A hand gripped Veradis' shoulder and he turned to see Nathair smiling at him. The Prince signalled for Veradis and Rauca to follow him. 'The council will begin tomorrow, the last king has arrived. Come and see.' He turned and marched quickly towards the stables, Veradis and Rauca trotting to catch him.

Nathair stopped just before the stables, staring at two men dismounting. Veradis almost laughed when he saw their mounts, more like ponies than horses, small and shaggy-haired; then he saw their riders and his smile vanished.

They were both short and lean, wearing loose-fitting breeches and only a sash thrown diagonally across their torsos, but it was their faces that drew Veradis' eyes. Their heads were shaven clean, apart from a single thick braid of dark hair, small black eyes glowering from beneath jutting brows. A latticework of crisscrossing scars covered the entirety of their clean-shaven faces, heads and upper bodies.

'Close your mouth,' Nathair said, nudging Veradis.

'Who are they?' he whispered.

'Sirak,' Nathair replied, 'from the sea of grass.' Veradis nodded, remembering tales his nursemaid had told him in his childhood, of betrayal and bitter rivalries between the horse-lords and the giants.

'Tomorrow should be very interesting,' he said to Nathair and Rauca.

Veradis looked around the feast-hall, stripped now of its rows of benches, the firepit boarded over. He was standing a little behind Nathair, who was seated at a massive table of oak that stretched almost the entire length of the room. Over a score of kings or barons had come, each with at least one person accompanying them – a counsellor, a champion or both – and over four score were seated around the great table.

Nathair was sitting beside Aquilus, a thin circlet of gold about the King's head. Seated on the other side of Aquilus was Meical, his counsellor, jet-black hair braided and clasped at his neck with silver wire. He studied all who came into the room. Veradis' eyes were continually drawn back to the man. He was tall, even sitting that was clear to see – possibly taller that Krelis, who was the largest man that Veradis had ever seen – and close up it was apparent that this man was no stranger to combat. Part of his left ear was missing, four clean scars running from his hairline to his chin, looking like *claw* marks. And his arms were strewn with more silvery scars. Even his knuckles were ridged, knobbly, looking as if he'd spent his life in the pugil-ring.

A woman swept in, aged but straight-backed, white hair flowing across a checked cloak of black and gold, a thin band of silver around her neck. She was not the only one in the room to wear a crown around her neck, while others wore them as rings about their arms.

Behind her paced a slim man, young, a swaggering confidence in his walk. His gaze swept the room, cold and arrogant as a hawk.

Surely her first-sword, Veradis thought. *Watch that one.*

The slim warrior pulled out a chair for the lady, who sat with a smile, filling the last chair at the table.

A hush fell over the room as Aquilus stood.

'People of the Banished Lands, whether you be king, or baron come to speak for your king, welcome to my hall.' He went on to welcome each person individually, the tide of strange names and places soon flowing over Veradis' head, with only a few standing out in his mind. Brenin, Lord of Ardan, because the old warrior who had bested Rauca stood behind him, and also Romar, the King of Isiltir. Two men attended him, one sitting either side – the two from the sparring court yesterday, he recognized. The red-haired one was named Kastell, the dark-haired, Jael.

Other names rang out and the lady who had entered the hall last was named as Rhin, Queen of Cambren.

'This is a momentous occasion,' Aquilus said. 'One that has not happened since our ancestors first set foot upon these shores, since Sokar was named high king. I am honoured that so many of you have remembered your ancestors' oaths and come.'

'It was hard to resist,' said Mandros, King of Carnutan, 'though a long way to come for such cryptic hints – dark times, a new age, signs and portents – I for one am intrigued. What is this all about, Aquilus?'

A silence fell. Nathair tapped his fingers quietly on the smoothed oak of the table.

'War is coming,' Aquilus said. 'An enemy that would conquer the Banished Lands, destroy us all.'

'Who?' a fat, red-haired man shouted out. Braster, King of Helveth.

'Asroth,' Aquilus said. 'The God-War is coming. Asroth and Elyon will make the Banished Lands their battleground.'

Silence. Motes of golden dust danced in the sunshine that washed through the tall windows.

Someone laughed: Mandros. 'You cannot be serious,' the King of Carnutan said. 'I have ridden a hundred leagues for this: fireside tales my mam told to make me stay in bed at night.'

Do not trust him, a voice murmured in Veradis' head.

'There have been signs,' Aquilus said. 'I know you will have seen them. I do not believe my kingdom is the only one to have experienced these things.'

'What things?' Mandros snorted.

'The giants, attacking in force for the first time in generations. Lawless men multiplying, raiding, killing. Creatures, beasts prowling the dark places, bolder than ever before. And worse. The giant-stones, weeping blood. Tell me you have not heard these things.'

'Tales for campfires,' Mandros said.

'*I* have heard these things,' another man said, a gold torc around his neck. Brenin of Ardan. 'There are giant-stones in my realm. I have been told of blood flowing from them, like tears, seen by men I trust.'

'The giants have become a plague on my borders,' someone else spoke, a broad-shouldered man, Romar of Isiltir, Veradis thought. 'On my journey here I was forced to battle against the Hunen, raiding out of Forn Forest. They have stolen a great relic from me, an axe. One of the seven Treasures of old. And what you say about beasts – draigs have been seen prowling my hills for the first time in generations.'

'Dark tales are told in my court,' Braster said, tugging at his red beard. 'As you say, of giants and draigs and worse. I have had reports, sightings of white wyrms on my borders, in the mountains, and in the fringes of Forn Forest.'

Mandros shook his head with contempt. 'The white wyrms are straight out of our storybooks. They do not exist.'

'Yes they do,' Benin said, gesturing to his first-sword. The old warrior stood, heaved a sack up and emptied it onto the table. A head rolled out, as big as a war-shield. It was reptilian, with long fangs and blood red eyes, the flesh around its neck torn and stinking. Its scales were flaking, decaying, but it was clear to all that in life they must have been a milky-white.

Gasps were heard around the table.

'There has been no record of the white wyrms since the Scourging,' Aquilus said. 'The tales tell that they were bred by the giants, used in the War of Treasures.'

'You all forget one thing,' a new voice added, Rhin, Queen of Cambren. 'All this talk of a God-War. For that to happen there must be *gods*. Elyon has turned his back on us, on all things: men, giants, the beasts of the earth, on all his creation. That is, if our loremasters speak the truth. It takes at least two sides for a battle. Elyon is the absent god. He is *gone*. So there can be no God-War.'

'There will be a war.' For the first time Meical spoke, Aquilus' counsellor. His voice was clipped, precise, controlled. 'Asroth seeks to destroy all that Elyon created. He seeks to destroy you. Every one of you. Elyon's presence is not required for that. And you will either die meekly, fooled by him, or you will resist, fight back.' He stared at Rhin.

'A king may be absent and yet those faithful to him will still do battle for him,' Aquilus added. 'And Elyon will not be absent always. If our loremasters speak the truth.'

Rhin smiled and dipped her head to Aquilus, as if acknowledging a touch on the sparring court. Her gaze drifted to Meical, the smile fading.

'Even if these things are happening, which is debatable,' Mandros said, 'why conclude they are the forerunners of this *God-War*?' His lips twisted. 'We are not superstitious children, surely. Bad things happen sometimes, that is the way of the world. Why call them *signs*?'

'Because of this,' Aquilus said, gesturing to Meical.

The counsellor pulled a book from his cloak, thick and leather-bound. 'I found this in Drassil,' he said. 'It was written by Halvor, the giant, during the Scourging.'

'Hah,' Mandros burst, slapping the table, 'you go too far now. A book over a thousand years old. *Drassil*, an imaginary city. Aquilus, please, you insult us.'

Veradis looked around the table. Heads were nodding in agreement with the King of Carnutan, but there were also many that were silent, even *scared*. He could scarcely believe what he was hearing. His head was whirling with all this talk of gods and wars and signs.

'Once I thought as you do,' Aquilus said to Mandros. 'I have had cause to rethink. Please, all of you, listen now, judge after.'

Mandros pulled a sour face and leaned back in his chair.

Meical opened the leather cover. 'This was written by Halvor during the Scourging,' he said. 'It gives an account of our oldest histories: the starstone, the death of Skald, the first giant king, and the following War of Treasures, ending in Elyon's wrath. That part is lucidly written, but spread amongst it, scattered, is other writing, different. It could almost have been scribed by another's hand. But the lettering is the same.'

'Read to them, Meical. Of the avatars.'

Meical turned pages, the parchment creaking. He paused, finger tracing the script. 'Here is the first part. War eternal between the

Faithful and the Fallen, infinite wrath come to the world of men. Lightbearer seeking flesh from the cauldron, to break his chains and wage the war again.'

Mandros snorted. 'Tales we are told on our mother's knee,' he muttered again.

Meical seemed oblivious, engrossed in the book. 'Two born of blood, dust and ashes shall champion the Choices, the Darkness and Light.' He paused, turned more pages. 'This is not written clear to see, you understand,' he murmured as he searched through the book. 'This script is almost hidden, spread from beginning to end. It has taken me moons to work just a little part out. Ah, here is more. Black Sun will drown the earth in bloodshed, Bright Star with the Treasures must unite.' Again he stopped, carefully turned more pages, eventually continued his halting reading: 'By their names you shall know them – Kin-Slayer, Kin-Avenger, Giant-Friend, Draig-Rider, Dark Power 'gainst Lightbringer.' And so he went on: read, pause, search. Read again. 'One shall be the Tide, one the Rock in the swirling sea. Before one, storm and shield shall stand; before the other, True-Heart and Black-Heart. Beside one rides the Beloved, beside the other, the Avenging Hand. Behind one, the Sons of the Mighty, the fair Ben-Elim, gathered 'neath the Great Tree. Behind the other, the Unholy, dread Kadoshim, who seek to cross the bridge, force the world to bended knee.'

After this there was a heavy silence, broken by Braster. 'That doesn't sound good,' he muttered.

'There is more,' Aquilus said, and Meical read on.

'Look for them when the high king calls, when the shadow warriors ride forth, when white-walled Telassar is emptied, when the book is found in the north. When the white wyrms spread from their nest, when the Firstborn take back what was lost, and the Treasures stir from their rest. Both earth and sky shall cry warning, shall herald this War of Sorrows. Tears of blood spilt from the earth's bones, and at Midwinter's height bright day shall become full night.'

No one spoke. *Tears of blood*, thought Veradis. *Surely the weeping stones* . . . Until that point, Meical's reading had reminded Veradis most of old folktales, but those last words had hit him hard. How could that have been written *generations* ago? He suddenly felt a coldness spreading within him, like a fist clenching about his heart.

'This is madness,' Mandros declared. 'I will listen to these faery tales no longer.' His chair scraped as he stood and marched from the room, a younger man trailing him, his son.

'What does all of that mean?' Braster said. 'Most of it sounded like riddles to me.'

'That is why I have called you all here,' Aquilus said. 'To discuss the meaning of these words, and to decide on a way forward.'

With that they set about debating the meaning of what Meical had read, its reliability, what to do if it was true, back and forth, back and forth until Veradis' head was spinning. Highsun's bell came and went, the table filled with food and then cleared, wine cups filled and refilled. The light was dimming, wall sconces were being lit when Braster spoke up.

'So what would you have us do? We cannot march against an enemy that we cannot see. I know there has been much talk today of this Black Sun, Asroth's champion, but where is he? *Who* is he?'

'I do not know,' Aquilus said. 'But I propose this. That we agree to aid each other against our enemies, whether they be lawless men, corsairs, giants, or a horde of wyrms and twisted beasts from out of Forn. And that we also agree, when this Black Sun does reveal himself, that we unite and fight against him together.'

'And who would lead us?' Rhin asked. 'You?'

Aquilus shrugged. 'The Bright Star, when he steps forward.'

'Or *she*,' Rhin said.

Aquilus smiled. 'Until the Bright Star is revealed to us, whomever we choose shall lead us. I am high king, but I will not stand in the way of this alliance. Maybe there will be a clear choice, when a leader is needed.'

He stood and leaned on the table.

'All has been said that can be said. Now is the time of choosing. If you wish to join me, stand with me now.'

There was the scraping of chairs on stone, as kings and barons stood.

Veradis counted, frowned. Only five had stood: Romar, King of Isiltir, Brenin of Ardan, red-bearded Braster, Temel of the Sirak and Rahim of Tarbesh.

'I will wait,' a seated king said. Owain of Narvon. 'Until

Midwinter's Day. Let me see this sign that you have spoken of, that is foretold. Then I will decide.'

Aquilus nodded.

'For those of the same mind, this alliance stands open to you. Those that stand with me now, we shall meet again on the morrow. For the rest of you, I thank you for journeying so far from your lands. Elyon speed you home. But not today, I hope. A feast has been prepared for you all. Dine with me this evening, whatever your choices in this room today.'

Soon after this, Veradis was standing in King Aquilus' chambers. Prince Nathair was sipping from a cup of red wine, a heavy silence on him. Meical stood by a window, staring at the sun sinking behind distant mountains.

'Why were the Vin Thalun not invited to this council, Father?' Nathair suddenly asked.

'Because I do not trust them,' Aquilus said. 'We've had this conversation.'

'If trust were the criterion, I would not have invited most that sat in the council chamber today,' Nathair muttered.

Aquilus sighed and focused on Nathair. 'What is your point?'

'I do not trust Mandros, or Rhin, or Braster. Or any of the others. They all have their secrets, their own agendas. And, for all you know, any one of them could be this *Black Sun*, or at least serve him. Mandros seemed set on undermining everything you said.' Nathair sucked in a long breath, closing his eyes. 'Your alliance is about who is *useful*, surely, and the Vin Thalun are more useful than most: ships, a fleet even, a network of contacts throughout the Banished Lands, great strength in warriors. They should have been here.'

'The Vin Thalun have raided, murdered amongst most of those gathered here today. Most likely they still do. Those here would not tolerate such as the Vin Thalun in their company.'

'Their petty grievances are their own. It is beneath us,' Nathair said.

'This alliance is *everything*.' Aquilus growled. 'I will not put it at risk by inviting corsairs to the table.'

'Even if that means making an oath-breaker of me? I made a treaty with them.' Nathair scowled at Aquilus, but his father did not answer. 'And what is the point of making an alliance with those gathered here. Most of them could not agree to *anything*. Better an empire than an alliance. At least if you ruled them you would not have to tolerate their squabbles, their whining.'

Aquilus passed a hand over his eyes. 'The closer to rule you come Nathair, the more you witness squabbles and whining. At least I am in a position where I can influence them, to a degree. As for the Vin Thalun, they will betray us.'

'And if you are wrong?' Nathair asked.

'Enough,' Meical grunted, turning from the window. 'Your father has spoken.'

'I do not recall addressing *you*.' For a moment the Prince and Meical stared at each other, a sudden tension in the room. Instinctively, Veradis' palm strayed to his sword. Then Nathair turned and left the room, Veradis close behind him.

CHAPTER NINETEEN

CYWEN

Cywen was loitering with her brother in the courtyard outside the feast-hall, engrossed in picking dirt from under her fingernails with one of her knives. It had been hard to get a clear story from anybody, but what *was* definite was that the wounded man on the litter was the last survivor of the outlaws in the Baglun Forest. Two riders cantered into the courtyard, drawing up sharply before the hall's steps.

A tall warrior dismounted and held the other horse.

'I can manage,' the other rider snapped. Brina, the healer. Despite her age, she swung nimbly down, silvery hair spilling over a black shawl.

Her gaze swept imperiously around the courtyard, then she took a bag that was hanging from the pommel of her saddle and bustled up to the feast-hall's doors, the two warriors on guard quickly opening them for her.

Cywen darted forward to look inside and caught Princess Edana's eye. She hurried over to them.

'Hello,' she said, smiling at Cywen and Corban. She glanced over her shoulder back inside the hall. 'I can't stay out here, I don't want to miss anything.'

'What's happening in there?' whispered Cywen, Corban hovering near her shoulder.

'Walk with me,' Edana muttered, striding quickly out of the courtyard, shadowing the eastern rim of the hall and keep. 'You will have to be very quiet; if Mother finds out she'll skin me.'

'Finds out what?' Corban asked.

'That I've let you into the fortress to listen.' She stopped, opened a narrow door and guided her two companions through a series of wide corridors.

'Wait here,' she whispered, one hand on the iron ring of a large oak door. 'The feast-hall is on the other side. I'll leave the door open a little so that you can hear what is said.'

Cywen grabbed the Princess' hand.

'Thank you.'

'Well, what are friends for?' Then she slipped into the hall.

'. . . are sure they are all dead?' Cywen heard Queen Alona's voice.

'Aye,' Pendathran grunted. 'All but this one. And he may not see the morning.'

'Are you sure there were no others?' Evnis this time.

'Aye. My huntsmen have covered every handspan of that cursed forest. Not only my nephew Marrock, but also the newcomer Halion. It was he that found their trail.'

'Well, brother, congratulations are in order, although my husband will be unhappy if no one survives to serve his justice to.'

Pendathran muttered something, but Alona spoke over him.

'You have done what you had to do. You and your men must need food and rest. Brina, will he live?'

'Would you recover from a hole between your ribs in this cold draughty room?' the healer snapped. 'I have herbs for a poultice, and hazel bark to dim the pain and draw out the fever, but it may be too late.' She shrugged. 'We will know better in the morning.'

'But Pendathran said he may be dead by morning,' Evnis said.

'Aye. Then you will know, will you not?'

Silence.

'Do all that you can, Brina. Come, Pendathran, escort me to my chamber, I would talk more with you. Evnis, see to Brina's requests and arrange some food for the warriors.'

'Yes my Queen.'

Pendathran's gruff voice spoke out. 'Tarben, Conall. First guard. Watch him well; Darol had many friends.'

Cywen and Corban hugged the wall, hearing footsteps approach. They looked up and down the corridor. Too far to run, no cover to hide behind. A moment's panic seized them both – to be caught eavesdropping on the Queen. Then Princess Edana appeared in the doorway.

'Quickly,' she hissed as she ran down the hall. The corridors twisted and turned, tapestries rippling in the wake of their passing. They rushed up a wide stone staircase, Edana shoved a door open and they ran inside, the Princess pulling the door closed behind them.

A huge bed of oak dominated the room, clothes strewn about the floor.

'This is my chamber,' Edana whispered. 'This way.' She walked to a large window, opened its shutters, stepped over a stone sill and crouched on the balcony beyond. 'My mother and father's room is next door. This is where she'll bring Pendathran.' They shuffled along, crouching under another window.

It was only moments before they heard the door open and shut in the room beyond. Drink was poured from a jug, chairs scraped.

'Did you have to kill all of them?' Alona asked.

'Aye, sister. They fought well. Tried not to kill them all, that's why we lost so many men. It's harder than you'd think, you know, trying to take men alive.'

Queen Alona snorted.

'It was a hard fight. The new lads, Halion and Conall, turned it, though I don't think they thought much about taking anyone alive. They are two to watch, I think.'

'How so?'

'Well, I'd be happy for either one to be my shieldman. If I trusted them.'

'That good?'

'Aye. Halion, the older one, he's a thinker. And he's led men before, that's obvious. My lads took straight to him.'

'What about the other one?'

'Conall. He's the complete opposite. No thought at all, fights like a summer storm. But he's deadly. May even be a match for Tull.'

Alona sucked in a breath.

'Who are they, sister?'

'Brenin would not say,' she sighed. 'When I asked him, he told me little. Said he'd given an oath. You know how he is.'

'Aye. So he'll take whatever they told him across the bridge of swords with him. Ah well. There's something about them – both used to giving orders, not so used to taking them. And little trust in either one.' There was a pause, the sound of gulping, a cup slammed down hard. A chair creaked. 'Well, sister, I am for some food and ale now.'

'Thank you, Pen. Brenin will be grateful, as am I –' she paused – 'and Rhagor would be proud of you.'

The footsteps to the door stopped.

'Not a day passes that I do not think of him,' Pendathran muttered. 'I pray that brigand survives. My heart tells me they were Braith's men, but it would be good to know for sure.'

'I think, if this man survives and proves you true, then our King will deal with Braith and his brigands once and for all,' said Alona.

Pendathran chuckled. 'The thought of that, dear sister, brings joy to an old man's heart.'

'*Old*, get out of here, you bear, there are many more years left in you yet, I think.'

Still chuckling, Pendathran left the room.

Cywen and Corban followed Edana back through her chamber, and without a word slipped down deserted corridors and a steep stairway until they were back at the door where they had entered the fortress.

Cywen and Corban whispered their thanks, knowing the risk Edana had taken sneaking them in. She just grinned.

'I can trust you to tell no one, can't I?'

They nodded solemnly.

'Where are you going now?' Edana suddenly asked. Corban looked up at the sun, well past its zenith, but there was still plenty of daylight left.

'Let's go and see my new colt,' he said.

'All right,' said Cywen, 'but we won't be able to stay long.'

'What colt?' Edana asked, and Corban quickly explained his gift. It was not long before the three of them were hurrying down the path that led from the fortress to Havan, Edana with the hood of her cloak pulled up.

'I'm not supposed to leave the fortress without Ronan, my shield-man,' she explained.

Children were playing in groups around the main street of the village, dogs running and barking at their feet. A familiar figure was sitting forlornly on a large stone by the roadside.

'Dath, what are you doing?' Corban called. 'What's happened to you?'

'Oh, nothing. I fell,' said Dath, hand going to his cheek.

Edana stepped forward, pulling her hood back. Dath's mouth opened and closed like a fish as he recognized her.

'This doesn't look like it was caused by a fall. The skin is broken here, by something sharp.' Edana gently touched the mark on Dath's face.

'My da's ring,' Dath muttered. 'He won't even remember doing it tomorrow. I'll just tell him I fell, hit my face on the ship's rail.'

'Why did he hit you?' Edana asked.

Dath shrugged. 'He missed the tide this morning, been drinking usque all day since.' He looked away. 'He says I remind him of Mam. Don't know why that makes him angry. As I said, he won't even remember tomorrow.'

'Then you should tell him what he's done. When he's sober. It's— it's not right,' Cywen blurted.

'Well, it's not your concern, is it?' Dath snapped. 'And don't be so quick to judge what's right and wrong. You've still got your mam.'

An uncomfortable silence hung in the air. Corban coughed.

'Come with us, Dath,' he said. 'I've been given a gift. A colt foal. Come and see him with us.'

They were on their way to the paddock, their shadows stretching far in front of them, when they heard riders on the road behind. They scrambled down the stony embankment, standing in the grass and flowers of the meadow as a rider came into view.

It was Brina, the healer, galloping hard. Dath made the sign against evil. 'She makes my blood cold,' he muttered.

'I thought she would have stayed in the fortress tonight,' Edana murmured as Brina disappeared into the distance.

'She has to be within her own walls at night, because of her *spells*. So that the spirits she controls don't escape.' Dath looked at their expressions and scowled. 'You must have heard the stories. Strange noises, *voices* coming from her cottage at night, and nobody in there but her.'

'She's a healer, not a witch,' Cywen said, but still looked apprehensively down the empty road as they continued to the paddock to see the foal.

'What are you going to call him, Corban?' Edana asked as they reached mother and foal.

'I don't know yet. Gar said I shouldn't rush his naming, that I should wait until something fits him.'

The colt looked up, towards the road, then bolted.

Cywen saw two figures duck under the paddock rail. At first she could not make out who they were, the sun sinking low in the sky now, then one of the figures shouted and she saw a flash of blond hair.

It was Rafe, his fellow bully Crain behind him.

'Oh no,' she heard her brother whisper.

The mare looked at the new arrivals, then trotted after her foal. Cywen rose and walked towards Rafe. Her companions followed her, Edana pulling up the hood of her cloak.

'Look,' cried Rafe, 'it's Cywen the brave and her cowardly brother.' Crain laughed loudly, staggering a little.

'Usque,' muttered Dath, sniffing.

Crain lifted a clay jug to his lips and slurped noisily, wiping his chin with the back of his hand. 'That's right,' he said. 'Want some?'

Dath shook his head.

'See, I told you it was them,' said Rafe, slapping Crain across the chest. He bowed low, arms outstretched. 'I wanted to thank you for your gift, Corban. The finest practice sword I have ever had the pleasure of using,' Rafe said, holding the wooden sword high.

'I am glad you like it,' Corban said. Cywen frowned. Ban had never mentioned anything about a practice sword to her.

'The spoils of war,' Rafe gloated.

'You're a thief and you should give it back, if you have any honour,' Dath muttered.

'Honour? And this from a fisherman's son,' Rafe said. 'Well, not even that any more, eh? Just a drunk's son, now, aren't you. Your da give you that mark on your cheek?'

Dath's fists bunched, then Edana pulled down the hood of her cloak.

Rafe took an involuntary step backwards. 'W-what're you doing here? With . . .' he trailed off, gesturing to Cywen, Corban and Dath.

'You should not be so quick to insult people about their father's habits when your own bruises have only just healed,' Edana said.

Rafe's empty hand jerked towards his cheek, stopping halfway. He opened his mouth to speak but Edana carried on.

'And did you steal that practice sword from Corban? If so, you must return it. Immediately.'

'I did not *steal* it,' he said, spitting the words out. 'I won it, in a contest. If he wants it back he must earn it.'

'What do you mean?' Cywen said, her anger rising.

'I mean,' Rafe said, turning his head to smirk at her, 'that if your *brave* brother wants his stick back, he will have to complete a task.'

'What task?' she asked.

Rafe tapped his chin a moment, then a smile spread across his face.

'He must sneak into the healer's cottage, and bring me a trophy as evidence.'

'Oh, that's ridiculous,' Edana said. Dath sucked in a deep breath.

'I'll do it,' Corban blurted.

'No,' said Cywen and Dath together.

'You know what she can do to people, Ban. She could put a spell on you, or, or, take your soul, or something,' Dath said.

Cywen saw her brother's gaze shift fleetingly to Edana, then his shoulders rose as he drew a deep breath.

'I shall do it to win my practice sword back, and to prove that I am no coward.'

'Good,' Rafe cried, laughing. 'Come, then. We shall wait nearby while you brave the witch's lair.'

CHAPTER TWENTY

VERADIS

Veradis galloped through the gates of Jerolin, hard on the trail of Prince Nathair.

After the disagreement with his father, the Prince had stormed from the tower and headed straight for the stables, Veradis following. He had seized a fully harnessed horse from a stable boy and ridden from the fortress. Veradis had taken a little longer to organize a mount but caught up on the road that skirted the lake, both of their mounts blowing hard. They slowed to a canter.

'My father . . .' Nathair said after a while, 'he speaks of truth and honour, of championing Elyon against the darkness of Asroth, and yet he cannot see his own dishonour. Cannot or *will* not. He is so consumed with this alliance. And he fawns at that worm's feet like a newborn puppy.'

'Worm?' Veradis said.

'Counsellor Meical,' Nathair growled. 'Honour. Father has always spoken so highly of it to me, how it must be the foundation of all actions and decisions. And yet, when it comes down to it, my honour, my *oath*, seems to count for nothing. I know the Vin Thalun have been Tenebral's enemy in the past, but I gave my word.'

'I agree with you,' Veradis said. 'Although I can also understand the King doubting the Vin Thalun. I have lived on the coast, Nathair, and we feel the corsairs' bite more often than you. That they would just stop is difficult to imagine.'

Nathair nodded, took a deep breath.

'We are on the brink of a new age, Veradis, where much will be swept away and much will change, as my father so readily tells me. Yet when it comes to it he is not quite so willing to embrace that change.

All he can think of is this council and of forging this league. He has dreamed and imagined it as he hopes for it to be for so long that he does not see the truth of how it really is. And *these*,' Nathair snorted, gesturing at the banners rippling around the fortress, 'they are only here to serve themselves. They cannot see beyond their own borders. How can my father imagine they would unite with him? Better to rule them than bicker with them. If the need is as great as my father believes then we cannot risk these fickle kings. They change their minds with the wind. What then?' He was looking at Veradis again.

'I don't know,' Veradis said. 'I have spent more time with my sword and spear than I have in my father's council chamber. There seems much wisdom in what you say. But we must trust our king, must we not. What else is there?'

Nathair looked intently at Veradis and slowly nodded.

'What do you think of this *God-War*?' Veradis asked. He could hardly believe the talk of the council. He liked the old tales well enough, and knew that there was truth in the stories of the Giant Wars, and the earth showed the signs of Elyon's Scourging, plain as the back of his hand. But a *war* between Asroth and Elyon – he could not even imagine it.

'I believe in the Gods, if that is what you mean. As to this book that Meical brings us. Much as I dislike him, perhaps it is true. There is much I don't understand, but some of it – the giant-stones *have* wept blood, have they not? That cannot be denied. And Brenin had a wyrm's *head* in a sack . . .'

'True enough,' Veradis muttered, feeling a shiver sweep him at the memory of Meical reading those words from the book.

'Midwinter's Day,' he said. 'When day shall become night. That will decide it in most minds. But my father believes it now, without any doubt.' Nathair glanced sidelong at Veradis. 'As do I. For my own reasons.'

'What reasons?' Veradis asked.

'Another time.'

They had reached the point where the road forked, and saw a stream of people hurrying from the lakeside village into the forest. Veradis leaned down and beckoned to a young boy.

'Where is everybody going?'

'There's a strange sight in the forest,' the boy replied breathlessly.

'What sight?'

'*Creatures*, I don't know.' The boy shrugged as Veradis dismissed him. Veradis looked at Nathair, who raised an eyebrow and with a click of his tongue urged his horse into the forest. They passed many of the crowd on foot, and soon they rode into a wide, open glade and pushed to the front.

There the ground was black, seething with frantic movement.

They were ants. Thousands of them, thousands upon thousands. The biggest that Veradis had ever seen, each one easily the size of his small finger. They marched in a wide column, as wide as a man lying with arms stretched overhead, a writhing, boiling black mass that issued from one side of the glade and disappeared into the forest on the other, in permanent, remorseless motion.

'I have heard tales of such a thing, deep in the heart of ancient forests,' he whispered to Nathair, 'but never did I truly believe them.' The Prince did not answer, just crouched to see the ants better, an intense, almost rapt expression on his face.

An isle of green grass separated the crowd from the column of ants, no one being overly keen to get too close. Veradis saw the boy that he had spoken to on the road standing nearby.

Knees and elbows began to dig into Veradis' back as the crowd swelled. The thought of being pitched face first into the marching black carpet in front of him was not appealing, so he jostled back a pace.

Another ripple ran through the crowd as more joined the back, trying to squeeze their way through. The boy from earlier suddenly lurched forwards, knocked by bodies behind him, and his foot came down on the edge of the marching column. Instantly a black tide swarmed up his leg. The boy tried to jump back, but the press of bodies behind stopped him. He screamed and flailed at his leg. Blood was welling in rips that the insects had torn in his breeches, their mandibles tearing through cloth and flesh.

Veradis leaped past the Prince, who glanced at his friend briefly, his eyes drawn immediately back to the mass in front of him. Veradis swept the boy up into his arms, almost instantly feeling stinging pain as the ants surged onto him.

'To me, pass the boy to me,' a voice shouted, a young, red-haired man gesturing at him.

Veradis swiped at the boy's leg, knocking scores of ants onto the ground, people suddenly pushing away from him. *Now they're moving.* In the new space Veradis lifted the boy over his head and passed him to the red-haired warrior.

Further up the line a dog barked, a scraggly, wire-haired ratter. Even as Veradis looked, it was knocked sprawling into the ants. For a moment they just swirled around the dog, like a boulder in a river, but then the black tide swarmed up its legs, engulfing it. The whine turned to a frenzied howling as the dog stumbled to the ground, tried to rise, snapping, foam in its mouth turning pink. In a matter of seconds it quivered and then lay still.

Cursing, Veradis turned and stormed into the crowd, pushing his way through, glaring at people as they fell about him.

He found the red-haired warrior tending to the boy in an empty part of the glade and realized it was Kastell. He had sat with Romar, Isiltir's King, at the feast. Methodically he was plucking insects from the boy, crushing them in his big hands. An older warrior, grey-haired, crouched beside him and tried to calm the boy, who was crying, chest heaving in great, racking sobs.

'My thanks. There were not many back there inclined to help,' Veradis said.

The warrior nodded.

'I have seen you before,' the grey-hair said. 'You are the Prince's man?'

'Aye. Veradis.' He extended his bloodied hand.

'Maquin. And my friend here is Kastell. A strange sight, eh?' he said, gesturing to the column of ants.

'Aye. One I've never seen before.'

'These are the times for strange sights, it would seem. Judging by today's council,' Kastell said.

Veradis smiled. 'I saw you in the practice court yesterday. It would have gone the worse for you without that well-timed knee below the belt.'

'I did not mean for that to happen,' said the big youth, scowling.

'It was well done, I would say,' Veradis replied, and Maquin grunted an agreement. 'Your opponent – he had it coming. He may not be so quick to laugh at you next time.'

'Maybe. Maybe I have made things worse.'

'How so?'

Kastell was silent.

'His opponent was Jael, nephew of Romar, Isiltir's King,' Maquin said.

'Jael is my cousin,' Kastell said. 'His reputation in my homeland is not for forgiveness. I should not have struck him as I did. And especially not in front of such an audience.'

'Long overdue, though,' growled Maquin, and Veradis laughed.

'You should stay out of things,' Kastell said to Maquin with a scowl, 'otherwise Jael will mark you as well.'

'When you were six years old I carried you to Romar on my saddle. I have been your shieldman longer still. I think Jael already has me marked,' Maquin said.

'Aye, well, you should still be more careful. It is better not to catch Jael's eye.'

'Wise words from the man that kicked him in the knackers.'

Veradis laughed.

'Don't encourage him,' Kastell said. 'And just because you are a giantkiller now, it doesn't make you invincible,' he added to Maquin.

Veradis held his hands up. 'I did not want to start a disagreement. Only to say that I thought you fought well.'

Kastell nodded and smiled.

'And it seems there are some tales worth listening to here,' Veradis added. 'Giantkiller?'

'It was a lucky throw,' the old warrior said. 'Kastell could see the colour of the eyes of the giant he killed.'

'Oh-ho, *two* giantkillers. This must be a tale indeed.'

The boy on the ground whimpered.

'Another time,' said Maquin. 'Find us at the feast tonight and we'll share a jug. But now we'd better get this lad back to his kin.'

The two warriors carried the boy from the glade. Veradis studied his arms, grimacing at the mass of cuts and drying blood, then went to find Nathair.

The Prince was still at the front of the crowd, crouched in the grass, as engrossed in the macabre procession before him as when Veradis had left.

Suddenly the end of the marching column appeared, the insects receding from the far side of the glade as if a long rug were being rolled up.

Veradis watched silently as the crowd left the forest glade, until he and Nathair were the only two left.

The ants had flattened the ground they had marched over, leaving the impression of a wide, oft-walked path. All that remained of the dog was a mass of torn bloodied fur and bone.

'They eat as they march,' said Nathair, watching Veradis. 'Amazing. Quite amazing. Did you see them, Veradis, the ants? How they overpowered something so many times their size and strength?'

'I did,' said Veradis, shivering at the memory.

'We could learn from them,' Nathair whispered.

'What do you mean?'

'When we go into battle we fight warrior against warrior, sometimes with shield-brother, but often without. Our wars are like a thousand duels on a battlefield, all happening at once.'

'Aye. It is the way it has always been done.'

'But what if we fought like the *ants*, Veradis, as one body, all aiding each other?' He paused. 'We would be unstoppable.'

Grease dripped down Veradis' chin as he bit into a thick slice of meat. He was sitting at one of many long tables that had been set up in the practice court outside the keep. The night was warm, a half-moon and stars shining down from a cloudless sky. He had searched out Kastell and Maquin and shared a jar of wine with them. They had been good company, though King Romar had called them away early. Now his brother-in-arms Rauca was sitting next to him, trying to talk and gnaw on a rack of ribs at the same time. Veradis was not really listening. He was thinking about Nathair and events since the council had ended.

Rauca slapped Veradis on the shoulder and pointed to the open doorway of the keep. Prince Nathair was standing there, dressed in black with the eagle of Tenebral carved on a leather cuirass. He caught Veradis' eye and beckoned to him.

'Are you well?' Veradis asked him.

'Aye, my friend. My apologies for my mood earlier. I love my father, I just do not understand some of his decisions. I have thought on what you said, though, and you are right. We must trust our king; but I will not sit idly by and watch while all he has worked for turns to ashes. I must work to further his cause, and indeed my own, for I will be king after him, will I not?'

'Aye, Nathair. Of course.'

'Then come, let us play the game that is before us,' he said, flashing a smile.

Nathair led him into the courtyard, singling out kings and barons, methodically speaking with them all. Nathair was courteous and friendly to all, whether they had agreed to ally themselves to Aquilus or not, talking to them of their concerns with the alliance, and also about their own worries within their realms. Mandros of Carnutan was one of a few who refused to be charmed by Nathair, so the Prince instead turned to Mandros' son, Gundul, a round-faced youth who laughed loudly at all of Nathair's jokes. The Prince invited many out hunting with him the following day. Gundul agreed, as did a handful of others – including Jael, who had fought Kastell in the practice court.

He is made to be king, Veradis thought as he watched Nathair throughout the evening, charming, interested and knowledgeable in all subjects.

As the night grew late, and some were beginning to head to their beds, Nathair led Veradis towards a royal group gathered in the gardens that bordered the weapons court. Veradis recognized Brenin of Ardan, along with Rhin and Owain.

Brenin gripped Nathair's arm, and Veradis noted his muscular build. *Not a soft king, like so many of these others*, he thought. He nodded a greeting to Tull, the King's first sword.

The ageing warrior smiled at him. 'How is your friend, Rauca?' he leaned over and whispered.

'He is well, although his knuckles are still bruised, no doubt.'

Tull laughed. 'He fights well, but you don't get to live as long as I have without learning to use this.' He tapped a finger against his temple.

Veradis smiled, liking the old warrior.

'This is Heb, my reluctant loremaster,' King Brenin said, gesturing at the spidery old man behind him.

'Reluctant?' said Nathair.

'Oh, it's nothing personal,' Heb said. 'I like Brenin well enough, I just like the pleasures of my hearth more. And I hate long journeys.'

Veradis coughed to cover his laughter.

'Ignore him; he lies,' Brenin said. 'I would have had to tie him down to keep him away. He's far too inquisitive to have stayed in Ardan.'

Nathair took Rhin's hand and kissed it. Her skin was mottled, papery thin, blue veins standing proud. 'You look beautiful, my lady.'

'Flatterer,' Rhin said, though she smiled warmly, the flickering torchlight turning her lined face into a place of dark gullies.

'I speak the truth as I see it.'

'Really? A dangerous practice for a prince. If I were ugly, would you have told me so?'

'No,' Nathair grinned. 'I would have focused on some other virtue.'

'If you could find one.'

'All have something worthy about them, if you look hard enough.'

'Well said,' Rhin smiled. 'Keep looking for my virtues and I think you and I shall get along very well.'

'Please, Rhin, stop playing with the boy.' Owain spoke now, the King of Narvon. He was a dark-haired, sharp-featured man, his smile showing little warmth. His realm bordered both Rhin's and Brenin's, if Veradis remembered his maps right.

'I don't play at anything,' Rhin said, her eyes fixed on Nathair. 'Besides, he is doing very well for himself. So far.'

Veradis decided he did not like this Rhin. There was something predatory about her, about the way she looked at Nathair. *That's not right. She's so old.*

'Careful, Nathair, you are swimming in dangerous waters here,' Owain said, draining his cup. 'Before you know it, Rhin will sweep you away and have you handbound.'

'Hardly,' Rhin snorted. 'Variety is what keeps me young. Though for the right man . . .' She smiled.

'And how do things stand in your homeland?' Nathair asked her, his neck flushing red.

'Well enough,' Rhin laughed. 'As most of the realms that border my lands are ruled by one relative or another, so times are stable. A little dull, but stable. Apart from the giants in the north, of course. They are always determined to test my warriors' mettle. Still,' she turned to her champion, 'I am never in danger, even when the giants are feeling more ferocious, not while I have Morcant here to guard me.' She ran a long white finger down the curve of his cheek. He smiled back at her. Something about the gesture made Veradis blush.

'If what we heard in the council today is true, it will take more than one man's blade to keep you safe,' Nathair said. 'I must confess, I had hoped to see more support my father.' Nathair looked at Rhin and Owain. 'I do not remember seeing either of you stand today.'

'That is because I did not,' Rhin said. 'I am old, Nathair, and there are lessons that age has taught me. One is that rushing is overrated. Much of what your father said strikes a chord in me, but I am not yet convinced. Also, I felt a little unsure, shall we say, of your father's counsellor and his findings. There is something unsettling about him.' She smiled, brushing a strand of white hair out of her face.

'I am not the most trusting of people – one of my faults, I fear – but I find it hard to take the word of one man on such claims. So I shall wait, see what Midwinter's Day brings us. Besides,' she added, 'all of this talk of Gods and demons, maybe we do not need to look so far afield for conflict and war. There are those here that would be better served paying more attention to what goes on in their own realms, instead of wishing faery tales come to life.'

She's a clever one, Veradis thought. *Who was that intended for? Brenin, Owain, Nathair. All?*

Brenin raised an eyebrow but said nothing. Heb smiled, as if watching an entertaining game.

'Please, speak plainly,' Owain said. 'I have drunk too much wine to untangle your riddles.'

Rhin clucked her tongue. 'No tact, Owain. I am sure Brenin will explain it to you.'

Brenin chuckled. 'Leave me out of this.'

'Very well. Speaking plainly, I have heard that you both have had troubles of late.'

'Aye, true enough,' said Brenin. 'Lawless men, striking out from the Darkwood. Braith is at the heart of it with his band of outlaws, I believe, though I have not the proof yet. I hope it will be waiting for me when I return.'

'It is the same for me,' Owain grunted. 'All along the border of the Darkwood I am raided.'

'Maybe this alliance is the answer for you both, then,' Rhin said.

'Perhaps working together, and with King Aquilus' help you could deal with these lawless men.'

'I am capable of keeping my own lands safe,' Owain snapped.

'Really? And yet you are here, while your lands are raided, robbed. As are you Brenin.'

'Ever the same, Rhin,' Brenin said, shaking his head. 'You will not bait me, try as you might. I will not be part of your amusements.' With that he strode away, Heb close behind him. Tull nodded at Rhin's champion, then followed his King, winking at Veradis as he passed him by.

Soon the Prince excused himself, taking Veradis in search of wine.

'Dry work, this politicking,' Nathair said as they drained their cups.

'I am thirsty just listening to it,' Veradis said.

'What do you think?' Nathair asked.

Veradis shrugged. 'I do not know. In truth, Nathair, much of this talk bores me. I will gladly follow you around such gatherings, but only so that I know you have a sword to guard your back.'

Nathair laughed. 'You are a tonic to me, Veradis, amidst all this guile and bickering and these guarded words. But since you will not tell me what you think, let me tell you what *I* think, O sword that guards my back.' He bowed low.

'The kings of the Banished Lands are like children. They squabble and they swagger, but they will not stand together. My father is deceived by the dreams of his heart. He cannot forge an alliance here that will last. It is a fraying rope that will break when pulled tight, after tonight of that I am certain.'

'Then how will we stand against this Black Sun when he comes?' said Veradis.

Nathair looked about him, but they were far from anyone. Nevertheless he lowered his voice.

'Empire . . .' he breathed. 'There must be an empire. This land needs to be united and strong if we are to be ready when Asroth comes. That will never happen while the Banished Lands are governed by a score of bickering children. An empire, with an army such as the ants we saw, that fights together as one to defeat any foe in its way. I will make Father see this truth. Out of the ashes of his old dream a new one shall be born, and I will give my life to see it come to pass.'

CHAPTER TWENTY-ONE

CORBAN

The sun was just a line on the horizon as Corban stepped carefully amongst the trees surrounding Brina's cottage. The sound of running water drifted through the alder grove, a breeze rustling branches above him, all else quiet and still.

She is only a healer, he told himself, not for the first time since he had left his companions and headed towards the cottage.

How did I get myself into this? he thought, but then Rafe's sneer flashed in front of his eyes. He took a deep breath, pushed down his fear and peered out from behind a tree at Brina's cottage. Green turf capped the wattle-and-daub building, a thin line of smoke climbing faint against the darkening sky from its single chimney. A light flickered from an open window, spreading a warm orange glow into the twilight.

A shadow passed across the brightly lit window and Corban ducked behind a tree, holding his breath. When he had counted two score and ten he dared to look out again.

She must be in the room with the light in. So, I just need to climb through one of the dark windows, grab something and go. Without losing my soul. He shuddered.

He scurried across an open space of grass and wildflowers, throwing himself to the ground underneath the window. Eventually he steeled himself, gently tested the shutters and breathed out in relief when they opened. Quickly he climbed over the rim and slithered to the floor on the other side.

On the far side of the room he saw a small wooden bed. Next to it was a low table with dark objects scattered about, indistinct in the darkness. A thin rim of light outlined a doorway on the far wall.

He scuttled lightly across the floor, stooping, reached the low table next to the bed and grabbed the first thing that he found. Holding it up he saw it was a bone comb. Quickly he stuffed it inside his shirt.

'*STEALER*,' a voice rasped behind him.

Corban spun around. Footsteps thumped, and before he could make his legs move, the door flew open, flooding the room with light. Brina stood outlined in the doorway.

Corban felt hot and cold all at once, beads of sweat breaking out on his forehead.

'What are you doing?' Brina asked in a low, terror-inducing voice.

Corban opened his mouth but nothing came out. Then something moved next to Brina. Corban squinted and suddenly realized it was a huge black crow jumping up and down on a perch beside the door.

'*STEALER, STRANGER, STEALER, STRANGER*,' it croaked repeatedly.

'Thank you, Craf,' Brina said, stroking the bird's ruffled feathers. Slowly the bird's squawking subsided, but it still shifted its weight from one foot to the other, beady black eyes staring at Corban suspiciously.

'Now, boy, what are you doing in my house?'

'I-I am sorry,' Corban blurted.

'I did not ask you how you feel,' the healer snapped. 'What. Are. You. Doing. In. My. House?' She took a step closer with each word, until she stood almost nose to nose with Corban, who had backed away until his legs collided with Brina's bed.

Corban tried to say something, to explain, but all that came out was 'Dare', in a raspy voice.

'You sound like my crow,' the healer said.

'*Death*,' muttered the crow, drawing a squeak from Corban.

'Not yet, Craf. It is not sensible to rush into something quite so permanent.' She fixed Corban with her eyes. 'Well?'

'I'm here on a dare,' he managed to say this time, trying to take deep breaths as Gar had counselled him when panic threatened to overwhelm.

'Explain,' she said.

So Corban did, haltingly at first, but soon the words came tumbling out. Brina stood there, arms folded, listening to him talk about his colt, and Rafe, and his practice sword, and eventually the dare. When he had finished, the two of them stared at each other. Brina tapped her foot on the floor.

'*Death*,' rasped the crow again, staring balefully at Corban, who gulped.

'I think not, my bloodthirsty friend,' she eventually said. 'Not this time, anyway. But w*hat* to do, eh, that is the question.'

'*Wrong, wrong, wrong*,' uttered the crow, beginning to hop from one leg to the other again.

'Yes, you are right, Craf, he *has* done wrong, and he *should* make recompense. You do agree, boy, don't you?'

Corban nodded, a little uncertainly.

Brina laughed. 'Don't worry, boy, I won't turn you into a toad, or take your soul. Nothing quite so dramatic. I was thinking more along the lines of chores.'

'Chores?' repeated Corban.

'Yes, chores. You're not slack-witted, are you?' she frowned, leaning forward and peering intently at him.

He shook his head.

'Good. Well then, chores. The collecting of herbs, plants, roots, various items that a healer needs. And maybe some tidying up too. The days seem to be so busy and I often run out of time.'

Corban just stared at her.

'Well?' she snapped. 'Are you prepared to do this, as a means of making amends for the terrible upset that you have caused?'

Corban nodded. 'Yes,' he eventually managed, overjoyed that he was not going to die, suffer some lingering torment or spend the rest of his days hopping around and eating flies.

'Good. Then be here at highsun tomorrow. Now, I think you had better go. We've all had enough excitement for one evening.'

Corban looked around for a way out.

'Perhaps you should use the door this time,' Brina said.

He nodded again and she ushered him out. As he stepped across the threshold he stopped, fumbled inside his shirt, pulled out the bone comb and offered it to Brina. She looked at it for a moment and then shook her head.

'Bring it back tomorrow, I think.'

'I will,' he said. He stepped out of the house, then paused. 'Thank you.'

'Go on, be off with you,' the healer snapped.

He managed to walk calmly for a few steps, but then broke into a run and sprinted into the alder grove, heart beating fast.

A figure rose and ran towards him as he drew closer, and then Cywen threw herself on him, hugging him fiercely.

'I was scared for you,' she whispered.

'No need,' he grinned at her, and together they walked back to the rest of the group.

Dath and Edana hurried over to him first, Rafe and Crain following more slowly.

'Well, the hero returns,' brayed Rafe. He held the practice sword in one hand, the jug of usque in the other. 'Or *is* he a hero? Maybe you just sat in the woods and waited a while. How would we ever know?'

'You asked him to bring back a trophy,' said Crain.

'That's right, so I did,' said Rafe. 'Well, where is it then?'

Slowly, dramatically, Corban reached inside his shirt. He gripped the bone comb and pulled it out with a flourish, holding it high before him so that all could see, a look of supreme satisfaction on his face.

Dath gasped, as did Cywen. Edana just smiled at him.

'That's not the witch's comb, it's your sister's,' Rafe said, scowling. '*She* gave it to you just now, when she ran to you. You both had this planned all along. Don't think you can fool me with your cowardly ways.'

'It *is* Brina's comb. I did as I was asked,' Corban insisted. 'Now give me my practice sword.'

Rafe's scowl deepened, looking from Corban to the wooden sword in his hand. He drank from the jar and passed it to Crain.

'If you want it, come and take it.'

Not again, Corban thought, fear tugging at him, a coiled, icy snake flexing in his gut.

'Just give him his sword,' snapped Dath.

Rafe sneered at Dath and, quick as could be, backhanded him across the mouth.

Something changed in Corban then; he *felt* it. The ice melted in a blast of heat that flushed his face and bunched his fists. He lunged forwards clumsily, forgetting everything that Gar had taught him, and threw a fist at Rafe's head.

Rafe sidestepped, a little sluggishly, and Corban's fist swung through empty air. At the same time Rafe raised and snapped the practice sword out, catching Corban in the back of the knee, sending him sprawling face-first in the grass. With an animal snarl, Corban launched himself at Rafe, his sheer speed and ferocity catching the older boy by surprise, hoisting him into the air and hurling him to the ground. Corban stood over Rafe a moment, then a noise seeped through the blood pounding in his ears and he looked around. Dath was laughing, pointing at Rafe's surprised expression, and the others quickly began to chuckle. Only Crain did not laugh. In fact he looked furious. Then Corban heard a rustling, looked back at the empty spot where Rafe had been and instinctively ducked. The wooden sword whistled through the air where his head had been. He threw himself at Rafe. This time he was not so lucky. The practice sword, catching him on the right shoulder, knocked him off balance, and then Rafe's fist connected with Corban's face, striking him high on the cheek, just under the eye. His legs turned to porridge and he fell, pain exploding in his head. Rafe took a step towards him, sneering, raising the wooden sword high. Then, with a soft *thunk* a knife flew into the ground just in front of Rafe's boot.

'Not another step,' Cywen said, with another knife held high, arm bent back to her ear.

'You wouldn't dare,' sneered Rafe.

'Take another step and you'll find out,' she said, eyes glinting in the moonlight.

There was a frozen moment.

The tension went out of Rafe's shoulders and he laughed.

'Sister coming to your rescue again, coward,' he said to Corban, then turned and strode away, swaying slightly, Crain following behind him.

'Here, Ban,' said Dath, offering his hand and pulling Corban from the ground.

'You dropped this,' Edana said, holding out the healer's comb. He took it with a rueful smile. 'Let me see your face,' she said, and Corban winced as her fingers probed his skin.

'I'm sorry, Ban, please don't be angry with me, I thought he was really going to hurt you,' Cywen said.

'It's all right.' He was angrier with himself for being beaten again, but at least this time he had fought back, *and* he had managed to knock Rafe down. Also, Edana's face was extremely close to his as she examined his cheek, and he was finding it hard to concentrate on anything else.

'I think you'll live,' Edana said with a smile.

'Very good,' said Cywen sarcastically, 'you should think about becoming a healer.'

After his morning training, as Corban drank thirstily from the water barrel, Gar asked him about the bruise on his cheek. 'Rafe did it. We had a disagreement, last night.'

Corban went on to tell him about the dare, Brina's comb and the fight. 'I know I lost,' he said, 'but at least I didn't just stand there, too scared to move. And I felled him once.'

'That's something, lad. But *lost* as a youth often means a bruised face and some wounded pride. *Lost* after your Long Night usually means *dead*. And you felt anger this time, you say, more than fear. Well, letting your anger rule you will most likely kill you as quickly as fear. There are some that can fight in a kind of red haze of rage. I knew someone like that, once. As it goes, his rage always looked after him. But most likely anger will just flood your mind and make you clumsy, unable to think.'

'But how can I ever hope to win? Surely you would be inhuman to not feel *anything*.'

'That's right, lad, but it's about *control*. About who is the master. All men feel fear, all men feel anger. Use it. Harness it like a packhorse to give you strength, but don't let it cloud your mind and rule your limbs. Do you understand?'

'Aye,' nodded Corban slowly, 'I think so.'

'Good. When *you* control your emotions you can still think, and that saves lives. Part of a warrior's skill is assessing combat before you are caught up in it. Can you beat Rafe?'

'Not yet,' grunted Corban. 'Though I think I'd stand a better chance with a sword in my hand, after all that you have shown me. But anyway, I had no choice. Honour demanded I fight him.'

'You always have a choice. Sometimes it is possible to retreat *and* keep your honour intact. You can duel with words as well as with swords or fists, you know. Words have a power all their own. Still,' he added, seeing Corban's downcast face, 'he is older, bigger, much further along his training than you. You did well. Save for your wound. Your mam will be none too pleased about that.'

'I know,' said Corban ruefully.

'What happened to you?' Gwenith said as Corban sat down to break his fast, hands on her hips.

His da was staring at him, Cywen gazing into her bowl of porridge. 'I fell, Mam. It looks worse than it is.'

'I hope so,' said Thannon, 'for it looks very bad indeed.'

A large bruise surrounded an angry-looking gash on Corban's cheekbone, a brown-black scab not quite covering the cut yet.

Gwenith laid a plate of honey-cakes on the table, then gently touched Corban's cheek.

'Don't fuss, Mam, it'll be fine,' Corban mumbled.

'You fell?' she said.

'Aye, Mam. I was on the rocks down by the beach, with Dath. It was wet. I slipped.'

Gwenith stroked his face. 'You must take more care.'

'Aye, Mam.' Corban did not look up for a while. When he did, Thannon was staring at him.

'I could use your help in the forge, just for the morning,' his da said. Corban nodded, and soon they were walking the stone streets of Dun Carreg. When they reached the forge they silently fell into their normal routine, the hound Buddai draping himself across the open doorway.

Corban banked the edges of the fire, so the heat would be turned in on itself, then set to starting a flame, striking sparks from his flint into a small pile of kindling – twigs, straw, some dried moss and slivers of wood. When the spark took, he gave a steady, gentle pull on the bellows, flames springing up hungrily.

The work began: the coaxing of raw iron into shapes that it would hold for generations. There was something satisfying in that, Corban thought, as he pounded with a hammer where Thannon directed, sparks flying, sizzling and spitting on his leather apron. Thannon doused the length of iron in water and steam leaped up in a hissing cloud.

Time passed quickly, father and son lost in the rhythm of their work. Corban had just doused another length of iron, steam filling the room, when a shadow filled the doorway.

It was Vonn, Evnis' son. He stepped gingerly over Buddai.

'Good day,' he said to Thannon.

'And to you,' said Thannon.

'My da's smith is running low on dousing oil. He has sent me to ask if we might buy some from you,' Vonn said.

'I have plenty,' said Thannon, and pulled out two big buckets, wooden lids on top to stop the oil spilling.

'My thanks,' said Vonn, making to give Thannon some coins, but Corban's da held up his hand.

'I'll see your da after, we'll sort out a price then.'

Vonn nodded, pocketed the coins and picked up the buckets.

As he left the forge he paused in the doorway. 'I am sorry, for last night,' he said to Corban. 'I heard what Rafe did. It should not have happened,' Vonn continued, nodding at Corban's bruised face. 'Rafe has taken a disliking to you, but he is not always as you see him.' Corban stared at the ground. Vonn shrugged and walked on.

There was a long silence in the forge, then suddenly Corban found himself lifted from the floor and his head shoved into the water trough. He struggled but Thannon held him with an iron grip, then he was pulled out, water flying in a glistening arc.

'"*I fell, Mam,*"' Thannon said and shoved Corban's head back into the trough. When his da pulled him out this time he gave Corban a shove, sending him stumbling backwards, falling with a *thump* onto his backside.

There was another long silence, the only sound water dripping from Corban's bedraggled hair.

'Your mam deserves better,' Thannon growled. 'Whatever your cause, lies are a coward's way; and they are like poison. They bring death. Death of trust, Ban. Death of honour, death of respect. Two things,' he grunted, holding up two fingers. 'Truth and courage. Elyon gave us the power of choice. Choose those two and they will see you through. Maybe not easily, but . . .' He leaned back in his chair, shaking his head. 'Now, why did you lie?'

Corban took a deep breath.

'Because I was scared, ashamed. And I don't want you to think me weak, a coward.'

'Tell me,' said Thannon, iron in his voice.

He told his da the full tale, from Rafe taking his practice sword at the Spring Fair through to their encounter the night before. When he had finished Thannon just sat looking at him.

'Do you think your mam would love you less for knowing this, or me?'

'Love me less? No, but, *think* less of me, somehow, yes. Why not? *I* do.'

'Come, boy, it is time for a lesson. Let me teach you the power of words,' Thannon said, walking from the forge, Buddai following.

His da set a fast pace, marching through the stone streets of the fortress.

'Where are we going?' Corban said, trotting to keep up, a sick feeling growing in his stomach. As they marched past the stables Cywen spotted him, and in a quick glance over his shoulder he saw his sister and stablemaster Gar following behind.

The streets twisted and turned as they walked past the feast-hall, people looking at Corban and his dripping hair. Thannon eventually stopped before a large gateway.

Corban suddenly realized where they were.

Evnis' hold.

Most of the warriors were in the Rowan Field, so only one warrior stood guard in the courtyard. It was the man that had fought Tull in the sword-crossing at the Spring Fair. He was leaning against one of the gate columns. When he saw Thannon he stood straighter and gripped his spear more firmly. A red line ran across his nose where Tull had broken it.

Beyond the guard and the gateway was a small open courtyard, then a short set of wide steps leading up to a squat-looking tower. Corban peered around his da, saw Evnis standing on the steps, talking to Brina the healer.

The guard stepped in front of them. 'What is your business?' he asked, looking up at Thannon.

'I would speak with one of your hold. Helfach, the huntsman.'

Brina rode out of the yard, Corban trying to hide from the healer behind his da. Evnis saw them at his gates and walked over. Cywen and Gar caught up with them, his sister whispering in his ear.

'What are you doing?'

'Being given a lesson in the *power of words*,' he muttered, receiving a blank expression from Cywen, a faint smile from Gar.

'Stand down,' said Evnis as he reached the gate. 'Thannon, have you come for payment, for your dousing oil?'

'That can wait,' Thannon said, 'I would speak to your huntsman. We have business to talk over.'

'Really? Certainly, then.' Evnis sent the guard in search of Helfach and disappeared inside his tower.

Moments later Helfach appeared, a tall, thickset hound at his side, the guard behind him. Thannon strode forward to meet the huntsman, Corban reluctantly following.

Helfach was tall, although not as tall as Thannon, with broad shoulders and a narrow waist. He had a wide, flat face with pale, watery eyes.

'Come to see which of my hounds will begin the next hunt? Most likely Braen here,' he said amiably, patting the grey hound's wide back.

'No, Helfach. I would talk with you about Rafe.'

'What of him.'

'It seems he has had a disagreement, with my son.' He gripped Corban's shoulder in his big hand and pulled him forward so that Helfach could see Corban's marked face.

The huntsman stared a moment, then shrugged.

'So?'

Thannon took a deep breath and carried on. 'This is not the first time it has happened. Your son has seen almost two more namedays than Ban. He has had almost two years in the Rowan Field where Ban has not had one day.'

The huntsman said nothing, just stared back.

Thannon grunted. 'Your son is bringing dishonour on himself and your hold. It should end.'

'You should not involve yourself in children's squabbles,' said Helfach. He turned to walk away. Thannon's hand shot out, gripping the huntsman's arm. With a snarl, Helfach spun, wrenching himself free.

'Do not touch me, *blacksmith*. Your hound is chosen to lead one hunt and next you think you can come here, in Evnis' own court, and seek to lord it over me.' He spat on the ground at Thannon's feet. 'Go back to your iron and your ash.'

Buddai gave a low, rumbling growl and then Thannon's fist crashed into Helfach's face. He staggered back, falling to one knee.

Chaos erupted.

Everything happened at once. The two hounds leaped at each other, rolling away in a twisting, snapping mass of teeth and spittle. Helfach launched himself at Thannon, landing a heavy blow under the smith's ribs, making him grunt. There was a flurry of movement and a crashing sound behind Corban. He turned to see Gar with his boot resting on the guard's chest, the warrior lying prone on the floor with Gar holding the guard's spear.

Turning back to his da, Corban saw Thannon grab Helfach by his shirt with one hand and his breeches with the other, lift the huntsman over his head, ignoring the blows raining on him, and throw Helfach against the courtyard wall.

The huntsman crashed to the ground, slowly began to rise. Thannon stepped quickly over to him and threw a heavy hook at his jaw. This time Helfach fell and lay still.

Corban filled a bucket from a water barrel and threw it over the frenzied hounds. Thannon leaned in and pulled Buddai away by his thick collar. The grey hound limped over to Helfach, nuzzled him, then Evnis burst from his tower, staring around his courtyard.

'What is the meaning of this?' he demanded.

'I am sorry,' Thannon said, frowning. 'I did not intend for this to happen.'

There was a long silence.

'The power of words,' muttered Corban and Gar threw his head back and laughed.

Brina opened the door of her cottage as Corban rapped on it. She glanced up at the sun and ushered him in.

'Welcome,' she said as he delved inside his shirt, pulled out her comb and placed it on the table.

'My thanks,' he mumbled.

'*STEALER*,' squawked a voice in Corban's ear, making him start.

Craf was sitting in a dark alcove, beady eyes shining as he ran his beak through coal-black feathers.

'No, Craf, you are mistaken. He is returning my comb, so stealer is incorrect. *Borrower* might be more appropriate.'

'*BORROWER*,' the bird repeated.

'Yes, well. Did it serve its purpose?' Brina said to Corban.

'Not really,' said Corban, still eyeing the crow.

'But I thought it was required, as evidence.'

'Yes, it was. But some people only believe what they want to believe,' Corban said, touching his cheek.

'Ah, I see. Well, be that as it may, now that you are here, let's put you to work. Do you know your plants?'

He looked at her blankly.

'Plants, boy, plants. Can you tell the difference between vervain and foxglove, between hare's foot and wormwood?'

'Worm what?'

Brina gave an exasperated sigh.

'*Useless*,' muttered the crow.

'Today I shall show you. I hope that you have a brain in that battered skull, because next time you shall have to do it alone.'

'Next time? Alone?'

'Yes, boy!' she yelled. 'Next time. You don't think that one fleeting afternoon is all that is required to atone for breaking into my home and attempting to *rob* me? Do you?'

'No, no.'

'Good,' she snapped, and Craf opened and closed his beak with a loud crack, making Corban twitch.

'And can you please stop repeating what I say. You're behaving alarmingly like my crow.'

'*Alarmingly*,' said the crow.

Soon they were out in the alder grove, Brina pointing to various plants, talking in an almost constant flow as she plucked leaves or pulled them up whole, roots and all.

'. . . silverweed . . .' she said as she passed a plant to Corban, who carefully placed it in a hemp bag that the healer had supplied him with.

'. . . even though its flower is yellow,' she explained. 'It is named after its leaves, which are *green*, but, see these fine hairs on the leaves?

Well, they give the appearance that the leaves are edged in silver, and hence the name.'

'I see,' said Corban, nodding sagely, trying to give his best impression of being interested.

'And this is bittersweet. It has a small purple flower and red berries. Very good for old bones like mine.'

'Why were you at Evnis' hold?' Corban said, finally gathering the courage to ask one of the many questions hovering in his mind.

'His wife is ill. Very ill. I took him some seed of the poppy to help ease her pain. Surprised me, though,' she said, almost to herself. 'She looked better. Not healed, mind you, but better than the last time I saw her. And that does not usually happen to people in her condition.'

'Oh,' said Corban. 'But I thought you were at the fortress to see to the outlaw from the Baglun.'

'I was. But I can see more than one person in a day, you know. After all, I am a healer, so I try to heal people, when I can.'

'He's still alive, then?'

'Yes, boy. For now. And if he can avoid another blade in the back. Do you always ask so many questions?'

'Mam says I do,' he answered quickly.

'Well, that is not such a bad thing, I suppose. Annoying, but not bad.' And so the afternoon continued, Brina educating Corban on the appearance and properties of plants, Corban asking questions, not usually related to plants in any way, whenever Brina paused for breath. Eventually they returned to the cottage and Brina set Corban to sweeping, which took him a while to get the hang of, but it did not stop him asking questions.

As the sun was setting, Brina told Corban that he could go home.

'When shall I come back?' he asked.

'Let me see,' she said, tapping a tabletop with a long, bony finger. 'Once every seventh night should be enough. Give the dust a chance to build up for you. And allow me time to gather my strength for your barrage of questions.'

Corban smiled hesitantly, not sure if she was joking or serious. He nodded to her and walked away, heard Craf flutter onto Brina's shoulder as she stood in the doorway.

'*Annoying*,' squawked the crow.

'Yes, he is,' he heard Brina say. 'But in a pleasant kind of way.'

CHAPTER TWENTY-TWO

KASTELL

Kastell walked through the open gates of Jerolin into the wide plain that surrounded it. Already it was beginning to empty, banners furled, patches of yellow grass where tents had stood. Many had left for home the day before.

Home. That was a strange thought. He'd been away from Mikil for only a few moons, but so much had happened since he'd left, it felt more like years.

Maquin belched in his ear.

'Always good t'break your fast, lad, an' that was the best we'll have for a while, I'm thinking. Best make ready for the journey home, eh? Wouldn't want to be last in the saddle, give your cousin something else to moan about.'

Kastell snorted. Things had not been going well with Jael. He had avoided the practice court since his run-in with his cousin, but Jael had still managed to root him out, and more of the usual had followed – goading, mocking. Somehow, and only by the slimmest of margins, Kastell had managed to keep his anger in check.

'He left early this morning, again, hunting with his new friend, the Prince of Tenebral.' Kastell hawked and spat. 'They make a fine pair.'

Maquin laughed. 'Come, lad, you sound jealous. Anyway, Prince Nathair can't be all bad, not if his man Veradis is anything to go by.'

'Aye, true enough.' They had spent some time with the young warrior since meeting him in the forest glade, usually over a skin of wine, Kastell experiencing the strange new sensation of making a friend.

They headed towards their tents.

'So what now? Back to Mikil?' Maquin looked sidelong at Kastell. 'What else is there?'

'Plenty, for one with your skills, giantkiller.'

'Joining the Gadrai's a nice thought, if giantkilling gives entry to their band, but if it means fighting more of those Hunen, I think I'll take my chances with Jael.'

'You'd rather carry on like this, then?'

'As I said, what else is there?'

'Well, I'm not one for telling a man what he should be doing . . .' Kastell snorted.

'. . . but no good is going to come of this. There's trouble brewing between you and your cousin. Real trouble. Neither of you are bairns any more.'

Kastell sighed, but said nothing. How could he argue with the truth? They finished their walk to King Romar's encampment in silence.

As the tents were slowly dismantled and packed away a sound filtered through Kastell's thoughts. He looked up to see a handful of riders spill from the forest. Nathair was at their head, the carcass of a deer draped across his saddle. Jael rode close behind. With a loud farewell to the Prince, Jael rode into Romar's encampment, sneering at Kastell as he passed by.

Kastell looked away.

Another rider detached itself from the hunting party and headed towards Kastell and Maquin.

It was Veradis. He smiled as he approached them, slid from his horse, letting it graze freely on the meadow grass.

'Making ready to leave?'

'Aye.'

'You're back earlier than I thought,' said Kastell. 'Didn't think Jael would return here until all of the work was done.'

'Does he not like hard work?' said Veradis.

'Careful,' muttered Maquin, glancing around, 'remember where we are.' They were hidden from view behind a half-collapsed tent, but the sound of others labouring nearby was still clear.

'Well, Nathair has put in a good morning's work, I think. Caught a deer and charmed the sons of some kings a little more.'

'Work? What do you mean?' asked Maquin.

'Nathair works hard for this realm. He is championing his father's cause – Tenebral's cause. I know he is right, but I find it wearisome. Politicking is not my favourite pastime.' He smiled. 'Don't mind the hunting so much, though.'

'Politicking?' Maquin said.

'Nathair is trying to win more support for his father. You were there,' he said to Kastell, 'you've told Maquin about the council?'

'Of course,' Kastell grunted. His shieldman had been sceptical when he had told him of King Aquilus and Counsellor Meical's claims. *He* was sceptical. The gods Asroth and Elyon, the Kadoshim and Ben-Elim brotherhood, suns and stars. It was a lot to ask any man to believe. Still, Kastell had felt *strange*, almost excited, as that ancient book was being read. And those things it spoke of – the stones weeping, the white wyrms. They had *happened*.

'It is quite a claim,' said Maquin thoughtfully. 'Asroth's God-War against Elyon, here, amongst us. Do you believe it to be true?'

Veradis flushed at the neck. 'My King tells me it is so. There is no more.'

Maquin held up a hand. 'I mean no insult to you or your King. There is no disloyalty in having an opinion of your own.'

Veradis grunted, his shoulders easing slightly. 'Aquilus is a good king,' he said slowly. 'He is wise, has ruled Tenebral well for more years than I have drawn breath. I have not been close to him for long, but my father, who is critical of most that walk this earth, has only ever praised Aquilus. And if that is not enough there is Nathair. *He* I do know well, and trust with my life. He believes these things are happening, so I have no doubt that they are.'

'Good enough,' said Maquin. 'Dark times ahead indeed, then. Let us hope that Prince Nathair's efforts bear fruit.'

'Aye,' said Veradis, relaxing. 'Talking of Nathair, I told him I would not be long. I just wanted to see you both before you left, to wish you safe journey.'

Kastell gripped Veradis' wrist. 'If this alliance works the way you tell it, maybe we'll ride together one day.'

'That would be good,' said Veradis. 'Until then, watch out for that cousin of yours. And you stay out of trouble, grey-hair.' He grinned.

'Look to your own hide, pup. I've had some practice at caring for mine.'

Kastell watched as Veradis walked away. *So many years without a friend, and now I'm making them in all kinds of places.* He shrugged and set back to the packing.

'Here he is, lads,' a voice said behind him. Before he could turn, he was grabbed by the shoulder and spun around. A fist sank into his gut and he doubled over.

'Stay out of this, old ma— oof,' he heard through ringing ears. Maquin stood over another man, fists bunched. Others were rushing around the side of the tent, closing quickly, all faces he knew, faces from Jael's hold. Some fell upon Maquin, two running past the grizzled warrior to throw themselves at Kastell. He ducked a blow, sidestepped, managed to connect his own fist with a jaw and send the man on the end of it crashing to the ground. *Doing quite well, considering*, he thought, then he was grabbed from behind, someone pinning his arms.

'Jael sends his greetings,' a voice whispered in his ear and some-one began raining solid blows into him. His vision blurred and stars burst in his head, then he heard shouting, then that unmistakable sound of a sword hissing from its scabbard. Suddenly he was falling, the arms that had gripped him gone. He crunched jarringly to his knees, toppled slowly to the side.

More shouting and his eyes fluttered open. Booted feet were everywhere, other figures lying near him, one of them rising slowly – Maquin, he realized, blinking to clear his vision. Holding onto a tent pole, he pulled himself up, looking around.

Two men lay unmoving on the floor, two more stood together, facing Maquin, fists raised. One stood alone, a sword-tip at his throat.

Veradis was holding the sword.

Kastell staggered over to Maquin's side. Other men ran around the tent now, more of King Romar's warriors. They snarled as they saw their friends, some drawing weapons.

'Halt,' cried a loud voice. Romar himself cleared the part-collapsed tent, Jael at his heels. 'What is the meaning of this?' he bellowed. An awkward silence fell. Romar repeated his question, this time aimed only at Veradis.

'Best ask your own,' the warrior of Tenebral replied calmly, keep-ing his eyes on the man at the end of his sword-point. 'For myself, I was returning to the fortress when I saw these men set upon those two,' he gestured towards Kastell and Maquin. 'I do not know your customs in Isiltir, but here in Tenebral five against two is considered cowardly.'

King Romar looked from Veradis to his warriors to Kastell and Maquin, both with bloodied faces, and then finally to Jael.

'You can sheathe your weapon,' he said to Veradis, who took a step back, and smoothly slid his sword into its scabbard.

'My thanks,' mumbled Maquin through swollen lips.

'And mine also,' said Romar. 'Come, share a drink with me before we leave.' Veradis looked back at the fortress, then nodded.

'I will deal with you later,' Romar said to his warriors as he turned and walked away, Veradis following him. 'Jael, Kastell, with me,' he barked over his shoulder.

Silently the three men followed Romar's broad back until they were standing in a row inside a tent. The King of Isiltir filled four cups from a skin and handed them out. Kastell winced as the sour liquid stung his cut lip, but he gulped it down nevertheless. Fighting was thirsty work.

'Again, my thanks,' said Romar, tipping his head to Veradis.

'I am glad to have been of some help. Sometimes disagreements can flare into something worse.'

'Not all would have done as you did. Aquilus is fortunate to have men like you around him. A wise king surrounds himself with men of quality, such as yourself.'

Veradis bowed his head, looking uncomfortable.

'But what does that say about me, I wonder? Those I have close to *me* seem more inclined to fight each other than our true enemies.' He scowled at Jael and Kastell. 'And what have you to say?' he directed at Kastell, who shuffled his feet, looking at the rim of his empty cup.

'Just a disagreement. Nothing more,' he mumbled.

'Do not lie to me, boy. You are not very good at it.' He looked back to Jael.

'Do you think me a fool? Do you think I know nothing of this, this *bairn's* grudge you have fostered against your cousin?'

'You take *his* side?' Jael blurted incredulously.

'It is not about *sides*,' roared Romar, hurling his cup at the ground.

'I saw, Jael. I *saw* what you did to Kastell, in the practice court.' He drained his cup and poured another. 'I was ashamed. This. Ends. Now,' he growled.

'But . . .' said Jael.

'*NOW!*' bellowed Romar. 'You will both be lords soon. If I were to die it would probably be one of you two that would rule Isiltir until my son Hael comes of age. You will be leaders of men. You do not lead by shaming others.'

'But he shamed *me*. If you were there you must have seen what he did.'

'Aye, I did. There was wrong on both sides, but more with you, Jael.' He began pacing around the empty tent. 'I say again: this ends today. Right now. You are kin, bound by blood. This only brings shame on you both, on me, on our family.'

There was a long, uncomfortable silence.

'Now, start behaving like kin, and men.'

Another long silence.

'Yes, Uncle. You are right. We should put this childishness behind us,' Jael said. He held out his hand to Kastell, who hesitantly took it.

Romar smiled. 'That's better, lads. Well done.'

Romar slapped them both on the back. 'That is good. I have high hopes for the both of you. New times are ahead for us all, what with this alliance and . . .' he trailed off. 'Anyway, the two of you figure highly in my plans for the future of Mikil, and of Isiltir. Now, let us get this campsite cleared and begin the journey home.'

'Yes, Uncle,' said Jael. Kastell grunted, and they both left the tent.

'This is far from over,' hissed Jael as he walked away.

CHAPTER TWENTY-THREE

CORBAN

Corban slipped into the kitchen, face flushed and sweaty from his morning's training with Gar. His mam was standing by the oven, pulling out a tray of oatcakes. He ran a hand through his damp hair, chewing on his bottom lip.

'Can I speak to you, Mam?'

Gwenith placed the oatcakes on the table, brushed her hands down her woollen dress, and sat. 'Of course.'

He sat opposite her, absently digging at a piece of wood in the table with his thumbnail.

'Has this anything to do with the bruises on your da's face?' Gwenith asked. 'And the rumours I'm hearing – that he had a *talk* with Helfach?'

'I'm sorry, Mam,' he said slowly. 'I lied to you.'

She said nothing and he looked up at her now, his dark eyes meeting her gaze. 'About my face. I didn't fall on the rocks. I was fighting.'

'Who with?'

'Rafe.'

'Ah. I see.' Gwenith nodded to herself. 'Go on.'

And so Corban told her his tale, including Rafe's dare and his penance of afternoon chores with Brina. When he was done they sat in silence awhile.

'There is something else,' he said. 'In the mornings, when I go out early. I have been training. Training with Gar. He told me to tell no one, but I wanted to tell you. I don't want to lie to you any more.'

'Does Gar know that you have told me?'

'Yes, Mam. I spoke to him about it this morning.'

She looked at Corban, large brown eyes filling, and held out her arms. 'Come here, son.'

He wrapped his arms around her and nuzzled his head into her shoulder.

'You are a good boy,' she murmured, stroking his dark hair, 'better than you know.' A tear spilled out and rolled down her cheek.

'Why did you laugh?' Corban grunted as he rested a moment, hanging from a beam in the stables. 'In Evnis' courtyard. About the "power of words".'

'I believe Thannon intended a different outcome for his lesson. Your da would not be my first choice for a task requiring diplomacy. You see, Corban, the power of emotions . . .' Gar shrugged. 'I have not seen the man that could best your da in a fistfight. But anger ruled him for a while back there. And he has made an enemy now. For life.'

'So?' said Corban. 'What does that matter?' He dropped from the beam and rolled his shoulders.

'Maybe nothing. Maybe something. Thannon will need to watch his back from now on, that's all.'

Corban grunted, not liking that thought, particularly as he had been the cause of the conflict.

'Well, Helfach has stayed out of Da's way since. And I haven't seen Rafe at all.'

'Aye. Helfach is a proud man, a beating like that will not sit well with him. As for Rafe, I have heard that he is not able to leave his bed at the moment.'

Corban looked at the floor.

'Queen Alona should declare the next hunt soon. It will be interesting whose hound she chooses to lead it.'

'A hunt? It's my nameday soon. If the hunt is after then I will be able to go.'

'Aye, lad. True enough. And you know what else your nameday means?'

'Yes. The Rowan Field,' said Corban reverently.

The fourteenth nameday was the traditional day for boys to begin their warrior training. All began their training long before they reached fourteen, whether on their own with a stick and a defenceless tree, or with their da. Corban had spent many hours whacking the trees in his mam's rose garden, and Thannon had done his best to teach Corban some combat basics, though the blacksmith was somewhat lacking in technique, having little need. The Rowan Field, a great empty space at the northern tip of the fortress, was where it happened. It held an almost holy aura to all the boys in Dun Carreg. When he came of age, on his sixteenth nameday, he would attempt the warrior trial with sword, spear and horse. If he passed he would ride out to sit the Long Night, standing guard throughout the dark of night over those who had protected him. Then he would be a man.

'They will not teach you bladework as I do,' Gar said. 'They do things differently, where I was trained.'

'Helveth, you mean?'

Gar gave a curt nod.

'For one thing, you will be shown more with a shield. When I learned my weapons a warrior would grip a sword two-handed and attack rather than hold a shield and defend – we were taught the best defence is to attack.'

'Which is better?'

'You will make up your own mind. It will do you no harm to learn both ways. I will continue to show you my way until you ask me to stop, or I have shown you all I have to teach.'

'That won't be any time soon,' said Corban.

Gar grunted. 'You will be teamed to a warrior in the Rowan Field, one that will begin your training. Usually Tull takes those on their first day, finds out what they can do, then he passes them on to whoever is free. But Tull is not here. Tarben would be best out of those still at the fortress – if you can learn to block his moaning from your ears.'

Corban smiled.

'If that does not happen, try for one of the newcomers, Halion or Conall. I have watched them in the Rowan Field. Both know how to hold a blade, though for you Halion would be better. The older one.'

'Why him?'

'He is a thinker. He will teach you to use this.' The stablemaster prodded Corban's temple none too gently.

*

Days settled into a routine for Corban, the spring sun growing in its strength and lengthening the days, summer's heat building early. He trained with Gar most mornings, and even though his body complained, he always came away with a sense of satisfaction. He was starting to feel a little stronger in his exercises and a little less clumsy in his sword dance.

The rest of his days were filled with hot sessions in the forge, hours in the paddocks with Cywen and Gar, building a bond with his colt, and regular afternoons in and around Brina's cottage.

Gar had told him not to attend his usual pre-dawn training at the stables. *It is a special occasion*, he had said. So Corban had risen at sunrise and broken his fast with his family, although he hadn't had much of an appetite. His thoughts kept drifting to the Rowan Field. He had looked forward to this day for so long, *longed* for it; but now that it was here, he'd rather wait a little longer. This business with Rafe had tainted it. He felt a pressure building behind his eyes and in his chest as his time to walk into the Field rapidly approached. Until finally Thannon ushered Corban out of the cottage door.

They walked in silence, his da leading Corban past the feast-hall, the keep, the well passage, past stone buildings busy with people, then past stone buildings empty and dark.

He heard the *clack-clack* of wooden swords striking each other before he turned a corner and saw the Rowan Field opening up before him. Green grass flashed bright in the sunlight at the end of a long path, rowan trees edging both sides of it, their branches crisscrossing overhead to form an arched tunnel. He stopped.

So here he was, staring at the entrance to the most esteemed warrior training ground in all of Ardan, a place of mythologized grandeur that had a special place in the hearts of every boy in the realm.

Thannon rested a large hand on Corban's shoulder.

'Here you are, son.'

Corban nodded silently, took a deep breath and walked into the shade of the trees.

A huge field unrolled before him, ending in the high stone walls that ringed the outskirts of the fortress. The sound of the sea and the calling of gulls underlay everything else – the noise of men sparring, practice sword beating against practice sword, or shield, or leather, or flesh. Corban felt the thud of hooves through the ground, saw at the far edges of the field warriors riding at each other, or running beside cantering horses. Closer stood rows of thick tree trunks, driven into the ground. Men were lined before them, some drawing bowstrings, some casting spears at the wooden targets. Closer still, men sparred in pairs, some with shields strapped to their arms, others with wooden swords held in two-handed grips, the grass worn and patchy. Around them were small clusters of men watching the contests.

As Corban gazed around the field a warrior approached them. He was tall and gangly, long brown hair tied back from his face.

'Name's Tarben,' he said as he drew nearer, nodding to the blacksmith. 'This your first time in the Field?' he directed at Corban.

'Yes.'

'This is my son,' Thannon said.

'Normally Tull runs things round here, so it would be him that would welcome you to the Field, but as he's away, playing at Elyon knows what, it's fallen to me to be the overseer of the Field.' Then the gangly warrior drew himself up straighter and spoke in a loud, clear voice. On the edge of his vision Corban saw heads turn amongst those watching the sparring, looking over.

'Welcome, Corban ben Thannon, to the Rowan Field of Dun Carreg. May you learn the ways of a warrior while you are here, and may truth and courage guide your hand.' He grabbed Corban's arm in the warrior's grip.

'Good,' the gangly warrior said, shoulders slumping. 'Now that's over. You staying, big man?' he asked Thannon.

'Not today.' Thannon hesitated. 'He's my son. Any problems, I'll not be happy.'

'Aye, that's been made clear already. Have no worries,' Tarben said quickly. 'There'll be no trouble in the Field while I am here.'

Thannon grunted, slapped Corban's shoulder and walked away.

'Come on, lad, follow me,' and Tarben set off, striding briskly towards the mass of sparring warriors.

'Mounted combat over there,' Tarben said with a wave of his arm, 'spears and bows over there, but Tull always starts the new lads on swords. Worked well enough for him, so let's stick with it, eh?' They pulled up before a row of wicker bins, the hilts of practice swords of all shapes and sizes protruding from them. Tarben took a long, appraising look at Corban, then delved into one of the bins, pulled out a battered wooden sword and passed it to Corban.

'How does that feel, lad?'

Corban swung the weapon, feeling the smooth wood of the handle, worn by countless years of use.

'Good enough,' he said.

'Right. This is what's going to happen, see. First, I'll test you out a bit, see what you can do, then I'll set you up with a warrior that'll train you.' He walked into the sparring area, searching for a clear space.

Corban followed, glancing furtively about him. Mostly the people around him were concentrating on their sparring, but here and there he spied faces turned his way, eyes focused on him. Then he found Tarben standing ready in front of him, weapon raised. Filling his lungs with a deep breath, he stepped into the first stance of the sword dance and raised his weapon, one of Tarben's eyebrows rising.

'Begin,' said the tall warrior.

Neither of them moved, Tarben's eyebrows lifting again. The tall man grunted and stepped forward. Corban stood side-on, sword held high as Gar had shown him. Tarben aimed a blow at his head. Corban blocked it, clumsily, nearly losing his grip on his weapon. Tarben slashed at Corban's ribs. He blocked it, more comfortably this time. Another swing at his thigh – blocked. Tarben lunged, sword aimed at Corban's chest, he blocked it, sweeping the wooden blade away as he slipped into another stance from the dance, moving around Tarben, trying to expose the warrior's left side. Then he struck at the tall man. Tarben blocked him, and so it went on: strike, block, strike, again and again, Tarben's attacks increasing in speed, the blows falling harder and harder, making Corban's wrists ache and his shoulder throb, then he slipped. Tarben cracked his elbow and his own weapon went spinning from his fingers. Tarben stood there staring at him, face shiny with sweat.

'Tarben.'

They both turned, saw a warrior walking quickly towards them, coming from the rowan path. It was Marrock.

'Pendathran wants to see you. In the feast-hall,' he said.

Tarben sighed. 'All right, give me a moment,' he muttered, rolling his eyes. He walked away, heading towards a warrior who was standing on his own, watching the sparring. Corban saw a handful of people detach from the crowd gathered round the sparring ring. They began to walk over to him, Rafe at their head. One side of his face was mottled a dull green and he walked with a slight limp. Corban recognized some of the faces around him: Vonn, Crain, others he did not know.

'So, the coward dares stand in the Field,' Rafe said.

Corban looked at the floor.

'Well, coward? Got nothing to say? Maybe because you haven't got your sister or da around.'

'I'm sorry about what happened,' said Corban, looking at Rafe's bruises.

'Sorry. *Sorry*,' hissed Rafe, a vein throbbing in his neck. He took a step towards Corban.

'What's this?' said a voice, not loud, but firm nevertheless. It was Halion, one of the two newcomers. The warrior looked at them, at Corban standing on his own, Rafe at the head of a handful of others, face twisted with anger.

'Enough,' said the newcomer. No one moved.

'I said, *enough*.' He placed himself in front of Rafe. 'This is the Rowan Field; grudges come no further than the trees.'

Rafe scowled at the warrior, then turned silently and walked away, the others following him.

'What was that all about?'

Corban said nothing.

Halion sighed. 'No business of mine, eh?'

Corban nudged the grass with a toe.

'Tarben has asked me to help you in your training. Told me a few things about you, Corban.'

'What things?'

'That this is your first day in the Field. That you fight like you've been here longer.' He had a practice sword in his hand, longer and heavier than the one Tarben had used. He dug the tip under Corban's weapon still lying on the ground and flicked it back up to Corban.

'Let's see if I agree with him,' he said.

They sparred for a long while, Corban losing all sense of time as everything came down to Halion's wooden weapon, its tip stabbing, edges slashing, testing, probing. Corban blocked and attacked as best he could, but no matter how hard he tried, he could not get close to the dark-haired, solemn-faced warrior who fought with an efficiency of movement that reminded him of Gar. Then suddenly Halion stepped back, lowered his sword and held a hand up. He leaned on his practice sword, looking intently at Corban.

'Well, I'm not from these parts, but I think I must agree with Tarben.'

Corban smiled tentatively, in between deep, ragged breaths.

'So, who has trained you?'

Corban shrugged. 'Family, friends.'

'Oh, aye, we all do that before we set foot in the Field, but there's more than that here. You use a style I've never seen before. Who has trained you?'

Corban looked at the grass a moment, then raised his eyes and met Halion's sea-grey gaze. 'Where are you from?' he asked.

Halion's face went hard as flint. His fingers twitched, and for a moment Corban thought the warrior would strike him. Then the edges of his lips moved in the glimmer of a smile.

'So it's like that, eh? Tell me your secret and I'll tell you mine. Well, it may seem like a fair trade to you, but I think I'll just have to live without knowing your secret.' He passed a hand through his thick black hair. 'You know some, lad, but not all. So let us begin your training.'

The next time Corban looked around, the Field was much emptier. He was sweating; his sword arm like lead.

'People do not stay that long,' said Halion, seeing Corban looking around. 'Many have tasks – fields to tend, fish to catch, iron to forge. Some stay longer, mostly those that serve as warriors in the holds of barons here in the fortress.'

'How about you? Do you need to go?'

Halion snorted. 'No, lad. Brenin has taken me into his warband. A good man, your King. So we only help where it is needed, and commanded. Come harvest, I imagine I'll be spending a lot of time in the fields, my brother as well.' He nodded towards a group of warriors still sparring. 'But right now, there's not so much needs doing.'

Just then Tarben strode back into the Field, long legs quickly carrying him over to them.

'How'd the boy do?' he asked Halion, ignoring Corban.

'Well enough. He has potential, I would say. With a sword, anyway. He came here knowing something, like you said, but he's quick enough to pick up new things. Uses his head. I didn't try him with bow or spear, though.'

'Plenty of time for that. Well, if you're willing, you may as well stick with the lad. You're as good as any to teach him his weapons.'

Halion nodded.

'Good. That's settled then.'

'Where did you go?' asked Corban. Tarben looked at him for the first time.

'Found your voice then, boy?' A troubled look swept across the tall warrior's face. 'Well, no harm in saying, I figure. I'm about to tell everyone else. Fain, Evnis' wife, is dead. I'm supposed to tell all of his hold that are here.'

'When?' said Corban, thinking of Brina saying how well Evnis' wife had been doing, only a short time ago.

'Earlier today. There's other news that needs telling as well. Not so bad, though. The hunt's on. In half a ten-night, before you ask.'

CHAPTER TWENTY-FOUR

VERADIS

Veradis gazed absently at the river as he rode along its bank, the water churning and foaming around huge grey boulders. It had not been so long ago that he had ridden the same journey in the opposite direction, with his brother Krelis and a captive Vin Thalun corsair in tow.

It *felt* a long time ago. He had left Ripa looking to find his place in the world. Now he was returning, would be riding through his father's gates beside the Prince of Tenebral. More than that, Nathair had declared him his first-sword and captain of his ever-growing warband. He suspected this was mostly based on his suicidal leap through the wall of flame, although it was becoming clear that he had risen above all competition in the weapons court, apart from Armatus, the weapons-master, of course. But whatever the reasons, he felt a warm glow of pride deep inside. He was looking forward to seeing Krelis, even though he knew his brother would most likely break his back in one of his bear hugs. It would even be good to see Ektor, his other brother.

But most of all it was his father's face that he wanted to see. Not out of any love shared, but because he felt that he had finally *achieved* something that could not be denied.

'Is she pretty?'

He looked, saw Nathair riding beside him.

'You were smiling to yourself. Thinking about a girl, back home? One that you will be seeing soon?'

'No, lord,' Veradis said, shaking his head.

'*Lord*. I thought I had told you: there will be none of that between us.'

Veradis smiled ruefully. 'Habit. We are nearing my home now, where I was raised to call my own father "lord".'

Nathair raised an eyebrow.

'So no woman's arms to return to then?'

'No.'

'You surprise me, Veradis . . .'

He snorted. 'I like women well enough, it's just, they make me nervous. There *was* one girl, Elysia, the stablemaster's daughter . . .'

'Hah, see, I was right all along,' Nathair said, snapping his fingers.

'No, nothing came of it. She was always saying one thing but meaning another. It was confusing. Better a sword and someone to fight, I think.'

Nathair laughed.

'You may be one of the most skilled warriors in all of Tenebral, but you have much to learn, my friend.'

'Aye,' blushed Veradis. 'But what of you, Nathair?' He spoke quickly, trying to deflect this uncomfortable subject away from himself.

'Ah, a counter-attack, I see. No. No woman, or women. Not recently, anyway. I have too much to achieve. There is little room for anything else.'

A score of warriors rode behind them, handpicked from Nathair's rapidly growing warband. The river Aphros tumbled ahead, widening in the distance, snaking its way into a wall of trees on its journey to the coast. The forest rolled away into the horizon, and although he could not see it yet, he knew his home lay on its far side. He felt a fluttering in his stomach as he gazed on the forest, his eyes picturing the walls of his home. *Fear?* Then the sensation was gone.

Many *were* scared to enter the forest, with the ruins of giant-built Balara rising jagged on the horizon, standing on a bare hill to the north of the forest. Similar ruins were found throughout the Banished Lands, abandoned by the giants in their defeat. Some had been inhabited by men, as Jerolin had been, but many more had been left empty, men preferring to build in wood and thatch. Strange tales were told about the ruins of the giants' stronghold, but *he* had never been scared of entering the woodland, having been raised on its fringes. He had always enjoyed his times in the forest, usually hunting with Krelis.

Squawking, a handful of crows took flight from a stand of trees on the far bank. Veradis started, felt that brief tickling sensation in the pit of his stomach again. He stared at the copse of trees a while, mostly willows and alders, then shook his head.

Unmanned at the thought of going home. He snorted, angry with himself, and set his eyes back on the road ahead.

They made camp that night some distance into the forest, the river flowing glossy black beside them. At times Veradis could see the dark shadow of Balara's jagged tower framed by the moon through the swaying treetops.

He stamped his feet, fighting the drooping of his eyelids. A horse whinnied nearby, a twig popping on the fading fire. He paced silently along the perimeter of their camp, where trees had been cleared from the forest road that shadowed the river.

A sound caught his attention and he picked his way carefully around sleeping forms until he was standing above Nathair.

The Prince was mumbling in his sleep, limbs jerking. Veradis crouched, trying to hear better what he was saying.

Sweat beaded Nathair's face, his eyelids twitching, then suddenly they snapped open, a hand shooting out to grab Veradis by the throat. Veradis tried to prise Nathair's fingers apart, but they were unmovable. The Prince's eyes were wide, bulging, staring wildly at Veradis like some cornered, feral creature. He knew a moment of panic as his lungs began to burn, then suddenly Nathair's eyes cleared. The Prince loosed his grip and fell back with a sigh.

'My apologies,' Nathair mumbled, wiping sweat from his face.

Veradis massaged his throat. 'You were dreaming?'

'Aye.' Nathair sat up.

'You were talking, in your sleep.'

Nathair's eyes narrowed. 'What did I say? Did you hear what I said?'

'No. Not really. Something about – *searching*, I think. And something that sounded like *cauldron*. I am not sure.'

Nathair stared at Veradis a moment, then shrugged. 'I have dreams, Veradis. Troubled dreams. Often the same one.' He smiled, hesitantly. 'I have dreamed it as far back as I can remember, or variations of it; but of late it is becoming more urgent.'

Veradis stepped over to the dying fire, where a clay jug of wine had been left warming. He swigged some himself, the warm, sour liquid soothing his throat, and passed it to Nathair, who gulped greedily. 'What do you dream?' he asked.

Nathair looked about, checking for eavesdroppers. 'I hear a voice, asking for my help, sometimes see the shadow of a face. A noble face, I think, although it is never quite the same, never clear. But the *voice* is always the same. A whisper, yet filling my head with noise.'

'What does it say?'

'Always the same thing. He is searching, searching, and he asks me for aid. To find a cauldron, no, *the* cauldron, though why it is so important, I do not know.' He sighed deeply.

A memory tugged at the back of Veradis' mind. 'Did Meical not speak of a cauldron, during your father's council?'

'Aye. He did, though he claimed to know nothing of it when I questioned him. I do not know. But the voice is becoming more insistent.'

'Have you spoken of this to anyone?'

'No, you are the first. It would not do to have people think that the Prince of Tenebral is mad.' He rubbed his eyes. 'Do you . . . think me mad?'

'A few moons ago, maybe I would have,' Veradis smiled. 'Now, with all this talk of gods, demons, weeping stones and the mother of all wars –' he snorted – 'dreams and strange voices seem tame.' He smiled, but inside he *was* worried. He did not believe that Nathair was touched, and he had suffered unpleasant recurring dreams himself, usually about the dead mother he had never met. And even he heard voices sometimes. He always put it down to his conscience, but maybe it was more than that.

Nathair smiled and drank some more wine. 'It means something,' he said. 'Somehow, it is important.'

They sat there in silence a while, passing the clay jug back and forth until it was empty, the sound of insects filling the darkness, the wind sighing in the branches above them.

'We could ask my brother Ektor,' Veradis eventually said. 'He knows his books like none other.'

'No,' Nathair snapped. 'I would not speak of this to anyone.'

'We need not tell him of your dreams. Only ask him if he knows of this cauldron. He is very learned. Arrogant, aye, and spiteful, but learned. And the tower at Ripa dates back to the giants, and holds many ancient manuscripts. I think Ektor has read every single one of them. If anyone could help, it would be my brother.'

'Maybe,' Nathair nodded thoughtfully. 'Let me think on it in the light of day.'

Veradis stood, Nathair laying his head back on the ground. Returning to the edge of camp, Veradis gazed into the darkness, his eyelids no longer heavy.

Ripa appeared as the forest road spilled into a plain of rich grass, the breeze from the sea giving it an undulating fluidity. A town of timber and thatch sprawled between them and the fortress, grown large on the harvest of the sea and forest.

The sun was high, the day warm. Sweat trickled down the back of Veradis' leather cuirass, silver eagle standing out bright in the boiled and black-dyed leather. He rode beside Nathair at the head of their small column, women washing clothes in the river and children splashing around them stopping to stare at the warriors passing by. Veradis took a deep breath, a swarm of memories flooding him with the sounds and smells of home: gulls calling, salt on his tongue, fish laid out in the dozens of smokehouses that lined the river as it flowed languidly into the bay. Ripa was a wooden fortress that had grown up around a tower of stone, built long ago by the giants as a watchtower overlooking the bay. It was an ideal spot to guard against the raids of the Vin Thalun, as the view from the top of the tower commanded leagues across the bay and along the coast. Veradis remembered the look on his father's face as Krelis had told him of the Vin Thalun's plans, following his capture of the prisoner, the pride that his firstborn had unmasked such a grievous plot against the realm. He felt a brief twist in his gut, a sharp stab of jealousy. He fought it down, instantly ashamed. Krelis deserved the adulation his father lavished on him.

His eyes swept the dockyard, snapping back to the unmistakable outline of a Vin Thalun galley moored alongside the other ships, sleek and low, like a wolf amongst unwary sheep. He was halfway to drawing his sword and turning his mount before he realized what he was doing. Even though King Aquilus had made a peace of sorts with the Vin Thalun – they had even been seen trading in Jerolin, Nathair riding out to welcome them – it was strange to see them walking amongst the people of Tenebral, stranger still to see one of their ships moored here, where they had only ever been the *enemy*.

They finally rode into a hard-packed courtyard before the steps of a wooden hall. Veradis smiled at the gathering faces as he jumped from his horse, recognizing many. A lean, almost skeletal man stepped forward, Alben, his weapons-master. Veradis ran and embraced the man, who pounded his back in return. After a moment he stepped back, a wide smile sending more wrinkles bunching around the corners of his mouth and eyes.

'Welcome home, Veradis ben Lamar,' he said formally, looking the young warrior up and down. 'You have much to tell me, I think.'

'Well met, Alben. There is some to tell, aye, but later.' He moved to the side, allowing Nathair to be seen, and spoke loudly. 'I am sent with Nathair, Prince of Tenebral, to relay news from our King to my father. Where is he, Alben?'

'Your father is within, awaiting you,' the white-haired warrior gestured at the doors of the wooden hall. 'Greetings Nathair, Prince of Tenebral. Lamar, Baron of Ripa and Keeper of the Bay, bids you welcome.'

'My thanks,' replied Nathair, smiling warmly.

'My lord has commanded me to speed you to him, you and your first-sword.' Alben glanced at Veradis, who felt a warm burst of pride in his chest at the words. *He knows. So too then must Father*.

They were led up stairs to a circular room where two men were poring over a large parchment. Then Lamar, Lord of Ripa, looked up. Even stooped by age as he was, he was a big man. Age had had its way, though, in a fashion that Veradis had not noticed before. The skin of his face had a papery quality, hanging in places like melted wax, and, although still broad at the shoulders, his wrists and hands looked frail and bony, almost brittle. His eyes were bright still, sharp as a hawk's, just as he remembered them.

Beside him stood a slight man, much younger, pale-faced with dark greasy hair hanging in clumps. Ektor, his brother. He watched Veradis and Nathair enter the room, as a child would study insects caught in a jar.

Veradis froze for a long moment, daunted by his father's gaze, then he walked forward and dropped to one knee.

'Lord,' he said.

'Rise,' Lamar boomed in his deep voice. That, at least, was still unravaged by time.

'My Prince,' the ageing lord said.

'Lord Lamar,' Nathair replied, 'my father sends his greetings, and more. He has bade me inform you of the recent events at Jerolin. Of the council, of its conclusions.' His eyes shifted from Lamar to Ektor, who returned the gaze, unblinking, and gave a stiff bow.

The sound of heavy footfalls drifted from beyond the doorway, growing louder. In a flurry, the door burst open, filled almost completely by the frame of a huge man who rushed into the room and swept Veradis up into an embrace.

'Put – me – down – Krelis,' wheezed Veradis, bones *clicking* in his back.

'It is good to see you too,' Krelis chuckled, looking Veradis up and down.

'See here, Father, my baby brother has changed. You've had your nose broken – a good thing.' He ran a finger down the battered ridge of his own nose. 'I have heard tales about you: *giant fighting*? Are they true?'

'Aye,' mumbled Veradis, eyes flickering to his father.

'More than that,' Nathair said. 'He leaped through a wall of fire, fought a giant single-handed to save me, followed me where none other dared.'

Krelis dragged him into another embrace.

'I knew it, little brother. You are the best of us. Destined for great things.' He released Veradis, a huge smile splitting his black beard, moisture filling his eyes. 'Still can't grow a beard worth a damn, though.' He winked as he tugged at the straggly whiskers Veradis had grown during the journey south.

'Enough of your foolery, Krelis,' said Lamar, 'Prince Nathair brings us news from Jerolin. But, come, Nathair, unless you bring tidings of invasion, and I need muster my warband now, I bid you rest, wash away the dust of your journey. Eat with us this eve, and then tell us of your news.'

'That I will be happy to do.'

'Good, it is settled then. Alben will show you to your rooms.'

Veradis turned to follow Nathair, then stopped. 'Should I await your call, lord?'

Lamar frowned. 'Maybe on the morrow.'

Veradis nodded sharply, hiding his hurt and followed Nathair's fading footsteps down the tower staircase.

The rest of the day passed quickly, and all was well with the horses and men, so Veradis and Alben took a skin of wine, some clay cups and sat on the stairs to the hall, basking in the hot sun.

'Jerolin has been good for you, little hawk,' said Alben. He had called Veradis that as far back as he could remember. Alben had been his sword-master, as he had been for all of Lamar's children, training him from when he was only as high as the warrior's belt. Veradis sipped at his cup, looking at the fortress walls.

'You left an untested warrior, you have returned a leader; that is clear to see.'

Veradis snorted. 'It is Nathair who is the leader. We would follow him anywhere. He is a great man.'

'Aye, I'm sure that's true, but that doesn't change what else I see. And Nathair's words, just now . . .'

'Aye.'

'You bring honour on us Veradis, on Ripa. I am proud of you.'

Veradis snorted again. 'What of my father? He did not seem so proud.'

'Look around, your father is lord of all you can see. He has many cares.'

'Aye, right enough, but he is still my father.' Veradis shook his head. 'I should not expect so much, then I would not be so disappointed.'

'You know how you remind him of your mother,' Alben said. 'Out of all your brothers, you are the most like her.'

'And I killed her,' Veradis whispered. 'That is why he cannot bear to look at me.'

Alben tutted. 'Lamar loved your mother. Fiercely. When you love that strongly, reminders can be painful. It does not mean he has no love for you.'

Veradis snorted.

'I remember when you were a child, not much taller than my knee. You were always quiet, thoughtful.'

'You're confusing me with Ektor.'

Alben drank from his cup. 'No. I think not. Do you recall when you followed Krelis on one of his secret forays into the forest. He didn't even know you were there until he put his foot into a fox-hole and snapped his ankle.'

'Some of it, but not too clearly, truth be told.'

'Aye, well, that's not surprising. You could not have seen more than five winters. Anyway, you stayed in the forest all night, refused to leave him to the dark in case the spirits of the giants came and took him away. At first light you came back to the fortress. Your father was mad with worry. He grabbed you, held you as if he would never let you go. When Krelis told him that you *chose* to stay the night in the forest, thinking you were protecting him, his eyes fair glowed with pride. I saw the same look when we were brought the news about you becoming Nathair's first-sword.'

'He does know, then?'

'Aye. For some time.'

Veradis sighed, passing a hand across his face. 'I do not know the man you are talking of, Alben. I have seen him look at Krelis the way you describe, often. But never me.' He shrugged. 'But you are getting old. Maybe your wits are deserting you.'

Quick as a snake, the old man cuffed him round the back of the head, then the two of them laughed.

'Sometimes it is hardest to see what is right in front of us,' Alben said quietly.

'Some things have not changed. Still the riddles.'

CHAPTER TWENTY-FIVE

EVNIS

Evnis wept as the last stone was placed on Fain's cairn.

The book had helped, for a while; the earth power restoring some of Fain's strength for a time. Her smile had warmed him, kept the hatred at bay. But only for a while. Then her strength had failed, until she was only a shell of what she had been.

And now she was gone.

His son Vonn stood beside him, tall, keeping his grief within. *Does he look to me for comfort, for guidance? Right now, I do not care. I have too much grief of my own.*

A ring of his warriors stood about him, spears held high, with all from his hold, to sing the last lament. But even here his thoughts returned again and again to his book: just the merest hint that he had mastered so far was like a drug, calling, consuming. With an effort, he wrenched his will back to the cairn in front of him. To Fain. His hatred flared bright, and now there was another to add to his list.

King Brenin.

Vengeance, a voice whispered in his head.

I shall destroy him, he promised the voice.

CHAPTER TWENTY-SIX

CORBAN

Corban rested a hand over his eyes, shielding them from the sun as he gazed back towards the river Tarin, where he knew his da was standing before the gathered hunters of Dun Carreg.

Corban was about half a league from where the hunt was gathering, other boys near him arranged in a long, stretched-out line, facing the forest. All of them had entered the Rowan Field but were not of an age to attempt their warrior trials.

Their task was to flush or beat the game into the path of those come to hunt. Drifting in the wind he heard the single blast of a horn, then a distant roar. His heart leaped – the hunt had begun. With a jerk he jumped forwards, seeing the beaters' line lurch towards the forest. They reached the first trees and started banging their wooden rods together. The noise was immense. Distantly Corban heard an answering echo, the beaters on the other side of the hunters, then he was amongst the trees, the boys on either side of him flickering in and out of view.

Walk slowly, keep beating. It was easier said than done, but nevertheless, slowly, step by step, he made his way deeper into the Baglun, beating his rods together as much as possible. In a short time the line of beaters became separated by trees and undergrowth.

Some time later his belly rumbled. How long had he been walking and beating now? One thing he had learned about the forest was that time passed very quickly once you were inside it. He looked around, searching for somewhere to sit and eat. He heard the clacking of sticks, somewhere off to his right.

'Farrell,' he called out to a boy who had been nearest as he'd entered the Baglun, not wanting to eat on his own.

'Aye,' came the response, closer than he expected.

'Over here.' He moved in the direction of the voice. Soon they found each other.

'Hungry?' asked Corban.

'Starved,' said Farrell, the son of Anwarth, whom many called *coward*. Farrell was tall, broad and thick limbed, a shock of spiky brown hair framing a handsome, though sullen face. Corban had seen him in the Rowan Field, wielding a practice sword like a hammer.

He sat on a flat, moss-covered stone, Corban with his back to a thick-trunked tree.

'Bored yet?' asked Farrell through a mouthful of bread and cheese.

'No. I like being in the Baglun. But how long till we turn back?' Corban asked.

'Oh, we'll hear the horns. Why don't we walk together? Line's broken anyhow, and one of us could beat while the other uses *both* hands to make a path. Less blood for the thorns.'

'Makes sense,' said Corban with a grin, and they set off soon after. Corban took the lead, Farrell behind him. He saw deer tracks in soft earth near a stream, and further on the marks of something larger, but he could not tell what. Wolf maybe. He looked around, suddenly wary.

Deeper than I've ever been before, even when I got lost, Corban thought. Still, he was not alone this time; Farrell had done this before, and soon he switched with him. They came to a small stream cutting across their path. They jumped across, then Farrell pulled to a sudden stop and Corban ploughed into his back.

'What's wrong . . .' Corban began, then a low, deep growl silenced him.

Farrell took a step backwards, turned and bolted into the thicket, heedless of the thorns. 'Come on!' he yelled at Corban, grabbing his shirt and pulling. Corban staggered back and became tangled in the thorns as Farrell lost his grip. Then Farrell was splashing through a stream, leaving Corban snared, staring at what Farrell was running from.

Wolven. Half a dozen at least were in the glade before him,

snarling at him, baring dagger-long teeth. Each was easily as big as a pony. One of them growled.

Terror, mind-numbing, icy-cold terror, flooded him. He opened his mouth to scream, to call for help, but nothing came out. In the distance a horn called. Hounds bayed in answer, closer.

Behind him he heard movement, felt a presence. Farrell had come back.

'You should have kept running,' Corban whispered.

'What – you stand while I run? Don't think so. I'll not be called coward.'

'Better than dying.'

'Not to me.'

Before them was a small clearing, bordered heavily with thorn bushes and densely packed trees. In the centre of the glade reared the wide trunk of an ancient tree, in and about which were the wolven. Most were pacing, agitated by the sounds of the hunt, ears flat to their skulls, twitching. One was still. All were staring at him with their copper eyes. Then Corban saw movement on the ground.

Cubs.

On the forest litter, gathered together between two widespread roots, squirmed a handful of cubs. Above them stood their mother, her belly still loose, coat dull grey and striped bone white, teeth dripping saliva as she snarled at him. He looked into her copper eyes and remembered – although then she had been covered with thick black mud, and her belly had been swollen, heavy with pup. She was the wolven he had dragged from the bog. She took in a deep, long sniff, holding his scent.

Another wolven, huge and black, snarled and took a step towards Corban. Muscles bunched as it prepared to spring, but the she-wolven snapped at it, a short, staccato bark.

Corban's eyes remained locked with the wolven standing over the cubs. Then the trees opposite exploded as hounds, men and horses poured into the clearing. Corban saw Evnis, tall on his horse, a heavy spear in his hand. Behind him rode his son. Next came Helfach the huntsman, his hounds about him. Warriors followed them: ten, fifteen – more pouring in all the time.

There was a single moment of stillness, then the wolven threw themselves at the intruders, meeting Helfach's hounds with a snarling collision of flesh and bone.

There was blood everywhere. Corban saw a hound thrown through the air to crash against a tree, the sound of bones snapping as it slid lifelessly down the trunk. A wolven wrestled a horse to the ground, jaws clamped around its throat. Spears punctured the beast's side, the rider screaming as his horse collapsed on him, its eyes bulging white. Elsewhere a wolven stood over a warrior's body, canines dripping red, the man's face and throat a red ruin. Hounds circled another of the great beasts, snapping at its hindquarters. One jumped in, squat and grey, clamping its jaws around the wolven's throat. Razor-sharp claws opened the hound's belly, spilling its guts. Other hounds leaped in and the wolven sank to the ground, snapping, twisting, biting, taking life even as its own bled into the forest floor. A man screamed, a wolven biting into his arm and shoulder, blood spurting as he fell, the wolven on top of him, shaking his body like a rag doll. Helfach leaped upon its back, a long hunting knife rising and falling.

Then, suddenly, it was over, the sound of a man groaning, a dog whining, everyone taking deep, ragged breaths. Evnis slid from his horse and ran to the fallen rider, still pinned beneath his dead horse. It was Vonn.

'No,' mumbled Evnis as he cradled his son's head in his lap, the face pale, eyes closed. 'I will not lose another. Come, help me.' Men around him lurched into life to drag Vonn's body from beneath the horse's carcass, his leg broken.

'There's another,' cried a man, and all heads turned to look where he was pointing. In between two thick roots of a tree, crouched amongst the leaves of the forest, was the last wolven. She crouched over her cubs, almost blending with the foliage around her. With a snarl, Evnis flew back into his saddle, taking up his spear, and threw his horse towards the beast. She growled and stood, then bunched her legs and sprang at the onrushing horse and rider. Her growl suddenly became a whine as Evnis' spear pierced her, pinning her to the ground. She spasmed and then lay still. Evnis continued his charge, guiding his horse towards the huddle of cubs, trampling them, fur and blood flying around his horse's hooves, squeals and yelps cut sickeningly short. He reached the far end of the clearing and turned his horse.

Then others were entering the clearing: Corban saw Pendathran, Marrock, many others. Amongst the matted fur that had been the wolven cubs a flicker of movement drew his eye. Before he even realized what he was doing, Corban's feet were moving. He staggered over to the base of the tree. One cub still lived, nuzzling feebly at the body of one of the other dead pups. Instinctively Corban swept it up, cradling it like a newborn child.

Then he looked around.

All eyes were upon him. Eventually his gaze fell on Evnis, who was staring at him, his eyes narrowed.

'Put it down, boy,' he said quietly, though all in the glade heard him.

Corban said nothing.

'Put the cub *DOWN*!' shouted Evnis.

'No,' Corban heard himself say.

Evnis breathed deeply, closed his eyes for a moment. 'Put the cub on the ground and move away, or so help me, by Elyon above and Asroth below, I shall ride you down as well.'

Corban saw movement out of the corner of his eye. A man had taken a step towards him. Gar.

Evnis clenched his reins.

'*HOLD!*' shouted a loud voice. 'Hold, Evnis.' It was Pendathran.

'But these beasts may have taken my son from me. That cub must die.'

Pendathran frowned at Corban. 'He speaks true, boy. Let it live and it will grow, maybe take more lives amongst our people. Besides, its mother is dead. It is going to die anyway. Put the cub down, lad.'

Corban hugged the cub closer to him and shook his head.

'Do as you're told,' Pendathran snapped.

Corban looked frantically around the glade, but no one spoke or came to his aid. Gar watched him, his face an unreadable mask, but made no move to help. Pendathran clicked his horse forward.

'I claim King's Justice,' Corban blurted, looking defiantly between Pendathran and Evnis.

Pendathran pulled his horse up, scowling. 'You have the right, but you are only delaying the inevitable. And angering me into the bargain.' He pinned Corban with a glowering look. 'Are you sure?'

Corban nodded.

'So be it,' Pendathran growled and turned his horse away. Evnis rode back to his son, staring at Corban all the way. The wolven cub whimpered and nuzzled its nose into the crook of Corban's arm.

CHAPTER TWENTY-SEVEN

KASTELL

It took Kastell almost a moon to reach the borders of Tenebral, even though King Romar set a fast pace and the roads were good. Slowly the oak and chestnut woodlands of Tenebral were giving way to pine and fir as they climbed higher into the mountains that marked Helveth's border. Eventually they left the trees behind completely, cantering through lush meadows. Snow-capped peaks reared above them as the warriors rode into a narrow valley. They clattered across an ancient, time-worn bridge spanning a great chasm, a rent in the earth's fabric. A reminder of the Scourging, Maquin muttered to him as they crossed, when Elyon's wrath near destroyed the world. Kastell peered over the bridge, saw sheer rock disappear into darkness. How deep it was he could not tell. Not long after, they made camp for the night.

The following day, as they rode through deep valleys and around dark lakes of Helveth's southern border, King Romar called Kastell to ride with him. 'Do you believe in fate, lad, destiny, the will of Elyon . . . call it what you will?' Romar asked him.

'I don't know,' said Kastell. 'I suppose so.'

'Good,' Romar grunted. 'I do. The gods, Elyon, Asroth, the coming of the Dark Sun. I could not explain it to you, but in my heart, when Aquilus spoke of these things at the council. I *knew* it to be true. I felt it.'

Kastell grunted, not quite sure what to say. He had felt something, too, but he could not explain it. Did not understand it, even.

'And I believe you were meant to be here, nephew. It was no accident that I found you moments from death by giants as I travelled to the council. No accident.' He looked at Kastell and smiled, creasing his broad, lined face.

'I am glad your feud with Jael is at an end. I saw it when you were young, but was loath to intervene.' He frowned, shaking his head. 'I was worried. So I was glad for you when you left home with Maquin. But now you are back with us, and your feud is at an end. Fate. Maybe Elyon is taking a hand, even now.' He smiled at his nephew again. 'I am proud of you. Not even seen your eighteenth nameday and you are a giantkiller. Your father would have been proud.'

Kastell winced. He did not feel proud, or brave. Mostly when he thought about the giants all he remembered was terror.

'There are many here named giantkiller now,' was all he said.

'That is true, lad – myself among them. Although I must confess, when I crested that ridge and saw the Hunen running at you, my guts turned to water for a moment. But we rode them down, true. *But*, 'tis also true that it's easier to be brave when you've got four score hard men riding at your shoulder.' He laughed loudly and Kastell could not help smiling at that. He was inclined to agree.

Romar examined his nephew. 'You have changed, lad. Grown. What I said to you back at Aquilus' stronghold is true. I have plans for you. I have been talking with Braster, King of Helveth. We have agreed to strike out against the Hunen. To break the giants' strength once and for all.'

'Why now, Uncle?'

'All this talk at the council, it rings true with me. The giants have been a curse since the dawn of time. Elyon should have finished them at the Scourging. To end the Hunen will be a good start. I would leave my kingdom safer for my son. Hael is only eight summers, but a king must look ahead. And, besides, they have my axe, and I want it back.'

'When will you act?'

Romar shrugged. 'Soon. Not this year, but maybe next spring, summer. I have a mind to involve Aquilus in this. He proposed that we give each other aid, after all. If we are to venture into Forn Forest and give battle to the Hunen on their own ground, the more warriors the better, eh?'

'Into Forn Forest?'

'Aye, lad. I hardly think the Hunen will agree to march out and fight us on an open plain. We will have to go and root them out.'

Kastell nodded slowly.

'There are dark and dangerous times ahead, of that I have no doubt. I will need men about me that I can trust. Men that can lead, and not shrink from what must be done. You are one of those men.'

Stunned, Kastell stared at his uncle, mouth open. King Romar laughed again. 'Don't worry, lad, I don't mean today.'

'But I don't think there are many men that would be happy taking orders from me.'

'You'd be surprised. You are my blood-kin. If you give orders, men will listen. Until now you have not chosen to do so, but that can change quick enough. Look at Jael – he's been practising ever since he came to Mikil as a boy.'

Kastell grunted.

'Also, Maquin is good company for you, a more loyal shieldman you'll never find. But he could be more. He could be a leader of men. I see it in him. You could learn much from him.'

'He is my friend.' It felt strange saying that out loud.

'I know, for which I am glad.'

They rode again in silence. Soon after, Kastell dropped back down the line, thinking over all that his uncle had said. Then, as dusk began to settle, Jael fell back, leading a packhorse laden with many empty water skins.

'Making camp soon,' he said to Maquin, ignoring Kastell completely. 'Take the horse and some extra hands, find water, and fill the skins. And don't take too long, I'm thirsty.' He pressed the packhorse's reins into Maquin's hand and kicked his horse back to the head of the column.

Maquin gathered a handful of riders about him, including Kastell. Turning away from the column, they rode down a gentle slope into the woods to a stream they'd spotted. Three warriors had joined him and Maquin. An owl hooted amongst the trees.

Maquin knelt beside the stream and slipped on a moss-covered stone, falling back with a splash into the water. There was a moment's quiet and then everyone was laughing. Maquin held a hand up.

'Come, help an old man up,' Maquin said to the nearest warrior, Ulfilas, holding a hand out.

'When *I* called you *old man* I got a fist in the eye,' the warrior said. He gripped Maquin's forearm, hoisting him out of the stream. Maquin slapped him on the back in thanks.

My uncle is right, thought Kastell, *he is a natural leader*.

The owl hooted again, closer now, and Maquin paused, cocking his head as he stared into the twilight of the forest.

'What's wrong?' said one of the other warriors. There was a hissing sound, a thud, and a spear-point burst through the warrior's chest. He toppled into the stream.

The forest erupted around them, figures leaping out of the shadows. They were lean, desperate looking, covered in fur and leather. Iron glistened in the rain: Kastell saw spears, swords, long knives, an axe. Maquin and Ulfilas had drawn their swords, while the other warrior with them was wrestling with one of the attackers. They tumbled into the stream, arms flailing.

There were screams, the clash of iron on iron. Kastell lurched to his feet, slipping on moss. He reached for his sword as he stumbled towards Maquin and Ulfilas. A spear-point lunged at Maquin's side. Ulfilas swung his sword hard, chopping the spear in two, and Maquin's sword buried itself in the spearman's neck. He slumped to the ground, falling on top of other motionless shapes. Many others ringed them: too many to count.

Kastell reached the two men fighting mid-stream, water foaming. He raised his sword but couldn't make out friend from foe. Maquin yelled and he looked up – men were moving towards him, slower than the first rush, taught caution. A savage-looking man lunged at him. Kastell ducked and barrelled forwards, stabbing wildly. He felt his sword punch through leather and flesh. His momentum buried his sword up to its hilt; dark blood pumped over Kastell's hands, the slumping weight pulling him off-balance. With a great heave, he pushed the corpse away and leaped sideways as a spear plunged into the space where he'd been. He staggered, sweat falling into his eyes, saw a blurred movement and raised his sword instinctively, catching an axe blow aimed at his skull. Sparks flew as the axe and sword grated together. His eyes cleared, a grimy face filling his vision as his attacker leaned into him, shoulder to shoulder. Sour breath washed over him. Out of the corner of his eye he saw someone circling him. Bellowing, he thrust the man with the axe back to the stream's bank. The man stumbled, tripped, and Kastell's sword hacked down, chopping between neck and shoulder. His blade stuck. He wrenched, but it would not pull free.

Maquin and Ulfilas were still fighting back to back, standing knee deep in the stream. Then Kastell heard splashing behind him. Desperately he tugged at his sword again but it would not pull free. He let go of his blade and twisted away, pain lancing up his side as a spear-point grazed his ribs. Another fur-clad man stood in front of him. Through the chaos he heard Maquin shout his name, saw the man before him pull his spear back and set his weight for a killing thrust, saw the knuckles whiten as the man's grip tightened on the shaft and the twitch of muscles in the shoulder as the spear jerked forwards. Then, with a soft thud, the man stopped, a black-feathered arrow sticking from his throat. His spear slipped from his fingers and he dropped to his knees in the stream, toppling backwards, surprise on his face.

More figures appeared from the treeline, faces twisted, inhuman. They wore baggy breeches, their upper bodies bare, heads shaven, apart from thick warrior braids of black hair, intricate tapestries of scars covering them.

The Sirak.

With high-pitched howls they came out of the forest, short curved swords rising and falling. The men that had attacked Kastell and his companions screamed in terror, their wall around Maquin and Ulfilas collapsing as they ran in every direction, trying to escape the sudden death flowing from the trees.

None did.

Maquin and Ulfilas still stood, exhausted, leaning against each other in the stream. Maquin's face was covered in blood, a gash across his forehead, and Ulfilas dropped to one knee, blood seeping from a wound in his thigh.

He saw Maquin lean over one of the corpses, fingers moving quickly at the man's belt, then a sound in the distance caused them all to turn and look.

Riders appeared: Romar and Jael at the head of a dozen warriors. Jael levelled his spear upon seeing the Sirak and spurred his mount forwards. Maquin leaped into his path waving his arms frantically, calling out, '*Friends, friends, they are friends.*' Romar reined in his horse, crying out in a loud voice. Jael lifted his spear-point, pulling his horse up in a spray of forest litter and mud.

There was silence a moment, the only noise the blowing of horses, the patter of raindrops on the stream.

'What goes on here?' Romar growled.

'We were set upon,' said Maquin, wiping blood out of his eyes. 'By these . . .' he gestured around him at the dead bodies strewn along the stream bank. 'We were outnumbered, then these men came to our aid. They saved our lives.'

Romar looked at the strange rescuers. One stepped forward.

'I am Temel of the Sirak,' he said in a guttural accent.

'I am Romar, King of Isiltir. And I know you, from King Aquilus' council.' He glanced at the dead bodies all about him. 'My thanks for your aid, here. Please, our camp is not far. Come, eat with us so we may express our thanks.'

The Sirak nodded, a sharp, economical movement. 'We will go to our horses, meet at your camp,' he said and turned away, the other Sirak disappearing into the darkness behind him.

'Search their bodies,' Romar commanded, gesturing at the dead scattered around, 'I would know who they are.'

The attackers' corpses were piled together; the bodies of Isiltir's fallen warriors draped across horses. Kastell knelt by the water and washed blood from his hands. His side was throbbing. He lifted his shirt, saw a gash across his ribs, blood trickling from it. Maquin knelt beside him.

'Still alive then, lad. Someone must be smiling on us, eh?'

'Doesn't feel like it,' Kastell muttered, wincing as he doused the cut. 'That doesn't look good.' He pointed at a cut on Maquin's head.

'It's not deep, but I'm bleeding like a stuck pig. Scalp wounds always do. Looks worse than it is, though.' He ripped a strip of cloth from his shirt, soaked it in the stream, wrung it out and bound it around his head. 'Ah, by Elyon's teeth, but it's good to be alive.'

Romar called for them to mount up.

There were no clues amongst the corpses as to their identity.

Quickly they made their way back to the road and joined the camp. Soon the Sirak cantered in on small ponies, less than a score, Kastell counted. With Maquin and Ulfilas he went to have his wound tended.

Then, at last, he sought out meat and drink, thankful to be alive. The Sirak were sitting around a fire with his uncle and a handful of others. They had saved his life, those strange, fierce, terrifying-looking men. He wanted to give them his thanks, but he could see Jael beside Romar.

One of the Sirak rose and left the group, walking towards the fringes of the camp. Kastell watched him a moment, then stood and followed, still clutching a skin of watered wine, something he'd acquired a taste for while in Tenebral.

The Sirak stood beside an oak, relieving his bladder.

When he had finished, Kastell approached him. 'You saved my life,' he said. The Sirak just stared at him, black eyes gazing out under a jutting brow.

'At the stream. You . . . saved my life . . . my thanks,' he said haltingly, holding out the wine skin. A smile split the warrior's many-scarred face, making him appear even more gruesome in the firelight. He took the wine and drank.

'Bodil,' he said, cuffing liquid from his chin. 'My name. Bodil.'

'Kastell. How did you find us?'

'A strange place to meet, no?' Bodil laughed, a short, abrupt sound. Kastell nodded.

'We had been following those men. They were travelling same path that leads us home,' Bodil said, passing the skin back. 'We left Jerolin a day after you. We rode hard. We have been away from Arcona . . .' he paused, 'the, how would you say it, Sea of Grass. My homeland. We have been away too long.'

Kastell concentrated on the Sirak's words, his strange accent hard to follow. The Sea of Grass was the land to the east of Forn Forest. He had heard tell of the realm that sat upon a steep-sided plateau of rock, rising high above the trees of the forest, stretching for leagues without number.

'Not far back, maybe a league,' Bodil said, waving his hand at the forest, 'we saw tracks lead away from the road. My father is not very trusting, and he is not one to ignore someone else's trouble, so we followed. The rest you know.'

Wolven howled somewhere in the forest.

A voice called out from the campfire and Bodil stiffened.

'I must go,' he said. 'My father is calling.'

Kastell nodded. 'I just wanted to say thank you, for saving my life.'

Bodil smiled again. 'You are welcome, Kastell of Isiltir.' He walked back towards the fire.

Kastell leaned against the oak, sipping slowly at his wine. There was not much left. Maquin loomed out of the darkness, a clean bandage tied around his forehead.

'Here you are, lad. I've been looking for you.'

'I think you should see this,' Maquin said, pulling out a pouch from inside his shirt. He shook it gently, coin chinking.

'Where did you get that?' asked Kastell.

'Off one of the corpses at the stream,' Maquin said quietly, glancing around. 'I don't know what you think, but they seemed a ragged gang to me, not the kind to be carrying coin like this.'

'What do you mean?'

'Hold your hand out, lad,' and Maquin poured some of the contents into Kastell's open palm. They glittered in the firelight.

'Gold,' frowned Kastell.

'Aye, lad, and that's not all. Take a closer look.'

Kastell held one up, twisting it so that the light from the campfires illuminated it. 'I don't understand,' he stuttered. He was looking at the imprint on the coin, a jagged bolt of lightning. It was the crest of Isiltir.

'No? Then let me help you. We are a long way from Isiltir, are we not?'

Kastell nodded.

'And even if we *were* in Isiltir, who would have coin like this? The King. His kin.'

'Jael,' whispered Kastell.

'Aye. I don't think what happened by the stream was an accident. Those men were paid, and paid well, to do a job.'

Kastell glanced at Maquin, face serious.

'Joining the Gadrai looking more attractive now?' asked Maquin.

CHAPTER TWENTY-EIGHT

CORBAN

'What in Asroth's Otherworld is the King's Justice?' asked Farrell as he munched on a cold leg of chicken.

Corban was sitting in the back of a large wain, bumping along the giantsway, sitting with about a dozen other boys. All of them were eyeing him – or more accurately, the bundle of fur that poked out from under his arm – with varying degrees of curiosity and caution. Farrell was the only one that had actually spoken to him since he climbed into the wain, although all of the others were listening avidly to their conversation.

'It's an ancient law,' said Corban. 'If you invoke it then your griev-ance can only be judged by the king.'

'Asroth's teeth, I've never 'eard of that before,' whistled Farrell, spitting food everywhere.

'As I said, it's an ancient law. I don't think it's been used since Ard's reign.'

'How'd you know 'bout it, then?'

'Brina told me.'

'That *witch*?' spluttered Farrell.

'She's a healer,' Corban muttered distractedly. Dark clouds sat on the horizon and a strong, sharp wind was swirling about him.

Glancing down at the bundle of fur nestled in the crook of his arm, he sighed. *What am I doing?* he thought. *I must be going mad.* He remembered Evnis shouting at him in the glade and knew he had to do this.

The dead and wounded from the glade had been bound to horses and led slowly out of the Baglun, a rider sent ahead to fetch Brina and any other healers that could make it to the fortress that night.

Vonn had fainted when lifted from the ground. Corban remembered his limbs hanging limply as he was carried from the glade.

'So, what're you going to do with it?' Farrell said, nodding at the cub.

'I suppose that will be for Queen Alona to decide.'

'Aye,' Farrell nodded. 'I s'pose so.'

'Thank you,' Corban said, 'for coming back.'

Farrell grunted.

The fortress of Dun Carreg appeared in the distance. Iron-grey clouds were sweeping in from the sea, causing the day to darken early. The taste of salt was on Corban's lips, this far inland, and gulls were swirling along the coastline, white specks in the sky.

A storm was coming.

CHAPTER TWENTY-NINE

CYWEN

Cywen paced across the courtyard behind Stonegate. Something was wrong. Very wrong, and no one would tell her what. It was maddening.

A steady stream of riders had been returning to the fortress for a while, most of them grim faced and stern. She had rushed to the stables, leaving her self-imposed post at the gates, where she had been waiting for Corban's return. The place was heaving with activity, horses whinnying, harness clattering, voices thrumming in low, muted conversation. That was different – usually the clamour was deafening, warriors boasting of their feats in the hunt and looking forward to the evening's feast. As she entered the stables what little conversation there was seemed to stutter and die.

She set about unsaddling a warrior's horse, asking politely how the hunt had gone, but received a frosty silence and a hard look in answer.

No answers were forthcoming, so soon she gave up and returned to the gates.

The line of returning riders was thicker now. Then she saw the dead and wounded draped over horses, being led by weary-looking riders. Her breath caught in her throat. *Da, Corban, Gar, where are they?* She saw her da ride through the gates on Steadfast, his huge workhorse, then Gar – stony faced as usual – upon Hammer, Buddai padding along behind. She breathed a deep sigh of relief and rushed over to them.

'Where's Ban?' she said as she fell in beside them. Thannon looked down, grim beneath his beard. She took a step back.

'He'll be along soon enough,' Thannon said.

'He is well, then? When I saw some of those returning . . .'

'Aye, Cy, he is well, for the moment.' He passed a big, calloused hand across his face, relaxing slightly.

'What has happened?' Cywen asked.

'Not now, girl,' he muttered, glancing about him.

'But . . .'

He gave her a look that would have stripped bark from a tree. Her protest died on her lips.

'Go home, girl; we'll be along soon enough.' He fixed his eyes ahead, dismissing her, and she dipped her head meekly, turned and left the courtyard. Once out of sight, she retraced her steps and peered into the courtyard, checking that Thannon and Gar had ridden from view, then she ran back to the gate.

It was some time later that the wains carrying the beaters came into view, rattling across the bridge. Daylight was fading quickly, thick black clouds churning overhead, so she could not make out Corban in the press of shapes.

Then she saw him, sitting by the tailgate of the second wain. One hand on the rail, he jumped to the ground, holding his left arm tight to his side.

'Ban, what's going on?' she called as she ran over to him. 'Are you all right?' Then she pulled up short. Something had moved in the crook of his elbow. She saw a flash of pale white fur, flecked with black.

He did not answer her, just took a deep breath and began walking. She fell in beside him, almost trotting to keep up.

'Ban, what's wrong? Where did you get that pup?'

He sucked in a deep breath. 'It's not a pup,' he said, holding his arms out. Cywen gasped as she saw a long muzzle, fluffy-furred cheeks and copper eyes. Two sharp canines protruded from its lips.

'It's a wolven-cub, Cy. I found it in the Baglun.'

'Oh.' For a moment she could not think of anything else to say, then a flood of questions welled up in her mind. It must have shown on her face, for Corban stopped.

'Please, Cy, wait. Or I'll have to give the same account scores of times. I just want to go home. I'll tell you all when we get there.'

A warrior strode up: Marrock. He saw Corban and hurried over.

'The Queen would speak with you. Now.' Without waiting for

an answer, Marrock turned and strode away. Corban followed the disappearing warrior in silence. Cywen hurried after them.

It was dark now and fat raindrops were starting to fall. Sharp gusts of wind sent them stinging into Cywen's face. She pulled the hood of her cloak up.

Soon the feast-hall loomed out of the darkness and they marched through its doors; there was a spitted deer turning above a fire. They trod stone corridors for a while, then Marrock walked through another doorway. Alona was sitting in a dark wooden chair, draped with furs.

Standing before her were Cywen's parents Thannon and Gwenith, along with Gar.

'Are there any more from your hold that will be joining us, Thannon?' asked Alona. The smith flushed.

'No,' he muttered, shifting uncomfortably. 'Ban is not of age, and this is a serious matter. I should be present.'

'Most certainly, as should the boy's mother,' she said with a quick glance at Gwenith. 'The presence of his sister and my stablemaster is debatable, however. But,' she held up a hand to ward against the bubbling protests, 'I will allow them to stay. We will not be discussing any secrets of the realm, I think.'

Corban moved forward, standing immediately before the Queen. Cywen stood next to her mother. Corban began to say something, but Alona raised her hand.

'We must wait for one more,' she said in cold tones. Corban nodded and looked at the floor.

Long moments passed until footsteps were heard in the corridor. Evnis swept in, dirt and dried blood smearing his pale face.

'Evnis,' she said. 'Pendathran has told me some of what has happened. How is your son?'

'He is alive, my Queen. Brina is tending him. She met me on the road, has insisted on caring for him at her cottage. That is why I have been so long.' He took a deep breath, as if to say more, but then decided against it.

'So. Corban, you have claimed King's Justice.'

Corban lifted his gaze from the floor and nodded.

'Yes, my Queen.'

'Unfortunately, as you know, your King is not here. Are you content to settle for your Queen's justice?'

'Of course. Yes,' he said quietly. 'You are King Brenin's voice, while he is away.'

'Good. I shall hear all that is to be said, and when I give my decision, it shall be final. Is that understood?'

'Yes, my Queen,' said Corban.

'Evnis?'

'Of course,' the counsellor said.

'First, Corban, tell me. How did you come to know of "King's Justice"?'

'Brina has told me of it.'

'Brina. Really?' Alona raised an eyebrow.

'I help her sometimes. Gathering herbs, doing chores.'

'I see.' She looked at Corban thoughtfully. 'Evnis. May I hear your account of today's events.'

'There is little to tell, my Queen. A while after highsun the party that I was leading in the hunt entered a glade deep in the Baglun. There were wolven there. And this lad,' he said with a gesture at Corban. 'The wolven attacked us. We killed them all, sustaining grievous losses and injuries. My Vonn,' he paused, a tremor in his voice. 'Vonn was injured, though he lives. There were cubs in the glade. I killed them all, except the one that the boy holds. He refused a command from me to relinquish it, counsellor to the King, and then he refused an order from your brother, battlechief of Ardan. It is a simple matter – the cub must be destroyed. And this insolent child requires some disciplining.'

Cywen could not believe what she was hearing. With a conscious effort she closed her mouth. How had Ban got involved in this? And defied Evnis and Pendathran, two of the most powerful men in the kingdom.

'Marrock, how is it that this has come to pass? I have never heard of a confrontation with wolven like this, in our generation or any other.'

Marrock stepped forward, old scars he had received from a wolven livid on his cheek and neck.

'I am not sure, my lady. My experience with wolven is limited. But from what I know they are from the old days, if we are to believe the tales. The giants bred them as another weapon in their War of Treasures. Heb could tell us more. I know that they are wolf-like, though larger, of course, and said to be extremely intelligent. They are trackers, hunters, killers. I would hazard a guess that the cubs played a large part in making the wolven attack today. I looked at the glade. There was a large den, dug beneath a great tree. Usually cubs would not be moved until they were much older, and without the cubs I suspect that the wolven would have simply left.' He looked at the bundle of fur in Corban's arm.

'My guess is that the wolven would not move the cubs out of instinct, and so chose to stay. Then when they *were* discovered, they fought like demons to protect their young. And these wolven, they live their whole lives in a pack. Their bonds, I would guess, must be very strong.'

Alona nodded, then, slowly and deliberately, she turned her gaze upon Corban.

'Well?' she said. 'What have you to say?'

Corban looked uncertain and for a moment Cywen thought he would just hand over the wolven-cub, but then she saw him stand a bit straighter, recognized his stubborn expression.

'It, it is difficult to explain,' he said.

'Well, you must try, or the cub's life is most certainly forfeit,' Alona replied stonily.

He nodded. 'To understand what I have done, and *why* I have done this, I must . . .' he paused. Cywen saw fear or worry in his face. He took a deep breath. 'To understand what I have done, I must tell you of the last time I entered the Baglun Forest.'

Alona waved a hand in the air. 'Proceed.'

Corban told of his foray into the Baglun, of his hearing the howling, of finding and saving the wolven, and of being found by Gar. Cywen glanced around, saw shocked expressions on her mam and da's faces. Even Gar's normally steely demeanour was troubled.

'When I stood in the glade today, facing those wolven, I was scared. More than scared. Terrified. Frozen with terror. I thought I was going to die. Then she looked at me, the wolven, and I knew her. And she knew *me*. She remembered the swamp.'

Evnis snorted and Corban blushed.

'It's true, she did. And what happened to them – they were protecting their young, only what any here would have done.'

'Eight men died. Three horses. Almost my whole pack of hounds,' Evnis growled.

'I'm just saying, it was not the cubs' fault. They were innocent, and you trampled them.' Corban paused, gritting his teeth. 'When it was all over, when they were all dead, I saw this cub was still alive, so I grabbed it. I didn't really think about it, it just happened. But, when I looked at it, held it, felt it wriggling, it, it felt right. It *is* right, to protect the innocent, isn't it.'

'Yes,' Cywen whispered.

'If I'd have let Evnis kill it, I don't know, it just would have all been for nothing – pulling the mother from the bog, getting lost – all of it.'

Alona bowed her head. Silence settled in the room. The Queen stirred, gripping the arms of her chair.

'What would you do with this cub?' she asked Corban. Evnis' eyes bulged. Something – hope? – danced across Corban's face.

'I would care for it. Raise it. My da has bred and raised the finest hounds; no one would be able to do it better than he.'

'Whoa, boy,' spluttered Thannon, 'that is no hound you have in your arms.'

'But what if it was raised like one?' Corban enthused, carried along by the idea. 'What if you could raise it as you would a hound? They are not so different – just bigger and with longer teeth.'

The corners of Alona's mouth twitched.

'Your enthusiasm is compelling. Marrock, is this possible?'

Evnis made a disgusted sound in his throat.

The huntsman shrugged. 'I could not say with any certainty. Maybe. It is quite a risk. But . . .' He tapped the hilt of his sword with one finger. 'But perhaps this lad, with Thannon's help, is equal to the task.' He shrugged again.

Evnis opened his mouth, but Alona spoke before he did.

'Yes, it is a risk.' She held Corban with a stern gaze. 'But I feel inclined to grant this request. We need examples of mercy as well as harsh justice in these difficult times. Thannon, as head of your hold, are you willing to assist your son in this?'

Thannon glanced at Gwenith, who gave a quick nod.

'I am, my Queen.'

'Good. But,' she said, stern and cold again, 'if there is one incident where a subject of mine is harmed by this creature, it will be destroyed. Immediately, with no chance of reprieve. Those are my terms.'

'What?' choked Evnis. 'How can you even *countenance* this? These beasts are killers. Letting it live dishonours my son. How can you *do* this?'

'That cub did not savage your son, Evnis. And the others were trying to protect their young, nothing more, according to my huntsman.'

'Nevertheless . . .' Evnis began.

'Might I remind you that you swore to abide by my decision? It is final.'

Evnis stood there a moment, struggling to master himself. He bowed his head.

'If that is all, my Queen, I would tend to my son.'

Alona nodded and Evnis left abruptly.

Cywen shared a shocked look with her mother and father, then Corban surged forward, dropped to his knees before Alona and kissed her hand. He stood slowly, not knowing quite where to look.

'My . . . my thanks,' he stuttered. 'You will not regret your decision.'

'Time will be the judge,' Alona replied. She gestured towards the door and, recognizing the dismissal, Corban left. Cywen followed her mam, and for the briefest of moments saw Alona's gaze lock with Gwenith's, then they were in the stone corridors again.

Gwenith broke the silence as they bustled out of the rain into the warmth of their kitchen.

'I'll fetch some goat's milk. T'would be a shame for the cub to die of hunger after all you've done for it.'

Corban put the cub down on the floor, where it stood quite still, legs straight and stiff. He sat down beside it, holding his hand out near its muzzle. The cub stretched its neck out, sniffing, ears twitching. It was covered in thick white fur, darker stripes zigzagging its torso. Buddai uncurled from his spot before the fire, stretched, padded over to the cub and pressed his wrinkled black muzzle hard into its fur, taking deep, snorting breaths. The cub nipped Buddai, who shook his head. All watched to see what the hound would do. He collapsed onto the ground, pawing at the cub with his huge, heavy pads. The wolven-cub pounced at one of his ears, growling.

Thannon laughed.

'Fool hound,' he snorted, 'still thinks he's a pup. Well, lad, if Buddai is happy for the cub to stay, so am I. Is it a dog or a bitch?'

Corban shrugged and lifted the cub's back leg.

'Bitch.'

'What are you going to call her, Ban?' asked Cywen. Lightning flashed above the fortress, thunder rumbling almost immediately behind it. The kitchen door blew open, banging against the wall, rain sheeting onto the stone floor. Gar closed the door.

'Storm. I shall call her Storm.'

CHAPTER THIRTY

VERADIS

Veradis sat in the chamber where his father had greeted them. Now the table was cleared of maps; instead, jugs and cups were laid out. King Lamar sat with Krelis and Ektor either side of him, Prince Nathair and Veradis opposite. They had shared a meal in the great hall, all going well enough except for one incident with Nathair. He had made to sit in the chair beside Lamar, the one that always remained empty: Veradis' mother's chair. Of course his father had blamed him for not explaining the tradition to Nathair, and Veradis was inclined to agree. He had been distracted, in conversation with Elysia, the stablemaster's daughter, at the time. His father had been in poor humour ever since.

'Aquilus honours me by sending you, Nathair,' said Lamar.

The Prince inclined his head. 'My father values you, Lamar. He knows your loyalty.'

Lamar leaned forward. 'So. News of the council, I believe you said earlier.'

'Aye. The council. We are on the brink of momentous times. As you know, my father sent messengers to all corners of the Banished Lands, and most honoured his call. Only a handful did not come.'

Veradis watched his father's and brothers' faces as Nathair spoke of Aquilus' council, of Meical and the writings he'd discovered by the giant, Halvor. He told of the claims and mysteries spoken of in his book. Nathair finished with the proposal of an alliance of kings against the times ahead, and of the debate that raged back and forth.

Lamar's face gave away nothing, but he asked many questions, especially regarding the arguments made for and against the alliance, and particularly about who had spoken against Aquilus. Krelis exclaimed often, audibly muttering whenever Nathair described someone speaking against the King. Ektor said nothing, but was intent throughout.

'This Meical,' said Lamar. 'I have heard his name before, but never seen him. Tell me of him.'

'He is counsellor to my father, but rarely found within the realm. He has been absent for many years, gathering the information I have told you of.'

'What does he look like?' Ektor interjected.

'He is tall. Very tall. Dark haired, battle scarred,' Nathair said with a shrug. 'There is little more to tell.'

'What of his eyes? What colour are his eyes?'

'I . . . dark. I do not know for sure. Why?'

'Probably nothing,' Ektor said, waving his hand.

'Is there aught else you can tell me of him?' Lamar asked.

'Aye. My father trusts him utterly. It was only after his return that the messengers were sent out heralding the council.'

'And what of you? Do you trust him?'

Nathair leaned back in his chair. 'He is my father's counsellor, not mine. We do not confide in one another. But I bow to my father's wisdom. If my father trusts him, then I see that as good reason to do the same.'

'Aye, well spoken. Aquilus is no fool, that is one truth I know for certain.' Lamar looked weary as he leaned forward. 'So, this is news indeed. A God-War, fought before our eyes. More even, with us as their pawns. The evidence of the Scourging is left in the scars of the land, but still, it is hard to imagine, eh? Gods, angels and demons, here.' He clenched a fist, knuckles popping, and winced. 'But not before the coming of this *Black Sun*?' He frowned. 'I would like to see a copy of this book.'

'As would I,' said Ektor hungrily.

Lamar placed a hand on Ektor's shoulder. 'My son is most learned, and we have a collection of ancient manuscripts, here in this very tower. Ektor may be able to help in the understanding of these predictions.'

'I have heard of Ektor's reputation,' said Nathair, and Veradis saw something flicker across his brother's face. *Pride?* 'I am sure that can be arranged.'

'So, then, what would Aquilus have me do?' Lamar asked.

'Prepare. Train your warband for the coming war, and begin this alliance, helping those that stood with him at the council.'

'And how are we to do that, exactly?'

'My father will let you know. There is talk of a force needed to deal with the Hunen, the remnants of a giant tribe causing some kind of mischief in Helveth. It may be that my father will send a warband.' Nathair shrugged. 'It is only talk, at present.'

'You have given me much to think on,' Lamar said. 'If there is no more to tell, I think I will retire now. We shall speak more on the morrow.'

Nathair dipped his head and began to rise. 'My apologies, for earlier,' he said.

'Apologies?'

'Aye. About the chair. Veradis has since informed me of your custom.'

'It would have been well if he had informed you *before* the meal,' Lamar said.

'I have apologized, Father,' muttered Veradis.

'Apologized,' said Lamar, quiet and cold. 'Not to me. But anyway, how can you apologize for *forgetting* your mother? No amount of words can undo that.' He rose.

'You should not be so harsh, Lamar,' said Nathair. 'Veradis has risen far in Tenebral. Far indeed. He is my first-sword, and captain of my warband. You have much to be proud of. Why not think on those things, instead of dwelling on some petty mistake.'

Lamar tensed. '*Petty.*' He took a deep breath. 'Importance is oft a case of perspective. Risen far, you say. Maybe, but maybe too far, too fast. A child does not become a man overnight.'

'No, true enough. But perhaps your eyes expect a child, where a man now stands.'

Lamar gripped the back of his chair, hands whitening. 'Do not seek to instruct me, in my own hall, on how I treat my own kin. You are not king yet, Nathair. You are young, but your years are poor excuse for such arrogance.'

There was a moment's silence, Lamar's words hanging in the air.

He calls you a child, Veradis' thoughts whirled, *and insults Nathair, the one man to believe in you.* Anger flared deep within. 'You owe

Nathair an apology,' he growled, finding himself rising in turn, 'he is your prince, and is due your respect.' His heart was pounding, and suddenly Krelis was standing too. Lamar's gaze shifted from Nathair to Veradis, and for long moments they all just stood there.

'Respect,' Lamar eventually said. 'A pity you know so little of it.' He turned and left, Ektor rising quickly and following him. Krelis lingered a moment, then left too.

Veradis rode at the head of his small column of warriors, Nathair beside him.

The Prince had made the decision to leave at sunrise. *I have said all my father bade me, my duty is done*, he had said, so at first light Veradis had headed for the stables, ready to ride. There was more than one red-eyed, sore-headed warrior amongst his small band, but nevertheless, and much to Veradis' pride, they were all soon gathered in the courtyard before the main gates. As soon as they were ready, Nathair had walked from the hall, deep in conversation with Ektor. Krelis loomed through the doors behind them. He walked straight to Veradis.

'Farewell, little brother,' he said, offering his arm. Veradis had leaned forward in his saddle and gripped it.

'Last night, Father . . .' Krelis began, then shook his head. 'I think I will visit you soon. Until then, have a care.' His eyes flickered briefly to Nathair, and suddenly the anger of the previous night had gripped Veradis again.

'*Have a care*,' he said. 'I would remind you that I was sent to Jerolin, and have returned the better for it. I am no *child*, Krelis. I serve the Prince of all Tenebral.'

'Aye. You made that clear enough last night,' Krelis said, his voice quiet, meant only for Veradis.

'Is it a crime to serve your Prince?' Veradis said tightly. 'It is Father who should have a care. His words bordered on treason.'

Krelis' eyes narrowed, and he quickly released his grip on Veradis' arm.

'Be very sure you mean the words that come out of your mouth. You cannot unsay them.' Before Veradis was able to reply Krelis had taken a step back and raised his hand in farewell. He raised his own arm, fist clenched, and led his band of warriors from Ripa.

He had not looked back.

They were cantering along a worn track skirting the northern fringe of the forest. Nathair had insisted, saying that he would explain later. Veradis was not overly concerned – his mind kept returning to his brother's face and their harsh words. Never had he been at odds with Krelis before. Never.

They made camp before sunset, within sight of the broken walls of Balara, the old giant ruin.

'Leave your horse saddled; you and I will be riding out soon,' Nathair said. Veradis just nodded and helped the other warriors settle their mounts and make camp.

He ate a bowl of fish stew as the sun sank into the forest, high clouds glowing a soft pink. Soon after, Nathair called him.

'If we are not back by first light,' the Prince said to Rauca, pointing to the outline of the giant ruins, 'take everyone here, ride to that tower and kill anyone that you find there. Do you understand?'

Rauca frowned, but nodded.

'We are going to meet Calidus of the Vin Thalun, and another. His master, Lykos,' Nathair said as they rode into the darkness, the ground rising gently as they passed amongst the first trees of the forest.

'Is this safe, Nathair?'

The Prince shrugged. 'I believe so. Sometimes risks must be taken, if the rewards are great enough. Tonight I will further my father's cause.'

'But, what if they mean to kill you, or take you prisoner and ransom you?'

'Aye, there is that. But they could have done that already. Calidus made that point quite clearly, remember.'

'Still . . .' grunted Veradis, not liking it at all.

Nathair reined in his horse and dismounted. 'First I would talk with you, of something else.'

Veradis slipped from his saddle and faced Nathair, whose face was mostly shadow, eyes reflecting liquid starlight.

'My father's cause. Our cause. Do you believe it to be true?'

'Aye, Nathair.' The Prince stared at him in silence, so Veradis continued. 'I am not a thinker, like Ektor, but I am, I guess, a fair judge of people. I know King Aquilus, I know you. I follow your lead. I trust my King. And these are strange times, there's no denying. Stones weeping blood, white wyrms roaming the land.'

Nathair shook his head. 'No. Following my lead, my father's lead, it is not enough, Veradis. I must know what *you* believe.' He poked Veradis in the chest. 'Halvor's book. What it predicts, about the God-War. Do you believe *that*?'

Slowly, deliberately, Veradis nodded. 'I do.' And he was surprised, for, saying it out loud, he realized that he did, completely.

Nathair smiled, ran a hand through his hair, the silence growing. Eventually he spoke.

'My dreams. The ones I have told you of.'

'Aye.'

'I think I have some understanding of them. The voice that I hear, always the same. I believe it to be Elyon, the All-Father.' He paused. 'Do you think me mad?'

'No, Nathair.'

'The one spoken of in the prophecy, the *Bright Star*, Elyon's champion. I believe . . . I believe I am that man. That through my dreams Elyon is summoning me. When we met Calidus, when you leaped through a wall of fire for me. Afterwards I talked with Calidus a long while, in his tent. He knows. He spoke of the God-War, he told me I am . . . chosen.'

Veradis shivered.

'My father has been telling me of these times. Warning me of them. *Preparing* me for them. We are on the brink of the abyss, Veradis. I *must* have good men around me. *Great* men. You are the first of those. Already we have stood for each other's lives, you and I. You leaped through the fire for me, when no one else did. And I saw your loyalty to me last night, before all else, even your own kin.'

Veradis was silent. He wanted to look away, feeling suddenly awkward, but Nathair's gaze held him. The Prince drew a knife from his belt. It glinted in the starlight.

'I would make a blood-oath with you. You are Elyon's gift to me: the brother that I never had, my first-sword, champion, battlechief and friend. Bind yourself to me now, and Elyon will take us on to glory you have never dreamed of. We shall face Asroth's Black Sun and change our world. What say you?'

Everything that had happened over the last turn of the moon flashed through Veradis' mind. He saw his father's face, heard his words of the night before – *a child does not become a man overnight* – he saw Krelis' face, Ektor's, but above them all Nathair's words resonated. Somehow, utterly, he *knew* that Nathair was destined for greatness. He *felt* it, could almost hear a voice whispering it in his mind, urging him to bend his knee. But more than that, Nathair *believed* in him. Suddenly he was overwhelmed by this man before him: prince, leader, friend, and he sank to his knees.

'I would swear this oath gladly. I would bind myself to you and your cause, Nathair, now and until death.'

'Then stand, brother, for that is what you are to me now, and let us seal this oath with our blood.' He drew his knife across his open palm, then offered the hilt to Veradis. With a quick motion Veradis did the same, and they gripped each other's hands, standing there long moments in the darkness.

'We are blood-sworn now, bound while blood flows in our bodies.' Nathair smiled. 'Come then, let us go meet our destiny.' He swung back into his saddle and urged his horse forwards. Veradis stood there a moment, clenching his stinging palm, then he scrambled onto his horse.

The ruin of Balara rose up, a dark shadow framed in the starlight. Veradis felt a pang, being this close to the place of so many childhood terrors, but Nathair was determined to enter. The gateway was blocked with fallen rubble, so they rode around the walls and soon found a section that had collapsed. There was no path for the horses, so they dismounted and hobbled them amongst a stand of trees, then entered the ancient fortress of giants.

Nathair strode along a wide street, Veradis a step behind, eyeing the deep shadows to either side suspiciously. He saw a light up ahead, filling an arched doorway, and above it reared the broken tower, rubble littering the ground around it.

A man stood beside the door, a long spear in his hand. Veradis gripped the hilt of his sword but Nathair walked past the man and through the open doorway. The spearman was Deinon, the Vin Thalun he had taken to Jerolin in chains. The corsair dipped his head to Veradis, who grunted and followed Nathair into the tower.

Torches burned around the room, which was wide and round; crumbling stone and rotted wood were scattered across the floor. A stone stairway wound around the tower wall until it abruptly ended, stars shimmering beyond the jagged outline of the shattered wall.

Three people stood before them. Two he instantly recognized – the thin, grey-bearded face of the Vin Thalun Calidus, and his giant companion, Alcyon. The other one stepped forward. He wore a plain leather cuirass, sharp eyes staring out from a weathered face, all deep lines and brown skin. He extended a hand towards Nathair, a jewelled ring of office glinting in the torchlight.

'Welcome, Nathair. I am Lykos. I have waited long for this moment.'

Nathair gripped his arm.

'Lykos. I have come as you asked. I am glad of the treaty between us.'

'There was a time when it would have been impossible, when no one man could speak for the Vin Thalun,' Lykos said, voice smooth but with an edge of gravel. Veradis thought of wolves. 'But now the warlords of the Three Islands have bowed their knee to me. We are no longer a fractured people. We are a force, rather than an annoyance to greater realms.' He tugged thoughtfully at a braid in his beard, streaked with grey. Iron rings bound in it chinked together. 'I wanted to meet you, thank you for your part in the treaty. I am sure that without your efforts it would not have come about.'

Nathair dipped his head.

'And for what else? What other reason are we meeting here, in the dead of night?' Nathair asked.

'You do not know?'

'I think perhaps I do,' Nathair said quietly, almost a whisper. 'But I would hear you say it.'

'So be it.' Lykos drew a breath. 'For decades I have known that I would serve you. And I have been preparing the way. You are set apart, Nathair, chosen.'

Nothing differed in Nathair's expression or bearing, but suddenly Veradis sensed a change, a tension filling the room, setting his skin tingling.

'Why would you say such a thing?' Nathair whispered.

'Because I have dreamed it. And in my dreams I have been told of a coming darkness; but more than that. I have been told of a man who will change the world we tread, someone who will unite the whole of the Banished Lands under one banner. I have been told that man is you, Nathair.' Suddenly Lykos dropped to his knees.

'I am at your command, Nathair, and along with me the Three Islands of the Vin Thalun, and a fleet the likes of which the Banished Lands has not witnessed since the coming of the Exiles to these shores.'

CHAPTER THIRTY-ONE

CORBAN

Corban checked again the list of herbs and plants that Brina had sent him to collect: *goldenrod, heartsease, meadowsweet, poppy, monkshood, elder.* They were all in the sack he had slung over his shoulder.

Keep them separate, she had warned. Before he had been able to clench his mouth shut he had asked why. Some days Brina would answer half a dozen *whys* before her patience snapped. Other days, like this day, he could tell there would be a sting in the tail of any answer, even for a single *why*.

Because some are for a poultice, and some he needs to drink, she had snapped. *Now get you gone before the lad dies of waiting*, she'd finished as she held her cottage door open.

'*GET YOU GONE*,' Craf the crow had screeched as he left. He really hated that crow.

Now he was trudging back to the cottage, a knot of fear germinating in his belly at the thought of having forgotten something.

'Goldenrod, heartsease, meadowsweet, poppy, monkshood, elder,' he recited out loud. Storm cocked her head at him as she trotted through the long grass nearby. She had been stopping frequently to pounce at butterflies or leap around clumps of grass, slowing his return, but he had been quite glad of the distraction.

He and the wolven-cub had hardly left each other's sides since his return from the hunt, a ten-night gone. The only time he did leave her was during his trips to the Rowan Field. Thannon had insisted. *Let them get used to the idea before she is paraded before them*, he had said. *There'll be warriors in the Field that were close to those killed or hurt.* When Thannon decided on something it very rarely changed. And anyway, his da was right. Men had died in the Baglun Forest. If it had been one of his kin he might not have been able to think of Storm without distrust.

He bent down, rustled the grass in front of the cub. She crouched, pounced, grabbed his wrist and shook her head, Corban yelping. Her teeth were sharper than his mam's bone needles. He twisted his hand free, caught some of the fur of her cheek, and tugged it playfully.

Looking up, he saw a thin line of smoke rising from Brina's cottage, tall alders shielding it. He didn't want to go back. It was bad enough having to be around Vonn, Evnis' son, although now that the fever had taken him he didn't have to put up with his scornful comments every time Corban was in the cottage. Adding Brina's foul mood to the brew made lingering outside tempting, but he was sure that the longer he delayed, the worse the tongue-lashing would be when he returned.

'Come on,' he said resignedly to Storm, setting off again.

Two horses were grazing on the lush grass around the cottage, a man sitting with his back to a wall. He rose as Corban approached and moved in front of the door. It was Evnis' guard, his nose crooked from when Tull had broken it. His name was Glyn, Corban had learned. Corban tried to move around him, avoiding eye contact as he reached for the door handle, but the warrior blocked him.

'None may enter.'

'But, Brina . . .' stuttered Corban.

'*None*,' Glyn snapped, cutting Corban short, poking him hard in the chest with a stubby finger. Corban took a step backwards, looked at the ground, not sure what to do.

Storm made a noise, somewhere between a hiss and a growl.

'Should put this spear in your pet,' the warrior muttered, prodding the butt into the wolven-cub's ribs.

'Don't you touch her,' Corban heard himself snarl. Glyn prodded Storm again, harder. She whimpered, jumped away, snapping. Corban's hand snaked out and grabbed the spear shaft. Glyn tried to jerk it free but Corban held on with strength he had not known he possessed.

There was a moment's silence as boy and warrior glared at each other. Then the cottage door opened suddenly. Brina appeared, a larger form behind her.

'. . . under my feet,' Brina was saying. Her eyes narrowed as she saw Corban and Glyn, Corban still clutching the warrior's spear shaft. She poked Glyn with a hard, bony finger. He recoiled as if bitten by a snake.

'Get out of the way, you oaf,' she snapped at him, 'and let my apprentice through.'

Apprentice. Corban's eyes widened.

'He has herbs vital to Vonn's recovery. I hope that you haven't hindered him,' she added with a sharp look. Glyn took another step back.

'Enough of this,' Evnis said from behind Brina, emerging into the sunlight.

'I will leave Glyn here. If there is any change in my son's condition, *any*, send him at once.'

'I have told you, I do not want someone *else* littering my cottage. It is overcrowded as it is. And, besides, there is no need, I have some-one here that I can send if necessary.' Brina gestured towards Corban. Evnis looked disdainfully at him.

'Glyn will stay,' he said.

'Well, he will stay *outside*,' said Brina. She grabbed Corban by the shoulder, dragged him in and slammed the door, Storm just manag-ing to avoid her tail being crushed as she darted through behind.

'Well?' Brina said, rounding on Corban. He stared at her blankly a moment, then hurriedly passed her his bag.

Muttering, she turned to a pot suspended over the fire. She emptied the bag's contents, quickly separating them into two piles. Breaking some up, she began dropping herbs into the bubbling pot. Craf squawked, hopping from foot to foot, beating his wings. '*Potion*,' he muttered.

'How is it . . .' Corban said hesitantly, 'that Craf speaks?'

Brina and the crow looked at him, appearing unnervingly alike for a moment.

'That is a question I had expected from you some time ago,' she said.

'It is one I have thought to ask, many times,' he admitted.

'Then why did you not?'

Corban shrugged. 'It seemed rude.'

Brina threw her head back and laughed, a throaty, unsettling sound. Craf squawked and ruffled his feathers, flapped his wings once. Storm *hissed* and hid behind Corban's legs.

'How is it that Craf speaks?' Brina repeated when she had recovered. 'When the world was young, things were very different. You know this already, or should do,' she added, frowning. 'Before the Scourging there was a harmony, to the land, amongst and between the races: giant, human. There was a *balance*. Elyon set an order into nature, into *us*. To the giants and mankind was given a gift, a responsibility. We were the *overseers* of this world, with a duty to care for it, and all that dwelt in it. You have heard the term *Elemental*, I would guess.'

'I have, though I do not really understand what it means. Magic, I think.'

'Magic,' Brina snorted. '*Magic* is a word the ignorant use to explain what they do not understand. An *Elemental* refers to those that have some kind of command – or *authority* is maybe a better word – over the world around them. It is an ability to use the elements: earth, water, fire, air, and *command* them, to some extent. The giants still claim some knowledge of this, though it was not solely their province. Once, when the world was young, *all* were Elementals. It was part of the pact, part of the way of things. Elyon gave us *authority*, so that we could better care for the world in which we were placed.'

'What? You mean you, *I* could . . .'

'Yes, that is exactly what I mean. And along with this was the ability to communicate with animals. It was part of the order.'

'But then,' Corban said, 'how is it not so now? It is just a tale, surely.'

Brina shrugged. 'If it is only a tale, then how is it that you hear Craf speak?' Her eyebrows beetled as she stared intently at him.

'I . . . don't know,' he said.

Brina snorted.

'What happened, then?' he asked, a little grudgingly.

'You know of the Otherworld?'

'Aye, though again—'

'Yes, yes, you are *unclear* of the details,' she said with a scowl. 'The Otherworld is the realm of Elyon, and of Asroth. Some say we can see it, at times even visit it, in our dreams. A world of spirit.'

Corban felt a vague tugging, at the back of his mind, a distant memory struggling to break through.

'As you know, Asroth and his Kadoshim are not *best pleased* with their being confined to the Otherworld. Asroth would like nothing more than to walk the land we tread.'

'Why?'

'Because he hates us, Corban; hates all creation. It is the joy, the crowning glory of his enemy, you see. He is too cunning to fight Elyon directly, not again, so he would destroy Elyon's creation instead. Destroy me, you, all of us. A type of revenge, if you like.'

Corban felt suddenly anxious, as if watched. He looked about the cabin.

'Before the Scourging the giants were different,' Brina continued. 'They were not so warlike, more inquisitive, but still the usual happened.' She twirled a hand. 'Greed, corruption, jealousy, the thirst for *power*, as always. The giants made things, great things, from a star that fell from the sky. Somehow the things that they forged from it – a spear, a torc, a cauldron, other things – all were somehow linked to the Otherworld. Some amongst the giants, tempted, swayed by Asroth, I don't doubt, began to explore this link. Some kind of *doorway* was made, between our world of flesh and the Otherworld, the world of spirit. *That* was when Elyon stepped in, decided enough was enough, I suppose. And you most certainly *do* know the rest: the Scourging of fire and water, where the world was changed – giants, mankind, virtually destroyed, our ancestors fleeing, being washed up on the shores of the Isle of Summer . . .'

She ran a finger through Craf's feathers, smiling sadly at Corban. 'So, you see, once all animals spoke, all people were Elementals and lived in balance with this world. Much has been lost. What we have now is but a pale reflection, a fragment – and even that is fading with the passing of time.' She sniffed. 'That is the way of the world, I suppose. No point fighting it.'

'How do you know all this?' Corban asked.

'I learned my letters, I read, I listened. I still do. You should try it, boy. History is of value. If more of us took heed of the mistakes of the past, the future could be a different thing.'

'Mam and Da teach me and Cywen our histories,' he said, 'but you know so much, and about giants . . .'

'Sometimes boy, you ask too many things for an old woman to keep up with,' she said. 'It is hard enough answering your questions, let alone answering the same one twice. I just told you: I learned my letters. I read. I listened.'

Vonn groaned, twisting in his cot. Brina returned her attentions to the pot in front of her. 'You can go now,' she said over her shoulder, 'I have no more need of you this day. Return on the morrow.'

Corban met Cywen on the giantsway, near the paddocks.

'I've been waiting for you. Mam wants us to fetch her some eggs,' she said. 'Our chickens aren't laying.'

'What's wrong with them?' Corban asked.

'Mam thinks Storm has scared them half to death.'

'She's stopped chasing them,' Corban said defensively.

'Yes, now she just stares at them, hungrily,' Cywen grinned.

'All right. Let's get Dath, I want to show him Storm.'

They found Dath sitting against the door of his house, gutting and boning a barrel full of fish. Corban made him give Storm a slice of one. Dath's hand shook a little as he offered it, but the wolven-cub snatched it and swallowed it in a heartbeat, licking her lips and canines, which were already starting to protrude visibly.

'Everyone's talking about you and *that*,' Dath said. He was staying perfectly still as Storm sniffed his hand, licking a finger. 'She's beautiful,' he whispered, 'but is she, you know, *safe?*'

'Yes,' Corban said. 'Da's helping me train her, just like a hound. She's doing well.'

'More importantly, can you train her to bite Rafe?' Dath asked with a grin.

'I'd like to, but Alona said if Storm hurts anyone she'll be killed.'

'Shame,' Dath frowned.

Corban sat down beside his friend. 'Not out fishing, then?'

'No.' Dath's frown shifted to a scowl.

'Your da inside?'

'Mmhhm.'

Cywen kicked his foot. 'Why don't you come down to the shore and find nests on the cliffs with us – climbing's about the only thing you're good at.'

Dath looked up at them, sighed. 'I'll check on Da.'

A stale smell leaked out of the gap in the doorway as Dath slipped into his house. Corban heard muffled snoring, Dath's footsteps, then his friend was back.

'Come on, then,' he said brusquely, setting off towards the beach. 'He won't be waking up any time soon.'

'How is your da?' Corban said, catching up with his friend.

Dath shrugged. 'Not good.' A slight tremor shook his voice. 'I don't know what to do, Ban.' He blinked hard.

'What does Bethan think?'

'Bethan? She's never home any more. When she is, she and Da just argue. I think she's in there.' He pointed towards a row of smoke-houses that lined the path to the beach.

'You should come live with us,' Cywen said.

'Couldn't leave Da,' Dath replied. 'He needs me.'

'What, as a punch-post?'

'You don't know what you're talking about,' he snapped.

They walked in silence a while, following the winding path down to the beach.

Dath glanced to his right, to where his da's skiff was beached, slumped on the stones.

They turned towards the cliffs that Dun Carreg was built upon. The tide was out, so they splashed through the shallow surf, fist-sized crabs scuttling out of their way, and stopped beside the cliff's foot.

Corban stared into a large cave at the base of the wall of stone. The sea filled it, surf echoing out of the blackness, sounding other-worldly, booming. A narrow path disappeared into the gloom, slick with seaweed. Dath saw him gazing into the cave's mouth and screwed up his face.

'No eggs in there, Ban.'

Corban nodded. 'All right. We'll do the cave another time.'

'Not likely, that cave's cursed.'

'Dath, are you scared of *everything*?' Corban scoffed.

'Say that to me when we're up there,' Dath said, pointing at the nests perched high above on rocky outcrops. He began to climb the cliff face, his slight, wiry frame easily scaling the slick, pitted rock.

'Wait here with Storm for me,' Corban said to Cywen. She grinned, watching the wolven-cub stalking a huge crab.

Corban began to climb, much slower than Dath. He had never

been as good a climber as his friend, though he thought few probably were, Dath seeming to possess an unnatural ability to scale
anything effortlessly.

As he climbed higher, the breeze that had been refreshing when
his feet had been on the ground seemed far more malevolent; now
clutching at him, trying to snatch him away from the rock. At last he
reached a cluster of nests and filled his small bag.

Then a voice drifted up to him, calling his name and his stomach lurched as he realized how high he was. Cywen was jumping
about, waving her hands at him. He shouted for Dath, then began
the climb down, and in a short time he was standing at the foot of
the cliffs, his legs and arms shaky from his exertions. Dath was right
behind him.

'Storm's gone,' Cywen almost shouted at them. 'I tried to stop
her, went after her a way, but it was too dark to see. I kept calling,
but she wouldn't come.' Tears welled in her eyes.

'Where,' Corban interrupted.

She pointed into the cave.

'Oh, no,' gulped Dath.

Corban strode in, calling Storm, but the sound of waves crashing on rocks drowned his voice. Cywen was right, in only a few steps
all was darkness. He went on a little way, hands grasping cold rock
walls, but his foot slipped on slick stone and he nearly fell into the
channel of seawater, so he turned back. 'Where's Dath?' he said as he
emerged blinking onto the sand.

'Gone to get a torch.'

Soon Dath flew back across the beach to them, quickly sparked
a torch of dried rushes to flame.

Corban entered first, Cywen behind him.

'Ban,' Dath called, hovering at the cave's entrance. He was pale,
looking as if he was about to vomit.

'What's wrong, Dath?'

'I-I don't think I can come in there . . .' he muttered.

'Why not?' Cywen snapped.

'It's – it's *cursed* . . .'

Cywen snorted.

'Take our eggs, Dath. Take them to my mam.'

'Thank you,' Dath said, taking Corban's bag of eggs.

'Tell her we're helping Brina with something,' Cywen added.

'I will,' Dath called over his shoulder.

The cave burrowed further than Corban would have thought, narrowing as they went deeper, though the ceiling was too high for the torchlight to touch it. They found Storm standing over a rock pool. Even as Corban watched, her paw snaked into the water and scooped out a fat, silvery fish. It flopped about on the rocks for a moment, before the wolven-cub pounced on it and crunched into its head.

'Think she likes fish,' Cywen said, relief dripping from her voice.

'Aye,' Corban grinned.

Storm saw them, picked up the fish and backed into the darkness. They gave chase, their torchlight sending shadows flickering up glistening rock and across the dark swell of the sea. The path narrowed to almost nothing, winding and curling about tall rock formations. Suddenly the cave ended, walls closing in. Storm was crouched at the end of the path. The half-chewed fish lay discarded beside her. She seemed to be growling at nothing, just a wall of pitted rock.

'What's wrong with her?' Cywen asked.

Corban swept the cub up. She twisted, hissing at the wall in front of them.

'Don't be stupid,' Corban said, 'there's nothing there.' He tapped the torch against the wall, suddenly gasped as the torch and half his arm *disappeared*. He staggered forwards a few steps, off-balance, felt a pressure building in his head and chest, heard a humming. Then it was gone.

He looked about. A massive chamber opened in front of him, his back seemingly to a rock wall, Cywen nowhere to be seen. Distantly, he could hear her voice, calling his name. He reached a hand out to touch the wall behind him, saw it sink *into* the rock. With a gasp, he snatched his hand back, then did it again. Taking a deep breath, he stepped into the wall, the pressure and humming building again, Storm spitting and growling, then he was through, Cywen before him, mouth open.

'Follow me,' he said, and stepped through the wall again. He walked into the chamber, and in a few moments Cywen emerged from the wall, eyes wide.

'What was that?' she said.

'A glamour,' Corban whispered. 'Must be. All the tales tell of giants doing them. They built Dun Carreg. They must have built this, as well.'

They were in a massive chamber of rough-hewn rock, damp and dripping. A large archway was at the far end, stone steps leading upwards.

Storm was still hissing at the glamour-wall, ears flat to her head, so he took a dozen steps away from it before putting her down. She growled at the wall one last time, then set to sniffing about the cavernous chamber.

'Where do you think those steps go?' Cywen muttered.

'Up,' Corban shrugged. 'Only one way to find out.' They climbed for a long while, an endless spiral. Then they spilled into another hall, where a shape drew Corban's attention. Motionless at the centre of the chamber lay a coiled mass. The three of them approached cautiously. It was the carcass of a dead snake, huge, its body thicker than Corban and Cywen together, its skin a pallid white. Its head was gone, a pool of black, dried blood soaked into the rock floor. Storm sniffed at it and backed away.

'I don't like the look of that,' Cywen whispered.

'Me neither,' said Corban, glancing about at the shadows. 'What killed it, and do you think there are others?' He'd heard of snakes growing huge in far-off Forn, but never imagined anything like this.

He knelt, prodded the carcass with the butt of the torch. The skin was thick, a layer of something slimy coating it, mucus, jelly-like. 'What could have killed this?' he muttered.

'I'd rather not hang around to find out,' Cywen said. 'Let's get out of here.'

Corban frowned. The beast's head was gone, the cut looking clean, no signs of toothmarks or tearing. *Chopped off. By a weapon?* 'Agreed. But let's go up, not down. We've climbed so far, we must be near the top.'

Cywen looked at him dubiously, but nodded.

Another archway led out of the chamber, ever up. They took it. Passages branched off it now, smaller ones, twisting into darkness. Corban stared into each one, imagining white snakes coiling in the gloom, waiting to strike. He ran his hand against the tunnel's wall, in case they passed another glamour, and increased his pace.

Eventually the passage came to a dead end, the rock all around them hard to the touch.

'What's that?' Cywen said.

It was an alcove, fist-sized. Corban held the torch close and peered in. There was some kind of handle inside. He reached in and turned it. With a *hiss* an outline appeared in the rock – a doorway. Cywen pushed against it and it swung open. They crept through and found themselves still underground, a dark pit opening up before them, with a path around it.

'We are in the well-house,' Cywen said.

The well-house was where most of Dun Carreg's water was gathered, and a short passageway led up to the fortress. Pale light, *dusk*, Corban realized, marked their way out.

Cywen pushed the door closed and it snapped shut, its outline disappearing, just a rock wall.

'There must be another handle this side,' Corban said. They searched long and hard, eventually finding it in the actual well. Cywen had to hold Corban's feet while he lay on his belly and wriggled over the edge to reach the alcove, just a darker shadow in the well-shaft. He tried it to make sure it worked: as soon as he turned it the outline of the door appeared in the wall.

'Let's get home. The moon's almost out, Mam's going to skin us,' Cywen said.

Corban closed the door; even its outline disappeared. They crept into the fading daylight, the well's courtyard empty before them. Then they heard voices, footsteps, and darted into the doorway of an empty building.

CHAPTER THIRTY-TWO

CAMLIN

Camlin stared at the wall, watching as moisture pooled slowly into a single droplet. It rolled down the rock face, its course changing as it encountered pits in the surface, until it eventually reached a horizontal edge. Here it hung awhile, suspended, clinging to the rim until another droplet rolled into it. Swelling, it tore away from the edge and tumbled through the air to burst on the stone floor.

Camlin sighed. He hated it in here, just rock and stone, no trees or wind or sky.

Grunting, he stood from his cot, stretching his arms overhead. He winced as skin pulled tight around his wound, reached down, tentatively stroking it, reassuring himself that it had not torn open. Although she had a sour tongue, he had to admit the healer had done a fine job. He'd seen men die of much less, especially once the fever took them. That was not an end he wished for himself.

He grimaced.

'Made me well so they can kill me properly, most like,' he muttered quietly, pacing around the large stone room that had become his cell. 'Still, alive is alive.' He tutted. *Talking to yourself, you old fool. First step to madness, that is.*

He frowned, suddenly remembering Goran's face staring lifelessly at him from amidst a framework of wildflowers and meadow grass. That had happened a lot of late, remembering faces from the past: his mam and big brother, Col, both long gone now, other, nameless faces he'd killed in combat or ambush, and especially those of the crofter's family near the Baglun. He shook his head, as if to dislodge the memory.

Stretching out on the floor, he began doing push-ups until sweat was staining his linen shirt. Eventually, when his arms were quivering and he could do no more, he rolled onto his back and stared at the roof. It had been difficult at first, forcing his body to exercise, trying to regain his strength. He had been as weak as a baby, but solid hard work and stubborn determination was starting to pay now. His wound and fever had sheared what little fat had been on his body, along with a good portion of his muscle. It was the reflection of his face, which he had seen on his first walk past the well-pool, that had shocked him most: like a wax doll left out too long in the sun. Still, the effort was working; he was definitely stronger now, even if he had not put much of the weight back on yet. Given time, it would come. Especially if they kept feeding him so well.

As his breathing returned to normal he heard noises filtering through the window above him. People were shouting, and feet were echoing on stone. Clenching a fist, he banged on the thick oak door of his cell. 'What's happening?' he called.

No answer.

He resumed his banging, paused and then called out again.

'Be silent,' a muffled voice shouted from the other side of the door, none too pleasantly. He smiled to himself and pummelled the door some more, pausing periodically to call out.

There were no more answers, so he sat back down on his cot, set his eyes back on the tiny channels of water gathering into droplets on the stone. 'One,' he breathed out as the first droplet plummeted to the floor. You had to do something in this cursed room of rock to aid the time in its passing.

It was still daylight when the door to his room rattled and creaked open. Inside his cell it was semi-darkness, torchlight making his eyes sting. He resisted the urge to leap up, and forced himself to remain lying on his back, his only movement to link his hands behind his head.

A hulking shape was first through the door. He recognized the man immediately.

Pendathran. He had visited before, soon after the fever had left him. Camlin had answered none of the big man's questions, and he had left soon after, cursing and splintering the doorframe as he punched it on his way out.

Next through the door was Conall, the man who had felled two of his men back in the Baglun. Nevertheless, he respected the man and he had been one of Camlin's regular guards on walks around the fortress.

Light and air, the healer had said, *and he needs to move, or he'll die before you have a chance to try him.*

One last figure stepped through the doorway, tall and broad, though not so much as Pendathran, fair hair bound in a single warrior braid. Apart from a thick gold torc twisted around his neck, he was dressed simply in a white linen shirt and breeches.

This man was a leader. Camlin knew it immediately; the way Pendathran and Conall fell in behind him, the way the man stood and looked at him, blue eyes clear and piercing, there was something of Braith about him, although they looked nothing alike.

This must be Brenin.

'Stand before your king,' growled Pendathran. Camlin turned his head to look at the bear of a man and rolled up into a sitting position, trying to hide the effort it required, and looked intently at his thumbnail, picking at imaginary dirt.

'He's no king of mine,' he said.

Pendathran stepped forward, pulled his arm back. Camlin tensed for the blow, but it did not come. Looking up, he saw Brenin had laid a restraining hand on the bear's arm.

'True enough,' said Brenin, 'but I am still ruler of this land, and all that choose to enter it. And now you find yourself in the heart of my power. In a cell, surrounded by my shieldmen.'

Camlin leaned back on his cot and said nothing.

'I will not deceive you. On the morrow you will be tried before my people. The likely outcome is that you will die soon after.' Brenin stared intently at Camlin, and the world seemed to shrink to just the two of them. 'I would have answers from you. It is your choice whether you cross the bridge of swords and meet your maker with honest words or falsehood upon your lips. And let this be a further incentive for you to tell the truth. You have not felt the questioner's tools because my healer has deemed you too weak to take the strain of it. That is no longer the case. If I am not convinced that you are answering true then you will be put to the question tonight. You'll still die on the morrow, but it is yet to be decided how you will spend your last night.'

So then, an execution. And before that, torture. He had known it was likely, and that each day of breath was a gift, but still, hearing it spoken aloud, he felt cold.

'What would you know?' he said, glad that his voice remained firm, did not betray the fear gnawing in his gut.

'Is Braith your lord?'

Camlin drew a deep breath, the word '*No*,' forming on the tip of his tongue. But Brenin's words had sunk deep. He did not want to meet Elyon branded a deceiver. He had done things, aye, hard things, but *right* oft depended on whose side you were on. His chief gave orders, he followed them: there was no more to it than that. And no shame. He owed Braith his life.

'Aye, Braith is my lord. But know this,' he said, raising a hand, 'I will tell you nothing that may bring him harm.' For over ten years now Braith had ruled in the Darkwood, built them up into something much more than just masterless men waylaying travellers in a wood. He could remember clearly the day Braith had appeared, brought in by scouts, Casalu still their chief back then.

Braith had been popular from the first, having a way of making men feel special, as if they counted. It had not been long before the camp had started to split, Braith's supporters growing steadily. Casalu had got wind of a change and started sending Braith on the most dangerous jobs, but he had kept coming back.

Eventually Braith had challenged Casalu. They decided it the Darkwood way, tied to each other's wrist in a knife-fight. Braith became something different when he fought, something cold, savage. He had near taken Casalu's head off. No one had challenged him as chief in all the years from then till now.

'I thank you for your honesty,' Brenin said, dipping his head to Camlin. 'Your lord tried to kill me.'

Camlin raised an eyebrow.

'In the hills that border Carnutan and Ardan. Yester-eve.'

Camlin shrugged. 'Maybe,' he said. 'Braith does not take me into his counsel. Though how are you sure?'

'They were woodsmen, like yourself. It was an ambush, using bows.'

'Cowards,' muttered Pendathran.

'But, as you can see, they failed.'

'How do you know it was Braith?' Camlin repeated.

'We captured one of them. Tull – no doubt you have heard of my first-sword – can be very persuasive when he sets his will to it. The captive confessed.'

'Aye. Well, what of it? You have been trying to kill Braith for years. Only fair he gives like for like.'

'True. But do not think to judge us the same,' said Brenin, an edge of iron in his voice. 'I have hunted him only because he raids my lands, steals from my people, burns their homes, murders men, women, children. Would you accuse me of the same? Could you?' Brenin's eyes bored into him. Camlin tried to meet them, but found that he could not, and looked away.

'A good man, Braith, you say. Well, maybe to those that follow him. But he has little honour.'

Camlin wanted to answer, his dead mam's face flashing through his mind, his murdered brother, but he could find no words, so he just glowered at the King.

'Why did you come to the Baglun Forest?'

'The Darkwood is getting crowded. Me an' some of the lads fancied a change of scenery.'

Brenin's eyes narrowed. 'Please, answer fair or not at all.'

Strangely, Camlin felt a flush of shame. 'Answer's obvious,' he muttered, looking at the floor. 'Braith told us to come here.'

'Why?'

'There's truth in the answer I just gave. Darkwood's filling up. Braith's band has grown of late. Too many mouths to feed. So he decided it was time to branch out. We're woodsmen, and the Baglun is the nearest large span o' trees to the Darkwood.' He shrugged. There was more to it than that, much more, but he would be damned if he would betray Braith. Not now, not ever.

'There's more you're not telling me, woodsman,' said Brenin.

'Like I told you, Braith does not take me into his counsel. If there was more, he did not tell me.' This time Camlin raised his chin, met Brenin's gaze and did not look away. Finally Brenin sighed and nodded.

'One last thing, then. There was someone, either here or in the village, that was helping you. Who?'

Camlin's mind raced. Brenin could not know for certain, yet he did not feel inclined to lie to this man. Half-truths were well and good, but not outright lies, not after this man in front of him had put the fear of Elyon into his bones.

'There was someone. But I don't know who it was.'

'Is there anything you can tell me about this contact? It is likely to be in your favour. They may not be happy that you are still breathing, you being someone that could incriminate them.'

Camlin thought of the men that had ridden up to him in the meadow, the one with the broken nose. He thought of Goran, stabbed in the back by them. He should not have died like that. But these were Braith's contacts. It was for Braith to deal with their betrayal.

'Aye,' he said. 'I know that. But you're going to do their work for them. If I lose my head on the morrow, you'll most likely be putting smiles on their faces.'

'So I should keep you alive, you think, to cause them sleepless nights?' The King's lips twitched at the edges, some amusement lurking there.

'I've heard worse ideas, now that you mention it,' Camlin answered.

Brenin's face changed, became stern. 'You played a part in killing, *murdering*, people under my care. Men, women, lads too young to sit their Long Night.' He took a deep breath. 'I think the morrow will be your last day of breath.'

The words stung. He had known what he had done, and this was not the first time he had done it. But it was part of a *cause*. A necessary evil. Many such evils were undertaken in war, for the greater good. But it still did not sound right, hearing it said so straight and clear. And he had not ordered the deaths of women and children. That had been an accident. No point saying any such thing, though. As if these men would believe him. He'd made his choice a long time ago, right or wrong, the day Col and his mam had died. He'd take the consequences. He gave a curt nod.

Brenin rubbed his face, looking suddenly tired. 'My thanks for your help.' He looked around the cell. 'You have been treated well?'

'Aye,' grunted Camlin. 'Well enough. On your healer's orders I even get walked once a day. I've the makings of a good hound.'

Only Conall smiled.

'Have you walked today?' asked Brenin.

'Nay.'

Brenin looked at Conall.

'They should be coming for him soon enough; my watch is almost up,' said the warrior.

Brenin looked back at Camlin. 'Enjoy it,' he said, leaving the rest unsaid but clear enough. *It will most likely be your last.*

Camlin sniffed and Brenin swept from the chamber, Pendathran following, giving Camlin one last glower. Conall winked at him as he pulled the door too, the key rattling as it turned.

Camlin sighed and lay back on his cot. So that was Brenin. He'd heard much about the man, growing up in a village in Narvon within sight of the Darkwood, and then joining Braith's crew, back in the days when there were only a handful of them. Not much of what he'd heard of Brenin had been good. Couldn't say he'd seen anything to fault just now, but they'd only shared a few words. Still, he'd always prided himself on being a fair judge of men and he hadn't seen anything that stood up false in Brenin. Not liking that thought, he chose not to pursue it, instead rising and pushing his body to more exercise. *Work the body, rest the mind,* he told himself.

Not long after, he heard the slap of footsteps in the corridor outside, then muffled voices.

'Ready for our stroll?' he said to the man in front of him. It was Marrock, nephew to Pendathran, he knew that much. Camlin knew the procedure by now. He fell into step behind Marrock, hearing the footsteps of the other warrior, one that he had not seen before, echoing softly behind him.

Soon they were outside the keep as dusk fell, walking a road that Camlin had come to know very well. He took a deep breath, tasting salt on his tongue. The street before him twisted and turned, the sounds of people in the fortress fading. Finally the stone courtyard with the great pool opened up before him. The courtyard was silent, as always.

'Got your King back from the Baglun, then?' he said to Marrock as they paced around the edge of the court, mostly just to break the silence.

'Aye. No thanks to you,' grunted Marrock.

'I can't take the praise for that, not as I've been enjoying your hospitality here.'

'You and your kind is my meaning, which you well know,' said Marrock, giving Camlin a sour look.

Camlin was near to the pool now, so he took the final steps needed to reach it, scooped up the ice-cold water in cupped hands and splashed water in his face. As he blinked he saw the shadow of a movement behind a building. Frowning, he took a step towards it.

'Stand, woodsman,' Marrock snapped, 'or you *will* feel my blade, no matter what the morrow has in store. And I promise you, there will be a lot more pain involved than you will feel from the headsman's weapon.'

Camlin froze. Suddenly there was a whistling sound and then two arrows were sprouting from the nameless guard – one from his throat, the other his chest. Blood fountained outwards, spraying Camlin's face. The warrior plucked feebly at a feathered shaft, then fell forwards.

Marrock twisted as more arrows flew from out of the shadows. One caught him high in the left shoulder, sending him spinning, crashing to the floor. Figures appeared: one, two, both wearing dark cloaks with hoods drawn. Dark iron was in their hands.

Marrock lurched to one knee, reaching awkwardly to pluck the arrow from his shoulder. With a grunt it pulled free and he dropped it clattering on the stones, grasped his sword hilt.

What is this? Camlin thought, *Rescue attempt or an assassination?* All of a sudden, death on the morrow looked far more appealing than death *now*.

One of the hooded men reached Marrock, kicked his sword-arm viciously, the weapon flying out of his grip as he fell backwards, hitting the stones. The hooded warrior stood over him, sword raised and placed a foot on Marrock's chest.

'Stop,' cried a voice behind Camlin. He spun on his heels. Two lads and a pup stood on the far side of the pool. No – one lad, one lass. He blinked, shook his head. And it wasn't a pup, it was a wolven-cub. This night was getting stranger by the moment. If not for the sense of death breathing down his neck he would have laughed.

The hooded men shared a look, unsure what to do. The lass reached to her belt, a knife appearing in her hand.

One of the hooded men strode forward, pushed his hood back. 'You're skinny as an ice-hare, Cam,' he said.

Camlin's mouth moved but nothing came out. The man that had spoken to him was tall, fair-haired, a neat scar running from eyebrow to chin.

'Braith,' Camlin breathed. 'Why have you come?'

'To save your fool hide, of course. What else? Heard you'd got yourself into a spot o' trouble.' They both grinned.

The lad, lass, and cub were still standing in the same spot, the other hooded warrior training an arrow on them.

'Can't have any witnesses,' Braith said.

Fear sparked in the boy's eyes, but nevertheless he stepped in front of the lass.

'Hold,' Camlin heard himself saying, moving between Braith and the lad.

'What, man? We can't just walk away. If you'd forgot, we're in the middle of Dun Carreg. And we've still got a fair bit to go 'fore we can breathe safe. It's the only choice.'

The faces of his mam and Col swam before Camlin's eyes, along with the crofter and his family. 'No more innocent blood,' he said.

'This is not the time to grow a conscience, Cam,' Braith grunted, his companion's arm starting to quiver under the pressure of his drawn bow. 'Just look away.'

'No, Braith.' He drew a ragged breath. 'I am thankful for your coming, more than I can ever show, but I'd rather walk right back to my cell and face the headsman on the morrow than see their blood spilt.'

'Braith?' muttered their companion, his arrow still trained on the lad.

'Leave it,' snarled Braith, lowering his own bow. 'So what would you suggest we do?' he asked Camlin in clipped tones.

'Good question. You there,' said Camlin, walking towards the youths. 'Seems we have a situation here,' he said quietly, for only their ears. They were both staring wide-eyed at him. 'I'm about to leave here pretty sharpish with my friends, see. And they're not inclined to believe that you're just going t'walk away, not say a word to anyone 'bout what's gone on here.'

'You're not supposed to leave,' said the lad, still standing in front of the lass, though he'd had to put an arm out to hold her there. 'You killed Dylan. You're to be judged.'

'Hush, lad,' said Camlin, raising a hand. 'Talk like that'll get you killed.'

A long, drawn-out groan filled the courtyard. It was Marrock. He was crawling towards his sword, face pale, blood pumping steadily from the wound in his shoulder. Instantly Braith and the other woodsman trained arrows on the wounded warrior.

'No.' This time it was the lad, stumbling forward, arms waving.

'That there's Marrock,' Camlin said, low and quiet to Braith. 'Marrock – Rhagor's boy.'

Braith eased the draw on his bow slightly. Camlin felt the stirrings of a plan.

'Let's take him.'

Braith just looked at him, waiting for him to say more.

'Marrock, as hostage. He's held in high regard here. Rhagor's son, nephew to Alona and Pendathran.'

Braith nodded slowly, the idea growing in his mind. 'Aye. Might be useful, 'specially if we find ourselves in a tight spot. Sometimes, Cam, you surprise me.' He lowered his bow, covered the ground between him and Marrock speedily, lithely, like a cat. 'Bind and gag him,' he ordered his companion. 'And treat his wound quick, 'fore he bleeds to death.'

'Aye, chief.' Camlin moved to help as well, checking behind him as Braith approached the lad and lass.

'Boy,' said Braith, 'you know this man?'

'Of course,' nodded the dark-haired lad.

'I will have your silence, or his death will be on your hands,' Braith said, gesturing towards Marrock. 'I want your word on it. If you hold your silence, I will release him.'

'Alive?'

'Aye. Alive.'

'When?' said the boy, bracing himself before the larger man.

Braith's eyes narrowed. 'You're in no position t'haggle, boy. If it weren't for my friend's attack o' morals I'd have killed you already.'

'When?' the boy repeated, trying to hide the tremor in his voice.

Braith rolled his eyes. 'When we are far enough from this cursed place. By sunrise ought t'do it.'

The lad looked between all gathered there. The wolven-cub was still at his feet, regarding Braith with fierce copper eyes. Eventually the lad sighed, knowing he had little choice.

'You have my word.'

'Good.' Braith spat onto the palm of his hand, stared at the lad, who looked at him blankly a moment, then spat into his own palm and gripped the woodsman's outstretched hand.

Braith smiled. 'It's a bargain,' he said, 'Darkwood style. Break it an' you'll have Asroth snapping at your heels, along with all the dread legions of his Kadoshim.'

The boy went pale and Braith smiled again, not kindly. 'I'll see you again,' he said. 'Let's go.'

It was dark now, as Braith, Camlin and the other woodsman steered Marrock into a side street. 'You sure you only came back for me?' Camlin said to Braith, who glanced at him, raising an eyebrow. Suddenly, quick as a viper, Braith had Camlin pinned against a wall, knife pricking under Camlin's chin.

'What have you said, Cam? What've you told – about me, the Darkwood?'

'Nothing, Braith. Nothing, I swear. Nothing they don't know, anyway.'

'Have you told who my contact is here in the fortress?' Braith's eyes were cold, suddenly dead, a killer's eyes.

'No.' He tried to shake his head, felt the knife cut into his flesh, felt blood trickle down his neck.

'If I find out you're lying to me, you know it'll go bad with you. Best all round if you tell the truth now.'

'I swear it, Braith.'

'Have you been put to the question?'

'No. Think that may've been coming later tonight. Brenin's only just returned.'

'I know.' Braith took a step back, sliced open Camlin's tunic, checked his torso. He lifted Camlin's hands, counted fingers, looked for fresh scars or burn marks. Then, suddenly, he smiled. 'Had to ask, Cam,' he said. 'Come on then, we haven't got all night.'

'How do we get off this rock?' Camlin whispered with relief, his fear receding.

'The fun is only just beginning,' Braith said, flashing a smile. Braith often won men over with that first smile. It said *you are the only person here*, and seemed to hold all the charm and power of a blood-oath. Camlin found himself smiling in return. 'Fortunately for you, I have friends in unlikely places. We've got a long walk in the dark ahead.' Braith gripped Camlin's shoulder. 'You know, my friend,' he whispered, 'sometimes you can be a great deal of trouble.'

CHAPTER THIRTY-THREE

VERADIS

Veradis whistled through clenched teeth. He was standing in the main stable block at Jerolin, huge pillars of black stone rising high above him, braced by lengths of timber wider than two men standing back to back. Birds flittered in and out of view, chasing each other around the beams.

He was with Nathair, both of them staring admiringly at a huge white stallion, which reared and neighed, ears back. A tremor passed through the floor as its hooves thudded down to the ground.

'He's fair, I'll say that,' said Valyn the stablemaster.

'Fair,' laughed Nathair. 'Tell me he's not the finest animal you've ever laid eyes on.'

'Not many could match him,' the stablemaster admitted, 'though one that equals him is stabled here right now. Not as big-boned, mind, but a little taller, and faster, I'd wager.'

'What?' said Nathair, genuinely shocked.

'Aye. Belongs to your father's friend. That Meical.' He nodded towards a stable. Veradis could see the glimmer of a silvery mane, but nothing more.

'Even *he's* not this stallion's better, though,' Valyn said, seeing Nathair's face darken. 'And in truth, apart from Meical's horse, I don't think I've ever seen this animal's equal.' He stepped forward, held his hand out for the stallion to sniff, a decidedly flustered-looking stable boy holding on to its bridle.

'So, come on, Nathair, how have you come by him?' said Veradis. 'He wasn't bred hereabouts.'

'He's a gift. From Jael of Isiltir.'

Veradis was blank a moment, then a dark-haired, handsome face appeared in his mind's eye. 'Ah, the nephew of King Romar. I remember him.' He thought of Kastell, kneeing the man in the knackers in front of the best warriors in the Banished Lands. He smiled, but did not share his memory. 'You must have made an impression on him,' he said instead.

Nathair smiled. 'It would seem so.'

'Easy, lad,' said Valyn, resting a hand on the stallion's chest, running the other down its foreleg, coaxing him to lift his hoof.

He did, but as Valyn bent low for a closer look the stallion's head darted back, Valyn only just managing to jump out of reach of its snapping teeth.

He was laughing as he rejoined Nathair and Veradis. 'Well, he's got spirit, that's for sure.'

'You're not going to let him get away with that?' said Veradis. He prided himself on his knowledge of horses, and backbiting was one habit he'd always been taught to master as soon as it appeared.

'I've a mind to let him off,' said Valyn. 'He's come a long way, new surroundings – the best of us act up sometimes. Besides, attitude like that can suit what you're looking for,' he said to Nathair. 'I think you've found yourself a warhorse. The best ones aren't often the most easygoing. Time'll be the judge.'

Valyn's attention shifted, Veradis and Nathair following the stablemaster's gaze.

Meical was standing in the stable entrance, a dark form outlined by the sunshine. He nodded to Valyn, strode towards where his horse was boxed.

'Can I help you?' Valyn called. Meical shook his head, then he saw Nathair.

'Your father has sent runners for you. He wishes to see you in his chambers. Now.'

Nathair walked across the stable, following Meical. 'Veradis, make sure there are no ears, nearby. I would have some privacy with Meical.'

Nathair opened the box; inside, Meical was adjusting a saddle-rug on a tall dapple-grey horse. Its dark, liquid eyes regarded the Prince. Valyn was right, the animal *was* impressive – regal, almost, more fine-boned than the white stallion from Isiltir. Veradis positioned himself by the open gate, with a good view of the stable

as well as Nathair and Meical. There was something about Aquilus'
counsellor that he did not like.

Meical paused as the Prince entered the box, eyes flickering
across Veradis, then back to Nathair. Not for the first time Veradis
was struck by the counsellor's height. *He must be taller even than Krelis*,
he thought, *though not so wide*, and he had thought Krelis easily the
largest man he had ever seen in all of Tenebral. He remembered
his father's and brother's questions about Meical, back in Ripa, and
Ektor asking the colour of Meical's eyes. He looked, but the stable
light was poor. They were dark, of that he was sure, but he could not
tell more.

'How goes it with the giant's book?' Nathair asked.

Meical stared at Nathair. His face was clean shaven, battle
scarred, though otherwise unlined. Something about him whispered
age. Long black hair was pulled back from his face, tied with silver
wire high at the back of his head.

'Slowly,' Meical said.

'Do you know who the Black Sun is yet? Where he will strike
from?'

Meical regarded him with his dark, liquid eyes. 'I cannot say, yet.'

'Cannot, or will not? I am the Prince of Tenebral, your ally. You
can talk to me of these things.'

'Aye, you are prince, not king. Your questions are best asked of
your father.'

'Who are you?' Nathair whispered, 'that my father trusts you so?'

Meical returned his attentions to his horse, lifting a saddle onto
the animal's back. A dismissal.

A shiver ran through Nathair, then he turned and walked away.
Veradis' eyes lingered on Meical, who returned the gaze, unblinking.
Veradis was the first to look away. Quickly he followed his Prince
from the stables.

He caught up with Nathair as he entered the keep. Veradis felt
he had come to know Nathair well, and there were times to ask questions of him. Looking at his face, this was not one of them. They
climbed a staircase and passed into a short corridor, heavy tapestries
stirring in their wake.

Nathair rapped his knuckles on a wooden door and pushed it
open, not waiting for an answer.

King Aquilus was within, sitting on a carved oak chair. Peritus, his battlechief, stood before him. Fidele was there also, half-clothed in shadow as she gazed out of a narrow window. 'Father, you sent for me. Mother,' he added with a glance to the Queen.

Fidele smiled.

'Peritus has returned to us,' the King said.

'I would speak with you both. Of the way ahead.' He smiled at Veradis. 'You have become my son's shadow, so much so that I almost forget you are here, Veradis ben Lamar.' Veradis returned the smile, liking the sound of his words. 'I am sure I do not have to remind you that the things we talk of remain between us only.'

Veradis nodded.

'Good. Now, Peritus, tell us of your journey.'

Peritus was a slight man, dark haired, thinning on the crown, with sun-darkened skin. Despite his size, Veradis knew he carried a fierce reputation. The hem of his cloak was dark with mud, as were his boots, his clothes dusty and travel stained.

'I have travelled the northern borderlands, stopping longest at Baran,' Peritus said. 'Marcellin was a good host, as always. He bids me tell you his oath stands till death, and that your will is his.'

'Good,' said Aquilus.

'The rest of my journey was much the same. All of the barons that I spoke with pledged their loyalty to you and your cause.'

Aquilus nodded slowly, then looked to Nathair. 'And you, my son, for Peritus' benefit, tell us of your journey.'

'My tale is much the same as Peritus', as you know. Lamar of Ripa agreed to prepare for war and renewed his oaths to you. The barons that I met with, well, they are more concerned with crops, weather, the extension of their lands, and lawless men, but their oaths to you stand. They will come at your call. Tenebral stands united behind you.'

'That is as it should be. But we must not sit idly by and just wait for Midwinter's Day. Many will join us then, I am sure. Though not all.' Aquilus stood, and began to pace around the room.

The King's eyes were sunken and dark, and Veradis noticed much more grey in his cropped hair and beard. *He carries a great burden.*

'Asroth's champion is a mystery to us,' Aquilus continued. 'Who is he? Where? We know not, so we must do all that we can in the time that is left to us. Nathair, how does your warband fare?'

'Well, Father. They train hard, every day. Numbers are growing.' Nathair looked to Veradis. 'How many?'

'Just short of a thousand strong.'

Aquilus' eyes widened. He laughed and slapped Nathair's shoulder. 'Well done, my son. You have taken my words seriously.'

'Aye.'

'It is no wonder our barns are emptying quickly. No matter. But we must find work for them to do, to earn their keep and to cut their teeth.'

'Tenebral is as peaceful as I have ever seen it,' said Peritus.

'Aye, that is so. Particularly as the Vin Thalun have kept their agreement within our borders.' Aquilus' eyes flickered to Nathair. 'So we must look elsewhere to give your men some experience of combat.'

'What do you mean, Father?'

'The alliance that was forged in the council. There were only a handful that stood with us outright, but already I have had requests for aid from Braster of Helveth, Romar of Isiltir and Rahim of Tarbesh. Brenin of Ardan spoke to me of trouble on his border. I think he would welcome help,' said the King.

'Braster and Romar share a border with each other, marked by Forn Forest. They have agreed to join forces in crushing the Hunen, a giant clan that lives within. They have asked me to be a part of their endeavour, to send men to aid them. I am of a mind to do so.'

'When would this happen?' asked Nathair.

'Not this year. Next spring, most likely. And Brenin's realm is not much further than Isiltir, so we could send a warband and then split it. One to fight against these giants in Forn Forest, one to help Brenin against the lawless men that trouble his border.'

'Trouble lurks in the dark places,' Peritus muttered.

'So it would seem,' said Aquilus.

'And King Rahim of Tarbesh?' asked Nathair.

'He, too is having trouble with the remnants of a giant clan. There is a band of land stretching across his kingdom that has become too dangerous to cross. No forests, though,' he smiled at Peritus.

'And when would you send aid to Rahim?' Nathair persisted.

'Perhaps this year,' Aquilus said, tugging gently at his short beard. 'Perhaps soon. Their land is to the south-east, much of it desert, so winter would not hinder our warriors as it would in a northern campaign.'

'I would be proud to lead men to Tarbesh, to represent you, to further the alliance and our cause,' Nathair said eagerly.

'It is a strange land, I have heard,' Aquilus said. 'Blistering heat in the day, nights of bitter cold. I was thinking to send a more experienced warband to Tarbesh, with men who have sat a campaign before. I thought to send you north come spring, Nathair, to Isiltir.'

'Do you doubt me? Do you doubt my men? We are more than equal to the task,' said Nathair.

Aquilus looked at him searchingly, then shifted his gaze to Peritus. 'Perhaps. I will meet with your men, watch your training, of which I have heard much.' He raised an eyebrow. 'Then I will decide.'

Nathair bowed his head. 'As you wish.'

'Peritus,' said Aquilus, 'you still carry the dust of your journey. Please, relax this day. Join me on the morrow. We shall view my son's warband together.'

'As you wish,' said the battlechief and, with a nod to Nathair, left the room.

'Nathair, there is another matter that I would speak of with you.' The King frowned. 'A messenger came this morning from our border with Carnutan. He had interesting news. There have been more raids, by the Vin Thalun.'

Nathair said nothing.

'Over the last moon the Van Thalun have caused more death and destruction than ever before.'

'What of it, Father?' Nathair said with a shrug. 'They have kept their word to us. No raids have taken place within our borders.'

'Aye, true.' The King took a deep breath, exhaling slowly. 'But the Vin Thalun are raiding as far west as Carnutan. That has *never* happened before.' The King's fingers tapped on the arm of his chair, the room otherwise quiet and still.

'If you looked hard enough, you could almost see a pattern emerging here,' Aquilus continued. 'The lands raided during the last moon: only Carnutan, a realm that opposed me in the council, and Mandros of Carnutan louder than most. And what of Tarbesh? A realm that stood with me in the council, but that has oft been raided by the Vin Thalun in the past – *nothing*!' Aquilus stood suddenly. 'Tell me true, son. Have you played a part in this?'

Father and son stared at each other.

'Nay,' said Nathair eventually, holding Aquilus' gaze. The King sighed, looked away, the tension dissipating.

'Good. That is good. But if I have thought of this, others will not be far behind. Mandros most certainly; he mistrusts all at the best of times, and it is no secret that you have championed the Vin Thalun and our treaty with them. *They* could be trying to sow discord here, to undermine the alliance before it truly begins.'

'Surely not, Father.'

'In the past I would have agreed with you, but their new leader, this Lykos. I have heard troubling things of him. It was quite a feat of itself to unite the islands, eh? Panos, Nerin and Pelset were always a thorn in the side of the mainland kingdoms, but no more than that. Now that they work together, they are capable of considerably more.'

Veradis was growing increasingly uncomfortable. He knew that things had been hidden from Aquilus, but lying outright was a greater step. He swallowed. *It is for the greater good*, he told himself. His eyes touched on Fidele. She was watching Nathair intently, *studying* him.

'Father, why is it that you care so much about the opinions of such as Mandros. They are beneath you. We do not need him, or any like him. *We* are the instrument of Elyon's justice. *We* will take the war to Asroth, and the likes of Mandros will matter not at all.'

Aquilus shook his head. 'Nathair, you are young, your principles fixed, but you have much to learn of politicking. You still possess the naivety of youth. And the pride.' He sighed. 'Asroth's champion, this *Black Sun*, will not be some mountain brigand that can be swept aside in a day's combat. We must marshal all of the strength available before he reveals himself. We *need* the likes of Mandros. *Every* realm that does not stand with us will most likely stand *against* us.'

Nathair snorted. 'I do not agree, Father. Mandros and his ilk are more trouble than they are worth. I have a *feeling* about Mandros: he is *wrong*, somehow. Have you considered that he could be in league with this Black Sun? Could even *be* him. Asroth is cunning incarnate, the tales tell us – he would not be likely to let you raise this alliance unhindered.'

'You are not *listening* to me,' Aquilus pounded the arm of his chair. Then his voice dropped. 'I am not so interested in your *agreement* or your *theories*. It is your *loyalty* that concerns me. I will not have you opposing me thus at every turn. I am king, Nathair, and my word is law. Remember that.' He now looked weary, bowed his head and walked to the open window beside his wife. 'And my word on *this* matter is that you will distance yourself from the Vin Thalun. I do not want you linked to them, in any way. Is that clear to you?'

Nathair's shoulders tensed. 'Aye, Father. Your will is clear to me.'

Aquilus grunted. 'That is all. I will see you on the morrow.'

CHAPTER THIRTY-FOUR

CORBAN

Corban grunted as Gar's practice sword cracked his knuckles, his weapon dropping into the hard-packed dirt of the stable.

'What's wrong with you?' Gar asked as Corban bent to retrieve it.

'Nothing,' muttered Corban, wincing as he flexed his hand. The knuckles were red and already swelling. He grimaced. In truth there was much wrong. He had slept little, wondering all night if he had done the right thing, allowing the brigands just to walk away. Cywen had made her thoughts on the matter clear before Braith and his companions had even disappeared from view, scolding him for a fool. But what else could he have done? Died a warrior's death, yes, but Cywen and Marrock would have done so too, and the outcome would have been the same: the brigands slinking off into the darkness. They had talked about going straight to King Brenin, or their mam and da, but eventually decided against it. Telling any adult would most likely result in the alarm being raised and Marrock being executed. He did not doubt for a moment that Braith would do it. At least this way there was a chance that Marrock would live.

He sighed, gripped his practice sword and faced Gar again. Trying to clear his mind, he inhaled deeply, held his breath, feeling pressure build in his chest, then blew out slowly, as Gar had taught him.

The stablemaster nodded to himself, watching.

He misses nothing, Corban thought, then all else was banished from his mind as he set about determinedly attempting to keep his knuckles from further harm.

'There's something on your mind,' Gar said, breaking the silence as they rested after their training session.

Corban looked up, but said nothing.

Gar shrugged. 'Your business is your own. But you must try harder to focus. It affected your training today.'

Corban dipped a ladle into the water barrel and took a long drink. 'Easy for you to say,' he muttered under his breath.

'Aye. It is,' said Gar.

Corban blinked, feeling a flush of embarrassment.

'Most things of worth don't come easy,' Gar continued, 'and *anything* that can save your life on the battlefield *is* of worth. But you got the better of your distraction, after a while. That is good. Just do it more quickly next time; save your knuckles some pain.'

'Huh,' Corban exclaimed sourly.

'How goes it in the Rowan Field?' asked the stablemaster.

You know well enough, thought Corban. He had often caught sight of Gar watching him train in the Field, standing in shadows.

Halion had taught him much, and he was now beginning to feel more at home with shield and spear, although it was with the sword that he was excelling, felt like it was becoming part of him, an extension of his arm, rather than just a heavy stick. Nothing had been said, but he could tell that he was doing well, just by the way Halion would raise an eyebrow during sparring, or sometimes he would look around during a pause in training to find eyes on him from amongst the older warriors. Much of his progress was thanks to Gar, he knew.

'My weapons training is going well,' he said. 'Halion says little, though more than you. I think he is pleased with me.'

Gar grunted, said nothing more.

'Why do you not train in the Rowan Field?' Corban asked, giving voice to a question that he had long wondered about.

'I cannot fight with a warband. My leg, my wound . . .' Gar turned away, cupped some water from the barrel in his hand and drank. 'There is little point training with warriors when you cannot fight beside them.'

Corban looked sceptical. 'I suspect your wound is not as bad as you think. It does not stop you killing *me* ten score times every time that I spar with you.'

'*You* are a fourteen-year-old boy, not a full-grown warrior.'

'But still, I watch others in the Field, Gar. Halion can best most of them, probably all, and you are at least his equal. You would be given more respect if people knew. They would not think of you as just a stablemaster.'

'*Just* a stablemaster.' Gar frowned. 'I do not desire other men's respect. And *stablemaster* is good enough for me.'

'But . . .'

'Enough,' Gar's patience was at an end. 'I made my decision a long time ago. I will not change it now.'

In silence they unwound the padding from their practice swords – Gar had become concerned about the noise their sparring had been making and so insisted on covering the wooden swords in tightly bound lambskin.

'How is your wolven-cub?' asked the stablemaster.

Corban could not help but smile. 'She is well. I left her snoring with Buddai before the fire,' he said. Usually Storm woke when he did, but not this morning. He always left her behind when he trained with Gar, anyway, as he often went straight from the stables to the Rowan Field. Halion liked to start early, and that meant an earlier finish, leaving more time in the day for other things. There would be no training in the Field today, though. Halion had left before dawn with a search party hunting for Marrock and the escaped brigand.

His stomach growled. 'I think I shall go and wake her,' he said and bid Gar farewell.

Corban stepped quietly into the kitchen. Thannon was sitting on a chair by the fire, chin resting on his chest. Wisps of his black beard rose and fell around his mouth as he snored rhythmically. Buddai looked up from his master's feet, tail thumping softly on the stone floor at the sight of Corban. Storm appeared from behind the hound and bounced over, a bundle of soft white fur slashed with darker stripes. He crouched and she rubbed her muzzle against him, nipped at his fingers with her sharp cub's teeth.

'Shh,' he whispered, not wanting to wake his da. He stroked Storm gently, calmly. Her white baby fur was soft and fluffy, coarser hairs already beginning to grow through, flecked with black.

Thannon woke as plates banged onto the kitchen table, and Cywen came in from the garden, a dozen or so eggs scooped in her shirt.

There was not much conversation during the meal. All were tired, having slept little. The alarm had been raised in the dead of night, when the brigand's guard had been changed and his cell was found empty. It was not long after that news spread of a dead warrior near the well-pool, of Marrock and Camlin gone. Corban put his energies into demolishing the cheese, eggs and warm bread that was placed in front of him.

'Any word?' asked Cywen. Corban stared at the contents of his plate, resisting the urge to look at his sister. He could feel her eyes on him.

'None yet,' said Gwenith, her back to them as she bustled around the ovens.

'It's early still,' said Thannon. 'Tracking'll be easier, now sun's well up.'

At dawn, thought Corban. *Marrock should have been released at dawn*. Raising his eyes, he caught Cywen's gaze; it told him she was thinking the same thing.

Braith had given his word. *Darkwood style*. He shuddered, remembering the woodsman's eyes, his grip and his promise of retribution if Corban broke his word. Despite all that he had heard of the chief of the Darkwood outlaws, he had believed him. *Fool. I am a fool*, he told himself.

'I'll be off to Brina's,' he said, chair scraping on the flagstones as he stood quickly. 'Get my chores out of the way.'

'I'll walk some of the way with you,' said Thannon. Gwenith slipped some food wrapped in waxed paper to him as he left with his da, Buddai and Storm trotting out behind them.

'Where are you going, Da?' asked Corban.

'Could do with checking on Steadfast. He's in the paddocks, near your colt,' said the huge blacksmith. Corban looked up at him as they made their way to Stonegate, an eyebrow raised.

'All right, truth be told I'm not so happy about you walking the countryside on your own right now, what with escaped brigands from the Darkwood about.'

'They're long gone by now,' said Corban.

'How do you know that, lad?' said his da. Corban's heart lurched in his chest, but then Thannon carried on. 'They may've gone to ground somewhere nearby. Wait for the fuss to die down, make their way back to the Darkwood when eyes aren't watching for them. It's an old trick, I'd not put it past that brigand. What I want to know is, where's Marrock?' He went on, not expecting an answer from Corban. 'Dead, most likely. Lying behind a wall or in the bay with his throat slit.'

Corban felt sick.

They walked in silence a while, passing under the arched pillars of Stonegate, out across the ancient stone bridge. Goats roamed across the hill as they descended, searching for grass and vegetation on the wind-blasted ground, gorse bushes flowering yellow in the summer sun.

'Have you named your new colt yet, Ban?' Thannon asked.

'No. Not yet.' It had not been from lack of thought on the matter. He had spent much time with his colt, both with Gar and Cywen, and alone. Many nights he had fallen asleep to lists of names: Swift-foot, Hunter, Keensight, Light-tail, even Windwalker, after the stallion that had belonged to Sokar, their ancient ancestor, first king of the Banished Lands. Nothing seemed to fit.

'Gar has told me that the name will claim the horse, and not to rush it,' he said, 'but it has been a long time, and I'm growing tired of calling him "Boy."'

'Well, there aren't many that know horses better than Gar. I'd take his advice.'

'Aye,' Corban agreed.

They continued down the hill, walking quickly through the village and out towards the giantsway, children playing in the street stopping to stare as Buddai and Storm trotted behind them, Storm bouncing around the hound, slipping between his legs as they played. Thannon chuckled.

'Used to all the eyes on you, yet?' he asked, looking at the wide-eyed children.

'No,' said Corban. 'I hope people will get used to her soon.'

'That may take a while,' said Thannon. 'There aren't many places where a wolven walks amongst men in the light of day. And she's only going to get bigger.'

Corban had not really thought too far ahead about Storm, but his da was right.

'I don't care,' he said. 'She's here now, and that's how it's going to stay. People will have to get used to it.'

'Aye, lad, no doubt about that.'

He'd had to remind himself that the cub was not a hound pup, but something altogether wilder, more dangerous. Only once so far had he caught a glimpse of that. He had been walking back from the village, with some smoked fish his mam had sent him to get, trailed by a few dogs from Havan. He'd thrown a scrap of fish to Storm, but one of the dogs had darted forward and tried to take it from her. She had dropped the scrap, pounced on the dog, which had been almost twice her size, all snapping teeth and white fur. The dog had run off, tail between its legs, whining.

The paddocks came into view, Havan receding behind them. Corban could see his colt, standing quiet in the shade of a hawthorn bush.

'I'm going to check on Steadfast. You'll be all right from here, Ban?'

'I was all right to begin with,' said Corban. Brina's cottage was not much further along the road. He could see a thin wisp of smoke rising from behind the trees that hid her cottage.

The sound of wheels crunching on stone drifted faintly behind them, and they both turned to see two horses pulling a large wain. It was coming their way, leaving Havan. Thannon stared at it a moment, then looked back to Corban.

'Maybe I should walk with you to the healer's cottage,' he said.

'I'll be fine. I'm not a bairn, and, besides, I have Storm to protect me.'

Thannon chuckled. 'No doubts she'd try, but she needs to grow a bit, yet. Take Buddai, ease your old da's mind. Then I'll stop fussing over you as if I were your mam.'

'Fine,' said Corban. His da smiled and left the road, told Buddai with a flick of his wrist to stay with Corban. The hound watched his master a moment, then bounded after Corban and Storm.

The path through the trees to Brina's was trampled, the constant coming and going of guards set by Evnis to watch over Vonn having churned the ground. Corban saw the guard sitting in the shade, back against a tree, his horse cropping grass. Another horse stood nearby, its reins wrapped loosely around the branch of a willow near the stream.

Corban knocked on Brina's door, heard raised voices inside. The door flew open and Brina's wrinkled face appeared.

'What now? Oh, it's you,' she said, squinting at Corban. 'Well, you may as well come in. Why not, everyone else has. It's like the Spring Fair in here.'

Corban stepped through the doorway, unsure whether to smile or not. Buddai padded warily in behind him, sniffing the air, Storm hidden between the great hound's legs.

An old man stood in the middle of the room, grey haired, thin. Corban blinked as he recognized Heb, the loremaster. His eyes flickered over Corban and he raised an eyebrow, looking at Brina.

'My apprentice,' she said with a wave of her hand.

Heb raised his other eyebrow. '*Apprentice*. Very well. As I was saying, it is not safe here, Brina. No one knows how the brigand escaped, how many aided him, where he is.' The loremaster sat in a wooden chair, fingers steepled under his chin. 'You trouble me, living alone, so far from protection.'

Brina's face changed colour, purpling as if she were choking on a stone.

'Not safe . . .' she managed to splutter. '*Protection* – I have managed well enough for a score of years, and without any of your newfound *concern*.' She spat the word as if it were poison. 'It is bad enough having to put up with idiots with sharp sticks lurking on my doorstep day and night: why would I choose to live in a fortress *full* of idiots?' She smiled humourlessly. 'Do you miss my company?'

'Company? Stone the crows, woman, time in your presence ages me,' said the loremaster, standing to pace around the room. Craf squawked above their heads. Heb glanced up, the scruffy-looking crow watching them from a beam, his beady black eyes shining.

'You are as stubborn and stiff-necked as ever,' muttered Heb. 'Age is supposed to mellow a person.'

'Hah, as it has you?'

Heb held a hand up, took a breath. 'Would you not consider it? I would sleep better knowing you were within the walls of the fortress.'

'Dun Carreg is no place for me. I like trees and grass, not rock and stone.'

'Think on what I have said, Brina. There is wisdom in it, you know that.'

'Pfah. Wisdom. What would you know of that?' the healer muttered.

'I give up.' Heb raised his hands and strode towards the door. 'Be careful how much time you spend with this woman,' he exclaimed to Corban, 'she can be bad for a man's health.'

The door closed with a bang, leaving Corban and Brina staring at each other.

'*Bad man*,' muttered Craf.

Corban looked away, flinching from the healer's glare. Vonn lay on his cot in the next room. He was pale faced, eyes sunken, but the fever had left him.

'What would you have me do?' Corban asked.

'I have little need for you today, no herbs need collecting. There is always sweeping, though. Yes. Where *does* all the dust come from.'

Corban fetched the broom.

'And don't let your hound eat my crow,' said Brina, eyeing Buddai suspiciously as he sat staring up at Craf, a line of drool hanging from the fold of one of his jowls.

He'd choke, thought Corban, but managed to stop himself from speaking the thought out loud. He pointed and Buddai curled up near the front door, Storm worrying at one of his floppy ears.

Vonn was propped up with pillows, watching Corban as he began sweeping in his room.

'You're missing some,' Vonn said, pointing into a corner. Corban ignored him.

'Boy, boy, I am talking to you.'

Corban looked over at him.

'That's better. Now, just there, under the table – you haven't swept there.'

Corban grunted, swept where Vonn was pointing. He deeply begrudged doing Vonn's bidding, but Brina *had* asked him to sweep, and he knew without doubt that, no matter where she was in the cottage, she would be listening.

Just then Storm walked into the room, tiring of Buddai. She saw the stiff rushes of the broom sweeping back and forth and leaped on them. Corban laughed as the broom handle was wrenched from his fingers.

'You,' said Vonn.

'What?' said Corban, turning. Vonn had pushed himself into a sitting position, blond hair dark with sweat, strands clinging to his face.

'It was you, in the Baglun?' Vonn stared from Corban to the wolven-cub.

'Aye. What of it?' said Corban.

'You *dare* set foot here, and bring *that* with you?' Vonn pointed an accusing finger at Storm.

'Aye, I do.'

'You have much to answer for. Were I not confined to this bed I would teach you a lesson myself. Right now.'

'I have done nothing wrong,' said Corban.

'Nothing wrong? Other than protect the animal that caused the deaths of brave men, caused my own wounding, maybe. I think you have done *much* wrong. And when I am healed, I will come find you to seek a reckoning.'

'I have done nothing wrong,' Corban repeated, feeling anger and fear struggling within. It was well known that Vonn was skilled with a blade.

'My father thinks differently,' said Vonn.

'Aye, and the Queen thinks differently to *him*,' Corban retorted.

The two of them were silent for long moments. 'Sweep your own room,' Corban muttered, then stalked out, Storm following.

He began sweeping elsewhere, so violently that the dust rose in a cloud about him, but he did not notice. Brina sat in a chair, poring over a leather-bound book. She also kept an eye on Corban amidst the cloud that surrounded him, but she said nothing.

Soon after, the sound of shouting came through the open windows. Corban ran to the door, Brina just behind him.

The warrior posted to guard Vonn was on the far side of the alder glade. Corban could just see him holding his spear in the air and whooping loudly. In the distance was the sound of horses' hooves, lots of them.

The warrior stood there a moment longer, silent now, then turned and made his way back towards them.

'What goes on?' said Corban.

The warrior looked at him but said nothing.

'Well?' snapped Brina. 'Are you deaf? The boy asked you a question.'

'It was the search party, returning to the fortress,' the warrior said, still ignoring Corban, looking at Brina. 'Marrock rode with them.'

CHAPTER THIRTY-FIVE

VERADIS

Veradis took a deep breath, savouring the smell and taste of brine in the air, even though it whipped into him, stinging his face and bringing tears to his eyes.

He walked the deck of the ship easily, unconsciously allowing for the shift and roll beneath his feet. Others were not faring so well.

Bos clung to the side of the ship, bent double, spittle flying in a stream from his mouth. Other men in similar poses were dotted around the ship's edge. Veradis smiled. He had grown up on the bay, so the deck of a ship was more than familiar to him, but many of the warriors in Nathair's warband had come from further inland. For many this was the first time they had *seen* the ocean, let alone journeyed on it.

He looked grim. This would be an opportune time for the Vin Thalun, whose ships they travelled in, to turn on them. *No*, he thought, *Nathair is right. If they wanted him dead they could have done the deed many times over.*

He reached the prow of the ship, the sun rising on the horizon before him, turning the sea to shimmering gold.

Half a ten-night they had been at sea. Earlier, the coastline of Pelset had been visible, the most easterly of the Vin Thalun's three islands. Now they were well into the great expanse of the Tethys Sea, nothing between them and Tarbesh but water.

He glanced over his shoulder, spying the other ships in their fleet as black dots in the glare of the sun. Eight hundred of Nathair's warriors were on those ships, only five or six score left at Jerolin to gather in and train any new recruits while they were away. He smiled at the memory of King Aquilus and Peritus, standing amazed as they had watched the warband train.

It had been something to see.

A third of the warband, some three hundred or so men standing shoulder to shoulder, the line three score long, five men deep. The other two-thirds of the warband, ordered to mass and attack as was common in the Banished Lands, an unorganized swarm. They had charged the still line of warriors, screaming war cries, wooden swords and spears raised. When only twenty or thirty paces had separated the two groups, the line of warriors had raised great round shields, forming a wall of oak and iron.

The charging warriors smashed into it. The wall had trembled, bent at the edges like a newly strung bow, but held firm. After long moments of battering ineffectually against the shields, battle-cries turning to grunts as men strained and pushed, a single blast of a horn went up from behind the shield wall, and, as one, they took a step forwards. Then another. Men began to fall before the wall of shields, unable to move back or manoeuvre in the tight press.

'How do they wield a blade in that crush?' Aquilus had asked.

Veradis and Nathair, along with Aquilus, Fidele and Peritus, had viewed the mock battle in the glade from a small muddy knoll recently stripped of trees. Veradis remembered Nathair's smile.

'The attacking warriors cannot, Father,' Nathair had said. 'The wall of shields forces them too close. They cannot separate into hundreds of individual duels, as has been the way, and so their swords and spears are too long. The shield warriors, though, have been equipped with these.' He drew a short sword from his belt, sheathed where he usually carried a knife. Nathair had commissioned a team of smiths to make the weapons in secret, and wooden counterparts had been fashioned for the warband to train with. 'These are more suited to this combat. See how they are thrust between the shields. They do not need room to swing a blade, only stab what is in front of them.'

Aquilus glanced at Peritus, who watched the battle in silence. He nodded, once.

'Your men are at risk of being flanked,' the battlechief had said, pointing to the glade.

'Aye, but watch.'

The shield wall had curved at the flanks as the attacking warriors sought to overwhelm or surround them. A horn blew again, two short successive blasts this time, and warriors from the centre of the back row moved quickly to strengthen the flanks. At the same time riders had filled the glade, two groups of horsemen appearing from the trees, each a score or so strong. They flew at the warriors who were trying to breach the shield wall's flanks, turning at the last instant to rake the massed warriors with spears and long swords.

The outcome was clear enough.

'It works well in partnership with mounted warriors,' Veradis said.

'I have seen enough,' said Aquilus.

Nathair raised a hand in the air. The horn sounded again, and instantly the mock conflict had stopped, the men in the shield wall helping fallen comrades regain their feet.

'Well, Father. Do you not judge us ready?'

Aquilus had sucked in a deep breath. Veradis could still remember the smell of the glade, the air damp with morning dew, the smell of rotting leaves, rich forest loam, sweat, horses, all mingling.

'It is impressive, Nathair. What say you, Peritus?'

'As you say, my King. You use the terrain well, Nathair,' the battlechief had said, 'but here it is in the favour of your wall of shields; that would not always be so – woodland battle, a more open space, where the attackers are not so hemmed in, high ground.' He had shrugged. 'I am uncomfortable with some of the things I see here. These men are warriors, yet they are being herded as cattle. And your weapons: I would prefer to fight warrior to warrior, know that my skill with a blade had kept me alive.'

'A craftsman brings the right tools to complete the task,' Nathair said. 'And if the right tool does not exist, then he would make it. This is no different. The task is to *win*, to defeat Asroth's Black Sun, is it not, Father?'

'Aye, that is so,' Aquilus had agreed, frowning.

'Defeat in the coming war cannot happen. We must do all that is within our power to ensure victory,' continued Nathair.

Peritus had been silent awhile. 'There is truth in what you say. And your methods are effective – of that there is no doubt. How would your wall of shields fare against a charge of horse, do you think?'

'Just as well. A horse will not charge a wall of stone or timber, or a forest where there is no gap between the trees. This is no different.' Nathair had smiled.

'You say that, but you do not *know*,' the battlechief said. 'It looks impressive, but your warband is made up of untried warriors, most of them not long past their Long Night. How many veterans of campaigns are in your ranks? None. In times of danger, panic, experience holds a line better than youthful passion.' Peritus had looked at Aquilus and shrugged, ignoring Nathair's gaze.

There had been a long silence before Aquilus gave judgement.

'You shall go to Tarbesh,' the King had said. 'We shall begin organizing it today, for I would have you back with me by Midwinter's Day.'

'Aye, Father. My thanks,' Nathair had said, his joy spilling onto his face.

The Queen had lingered as Aquilus and Peritus had ridden from the glade.

'You are growing into a rare man,' she said to Nathair. He had just smiled at her. 'Remember your father's words. Follow his will, and all will go well for you; for us.'

'What do you mean, Mother?' Nathair had asked.

She stepped forward, cupping his cheek in her hand.

'I think you know, my son. Remember, you are all I have. I would not see you fall from your father's grace. You have a sharp mind, a *strategic* mind, but you must curb your enthusiasm. You have new ideas, that is clear.' She had gestured to the warband. 'Some can help the cause now. Some, maybe, must wait for another day. Others should be laid aside, perhaps permanently.'

'Such as?'

'Your association with the Vin Thalun.'

'Mother, I am a child no longer,' Nathair had said, rolling his eyes.

'No, but a son should obey his father, no matter his age, a subject should obey his king.' She had looked at him sternly, then turned to leave. 'Look after my son,' she said to Veradis.

Only a few nights passed, and then they had left Jerolin. Nathair rode at the head of eight hundred men with Veradis beside him.

Rauca was just behind, holding a banner displaying the eagle of Tenebral.

They had followed the river Aphros for a ten-night, and Veradis remembered the tension building in him as the first trees of the Sarva came into view, the knowledge that he would face his father soon a growing pressure within. But then Nathair had changed course, travelling south towards the coast.

The Vin Thalun were waiting, Lykos standing on a beach of shingle, alongside Calidus and his looming guardian, Alcyon. A fleet of ships was anchored at their backs.

'Your father will not be pleased,' Veradis had said to Nathair. 'Nor your mother.'

Nathair had grinned. 'What they know not will wound them little,' he had said. 'Besides, Father wants me back for Midwinter's Day. By travelling this way I will ensure that.'

'And what of flapping tongues? We have close to a thousand men here.'

'This will be a test of their loyalty,' Nathair said sternly. 'This is *my* warband, they are my men, not my father's. I shall make this clear to them.'

Veradis had shrugged, relieved at not having to see his own father, and in half a day all of the warband, horses and supply wains as well, had been loaded onto the Vin Thalun's ships.

The sound of footsteps brought Veradis back to the present. He turned his head and saw Nathair approaching.

'A good thing we are not fighting a campaign at sea,' the Prince said, gesturing at the sick warriors scattered around the ship's edge, vomiting.

'Aye,' grunted Veradis, part of him still concerned about that possibility.

'We will save at least a whole moon of hard riding, travelling like this, and the same if we return this way. No more than five nights, and we should be on solid ground again.'

'Are you so keen to face the giants of Tarbesh?' said Veradis.

'Indeed.' Nathair waved his hand, bit into a plum, dark juice dripping to the deck. 'They will fall before us. The Banished Lands have not seen our like before, Veradis. Destiny calls us; we will not fail.

This will be a fair trial for us.' He gave a ferocious grin. 'My father was right: we need combat to sharpen us. He is wise, in some things.'

But not all, Veradis thought, finishing Nathair's unsaid sentiment.

'This fixation he has about the Vin Thalun; he will come to see it is unjustified. I will change his mind. He is a man of reason – and we must think of the future, not the past, is that not so?' Nathair bit the last flesh from his plum and cast the stone into the sea.

'Aye.'

'Just look about us. They are a great asset, these Vin Thalun. Not only has this saved time on our journey, but also now we will arrive in Tarbesh rested, not weary from a hard road. And there are so many more possibilities, so much more potential – the speed with which we can move warriors, the element of surprise attacks. So much more.'

Rested? Maybe not all of us, thought Veradis, glancing at a warrior vomiting bile over the ship's rail. Still, overall he could not fault Nathair's logic.

'And there is more to their worth,' Nathair continued, talking more quietly now. 'I set Lykos a task, asked him to gather information for me.'

'About what?'

'You remember the book Meical read from, at my father's council.'

'Of course. Many things were spoken of.'

'Yes. I have talked of some of it with Lykos and Calidus. They are helping me to understand it.'

Veradis frowned, not sure he liked the sound of that. 'What of your father and Meical? Why not ask them?'

'I have tried. Meical will say nothing to me, and Father only says *soon* . . . But *soon* will be too late. So I must take help where I can find it. Lykos has built up quite a network of – what shall we call them . . .'

'Spies?' Veradis offered.

'Informers. And Calidus seems to know much about everything. Do you recall *white-walled Telassar* that Meical's book spoke of, and the *shadow warriors*?'

'Aye. It all sounded like riddles, to me.'

'And to me. But Lykos has told me of Telassar. It is a fabled city, hidden by a glamour, home to warriors fiercely devoted to Elyon: shadow warriors, the Jehar, they call themselves. They know of the coming God-War, have spent their lives preparing for it, preparing for the Bright Star.' Nathair looked around him, lowering his voice. '*I* am the Bright Star, Elyon's chosen, so they will fight for me.'

Veradis nodded. 'That would all make sense,' he said, 'except for one thing. Where are they? Fabled cities are often just that – fabled. And if they are hidden by a glamour, how will you find them?'

'Yes, good questions. As to where this fortress is, Lykos has heard word it is in Tarbesh.'

'Ah.'

'Exactly. So the time we are saving on our journey can be put to good use. I *will* find this Telassar, and talk to these shadow warriors.'

'Before or after we have dealt with Rahim's giants?'

'After.' Nathair flashed a smile. 'We shall take council on that now. I have asked Lykos and Calidus to join us here, as soon as they are able.'

'And the giant. Are you not troubled about taking aid from such as he?'

'Troubled? No, Veradis. Never take your eye from our goal, my friend.'

'The goal. And what is that, in the end?'

'Victory,' Nathair whispered. 'I will use man, giant or beast to attain that goal. For the greater good I will do what is required.'

Veradis heard the creak of a door, turned to see the hulking shape of Alcyon emerge from the hold, Lykos and Calidus walking in the giant's shadow.

There was something wolf-like about Lykos, Veradis thought, as the lord of the Vin Thalun approached them, iron rings clinking in his grey-streaked hair. His walk was graceful, confident, speaking of years on the deck of a ship. 'My lord,' the corsair chief said as he drew near. Many in the warband had been surprised to hear Lykos refer to Nathair so.

'Greetings,' said Nathair. 'As you know, I go to the aid of King Rahim. He is plagued with giant raids. Can you tell me anything that will ease my task?'

'Ever since we spoke of Telassar,' said Lykos, 'I have sent many men to Tarbesh, seeking to find your fortress. In the process my spies have travelled far and learned much.'

'Tell me.'

'They report to Calidus. He has been my ears for many years now, and has served me well.' He waved a hand at the gaunt man.

'A river marks the eastern border of Tarbesh,' Calidus said, 'marking the boundary between Rahim's realm and the Shekam giants. The Shekam have been crossing the river of late, raiding Rahim's lands. It is a familiar tale, I hear. The giant clans that are left are becoming bolder throughout the Banished Lands.'

'Aye, I have heard that also,' Nathair said. 'Do you know anything of how these giants, these Shekam, make war?'

'There is one more knowledgeable than I on that subject,' Calidus said with a grin and nodded to Alcyon.

The giant took a step forward; Veradis felt a slight tremor in the deck.

'You know of the Shekam?' Nathair said, looking up at Alcyon's broad, angular face.

'Aye,' the giant rumbled, his voice harsh and low pitched. 'All the clans had many things in common: like most, their weapons of choice are the axe and hammer. There are differences as well, I remember. The Shekam often fought mounted.'

'*Mounted*,' Veradis said. 'But a horse could not carry a giant.'

'Aye, prince's man,' Alcyon said, turning small, dark eyes onto him. 'They ride draigs.'

'Draigs,' Veradis spluttered, eyes widening.

'Aye. Draigs,' the giant repeated, the edges of a smile touching his mouth, making his drooping moustache twitch.

'I did not think giants rode anything,' Nathair said.

'Most do not. We can match your horses, over distance.' The giant shrugged. 'But the clans are warlike by nature. We were fighting each other long before your kind ever came to these lands, and advantages of any kind were sought. The Jotun in the north rode bears. I do not know if they still do, since your kin drove them across the Bone Fells, but I suspect so. The Shekam ride draigs.'

Veradis nodded, his mind filled with the coming conflict. He knew that the giant clans had been defeated before, and that there were more of them then, far more, so the task they faced was surely achievable. But giants on *draigs* – now, that was an unsettling thought.

'Is there any more you can tell us, Alcyon?' Nathair asked.

'Aye. Your greatest risk will be from Elementals. They are likely to be amongst their ranks.'

Veradis' eyes grew wide again. 'Sorcerers,' he muttered.

'Aye. Wielders of the earth power,' Alcyon rumbled.

'This task is becoming more than a campaign on which to "cut our teeth," Nathair,' Veradis muttered.

'Indeed,' replied the Prince. 'How can we combat these Elementals?'

'Do not be troubled,' said Calidus, 'Alcyon and I will accompany you. We are also familiar with these powers.'

'You are sorcerers?' said Veradis.

Alcyon said nothing and Calidus just smiled.

The rest of the journey passed quickly enough: the weather was hot, tempered by a constant wind that sped their progress, the sun filled cloudless blue skies, baking the skin of all that stood on the decks. After the passing of five more nights, Veradis found himself standing once again at the prow of the ship, looking at a dark smudge on the horizon.

'Tarbesh,' he muttered quietly, excitement building within him, a weightlessness dancing in the pit of his stomach.

As the day wore on, the land on the horizon grew until he could see the coast clearly. There were craggy cliffs of dark, reddish rock and sand with a covering of sun-blasted grass, here and there stunted olive trees with pale bark, looking like a twisted mass of tendon and sinew.

The small fleet turned north and followed the coastline until they came to a large bay where a river flowed into the sea. Here the land was greener, with groves of tall cedars flanking the river. By nightfall Nathair's warband was ashore. They made camp beside the river, and in the morning Lykos bid them farewell.

'I shall return on the last night of the Reaper's Moon,' he said. 'If you are not here we shall wait for you, or until you send word. I shall see you back to Tenebral and Jerolin in good time for Midwinter's Day.'

Nathair turned and swung into the saddle of his white stallion. Horns blasted, and with a great sound the warband moved out.

'How long till we reach Rahim's fortress?' Nathair asked Calidus.

'Four, five nights, no more.'

'Good.' The Prince turned in his saddle, looking at his warband. Veradis felt his spirits soar as he spotted Rauca in the mass of mounted warriors, holding Nathair's standard aloft, the eagle of Tenebral snapping in the wind. He raised his hand to his friend, a broad grin splitting his face. He had never felt more alive.

Nathair grinned at him fiercely, and Veradis knew the Prince felt it too. Destiny leading them, just as Nathair had promised. They both faced forward and spurred their horses on.

CHAPTER THIRTY-SIX

CORBAN

Corban was sweating by the time he passed through Stonegate into the shadowed cold of Dun Carreg. He looked only at the ground before his feet, fearing accusing eyes were watching him.

What will Marrock say? Does everyone know already that I let the brigands escape?

Buddai loped at his heels, Storm tucked under his arm. He had been desperate to get back to the fortress and had run all of the way, although he was equally terrified of what he would discover upon his return.

His first reaction on hearing that Marrock lived had been a sharp joy, utter relief.

Braith had kept his word and released Marrock.

Or maybe Marrock had escaped.

So many questions.

Where should he go? Surely Marrock would have been taken straight to Brenin. But that would have been some time ago, by now. Time enough for word to have spread through the fortress of Marrock's return, and also time enough for many to have heard Marrock's account of all that had happened, including Corban's part in it all.

He looked up and saw the grey stone of his home. So this was where his feet had taken him. The door was open, his mam standing there. A pressure began to build in his chest, as if his heart were expanding, becoming too large for his ribcage. He did not like the way his mam was looking at him – frowning, her mouth a straight edge, lines of worry around the corners of her eyes.

Storm wriggled under his arm. He put her down and she ran ahead with Buddai, both of them slipping past his mam's legs.

She did not move when he reached the door. He stood still, his gaze slowly rising until their eyes met. Gwenith reached out and ran her long fingers through his hair, brushing it away from his forehead where it had stuck with sweat.

'You have a visitor,' she said.

'Where?' he stuttered, trying to peer past her into the kitchen.

Gwenith stepped out of his way, although he did not move. He felt as if he had stepped into one of the Baglun's bogs.

'Out back, in the garden,' Gwenith said. With a wrench of will, he stepped into the kitchen, not even asking who was waiting for him, and strode to the back door. He pulled it open and walked through, passing under his da's giant war-hammer that hung above the door. Storm squeezed through as he closed it behind him.

Marrock was sitting on a tree stump by the woodpile, looking his way, Cywen silent and still beside him. She had a knife in her hand, had probably been practising her throwing when Marrock arrived. Corban froze a moment, blinking in the sunshine, then walked towards the huntsman. Marrock rose as Corban drew close. He was pale, the scar on his face standing out pink and livid. A bandage was wound tight around his back and shoulder. They gazed at each other in silence, then Marrock gestured for Corban to sit.

'He did his best for you, and for me,' Cywen blurted. 'You'd be dead if he'd done aught else.'

'Hush, lass,' said Marrock, raising a hand. He winced as he sat back down, facing them both.

Defending me still, even though she thinks me wrong, thought Corban, glancing gratefully at his sister.

A heavy silence fell on them as they sat there, Marrock looking at them, Cywen frowning in return, Corban's eyes flitting between them both.

'I am in your debt,' Marrock said, intense blue eyes boring into Corban. 'You saved my life.'

Surprise. An instant relief of pressure somewhere between his shoulder blades and the base of his skull. *He does not blame me.* Then worry descended again. *Who else knows?* Corban tore his eyes away from the huntsman, looking at the thick grass by his feet. He did not know what to do, what to say, so he stayed silent and did nothing.

'How did you come to be there? At the pool?' Marrock asked.

Corban shrugged, eyes darting to Cywen. They had argued about this as well. Cywen had thought they should go straight to Brenin, tell all, including the whereabouts of the secret door and tunnels beneath the fortress. Corban had thought otherwise.

He could not even explain *why* he felt so strongly about keeping the tunnels secret; he only knew that he did, and swore he would only ever know Cywen as 'oathbreaker' if she told.

'Happenstance,' he muttered.

Marrock exhaled, leaning back, looking between Corban and his sister. 'Happenstance? Well, Elyon must have some great task saved for me, to bring you along at such an opportune moment.'

Corban shrugged again. He took a deep breath. *Best to know, one way or the other.* 'Have you told anyone. Of our involvement?'

'Aye, lad. I have.'

Corban tried to swallow, but his mouth was too dry. Suddenly his throat seemed to constrict, tightening, his pulse ringing in his ears. *Well, so be it*, he thought, trying to remember Gar's counsel, breathing slow and deep through his nose.

'But only the King and my uncle know,' Marrock continued. 'In fact, Brenin had us swear that no one else should hear of your involvement.'

Silence, broken only by the small sounds of the garden, wind sighing through the branches of the apple trees.

Relief swept through him.

'You were courageous – both of you,' the huntsman said. 'Far beyond many warriors I have seen. I would have your names lauded from the highest towers, but Brenin is of a different mind. He believes if word spread of your involvement it could be misunderstood. Brenin would not have your bravery rewarded with scorn, or worse. So.' He smiled, his scar creasing. 'It shall remain our secret. Have *you* told anyone?'

'No,' Corban and Cywen answered together.

'Good. Then let it remain so.'

'Did you escape?' asked Cywen.

'Escape? Nay, lass. Much as it pains me to say it, Braith kept his word. He let me go, at dawn, just as he said he would.' Marrock lifted a hand, ran it through his hair. 'Did you see Braith's scar? Running from here to here.' He placed a finger beside his left eye, tracing it slowly down to his jaw line.

'I did,' said Corban.

'My father, Rhagor, gave him that scar, so Braith told me. He spoke of my da.' He fell silent, closing his eyes. 'They fought in the Darkwood. Braith said no man had ever so much as tickled him with a blade, until my da. Braith slew him that day, in the Darkwood.' An expression of utter desolation swept Marrock's face, quickly hidden.

'Where did you learn to throw a knife like that, lass?' he asked, blowing out a short breath, smiling again.

'My mam,' Cywen said, grinning shyly in return. 'She taught me over there.' She pointed at an old tree trunk back near the rose-bushes. It was splintered and pitted from a thousand knife blades. 'I don't let many know I can do it. Most men don't seem to like me being able to throw a knife. Makes them uncomfortable, Mam says.'

Marrock snorted. 'Well, I for one am glad you've acquired the skill.'

Cywen smiled.

With a big sigh, Storm flopped down at Corban's feet, her back leg coming up to itch her ear.

'How do things go, with your cub?' Marrock asked, looking at Storm.

'Well, I think,' said Corban. 'We're training her as my da did Buddai.'

'And how goes that?'

'She's not eaten any chickens yet,' said Corban with a grin. 'That day, the day of the hunt, when I stood before Alona. You spoke for me. If you had said different I don't think she would be here now.' He ran fingers through the cub's thickening fur. 'Why?'

'In truth, lad, I do not know. Keeping a wolven is not the most . . . sensible . . . decision. I just had a feeling. Sometimes you *know*, something speaks to you.' He shrugged. 'I'm mighty glad I *did* support your case. You might not have been as inclined to speak up for *me*, at the pool, if I hadn't.'

'Yes he would,' snapped Cywen, 'Ban's not like that.'

Marrock held his hands up, smiling now. 'I dare say you're right, girl. There is certainly more to you than meets the eye, lad. You have stood before Braith, the most feared outlaw in Ardan, and had the courage to bargain with him. You have a wolven at your heel, and a warrior for a sister.'

Cywen grinned fiercely.

Marrock stood. 'I must go, my wife is fretting about my health, and is most willing to tend me. Remember, I am in your debt. Both of you. You saved my life.' He held out his hand to Cywen, gripping her forearm in the warrior's embrace, which drew another huge grin.

'Look after your cub, lad,' he said to Corban as he gripped his arm. 'Not all are happy about her being here. Evnis has many followers in the fortress.'

Corban stepped out of the shade of the rowans into the Field, paused and sucked in a deep breath before he walked on, striding towards Halion. He kept his eyes fixed on his weapons-master, nevertheless felt ripples of attention begin to flow around him, heard muttered whispers and gasps.

He had brought Storm to the Rowan Field.

A ten-night had passed since Marrock's reappearance and life had almost gone back to normal. Vonn had recovered enough to return to his father's hold, so Corban was free of Brina's chores for a while. Something had happened to him when Marrock had returned. It had been strange, almost uncomfortable, hearing Marrock talk of him that day and using words such as 'courage' and 'bravery'. All that *he* remembered of the night by the pool was utter terror, as if his guts had turned to water. But nonetheless, he *had* stood up to Braith, bargained with him even. That must count for something, even if he knew deep down he truly hadn't acted out of any bravery.

And now he was tired of hiding Storm away. He had told his da as they broke their fast earlier that morning that he was going to take Storm to the Field. He had expected an explosion, or at least a flat 'No,' but neither had happened. Instead Thannon had just looked at him, frowning from under bushy eyebrows.

'As you wish,' was all his da had said, and then returned to the pile of oatcakes before him.

He looked down at Storm, padding beside him. She had grown already, just in the score or so of days since he had brought her out of the Baglun. She was taller, less fluffy, dark stripes marking her white fur. He knew that bringing her here would stir painful memories for some, but it was not her fault. She was *his*, and he was proud of her.

'Get that Asroth-spawn out of the Field.'

Corban looked up. A handful of people had drifted between him and Halion. Some younger, not sat their Long Night yet, but there were others, older warriors. He recognized Rafe's face walking amongst them.

Corban snatched a glance around him. Many were watching. '*That* does not belong here,' said a faceless voice from the group growing before him. Beyond them he saw Halion begin to stride towards him.

Corban tried to move around the small crowd, but Rafe stepped forward, blocking his path.

'Get out of my way,' Corban muttered.

'You heard, blacksmith's boy,' said Rafe. 'Take that *thing* out of here. You're fortunate Vonn is not returned to the Field yet.'

Deep breath, Corban told himself, feeling the familiar churning begin in his gut. He breathed out slowly.

'No,' he heard himself say, pleased that his voice did not tremble. He pushed forwards.

Rafe bunched a fist and swung, but Corban had been waiting for it. He ducked, stepped onto one of Rafe's booted feet and pushed him hard, both hands, in the chest. Instinctively Rafe tried to right his balance, but his pinned foot betrayed him and he tumbled to the ground.

Before Corban could move on, a strong hand grabbed him, spun him around. It was a warrior this time, broad and squat, powerful arms, a sneer curling his lip. Glyn. He hefted Corban until he was standing on tip-toes. Storm growled and the warrior drew back his leg to kick the cub.

'Put the lad down, Glyn.'

Halion stood at the edge of the crowd, appearing quite relaxed, apart from the lines around his mouth.

'Stay out of this,' the warrior grunted, glaring at Halion.

'This is the Rowan Field, Glyn. Grudges come no further than the trees, remember.'

'Not this time. You're not from round here – you would'na understand. Walk away.'

'No.'

Glyn released Corban, shoving him back a couple of paces and turned to face Halion. The tall warrior raised his hands, palms open.

'No need for this to go further, Glyn. Our heart rules us all on occasion. Let's leave it at that, eh?'

'Do not seek to instruct me, outlander,' said Glyn, taking a stride towards Halion, who did not move, other than a slight adjustment of his feet.

'What's all this?' a deep voice called from beyond the group. Over the gathered heads Corban saw a tall, wide form striding towards them. It was Tull.

The crowd parted before Brenin's champion until he stood towering over Corban. Rafe had scrambled to his feet and sidled a few steps away.

'What's all this?' Tull repeated, glancing at Corban before his eyes rested on Halion and Glyn. Halion said nothing, returning Tull's gaze.

'Someone answer me, 'fore I feel the need to start cracking heads,' the ageing champion growled.

A ring of people were formed around them now. Conall, Halion's brother, was pushing to the front, a scowl on his face.

'He's brought that devil-dog into the Field,' Rafe blurted from behind Glyn. Tull's head snapped around, like a hunting bird sighting prey, fixing Helfach's son. 'He mocks us, mocks the warriors that fell in the hunt,' Rafe stuttered, looking at the ground.

'The boy speaks true,' muttered Glyn, and other voices in the crowd echoed him.

Tull held his hand up, looking around, his eyes eventually falling on Corban and the cub at his feet. A heavy silence descended as the King's champion appraised him, and Corban was acutely aware of eyes on him. Almost certainly most of the Field would be watching this exchange. He cursed himself for a fool. *What have I done?*

'Lad, did you not claim King's Justice and stand before our Queen Alona?' Tull said loudly, for all to hear.

'A-aye,' Corban said.

'Speak up. If you're bold enough t'talk in front of our Queen, surely you're bold enough t'talk in front of this rabble.'

'Aye,' said Corban, louder.

'And did she not pass judgement on you?'

'She did.'

'What was her judgement?'

'That, that I was not responsible for the harm done in the Baglun. And that I could keep the cub.'

Tull grunted. 'Did any not hear?' he boomed.

Silence.

'King's Justice says this cub stays with the lad, and he can take it wheresoever he pleases. Any man, *anyone*,' Tull said, his eyes sweeping the crowd and coming to rest upon Rafe. 'Anyone here fault our Queen's judgement?'

Again, silence.

'Good. As it should be. I'll be reminding you, I am the King's sword. I'll disregard the insult that's been made here. But only this once.' He stood in silence, glowering at the group that had waylaid Corban. One by one they sidled away, until none was left.

Tull turned his eyes to Corban, frowning. 'I'll be watching you,' he said, then marched away.

'You all right, lad?' Halion asked. Corban was watching Tull's back.

'I . . . I'm fine,' Corban mumbled.

'Good. Come, then.'

They walked to a weapons rack, both searching for a practice sword to their liking. Something made Corban glance over his shoulder. Two figures stood in the shadows of the rowan trees: one a hulking mass, the other not quite so tall, slimmer. They moved away, and Corban blinked, then they were gone.

'Are you sure that you are well?' Halion asked him again as they found a space to begin their training. 'You look pale.'

Corban blew out a hard breath. He *did* feel a little light-headed.

'I didn't expect that,' he said.

'No?' Halion raised an eyebrow.

'No. I'm accustomed to staring, harsh words. But that . . .'

'Strong feelings, lad, oft are displayed in strong actions.'

'Aye. So I see.'

'Why did you do it? Bring the cub here?'

Corban looked down, watching Storm as she lay in the grass, her copper eyes considering him in return.

'Because it doesn't feel right, hiding her away as if she's done something wrong,' he said. 'She deserves better. And I've done nothing wrong either, and will not act as if I have.' He smiled at Halion. 'My thanks.'

'What for?'

'For speaking for me. No one else did.'

'You're welcome, lad. Come, let us begin.' The tall warrior raised his weapon, then lunged at Corban, striking at his head and chest. Stepping quickly backwards, Corban managed to block the blows, then there was a flurry of movement and Halion fell back, crying out. He was hoping on one leg, shaking the other frantically.

For a moment Corban could not tell what was happening, then he saw a bundle of fur attached to Halion's calf. Storm had latched on and was refusing to let go. Halion stopped jumping about and Storm planted her feet on the ground, jaws still clamped around Halion's leg. Only her copper eyes moved, looking up at the tall warrior. She growled, deep in the back of her throat.

There was a moment's silence as Corban rushed forwards, then Halion began to laugh.

'Storm. Here,' Corban said sharply, and the cub stepped back to him.

'Can't blame her, I suppose,' said Halion as his laughter calmed. 'She thought I was attacking you. Mind you.' He wagged a finger at Corban. 'It might be funny now, but she's going to grow as big as a pony. I would not find *that* amusing.'

Corban began laughing too, picturing the thought.

'We've taught her not to bite chickens,' he said, 'so I'll just teach her not to bite you.'

'I'd appreciate that. But don't stop her protecting you. It could prove to be quite advantageous.'

'I won't. I'm teaching her "Friend" and "Foe".'

'What do you mean?'

Corban walked over to Halion and knelt beside him, then called Storm.

'Hold your hand out,' Corban said to Halion, who squatted and did as instructed. Storm sniffed the warrior's palm with her long muzzle, then growled.

'Friend,' said Corban. The growling stopped.

Halion snorted. 'Come, lad. She's not *that* clever.'

'My da says she is. He teaches his hounds this, though he said it takes them much longer to pick it up. Even Buddai. Said she's very bright, and can pick out a scent better than any hound he's come across.'

Halion raised his eyebrows, but the disbelief in his face faded a little.

Suddenly he looked beyond the cub, eyes narrowing, then stood, strode quickly towards the warrior weapons court. Corban hesitated a moment, then followed him.

The weapons court was really just a square expanse of stone in the Field. It was the place where warriors sparred. Only those that had sat their Long Night were allowed to set foot on the stone.

As Corban hurried after Halion he saw Tull standing out on the Field, like an old oak amidst saplings, two smaller figures before him. He blinked as he recognized Dath standing beside his da, Mordwyr.

Of course, he thought, feeling a flush of joy. *Dath's nameday*. His friend's face was tight with excitement and concentration. Corban saw him grin as Tull took his wrist in the warrior embrace. *At least I'll have one friend in the Field.*

Halion reached the weapons court and stopped, folded his arms and stared.

Two men were sparring, if you could call it that. One man was a whirling blur, in constant motion, the other clearly outclassed, struggling desperately just to defend himself. It was Glyn.

The blur of motion around him stopped, the warrior laughing. It was Conall, Halion's brother.

'Guard your head, man,' Conall said, smiling as he struck at Glyn. 'That's it. Now, right thigh,' he shouted, 'gut, left shoulder, throat.' A split second after he spoke, his practice sword would whip out, slashing exactly where he had called. Warriors around the court began to chuckle, although others were frowning.

'Left knee,' Conall called, but this time his weapon caught Glyn on the wrist with a loud crack. Glyn's practice sword dropped from numb fingers and the tip of Conall's weapon was suddenly at Glyn's throat, pressing upwards, under the chin. Conall sneered, took a step forwards, pushing Glyn back.

'Next time you speak to my brother,' Conall snarled, 'you should be more polite.' He pushed forwards again, and Glyn tripped as he stepped back, falling heavily on his backside.

Conall hawked and spat at the man's feet, then turned and stalked away. He grinned as he saw Halion, changing his course to approach his brother.

Corban watched Glyn rise slowly, rubbing his throat, cheeks flushed, giving Conall's back a murderous look.

'Do you think he enjoyed the lesson, Hal?' Conall said, breathing deeply, but still grinning broadly. Halion just watched him approach, until Conall reached him, wrapping an arm around his brother's shoulder. 'He'll treat you better, next time you meet.'

'I can fight my own battles, Con,' said Halion.

'You are too soft, big brother,' Conall said, steering Halion away from the court. Corban and Storm followed them.

'He insulted you, called you "outlander".' Anger flashed across Conall's face, then the grin returned. 'He'll not be doing that again, I'd wager.'

'Maybe not,' Halion said, 'but you've made no friends out there today.'

'*Friends?* I care not for friends. You are all I care about. My brother. Just the two of us, remember?'

Halion's face relaxed. 'I know, Con, but do not forget, we are here by Brenin's grace. Do not abuse that.'

Conall looked grim. 'I will brook no insult, to myself or my kin, regardless of whose *favour* I jeopardize.'

'Have a care, Con. I, at least, have a mind to stay here. Your tongue and temper . . .' Halion looked around, taking a deep breath. 'As I said. I can fight my own battles.'

Conall pulled his arm away from his brother, then left abruptly with a glare, heading for the arch of rowan trees.

Halion stood and watched until his brother had disappeared from view. He sighed, looking down at Corban.

'Come, lad. Let's finish your training.'

CHAPTER THIRTY-SEVEN

VERADIS

Veradis shifted uncomfortably in his saddle, sweat trickling down his spine. He passed a hand across his face, flicking the dampness from his fingers. His horse whickered and he leaned forward, patted her neck.

'Damn heat,' he muttered.

'Aye,' grunted Nathair, one hand shading his eyes as he looked into the distance.

They were scouting ahead of the warband, sheltered in a dip two-thirds of the way up a steep grassy slope, looking over a wide, dark river: the Rhetta, he recalled Calidus telling him. He glanced quickly at the Vin Thalun, who sat a horse a few paces behind, the giant Alcyon standing silently beside him.

'So, where do they cross?' Nathair said quietly.

Veradis shrugged and winced absently as his coat of mail chaffed his shoulders. 'Rahim said there is only one natural ford, a league or so north of here.'

'Aye, but that is guarded, so they must cross elsewhere.'

Veradis squinted, his gaze following the sluggish course of the river, in the distance glimpsing the faint outline of a tower, the smudge of buildings around it. Rahim's bastion – built to fight the Shekam's raids, although little good it had done. 'They are giants. Maybe they use sorcery,' he said.

Nathair said nothing.

The river looked black from here, like congealing blood in an open wound. The land on their side of the river was green, lush, dotted with trees and flecked with bright flowers. A small village, single-storey buildings carved from white stone, clustered around a dirt track that led away west. There was no movement anywhere, the village empty and abandoned because of the Shekam's savage raids. And on the far side of the river the land was marsh. Veradis took a deep breath and pulled a face. There was a sickly sweet scent in the air, as of food left out too long in the sun.

'To slay these giants, we must find them,' he said, as much to break the silence as anything else.

Nathair gave him a sour look. 'The obvious I am well aware of. But *how* to find them. We could stretch our warband the length of the river, but then we would be spread too thin for combat.'

'My lord,' said Calidus, and Veradis felt a stab of annoyance. There was something about the Vin Thalun's insinuating voice that was beginning to grate on his nerves. He looked at the old man, studying him a while. His frame was lean, but muscle stood firm and knotted on his arms, his back straight, a strength in him that belied his silver hair. His eyes glistened in the glare of the sun. Veradis squinted, looking closer. *What an unusual colour*, he thought. They were amber, like a wolf's.

'Aye,' muttered Nathair, still gazing into the distance.

'We can help you, in the locating of any Shekam that cross the Rhetta.'

'How?'

'You remember we discussed the use of our particular skill?'

'Speak plainly, man. Do you mean the earth power?'

'Aye.' Calidus' mouth twitched at the edges. *Annoyance?*

'Then, yes, I remember very well.'

'Alcyon and I shall stand vigil. We will know when the Shekam cross the river.'

Nathair looked at him. 'You can do this? You are sure? I would not wish to camp out, roasting my warband in this heat, only to have you fail me.'

'We will not fail you.'

Nathair was silent a long moment. 'Good. Then we shall wait upon your word.'

More waiting. It had been almost twice a ten-night since they had set foot on the shores of Tarbesh now. Midsummer's Day had come and gone, and the Meadow's Moon passed into the Draig's Moon.

They had spent a handful of days at Rahim's fortress, where the

King of Tarbesh had held a feast in their honour. Then the warband had marched again, heading ever east. It had been clear almost immediately that Nathair's presence here was considered more token than genuine remedy to the giant problem, although Rahim had sent some two hundred men from his own warband as escort, under the command of his battlechief. Nathair pulled on his stallion's reins and cantered back up the slope with Veradis following. On cresting the ridge they saw their warband spread across a gentle valley with Rahim's camp alongside, hide tents and cook-fires dotting the grassland.

Dawn was not far away. Veradis shivered. Strange how the days in this land were so hot, and the nights so cold. He blinked hard, eyes stinging from tiredness. Leather creaked behind him and a horse whickered gently. Glancing over his shoulder, he glimpsed figures close to him – just – as solid, impenetrable shadows in the darkness. Some four hundred warriors were spread behind him, he knew, but he could only see a handful.

They had ridden hard for what must have been half of the night. Earlier he had seen the giant Alcyon march into Nathair's tent, Calidus cradled in his arms, and had rushed after them.

'The Shekam have crossed the river, over a score of leagues to the north,' the giant announced. They were headed south-west, so the warband could intercept them if it moved quickly. Calidus was exhausted from his *scrying*; some sorcerous effort, no doubt. Veradis felt the hairs on his neck stand on end at the thought of it, but still, here they were now, moments away from confronting the Shekam. *If* Alcyon and Calidus could be trusted.

A huge shadow loomed out of the darkness.

'It is time,' the giant rumbled.

Veradis dismounted, handed his reins to the warrior beside him, then turned and followed the hulking shape of the giant.

They climbed a steep ridge and Alcyon dropped to his belly, crawling the last few paces to the crest. Veradis followed suit, grunting as sharp stones dug into his arms and knees. He drew alongside Alcyon and peered over the ridge, not that it did much good. Although an edge of grey was seeping into the air around him, the sky above turning a deep purple, the valley below was still cloaked in darkness.

'Where?' Veradis whispered.

'From the east. Patience, little man.'

More waiting. He wished the battle would just begin – the waiting was worse. He wiped sweaty palms on the coarse grass beneath him, looking across the vale to the vague outline of the opposite ridge, where he knew Nathair and his four hundred men were hidden.

The darkness was thinning in the valley now, dispersing between solid clumps that slowly became recognizable: large boulders littered the slopes and valley floor, the odd stunted, twisted tree. He could hear the gentle trickle of water in the distance, where, he guessed, the village that the Shekam were bent on raiding was situated.

Not this time. He smiled humourlessly.

'They will come from there,' Alcyon rumbled, pointing. Veradis looked at the giant's arm. At the wrist, flowing from beneath a leather band, a dark tattoo swirled up it, circling great knots of muscle and sinew. Curved thorns were etched into the skin, the tattoo resembling a vine creeping up Alcyon's arm. It disappeared at his elbow, covered by a half-sleeve of chainmail.

'Why do you have that?' Veradis asked, without thinking. The giant looked at his arm and grunted.

'That is my *Sgeul*; my *Telling*, in your tongue.' His voice was cold, flat.

'Telling?'

'Aye. The lives I have taken.'

Veradis swallowed. 'You mean, each thorn . . .'

The giant grunted again.

With an act of will Veradis stopped himself staring at the giant's arm, from trying to count the thorns, and gazed back into the valley. He could see a thick wall of mist in the distance, in the direction that Alcyon had pointed. Veradis blinked. It was moving towards them, expanding, rushing like the tide up the valley's floor.

'They are come,' Alcyon whispered.

Veradis felt a faint tremble in the earth beneath him, then the muted sound of – drums? Surely not. The mist was immediately below him now, spreading on towards the village, like broiling storm clouds driven by a gale.

'That mist . . .' he mumbled.

'Do not fear, little man. Be ready,' Alcyon said. He began whispering, so low that Veradis could pick out no words, just a constant droning. He looked over his shoulder, saw his warriors, faces pale, anxious, all looking at him. In the valley the mist slowed as if hitting a barrier, churning sluggishly, then stopped. The drumming sound he had heard was closer now, a little louder, but still muted. It came from within the mist.

The sun had risen, spreading across the horizon, a molten half-circle joined to the land. The mist below began to bubble and seethe, like boiling water, then it thinned, evaporating into the air, revealing huge shapes within. Alcyon dug his fingers into the ground, clenching handfuls of dirt. Wisps of smoke or steam curled up from his hands. He had not stopped whispering. As the mist thinned, his voice rose sharply, then abruptly fell silent. He slumped to the ground, face pale, glistening with sweat.

'Strike now, Prince's man,' he grunted. 'I will join you soon.'

Veradis stumbled back to his horse and leaped into the saddle. Raising an arm, he dug his heels into his mount's ribs, broke for the ridge, four hundred mounted warriors following him.

His breath caught in his chest as he crested the rise. He had heard old men tell tales of draigs and seen drawings of them, but never viewed one in the flesh. The tales were no exaggeration.

The beasts were huge, reminiscent of the lizards that he had seen sunning themselves on walls at Rahim's fortress, but a thousand times larger. Their bellies were low to the ground, four bowed legs holding them up, splayed feet with curved claws like the swords of Rahim's warband. Long, wide tails flicked behind them, but it was to their heads that Veradis' gaze was drawn. Broad, flat skulls, long, square-tipped jaws full of razored teeth, the eyes small, dull, black. On their backs rode giants, dwarfed by the great beasts.

The valley floor seethed with them, like a nest of snakes, almost impossible to count. Alcyon had said at least three score had crossed the river. Surely there were more here.

He took a deep breath, squeezed his eyes tight. *Remember the plan.* He heard Nathair's last words echo in his mind. *The ants, remember the ants.* He pulled hard on his reins. His horse reared, neighed wildly, and he joined his own voice to it, screaming with all his might.

'*NATHAIR!*'

The call was taken up behind him as he thundered down the slope.

In the valley below, shouts of surprise rang out, then came strange-sounding horn blasts. Draigs roared, setting the very ground trembling as the giants and their mounts turned to meet their attackers.

Only a few hundred paces between them now, then a horn blew out behind Veradis, this time a call he recognized. He turned his horse to run parallel to the giants. A quick glance saw those behind do the same; somewhere there was a crash, a horse shrieked.

He reached for his spear, hoping all those behind him would be doing the same, found its smooth, worn shaft couched below his saddle. He cast it arcing into the air, followed by hundreds of others. They rose high, seemed to hang suspended a long moment, then plummeted to the valley floor. Many bounced from the thick-scaled hides of the draigs, or stuck quivering in leather-padded armour, but many more found their mark.

There was screaming such as he had never heard before. A great cloud of dust rose up from the valley floor, shapes rose and fell, giants tumbled from the backs of draigs, draigs crashed to the ground, some roaring in agony, others silent.

He dug his heels into his horse, urging her to climb the slope, racing away from the valley floor. Before he reached the crest of the ridge he leaped from his horse, slapped her hindquarters to make her run on, then turned, pulling his great round shield from his back, tugged his short sword from its scabbard, warriors all about him doing the same.

Dragging in a deep breath, trying to slow the pounding of his heart, he gazed into the valley.

Many draigs and giants were down. A few of the great lizards, riderless, were charging on down the valley towards the village, bellowing. Voices drifted up in the harsh, guttural tongue of giants. Draigs with riders scuttled forward, surprisingly fast for their bulk, forming a crude line that swept up the slope towards him – more than a score of them. *Too many*. Behind them he glimpsed giants on foot, taking great loping strides, pulling axes and great war-hammers from their backs. Tremors passed from the ground into his boots, up his legs.

'*SHIELD WALL!*' he screamed, taking a few steps forwards, trying to place himself at the front and centre of his men. All about him bodies pressed close, shields slamming together with dull thuds.

So far the plan had worked perfectly. Many giants had been felled, with no warriors of their own down. Nathair was right. Using ranged weapons and staying alive was much better than looking a giant in the eye and dying. *Still plenty of chance for that*, though, he thought.

Now was the time of telling.

The draigs seethed up the slope, bowed legs powering their huge bulk forwards, raking claws sending great sprays of gravel and dirt arcing into the air.

Three hundred paces between them and his wall of shields and men. He could feel, *smell*, the fear leaking from those around him, from himself. His guts churned and his legs felt weak, empty of all strength. Every instinct within him screamed to turn and run.

'Now, Nathair, now,' he muttered.

Two hundred paces. The ground was shaking, the oncoming draigs a great tidal wave approaching them. He could make out minute details: a chipped tooth in a draig's gaping mouth, speckled green and brown scales on another's neck, swirling tattoos on giants' arms – their Telling, he thought. *Where is Alcyon? Where is Nathair?* He tried to swallow but his mouth was dry; he coughed instead.

One hundred paces. Horns blew, somewhere in the distance, a great roaring, like the sea whipped by a storm. It *must* have been loud for him to hear it over the charge of the onrushing draigs. Many of the great lizards faltered, slowed, the giants in their saddles turning. The noise behind them grew: weapons clashing on shields, the roar of warriors' voices, frantic horn blasts. Veradis peered over his shield rim, glimpsed through the enemy Nathair's warband streaming over the ridge on the far side of the valley.

You will be the anvil, I the hammer, Nathair had said to him. Giants struggled to turn their mounts, realizing the trap they were plunging into – to be ensnared in the shield wall and then charged by horsemen from the rear. Harsh voices called out, then many of the great lizards turned and thundered back down the slope to meet Nathair's charge. A handful of draigs still powered up the hill, bent on the foe in front of them, giants on foot following behind.

Veradis grimaced. He had hoped more would turn. All, in fact. He sucked in a deep breath, braced his feet and waited for the storm to hit.

Draigs ploughed into the wall, sending a concussive explosion rippling through the massed men. Bodies, shields, blood, all flew through the air wherever draigs connected with the wall. Veradis felt terror threaten to overwhelm him. *Nathair was wrong*. The shield wall was not enough to turn the draigs.

The great lizards smashed through the wall, scattering men, trampling them into unrecognizable heaps of flesh and bone, giants seated on huge saddles, lashing about them with long-shafted hammer and axe, then the lizards were through the other side of the wall, their momentum carrying them across the ridge.

'*REGROUP*,' yelled Veradis, although he was not sure if anyone heard him above the screams of dying and injured warriors. The lizards were on the far side of the ridge, no doubt turning to wreak more death amongst his men, but he could do nothing about that. More pressing were the score or so of silent, grim-looking giants charging up the slope towards him.

'*SHIELD WALL!*' he screamed, and at least those about him heard, for he felt men draw close, then the giants were upon them.

Bodies slammed into the wall. The line wavered around Veradis, men grunting, setting their feet, leaning against the great pressure of giant flesh and bone. An axe slammed into the shield of the man next to Veradis, splintered wood spraying into their faces, then the warrior was gone, dragged forwards as the giant wrenched on his axe. Another warrior moved up and filled the gap.

A huge blow smashed into Veradis' shield, numbing his arm and making his legs buckle. He glanced over the rim of his shield, saw small, fierce eyes set in a giant's angular face towering above him, heaving a huge war-hammer over his head, readying it for another blow.

Veradis lifted his shield, blindly stabbed with his short sword under the iron rim, heard a howl, felt hot blood gush over his hand. The giant's grip on his war-hammer loosened, the weapon dropping to the ground as fingers clutched frantically over its thigh, trying to staunch the jet of blood. With a thud the giant fell to his knees and Veradis stabbed again, his blade sinking into the giant's throat. He pulled it out as his foe toppled backwards. He snarled wordlessly and hefted his shield. Another giant loomed before him, chopped at his shield with a great double-bladed axe. The blade stuck, Veradis gripping his shield with all his might, blinking at the axe blade's edge, only a handspan from his eye. There was a pushing and shoving behind him now, men shouting. Panic stung him: was that a giant's voice *behind* him? Were the draigs back? Then the giant in front of him heaved on his axe, pulling him stumbling forwards, out of the shield wall. He slipped in blood, fell to one knee, lifted his short sword in a vain attempt to block the axe-swing he knew would be coming. There was a chopping sound, a gurgle, and then a giant's head rolled in the dirt before him.

'Here, little man,' a voice rumbled behind him. He twisted round, saw Alcyon standing above him, his great longsword in his hand, blood dripping from its blade.

'The b-battle . . .' Veradis panted.

'Is all but done,' Alcyon said. 'Look.'

Veradis passed a hand over his eyes, wiping blood and sweat away. Alcyon was right. The shield wall had held against the giants' charge, over a score of the huge warriors dead along its length. Further away, the sounds of battle still raged. He walked to the ridge of the valley, Alcyon following.

The draigs that had burst through his shield wall to such devastating effect were fleeing, a dust cloud rising about them. Even as he watched, they were dwindling into the distance.

Turning, Veradis looked down to the valley's floor. Some of the giants and draigs were retreating back down the valley; the few standing and fighting were beset by a flowing tide of warriors on horseback. *Remember the ants*, Nathair had said, and from here the draigs and horsemen looked strangely similar to the ants he had seen that day in the glade, swarming over the dog.

His eyes picked out one warrior, gripping Nathair's standard. Rauca still lives, then. Good. Then he saw Nathair, unmistakable on his great white stallion, thrusting a spear into the mouth of a draig. The beast roared, reared backwards, crushing a handful of riders in its ruin. And as suddenly as it had started, the battle was over. He breathed a great sigh of relief. Nathair had been right – the surprise, the tactics, their own Elementals – all had combined to win the battle. But it had been so close, balancing on a knife's edge. If the giants and draigs had turned, attacked his shield wall from the rear instead of fleeing . . .

But they hadn't. The battle was won, the victory theirs.

Veradis looked along the slope, saw warriors looking at him, others on their knees, tending comrades, weeping, groaning, the wounded calling out. Many more were strewn about the ridge, unnaturally still. He felt his whole body begin to tremble and looked down at his hands. He still gripped his short sword, blade, hilt and hand black with drying blood. Thrusting it into the air, he screamed a victory yell. Those about him looked, did the same, more and more joining, like ripples from a rock cast into water. The shouting changed, became a chanted name.

'*NATHAIR, NATHAIR, NATHAIR . . .*'

CHAPTER THIRTY-EIGHT

CYWEN

Cywen gritted her teeth, sweat trickling into her eyes, stinging, making her blink. She shook her head, trying to clear her vision, and felt Corban's weapon thump into the join between neck and shoulder. Not that it was really a weapon, but a branch that they had tried to shape to resemble a practice sword.

She scowled, flung her own stick to the ground and held a hand up.

'One moment,' she muttered, trying to catch her breath.

Corban nodded, a smirk twitching at his mouth as he took a step back.

They were in their garden. The sky was a searing blue, cloudless, the sun high, hot, even though Midsummer's Day was long past. She wiped sweat from her face and sat with a thump in the grass. Storm was nearby, oblivious to her, a coiled spring of soft fur as she stalked a clump of grass and goldenrods. Ears pricked forward, hugging the ground, she pounced. A toad leaped into the air, through her clumsy paws, and disappeared into more grass.

Corban tapped a skin of water against Cywen's arm. She scowled at him again, but took the skin and gulped thirstily.

'You're supposed to be grateful,' he said, standing above her.

'For what? A new bruise?' She rubbed her shoulder.

'No. For teaching you the ways of a warrior.' He spoke as if talking to a child.

'*Warrior,*' she snorted, raising an eyebrow at him.

He pulled a face at her.

'I am grateful,' she grinned, holding out a hand for him to help her rise. 'It's just annoying. How easily you beat me.'

'It makes a nice change for me,' he said with a smile. 'I've more than enough of my own bruises.'

It *was* frustrating, feeling that you were learning something, progressing, becoming better, yet never getting closer at touching her pretend blade to any part of Corban. In fact, if anything, the gap between them was growing wider.

He must actually be learning something, she thought, looking him up and down.

He's changing. The thought struck her suddenly, as she stood there. Not just his *shape*, although that was obvious – arms growing thicker, shoulders broader, face more angular. But in other ways, inside. Even today. He had returned from the Rowan Field quiet, thoughtful, but less troubled than she had seen him for some time. His smile seemed different, *deeper*.

'Come, then,' he said, setting his feet and raising his stick.

She retrieved her own, then looked up. Taking a few paces backwards and to her left, she set her back to the rose wall, stood in the shade of a squat tower that loomed over the garden, the sun behind her.

Corban chuckled, knowing she was trying to use the sun to blind him, as he had taught her, and attacked her anyway.

She did better this time, remembering how Corban had told her to use her feet, to keep her balance when lunging, how to avoid overstretching. She still didn't touch him with her pretend weapon, though, not even coming close, but she did avoid being whacked for longer than the last time.

That must count for something.

Eventually, though, the frustration became too much. She rushed him, certain that she had him . . . only to end up face first in the grass with dirt up her nose and laughter rising behind.

She turned her head, a curse forming, but Storm bounded over, sniffed her ear with a wet nose and pawed her face.

'You let your emotions rule you,' Corban said.

'Idiot,' Cywen muttered.

He turned away and looked up at the sun, shading his eyes. 'Enough for today. Keep practising, Cy. You're doing well.'

'*Ban* . . .' she said, following him, but he ignored her, walking quickly towards their house.

Their da was in the kitchen, helping himself to a slice of meat and a cup of mead.

'Da, I wanted to ask you something,' said Corban.

'Aye.'

'Why did you not stop me from taking Storm to the Field this morning? After you had forbidden me for so long?'

Thannon swung his gaze onto Corban, was silent awhile. Then he shrugged.

'I judged you ready,' he said. 'I knew it would not go easy on you, so you had to *want* it. *Really* want it.' He smiled. 'You had a look in your eyes this morning.'

Corban frowned, eyes crinkling. 'Is that why you came? With Gar.'

'You saw us, then?'

'Aye – spying in the shadows.'

'It was not like that, Ban.' Thannon reached out a huge hand to ruffle Corban's hair, but stopped halfway. 'It was something you had to do. And I'm proud of you, lad. But sometimes, these things can get out of hand right quick. If we'd walked with you into the Field, how would you have felt?'

Corban thought about that a while. 'Like a bairn.'

Thannon nodded. 'Some things a man has to do by himself. But I wanted to be there, watch you. And that way, if things *had* got out of hand. Well . . .'

Corban smiled. 'Not the *power of words* again.'

Thannon chuckled. 'Something like that.'

Cywen looked from face to face, frowning. 'What's going on? What are you two talking about? What happened in the Field today?'

Corban just smiled at her. 'I'll see you after,' he said, and Thannon stepped out of the way.

'Where are you going?' Cywen called after him.

'Think I'll go and see Dath. It was his first day in the Field today.'

Cywen ran her thumb along the tip of her knife, pulled it back over her shoulder, focusing on the wooden post. A moment later the knife blade was deep in the post, its hilt vibrating with the force of her throw. She smiled, pleased with the accuracy, drew another knife from her belt and did it again. And then again.

Someone clapped behind her. She spun around, pulling another knife.

It was Princess Edana, Ronan at her shoulder.

'What are you doing?' Cywen snapped, despite herself, sheathing the blade. She didn't like the thought of people being able to sneak up on her.

'I knocked, but there was no answer,' Edana said. 'You must have been concentrating very hard.'

'I was,' Cywen said, marching to the post and pulling out her knives.

'Be careful, you might cut yourself,' said Ronan, Edana's shieldman. He was grinning.

Cywen whirled; in a blur she sighted and threw the blade in her hand. With a soft *thunk* it sank into the tree Ronan was leaning against, about half a hand above his head.

'Careful, girl,' he spluttered, ducking. His grin had gone.

'I only cut what I mean to,' Cywen said, trying to keep a smile of her own from her face.

'Can I see?' Edana asked, looking at the knife in the tree.

'Of course.'

Ronan wiggled the blade free, whistling as he ran his finger over its edge. 'It's weighted strange,' he said.

'It's made for throwing, not stabbing. My da makes them.' Inside she winced. Her mam had taught her to throw a knife, but her da had told her to keep the skill to herself, said others wouldn't like her being so skilled with a weapon. Said it wasn't *womanly*.

'Your brother has caused quite a stir, taking his wolven to the Rowan Field this morning,' Edana murmured as she studied Cywen's knife.

'What?' said Cywen.

'You don't know?'

'Nobody tells me anything,' Cywen muttered sourly. 'What happened?'

Edana told her.

So that's what he and Da were talking about. Cywen felt a grin spill onto her face.

'Your mam is at the keep,' Edana said.

'What?'

'Gwenith. Your mam. I saw her in the keep. She was talking to my parents.'

'She's never done that before. What about?'

'I don't know.' Edana shrugged. 'I thought you might.'

Cywen shook her head. Her mam, seeking an audience with Brenin and Alona. *Why?* But she *had* looked troubled, of late. 'You are a most useful friend to have,' Cywen said, smiling at the Princess. 'My very own spy in the keep.'

Edana grinned. 'Where is your brother?'

'He went to see Dath by the boats.'

'Maybe he knows why your mam was in the keep. Let's go and ask him.'

Ronan took the knife from Edana and handed it to Cywen. 'That's quite a skill you have there,' he said.

Cywen stared at him a moment, saw the summer sun had dotted his face with freckles. *He looks so young*, she thought.

'See something you like?' he said, grinning again.

Cywen looked away, scowled, feeling her cheeks flush.

'To the beach,' Edana said.

They rode out of the fortress and took the track that led down to the bay.

'There they are,' said Edana.

Two figures were standing a little way off, near one of the boats. One was sitting on a smooth, table-like slab of rock, a small shadow at its feet. *Storm*. The other was throwing stones into the bay. They both turned as they heard the approaching horses.

Cywen lifted her hand, smiled at her brother and saw him wave in return.

They dismounted, Ronan minding the horses as Cywen and Edana joined Corban and Dath.

'Cy. My lady,' said Corban. Dath just stared at Edana, which for some reason annoyed Cywen.

'Oh, none of that,' said Edana, her lips pursed. 'My name is Edana, not "lady". We were looking for you.'

'Aye. Well, you have found us,' Corban said with a faint smile.

'Edana saw Mam,' Cywen said. 'At the keep, with the King and Queen. Do you know why she was there?'

Corban shook his head. 'No.' He frowned. 'Why? Mam's never done that before.'

'That's what I said.'

'We'll ask her tonight.'

'No, Corban,' said Edana. 'Your mam took pains not to be seen – cloak on, hood pulled up, and she was led into the keep by my *mother*. Not Evnis or Heb, no other guards. If you ask her, it will probably lead back to me. Then your *spy* would be discovered, and that wouldn't do at all, would it?'

Storm appeared from behind a boulder and padded over to Corban, standing by his heel. Edana bent down. Storm stayed where she was, considering the Princess with copper eyes.

'Friend,' Corban muttered, and the wolven-cub padded forward, sniffing Edana's outstretched hand.

'She's beautiful,' said Edana, beaming.

'Aye, she is. Shame not everyone agrees with you.'

'I heard about your morning. In the Field.'

'Oh aye.'

'You should have seen him,' said Dath. 'Ban, all on his own, standing up to at least a score of them, warriors an' all.'

Corban coughed, blushing suddenly, and looked at his feet.

'And he put Rafe in the right place – knocked him on his arse,' Dath continued, laughing now.

'Enough, Dath. It wasn't like that, anyway.'

'Yes, it was,' said a voice from behind them. Ronan strode closer. 'And I'm not the only one who saw. Took some stones to do that.'

Corban just grunted.

'How was your first day in the Field, Dath?' Cywen asked.

'Good,' said Dath, skimming a stone into the bay.

'Your da must have been proud.'

'Well, he was there, at least.'

'Who's your weapons-master, boy?' asked Ronan.

'Tarben,' Dath said, turning now. 'He knows how to use a blade.' Reverence dripped from his voice.

'Aye, to be sure. And if his skill with a blade *doesn't* kill his foe, he has a secret weapon,' said Ronan, grinning.

'What's that?' asked Dath.

'His tongue. Once he starts moaning, he can suck the joy of life right out of any man. Makes you want to lay down your blade and let him kill you. I've heard it's ancient sorcery, passed down from the giant Elementals.' They all laughed except Dath, who looked a little offended.

Ronan winked at Cywen and she felt her cheeks colour again. She looked away, struggled for conversation.

'It is good to have your da back from Tenebral,' she said to Edana.

'Yes, it is. Mam is smiling again. Although he has been different.'

'Different?' said Cywen.

'I've never seen him so angry as when Marrock was taken.'

'And my lord,' said Ronan. 'Pendathran thought he had lost his brother's-son. And to the same killers.'

'Marrock is back now. And Father is planning to deal with Braith. Once and for all.'

'What do you mean?' Dath asked.

'I've heard him talking with Pendathran. My father is talking of clearing the Darkwood, once and for all.'

'How?' said Ronan. He shook his head. 'He cannot do that – the Darkwood does not lie only in Ardan. It spans a border with Narvon, leagues long. Owain,' he hawked and spat, 'he will not lend his aid. Braith will just hide his men in those parts of the Darkwood that cover Narvon. Brenin cannot take armed men there.'

'Not *yet*. But Father thinks the situation will change. It is to do with his journey to Tenebral. I couldn't quite understand what he meant. But he is asking for a gathering on Midwinter's Day, with Rhin, Owain and Eremon.'

'Where? Here?' said Ronan. 'They will never come, not so far into Ardan. Owain judges others by his own heart. He would fear treachery.'

'Not here,' said Edana. 'At the giants' stone circle.'

Many stories surrounded the huge ring of stones, holy place and ancient meeting ground of the Benothi giant clan.

'Maybe,' muttered Ronan. 'It still lies within Ardan, but within sight of Narvon's border. And close to the Darkwood, which I like even less.'

Edana shrugged. 'Father is sending out riders, inviting them all: Owain, Rhin, even Eremon from Domhain.'

'Why?' said Corban, frowning. 'What is he hoping to achieve?'

'I'm not sure. I wasn't supposed to hear, you understand, I was . . .'

'Spying,' said Corban with a grin. Edana shrugged and smiled back.

'And why would Eremon of Domhain come? Braith and the Darkwood are far from his borders,' Ronan said.

'There is more to it than outlaws in the Darkwood,' Edana said. 'It has to do, I think, with a prophecy, or *something* that Father heard in Tenebral.' She took a deep breath, frowning. A cold breeze gusted off the bay. 'He mentioned a *sign*, on Midwinter's Day, and a . . . a Black Sun.'

CHAPTER THIRTY-NINE

VERADIS

'We are close,' Calidus said over his shoulder, guiding his mount forwards. Alcyon strode in his customary place, alongside the Vin Thalun.

'How close?' Veradis called out, Nathair riding silent beside him.

'It is difficult to say, with certainty,' Calidus said. 'Telassar has not remained hidden throughout the ages just because of these mountains.'

Veradis looked about him. They were picking their way along a narrow path beside a chattering stream, peaks rearing all about them.

'What do you mean?' Veradis said, cupping a hand to his mouth to make himself heard.

'There is a glamour upon this place. Earth power has been used to keep the fortress of the Jehar hidden. That is how I know we are close. I can feel the glamour.'

'If that is so, how will we ever find it?' Veradis called.

Calidus reined in, turned in his saddle, white teeth glinting in what passed for a smile. 'Need I remind you? Alcyon and I are versed in the earth power too.'

'I remember well enough. I'll not be doubting you on that score again.' Veradis glanced at Nathair. The Prince's face was grim. A dark mood had fallen on Nathair with the passing of each night since they had left Rahim's fortress.

Calidus clicked his horse on again, and they continued on down the narrow track.

At least it is cooler, thought Veradis. The heat of this land had been starting to wear on him, but he had felt his spirits lift ever since they had entered this range of mountains, two nights past now, the temperature dropping as they climbed.

He looked over his shoulder, saw the stream disappear down a narrow gully, and frowned. He did not like travelling with so few men about Nathair. Mountains were a breeding ground for brigands, and the narrow paths they had taken through them were ready-made for ambush. Calidus and Alcyon counted for something, but even *they* could not stop an arrow in its tracks.

After the battle with the giants, Nathair had led his warband back to Rahim's fortress, where they had been greeted with shock and celebration. Three nights of feasting had passed, Rahim heaping praise and gifts on Nathair and his men. Then they had set out west, Nathair saying he wished to return to Tenebral with the good news of their victory. One day's ride from the walls of the fortress, though, and Nathair had placed Rauca in charge of the warband, charging him with their safe passage back to the coast and the meeting place with Lykos and his fleet. Rauca had been flushed with pride.

'We are to Telassar,' Nathair had said to Veradis.

No matter how hard Veradis had protested, the Prince refused to take any men with them, other than Calidus and Alcyon.

'I will not appear at their walls with a warband at my back. I mean to win them, not estrange them,' Nathair had said.

So here they were, wandering Elyon knew where in the middle of a strange country, deep within an unknown range of mountains, which apparently had some kind of sorcery cast over them, following a giant and a pirate spymaster.

Veradis studied Alcyon, who was sitting on the far side of the campfire, orange flames making shadows dance and flicker across his angular face, merging with the tattoos that spiralled both his arms.

I owe him my life, he thought, not altogether comfortable with the idea. Still, it was better to be alive and indebted to a giant than to be dead. He took a large gulp from a skin of wine. He could still see the giant towering over him, still remember the sickening sensation in his stomach as he had waited for the giant's axe to fall, then seeing its head rolling in the dust before him.

'I have not thanked you,' he said over the flames.

Alcyon looked up, his eyes small pinpricks as the firelight flickered over his face.

'For what?' the giant rumbled.

'Saving my life. On the ridge.'

Alcyon grunted. 'It was a battle. We do what we have to do.'

'Aye. Nevertheless, you have my thanks.'

Alcyon shrugged, grunted again.

Calidus chuckled, a high, thin sound, like air sucked through a hollow reed. 'My giant is unaccustomed to such praise.'

'*My* giant?' said Nathair. He sat slightly apart, hands clasped around knees drawn up tight to his chest.

'Alcyon is . . . indebted to me, shall we say,' the Vin Thalun said.

'Have you ever ridden a draig?' Nathair asked the giant.

'Nay,' said Alcyon. 'I am of the Kurgan. It was not our way.'

'They were quite impressive, would you not say?'

'Aye,' muttered the giant, 'but you slew them, regardless of how impressive they appeared.'

Nathair laughed, the first time that Veradis could remember since Rahim's fortress. 'But we were a thousand strong, with Rahim's warriors, against only four score of them.'

'True enough,' agreed Alcyon.

'And it only took a handful of them to kill five *score* of my men,' Veradis added, remembering the devastation the draigs had caused as they had rampaged through his shield wall, scattering all in their path like so much kindling.

'I would like one,' Nathair said.

'*What?*' spluttered Veradis. Alcyon and Calidus said nothing, but they both suddenly appeared animated, eyes focused on the Prince.

'Do you think it possible, for me to ride one?'

There was a long silence, broken only by the popping of twigs in the fire.

'Yes,' Calidus said eventually. 'Giants are bigger, obviously, but a saddle could be fashioned to accommodate a smaller frame. Also, the ones that we fought, they would have been old, fully grown. Draigs grow quickly at first; they are adolescents in little more than a year. One would be big enough then for you to ride it, and although they continue to grow, from then on the process is much slower. Those that you saw, large enough for a giant to ride, would have been ten years old, maybe more.'

Nathair nodded thoughtfully. 'And how would I get one? I would imagine they are hard to catch. How are they trained?'

The edges of a smile touched Calidus' lips. 'If they are walking, then it is already too late,' he said. 'You must have them in the egg, be there when they hatch, let them have your scent as you give them their first taste of meat. They are fiercely loyal. Only one person will they ever suffer to ride them, and that is the person who feeds them, rears them.'

'So. Where would I find a draig's egg?'

'The swampland you saw, on Tarbesh's border,' growled Alcyon.

Veradis wrinkled his nose, remembering the swamp beyond the river Rhetta.

'There are other places, throughout the Banished Lands: Forn Forest, parts of Benoth, the Kavala Mountains,' said Calidus.

Alcyon rose, walked to Nathair and kneeled before him. 'You have my oath, Prince of Tenebral. I will find one for you.'

Nathair laughed loudly. 'Alcyon, my thanks would be beyond measure. Can you imagine riding a draig into Jerolin?' he said, slapping Veradis' leg.

'If it would squeeze through the gates,' Veradis muttered.

'Alcyon,' Nathair continued, 'you would be a friend indeed if you would do such a thing for me.'

The giant nodded curtly, his gaze flickering to Calidus. He resumed his place by the fire.

Silence fell over them for a while. The fire guttered low as they passed the skin of wine around.

'I believe we will see Telassar on the morrow,' Calidus said, startling Veradis.

'Are you sure?' asked Nathair.

'There has been a shift in the glamour. Its presence is beginning to fade.'

'Uh,' grunted Nathair, his mood darkening. 'Calidus, do you know anything of this fortress of Telassar, of the Jehar? Now that I find myself here, I feel suddenly apprehensive, as if I carry a great weight.' Nathair avoided the Vin Thalun's eyes as he spoke, gazing instead at the embers of the fire.

'Yes, I know something of Telassar, and its people. Mostly tales and rumours, but I have found much truth wrapped up within such stories before.

'The Jehar are of the Old Blood. A people that dwelt here before

Elyon's Scourging – they survived both fire and water when the giant clans and the race of men were decimated. I say *survived*, but maybe they were *spared* – I know not,' he shrugged. 'All that is told of them is that they are fanatical. They live to serve Elyon, and they are reputed to be warriors without equal, trained from when they can stand.' He smiled, teeth and eyes reflecting red in the glow of the dying fire. 'I know not how much truth is in these tales. But *some*, at least.'

'How do you know so much?' Veradis asked.

Calidus shrugged. 'I am Lykos' eyes, his ears. The Vin Thalun's network of information-gatherers . . .'

'Spies, you mean,' said Veradis.

'Aye, spies. They are everywhere. Remember, the Vin Thalun are sailors; the whole of the Banished Lands coast is open to them. And also, before I served Lykos, I travelled much. There is little that I do not know or cannot discover, if I set my will to it.'

'*Before* you served Lykos. What did you do then?'

'Ah, Prince's man, that is a tale for another time.'

'If you know so much,' Nathair said, 'perhaps you can tell me who Asroth's avatar will be. The Black Sun.'

Calidus grimaced. 'I wish I could. Asroth is cunning, first and foremost, the old tales say. It is a question I have long pondered.' He shrugged. 'We should look to any that oppose you, that oppose your father's alliance. That would be the obvious starting point, though I think the Black Sun would not reveal himself at this point, not unless he could strike a decisive blow. But perhaps his servants . . .'

'Mandros,' Nathair whispered. 'He has opposed my father, mocked him, even. Do you think it could be him?'

'Possibly,' Calidus said. 'At the very least he is likely in service to Asroth's cause. He sows division amongst those your father would reach, belittles the truth of our cause.'

Nathair snapped a twig and threw it on the fire.

'When you stand before the Jehar on the morrow,' Calidus said, 'remember what I am about to tell you. The writings of Halvor, the giant, mention certain criteria that the champions shall be known by. *Kin-Slayer, Kin-Avenger, Giant-Friend, Draig-Rider*. You are already friend to a giant,' he gestured at Alcyon, 'and you have just spoken of riding a draig.' He chuckled. 'You *are* the prophecy, Nathair, living and breathing.'

'You know of the giant's prophecy?' Veradis said.

'Of course I do,' Calidus said, winking at him. 'Wouldn't be much of a spymaster if I didn't, now, would I?'

Veradis snorted. 'And the Jehar, they have heard it as well?'

'Yes. Their ancestors have lived through the Scourging, remember, so they are aware of Halvor's writings. If my sources are correct, they have disagreed, I understand, over the interpretation of the prophecy. It is vague, in parts.'

'More like riddles,' Veradis said.

'Good for the brain,' Calidus said, tapping his temple. 'The Jehar, they have a name of their own for Elyon's Bright Star. They call him the Seren Disglair. And remember one other thing. This you must say: the Ben-Elim, Elyon's warrior-angels, they will stand behind the Bright Star.'

'The Jehar know of the coming war, then?' Nathair said quietly.

'Yes, if the tales are to be believed. It is what they live for, have trained for. They *yearn* for it.'

Veradis looked at the faces around the campfire. Alcyon was gazing at the ground, face hidden in shadow. Calidus and Nathair were staring at each other, Nathair wide-eyed, Calidus calm but intense.

'I know who you are, what you will become,' the Vin Thalun whispered. 'That is why I serve you.' His voice trembled slightly.

Nathair nodded. 'Come, then. We should sleep, and let us see what the morrow brings.'

'We are here,' said Calidus. The Vin Thalun was sitting his horse at the head of their small column. Veradis squinted and leaned in his saddle to look past Calidus, but all he could see was more of the valley they had been riding through since daybreak, mountains all around.

He frowned as they moved on again. Calidus had just disappeared. He blinked, then Alcyon vanished too. He stared hard, could just make out two shadowy figures. The air before him and Nathair shimmered, the dim outlines of Calidus and Alcyon appearing as if through a veil of water.

Nathair looked at him, shrugged, then kicked his horse on. Veradis followed quickly. His skin tingled as he passed through the shimmering barrier, then he too was through.

The mountains were gone, replaced by a lush green vale. A river flowed out of the mountains, twisting in great curves through the vale until it reached a body of water that filled the horizon, sparkling in the sun as if dusted with silver.

Tilled fields filled the valley, rolling up to the walls of a fortress, white stone gleaming. 'Behold, Telassar,' said Calidus with an elaborate sweep of his hand.

'Where are we?' Veradis murmured.

'That,' Calidus said, pointing to the body of water that filled the horizon, 'is the Inland Sea. We are in the far north of Tarbesh, in the Hidden Vale, ancient and secret home of the Jehar.' A smile of satisfaction flickered on the Vin Thalun's face, but he said no more. Veradis glanced behind, could see no sign of the trail they had ridden in on, only sheer-faced cliffs climbing into clouds high above.

'Come, then,' said Nathair, kicking his white stallion on. Quickly they fell in behind the Prince, winding their way towards the white walls of Telassar.

They were still far from the fortress when a horn-call rang out and they spotted a group cantering towards them.

Veradis studied the riders as they drew near. Their horses were tall, long legged, finer boned than those he and his companions were riding. They had an easy grace about them that made him think of his own mount as clumsy. The riders were all dark haired, clean shaven, long hair tied back at the nape, sword hilts rising above their backs. Veradis blinked, realizing some of them were women. When only a dozen paces separated them, they reined in, raising dust from the road.

One of the riders spoke. It was a language that Veradis had never heard before, harsh and guttural, but Calidus replied in the same tongue. The warrior frowned, then spoke again, this time in the Common Tongue.

'Who are you? What is your business here?' He spoke slowly, carefully.

'I am the Seren Disglair,' said Nathair, spreading his arms wide. 'I would speak with your lord.'

The rider rocked back in his saddle. Murmurs spread through the riders at his back, followed by a stunned silence. Veradis saw shock, fear, disbelief, awe sweep their faces.

'The Seren Disglair?' said the rider that had first spoken, leaning forward in his saddle.

'I have travelled far to find you. I must speak with your lord.'

The warrior turned to his companions and spoke with them in his guttural tongue, then the leading warrior gave an order, and one of their number sped back towards the fortress.

'I am Akar,' the warrior that had greeted them said. 'Please, come. I shall escort you to Sumur, Lord of Telassar.'

As they approached the fortress, Veradis saw men, women and children working the fields. All stopped to watch, and soon the group passed through wide gates into a huge open courtyard. To one side row upon row of men and women were standing, all moving in a kind of synchronized pattern, almost like a dance. They held long, wooden practice swords, slightly curved, shaped like the one strapped to Akar's back.

To the other side, people were sparring, the familiar *clack-clack* sounding oddly reassuring in this unfamiliar place.

Veradis felt himself straightening in his saddle, felt eyes burning into him as word of Nathair's claim spread through the crowds.

Their escort led them through twisting streets lined with huge trees, drooping, wide-leaved branches giving shade, and single-storeyed buildings, all carved out of the same bone-white rock. Faces appeared at doors and windows, most glances first drawn to Alcyon, striding behind Calidus. Veradis smiled to himself. *No chance of a subtle entrance with him around.*

They dismounted quickly amidst a growing crowd, leaving their horses to a churning mass of stable boys, all eager to take their mounts.

'This way,' said Akar, waving a hand. He led them through an arched gateway into a garden, leaving the crowds behind. Stone pillars broke up the verdant surroundings and everywhere there was clinging vine, dark orchids, purple iris and other brighter flowers that Veradis did not recognize.

'How do you know their tongue?' Veradis whispered to Calidus as they strode down a wide path that dissected the garden. 'It sounded like some form of giantish.'

Calidus glanced at him, his thoughts clearly elsewhere.

'That language was the Common Tongue, before the Scourging.

It was shared by giants and men alike. Your kin the Exiles changed many things when they returned here from the Isle of Summer.'

Veradis grunted.

A high-domed building lay ahead, a warrior opening its dark polished doors for them.

They stepped into a high-vaulted room; a gentle breeze blew through many windows. A tall man stood in its centre, waiting, his jet-black hair bound at the nape like the other warriors Veradis had seen. A loose-fitting shirt of black linen ill concealed a broad frame. This man was clearly a warrior. Dark eyes gazed out intently from under a protruding brow, resting briefly on each of them. Veradis felt a weightlessness in his stomach, a slight tingle of fear. Although he seemed unsettled, there was something feral about this man.

Akar spoke quickly in their harsh tongue. The man answered, staring again at Nathair. 'Welcome.' He touched a hand to his forehead. 'I am Sumur, Lord of Telassar.'

'Well met,' said Nathair, stepping forward, smiling broadly. 'I have travelled long and far to find you.'

Sumur's eyes swept across them, pausing briefly on Alcyon.

'We are unused to guests here. How did you find this place, and why are you here?'

Nathair smiled. 'Surely our escort has told you.'

A silence settled, Sumur regarding each one of them in turn.

'I have been told of your claim.' Sumur nodded slowly. 'But you have not answered the question I asked of you: how did you find this place?' There was an edge to his voice now.

'Elyon guided us,' Nathair said.

Sumur snorted. 'A little more detail, please.'

'I am Nathair ben Aquilus, Prince of Tenebral. I found this place,' Nathair said with a sweep of his hand, 'because I am the Seren Disglair, and so was *meant* to find it.'

'So you say.' Sumur clapped his hands, gesturing to the cushions behind him. 'Please, sit. Some food and drink for our weary travellers. I would not have it said that the Seren Disglair walked into my home and was treated discourteously.' He smiled thinly.

Men and women suddenly appeared. They brought scented water and cloths to wash their guests' hands, then bowls of figs and peaches, plums and olives, warm flatbreads and jars of wine. They were all dressed similarly to Sumur and Akar, though none had a sword strapped to his back. All of them stared at Nathair.

Veradis ate a little, sipping at a cup of red wine, eyes fixed on Sumur. *He is nervous*, he thought, *and rightly so. The champion of a god has just walked into his house.* He shifted his weight on the cushion he was sat in, feeling awkward and uncomfortable, vulnerable. After a while he gave up wriggling and stood up.

Alcyon tried to eat from a bowl of figs, but his thick fingers could not pick anything up. In the end he lifted the whole bowl and tipped its contents into his mouth.

When they were done, the small tables were cleared, fresh wine brought.

'Let us cut to the heart of the matter,' Nathair said once the last attendant had left the room. 'I have appeared, making great claims. You are wondering if I speak the truth.'

Sumur smiled. 'Just so,' he nodded.

'Then let me seek to persuade you.' Nathair stood, began to pace about the room. 'I am *here*. Why would I come here, if not at Elyon's bidding? I have found this place. The Hidden Vale, which has remained secret for countless generations. How would that be possible, unless Elyon has brought me here?'

'There are ways, though they are difficult,' Sumur said. 'You are not the first to find us.'

Nathair raised an eyebrow at that. 'Halvor has written of these days, of me. You only have to look and see to recognize that.'

'The prophecy has been wrongly interpreted before,' Akar said. 'Sword brothers have left here, convinced by another's words. They were wrong. We must be sure.'

Nathair frowned. 'The giant-stones have wept blood, white wyrms roam the land, the Treasures are stirring.'

Veradis heard something, not quite a voice, but *something*, so faint. He looked at Calidus, saw the man's lips moving, forming silent words, his hands taught, knuckles white. A bead of sweat ran down his forehead. Suddenly Nathair seemed to *grow*, somehow, his presence, his voice appearing to fill the room, booming.

'I am the Bright Star,' Nathair declared. 'Elyon comes to me in my dreams, has told me this is so. Look at my companions – *Giant-Friend*, they call me.' He gestured to Alcyon. 'I am the Seren Disglair, chosen avatar of Elyon. All who resist Asroth shall gather behind me, even the Ben-Elim, the warrior-angels.'

He fell silent, breathing heavily, fists clenched, eyes burning.

'Enough of this,' Calidus said. The old man stood, looking taller to Veradis, his back straighter, shoulders broader. 'The Seren Disglair does not *negotiate*. He *is*. And his followers will know him. As I do.' Suddenly Calidus *changed*. It was as if he had been wreathed in mist, for now his travel-stained clothes were replaced by a coat of gleaming mail, his eyes blazed amber, and *things* were growing from his back, *wings*, Veradis realized, great wings of white feather. They extended across the room, flexed, the wind of them staggering Veradis, spilling the jug of wine.

'The Ben-Elim,' whispered Akar.

Sumur stood open-mouthed, staring, then dropped to one knee before Nathair. 'I am yours, my lord. The swords of the Jehar are yours.'

CHAPTER FORTY

KASTELL

Kastell lay back in the grass, fingers laced behind his head, eyes closed. He took a deep breath, drawing in the fresh scent of grass mingled with white meadowsweet and moist, rich earth.

It was good, being back here. Peaceful.

He had begun to feel claustrophobic since his return to Mikil, hemmed in by crowds of people and stone walls. Blowing out a long breath, he felt the tension easing from his body. Things were supposed to be different now: he had slain a giant, crossed mountains, traversed realms, seen far-off Jerolin, fought alongside the Sirak, been included by his uncle in important plans, made *friends*.

But now that he had returned, things seemed to be slipping back to how they had always been – people whispering about him behind their hands, sniggering and pointing, warriors he had befriended on the road avoiding him. And since the battle by the stream and Maquin's discovery of the bag of gold, he had felt a tension building, a shadow following him, like crows hovering behind a warband.

He had seen little of Jael, did not trust him now, knew that he was plotting against him.

Grass tickled his ear, and he opened his eyes, leaned forward. He was sitting on the slope of a small dell with a cairn standing at its base, grass and wildflowers growing in gaps in the stones. The bones of his mam and da were in there, cold, damp. He sighed. It had been a long time since he had been here.

'What should I do, Da?' he whispered.

Distant sounds of the fortress drifted down to him, carried by a strong, swirling breeze. But one sound was getting closer, a rider coming this way. Kastell scrambled up, reaching for his sword as a horseman crested the ridge of the dell. But it was only Maquin.

'I've been looking for you,' Maquin said as he slipped from his saddle. 'Thought I'd find you here. Jael is up to his tricks – I overheard talk today, over a jug of ale. Said you were behind the axe being stolen, that you were trading it with the Hunen, but the deal went wrong. Apparently the Hunen tried to kill us, but we escaped.'

'What? But, that's not true . . .'

'I know. I was there, remember.'

'Who was saying these things?'

'The man I heard was Ulfilas. One of Jael's men, of course.' He rubbed his knuckles and winced. 'He'll think twice before he says it again, though. But I'm sure he's not the only man Jael has put to spreading these rumours. Have you thought any more on joining the Gadrai?'

Kastell frowned. 'Aye. Just about every moment that I'm awake.'

'What's stopping you? I've seen how you've been treated since our return. And always by Jael's lads.' He hawked, spat.

A large part of him did just want to leave, to move on, to recapture the freedom that he had felt whilst on the road. But there was something keeping him in Mikil. He took a deep breath and decided just to come out with it.

'Do you remember on the journey back from Jerolin, when King Romar had me ride with him a while?'

'Aye, lad.'

'Well, he spoke of next year. Of taking men from Isiltir to join with Braster of Helveth, to attack the Hunen, root them out of Forn Forest. Romar said he wanted me to, to . . .' He paused. *Why was this so difficult to say?* He sucked in a deep breath. 'He wanted me to be involved in the campaign, to lead some of the men of Isiltir. Along with Jael.'

Maquin just looked at him, silent, and waited.

'My uncle has never asked anything of me before. He took me in after Da . . . He took me in, provided for me, never asked for anything in return. I would not let him down in this.'

Maquin nodded slowly. 'I see,' he said, then frowned. 'But, lad, he thinks that you and Jael are reconciled, that your bad blood is behind you.'

'Aye, he does.'

They stood there in silence for long moments, staring at each other.

'Kastell,' Maquin said. 'I am your shieldman, not your da, so I cannot tell you what to do, but I also count myself as your friend, so I'll give you my thoughts. You can do with them what you will.'

Kastell grunted.

'I understand you wanting to please your uncle, not let him down. But this thing between you and Jael – it is no childhood prank or grudge any more. I remember the stream, lad.' He raised a hand to the thin scar on his forehead, tracing it gently with one finger. 'I fought with you, saw men *die* over this *feud* between you . . .'

'It is not *my* feud,' snapped Kastell. 'I have done nothing wrong.'

'Aye, lad, aye,' Maquin said, holding up a hand. 'I know – other than kicking Jael in the knackers in front of the finest warriors the Banished Lands have to offer, that is. But that aside, whether you are in it willingly or no, you'll still be the one that has your blood spilt, sooner or later. You and Jael are close to being Romar's *heirs*. One of you will be *lord* here, and I know you have never wanted any part of that, never sought it. But Jael is a different creature; he thirsts for it, and in his eyes you are a rival. You are living in the den of your enemy, and he is only going to grow more powerful.' He sighed and shook his head. 'This is not going to end well, lad.'

Kastell grimaced. 'I do not want to run away.'

Maquin shrugged. 'You would not be running away; you would be joining the *Gadrai*. Every warrior's dream.'

'You think I should go, then?'

'Aye, lad. But not *you*: *we*.'

Kastell shook his head. 'I cannot take you from your home. Romar spoke to me of you, as well, Maquin. He told me you are a *"leader of men"*. He has plans for *you*, also. Great plans. I would not see you throw it all away to hold my hand, to protect me.'

Maquin raised a hand to his chin, rubbing his close-cropped beard. 'You insult me,' he said quietly. 'I have been your shieldman since before you could walk, swore an oath to your da, on our blood. And you tell me to abandon you, to walk away.' He grimaced, his eyes suddenly wet, and brushed angrily at them. 'You are like a son to me, and I fear for you. Let me make one thing clear.' He pointed a finger at Kastell. 'The only thing that will part me from you is death.' He stood there in silence a long moment, then dropped his hand and looked away. 'Besides,' he said, 'the Gadrai has been a dream for me too, you know.' He looked over his shoulder, back towards Mikil, though it was hidden from view. 'This place seems different, since we returned. Smaller.'

'I'd agree with you there.'

'It's about time for a change.' He closed his eyes a moment, the lines in his face deepening. 'My Reika crossed the bridge half a score years ago now. We had no children. I have no ties here, no reason to stay. This would be good for me, too. Better'n growing old and stiff inside those cold walls.' He waved a hand over his shoulder.

'I don't know, Maquin,' Kastell sighed. 'You make it sound so simple. I'll think on it some more.' He looked at the ground. 'I've had a mind to go and see Jael. Talk to him about this. See if it can be settled calmly.'

Maquin snorted. 'Stranger things have happened. But have a care. Keep your wits about you, *and* a leash on your temper. He's crafty.' He sucked in a deep breath, eyes drawn briefly to the cairn. 'Well, I'm for heading back, lad. Coming?'

Kastell nodded. 'I think I will.'

Kastell paced through Mikil's streets, long shadows cast by the sinking sun.

After returning to the fortress, he and Maquin had swiped a skin of mead from the feast-hall and sat on the outer wall. It had been good just to look at the sinking sun and drink, to talk and even laugh a little with Maquin, for a while forgetting the dark shadow that seemed to hang over most of his waking moments. Too soon, though, the feeling had returned and Kastell had excused himself, returning to his cold cell in the complex that Romar had given him as his hold. Only Maquin and a serving lady filled the cold rooms, whereas Jael had filled his complex with servants and followers. Kastell sat there long into the evening, thinking on Maquin's words in the dell.

The old warrior was right, it *was* time to do something, right or wrong, instead of just waiting for the hammer to drop.

*

He passed through a tall, wide archway into the weapons court.

It was almost empty, a few men sparring, others clustered in small groups, watching. The weapons racks stood full with wooden swords and spears. Kastell paused a moment, then saw the man he was searching for.

Jael stood with a small group of men, three or four, all watching two warriors sparring. Kastell breathed deep, straightened his back and strode towards them.

Jael heard him approaching, and his hand moved nearer his sword hilt.

'Jael,' said Kastell as he reached them.

Jael just stared, his companions turning now. One of them was Ulfilas, the warrior that had fought with him by the stream, also the one Maquin had heard spreading rumours. He nodded to the tall man, who grunted, eyes flitting to Jael.

'Jael. I would speak with you.'

Jael snorted. 'What is this? Some ruse?' he said, much louder than necessary. 'All know that you bear me ill will, resent me.'

'What?' said Kastell, frowning. He felt a muscle twitching in his jaw. 'I would speak with you, alone,' he repeated.

'Very well,' said Jael, smiling graciously. 'Walk with me.' He strolled leisurely away, not looking to see if Kastell followed.

'We must talk,' Kastell said softly, walking quickly to catch up with his cousin.

'*Must?*' said Jael.

'Aye. *Must*,' said Kastell. 'This rift between us. I would put it behind us.'

'Rift? I know not of what you speak.'

Kastell felt his fist clench involuntarily. *This is going to be harder than I thought.* With a slow breath he unclenched his fingers.

'Come, Jael. Let us not play games. I know that you mean me harm, that you hired those men, by the stream, in Helveth.'

Jael's head swung around, studying Kastell with heavy-lidded eyes. 'You have no proof,' he eventually said.

'I have a bag of Isiltir gold with Romar's crest on it,' Kastell retorted.

'Pfah. That means nothing.'

'If that is so, then it would do no harm for me to share my information with Romar.'

'Do as you wish. I care not.'

They walked in silence a short distance, then Kastell stopped. Jael turned, hands clasped behind his back, that maddening false smile still fixed on his face.

Briefly, out of the corner of his eye, Kastell saw Ulfilas and the men with him. They were watching him closely.

'I know not why you dislike me so,' Kastell said. 'If I have wronged you, I am sorry.'

'*Sorry*. *Wronged* me,' hissed Jael, still somehow managing to maintain his smile. 'Aye, you have wronged me. And it is too late for *sorry*. Too late by far.'

'What is it that you think I have done?' Kastell said, frowning.

'You shamed me, Kastell,' Jael said quietly. 'Before the greatest warriors in all of the Banished Lands; before kings, before the champions of kings and before the *sons* of kings. Surely you do not think I would let that just *pass*?'

'But, this grudge against me. It did not begin in Jerolin.'

'True, true,' said Jael, waving a hand. 'But then I was merely repaying you for your father's transgressions. *Now*, well, it is an entirely different matter, and a far more serious one. You shamed me before Nathair, the future King of Tenebral. He saw what you did to me, and I cannot let him perceive me as *weak*.'

'My father's transgressions? What do you mean?' Kastell growled, feeling his temper rise. This was moving far too quickly. But his da had been mentioned.

Jael frowned, looking at him intently, then laughed. 'You really don't know? Well, I do not think that now is the time to talk on *that* subject.'

Kastell breathed deep. Things were going off track. But his *da*. What did Jael mean? He blinked hard, shook his head, with an effort recalled the things he had wanted to say. 'Romar has plans,' he said. 'For next year, fighting the Hunen. Those plans involve both of us. For the sake of Isiltir, we must lay our grudges aside.'

Jael clapped gently, slowly. 'For the sake of *Isiltir*,' he chuckled. '*Isiltir* does not *need* you. My uncle does not *need* you. He just pities you.'

A rage burned inside Kastell now, flushing his neck and face. He felt his fists bunch. A distant voice in his head whispered that Jael was goading, *provoking* him, and with an effort of will he forced himself to breathe deeply, to smile, even though it came out more like a grimace.

'You are a useless, ugly, slow-witted idiot, Kastell,' Jael continued, smiling broadly now, 'just like your da.'

Kastell took an involuntary step forward, realized what he was doing, forced himself to stand still. 'No, Jael,' he growled. 'I am no longer a bairn that you can play like a puppet. Pull this string and he will do this, pull that string and he will do that. No more.' He wiped sweat from his face.

Anger clouded Jael's eyes, contorted his mouth, just for a moment, then the smile was back.

'I see. Well, when the puppet does not respond to the master's will, then the puppet's strings are cut and it is thrown on the fire.' Jael took a pace forward and leaned close to Kastell. 'Make no mistake,' he whispered, 'I *am* the master here. And, I promise you, one day soon, your strings *will* be cut, and you *will* burn.' He paused, sniffed. 'And, I fear, those close to you will be burned by the same flames.'

'What? What do you mean?' said Kastell.

Jael smiled. 'Work it out, halfwit. You only have *one* friend. Poor judgement can lead to an early grave, you know.'

He speaks of Maquin.

With a snarl, Kastell found himself lunging forwards. He grabbed Jael and heaved him backwards, throwing him into a stone wall. Jael grunted and then Kastell was on him again, hands around Jael's throat. There was a roaring sound in his ears, his vision distorted so that he saw Jael as if through a mist, eyes bulging, ineffectually swatting at his arms, but nothing could move him. Distantly he heard shouting, felt a sharp pain in his back, hands pulling at him. Jael's legs gave way, and his cousin began to sink slowly to the floor, Kastell still squeezing. Somewhere behind him a voice filtered through the red fog.

'. . . him go, you'll kill him, fool, let him go, or die.'

He saw his hands open slowly, releasing Jael, who slumped to the ground, gasping, retching, sucking in deep, ragged breaths. Men rushed forwards, lifting Jael.

Stepping back, Kastell felt the pain in his back again and turned to see Ulfilas with a knife in his hand, the tip, about half a finger long, stained with blood.

What have I done?

Jael pushed his helpers away, standing unsteadily on his own. 'You . . .' he rasped, pointing. 'This is the end for you.'

Kastell grimaced, turned and stumbled away. Men shouted, reaching for him.

'No,' creaked Jael. 'Let him go. My uncle will deal with him now.'

Kastell thumped on Maquin's door, trying to control the panic that was bubbling inside him.

He'd checked Maquin's favoured haunts but there was no sign of his friend.

Eventually he tried Maquin's cell in his hold, although he knew it was still much earlier than his friend usually liked to retire. He banged on the door again, harder, and heard footsteps. The handle rattled and pulled open, Maquin's frowning face staring out at him.

'Asroth's teeth, lad, what's wrong with you?'

Kastell threw himself at the old warrior, hugging him tight. Maquin grunted, then Kastell suddenly released him and stepped back, looking at the floor.

'You're – alright, then.'

'Aye, lad,' said Maquin, his expression hovering between frown and smile. 'Shouldn't I be?'

'I've been to see Jael.'

'Ah. Good. How did it go?'

'Not well,' Kastell mumbled. He dragged in a deep breath, stood straighter, meeting Maquin's eyes. 'I'm for the Gadrai. If you still wanted to ride with me, I'd be happy.'

Maquin grinned and slapped Kastell's shoulder. 'Well done, lad.' He peered into Kastell's eyes. 'No reconciliation with your cousin, then?'

'No,' grunted Kastell.

'I didn'a hold much hope. Still, at least you tried, lad.' He scratched his chin. 'So, when do you wish to leave?'

'Now.'

'*What?* But, we've things to arrange. What about Romar? You should speak with your uncle, surely.'

'I already have,' said Kastell. His uncle had not been happy. Far from it. Kastell would have felt better if Romar had raged at him, but instead he had just looked at him, disappointment writ plainly on his features.

'Why?' Romar had asked. 'Why would you leave, when you know my plans for you?'

Kastell had known that Jael would be pounding on Romar's door soon, telling him of what Kastell had done in the weapons court, so he had tried to explain. It had come out confused, serving only to harden Romar's attitude.

In the end his uncle had taken a quill to parchment, sealed it with hot wax, and stamped an imprint of his ring into it. 'Give this to Vandil. He is lord of the Gadrai, or Orgull, his captain. No one else. Do you understand me, boy?' Romar had said. Kastell just nodded. Romar had hugged him tight, crushing the air from his lungs, then opened the door and ushered him out.

Maquin frowned. 'There's more to this tale than you're telling.'

'Aye, there is. Come, I'll tell you while you pack.'

CHAPTER FORTY-ONE

CORBAN

Corban shivered and pulled his cloak tighter about him, waiting for Cywen. He looked up, towards the giantsway as a rider appeared out of the rain, draped in a sodden red cloak. *Another messenger from Narvon.*

Ever since the day Edana had told them of her father's plans about Braith and the Darkwood, and of this *prophecy*, of a *war*, the giantsway had been thick with messengers.

Time had passed since then, the Reaper's Moon turning to the Hunter's and then the Crow's Moon. The last day of summer was marked by Samhuin, already a ten-night gone. Brenin's messengers had left soon after Edana had told them of the King's request, inviting fellow rulers to the stone circle on Midwinter's Day. Most messengers had returned already. According to Edana, all the kings had assented, even Eremon, the ruler of distant Domhain.

'All well at Brina's?' Cywen said cheerily as she approached.

'Aye,' he muttered. He hated the rain: hot, cold, snow, he took in his stride, liking something of all of them, but the *rain*. 'Must we do this today?' he grumbled.

Cywen frowned but did not stop, ducking under the paddock rail. 'Horse training doesn't heed the weather, Ban,' she said, sounding annoyingly like Gar.

'Huh,' he said, not entirely agreeing, but following her anyway.

Storm rose silently and padded at his heels. Cywen stopped a score of paces into the field, waiting for them to catch up. She rested a hand on Storm's neck, sinking her fingers into the wolven's fur. She did not need to bend to reach Storm now. The wolven could hardly be called a cub any more, so rapidly had she grown – a shade taller than Buddai already, her head level with Corban's waist. She had lost her puppy fur, her coat coarser, thicker, dark blazes running jaggedly down her torso, looking like claw marks on pale flesh.

'Here,' Cywen said to him, holding out a rope halter. 'Remember, take your time. Are you sure you remember what to do?'

Corban ignored her. 'Come, boy,' he called, clicking his tongue.

'Isn't it about time you named him?' Cywen said quietly.

He ignored her.

His colt was standing beside its mother, taking shelter from the rain under an oak that dominated the centre of the field. He neighed and trotted towards them.

Corban reached into his cloak, pulled out a slice of apple and held it out. Crunching the apple, the colt bent its neck and sniffed Storm's head. The wolven stood still, not looking at the young horse. Corban chuckled – she'd had a kick a few moons back, when she used to chase everything that moved. The colt had tolerated that, thinking he had a new playmate, but when she started nipping at his heels Storm had received a hoof-shaped warning. Since then she had just ignored the colt.

Slowly, he raised the halter. The colt eyed it suspiciously. Corban had done this many times at the fortress, but this was different. It was his horse's first time with a halter, and he knew how important it was that he did this right. He gently slipped the halter over its head. The colt jerked back sharply, ears flat, but the job was already done. It danced backwards, startled by the unfamiliar halter rope, which bounced against its flank. The colt broke into a gallop around the field, bucking as it ran.

'Don't worry, Ban,' Cywen said, coming up beside him. 'That was well done; he'll come around soon. Be patient.'

They headed back towards the shelter of a small clump of hawthorns, near the paddock rail. Corban heard a call and looked up.

Three riders were on the giantsway. Corban squinted, wiping rain from his face, then the front rider pushed the hood of his cloak back. It was Vonn, Evnis' son. He spurred his horse off the road and down the steep embankment, cantering to the paddock. His two companions followed.

Corban sighed, his mouth suddenly feeling dry.

Vonn had never made good on his threat in Brina's cottage to find

Corban and teach him a lesson, not after Tull's words in the Rowan Field that day. No one wanted their head cracked by Brenin's first-sword. In fact, things had been much better for Corban since then. Even Rafe had confined himself to angry glares and the occasional harsh word.

But they were quite a way from the fortress and village now, with no one around. Corban felt worry stirring deep in his gut.

'Ho there, wolven-boy,' Vonn called out, his face stern. He reined in his horse, dismounted and ducked under the paddock rail. His two companions followed. Corban groaned as he recognized them – Helfach and Rafe. The huntsman's hound, Braen, padded at their heels.

The three of them filed across the paddock, stopping a dozen or so paces away from Corban and Cywen. Storm shifted beside Corban, her weight nudging against his leg.

'Well, well,' said Vonn, his expression hard, 'I have long hoped for an opportunity to talk with you, privately.' He looked around, emphasizing his point. 'Elyon must favour me.'

Corban just stared at him.

'What, nothing to say, now that I am not confined to my bed? I remember you being more vocal, at the healer's.'

'What is it that you want?' Corban said, pronouncing each word slowly, so that his voice would not shake.

'Want? Now there is a question,' said Vonn, a grim, humourless smile flickering across his lips. 'Merely to remind you of our words at the healer's.'

'I remember them well enough,' Corban said.

'Do not think that I spoke lightly, or in the grip of some fever. I mean to fulfil my promise to you. Even if I have to wait until you have sat your Long Night, and we can speak differently, as warrior to warrior.'

Corban sighed. 'I *had* hoped your words came from your fever. I would be happy to lay them aside.'

Vonn laughed, little humour in it. 'I am sure that you would. But I, however, am not *happy* to lay them aside.' He reached down and rubbed his knee. 'My leg still aches, more in this rain, because of you.'

'I did not cause your horse to fall upon you,' Corban said.

'I remember events differently.'

Corban held a hand up. 'There is little to be gained in this bickering. King's Justice has spoken about my wolven, so whether you agree or no, there is naught you can do. Better for all, I think, if we just put the past behind us.'

Helfach snorted. 'Better for *all*. Better for *you*, more like,' he spat.

Corban sucked in a deep breath, trying to master his emotions. He clasped his hands together and laced his fingers to stop them from trembling.

'Look at him,' Helfach continued, a sneer twisting his mouth. 'He's *scared*. He has'na got Tull, or that outlander standing at his back. My son has told me of the boy's cowardly ways.' He glowered at Corban. 'Is that not right, boy?'

'He thinks he has all the protection he needs,' Rafe added. 'His sister is here. She's well practised in fighting battles for him.'

'Shut up,' Cywen snapped. Rafe leered at her.

'Hush, Cy,' said Corban. He ignored Rafe, felt the fear inside him start to shift, into something colder. He looked pointedly at Helfach. 'You left out one of my protectors. You left out my da.' He met Helfach's glare with one of his own. 'Why is that?'

Helfach blinked and looked away, obviously remembering the day in Evnis' courtyard, when Thannon had confronted him, beaten him unconscious.

His hound, broad-chested and squat, growled, sensing a change in his master.

Storm bared her teeth, a deep rumbling response growing in her chest. Corban laid a hand on her neck, felt her hackles standing on end. He clicked his tongue and the rumbling stopped.

Suddenly Alona's words returned to his mind, like a bell, sharp and clear. '*If there is one incident where a subject of mine is harmed by this creature, it will be destroyed.*'

He swallowed, fear again spiking within.

'Cy,' he said, 'take Storm away.'

'What? *No*. Why?'

'Just do it. Please.'

She stared at him, puzzled, then nodded and walked away, calling Storm. The wolven did not move, stood motionless beside Corban, muscles tensed.

'Go,' said Corban, snapping his fingers and pointing. Storm turned reluctantly, and walked after Cywen.

'Why have you done that?' Vonn asked, frowning. Corban ignored him, watching until his sister and Storm reached the oak where the colt's mother still stood.

'Answer your betters, boy,' Helfach grunted.

Corban's mood changed then, quickly, suddenly. He turned to face them. 'You say I am different, without my *protectors* here. Well, what of *you*? You are different too: aye, bolder. Why is that, huntsman? You are mighty brave, all three of you. Would you be the same, if my da were here, or Tull. Tell me?' He snorted. 'And you call *me* coward.'

'I only came to tell you there will be a reckoning between us one day, when you are an age to face me,' Vonn said, angry, but there was something else in his eyes. *Shame?* Helfach, though, turned slowly purple, eyes bulging, a vein in his neck throbbing.

'How dare you?' he snarled. '*We* may be forbidden to touch you, but what can I do about a hound turned wild? Braen.'

The hound growled, baring his teeth.

'Helfach, what are you—' Vonn began, but then it was too late. The hound launched itself. Corban let out a strangled cry and turned, tried to run, but the hound crashed into his back, jaws snapping. Corban sprawled forwards, fell to the ground, the hound snarling, caught up in his cloak.

'No!' Corban heard someone shout. Vonn? The hound was rolling in his cloak, tearing at it. Cywen yelled his name. As he rolled on the grass and scrambled backwards he glimpsed her running towards him, Storm speeding before her, then the hound was on him, scrabbling up his chest. He grappled with it, digging his fingers into the thick cords of muscle around its neck, but it broke his grip easily and sank its teeth into his arm. He screamed, wrenched away, felt droplets of blood splattering across his face. The hound lunged for his throat, jaws gaping, teeth clicking a hairsbreadth from his flesh, hot, fetid breath blasting his face, huge feet pinning him to the ground.

A roaring thunder grew, filling his ears, drowning the frenzied growls coming from the hound. He heard a wild neighing, felt a jarring, bone-crushing impact, a high-pitched whine, then suddenly the weight of the hound was gone.

Hooves thudded down around him, his colt filling his vision, rearing, forelegs lashing out. There was a sickening crunch, then the colt's feet thumped to the ground. It stood over him, nostrils flaring, hot air shooting out in great cloudy blasts. Then Storm was there, nuzzling him, licking, standing beside the colt, between him and his attackers, crouched, snarling, long teeth bared.

He rolled over, felt Cywen's arms around him, helping him stand. His arm was throbbing, blood pulsing from his wound in time with his pounding heart, the rain sending it in red rivulets down his sleeve.

Vonn made to approach him, but Storm snapped, snarled, and he stopped.

Helfach was kneeling in the grass, cradling his hound's head on his lap, Rafe standing behind, frozen, staring.

'You . . . you killed him,' Helfach gasped, tears streaming down his cheeks.

'No,' Vonn said. 'You killed him, Helfach. Come. I will help you carry him.' He hooked an arm around Helfach as he looked at Corban. 'I am sorry,' he said haltingly. 'Are you—? Your arm. You must go to Brina.'

Corban nodded, numb, and watched the three of them carry the limp corpse of the hound out of the paddock.

'Ban, your arm,' Cywen said, hugging him, ripping the hem of her cloak and tying it tight just below his shoulder.

'What happened?' Corban mumbled, feeling suddenly sick and dizzy.

'We tried to reach you, when the hound attacked. But we were too far away, even Storm was not fast enough. Ban, it nearly killed you – *could* have killed you . . .'

'What happened?' Corban repeated, firmer.

'Your colt, Ban. He just raced past us, from nowhere, threw himself into the hound. He killed it, Ban, defending you.' She blew out a breath and shook her head. 'I've never seen the like before. I've heard tales, of full-grown horses doing things like that, *war*horses, but never seen, never heard of a *colt* doing such a thing.'

Corban nodded, walked forward unsteadily. Storm nuzzled his hand. He wrapped his good arm around the colt's neck and laid his head against it.

'I shall call you Shield,' he whispered.

CHAPTER FORTY-TWO

VERADIS

Veradis smiled as he crested a gentle rise in the land and saw Jerolin rise out of the plain before him, its central tower of black rock pointing to the sky like a scorched, accusatory finger.

Small figures were busy on the lake shore, beneath the fortress, the day's catch being unloaded from scores of fisher-boats. The sky was clear, a deepening blue as dusk settled around them.

He looked over his shoulder, saw the warband spread across the slope and plain behind him; he took a deep breath of the cold, sharp air.

'It is good to be back, eh?' he said to Nathair and Rauca, who were sitting their horses beside him. Rauca gripped Nathair's standard in leather-gauntleted hands, the eagle pennant snapping in the wind.

'Good to be back,' Nathair echoed, shifting his weight in his saddle.

'Aye,' agreed Rauca, a grin splitting his face and short dark beard.

Without another word, Nathair spurred his horse on, cantering down the gentle slope. Veradis and Rauca followed him, the warband spilling over the rise behind them.

The journey home had been quick and uneventful. The memory of finding hidden Telassar, of Calidus' revelation, of the Jehar warriors swearing their allegiance to Nathair was all blurred, somehow. Since that moment everything seemed to have changed, to have fallen into place. Seeing Calidus unveiled had sealed *everything*, although he had reverted to the bowed old man before they had left Sumur's chambers, swearing them all to secrecy. Veradis knew now, beyond all doubt, that Nathair was Elyon's chosen, that he rode with a man who would change the world. Just the thought made his heart swell with pride. They had ridden from Telassar with Sumur's promises ringing in their ears, that he would gather the Jehar's might, prepare them for war and then march for Jerolin.

Within a ten-night of leaving Telassar, Veradis and Nathair had rejoined their warband, finding them camped in a bay on the coast. Lykos had been there too, waiting with a fleet to ferry them back to Tenebral.

Their passage home had been swift, although the weather was changing for the worse, so enfeebled warriors clustered the ships' rails. Veradis had walked amongst them, thanking Elyon for his upbringing on the coast and berating his giantkillers for letting the weather cow them where giants and draigs had not.

Alcyon had left them before they had boarded Lykos' ships, bowing to Nathair and nodding a farewell to Veradis. It was strange; he felt that he almost missed the giant's company.

He snorted to himself, laughing quietly.

Lykos had returned them to the same quiet bay where they had first met him. Since then they had ridden another ten-night, a mounting excitement and desire for speed amongst the warband. Now they were back, Nathair ordered horns to be blown, announcing his return, an answering blast echoing from Jerolin's battlements. Veradis felt his back straighten when they entered the crowded courtyard to cheering, a smile spilling across his face. This was something indeed.

Valyn was at the stables, armed with a host of stablehands to help warriors tend their mounts. He grinned at Veradis and pulled him into an embrace.

'I'm glad you're back, lad, and in one piece.' The stablemaster stepped back. 'You've some tales to tell, I'd wager.'

Veradis just nodded, smiling broadly. He hadn't realized how much he had missed the stablemaster.

'Well, enough of that,' Valyn said, 'I've work that needs tending. We'll talk, eh? Later?'

'Aye,' said Veradis. 'Later.'

Veradis set to, stripping down his horse's saddle and tack, but he was only part-way done when a hand gripped his shoulder.

'Come,' Nathair said to him, 'I am eager to see my father, and I would have you beside me.'

Veradis had found a stable boy to tend his horse and followed Nathair to the keep. As Nathair and Veradis crossed the empty feast-hall, footsteps echoing, a door opened. King Aquilus hurried through, Fidele just behind.

The King saw Nathair, crossed the room in several strides, almost running, and grabbed Nathair in a crushing embrace. Queen Fidele joined them, arms about them both, smiling, stroking Nathair's face, his hair, tears glistening on her cheeks.

Veradis looked away, feeling as if he were trespassing. He thought of his own father and felt a stab of something, deep inside. Jealousy? The feeling shifted rapidly into shame, edged with anger. He stared at the stone floor.

Eventually the three figures parted, Nathair's cheeks colouring, a hesitant smile flitting across his face.

'I am back,' he said.

'So we see,' Aquilus laughed. 'Come. You must have much to tell.'

Nathair nodded, still smiling.

Soon they were seated in a room in the tower, a platter of food and a jug of wine on the table they were sitting around.

'Rahim sends his greetings. And his thanks,' Nathair said.

'I am sure he does,' said Aquilus, looking at Nathair proudly. 'How many were in this giant warband?' he asked, not for the first time.

'Four score,' Veradis mumbled, his mouth full of salty cheese.

'And they were mounted. On *draigs*?'

'Aye,' Nathair said. 'Veradis drew them onto a valley slope, weathered the brunt of their attack. You should have seen him, Father,' the Prince added, squeezing Veradis' shoulder. 'He has earned his title, thrice over.'

Veradis coloured under the approving looks of King Aquilus and his Queen.

'I charged them from behind,' Nathair continued. 'Veradis was the anvil, I the hammer.' He slammed his hand against the table with a crack, making his cup of wine jump.

Aquilus shook his head. 'Son, if I had known how many – and *draigs*. I never would have sent you.'

'No, you would not,' Fidele said, scowling at her husband.

'You have surpassed my hopes,' Aquilus continued. 'Well, the plan was for you and your warband to cut your teeth. I think we have accomplished that.'

'Ah, you remind me, Father,' Nathair said, reaching into a pouch at his belt. He held his hand out. A long, curved tooth sat there, longer than his palm was wide. 'It is a draig's tooth. A memento, Father, of the first campaign that you entrusted me to lead.'

Veradis' hand crept to his hip, a finger tracing the tooth that Nathair had given to him, set now in his sword hilt. The prince had given them to all of his warriors, the night before they had boarded Lykos' ships and left Tarbesh. Somehow it bound them even tighter to Nathair – if that was possible – filling them with a fierce pride. At the same time Nathair had sworn them all to secrecy concerning the Vin Thalun fleet.

Aquilus took the tooth, holding it up before him. 'Thank you,' he murmured.

There was a knock on the door.

'Enter,' Fidele called. Peritus swept into the room, smiling at them all. Aquilus gestured to a chair, and the battlechief sat. Veradis returned the greeting, but less warmly, remembering the doubts Peritus had voiced the day he had viewed the warband training. Nathair was colder still.

The King told Peritus of the campaign, the battlechief nodding and grunting as the tale unfolded.

'So, you see,' Aquilus said, 'your doubts were unfounded.'

'Aye. And I am glad they were,' Peritus said. 'I was only concerned for your safety,' he said to the Prince.

Nathair snorted. 'When is battle ever safe?'

'True enough. We can never *know* what may befall us in battle. But there are sureties that we can seek. That is Elyon's gift to us, no? Intellect. Choice. But, regardless, I have been proved wrong, and am glad about it.'

'Think nothing of it,' Nathair murmured. 'The man has not been born who is right *all* of the time.'

Laughter rippled around the room.

'I am surprised, though, at your speed. I had not reckoned on your return for at least another turn of the moon.'

'I was eager to return,' Nathair said. 'I drove my men hard, perhaps harder than I should have, but they are none the worse for it.'

He stood and groaned, stretching. 'I am for some hot water,' he said. 'Strip this dirt from my skin.'

'Of course,' said Aquilus.

'Come, Veradis,' said Nathair, turning and walking to the door. Veradis followed him.

'Nathair,' Aquilus called out; the Prince stopped, turned his head. 'I am most proud of you.'

Nathair stood there, eyes closed a moment, savouring this praise. 'Thank you, Father,' he said, then left.

Veradis walked quickly away from the weapons court, fastening his cloak around his shoulders as he went. A thin layer of snow now crunched under his boots and he pulled the cloak tighter. He was still sweating, blood pumping and various aches and pains only now making themselves known. He took a deep breath, slowly calming after his exertions on the court and touched a knuckle to his cheek, the skin swollen.

He ducked through the doors to the keep and slammed them shut on the snow, a blast of hot air hitting him as he walked into the feast-hall, carrying the smell of roasting meat, gravy, wine, sweat. It was always busy of late, the fortress filling with people gathering for Midwinter's Day. Where had the time gone? Three turns of the moon had passed already since Tarbesh; only six more nights until Midwinter and all that brought with it.

Quickly he filled a plate and found a space to sit alone with his back to the entrance.

The room grew noisier as more people came in. He heard footsteps, felt a slap on the shoulder and Rauca dropped onto the bench opposite him.

'There's a crowd still standing in the weapons court, freezing their knackers off, waiting to congratulate you,' the warrior said.

'Huh,' grunted Veradis.

'Why'd you sneak off?'

'I was cold, hungry, didn't see a reason to stay.'

'No reason to stay,' said Rauca, leaning forward. 'You just bested *Armatus*, man. I couldn't think of a *better* reason to stay. He's been weapons-master since I was twelve years old, and unbeaten long before that.'

Veradis shrugged. 'He's past his best, and this cold slows and stiffens old bones.'

Rauca shook his head. 'Past his best or no, there's no one else in all of Tenebral that's able to put a sword-tip to the man's throat. You should be enjoying your newfound glory, not looking like you're about to start weeping into your plate.'

'Aye,' Veradis sighed. Rauca was right, he knew, but something about the whole contest had tasted rotten.

Since Nathair's return to Jerolin there had been a growing, unvoiced tension between the Prince and Peritus, and this had spilt into their warbands. Armatus, the weapons-master, was a childhood friend of Peritus and had spoken out a few times against Nathair's new methods of training. Nathair had steered today's sparring contest between Armatus and Veradis, and although there had been no official recognition of the bout, almost every warrior within a five-league ride of the fortress had tried to view it.

Veradis would do anything for Nathair, give his own life, but there was something about this that he had not liked. He had felt manoeuvred. And, besides, he liked Armatus, and had felt little joy in beating him.

He raised a hand to his cheek and probed where Armatus had struck him. 'He gave about as good as he got,' he winced.

'No,' Rauca said firmly, shaking his head. 'I don't think so.' He winked at Veradis. 'You'll have a reputation to defend now. Every warrior that thinks himself handy with a blade will be wanting to make a name against you.'

Veradis grunted again, not liking where that thought took him.

A door banged nearby and he looked up. King Aquilus strode through the hall, stern faced, weary looking, the skin under his eyes tinged grey, the lines in his face more pronounced.

'Much rests on Midwinter's Day,' Rauca muttered, watching the King pass through the hall.

'Is there word of Mandros yet?' Veradis asked. The King of Carnutan had been invited back to Tenebral, to be in Aquilus' company for the witnessing of Meical's prophecy.

Rauca shrugged. 'I'll believe he's coming when I see him before me.'

Veradis nodded. He was not sure he wanted Mandros in the same place as Nathair, anyway, not with this talk of Mandros being a servant of Asroth . . .

'If he does come, I'm sure he'll be well guarded,' Rauca said, 'not that his shieldmen would be a problem to you.'

Veradis shook his head. 'Have you received a blow to the head? I am not one of the Ben-Elim.'

Rauca rocked in his chair, spluttering laughter. 'My friend, I do not think you see yourself as you really are. True, you are not as handsome as me . . .'

Veradis snorted.

'. . . and that broken nose you sport has not helped you there. But . . .' Rauca leaned forward now and gripped Veradis' wrist. 'Something happens to you when you draw a blade, even if it is only made from wood. You become *fearsome*.' His face grew more serious, intense. 'There is no one I would rather stand beside in battle, living or dead, than you.'

Veradis looked away.

'Asroth's teeth, man, you even stood your ground against a charge of angry draigs. I almost wet my trews, and I was only sneaking up behind them and prodding them with my spear.'

'I was too scared to move,' Veradis said, smiling a little. 'Besides, I was one of four hundred men. We all did what we had to do.'

'Aye, aye,' Rauca said, leaning back in his bench and shaking his head. 'You are a rare man indeed, Veradis ben Lamar. If I was you, I'd be standing on this table, proclaiming my greatness to all who would listen, and enjoying the attentions I'd won.'

'Then 'tis good you are not me,' Veradis said, smiling now.

'Aye, you are probably right.' Rauca bit into a leg of lamb, tore a strip of meat, juices trickling into his beard.

'So, where would you rather go?' he mumbled, mouth full.

'Go?'

'In the spring. To fight giants in Forn Forest or outlaws in . . . Where are they?'

'Ardan,' Veradis said.

'Yes, Ardan. Well?'

Veradis shrugged. 'I'll go wherever Nathair chooses.'

Rauca snorted. 'I know that. But where would you *rather* go? Forn is the darker campaign, eh? More giants. A harder task than rooting out brigands hiding in treetops.' He slurped from a cup of wine. 'But more glory fighting giants than men, I would guess.'

'Aye. I suppose so. I would not mind going to Forn Forest, though. I grew up beside the Sarva – one forest is much like another, I would think. And I made some friends who came from Isiltir, during the council. It would be good to see them again. You?'

Rauca shrugged. 'Remember that old man who taught me a lesson on the weapons court?'

'Aye. How could I forget.'

'He was from Ardan. Tull. I'd like a chance to even the score with him.'

'You sure you can?'

Rauca laughed.

'No point worrying about it,' Veradis said. 'We're warriors. We'll go where we're pointed.'

'Aye, true enough.' Rauca stood and cuffed his mouth. 'Talking of warriors, there's a fair few waiting for us. Time we went and knocked some more sense into our Prince's warband, eh?'

Veradis nodded, rose, chair legs scraping on the stone floor. The two friends walked from the hall into the soft-falling snow.

'You did well today,' said Nathair, reclining in an oak chair, torch-light flickering on the dark, shiny wood.

'I . . . thank you,' Veradis said, not meeting Nathair's eyes. He looked around instead.

They were in Nathair's chamber, a large stone room situated in Jerolin's tower, unshuttered windows looking out over the lake and plain. Night had fallen, lights from the village reflecting a faint glow from the snow-covered plain.

Long tapestries hung on Nathair's walls, from roof to floor. There was little furniture, other than an ornately carved bed, the two chairs they were sitting in, and a table with a platter of nuts and a jug of warmed wine standing on it.

'I have been unhappy with how Peritus has been disrespecting my warband. We have *earned* respect, have we not?' The Prince's hand rose to the long draig's tooth that hung on a leather cord about his neck.

'Aye, we have,' said Veradis.

'It would have been unseemly for me to stand against Armatus, or any of Peritus' supporters, but something had to be done. A statement had to be made. And what a statement.' The Prince took a handful of nuts from the bowl in front of him.

A silence grew between them, Nathair looking out of the window, systematically cracking nuts and eating them. 'Much will change after Midwinter's Day,' he eventually said. 'Once the prophecy has been fulfilled, things will be set in motion, choices made, and only half a ten-night away . . .'

'Is there news of Mandros?' Veradis asked.

Nathair sneered. 'No. He may come, he may not. I care little either way. I do not understand why Father runs after him, seeking his approval.'

'It worries me,' Veradis said, 'what Calidus said about him – serving Asroth, the Black Sun . . .'

'Maybe it *is* better that he come here. Friends close and enemies closer, isn't that the saying?' The Prince shrugged, worried. 'I have thought often of our time in Telassar and Mandros' behaviour.'

Veradis nodded. 'As have I.'

'The Jehar spoke of another that had come to them, making claims. Do you remember?'

'I do. But they spoke of sword-brothers deceived, of men that left Telassar. Looking for the Bright Star, I suppose. Looking for *you*.'

'Well, they have not found me,' Nathair said with a smile. 'But it troubles me. Warriors of the skill of the Jehar, loose in the Banished Lands, serving someone *else*.' He sighed. 'We need to find them.'

'We must talk to Calidus,' Veradis said.

'Aye. But he is not here, and my father, with his feelings about the Vin Thalun, means that it would not be wise to bring Calidus here, at this moment.'

'Nathair, perhaps you could speak of this with your father?'

Nathair shook his head, a single, curt movement.

'But, why not? Surely it would make things easier on you. It is *you* that he is waiting for, after all, he just does not know it yet. Tell him.'

'No.'

Nathair drew in a deep breath, his body tense. 'I spoke to you once, of living under someone else's shadow. Do you remember?'

343

'Aye. On the journey when we met Calidus.'

'Yes. That shadow was, *is*, my father's imagining of the Bright Star. This fabled person that he has spent his life waiting for, preparing for.' He smiled. 'Ironic, don't you think, that it is me?'

'Tell him,' Veradis urged again.

'No. I cannot. Father has believed for so long that this person is a stranger, that he will come to *us*. He would not believe me. Things are good between us, better than they have ever been. I have longed for him to look at me as he does now . . .' he trailed off. 'I would not risk that. Not yet . . .'

Veradis could understand that, thought suddenly of his own da. He had felt just as Nathair, once. No longer, though. His feelings for his father were buried deep, complex and without joy.

'But, he is *wrong*. It is you that Elyon has chosen; *you* that Elyon speaks to.'

Nathair shrugged. 'Aye. But he must realize this in his own time. The truth will out – as he is so fond of saying.'

'Yes, including how we travelled to Tarbesh. The men have kept your secret so far, but how much longer? It would be better if he heard these things from you, surely. And, Nathair, things would be so different if he realized, if he knew that you are the Bright Star.'

Nathair held a hand up. 'He has been set in this a long time, Veradis. There is time. I will *give* him time, before I need assert my station.'

A gust of cold air blew through the open window. Torchlight flickered across Nathair's face, sheets of darkness and light sweeping the contours of his features.

Veradis thought of Meical, his pale, enigmatic face, his dark eyes. The King's counsellor. *He* was the key to Aquilus' stance on the prophecy.

A soft tapping on the door startled them both.

'Enter,' Nathair called.

Fidele opened the door, closing it quietly behind her. She paused when she saw Veradis.

'I had hoped to speak with you,' she said to Nathair.

'Of course, Mother. I was just sharing a jug of warm wine with Veradis.' He smiled. Veradis stood and offered Fidele his chair.

'No, thank you,' she said. There was a tightness in her voice and face.

'What is it, Mother?' Nathair said. 'What troubles you?'

Fidele glanced at Veradis. 'I thought I would find you alone,' she said.

'Whatever you would say to me, you can say in front of Veradis. He is as a brother to me.'

'Very well, then,' she said, with the slightest of shrugs. 'I have heard unsettling things. Rumours.'

'Oh?' said Nathair.

'Of your campaign, in Tarbesh.'

Nathair remained silent, waiting.

The Queen drew in a breath. 'I have heard talk of sorcery, of giants, numbered amongst *your* warband; talk of enchanted mists, of a mysterious fleet of ships. I have heard the Vin Thalun spoken of.'

Mother and son stared at each other.

'Who has said these things?' he said. 'Peritus? You know he seeks to undermine me, fears my growing authority.'

'It matters not where I heard these rumours,' Fidele snapped. 'Are they true?'

'Where did you hear these things?' Nathair repeated. 'If there was truth in these, these *tales*, why are they whispered behind my back? I would see my accuser.'

Doubt touched Fidele's eyes. 'So, you deny them?' she said, her voice less firm. Hopeful.

'I deny nothing. I am a man grown now, a prince. A child no longer. I will make judgements, decisions as I see fit. And I would know who seeks to slander me, who seeks to drive a wedge between my father and me.'

The queen shook her head. 'Nathair, do not forget all that I said to you, before you left. If you have any involvement, any ties with the Vin Thalun, lay them aside. It will go ill with you, if, *when* your father knows the truth of it.' She stood tall, queenly now and cold. 'You are prince, not king. A son, not a father. Obey your King, obey your father in this. Do not seek to test him. These times are heavy enough on him without his own son . . .' She looked troubled. 'Do what is right,' she said, almost pleading now, then left.

'I shall,' Nathair whispered to the closed door.

CHAPTER FORTY-THREE

CORBAN

Corban squinted as he looked up at the cloudless sky, the sun a pale, watery, distant thing.

It was cold; his skin felt tight. Snow was coming, thick, heavy clouds gathering on the horizon beyond the distant line of the coast and out over the iron-grey sea.

This was not the weather to be travelling in, but here he was, six nights out from Dun Carreg, riding on the giantsway with King Brenin at the head of their column.

They were heading for Badun, a fortress close to the stone circle, to witness the prophecy that Edana had told him of, when day becomes night. Apparently Rhin, Queen of Cambren, as well as the kings of Narvon and Domhain would be there, come at Brenin's call to discuss the clearing of the Darkwood, along with other issues, all related somehow to the council in Tenebral that King Brenin had attended.

They had travelled east for five nights, skirting the surf-beaten coast of steep, sharp-faced cliffs and hidden coves. Today the road had veered southwards, passing around a treacherous space of marsh and bog. As the road sloped gently downwards Corban saw the fenland spread out before him, water sparkling in the weak sunlight like a huge dew-covered cobweb laid out upon the land, a hill and broken tower standing at its centre. He glanced to his side. Brina rode next to him, saying something unpleasant – if the expression on her face was anything to go by – to Heb the loremaster, who had ridden close to her since they had set out at daybreak.

There was a dark blur on the horizon.

'What is that?' Corban asked.

'That is the Darkwood,' said Heb.

The shadow that was the Darkwood stretched from the coast across the horizon as far as he could see. *Braith is in there. And Camlin, if they made it*, Corban thought, gazing at the distant forest.

Instinctively his eyes sought out Marrock and found him further up the grey-cloaked column, riding beside Halion and Conall. Not much further on, King Brenin rode at their head, the hulking forms of Pendathran and Tull flanking him, his daughter Edana just behind, shadowed by Ronan as always. 'How does your wolven cope with our journey?' Heb asked, pulling him out of his thoughts.

He glanced down at Storm, who loped alongside him, head down, muzzle close to the ground.

'It has been no problem to her,' Corban said. 'I think she likes it.'

The wolven had run alongside him every day, matching their speed effortlessly; but that did not surprise him: she was still growing, her shoulders only a few handspans below his horse's back. He leaned in his saddle, his fingertips just brushing the coarse hairs of her neck. He was glad of her company. The nights were cold, but he was sure that he was by far the warmest every night, with Storm curled up close to him.

He shivered and pulled his cloak tighter. When Princess Edana had first told of the journey to the stone circle, he had longed to go, and had not believed his good fortune when Brina had told him she required his assistance. He was not so sure now – six nights sleeping in the cold and days in the saddle had done much to erode his enthusiasm.

Still, they were close to their journey's end, and he was beginning to feel that first excitement spark inside again.

His mother had not wanted him to go, had forbidden him, in fact, until Brina had spoken to her. Officially Brina was going because she was King Brenin's most renowned healer, but Corban knew that she wanted to go, so that was that. And as her apprentice he would have to accompany her. Once Brina had spoken to his mam about it, then suddenly Gar *had* to go, to look after Brenin's mount, but he suspected it was more about looking after *him*. At least Gar coming meant that Cywen did as well. She had looked as if she'd swallowed a bee when Corban told her he was going and she was not, but the stablemaster's sudden decision had given her just the leverage she needed. Gar in turn had gathered stablehands for the trip, and Cywen had managed to have Dath included. To Corban it felt as if half of Dun Carreg was riding to Badun.

He glanced over his shoulder at Gar on his piebald stallion, but could not see Cywen or Dath amongst the press of warriors.

The day passed slowly, snow beginning to fall, and as dusk eventually spread around them the snow grew thicker, clinging insistently to the land. It grew darker and torches were lit, Brenin choosing to ride on as their destination was close.

Suddenly there was a call from the front of the column and the line halted. There were riders in the road ahead – two? huddled closely around Brenin.

They stood there a while, snow settling on Corban's shoulders and the cold seeping through his cloak until the column lurched forwards. The riders fell in close to Corban. One was clearly a warrior, a scabbard poking out from under his cloak. Corban saw his face briefly in his cowl, pale, with dark, sunken eyes. The other appeared to be a woman, slighter of frame. Corban caught a hint of red hair in the torchlight.

Not long after, they saw lights in the distance. Badun, last dwelling within Ardan before the Darkwood and the Kingdom of Narvon.

'No time for that,' Gar said to Corban as he saw him reaching for a honey-cake. 'You can break your fast later; I need another pair of hands. *If* Brina can do without you for a while?'

Brina snorted, waved a hand dismissively at Corban, and so he found himself trudging through the snow, following Gar's limping gait, Storm leaving a trail of pawprints behind them.

The fortress of Badun had grown large because of its position guarding the giantsway that led through the Darkwood into the kingdoms of Narvon and Cambren beyond.

Dath and Cywen stood at the doors to a huge barn, filling buckets of water from a barrel. Cywen smiled at Corban as they drew near.

'You have an audience,' she said, looking over his shoulder.

A group of children had gathered and were following at a distance, pointing and whispering.

'Not me. Storm,' Corban said. People had grown accustomed to the wolven at Dun Carreg and Havan, but here was a different matter. It was only because he rode with the King that he had even been allowed to enter the fortress, many warriors scowling and making the sign against evil as he had passed through the gates. Not all thought it so terrible, including most of the children that lived at Badun, apparently.

'You are making a name for yourself,' commented Gar.

Corban shrugged and began helping Cywen.

The feast-hall was emptying when Corban arrived with his sister. But close to the firepit sat the Princess, Ronan filling a plate for her. Edana beckoned to them.

'I'll get yours,' Ronan said, smiling at Cywen.

'Father's grumpy,' Edana said, nodding towards a corner of the hall. King Brenin stood with a small group of men: Tull and Pendathran were there, along with Evnis and Vonn. Corban had been thankful to see little of the counsellor's son since that day in the paddock, when Helfach's hound had been killed. Brenin was talking to a tall, blond-haired man, his long warrior braid touched with silver. He had an open, likeable face, and was smiling at the King.

'Is that . . .'

'Gethin,' said Edana, nodding.

Corban frowned. Gethin was Lord of Badun, but he was also Evnis' elder brother, and so Corban automatically disliked him regardless of his appearance.

Ronan put a bowl of porridge in front of Corban, berries and cream for Edana and a plate of hot oatcakes, bacon and thick-buttered bread before Cywen. Corban looked between his bowl and the other bounty on offer, frowned. Cywen smiled a thank you at Ronan.

'King Owain is here,' Edana said quietly, 'with his son, Uthan. The others haven't arrived yet.'

'But Midwinter's Day is tomorrow,' said Cywen.

The Princess nodded. 'That's why Father is grumpy. He thinks Rhin plays games with him, though King Eremon has not arrived either. But he has much further to travel, all the way from Domhain, beyond Narvon *and* Cambren. And he is *ancient*, apparently.'

'Do you think they'll agree?' Cywen said. 'To your father's plan?'

'I don't know.' Edana shrugged. 'Owain *should*, as Braith raids his borders too, but he often likes to disagree with Father just for the sake of disagreeing. As for the others: Rhin and Eremon have less cause to commit to clearing the Darkwood. After all, Braith does not raid *their* lands.'

'There is more to it all than clearing the Darkwood, though, isn't there?' Cywen said. 'This prophecy . . .'

Edana nodded. 'Father said that day will become night, at high-sun tomorrow, whatever that means. I cannot imagine such a thing.' She toyed with a spoonfull of berries on her plate. 'It is supposed to signify something about a war between Elyon and Asroth, about it being fought here in the Banished Lands.'

'Who are *they*?' Cywen whispered.

Two figures had entered the hall, those that had joined them on the roadside. The man was young, pale-faced, dark rings under his eyes, a warrior braid in his hair. His eyes read the room as he ushered his companion to sit – an older woman, red-haired with streaks of grey.

'I'm not sure who they are. I asked Father, but he wouldn't tell me.' Edana ducked her head closer, conspiratorially. 'I think they asked Father for Sanctuary.'

If these two had come to King Brenin seeking Sanctuary, they would not be the first to be drawn by his reputation. Halion had told him that he and his brother had done the same. The weapons-master had been most tight mouthed, though, about what exactly they were running from.

'So, we must wait and see if Rhin and Eremon arrive, if your father's hopes are to succeed.' He pushed cold porridge round his bowl.

'Aye,' muttered Ronan.

'Much depends on them,' Edana said.

A column of riders filed out of the Darkwood; Corban counted some four score as he stood on the wooden palisade that ringed Badun.

'There's Queen Rhin,' Edana said, pointing, as they drew nearer to the town's open gates. 'There, with the white hair.'

Rhin rode close to the front, a half-dozen warriors before her, tall spears couched upright in their saddles. A warrior rode beside her, young, handsome, exuding confidence. He laughed as the Queen commented on something, more akin to a courtier on an excursion, than guard to the Queen of Cambren. 'I don't see King Eremon,' Edana muttered.

'He is not come, but he sends others in his place,' Ronan said. 'Those on the grass – they wear the green of Domhain.'

The rider at the front of the group, cantering ahead of the others, was old, grey hair streaming behind him. He did not wear the torc of a king about his neck, only a thin band of twisted silver around his arm. As Corban watched one of the riders with him lifted a banner bearing the outlines of black wolves on a red field.

'Rath,' Ronan breathed.

Corban had heard of the old warrior, battlechief once to Eremon. Giants had raided out of the north, slain all in his hold. Rath had sworn vengeance, pledged himself to the defence of Domhain's northern border, so that he might have more chance to avenge himself on the giants who had slain his kin. If the tales were true the old warrior had fulfilled his oath many times over.

The men that rode with him, the Degad, were as famous for their prowess as he – rumoured to be as fierce and savage as the giants they hunted.

Rhin looked up as she reached the walls, a faint smile visible as she passed from view.

CHAPTER FORTY-FOUR

EVNIS

It is good to be alone. Pretending to like my brother is so draining. Evnis stood with hands clasped behind his back, staring at the cairn. His mother was in there, beside his father, long dead, just bones now. His mouth twisted and he spat. He wished she still lived, so that she could see his triumph, his ascension. First he would eclipse Gethin, his fawning brother, seeking to match his daughter to Uthan, King Owain's son. Once that would have angered him, but no longer: let him have his small victories. Greater things were in store for Evnis, of that there was no doubt. He had made his bargain, sworn his allegiance many years ago, in a dell in the Darkwood. And now he was counsellor to a king, had the earth power at his fingertips, and more . . .

The necklace, with the black stone. It scared him, but called to him, too. He had studied it, searched the old manuscripts, even talked to that fool Heb. He was sure, now, what it was. One of the seven Treasures, Nemain's necklace. It had great power, but how to tap it, use it . . .?

He squeezed his eyes shut. He was tired, sleep becoming elusive of late, and when he did find it, there were always the dreams, troubling dreams that he would wake sweating and anxious from. He must keep his wits about him; there was so much to do.

Seeing Rhin had been good, seeing her riding through the gates of Badun seemed to make all the plans and schemes real, suddenly. She had smiled at him, though not in the way she used to. That was reserved for the young warrior riding at her side. *Probably for the best*, he sighed. *Rhin's appetites are voracious. I doubt I could keep up, any longer*. Besides, it would feel like a betrayal to Fain, even though she was dead.

He felt the pain of her loss again, suddenly, just at the thought of her. Would it ever diminish?

He heard voices and stepped back into the shadows of his parents' cairn. Two men, warriors, coming closer. Halion and Conall, he realized. Two men he wished were in his service. He could always use good swords. But the elder, Halion, seemed unapproachable. He'd met the man's like before, morally *inflexible*. His brother, Conall, however. Now there was a man that could be worked on. Pride is a brittle master.

'I will not run and hide like some *girl* . . .' Conall was saying.

'Use your head, Con,' his brother said. 'We cannot let him see us. No one knows where we are, who we serve, and it needs to stay that way . . .' Then they were past him, continuing their hissed conversation.

Interesting . . .

Evnis allowed the shadows to mask him a while longer, then started walking. *I must get word to Rhin, of Brenin's latest act of charity. She will be eager to hear about the two who rode in with Brenin, having begged him for Sanctuary. Sanctuary from Rhin.*

CHAPTER FORTY-FIVE

CORBAN

Brina had been given an empty cottage to stay in whilst they were in Badun and, after seeing the cramped sleeping quarters of most of their party, Corban was, for once, grateful to be linked to the healer. That sense of gratitude had been short lived, though, as she had made him sweep the cottage from top to bottom.

She had told, rather than asked, Cywen and Gar to share the small cottage with her and Corban and they were also only too happy to obey.

Corban stepped into the night, following Gar and his sister, Brina close behind him. Corban was sure he heard a rustle of feathers and saw a black, beady eye from the raftered shadows within the cottage as the door snapped shut.

Soon the thick wooden walls of the feast-hall loomed out of the darkness, pitch-soaked torches burning bright around the wide doors. They were some of the first to arrive, Brina keen to eavesdrop on the high table.

The hall started to fill, people trickling in at first, then in greater numbers and soon it was thrumming with conversation and laughter. Dath rushed in and sat with Corban, as did Tull with a clutch of Dun Carreg's warriors about him. Then those at the high table took their places, after kings Brenin and Owain.

Rhin was the last to enter, a sable cloak about her shoulders, trimmed in white fox fur. The Queen of Cambren claimed her place at the high table, then made a show of insisting that her debonair young champion take a seat beside her. He was quick to ascend. Corban heard grumbling ripple through the hall, saw warriors frown.

Champions were not supposed to sit at the high table; it was a privilege reserved for lords and their close kin.

Ronan pushed a way through the feasting crowds, making a path for Edana. When she was seated the young warrior scanned the room, came and sat on the other side of Corban, winking at Cywen. The warrior smiled as she flushed red.

Then movement at the back of the hall caught Corban's attention, a hooded figure entering late, standing in shadow. Rhin's champion rose and made his way through the hall, left with the newcomer. Suddenly a loud banging filled the hall, drawing all eyes to the high table. Lord Gethin was standing, cracking a spoon on the base of a wooden plate.

'Welcome to my hall and my table,' Gethin said in a loud voice. 'We stand in the highest company the west has to offer, upon the eve of a momentous occasion.' His eyes flickered to Brenin.

'I have an announcement, something that will add to the joy of this gathering, I hope.' He looked to the young woman that had followed him to the table. 'Stand, Kyla,' he said.

Hesitantly she did, eyes downcast. A chair scraped further along the high table and Uthan stood also.

'Today, my daughter has been betrothed to Uthan ben Owain,' Gethin said with a grin. Many in the hall cheered, cups banging on tables. But King Brenin's face pinched into a slight frown. Quietly Rhin's champion returned to his chair, leaning over to whisper in the Queen's ear. Her expression clouded.

'They will be handbound in the spring. I hope their union will be a mark of closer relations with our kin in Narvon.' Gethin looked at King Owain, who nodded.

Beside Corban, Heb the loremaster muttered something to Brina.

'Circles within circles,' she said.

Suddenly Rhin stood, her chair falling behind her.

'Where are they?' she hissed, pointing a clawed finger at Brenin. He looked back at her, meeting the venom in her glare, but said nothing.

'Do not play me for a fool,' Rhin said, almost spitting in her fury, 'I knew you when you wet your bed every night.' Chuckles sprinkled the hall. 'Do not cross me in this. I know they are here. You will give them over to me. Now.'

Brenin closed his eyes and blew out a slow, deep breath. When he opened them again his face was firm, resolute.

'They are not your property, Rhin. And they have asked me for Sanctuary.'

Rhin's face was cold, almost frightening. 'Have you granted it?' she whispered, though all in the hall heard.

Brenin nodded. 'Aye.'

There was a moment of silence, Rhin absolutely still. 'Very well. The Court of Swords will decide this. Morcant,' she said, glancing at her champion.

He rose fluidly, smiling. Suddenly Tull was on his feet as well, stepping into the space between the crowd and high table.

'What? No, no. Rhin, you must not do this,' Brenin said, standing as well.

'*Must not?* You forget yourself.'

'But tomorrow – our pact . . .'

'You should have thought of that,' she snapped, cutting him off. 'I will have what is rightfully mine. And I will not bargain or plead with you, Brenin.'

Brenin opened his mouth, but Rhin's tirade could not be staunched. 'You summon us, *me*, like vassals to your gathering. Well, I came, but you go too far, you and your *honour*. You shall reap what you sow. Surely your father taught you that.' She fastened her eyes on her champion.

The young warrior nodded, and moved to face Tull.

'The Court of Swords will decide this matter. Now,' Rhin said.

Brenin scowled, gripping the table. 'So be it.'

Tull strode forward, drew his own sword and touched it to Morcant's waiting blade, accepting the challenge.

Morcant laughed. Tull shrugged and stepped backwards, eyes on Rhin's champion. The air whistled as he chopped his sword through the air, rolling his huge shoulders.

The room exploded into noise as people jumped from their tables, forming a half-ring around the two men. Coins chinked as wagers were exchanged. Corban stood in the front row and people took care not to jostle him because of Storm, who eyed the two warriors with suspicion.

Corban could not believe what was happening. His heart was pounding in his chest; he had never seen a duel before. Plenty of sword-crossings and sparring sessions with padded or wooden blades, but not with sharp, death-dealing swords of iron. He was suddenly scared, and excited too. Tull's reputation was massive, and seeing him in the flesh it was impossible to imagine him ever being bested, yet there was something about Rhin's champion. His confidence was unnerving.

A hush fell as the two champions approached the high table. Tull bent, grabbed a handful of ash from the corner of the firepit and rubbed it into the hilt of his sword. They bowed to Rhin and Brenin, then turned to face each other.

Corban expected them to rush each other, to beat at each other, but they didn't. Morcant walked slowly around Tull, the older man turning with him, his sword-tip held low. Suddenly Morcant darted forwards, sword snaking out, almost faster than Corban's eye could follow, but Tull met the lunge with little effort, turning his block into a swing of his own, his blade whistling through air as Morcant danced lightly backwards. He settled back into his slow walk around the big champion, lunging in, fast as a striking snake once more, then again.

'They seek each other's measure,' Gar whispered to Corban. He nodded, but could not speak or move his eyes from the contest before him. Then Morcant was moving forwards, not with a single stroke as before, but a blurring combination of slashes and lunges. Tull met each one, stepping backwards until he was close to the ring's edge. Corban could see sweat on the big man's bare shoulders, stains on his leather vest.

Tull grunted with each block, feet planted, then stepped nimbly aside, Morcant's blade slicing through air. Rhin's champion staggered forwards a half-step, and suddenly he was on the defensive, retreating before Tull's looping, powerful strokes. Corban resisted the urge to cover his ears as the iron blades clashed and rang.

Brenin's champion was almost a head taller than Morcant, strong as an ox but also fast for a big man. His attack was relentless, and suddenly Morcant's mocking smile was gone, his face drawn in concentration as he met each of Tull's blows, every one powerful enough to gut a boar. But Rhin's champion was quick, with an iron strength in his leaner frame. He parried an overhead slash, pushing Tull's sword away and down, stepped close, inside the big man's guard and spun away, cutting backwards with his blade. The tip cut into Tull's waist, drawing the first blood of the contest. Corban gasped.

'You bleed like the rest of us, then,' Morcant said, his smile returning.

Tull touched his fingers to his waist, drew them away red, snarled, attacked again. Morcant retreated under another withering barrage, somehow managing to fend off the flurry of great two-handed strokes. Tull slowed briefly and Morcant lunged, forcing Tull backwards again.

The two warriors fought back and forth across the ring, Corban losing all track of time, flickering flames from the firepit making the warriors look like fiends, like Asroth's Kadoshim themselves. Eventually they broke away from each other, stepping back in some unspoken agreement. Both were sucking in great lungfulls of air. Tull's waist was soaked with blood, a thin line of red ran down his shield arm, from shoulder to elbow. Morcant was unmarked.

Tull snorted, gathered his energies. He battered Morcant backwards, then swung an overhead blow. Part-way through, he suddenly released his blade, snatched it with his left hand and slashed it diagonally instead of vertically. Somehow Morcant managed to change the angle of his block, but Tull's blade still raked him from shoulder to navel, leaving a welling red line in its wake.

'Ah-ha, old man,' Morcant said, stepping out of range. 'You are too famous for your own good. I have heard of all your tricks.'

For the first time Tull seemed hesitant. Corban glanced at Brenin, tearing his eyes away from the two champions. The King's face was taut, worried.

Iron clashing on iron drew him back. Morcant was pressing the attack now, his sword slashing and lunging in a blur. Tull retreated, an edge of wildness, of desperation in his movements as he blocked and turned the hail of blows. Blood welled on his forearm as Morcant's blade nicked him, then across his chest, his thigh. His back slammed into an oak pillar. Morcant slashed again, sparks flying as their swords grated until they were standing chest to chest, wrist to wrist, locked for a moment.

'Soon, old man,' Morcant grunted.

With a heave, Tull shoved Morcant away. Rhin's champion staggered back out of range, but Tull did not follow. Instead he leaned one hand on his thigh, braced his sword-tip into the floor, dragging in deep, ragged breaths.

'I must – confess,' he gasped, 'you are – quite good.'

Morcant smiled, stood tall. He was weary, but not as tired as Tull. 'Ready to die, old man?'

'Not yet,' Tull said through gritted teeth. He flicked his wrist, his sword-point flinging rushes and earth into Morcant's face.

Rhin's champion grasped at his eyes, stepping backwards, raising his sword to protect his head and chest, but Tull did not strike there. He stepped forwards, swinging his sword low and hard into Morcant's booted ankle. There was a loud crack, Morcant wobbling for a moment, then he crashed to the ground. Tull leaped forwards, trod hard on Morcant's sword wrist and levelled his blade at the fallen man's chest.

'My King?' Tull said, not taking his eyes from Morcant's.

There was utter silence, broken only by the loud breaths of the two champions and the crackle of flames. Corban's palms were clammy with sweat. He held his breath. All eyes turned to Brenin, knowing Tull asked his lord's sentence.

The King of Ardan bowed his head, looked at Rhin.

'Let him live,' he said.

Tull was still a moment, then he shrugged, spat blood and saliva into the rushes by Morcant's head.

'As you wish,' he said, lifting the tip of his sword away from Morcant's chest. He traced a line up the man's neck, over his chin, rested the point on his cheekbone, flicked his wrist, cutting a deep line below Morcant's eye.

'Here endeth the lesson,' Tull said, then turned and limped from the hall, Tarben and a handful of warriors from Dun Carreg hastening after him.

Rhin glared at Brenin and pulled her cloak about her. 'I seem to have lost my appetite,' she said, and left, not even glancing at her fallen champion.

CHAPTER FORTY-SIX

VERADIS

Veradis brushed his horse's flank, the slow rhythmic movement helping to calm him. He felt anxious.

It was Midwinter's Eve. Four nights had passed since he had witnessed the confrontation between Nathair and Fidele. Nothing related to Fidele's warning had actually *happened* since then but its potential seemed to hover over Veradis like a bad dream, always there and just out of view.

The things that Fidele had said were true, and so it was surely only a matter of time before Aquilus heard the same rumours and confronted Nathair.

The truth will out.

That was not a confrontation he wanted to witness. Nathair had said that he was going to tell Aquilus, talk to him about the Vin Thalun and their uses. He was just waiting for the right time. Veradis hoped it would be before Aquilus heard from some other source.

And then, tomorrow was Midwinter's Day. Would the sun *really* turn black?

He had never doubted Nathair, and that included the prediction of tomorrow's events. And of course he had *seen* Calidus transformed, although the memory of it felt distant, insubstantial, somehow, like a fading dream. And tomorrow was so central, so pivotal to everything that had happened since Aquilus' council, as if all led to this one moment. This moment that would mark the beginning of – what? A new age, Nathair called it. Word had reached them that all over the Banished Lands kings and queens were gathering. But what if the sun did not turn black?

He had heard tales of similar omens. A blood-red star in the sky, falling to earth had supposedly heralded Elyon's Scourging, when the world had been a different place, even a different *shape*, but that was just a tale. Over a thousand years the Exiles had dwelt in the Banished Lands, with no talk of wars between Elyon and Asroth, no unnatural signs in the sky.

He sighed and rested his head against his grey's neck. 'What will the morrow bring?' he muttered. He shook himself and set to pulling knots from the horse's mane.

What will be, will be, he thought. *One thing is sure: come what may, I am the Prince's man. I will follow his lead.*

The sun rose into a clear sky on Midwinter's Day, a bitter wind blowing from the mountains, the land froze iron hard. It was mid-morning when Veradis stood in the hall outside Nathair's chamber. He waited there a while, then straightened his shoulders and knocked on the door.

Nathair answered quickly. A sable cloak draped his shoulders, the white eagle of Tenebral standing bright on a black polished breast-plate. His short sword hung at his hip.

'Ready?' the Prince said, grinning at Veradis.

'Aye.'

'Are many gathered?'

'Some, though your father has not yet left the keep.'

'Good. Come, then,' Nathair said, striding down the hallway.

They found Aquilus and Fidele in the feast-hall, a small crowd gathered about them. Peritus was there, as was Armatus, the weapons-master. Although Veradis had bested him recently, the grizzled warrior was still King Aquilus' first-sword.

King Mandros of Carnutan stood in conversation with Aquilus, a sour look etched on his face. He had arrived late the previous day and still looked worn from the journey, dark rings under his eyes. News of their first meeting had spread through the fortress, Man-dros all but accusing Aquilus of setting the Vin Thalun loose on his realm. Veradis eyed him suspiciously. He did not like the thought of enemies allowed so close to Nathair and Aquilus. His gaze lingered on Mandros' sword.

A tall figure stood beside Fidele. Meical had returned.

The King's counsellor had been absent since before they had left for Tarbesh. It was unusual for a counsellor to be away so much, but it was Aquilus' choice to send him on such lengthy quests. When Veradis had mentioned it to Nathair he had only replied that his father was strong minded and took little counsel anyway. It was fitting, though, that the tall man should be here today. After all, it was he who had found the book that had drawn them all to this point.

Meical leaned forward and whispered something to Aquilus as Nathair and Veradis approached. The King swung round, eyes fixing onto his son.

'Father,' said Nathair, bowing his head. 'The day long awaited is finally here.'

'Aye,' Aquilus said curtly. 'Come, let us find a place on the walls, the better to see it.'

They filed out of the keep, a warrior escort waiting beyond, and made their way to the battlements that ringed the fortress, climbing the wide, giant-crafted steps to look out upon the plain and lake.

Scores of people stood on the lake shore, and the battlements and streets of Jerolin were crowded, everyone looking upwards.

The sun was high now, bright in a pale blue sky. Everything looked normal.

Veradis swallowed, his mouth dry. He looked around, saw stable-master Valyn standing further along the battlements, also staring skyward. He scratched his head, tried to stifle a yawn as he scanned the crowd, eyes coming to rest on Meical. He stood almost a head taller than anyone else in the crowd, the scars on his face silver in the daylight. Unlike most, he was not looking at the sun. He looked around the crowd, studying, measuring everything, everyone, his eyes eventually fixing on Veradis. Seeing the warrior watching him, he returned the gaze, his expression unreadable. Veradis thought of Nathair's words, of the part Meical had played in Aquilus' plans.

The dark-haired man looked away, gazing upwards.

Suddenly, almost collectively, the crowd gasped. Veradis' head jerked up, staring at the sun, shielding his eyes.

Through the glare he saw something, an indentation, on the sun's western rim. He blinked and rubbed his eyes. The mark was still there when he looked again, appearing like a curved finger caressing the sun's edge.

People cried out, pointing. Slowly, the black smudge grew,

spreading like a stain across the disc of the sun. He shivered, blew out a long breath and saw it mist in the air before him. It was colder, dramatically more than when he had climbed the steps to the battlement.

A sound, a movement caught his eye. Meical had staggered, was clutching at the black stone of the battlement. Beside Veradis, Nathair muttered something and leaned against him.

'Are you well?' Veradis said, suddenly worried.

Nathair collapsed.

CHAPTER FORTY-SEVEN

CORBAN

Corban gazed up at the sky, wondering what, if anything, was going to happen. The snow clouds were gone now, the sky a sharp blue, the sun pale and weak. He was stood close to the stone circle, amongst a crowd of onlookers. Brenin, Owain, Rhin and Rath were within the tall stones, though there was an icy gap between Rhin and Brenin.

Corban was still filled with the excitement of the duel between Tull and Morcant. Both men were standing close to the circle, though Morcant had his head bowed, the cut on his cheek stitched now, raw and angry.

Suddenly something changed. It was colder, Corban's goose-fleshing. People were shouting, pointing. He squinted at the sun, saw a shadow creeping across it, like a veil being drawn. He felt light-headed, dizzy, and he staggered. Cywen was beside him, caught his arm and snorted in annoyance. Then his legs were too weak to support him and he was falling, his vision fading.

He was alone, still at the stone circle. He walked into it, turning as he did so, looking all about. All was the same, yet different. Mist swirled about his feet. The sky was grey, the sun a leached, colour-less *brightness* behind thin clouds. The stones seemed taller, more ominous, somehow, the Darkwood an impenetrable shadow before him.

A figure appeared from those shadows, the man he had seen before, marching towards him, an urgency in his stride, his cloak billowing behind him.

'It is time,' the man said, smiling warmly as he drew near. 'I have given you all the time that can be spared. Will you help me?'

'Where am I?' Corban mumbled.

'The Otherworld. The place of spirit,' the man said.

'And who are you?'

The man smiled, his eyes creasing. 'Your friend.' A smell touched Corban, *decay*, thick and cloying. 'Help me.'

'I-I don't know,' Corban said.

The man grimaced, his mouth tightening. 'I have been patient, but I cannot wait any longer. You are not my only option, you know.' He gestured in the air.

Corban saw a figure, transparent but clear, a curly-haired man, handsome, with striking blue eyes. He was walking alone on a battlement, staring out into an empty plain. Cords, *chains*, were wrapped around the man's wrists and ankles, though loosely, moving with him as he walked. Corban felt a sharp stab of worry for the man. *He is ensnared, yet does not know it.* A wind gusted and the figure melted away.

'Others can help me, but I want *you*.' The last word was almost a growl. 'You must make a stand, fight for what is right. Fight for me. If not, you will fight for someone else, eventually. I will not let that happen.' Suddenly Corban felt scared.

'I have no use for cowards,' the man continued. 'Courage is what I need. I can see the fear in you, can smell it.' He took a long, languid breath, his tongue flickering out, as if *tasting* the air. 'You must face your fear, defeat it. Do not be afraid of the task I set you.'

'It is not the task that I fear,' Corban said, looking into those ancient, amber eyes. 'It is you.'

The man frowned. 'That is a shame.' He looked genuinely saddened. His hand reached inside his cloak, resting on a sword hilt. Corban saw he was wearing a coat of chainmail, dark and oily, but as he stared, it flickered, looking for a moment like *scales*.

'I have been patient. Decide. Now. Will you help me?'

'I will not,' Corban said, not knowing why; just that every sense within him was screaming '*No!*' at the man before him.

The man sighed, shook his head and drew his sword. Black smoke coiled around the blade.

Corban turned and ran.

Behind him the man screamed, full of rage.

There was a sudden rushing of air, the sound of beating wings, and figures dropped to the earth about him, the wind from their leathery wings almost knocking him from his feet. Six of them, all wearing dark mail, carrying smoke-wreathed weapons, sword, axe, spear. Their faces were human-like, though sharp featured, with slitted, reptilian eyes. They converged on him, barring his path.

'Please,' Corban whispered.

'Too late for that,' the yellow-eyed man said behind him.

A strange sound rang out from somewhere above – a horn call? Corban looked up, saw figures bursting through the clouds. They sped towards him, like arrows loosed from a bow, growing from pinpricks to man-size in moments.

'The Ben-Elim,' growled one of the figures nearby.

They alighted about Corban, broad wings of white feathers folding behind them; without a word they fell into savage combat with the creatures about him.

The ferocity of it stunned Corban. There was no posturing or negotiating, only a primal, feral violence. One white-feathered warrior hacked through a shoulder, the blow continuing through a leathery wing. The creature screamed, collapsed writhing to the ground, black smoke issuing from the wound. A head rolled on the floor before Corban; all about him the clash of arms, grunts and battle cries of combat. Two figures took to the air, clawing, gouging at each other.

Hands grasped Corban and suddenly he was being lifted into the air, great white wings propelling him skywards. He twisted but was held firm.

'Be still,' a voice growled in his ear.

He looked into a grim, battle-scarred face, dark, purple-tinged eyes staring back at him. A hand reached out, touched his temple and he heard whispered words, then all faded into darkness.

His eyes fluttered open. It was mostly dark, a soft light seeping into the edges of his vision.

Where am I?

He blinked, saw wooden beams condense, take shape in the darkness above, and realized he was lying on his back.

Slowly he lifted his head and rose onto his elbows, tried to move his feet, but found that he couldn't.

A noise broke out above him, a flapping, a squawking.

'*Awake, awake, awake,*' rasped a harsh voice somewhere up in the rafters. A door opened, footsteps, a face filling his vision.

Brina.

She pressed a cool hand against his forehead, her skin rough. Fingers touched his temples and probed his neck.

'You'll live,' she muttered, then smiled at him, which scared him more than anything else. He was far more accustomed to scowls from the old healer.

Something moved at his feet, scrambled up the cot he was lying on and then his face was engulfed in fur, hot breath, a wet tongue.

Storm. Smiling, he pushed her away and sat up. Cywen, Gar and Dath were hovering behind Brina, Dath's gaze flitting between Corban and the roof, where Craf was hopping about on a beam, scratching the wood and muttering incomprehensibly. Gar looked about as worried as Corban had ever seen him.

Cywen flung herself upon him, hugging him tight. He grunted, hugging her in return.

'I was so worried,' she mumbled into his neck.

'What – what happened?' Corban asked. 'How did I get here?'

'You just fell over, Ban,' said Dath, moving closer, reaching out to touch Corban's arm. 'Right there in the snow. The sun turned black, and then you just fell over.'

'Oh,' said Corban. Cywen released him from her grip and stepped back, wiping at her eyes as Brina bustled out of the room.

'We didn't know what to do,' Cywen said.

'Cy was screaming,' Dath added over her shoulder.

'We didn't know what to do,' Cywen repeated, shooting a glare at Dath. 'Gar threw you over his horse and galloped you here.'

'Where is *here?*'

'The house we've been staying in,' Dath said, sitting at the bottom of the bed.

Brina returned, holding a tray in her hands, a cup and bowl on it.

'Here, drink this,' she said, passing him the cup as she hooked a hand under his arm and hoisted him, none too gently, into a better sitting position. Gar hurried to help.

'What is it?' said Corban, sniffing suspiciously at the steam rising out of the cup. He wrinkled his nose.

'What do you think?' the healer snapped.

He frowned, sniffing again. 'Hemlock, and something else.'

'Huh,' grunted Brina. 'Hemlock and wormwood, if you must know. Now drink up. It will help.'

Screwing his eyes shut tight he took a sip, wincing at the bitterness of Brina's concoction, then held his nose and swallowed the lot. He thought he might as well, before Brina grabbed his nose and did it for him. He'd seen her do it too many times to those in her care.

'Good boy,' said Brina, smiling sweetly. 'Now, eat this.' She passed him the bowl and a wooden spoon. 'Just oats, before the questions begin again. To fight any fatigue.'

Corban nodded and began spooning the porridge into his mouth.

Cywen laughed. 'Well, Brina. You must teach me your secret. I have never seen Ban go along so meekly with something he does not want to do.'

'I've only just woken,' Corban mumbled, his mouth full. 'She's taking advantage of me.'

Dath laughed, but it trailed off as Craf fluttered out of the darkness above, alighting on a bedpost at the foot of the cot, right next to Dath. The fisherman's son eyed the crow warily.

Storm nuzzled Corban's hand, trying to stick her nose into the bowl of oats.

'She wouldn't leave you, Ban,' Cywen said. Corban scratched behind the wolven's ear and let her lick the last of the oats from his bowl.

'*STRANGER*,' squawked Craf suddenly in Dath's ear, causing him to leap from the bed as if he'd just sat on a roaring fire.

'Oh, hush,' said Brina, waving a hand at the crow. Dath had gone bright red, his eyes looking a little wild.

'How long have I been here?' Corban asked.

'Not long,' said Brina. 'You've been here as long as it takes to boil a pot and mash some oats.'

'What happened to me?' he asked.

'You fainted,' Brina said with a shrug.

Suddenly a memory struggled within him, faint, like a moth battering against wooden shutters. He heard the sound of *wings*, smelt something rotten, saw purple eyes. Then it was gone. He passed a hand over his face, pressed at his forehead.

'Can you smell something?' he wondered.

'Eh?' snapped Brina. 'No. And don't change the subject.'

'Is he well?' Gar asked, frowning deeply.

'Well, there is nothing seriously wrong, as far as I can tell. Other than his permanent ailments, that is: stubbornness, stupidity, spouting ridiculous questions, an ability to vex Elyon himself.' She folded her arms and smiled again. Cywen snorted in agreement.

Corban rolled his eyes. *The less time Cywen spends in this woman's company the better*.

'Why did it happen, though?' said Gar, still frowning.

Brina shrugged. 'Many people faint,' she said, peering at Corban. 'A shock, lack of food, water, air, many reasons.'

'See, Cy. I'm fine. And you don't need to be telling Mam or Da about this. There's no need to worry them, is there?'

'Well, I don't know, Ban.'

'Please, Cy. If it happens again, tell them. If it happens again, *I'll* tell them. But it won't.'

There's no point you two having this conversation,' said Gar. '*I'll* be telling your mam and da, as soon as we're home. And talking of *home*, you all need to make ready. King Brenin has concluded his council with the other rulers. He is leaving.'

CHAPTER FORTY-EIGHT

VERADIS

'And you are sure that you feel well, now?' Veradis asked Nathair, not for the first time. When Nathair collapsed on the wall Veradis had thought he had been victim to some attack – poison, or elemental magic. It had only been his utter panic over Nathair that had stopped him stabbing Mandros, then and there. He was convinced that the King of Carnutan was behind it.

Nathair had been carried to Aquilus' chambers and healers sent for. They had only just arrived when Nathair had woken, though. He had assured them that he was well and continued to do so every time that Veradis asked him, but he looked odd, somehow. Distracted.

'I cannot believe I missed it,' Nathair said, smiling. 'All this time, waiting, and then I go and faint, just as the sun turns black.' He shook his head. 'Tell me again, Veradis. It did happen, didn't it?'

'Aye. Just as Halvor's book said. Day became night. It was the strangest thing. It was not pitch dark, but close, and bitter cold, for a while.'

Nathair paced to a shuttered window, thrust it open and breathed deep of the cold air that came swirling in, rustling amongst parchments that littered tables and tall scroll shelves covering the walls of the room. Veradis stood in silence, watching the Prince.

Eventually Nathair turned. 'So, it has happened.'

'Aye.' Looking out at the pale sky the whole episode felt like a vivid, freshly remembered dream. 'What happens now?'

Nathair crossed the room, sat in a chair beside an inkhorn and scattered quills. 'First, I think it is time that I spoke to my father, about who I am. It is time.' There was something in Nathair's tone that caught Veradis' attention. Something resolute.

'You are sure?' Veradis asked. 'Now is a good time?'

'Yes. It must be. Time is running away.' Nathair nodded to himself. 'And after that, we take control of this war, Veradis. We stop waiting for things to happen. We *do*. I will not sit idly by and wait for Asroth's Black Sun to grow strong. I will take the battle to him.'

Veradis rubbed his chin, itching his palm on the short, stubbly beard that he had been cultivating. 'And how, exactly, will we do that?'

'Finish what we have begun. Forge a warband the Banished Lands have never witnessed – an *army*, a fleet. Bring the weak to heel. I must have a firm grip on the land if I am to fulfil the task Elyon has set me.' They fell silent as footsteps echoed in the corridor. The door opened and Aquilus entered, Meical behind him.

Nathair smiled at his father, but did not rise from his chair. Aquilus just stood and regarded his son a moment, looking weary beyond measure.

A silence fell.

'Meical has returned to us.'

'So I see,' Nathair said. 'A timely arrival.' He looked at Meical. The tall, dark-haired man returned his gaze in silence.

'Where have you been?' Nathair asked him.

'Tarbesh.'

Veradis felt his heart suddenly quicken in his chest, thudding against his ribs.

'Rahim was full of praise for you,' Aquilus said. 'Though he was most surprised with your methods. Using giants and sorcerers to track the Shekam, using a fleet of ships to speed your journey. Using the Vin Thalun.'

Nathair looked away, eyes flitting across the rowed scrolls on the walls.

'Have you nothing to say?' Aquilus asked.

'It was necessary.'

'*Necessary.*'

'Aye. Victory is what counted. I succeeded in the task you set me, Father. What matter the means?'

Aquilus quickly closed the gap between him and his son, slammed a clenched fist onto the table, tipping the inkhorn. A dark stain spread across the tabletop, ink dripping to the flagstoned floor.

'You lied to me.'

'I did not lie. I withheld some of the details, true, but only for a time. I was going to tell you,' Nathair said, a tremor creeping into his voice. 'Father, consider the *results*; consider the *possibilities* . . .'

'No,' Aquilus said, voice controlled now. 'You deceived me. You disobeyed me. I forbade your involvement with the Vin Thalun.' The King seemed to falter and reached out a hand, steadying himself against the table.

'Father, I . . . I am sorry. I did not mean to, I wish only to make you proud of me. All that I have done has been to win your favour . . .' Nathair's voice wavered suddenly, tears filling his eyes. He looked down to hide them.

'My *favour*?' said Aquilus. He shook his head. 'You know what we face, Nathair, know what I seek to achieve. We *must* be ready for the Bright Star.'

Nathair straightened and took a breath to speak, but Aquilus continued.

'How can I trust you? Allow you into my confidences?' The King sighed. 'Now, tell me the *truth* of what happened in Tarbesh. I must know it all, before we talk of what happens now.'

'What do you mean, *what happens now*?' Nathair said.

'Do as I command,' Aquilus growled, dangerously now. Nathair glowered at him a moment, then began to speak.

He told of their journey to Tarbesh, of Lykos and his fleet, of the information Alcyon and Calidus provided, though he took care to avoid any mention of Calidus' name. He told of Rahim's problems in finding the Shekam, of Calidus and Alcyon's aid in finding the giants, of thwarting their sorcerous mist, of the battle. He told all except their journey to Telassar. That he mentioned not at all.

'. . . so you see, Father, I have only ever had one goal, *your* goal, in mind: the defeat of Asroth and his Black Sun. I have just employed unusual means. Too often we are shackled by tradition, by *ways* of doing things. I say it is the *results* that matter. Sacrifices must be made for the greater good.'

'I have heard that phrase before,' Meical said, quietly, almost to himself. 'A long time ago. No good came of it then, either.'

'You speak out of turn,' Nathair said coldly. 'You are a counsellor. Speak when counsel is requested.'

Meical stared at the Prince, only the slight flaring of his nostrils revealing a hint of his anger.

'Meical is more, much more, than a counsellor,' Aquilus said.

'More? What?'

'I was hoping to talk to you of that,' Aquilus said. 'But not now, not after this. Truth and courage, Nathair, I have tried to teach you their value, have I not?'

Nathair just stared, dumbly.

'Trust, Nathair,' the King continued, both stern and sad. 'Trust is vital between us. It is the mortar that protects us from Asroth's schemes and deceit, that holds us together. And I no longer trust you. You – my only son.'

'That is ridiculous, Father—'

'Who was the Vin Thalun?' Meical interrupted.

Nathair paused, frowned.

'The one that guided you through Tarbesh, the giant's companion. What was his name?'

Nathair shook his head. 'It is of no import,' he muttered.

'What was his name?' Aquilus said.

'Calidus,' Nathair breathed.

Aquilus froze, speechless. He looked at Meical, who for the first time looked more than concerned, scared even. Then Aquilus lunged forwards and grabbed Nathair, shaking him. 'Do you know what you have done?' he snarled into his son's face. Before he knew it, Veradis was stepping forward, his sword half drawn. A hand clamped on his wrist, the grip like iron, spun him.

'Hold, Prince's man,' Meical said.

Aquilus released Nathair, who stumbled back against the table, devastation on his face.

'You would draw your sword on me?' Aquilus levelled at Veradis.

'I . . . no, my King.' He looked down, suddenly ashamed.

Meical released him. With a click he pushed his sword back tight into its scabbard.

Aquilus sighed, rubbed his eyes and walked to the open window. 'Veradis,' he said.

'Yes, my King?'

'I must speak soon with Mandros. Go, bring him to me.'

'Is that wise?' Veradis blurted. Mandros was the *enemy*, of that he was sure.

'He has seen day turn to night, seen Halvor's words proven true. He will be humbled, now, ready to join me.'

Not if he is a servant of Asroth, thought Veradis. *Not if he seeks to prepare the way for the Black Sun.* Veradis glanced at Nathair, saw the Prince nod.

'As you wish, my King.'

'Meical – I would speak with my son. Privately.'

Meical looked between king and prince. 'Come,' he said to Veradis, and together they left the room, Aquilus and Nathair regarding one another in silence.

'Your loyalty is admirable,' Meical said as the two men walked away. Veradis said nothing. 'Take more care that it is deserved, though.'

'Do you speak ill of Nathair?' Veradis stopped abruptly, turning to Meical.

'I speak the truth as I see it,' the tall man said.

'He is the Prince of Tenebral, and a better man you will not find.'

Meical shrugged. 'His decisions are questionable. The companions he chooses . . .'

'Calidus is beyond doubt. It is you that concerns me.'

'Me?' Meical said contemptuously. 'I live to serve Elyon, and his Bright Star.'

Veradis grunted. 'Your Bright Star is *here*, you fool. On the top floor of this tower.'

Meical's eyes narrowed. 'You cannot think . . . Nathair?'

'Ha,' Veradis spat. 'The truth has been before you all these years, yet you have failed to recognize it. I have an errand to run,' he said, heading away to Mandros' rooms. He did not look back until he reached Mandros' door. When he did, Meical was gone.

The King of Carnutan was a large-boned man, once heavily muscled but now turning to fat, a belly pushing over a thick belt twined with silver.

Veradis informed him of the King of Aquilus' request, and he came almost immediately, two warriors following. He still looked pale and shaken, as he had on the battlements, even after the sun had returned to normal. *Not so mocking, now*, Veradis thought.

Veradis led the way silently back up to the tower to Aquilus' rooms, passing Orcus, his personal guard.

'Your weapon,' Veradis said to Mandros. There was no way he was going to allow this man within reach of Aquilus or Nathair with a sword at his hip. He was still half sure that Mandros had somehow been behind Nathair's collapse at the wall.

The King scowled at him but unbelted his sword and gave it to Veradis.

Nathair opened the door to Veradis' knocking. 'Wait for me,' the Prince said as Mandros entered the room, then the door clicked shut. Veradis was left standing in the hallway with Mandros' two guards.

He leaned against a tapestried wall. It had been quite a day. He remembered Nathair's face during the confrontation with Aquilus. The Prince had been devastated, had even shed tears. At least Aquilus was not like Veradis' own father. Lamar would most likely have slapped him for such an unmanly display. Veradis felt a surge of sympathy for the Prince – so clearly driven by a need for his father's recognition, his approval. He knew how that felt, had built walls against that pain long ago, but it was still always there, like a thorn in his flesh. He squeezed his temples. Everything had gotten so complicated.

The King's door opened, Mandros bustling through it, still pale, looking more haggard, if anything. His hands shook as he took back his sword and belt from Veradis. He closed the door quickly behind him and hurried down the hallway, his two warriors walking fast to catch him.

As they disappeared down the stairwell Orcus looked at Veradis and frowned. The guard was right – something was wrong.

Veradis went to the study door, straining to listen. No voices, only silence, then a coughing. Panic welled up and he shouldered the door open.

Nathair lay against a thick table leg, propped on one elbow, blood staining his waist, pooling on the floor.

'Ve— . . . Veradis,' the Prince stuttered.

'Orcus!' Veradis yelled as he rushed to Nathair, kneeling. A knife hilt protruded from the Prince's side, just below the ribs. Nathair plucked feebly at it, eyelids fluttering, face as pale as death.

'Lie still,' Veradis said.

Orcus surged into the room, stood frozen for a moment.

'The King?' he said.

Veradis just stared at him.

'Where is Aquilus?' Orcus shouted.

'There . . .' breathed Nathair, waving a hand.

In shadows beneath the open window a crumpled figure lay.

'No,' Veradis whispered.

Empty, lifeless eyes looked back at him.

CHAPTER FORTY-NINE

CORBAN

'What did you mean?' asked Corban.

'When? About what?' Brina said, rolling her eyes.

'At the feast, when you said "*Circles within circles*." About Uthan and Kyla being betrothed.'

Brina shot him a look. 'Your ears are as honed as your talent for questions.'

'Thank you,' Corban smiled.

'It was not a compliment. I meant,' she began slowly, choosing her words carefully, 'that things are not as simple as they appear.'

'What does that—'

'Ah,' Brina snapped, holding a finger up. 'I was going to explain, but if you insist on filling every moment that I pause for breath with a fresh question, then this conversation will end now.'

Corban clamped his mouth shut with an effort of will.

'*Specifically* what I meant,' she carried on, 'is that Gethin is forging his own links with the Kingdom of Narvon. Uthan is King Owain's heir – so he will be King of Narvon himself one day, if he does not get himself killed first, and Kyla will be his queen. This is something that King Brenin may not be too pleased about. The brothers Gethin and Evnis are ambitious. They seek to elevate themselves and their kin within the kingdom, and beyond, it would seem. Evnis has been manoeuvring for Vonn to be betrothed to Princess Edana for years.'

Corban grunted. For some reason he did not like that thought at all.

Brina raised an eyebrow. 'Imagine that, Evnis' son married to a queen, Gethin's daughter married to a king. Not a great leap for their blood to be sitting on two thrones, eh?'

Corban nodded slowly.

'People are such selfish little creatures,' Brina sighed. 'Always seeking to further their own position, no matter how small or petty.'

'Not all are like that,' Corban said, feeling somehow offended.

'No? Well, maybe you are right. But look about you, Corban. Once you are aware of the particular shape and stink of human greed you will not fail to recognize an abundance of such behaviour. It can be quite depressing.'

'People see what they want to see,' Corban proclaimed, feeling almost wise.

Brina looked at him sharply. 'And where did you hear that particular gem of wisdom? Heb?'

'Aye,' Corban admitted begrudgingly. Brina just huffed and looked ahead.

They were on the journey home to Dun Carreg, Badun three days behind them now. A cold wind had blown down from the north on Midwinter's Day, and had not left, freezing the land, ice crystals in the snow sparkling around them. It was so cold that Corban's ears ached.

He was still in awe of all that he had seen at Badun. The duel between Tull and Morcant had taken his breath away, leaving him feeling both sick and elated, and then Midwinter's Day had come.

He wished he had seen more of it, from what Cywen had told him it had been amazing – and it was embarrassing that he had fainted. He was not looking forward to Rafe getting hold of that information. Somehow, though, he felt *different*, stronger. He had strange flashes of memory, as if something significant had happened to him, however unlikely it seemed.

He didn't know what had occurred between King Brenin and the other rulers – although Rhin had left soon after the sun had returned to normal. And now they were bound for Dun Carreg early the next day, the mysterious couple that had begged King Brenin's Sanctuary travelling with them.

Their journey back to Dun Carreg was uneventful, and Gwenith grabbed him and Cywen before they had even fully entered their kitchen, the smells of home assailing them. She hugged them long and hard, Thannon stepping in and wrapping his broad arms about them all, then she insisted on hearing every detail of their journey.

'Welcome home,' his mam said when they had finally finished. 'No more journeying for a while, I hope.' She hugged them both again.

Frost-stiffened grass crunched under his feet as Corban followed Halion to the edge of the sparring court.

'Shield-work, Corban, is not all about defence,' Halion said, gesturing at two men facing up to spar on the stone. 'Watch a while, and you will learn more than I can teach you with words.'

Conall was on the court, dark hair pulled tight at his neck and a grin on his face, shield and wooden sword held ready. He faced Marrock, who was taller, leaner, the scar on his face looking red and livid against his pale skin. The huntsman also held a shield and practice sword. They nodded to each other and Conall instantly lunged forwards, Marrock retreating hastily.

'You see,' Halion said quietly, 'how my brother uses his shield? Not just to block Marrock's blade. He seeks to knock him off balance, to open his guard.'

Corban nodded. As he watched, Conall caught a downswing on his shield, pushed up and back, shoving his shield's boss at Marrock's face. The huntsman jumped back, swinging his own shield into Conall's side as the warrior surged forwards, unsteadying him.

Halion grunted approvingly. 'The shield can be a weapon too. In battle it would be iron rimmed, iron bossed. Strike your enemy with it and you may end it all there. Shield-work limits your choice of sword, though. Some men prefer a longer, heavier blade, which must be wielded two-handed. That will give you extra reach, more weight to your blows. To use a shield you must wield a lighter blade, unless the man is an ox like your da, or Tull. Such as they can have the best of both worlds.' Halion looked Corban up and down, slapping his shoulder. 'Your labour in Thannon's forge will serve you well – strong arms and shoulders. You'll not be as big as your da, I think, but you'll be stronger than many.' He stopped. Halion did not usually say much, except when talking of sword-craft.

'Why did you stay away from the feast at Badun?' Corban asked, remembering they had not been present during the feast and duel.

'What? That was moons ago.'

'So?' shrugged Corban. 'Everyone was there, and you missed the duel. I wanted to talk to you about it.'

'I had my reasons,' Halion said, his mouth tight. 'Now pay attention.' He turned back to the contest between Marrock and his brother.

The two men were trading blows now, huge sweeps and fast lunges, blocking and striking repeatedly.

'Marrock is well matched against my brother,' Halion said. 'He is a strategist, while my brother is a force of nature. If he weren't so good his anger would have got him killed a long time ago. Some men are like that, Corban, you can see it in their eyes. That can be a weapon too. Men make mistakes when they are angry.'

'I know. *Anger is the enemy*, as G—' Corban paused. Halion glanced at him, but said nothing.

'Would Conall *choose* to fight with a shield?' Corban asked.

'Sometimes. If the situation dictates it. He favours using two swords, or a sword and a knife.' He grinned. 'As I said, he's not a patient man. He *is* fast, though, the fastest I've ever seen.'

As if to prove Halion's point, Conall increased the momentum of his attack, his sword arm blurring in Corban's eye. He swept forwards, lunging with his shield, tucked his sword tight behind it, hidden from Marrock's view. He swung his blade at Marrock's ribs, checked the strike as Marrock moved to block, angled his sword down in a half-circle, beneath Marrock's shield rim, then up, the tip of his blade digging into the huntsman's gut.

Marrock paused, looking slightly confused, then realized the contest was over. He dipped his head to Conall, who was grinning again.

'Many think swordplay is about who is the strongest,' Halion said, 'and often I suppose that is true. But for the masters – those that plan to live the longest – swordplay is about *deception*. About making your opponent think you will strike from the left and then striking from the right, making him think you will slash but lunging instead. *Deception*. That is how Conall just defeated Marrock: his sword was not where he had made Marrock think it was going to be, so Marrock's guard, his weight, his *focus* was elsewhere. And he used his shield to aid the deception. You see?'

'I . . . yes, I do.'

'The duel you mentioned at Badun between Tull and Morcant, well, even though I didn't see it I heard about every blow.'

Corban nodded enthusiastically. How could he ever forget?

'Tull won that through deception, remember, flicking the rushes into Morcant's face. He has a keen mind, Tull, as sharp as his blade. People think he just overwhelms his opponents because he is big, but that is not the case. He *thinks*. That is no small task when you are fighting to stay alive. Come, lad, now you've seen how a shield *can* be used, let's see how you get on.'

Corban followed Halion to the weapons racks. He had tried shield-work in plenty, but still did not feel wholly comfortable with it. His training with Gar was always with a two-handed practice sword. That was the favoured weapon of the stablemaster, and so that was what he felt most at ease with.

He glanced around the Field as he crunched across frozen grass, saw Tull standing tall before a handful of warriors that he was working with.

His mam had been different since his return from Badun. He would often catch her staring at him, an unreadable expression on her face. And she was touching him more; not that she had never shown him affection before his journey, but now she would gravitate towards him whenever they were in the same room, even if it was just her fingertips brushing the back of his hand. Maybe it was because of his fainting.

But she was not the only one paying him more attention. Wherever he was, he would see his da or Gar. When at Brina's performing his chores, which had somehow settled into a permanent arrangement, Gar would be nearby working with horses in the paddocks; and if not in the forge with his da he would often feel the big man's presence nearby, even when he was spending his meagre free time with Dath around the village. It was starting to annoy him.

'Make sure your grip is good; it can make the difference between a broken arm or no,' Halion said as Corban hefted an old, battered shield. Then they set to, Halion pushing Corban to think about every move, making him pay with a new bruise for every thoughtless mistake. It was not long before Corban's arm was numb, his shoulder throbbing from the blows that had soaked through the shield into his arm. Halion grinned wolfishly at him. 'That'll do for the day, lad.'

'Good,' Corban grunted, sweat stinging his eyes.

'You're doing well. More than well with a blade, and your shield-work is not bad, either. We need to focus on bow and spear, though.'

'Huh,' grunted Corban. 'A sword's good enough for me. *Warriors* don't use a bow – why do I need to learn?'

'Because warriors need to eat,' said Halion. 'You won't have food caught by other people for you all of your life. You will need to play your part. And, who knows? Maybe one day you'll have to bring down your own meals. You'll be glad of time spent with bow and spear then.'

Corban didn't answer. He knew there was sense in Halion's words, but he was hungry to learn with a blade. There was just no *honour* in a bow, unless you were a huntsman like Marrock. He had already tried it, with Halion standing behind him, and done quite poorly. He'd taken the skin off his forearm with more than one mis-timed shot.

He glanced over to the ranges at the far end of the Field, saw the tall, gangly frame of Tarben, the small, distinctive outline of Dath beside him, straight-backed, launching arrows unerringly at straw targets. The fisherman's son had taken remarkably well to the weapon, although he was not overly happy with his newfound abil-ity – he longed to be a *swordsman*. That was the only way he'd be taken into a baron's hold as a warrior, and that was his secret dream: to escape his da's boat, fishing, the sea, and to carve a warrior's life for himself.

'Not today, though, lad,' Halion said, seeing Corban's sour expression. 'We're done for the day. I'll see you on the morrow.'

Corban trudged out of the Field, Storm rising from beneath the first tree of the rowan lane as he approached.

Others were leaving the Field, walking on their own or in small groups. Corban paid them little attention until he heard Storm growl quietly. He looked up, saw Rafe with his usual companion, Crain. They were stooping as they walked, snatching up handfuls of gravel and stones and throwing them at someone in front.

Corban sped up, trying to see better what was going on.

In front of Rafe a tall, broad figure strode, head bowed as small stones ricocheted off his back.

Rafe was laughing. 'Just like his da,' the huntsman's son was saying. 'There's no room in the Field for cowards, or the sons of cowards, you know.'

The figure in front suddenly stopped and turned. It was Farrell, son of Anwarth, the warrior rumoured to have feigned his wounding in the Darkwood when Rhagor had been killed. Farrell's fists were bunched, face red and pinched. Tears stained his cheeks.

'What?' said Rafe, sauntering up to him.

Farrell was shaking. 'Just – stop,' he said, a tremor in his voice. He was younger than Corban, but he stood as tall as Rafe, and broader.

Crain stepped up beside Rafe.

'No,' Rafe said, 'I don't think I will. The Rowan Field is for the training of *warriors*. Why don't you spend your days at the village? Try gutting and washing fish with the other women.'

'W-why are you . . .?' Farrell stammered.

Corban reached the group. A deep, burning sensation was spreading outwards from his gut. 'Leave him alone,' he heard himself say.

'Oh ho,' said Crain, turning. 'Where are all these cowards coming from?'

Rafe just scowled at him.

Storm took a step forward, snarling, teeth bared. A line of spittle dripped from her mouth. Rafe and Crain took an involuntary step backwards.

'I don't think she likes your tone,' said Corban, touching her flank lightly.

'Think you're the *hero* now, rushing to the rescue of other cowards?' Rafe said. 'You two could form your own warband, only cowards accepted. Walk on, blacksmith's boy – you'll have yours coming, but you've a while yet. Two moons from now I sit my Long Night. Not even Tull will be able to save you once you've sat *your* Long Night. I'll be waiting for you.'

Corban shrugged. 'Leave him alone,' he said again, glancing at Farrell, who was staring at him. He tried to smile reassuringly and took a step closer to the big lad. Suddenly Farrell's hands were on his shoulders, spinning him around, hoisting him a handspan off the ground.

'Stay out of it,' the broad-shouldered lad said, vehemently, scowling at Corban.

Without thinking, Corban kicked both his feet, cracking Farrell in the shins. He was suddenly dropped and staggered back. 'I'm trying to help you,' Corban stuttered.

Farrell just glared at him, eyes screwed up, then he turned and ran, lumbering away.

Rafe and Crain laughed, walking on. 'You must try harder at making friends,' Rafe called over his shoulder, still chuckling.

Corban stood there a while, shocked, angry. He had only wanted to help – he knew what it was like to have Rafe single you out for attention. He set off, kicking his heels against the shingle. Then he remembered how he had felt when Rafe had first hit him during the Spring Fair, how scared, how angry, how *ashamed* that he'd done nothing. And then Cywen had stood up for him. *He* hadn't been too grateful at the time, either. He thought about that for a while. Maybe he'd try and talk to Farrell, apologize.

How he loathed Rafe. '*I'll be waiting for you,*' the huntsman's son had said. *Well, good.*

Looking up, he realized his feet had taken him to the stables. His sister stood in the paddock, a horse's foreleg rested across her knee as she scraped out its hoof with a small knife. He settled against a post a few strides from her, waiting for her to finish.

A strange sensation suddenly spread along his neck, down his back and arms, goose-fleshing his skin. He looked up quickly and saw Gar near the stable doors with a tall, dark-haired man, holding the reins of a huge dapple-grey stallion. The man had deep scars on his face, like claw marks. They were both looking at him.

'Who's that, with Gar?' he asked his sister.

'Huh?' grunted Cywen, concentrating on the hoof in her grip. She glanced up briefly. 'Oh, he rode in earlier. What did Gar call him? Meical, I think.'

CHAPTER FIFTY

VERADIS

Veradis stood on a shingle ridge, arms folded across his leather-bound chest, watching.

Two score ships sat anchored in the bay they had found, crewed by men he would, until recently, have regarded as his enemy. Now they were his allies, speeding him towards his heart's desire.

Mandros.

Orcus' call from Aquilus' study to apprehend the King of Carnutan had come too late. Mandros had fled, not even gathering all of his warriors in his haste to vacate Jerolin. Aquilus' eagle-guard had followed, but the gap had been too great and Mandros had been reckless in his flight, losing men to the steep slopes and snow-filled trenches of the Agullas, but increasing the distance between himself and those that hunted him. Almost a full moon later those that had set out to bring Mandros back had returned to Jerolin, heads low, empty handed.

Aquilus' burial had already passed by then, the barons of Tenebral gathered to pay their last respects as a cairn was raised above their dead king, and swear new oaths of fealty to a still weak and pale-faced Nathair. The knife wound had missed all of his vital organs, but the Prince had come close to bleeding to death in Aquilus' study, waiting for healers to arrive, his grip on Veradis' hand growing weaker and weaker.

Not for the first time, Veradis felt a flame ignite in his gut. A fierce rage had consumed him those first few days after Midwinter. He had felt such *shame*, standing idly by in a corridor while his King was murdered and his Prince and friend stabbed, left for dead. Since then all emotion in him had been distilled, transformed into the raw essence of a cold, permanent rage that he had never experienced before.

Mandros would pay.

He had been tempted to leave as soon as those hunting Mandros had returned without their quarry, but Nathair had still been weak and the passes through the Agullas Mountains were closed to more than a handful of men. It would take more than that to root out Mandros. He would be safely back in his kingdom of Carnutan, surrounded by his warbands, who'd be guarding the mountain passes into his realm. Lykos – whom Nathair had summoned soon after the attack – had agreed to ferry a force to the coast of Carnutan, but he had counselled against sailing throughout the Tempest and Snow Moons. So they had waited, planned, organized provisions, spoken of goals and strategy.

Nathair had given Peritus overall command of the campaign, much to Veradis' surprise.

'He has weathered many campaigns,' Nathair had said. 'No matter my grievances with him, he is good at this, and his anger against Mandros burns as bright as yours. Watch him, learn from him.'

Veradis had grudgingly agreed, and soon recognized the truth in Nathair's words. Peritus was a keen strategist and a man of immense organizational skills. And so it was that he found himself on a beach on the southern coast of Carnutan, watching hundreds of warriors bearing the eagle of Tenebral disembarking from a fleet of Vin Thalun ships.

They had begun unloading at sunrise, the first of a score of scouts and their horses, quickly fanning out beyond the beach. It was now almost highsun.

As he watched, a dozen men cried out. The wain they were guiding down a wide ramp lurched off its bearings. One wheel teetered in air before toppling into the surf below, scattering its cargo and sending a cloud of spray up about it.

He cursed to himself, calculating the extra time needed to try and recover the wain's cargo.

'Patience,' a voice said beside him. He turned and saw Peritus a few paces away.

Veradis nodded, turned back to watch warriors filing onto the beach. They were forming into two loose clusters. The smaller was his warband: around six hundred men, the survivors of their campaign in Tarbesh – each man carrying a draig's tooth. When added to Peritus' larger band the whole force numbered a little under three thousand swords. Not a large force to send into the heart of an enemy realm, but they hoped stealth would be their ally. Mandros would expect them to wait for the spring thaw and cross the Agullas Mountains in large numbers when the passes opened, but that was at least half a moon away still. Their scouts had reported a massing of warriors at Tarba, the fortress guarding the mountain pass into Carnutan itself.

They *did* have another warband gathering at Jerolin, ready to march through the mountains with the thaw, but hopefully they would have Mandros by then. The task now was to march north to Mandros' own fortress. Lykos had assured him that Mandros had fled there, gone to ground like a fox fleeing the hounds.

On the beach a man detached himself from Veradis' gathering warriors and raised an arm to him – Rauca. He strode purposefully up the shingle ridge dotted with thin, straggly clumps of grass, and stood beside Veradis.

'There'll be songs about us, one day soon,' he grinned. 'Lads will dream of being us, lasses will just dream *of* us.'

Veradis snorted, Rauca's grin broadening.

'Be careful they're not singing your cairn song,' Peritus said.

'No chance of that. I plan on standing right next to Veradis through every moment of combat.'

Veradis shook his head. In silence the three men watched the last warriors empty from the Vin Thalun ships, rolling a score of wains across the beach onto firmer ground.

The fleet of ships began to move, turned and Veradis nodded approvingly as he saw the ships split into two groups, one disappearing east, the other west.

'Why are they doing that?' Rauca asked.

'They are splitting to harry Mandros' fortresses along the coast,' Peritus replied. 'That way, if the fleet has been spotted, it will just be thought that they are corsair raiders.'

The battlechief turned to Veradis. 'It grates me to be aided by the Vin Thalun, but they have strategic merit, I must confess. Nathair has a keen head on his shoulders.'

'Aye,' Veradis assented. He did not want to think about that right now; it was too close to his last memories of Aquilus, railing at Nathair over his association with the Vin Thalun.

Nathair had not spoken of the final words he had shared with his father while they had been alone. He hoped there had been some reconciliation between them before the end. *The end.* His thoughts turned to Meical and the conversation they had then had outside the King's rooms. He had resolved to question the counsellor more, but discovered that Meical had left Jerolin soon after word of Aquilus' death had spread. Valyn told him that Meical had saddled his horse along with the warriors that had set out in chase of Mandros. The stablemaster presumed that he was riding with them, but he had not. That troubled Veradis: where had the counsellor gone? And why had he left so hastily? Nathair needed him.

He sighed, rubbing a hand over his eyes. 'Come, then,' he said. 'It's a long walk to Dun Bagul.'

They had chosen against bringing horses – Lykos could only muster two score ships, and horses took up more space than warriors, so they had sacrificed speed on land for stealth. Besides, wains set the pace, and most warriors preferred fighting on foot to a horse's back, Veradis' warband more so. He was looking forward to forming a wall of shields against other *men* instead of draigs and giants.

'Aye,' muttered Peritus. 'To Dun Bagul, and vengeance.'

'We are discovered,' Peritus said grimly as Veradis entered the battle-chief's tent, Rauca slipping in before the hide flapped shut and closed out the night.

Peritus stood bent over a table, a parchment spread before him.

'We have done well to come so far,' Veradis shrugged. They could not see the old fortress of Dun Bagul yet but it was close now, no more than a day's march.

'Aye. But now is the knife-edge. Mandros will have a warband about him, at least equalling our numbers, likely more.'

'Good. Then he may be tempted to leave his fox hole to fight us.'

'He will send word for aid.' Peritus jabbed a finger at the parchment before him. 'His nearest strongholds are Raen in the east, Iska in the west. We do not have the numbers to stop some of them getting through but *if* our Vin Thalun allies are right, their garrisons are low, most of their warriors sent east to await our expected passage through the mountains.' The battlechief stretched wearily. 'We must prise him from his lair, bring him to battle before aid can reach him.'

'Aye,' grunted Veradis. 'If he does not march out to meet us on the field I will shame him before his men, shout of what he did . . .' he paused a moment, a tremor running through him. *Murderer*, whispered a voice in his head. 'I shall challenge him to the Court of Swords – anything to get him out from behind his walls.'

'We could storm Dun Bagul,' Peritus said. 'It is not impregnable, but it would be costly, both in men and in time. Mandros is no fool, and until now has been no craven, either. Our best chance lies here.' He prodded at the parchment again, Veradis and Rauca coming closer, looking at the map spread on the table. Peritus traced a line across it. 'This river lies between us and Dun Bagul. There is no bridge, only a ford, unless we would walk half a ten-night out of our way. The ford is bordered by woodland on one side, hills on the other. It is a most excellent site to ambush us. Mandros will know this, and if he considers our numbers at least even, then I think it likely that he will seize his chance.'

Veradis smiled grimly. 'Let me lead the vanguard across the river.'

Peritus frowned. 'Even expecting an ambush, prepared for it, that will be a most unhealthy spot to be standing.'

Rauca laughed, a harsh sound that did nothing to break the mood. 'We are accustomed to unhealthy spots now. At least we won't have murderous draigs and giants tearing at us.'

'I don't know,' Peritus said. 'I am not inclined to return to Tenebral without our new King's first-sword.'

'You've seen our warband train,' Veradis said hotly. 'You know we are best suited to this task, to bear the brunt of any ambush, any charge – our wall of shields is made for just such a position.'

'Maybe so.' Peritus suddenly grinned. 'You have something of your brother in you, it would seem.'

Veradis grunted, unsure of what to say. Krelis had become firm friends with Peritus during his time at Jerolin – and he had spoken frequently of Aquilus' wily battlechief.

'All right, you cross first, as our vanguard. We shall march at dawn, take our time reaching the river and just hope Mandros acts on the information his scouts bring him this night.'

There was a tapping on the tent hide and a voice called through – Peritus' guard.

'Enter.'

Two warriors stepped into the tent, a man between them. He was dressed in worn leather, a dark cloak pulled about him. He pushed back his cowl, revealing a broad, plain face, ruddy cheeks and nervously darting eyes.

Veradis heard Peritus exclaim under his breath. He had seen this man at Aquilus' council.

It was Gundul, Mandros' son, staring nervously back at him.

Veradis stepped into the shallow water of the river, ice-cold water swirling about his legs, seeping through his boots and numbing his feet. A loose row of some three score men stretched either side of him. Gravel shifted under his feet and he swayed, feeling the weight of the shield on his back.

Before him, too far away, was the far bank of the river. Then there was a gentle slope leading up into woodland.

He tried not to stare at the trees, to search for the glint of sunlight on iron, and kept his eyes on the water. Risking a quick glance over his shoulder, he saw most of his warband had entered the river, Peritus' warriors spread in a more disorganized crush behind them.

'Can't go back now,' Rauca muttered beside him. 'Who's fool idea was it to march us first across this river, anyway?'

'Huh,' grunted Veradis, a grin tugging at his mouth, despite the fluttering weightlessness he felt somewhere deep inside.

His eyes swept forward again, drawn inexorably to the treeline half a hundred paces from the river's edge. If Mandros was in there, he would wait until the warband was partially out of the river so that they could be charged from both flank and front. A head-on charge would keep them in the river, but a surprise charge to the flank usually wreaked more damage. It could even decide the outcome.

Mandros. The thought of Carnutan's King banished all doubts. Mandros was clearly a servant of the Black Sun. The traitor had grabbed Nathair's own dagger, stabbed King Aquilus through the throat, then plunged it into the Prince's side. He should not have let

Mandros into that room. *Justice*, whispered the voice in his head. Justice would be done this day: dark, merciless, bloody justice.

Over halfway across now, forty paces left till they reached the far bank, thirty, twenty . . .

Suddenly a cry erupted from beyond the trees, a keening, deafening war cry. Men swarmed into the daylight, iron flashing as weapons were drawn, feet thundering as they charged down the slope towards Veradis and his men.

Veradis shrugged his shield from his back, yelling, 'Shield wall!' He drew his short stabbing sword, hefted his shield and felt it connect with a satisfying thud to Rauca's on his left and Bos' on his right. He had just a moment to set his feet on the unstable riverbed and glance over his shield rim at the onrushing tide of men. They looked confused at this tactic. Battle was not fought like this. His warband should have been charging for the riverbank to meet the enemy, the battle quickly fragmenting into a chaotic melee of individual conflicts. If not for the weakness in his knees he would have laughed.

Then the screaming onslaught slammed into the wall. Hundreds of shields crashed into each other, a thunderous cacophony. The wall trembled but held, the mass of charging men pushing their first rows into a compressed, seething mass of limbs.

Veradis bent his knees, shoulder against shield and grunted at the enormous weight of bodies. He stabbed beneath his shield's edge, time and time again. His blade bit into muscle, sinew, raked bone. Hot blood gushed onto his hand, his arm, and men screamed, bodies held upright before him only by the crush of men behind them. To either side of him his warriors did the same, dealing out death with deadly efficiency.

He shouted a command over his shoulder, heard the warrior behind him pass it on, and in moments there was a horn blast. All in the front line of the shield wall stepped forwards, shoving the press of men before them, then another and another. Sand and shingle underfoot changed to flesh, leather and wood as the dead were trampled. The river ran red about them, piles of bodies marking the tide-line where the wall of shields had held. Slowly, inexorably, Veradis and his warband ground their way forwards. Some in the front ranks fell, stumbling over the dead or dragged from the line by sheer weight of numbers, but the gaps were filled instantly. Then

Veradis felt the ground change beneath him, becoming more solid, and the riverbank also turned to red as men fell before the unbreachable wall of wood and iron.

Suddenly the pressure on his shield lessened. He saw the front ranks of his enemy had retreated up the bank: fear now in their eyes. Battles were often won in the battle-fury of the first charge, when the blood was up. This should have been a slaughter, catching an outnumbered foe floundering knee-deep in a swirling river. Instead it was overwhelmingly Mandros' warriors that had fallen.

Veradis felt new strength fill his limbs and advanced with renewed vigour, his warriors following.

It was easier going now. The ground was more solid underfoot, the warriors before him less wild in their onslaught. More of Mandros' men swarmed the flanks of his line as Peritus' men now emerged from the river, returning with relief to their usual combat style.

Heedless, Veradis' warband ploughed onwards. Then a wild shouting filtered slowly through the clamour of battle. He looked up to see a mounted figure near the treeline and blinked with surprise to see the woodland so close. The figure was Mandros himself, screaming a mixture of fury and panic, eyes wild as he urged his men on. *Kill him*, the voice growled in his head. A cluster of mounted warriors milled about Mandros, faces grim and focused.

He pressed forwards, stabbing furiously, outpacing his comrades-in-arms. Pain punched his side as a blade thrust behind his guard, but was turned by his shirt of mail. It slid down, bit into his thigh and blood sluiced down his leg. He stumbled, suddenly weak, then arms were grabbing him, lifting and pulling him back. He saw Mandros and swore, spat blood onto the ground at his feet. He was so close.

There was a baying of horns, high and to the right. For a moment the battle seemed to lull, all eyes following the sound.

Lines of warriors were forming on the rim of the hill that edged the battle, most of them on foot, a score or so mounted at their rear. Veradis saw one of them draw a sword and hold it aloft. Gundul, son of Mandros, gave a great war cry and his warriors surged down the hill, screaming as they came.

CHAPTER FIFTY-ONE

CORBAN

Corban blinked, staring at the man standing with Gar. 'Meical, you say?'

'Yes,' Cywen grunted, turning her attentions back to the horse in her grip. 'He's only just ridden in. I'm in love with his mount – look at him. I wager he's the fastest horse I've ever laid eyes on.'

Corban glanced at the stallion behind the dark-haired man: a dapple-grey, tall, fine boned, but almost immediately his eyes were drawn back to this Meical. Before he realized it, his feet were moving, taking him towards the stablemaster and his companion. Storm followed a pace behind.

Gar was saying something, but he trailed off as Corban approached them.

'Ban?' the stablemaster said to him.

Corban just stood there, unsure of what to say or do now that he was here. He could not quite understand why he had walked over in the first place.

'Ban, you want something?'

'I, uh, you have a fine horse,' he mumbled, staring at Gar's companion.

'Thank you,' the newcomer said. He was tall, very tall, the sun behind framing him as a dark silhouette. There was something familiar about this man, tickling Corban's memory like a spider crawling across his neck. They stood there regarding each other, the silence growing.

'This is Meical,' Gar finally said, looking uncharacteristically uncomfortable.

'Well met,' said Meical, a hint of a smile touching his lips.

Corban just nodded.

The silence grew again as they stared at each other. Meical's eyes were dark, seeming to pin him to the spot; not just looking *at* him, but *into* him, measuring him somehow. But then he smiled.

'You keep unusual company.' Meical looked down to Storm.

The wolven was standing pressed tight to Corban's hip and leg, as she often did when he was anxious or troubled. Her ears were pricked up, hackles standing as she stretched her head forward, sniffing. Meical squatted down, looking the wolven in the eyes, and offered his hand for her to smell. Her long canines, protruding at least a handspan from beneath her lip, touched his fingers, but he did not pull away. After a moment Storm snorted and scratched at the earth, then lay at Corban's feet.

'Her name is Storm,' Corban said.

'A good name.' Meical rose quickly, then swayed on his feet.

'Your pardon,' he said. 'I have ridden long and hard.'

'Come,' said Gar, 'let's stable your horse, he looks as weary as you.'

Gar glanced at Corban. 'Are you to Brina's?'

'Aye.'

'Best you be on your way, then, before I find work round the stable for you to do.'

'Huh,' grunted Corban, but stood where he was a little longer, that nagging memory again crawling across his skin.

CHAPTER FIFTY-TWO

CYWEN

Cywen wiped sweat from her eyes. The air was cold, crisp, a constant, sharp wind blowing off the sea, but she had been working hard. She'd spent most of the morning and well into the afternoon breaking a colt to saddle.

Gar grunted when she reported her tasks done for the day. He seemed distant.

'I need Hammer brought up from the paddocks,' he said to Cywen. 'If you leave now you'll be back in good time for the evening meal.'

Cywen frowned. It was a long walk to the paddocks. If she'd known earlier she would have asked Ban to wait, but he was long gone. She shrugged.

'Go on then, girl, be off with you,' Gar said, marching away. Cywen set off for Stonegate.

Part-way to the bridge she remembered she had forgotten to harvest vegetables before the evening meal. Her mam would not be happy, so, muttering to herself, she changed direction and ran home. It was empty, not even Buddai warming himself before the fire.

Quickly she started gathering greens, her mind drifting to Ronan, and his increasingly distracting smile. And he was always looking at her, though he tried not to let her see. She felt her own smile spreading . . .

A noise came from the kitchen – the garden door opening.

Instinctively Cywen ducked behind a tree. She glimpsed her mam peering into the garden, then the door clicked shut again.

What am I doing? she thought, frowning as she headed for the kitchen. But then footsteps sounded as several people entered the room, but quietly, which seemed strange. There was no greeting, only the scrape of chair legs, the sound of drinks being poured.

She peeked through the crack between shutter and wall and it took a moment for her eyes to adjust. Her mam was standing at one end of the table, looking almost scared. Sitting before her were Thannon, Gar, and the man who had ridden in earlier, Meical.

Gwenith drank from her cup, a tremor in her hand, and a tense silence grew.

'Where is the boy?' a rich, lilting voice asked – this Meical.

'At Brina's. She is a healer,' Gar said. 'Her dwelling is beyond the village.'

'And your daughter?'

'She is not here, I have checked. We are alone,' Gwenith said.

'Good,' grunted Meical.

'Why? Why have you come?' Gwenith finally said, breaking the quiet.

'King Aquilus is dead.'

Cywen could not see her da's face, but Gwenith's mouth fell open. Gar just stared.

'How?' Gwenith gasped.

'Slain. Murdered in his own chamber.' Meical bowed his head. 'It is a grievous loss.'

'Who?' said Gar.

Meical rubbed his eyes. 'I was told Mandros, King of Carnutan. He openly opposed Aquilus, was proud, arrogant. And he *fled*. But I suspect there is more to it. Asroth's hand is in this.'

'More to it? What do you mean?' Gwenith asked.

'I cannot say, yet. Perhaps I should have stayed longer at Jerolin, but when it happened, a terror fell upon me, such as I have never known. I had to see the boy.'

'But you said we would not see you again, until the time. The *danger* – what if you were followed?' Gwenith said, her voice rising.

'Peace,' Meical muttered, holding a hand up. 'I know your concerns. I felt them myself, but I *had* to see him – to know he was safe. And I have been careful: the passes through the Agullas closed soon after I travelled them, and no one can match Miugra's pace. I rode him harder than he has ever known, and I took precautions. I will not be tracked.' He leaned back in his chair, his face relaxing. 'The boy looks well.'

Gwenith smiled at that. 'He is. He is a good boy.'

Cywen could not believe what she heard as she eavesdropped, her legs stiff from standing still so long, trying even to breath quietly. She felt at sea: talk of Aquilus, Jerolin, Carnutan. Did they mean *the* Aquilus – the one who had called King Brenin to a council?

Suddenly, though, something *had* become clear. For some reason they were talking about Ban. *Her* Ban.

'How go things with him?' Meical said.

Gwenith just nodded and smiled, glancing between Gar and Thannon. 'He is special, of course – he is my boy. But ever since you came to us, told us . . .' She paused and grimaced. 'I have watched him, *tried* to watch him, with objective eyes. He is sharp-witted, strong, honest, for the most part. Kind. And he is happy, I hope. You are not here to take him?' she said suddenly. 'I will not allow that.' A fierceness crept into her voice.

'No one is taking our boy anywhere,' rumbled Thannon. His hand reached out and covered Gwenith's.

'I am not here for that,' Meical said, 'though I told you, the day will come when he must leave. Go to Drassil. But not alone. With you both, and Gar, of course.'

'Aye, so you say,' Thannon said. 'In truth, it has been so long since you came to us.' He sighed and rubbed a hand over his eyes. 'I am only a blacksmith, and all your talk, I do not know about any of that. And it was so long ago. Until recently I had thought it all a bad dream, but things have been happening. Strange things . . .'

'Yes. The darkness will be upon us soon.'

'Aye. Well. Corban is a good lad. I am proud of him. I could not have asked for more in a son. And I am scared for him . . .'

Gwenith made a sound in her throat and looked away.

'We have prepared him as best we can,' Thannon continued. 'Taught him his letters, the histories, the benefit of hard work, truth and courage, right and wrong, I hope. And Gar has kept another pair of eyes on him, trained him, for which I'm glad.'

'My thanks to you,' Meical said. 'Much was asked of you. Much still is.'

'He is my son, my blood, my heart, my joy, my breath. No one need *ask* anything. I will do all that I can for him. Protect him. Fight for him. Die for him, if need be.'

Meical grunted, nodding, then looked to Gar.

'And you? I have thought of you much over the years. Not an easy burden.'

Gar shrugged. 'Mine is the greatest honour. I have learned not all glory comes from the battlefield.' He shrugged. 'It is as they say: he is bright, strong, just. He has learned his weapons well – more than well. He *excels*.'

'Praise indeed,' said Meical.

'He had dreams,' Gwenith added. 'Bad dreams.'

'Has he spoken of them with you?'

'No. Never. He would cry out through the night. Awake sweating, fearful. But they have passed. He has not called out in his sleep for some moons now.'

Meical smiled. 'Good. Asroth's search for him has not been restricted to this world of flesh. But the fallen one has been thwarted. For a time, at least. And the wolven? Tell me – how has this come to pass?'

Gwenith raised her hands, palms up. 'Ban saved her, as a cub. He has raised her since, regardless of all opposition.'

'Huh,' Thannon grunted.

'Very good. He can never have too many guardians, and something tells me the wolven will guard him better than most. I will speak with King Brenin before I leave. I do not think we will talk again, until . . .' He stood, chair scraping. 'I wish I could stay with you, ease your burden, but my presence would draw attention. We must give the boy all the time we can.' He paused, looking troubled. 'It would be good for him to sit his Long Night here. Then he can be told. Be vigilant – things are moving at a pace that I had not foreseen. I think I must journey to Drassil, make sure all is in place.' He looked at Gar. 'Your father will hear of your faithfulness.' The stablemaster straightened in his seat, his eyes lightening.

Meical strode to the door, then paused. 'Trust no one,' he said. 'Even, even if Aquilus' own blood rides through Stonegate. Trust only Brenin.' Then he opened the door and stepped into the streets of Dun Carreg.

CHAPTER FIFTY-THREE

CORBAN

Corban trudged along the giantsway awhile, head bowed, returning from Brina's. A large wain blocked his path, piled high with skins, a tall hound walking beside it.

Corban stared at it as he walked, then suddenly quickened his pace – could it be . . .?

Storm took a step forward, a growl growing in volume and snapped her teeth at the hound.

This is not going well, Corban thought. 'Are you Ventos?' he called out, poking Storm at the same time.

'What?' said the man in the wain. 'Aye. I am Ventos. Do I know you?'

'We met last year, at the Spring Fair. I am Corban.'

'Well, I'll be . . .' Ventos wiped a palm across his face.

'Asroth's teeth, lad, you've just succeeded in scaring the Other-world out of me.' He blew out a long breath.

Ventos jumped down and took a few hesitant steps towards Corban before he stopped. 'I'd invite you to walk with me, but I think my horses would bolt and scatter my wares between here and the Western Sea if your wolven came a step closer.'

Corban nodded. 'Away,' he said curtly to Storm and waved his arm in a short, sharp gesture. Storm looked at him, copper eyes glinting in the fading sun, then loped away about a hundred paces, then stopped.

Ventos raised his eyebrows, watching Storm. 'That is one clever wolven,' he muttered. 'So it's true. I've heard talk of you ever since Dun Cadlas, and everywhere between here and there. I didn't *believe* it, of course – didn't know it was *you*, either. The young warrior that tamed a wolven . . .' he whistled.

'She's not what I'd call tame,' Corban said, grinning. 'Well met.' He held his arm out. The trader took it in the warrior grip.

'You've changed, lad. I wouldn't have recognized you. Apart from your scruffy hair and muddied clothes, that is.'

Ventos tried to assuage Corban's curiosity about events beyond Dun Carreg as they walked. They stopped before they entered the village, Ventos pulling a thick leather glove onto his left hand. He drew some meat from a pouch in his cloak.

There was a screech from above. Corban looked up, saw the shape of a bird swooping down. It circled overhead, swept low over the road and landed on Ventos' outstretched arm.

It was a huge hawk, head cocked to one side as it studied Corban, golden feathers flecked with blue and red catching the last rays of the sun.

'It is my pleasure to introduce you to Kartala,' Ventos said, bowing slightly, beaming.

'She's magnificent,' Corban breathed, staring at the huge bird, eyes drawn to its curved talons gripping the leather of Ventos' thick glove.

'I won her from the Sirak,' he said.

'Sirak?'

'Aye. They use hawks to hunt on their sea of grass, and are very skilled at it. Fortunate for me that they are not quite so skilled with a throw-board and dice.' He grinned and winked. 'She has been a good companion. Most helpful. My hound Talar can catch a hare with ease, but have you ever eaten hare all year round?' He shivered. 'It tends to lose its appeal. I trade for food, of course, but villages are not always where I would like them to be. Kartala has caught me all manner of game, even other birds.'

'Does she eat crow?' Corban muttered, thinking of Craf.

'Crow. Why?'

'No matter,' Corban sighed. *Too dangerous*, he thought, *Brina would poison me*.

'Well I'd best pay the baron of the village a visit. Torin, isn't it? See if there's a spot in the roundhouse for me to lay my head. Come see me on the morrow, eh?'

'Aye,' Corban said.

Hooves thudded on the road, coming from the village. Corban looked up to see a tall, dapple-grey stallion trotting towards them. Meical rode him, and again Corban felt that tickling sensation across the back of his neck.

Meical slowed, his gaze not leaving Corban, something fierce in his expression. He glanced at Ventos, gaze lingering on the hunting bird and then looked ahead, kicking his horse into a canter.

CHAPTER FIFTY-FOUR

VENTOS

The air was thick and heavy in the roundhouse, smoke from the firepit swirling sluggishly around the smoke-hole above. Grey light edged the doorway, signalling dawn's imminent arrival. Ventos pushed himself up, slowly, not wanting to wake anyone.

An orange glow still seeped from the firepit, enough to guide his feet and reveal the forms of others – members of Torin's hold or other travellers – huddled in sleep. He reached for his boots and picked his way carefully to the exit, slipping through the doors.

Quickly he made his way through the village until he came to his wain. Talar emerged from beneath it, stretched his long limbs and nuzzled against his master's leg. Absently Ventos stroked the hound's head as he lifted the lid of the driver's bench seat. He pulled out a small chest, withdrew a tiny roll of parchment, a quill and a sealed horn of ink. Carefully he broke the seal, dipped the quill and began to write.

When done, he tapped the parchment into a small case, then looked to the brightening sky, clicking his tongue. Soon his hawk swept down and regarded him with bright, intelligent eyes. Deftly Ventos tied the case to the bird's leg.

'Fly true,' he muttered, watching as the hawk launched herself upwards, wings a soft whisper in the air before she disappeared into the mist.

CHAPTER FIFTY-FIVE

VERADIS

Veradis knew a moment of absolute, limb-numbing fear as he gazed at the men charging down the hill, the sound of their onslaught filling his ears. They hurtled into the press of warriors along the base of the hill, an avalanche of flesh and iron. Chaos erupted, men screaming, dying. Within moments it became clear that the new warriors were targeting Mandros' men, not those of Tenebral. Veradis blew out a long breath he had not realized he'd been holding.

Gundul had kept his word.

Taken by surprise, Mandros' men began to fall back, those that could clawing over one another in their haste to flee the swords of their enemies. Many lay dead or dying after those first frantic moments, and Peritus' men threw themselves back into the conflict with renewed strength.

Gundul himself flew down the hill on his black warhorse, driving towards his father.

'*Mandros!*' Veradis yelled, moving forwards again, slower this time, making sure he kept with the shield line. They met resistance for a few moments and continued their death-dealing.

The treeline was only two score paces away now and the ground before it seethed with men. Veradis scanned the mass, searching for Mandros and saw him standing tall in his saddle, bringing his sword crashing down onto another rider's helm.

Veradis was suddenly consumed with rage. Mandros, *kingslayer*. Then he was charging forwards, using his shield to smash men out of his way, striking at anything between him and the King of Carnutan. Suddenly Mandros was before him, yelling wildly, trying to staunch the flow of his fleeing warriors.

Veradis lunged, raised his sword arm, then a horse ploughed in front of him – one of Mandros' honour guard. The warrior kicked out at him, sending him stumbling backwards. Then the mounted warrior was reaching for Mandros' reins, dragging the King's horse from the battle and towards the treeline, others filling the space between them. Veradis watched in fury as Mandros disappeared into the gloom of the woods, a handful of his honour guard about him. Others blocked the path, holding back Gundul and his warriors.

Veradis turned, eyes sweeping the battlefield. Away from the entrance to the woods, most of the fighting was done. Here and there small pockets of Mandros' warriors were still battling on, but most were dead or routed. He saw Peritus, down by the churned banks of the river and ran towards him.

'Mandros has fled,' he gasped as he reached the battlechief. 'Horses – we must ride if we are to catch him. He cannot reach Dun Bagul.'

Peritus nodded and wiped blood from his eyes, streaming from a shallow gash on his scalp. Within moments he had gathered a handful of mounted warriors and scouts. Veradis and the battlechief climbed into saddles, pounded up the slope of the riverbank and crashed into the battle. Mandros' rearguard were grim faced and fighting furiously, with the abandon of those who have already embraced their death.

Veradis grunted as he deflected a sword swing, slashed in return, opening a red line down a warrior's thigh. Peritus' sword stabbed forwards, under the horseman's ribs – he swayed, toppled bonelessly from his saddle and disappeared beneath churning hooves.

Digging heels into his horse's side, Veradis pressed forwards.

Then it was over, Gundul's sword buried in the chest of the last defender.

Veradis rode to Mandros' son and sheathed his sword. 'My thanks,' he said between deep breaths.

Gundul's eyes were wide, still caught up in the frenzy of battle. He stared at Veradis, suddenly recognized him and grinned fiercely.

'Nathair will know of this,' Veradis said. 'You have become a friend of Tenebral this day.'

Gundul nodded. 'My father—'

'I know, I saw him flee. We must take him before he reaches Dun Bagul, or . . .'

'He will not reach the fortress. I placed men further along the road on the far side of the wood. But my father is cunning. Now that I am revealed he may head *into* the woods, leave the road.'

'Come then,' said Peritus. 'Let's be after him. You have men that know the land?'

'Aye.'

'Then lead on, with all haste.'

Soon they were galloping along a road dappled with sunlight, trees looming around them until the column stopped for their tracker to examine the ground.

'Men left the road here – not all of them, maybe a dozen,' the tracker said, a lean, sharp-featured man. 'The rest continued on up the road.'

'We must split also,' Gundul said.

'Which way?' Peritus growled. 'Which way would Mandros have gone?'

'I think the woods. He will suspect the road will be blocked.'

'Then what are we waiting for?' Veradis said between gritted teeth, kicking his horse towards the trees, Gundul following.

The woodland was dense and navigating a horse rapidly turned from difficult to impossible. They dismounted and led their horses. Veradis saw that Rauca had followed him, along with Peritus and a dozen or so others. His simmering rage was fuelled by the slow going, by his fear that Mandros would escape them. He was almost glad when they abandoned their horses, and set off into the woods after Gundul's tracker.

The man was sure-footed, scanning the ground before him, occasionally touching a broken fern stem, scuffed moss on a boulder or tree trunk. Their group was silent, only the slap of feet on earth, grunting breaths and a growing tension charging them.

Veradis' thigh burned where he had been cut earlier, but he gritted his teeth, ignoring the pain. Then, as he stepped into a small glade, something crashed into him – the tracker, a spear-point buried in his chest. Veradis ducked and rolled to the side, unslinging his shield as he came to his knees, drawing his longsword as he reached his feet.

There were a handful of men before him, their backs to a great boulder. Mandros was in their centre.

Veradis charged forwards, a cold rage possessing him completely.

He tried to dodge a spear, taking it square on his shield and sweeping it away from him. Swinging his blade, he saw the spearman topple backwards, a red gash across his throat.

His momentum carried him on and he crashed into another man. They tumbled to the ground, Veradis' sword pinned between them.

Distantly he heard the sound of battle about him, saw booted feet as he rolled, wrestling furiously with his opponent. He butted his head forward, the iron rim of his helmet crunching into a nose. Blood spattered his face, then he was free and scrambling to his feet, reaching for his sword hilt.

His opponent was slower to rise, blood sluicing from his nose. Veradis' sword punched into the man's chest before he was upright.

There was combat all about him, the grate of iron on iron, men shouting, grunting and screaming. He glimpsed Rauca trading blows with a bull of a man, saw his friend hack into the big warrior's knee, then he saw Mandros, slashing at a smaller man – Peritus. The battle-chief was quicker, driving Mandros back with fast sweeps and lunges until the King slammed into the boulder at his back, Peritus' sword sparking as the battlechief chopped forwards. The two stood chest to chest a moment, then Mandros brought his knee up into Peritus' groin and clubbed him with his sword hilt. Peritus dropped to the ground, Mandros standing above him, sword raised.

Veradis darted forwards, lunged and sank his blade into Mandros' shoulder. The King cried out and fell back against the boulder, dropping his weapon.

With a jerk, Veradis ripped his sword free and held its blood-covered tip to Mandros' throat.

As quick as it had begun the battle ended. Only two of Mandros' honour guard were still standing, but they lowered their weapons upon seeing their King taken.

A hush settled over the small glade as all looked at Veradis, waiting.

He was staring at Mandros, seeing only him, remembering his face as he emerged from Aquilus' chambers and fled from the tower, remembering Nathair in a pool of blood and Aquilus' lifeless eyes.

'*See that justice is done*,' Nathair had said to him, standing on a windswept quayside before he set sail.

'Justice?' Veradis had answered. 'What exactly would that be?'

'Peritus will find Mandros, help you beat him. But Peritus is a politicker. He may see *uses* in Mandros, advantages.'

'What would you have me do?' Veradis had asked.

'A life for a life,' Nathair had said, his voice as cold as the winter sea about them. 'That is justice. No negotiation, no compromise.'

'I will see it done,' Veradis had sworn.

Yet now, with his sword at Mandros' throat, something held his arm. *Do it*, the voice whispered in his head, *kill him. It is what he deserves. He is a traitor. It is justice.*

Peritus rose slowly, Rauca helping him. 'Veradis,' he said. 'We have him. We have won. Step back, lad. You don't want kingslaying weighing on your shoulders.'

'No,' Gundul exclaimed, taking an involuntary step forward. 'Kill him. He deserves death.'

The world seemed to freeze, a heartbeat becoming an eternity, then Veradis took a step back and lowered his sword.

'I will not kill you,' he said, and saw relief filling Mandros' eyes. 'You shall be taken to Jerolin, brought in chains before Nathair. There you shall answer for your crimes.' *No*, hissed the voice in his head. *He is cunning, sly, he will squirm out of his punishment. And all of Carnutan lies between here and Jerolin. He will escape.* His knuckles tightened on his sword hilt, indecision making him twitch.

Mandros was cut, his cloak torn, blood caked on one side of his face, but he still held something of the manner of a king – in his eyes, in the set of his shoulders. He snorted. 'My crimes. I am guilty of nothing except foolishness, trusting where I should have been wary.'

'Be silent, kingslayer, else I reconsider my decision. Save your lies for Nathair.'

'He should be tried. Here, now,' Gundul said, licking his lips. 'There is too much risk while he lives.' He looked between Veradis and Peritus, eyes a little wild. 'Nathair promised me, and I have kept my part, won you your battle. But if he lives, men will rally to him. God's teeth, we are in the middle of *Carnutan*.' He looked away. 'If he is paraded through the realm it will make things difficult. For me. People should think him slain in battle, think me the peacemaker. If he lives I will appear . . .' He rubbed the heel of his palm into an eye.

'A traitor?' Mandros sneered. 'Cowardly? Weak?'

Gundul lunged forwards and backhanded his father across the jaw. 'I need listen to your *insults* no longer,' he screeched.

Peritus caught him by the arm and pulled him away.

Mandros wiped a trickle of blood from his lip, spat on the ground.

'So, you have made a deal with Aquilus' whelp, eh? Good, for at least now I know you will not enjoy the fruits you think your betrayal has earned you.'

'Be silent,' Veradis muttered through clenched teeth. He would not hear Nathair disrespected.

'Come, Mandros. It is over,' Peritus said. 'You are taken. By Elyon's grace we have marched into the heart of your realm and *taken* you. And now we shall march you out. You have wronged us, wronged Tenebral, wronged *me*. You shall have your chance to speak in Jerolin. Save your words for my King. He shall judge them, and you.'

'Your King. You mean the *son* of your King. He will be your ruin, Peritus. He shall be *Tenebral's* ruin.' He glanced between Veradis and Peritus. 'On my oath, I did not kill Aquilus. Nathair did.'

Peritus blinked, just stared at Mandros.

'I *said*. Be. Silent,' Veradis growled, feeling the familiar rage churning in his gut again. *His lies will spread poison*, the voice in his head reasoned, *and Nathair does not deserve to be slandered so. He almost died*. Veradis' knuckles whitened as he gripped his sword hilt.

'You speak from desperation, Mandros. It dishonours you,' Peritus said.

'Do I? You think I would strike down your King? In his own chamber? I am no fool, Peritus – you know that of me, at least. No. When I entered the chamber Aquilus was already slain, though I did not see him at first. Your precious Nathair showed me his father's corpse, then drew his own knife and stuck himself.'

'You lie. You *fled*,' Peritus said, but there was something in his voice now, almost a question.

'What would you have done?' Mandros said. 'Say that Nathair slew his father and stabbed himself, and trust that justice will out?

Me, in the heart of your kingdom, a dead king before me and his wounded son accusing me.'

You cannot allow him to spread these lies. He is Asroth's tool, it is what he does, will continue to do. He must be silenced.

'Maybe I was a fool and panicked,' Mandros spat, 'but running seemed the best choice.' He held Peritus' gaze. 'Nathair slew your King, not I.'

Kill him, the voice in his head screamed.

Suddenly Veradis exploded into motion. In a heartbeat he struck, his sword slicing deep into Mandros' neck. The King wobbled a moment, sank to his knees and fell forwards onto the ground, dark blood pulsing into the grass.

No one had moved, so fast and ferociously had Veradis struck. He stood over the dying King, nostrils flaring. 'It is over,' he said, glaring at the small band. Peritus was the only one who withstood his gaze.

'Bring his head,' Veradis muttered to Rauca as he strode into the forest, slamming his sword into his scabbard.

Tarba, a squat, brooding fortress of dark stone, stood outlined against the rising sun as Veradis cantered out of thick woodland into a gently rolling plain. Peritus and Gundul rode before him, deep in hushed conversation.

The fortress guarded the mountain passes that led to Tenebral. Veradis studied it carefully. It was well placed, on a low hill over-looking a wide plain before the first slopes of the snow-capped mountains. He breathed in deep – much depended on the events of this morning as war or peace would be the outcome.

Belo, cousin to Mandros, ruled the fortress. He was a shrewd and cautious man, according to Gundul.

It had taken them a ten-night to march from the site of their battle with Mandros and, if Peritus' plans were timed correctly, a warband from Tenebral should now be sitting in the nearby moun-tain passes, waiting for their arrival.

Peritus did not want a fight, though. He hoped the fact that Belo would have to face foes from two sides, as well as the presence of Gundul, *and* Mandros' head on a spear, would convince the Lord of Tarba to lay down his arms.

But as the sun rose higher, they spotted shapes moving on the slopes before the fortress, sunlight glinting on iron. The hillside was covered in a sprawling mass of men: Belo's warband.

Veradis glanced over his shoulder, at the warriors pouring out of the woodland into the meadow. His own warband had suffered remarkably few casualties from the battle by the river, losing fewer than thirty men. Peritus' followers had not fared so well – he had lost around five hundred warriors. Mandros' warband had paid a much higher price, of course: some two thousands of their number littering the riverbank as food for crows.

Gundul's warband had swelled their ranks, but even so they still could only muster some three and a half thousand swords. There were considerably more than that massed on the slopes before them.

Veradis blew out a long breath, preparing for the fight ahead. *If the day turns sour my shield wall will carve a path to the mountains, or die trying.* He knew even his lethal wall of shields would most likely fall before this many men, though. If the wall were flanked in sufficient numbers it would be picked apart. He shared a grim look with Rauca, who rode beside him, as a small mounted party headed their way.

'Belo,' muttered Gundul.

'Come, then,' Peritus said, 'let us see what Elyon holds in store for us. You'd best join us, and bring your trophy,' he said to Veradis, glancing at Mandros' head, displayed on Veradis' spear-point. 'Belo will wish to know who slew his King.'

'Is that wise?' Veradis said.

'A sight such as that – it will set their will or break it. As to whether it is wise or no, that luxury was taken from us in a forest glade.' Peritus lingered a moment longer, then cantered after Gundul.

Veradis said nothing, but grimaced. He regretted what he had done, felt moments of intense shame, or at least part of him did. Another part of him gloried in it, knowing that justice had been done, Aquilus avenged, and a powerful servant of Asroth taken out of the coming war.

Belo was a tall man, ageing but straight backed and sharp eyed. Half a dozen men rode with him, all sporting black horsehair plumes on their helmets. Belo's eyes scanned their party as they rode to meet him, hovering on the head atop Veradis' couched spear.

'It would appear I am somewhat behind the times,' Belo said, tearing his eyes away from Mandros' decaying features and nodding at the battlechief. 'Peritus. I did not expect to meet you under such circumstances. You must know I cannot let you pass, even with the King's son hostage.'

'I am no hostage,' Gundul spluttered, nudging his horse forward.

'Then, how do you explain this?' the Lord of Tarba said, eyes narrowing.

Gundul drew himself up. 'As you see –' his eyes flitted unconsciously up to Mandros' head – 'I am no longer just the King's *son*. I am King of Carnutan, now, and I have made peace with Tenebral.'

'Peace?' Belo snarled. 'Peace with your father's murderers.'

Veradis moved forward, 'Mandros fell in battle,' he said, 'which is more than can be said for our King, murdered in his own chambers without a blade in his hands.'

Belo turned cold eyes onto Veradis. 'And who, may I ask, are you?'

'Veradis ben Lamar,' he said, glowering at the old baron.

'Nathair's first-sword,' Peritus added. 'Come, Belo, I have heard you are wise. Your King is dead, has paid the just price for his iniquity. Gundul has chosen wisdom, making peace with us rather than starting a costly war. And now you hold the pass to Tenebral, but you have one warband before you and one behind you, yes?'

'So it would seem,' Belo said, still looking at Veradis.

There is a warband of Tenebral in the mountains, then, just as Peritus planned, Veradis thought.

'But more than that,' continued Peritus. 'Your *King* orders you to stand down. Would your first act under your new king be one of betrayal?'

Belo sat silent for long moments, weighing Peritus' words. '*If* Gundul is no hostage, then there would be no harm in his accompanying me to my walls, where we can discuss, in somewhat more detail, the circumstances of this unusual situation.'

Another silence followed as Gundul glanced at Peritus.

'Of course,' the battlechief nodded.

'Good. Come, then, my King.' Belo waved an arm to Gundul.

Veradis grimaced, suspecting trickery. 'Do not converse over-long,' he called out to them as they cantered back up the slope. 'Our patience is not without end.'

Peritus frowned at him. 'You have much to learn,' he muttered.

'Maybe so. But we are not the wrongdoers here – I will not sit by and wait on Belo's pleasure.'

'Not the wrongdoers?' Peritus' eyes flickered to Mandros' head. 'There is more to this than right and wrong, I fear. And I for one would rather be courteous and perhaps live a little longer. Come, we'll let the sun rise a little higher at least, before we rush to battle.'

Veradis returned with Peritus, though with an uneasy heart. He did not trust Gundul: the man had betrayed his own father, so there would be no question of loyalty for loyalty's sake. It just remained to be seen whether Gundul believed it in his favour to remain at peace with Tenebral. That was an uncertain question, now that Veradis had removed Mandros from the board.

He shrugged to himself; he would almost welcome a battle. Since the death of Mandros he had been surprised to still feel so *angry*, the sensation lurking somewhere in the back of his mind. He'd thought it would have been quenched, now justice was served, but instead it remained, unfocused, a mist shrouding his thoughts.

Perhaps it was because of the manner of Mandros' death, the words he had uttered, trying to blacken Nathair. He had not wanted it to end that way, had not wanted Mandros' death on *his* shoulders. But it had been necessary for the greater good. At the memory of Mandros' *lies* about Nathair he felt his anger rise again. He ground his teeth, slid from his horse and settled on the ground beside Rauca and Bos.

Sometime later a small group of riders approached, Gundul on his black charger amongst them.

'Well?' grunted Veradis, his eyes fixed on Belo.

The ageing warrior held his gaze a moment, then dipped his head and looked to Gundul.

'Our peace stands,' Gundul said loudly, standing in his saddle. 'Be assured, you are both welcome and safe whilst in my lands. Clear passage to the mountains is yours.'

A cheer rose behind Veradis, although for an instant he felt almost disappointed.

'My thanks,' Peritus said to Gundul, though his gaze rested on Belo.

'I am but my King's servant,' the warrior replied. 'Come, if you are ready. We shall escort you to our border.'

Peritus turned to organize the march.

'Veradis,' Belo called, quietly.

'Aye.'

Belo leaned low in his saddle, speaking quietly. 'I would not display your trophy so proudly, if I were you. Gundul is King now, but oaths given to Mandros have stood for more than a score of years. Some may find it hard to put so many years behind them so quickly. They may object to a *kingslayer* passing through their midst.'

Belo turned and rode away before Veradis could form an answer.

It did not take long for Peritus to arrange the movement of their warband and soon they were on their way. Before he left, Gundul promised a new closeness between their realms and thrust a rolled parchment into Peritus' hand.

Soon a line of mounted warriors appeared on a ridge above them, all wearing the eagle of Tenebral on their shields. The warband that Peritus had arranged.

A giant of a man rode down to greet them. It was Krelis.

'Well met, little brother,' he said as they drew close.

Veradis could not help but smile, even though at their last meeting they had not parted well. He suddenly realized how much he had missed his brother. Leaning forward, he gripped Krelis' arm tight.

'Nathair has seen fit to place a few thousand swords behind me. Are they needed?'

'No, they are not,' Peritus said, grinning at the huge man.

'Still causing trouble wherever you go, eh?' Krelis said to the battlechief. He slapped Peritus' back good-naturedly, nearly knocking the man from his saddle.

'Not this time,' Peritus said. 'Your brother is the one to watch on that count. He begged to be the first one to walk into an ambush – through a river.'

'He never was the brightest of us,' said Krelis, grinning again. Veradis felt himself blush, feeling good for the first time since before Aquilus' death.

'And Mandros,' Krelis said, looking up at the head on Veradis' spear. 'He has answered for his crime, then.'

'Aye,' Peritus grunted.

'Did he die well?'

'Well enough,' Peritus muttered. Veradis looked away. 'Your brother did the deed.'

'Good. That is fitting,' growled Krelis. 'Aquilus was a great man. A great king.' He sighed and wiped a huge hand across his eyes. 'Well then, that is that. I suppose it is back to Jerolin for us.'

'Aye,' agreed Peritus.

'Come, then. I've had enough of these mountains,' Krelis rumbled. Together they began the journey back to Tenebral.

Veradis rode into the courtyard of Jerolin with Krelis and Peritus, and saw Nathair standing at its far end. Fidele was beside him, with rows of the eagle-guard standing behind in polished leather and iron.

The three men slipped from their saddles and dropped to one knee before Nathair.

'Rise,' said the new King of Tenebral.

Veradis thought him still pale, drawn around the eyes, but much improved from when he had last seen him.

'Welcome home,' Nathair said, gripping Krelis' and Peritus' arms in turn, then embracing Veradis before stepping backwards and regarding them all. 'Elyon has answered my prayers. My battlechiefs have returned to me, through countless dangers.'

'I only sat on a grassy slope for a ten-night,' Krelis interjected. 'It was these that risked life and limb – worst I got was a damp arse.'

'You would have risked all, though, if the need arose,' said Nathair, smiling. 'And just your presence played a great part in persuading Belo to grant safe passage, of that I am sure.' He paused a moment, reached for his mother's hand and squeezed it tight. 'And my father is avenged?'

'Aye. He is,' Peritus said, a tremor shaking his voice.

'Where is Mandros?' Nathair said. Veradis stepped over to his horse, untied a hemp sack strapped to his saddle and threw it to the ground at Nathair and Fidele's feet.

Mandros' head rolled out, the skin mottled, flesh peeling and hair falling out in clumps, but still recognizable as the King of Carnutan.

Fidele wrinkled her nose but did not step away.

Nathair nodded slowly, stared at the severed head, a sense of triumph in his eyes. Eventually he sighed. 'Come. There must be much you have to tell. To my chamber and some food and wine.'

Then a horn blast sounded out from the battlements and they moved to view the gate.

A huge figure was striding across the meadow beyond the fortress walls, through Peritus' and Krelis' combined warbands, warriors parting about him. It was Alcyon.

'A day for welcome arrivals,' Nathair murmured.

The giant nodded to Veradis as he drew near, then turned to Nathair. Dropping to one huge knee, he fumbled inside his cloak and drew out an egg, larger than a head. It was coloured in rippling, shimmering shades of blues and greens. The giant held it out in cupped hands to Nathair.

'My lord,' Alcyon rumbled. 'I have done as I promised. My gift to you: a draig's egg.'

CHAPTER FIFTY-SIX

CORBAN

The year 1141 of the Age of Exiles, Hound's Moon

'That's it!' Corban yelled. 'Nicely done, Dath. Now take the fight to her.'

Corban was standing in his garden with his arms folded across his chest, watching Dath and Cywen hack at one another with wooden sticks. Dath was limping slightly, and had a red mark blooming on one cheek. Cywen was unscathed.

Dath lunged forwards, swinging his stick a little wildly at Cywen's ribs. She stepped nimbly backwards, blocked his strike and swept her own weapon whistling down towards Dath's knee.

There was a loud *crack*, then Dath was rolling in the grass and Cywen was holding up what was left of her makeshift weapon.

Corban stepped in, trying not to smile. *Poor Dath.* It felt a little strange, teaching his friend and his sister their weapons, but there was something about it that he liked – probably being able to tell Cywen what to do with more effect than usual. And Dath had been desperate.

A warband had left Dun Carreg a moon ago, led by Pendathran, heading for Badun and then the Darkwood. It was the beginning of Brenin's move against Braith and the Darkwood brigands. Over two hundred warriors had ridden out with Pendathran, amongst them Halion and Tarben, leaving both Corban and Dath without weapons-masters in the Rowan Field.

Tull had stayed behind, gathered all of the lads together that found themselves suddenly teacherless and taught them as a group. Dath had become more and more embarrassed pitting his sword skills against others of his own age – it had highlighted his slow progress. In a moment of shame and rage he had asked Corban to help him while Tarben was away. So he was joining in with the training sessions Corban devoted to his sister.

'Am I the worst swordsman that has ever lived?' Dath muttered as Corban hoisted him off the ground.

'I've been teaching Cy for a while, now,' Corban said. 'Since before you set foot in the Field. And she's better than most our age.'

'Humph,' Dath grunted, rubbing his knee.

It probably didn't soothe his friend's battered ego, but it was the truth. Cywen learned quickly, her balance was good and she was *fast*: traits that were the bedrock for any swordsman, as Gar had told him many, *many* times.

'Come on, Dath. I might let you win next time,' Cywen said, grinning. He scowled and retrieved his practice stick.

'Don't gloat,' Corban said to his sister. 'It's not the way.'

Cywen rolled her eyes and stuck her tongue out at him.

'Be polite,' he said, 'or I won't teach you any more. Mind, you could always ask Ronan for lessons.' He had seen the glances between Cywen and Ronan, how she had watched the red-haired warrior ride out through Stonegate with Pendathran's warband, oblivious to all else. He grinned to see her blush.

She scowled at him, selected a new stick from their collection, then set her feet for another attack.

'If he comes back alive from the Darkwood,' Dath said.

Cywen lunged forwards and whacked his head.

'Ouch. What was that for?'

'Wait,' Corban said, 'prepare yourselves. And no cheating.' He walked away, stopping beside Storm, who lay spread on the grass, eyes fixed firmly on the chickens scratching at the ground on the far side of the garden. Corban sat down, and leaned into her. He took a deep breath, filling himself with the scents of the garden: flowers, grass, earth, fur, all mingled.

'Come on, then, Cy,' Dath said. 'Scared?'

Corban looked up, saw his sister staring at him, her expression unreadable. She had been doing that a lot, lately. She looked as if she wanted to say something, but instead just frowned.

''Course not,' she said to Dath and launched herself at him.

*

Corban watched as Rafe drew his arm back, held his breath, sighted along his spear's edge, then let fly.

The spear arced through the air, a black blur in a clear blue sky, then thudded into the straw-padded target.

'Six,' Tull called in his deep, booming voice.

Rafe was taking his warrior tests in the Rowan Field. Many were paying it no attention, continuing with their training as always, although a small crowd had stopped to watch. Corban was one of them.

One more hit and Rafe would have completed the first part of the tests, and earned his spear. Helfach's son strode to the target, jerked his spear loose and turned on his heel, face drawn. He counted off two score paces, turned, sighted, let fly again.

'Seven,' boomed Tull.

'Huh,' grunted Dath quietly. 'I was hoping he'd miss.'

'Aye,' muttered Corban.

They were standing with a small group of lads, those whose weapons-masters had accompanied Pendathran to the Darkwood. All were watching Rafe enviously.

The huntsman's son smiled as he pulled his spear from the target and turned to Tull, who was striding towards him, holding out a bat-tered shield. Rafe's smile faded.

'The running mount next,' Dath whispered.

As Rafe hefted his shield, adjusting his grip, Tull turned and waved to Gar, who was standing some way off, holding the reins of a tall dun mare. Rafe closed his eyes and sucked in a deep breath, then nodded.

Gar clicked his tongue, set the mare into a trot and let go of the reins. He said something and the mare broke into a canter, straight towards Rafe.

He started running, pacing himself to match the mare as she reached him. For a moment they were moving side by side, then Rafe put on a burst of speed, angled closer to the horse and reached for its dark mane with his free hand, shield and spear clutched tight in the other. He gripped a handful of horsehair and launched himself into the air, legs seeking purchase on the soft hide saddle. For a moment Rafe wobbled on the horse's back and Corban thought he was going to fall. Then he straightened and found the mare's reins, eyes searching the crowd for his da as he punched his shield and spear into the air.

Helfach was standing alone, a fierce pride etched on his face. He raised his arm as his son looked to him, and clenched his fist.

Few of Helfach's comrades were left in Dun Carreg, as most of Evnis' hold had ridden out with Pendathran's warband to help clear the Darkwood of brigands. Due to the dangers of travelling through the forest, Brenin had forbidden the handbinding of Evnis' niece to Uthan, so Evnis hoped he and his warriors could help speed this clearance. The brothers Gethin and Evnis were none too pleased about this delay, according to Edana.

So Helfach stood alone in the Rowan Field, watching his son take the tests of a warrior. From the look on his face, though, he would not have known if he were in the midst of battle. His eyes were fixed on his son as Rafe grinned fiercely and drew the dun to a stop, turf spraying around its hooves.

Others watching cheered, banged weapons on shields, and Corban found himself joining in. Although he despised Rafe, there was something special about this moment, almost sacred.

Corban looked about, saw the hulking frame of Farrell standing on the edge of their group. He had seen the blacksmith's apprentice a few times since that day with Rafe, but had felt uncomfortable every time, had avoided his eyes, even pretended not to see him.

He took a deep breath and sidled through the crowd until he stood next to Farrell.

'One day we'll be doing that,' Corban said, looking up at Farrell, who stood about a head taller than him.

Farrell regarded him a moment. 'Aye,' he grunted, then turned back to watch Rafe.

They stood in silence for a while, watching Rafe dismount, move on to test his skill with a sword against Tull. Corban cleared his throat.

'I am sorry,' he said awkwardly. Farrell looked down at him again, but said nothing. Corban felt his neck begin to flush. 'I meant no insult,' he said. 'That day with Rafe. I have been the subject of his attention, before. It just made me angry, seeing him do it to someone else.' He stopped.

The big lad was still looking down at him. Slowly he nodded, an acknowledgement.

The sound of sparring pulled their attention back to Rafe. He was attacking Tull, Brenin's champion standing with feet planted, fending off Rafe's slightly frantic attack.

Tull was taking the huntsman's son through all of the forms, testing that he knew all that an unblooded warrior should. The conflict lasted a while, Rafe circling the big man, lunging, slashing, feinting with his practice sword.

Part-way through, Tull halted Rafe, who was then handed a shield. He hefted it a moment, then the sparring began again, this time Tull pressing forwards, probing Rafe's defences.

Eventually Tull held a hand up. 'It is done,' he rumbled, beckoning to Helfach.

Rafe's father stepped forward, carrying a sheathed sword. He stood before Rafe, who sank to one knee.

'Rafe ben Helfach,' Tull boomed. 'You came to the Field a boy, you are leaving it a man, a warrior. Now rise, take your sword, and hold as tight to truth and courage as you do your blade's hilt. Take strength from all three through your Long Night: truth, courage and blade.'

Rafe stood, facing his father, Helfach holding the sword by the scabbard, hilt offered to his son. Rafe gripped it, slid the blade free and held it high.

Cheers rippled through the small crowd, loudest in a group near to Corban and Farrell where Rafe's friends stood.

'Now make your oath,' Tull said, and Rafe pledged himself to Elyon, Ardan and King Brenin. He finished by cutting his palm with his sword, blood dripping onto the ground out of a clenched fist.

Helfach placed a new-made torc around his son's neck and then embraced his son, pounding his back. Slowly the crowds began to disperse. Rafe eventually stepped out of his father's grip and, after a few words, strode towards his gathered friends.

'Here, I have no more need of this,' he said, tossing his practice sword through the air to Crain.

Corban stood and watched, remembering with sudden clarity the day Rafe had taken it from him.

Rafe glanced at him and winked. Corban turned away.

Soon after, Corban and Dath were trudging through wide stone streets, making for Corban's home, where Cywen would be waiting for them. Storm padded a few paces behind.

'Do you think he'll get through his Long Night?'

'Who?'

'*Rafe*. He sits his Long Night. *Tonight*.'

'Oh. Aye, why not?'

The Long Night was the final seal on the warrior tests, when a boy truly became a man. Rafe would have to leave the fortress before sunset, armed with his new sword, spear and a small sack of provisions, to spend the night on his own in the open, somewhere beyond the safety of Dun Carreg and Havan. The Long Night was supposed to be spent in vigil, unsleeping; a silent, solitary contemplation of those who had raised and guarded them through childhood.

'I don't know,' Dath muttered. 'I just wish he would fail it, somehow.'

Corban shrugged.

They reached his home, Corban throwing Dath a chunk of honey-bread still warm from the oven as they passed through the kitchen. He caught a glimpse of Cywen through the window, standing at the far end of the garden near the rose-wall.

'Go through, Dath. I'll just get our practice sticks.'

They had collected a stockpile of sticks that they used for their training, ones that closest resembled a sword, and Corban kept them rolled in a cloth in his chamber, so they would not rot from rain and frost. As he sped down the corridor he saw his mam and da's door was open, sunlight streaming through an unshuttered window and pouring out into the hall. He drew to a sudden stop and peeped in. His mam was sitting on the edge of her bed, her back to him. Without thinking, he stepped into the room.

His mam jumped, surprised, and twisted round. 'Oh, it's you, Ban,' she murmured, wiping her cheek.

'What are you doing, Mam?' he asked, peering over her shoulder. She had an old piece of fabric on her lap, alongside a piece of wood. He smiled at seeing the wood – a carving he had attempted when little more than a bairn. It was supposed to be a star, he dimly remembered, though poorly done and abandoned before it was finished. He had not known his mam had kept it.

'Just remembering,' his mam said with a sniff. She put an arm around his waist and hugged him.

'What's that?' he said, pointing at the fabric.

'Your sister's first effort at stitching.'

'It's not very good,' Corban observed.

'No,' his mam agreed.

'But . . . why is it making you cry?'

His mam's grip tightened. 'Time passes too quickly.' She rested her head against his waist, and he stroked her hair. 'I love you,' she whispered.

CHAPTER FIFTY-SEVEN

VERADIS

'Not long, now,' said Calidus.

Veradis leaned forward, peering over Nathair's shoulder. The new King was kneeling on the ground, staring intently at a large egg nestled before him in mounds of straw.

As Veradis watched, a thin crack, no wider than a hair, appeared amidst the blue and green of the shell. It spread quickly, cobwebbing out from a central point that soon became a hole, growing before his eyes.

Thick, clear fluid leaked from the hole, then the shell began to push outwards. There were a series of audible *cracks* and suddenly a flat muzzle was visible.

'Help it, Nathair,' Calidus said sharply, 'this must be done by one man alone.'

They were in a stable box, with Valyn, a larger crowd gathered beyond the stable gate.

Nathair began pulling bits of shell away, widening the hole, his hands soon slick with the jelly-like fluid oozing from the egg. The creature within thrust its snout through the hole, its head following, getting stuck at the shoulders. It twisted about, jaws snapping, trying to free itself.

Nathair dug his fingers into the shell, around the creature's shoulders, strained, and with a *snap* the egg broke and fell away, leaving a slimy, lizard-like creature standing in its ruin, about half an arm in length, from snout to tail-tip.

Veradis shivered, suddenly remembering seeing this creature's kin charging up a hill slope towards him. It bore the same broad skull, flat muzzle and thick tail. Needle-like teeth glittered as it opened its mouth, letting out a strange, dog-like bark.

'Feed it, quickly,' Calidus said.

Nathair reached behind him into a wooden bucket and pulled out a handful of raw meat. He opened his palm before the muzzle of the baby draig, which was sniffing loudly, its head twitching from side to side with eyes shut tight. It caught the scent, head lunging forwards. A long tongue snaked out of its mouth, licked Nathair's hand and the meat, and it started eating noisily.

'Now give it the remains of its shell,' Calidus said quietly, as the draig ate the last meat from Nathair's hand. Obediently the King of Tenebral did so and the draig crunched up pieces of shell, Nathair guiding them into its mouth, slime hanging in thick tendrils from its jaw.

'Ugly beast,' Valyn whispered in Veradis' ear. He smiled.

When the draig was done, it scratched at the straw, turned in a circle and promptly went to sleep.

'Well done,' Calidus said as Nathair stood and they all retreated from the stable box. 'He will be bonded to you already, but you must continue to feed it. You and only you.'

'Aye. Did you hear that, Valyn? No one else is to enter this box but me. I want a guard set to watch it, and word sent whenever it needs feeding.'

'Aye, my King,' Valyn said, dipping his head. 'Uh, if you don't mind me asking,' he muttered, 'how often, exactly, does it *need* feeding?'

Nathair looked to Calidus, who frowned. 'I'm not sure.' The Vin Thalun shrugged. 'I would imagine the draig will let you know.' He smiled.

'Use your judgement, Valyn,' Nathair said. 'Now, fetch me a bucket of water for my hands.'

The crowd that had gathered to watch dispersed quickly, and soon Veradis was left with Nathair, Valyn, Calidus and the giant.

'Draig-Rider,' Nathair said, grinning. 'Alcyon, I am in your debt.'

The giant said nothing, just dipped his head.

'You must teach me all you know of these beasts,' Nathair said to Calidus as they left the stables, Valyn peering over the stable door at the sleeping draig.

'Of course,' Calidus said.

'Good. Very good. Now, I have a task to attend to. My mother has asked for me, and she is still fragile. I will summon you all later. There is much I need to discuss with you. It is time, I think, for a Council of War.'

Sunlight streamed through the open window, a shaft of light slicing into the gloomy room. Veradis grimaced, looking out onto the lake and plains beyond the fortress. It was a little past highsun, thin clouds high above blunting the full heat of the day. The mountains were a ragged, white-tipped outline in the distance. He sighed and turned away from the view.

The last time he had been in this room he had discovered Nathair lying in a pool of blood and Aquilus dead beneath the window.

He squeezed his eyes shut.

'Are you well, Veradis?' Nathair asked.

'Me? Aye, well enough.' He poured himself a cup of wine from a jug on the table and offered some to Lykos, who was reclining in one of a few chairs arranged around the table. The Vin Thalun held his cup out.

There was a knock on the door, and Peritus entered without waiting for an answer. Following him strode Calidus, with the hulking shape of Alcyon close behind.

'Please, sit,' Nathair said, waving a hand. Veradis sat next to Peritus, who acknowledged him with a twitch of his lips.

'This is a Council of War,' Nathair said, addressing the room. 'Things have been difficult for me, since Midwinter's Day. The effects of my wound lingered much longer than I expected. But my father is now avenged, and I am fully recovered. It is time to start *doing*, rather than *waiting*.'

'What do you mean by "*doing*", exactly?' asked Peritus.

'My father set things in motion. I would see his plans, his dreams, come to fruition. He planned for aid to be given to those who stood with him in his alliance: to Rahim of Tarbesh, Romar of Isiltir, Braster of Helveth, Brenin of Ardan.'

'Aye,' Peritus grunted.

'Rahim has received that aid. The others have not.'

'When will we leave?' Veradis said, feeling a flicker of excitement.

Nathair smiled. 'Patience, my first-sword. There is much to arrange.' He looked at Peritus. 'I would not have my personal war-band split between these tasks.'

'You are King of Tenebral, now,' Peritus said. 'Its warriors are yours to command.'

'Yes, and the warriors of my realm shall fight, make war, as I see fit.'

Peritus frowned.

'You saw my wall of shields in action, did you not?' Nathair lev-elled at the battlechief.

'Aye, I did. It was efficient.'

Nathair snorted. 'Efficient? Veradis returned less two score men than he set out with. Your warband lost over five hundred swords, and Veradis led the *van*.'

'I know it well. He is a brave lad,' Peritus added.

'Brave. Aye, he is. But that is not what I speak of. Peritus, I do not have a limitless supply of warriors – Tenebral does not. I can ill afford to lose more, *unnecessarily*. If you had trained your warband in the shield wall, how many would have fallen? How many would have made the journey back with you, lived to fight another day, that are now corpses, lying cold on the bank of a river?'

Peritus mumbled something, looking away.

'So I have made a decision.' Nathair stood. 'All that would hold a blade in my realm, that would call themselves a warrior of Tene-bral, must learn this new way of making war. They must learn the shield wall.' He fixed his eyes on Peritus. 'I will brook no dissent on this matter.'

'Yes, my King,' Peritus said, his face now a blank, his thoughts hidden.

'Good,' Nathair said, smiling suddenly. 'You will see, Peritus – the shield wall will help us win our war against Asroth and his Black Sun.'

'Aye, my lord. How, exactly, do you mean to execute this plan?'

'Veradis shall choose a few score men that were with him in Car-nutan, those he deems capable of leading as well as teaching. They will be sent to my barons and will train their warbands. They shall be the foundations of a new breed of warrior, forging warbands the like of which has never been seen in the Banished Lands before. We are mustering for war.'

Veradis felt his blood stirring at Nathair's words. He could almost see the warriors locking shields, thousands instead of hundreds.

'When?' he said.

'Immediately. Give some thought to the men you would choose. As soon as that is done they will leave.'

Veradis nodded thoughtfully. 'If your warband is being split to train new men, how will we be able to aid Braster and Romar, or Brenin?'

'You see to the heart of it, my friend. The answer is we must wait a while, until these new warbands are ready.'

Veradis frowned. 'How long?'

'Two moons, at the earliest. Maybe longer.'

'But summer will be past by then, and with a long journey, we would be arriving at winter's beginning.'

'Possibly. If that is the case, then we may have to wait for next spring.' Nathair shrugged. 'There is much else to do, Veradis. Do not fret: I will not have you sitting idle in these cold walls. But if the training goes well you may yet see more battle before the year is out.'

Veradis looked doubtful. 'Helveth we can reach, but Ardan – that is a long way.'

'Aye, it is,' Nathair said. 'By foot.' He looked to Lykos, who was lounging in his chair, long legs stretched out.

'I could get a warband to Ardan easy enough,' the corsair said. 'Though the further north we sail the more treacherous the waters become. Earlier would be better. Hunter's Moon would be the latest it could be left.'

Nathair nodded.

'You have been of great service to me thus far, Lykos.'

The Vin Thalun dipped his head.

'You and your fleet are central to my plans. Already the speed you have gifted me has proved vital.'

'We can do more than ferry your warriors. We would gladly fight for you, shed our blood for you. We believe in your cause, believe in *you*.'

Peritus looked at the Vin Thalun, his eyes creasing.

'I know. And you will have many opportunities to do just that, my friend.' Nathair looked intently at them all. 'The Vin Thalun are welcome here, are a valuable ally. We should do what we can to help them, for helping them helps me, us, our cause.' He stood straight again, focusing on Lykos. 'How many men can you transport?'

'Now? Some three thousands, no more.'

'We will build you ships. Tenebral has vast forests, and I will need to move more than three thousand at a time ere this war is finished. Bring your shipbuilders here, to oversee the work. Together we shall build a fleet.'

'It shall be done,' Lykos said, the iron rings in his hair clinking gently as he nodded.

Nathair paced to the window, staring out over the lake and plain.

'My father expected many to join his alliance, once Midwinter's Day had passed. That has not happened. Carnutan is in hand now, of course, after the recent events. Gundul I can count on.'

Whilst he benefits from you, thought Veradis.

'But from the rest – silence. I have sent out riders. I would know where the realms of the Banished Lands stand. If they will not stand with me, then I must consider them against me.'

'Perhaps Aquilus' death has troubled them,' said Peritus.

Nathair frowned. 'Why should that change anything? My father may be dead, but the alliance should stand – the sun darkened on Midwinter's Day, did it not?'

'Aye, my King,' muttered Peritus.

Nathair looked frustrated. 'But you are most likely right. The kings of these lands are contrary. Even Romar, who pledged his aid at the council, is sounding hesitant. I have received a parchment from him, asking for a *detailed* explanation of the events around my father's death. He even expressed, what was it . . .?' He rummaged on the table they were seated around, pulling out a rolled parchment. 'Ah, yes. He expressed his *disappointment*, regarding Mandros' death before a trial.' Nathair screwed the parchment up, threw it on the floor and returned to the window. 'We shall do what we can, prepare for war. Then we shall do what we *must*.'

A silence settled upon the room, growing until it seemed Nathair had forgotten they were there. Peritus shifted in his chair, a leg scraping. Nathair blinked, movement beyond the window catching his gaze.

'A rider has just passed through our gates. One of the messengers I have been speaking of, I think. Peritus. Go, see what news he brings.'

Peritus rose and left without a word.

Nathair returned to the table.

'My friends,' he said, 'you four shall be my inner circle, those that I trust without question. Others will be useful.' He glanced at the door where Peritus had just departed, 'But none do I trust as I trust you.' He bowed his head, and looked troubled. 'Elyon speaks to me. I dream, almost every night now. I must find the cauldron. I have been told it is vital to our cause – a weapon. Can you help me?'

'In any way I can, my lord,' Lykos said. 'You have only to ask and I will attempt it.'

Nathair nodded. 'I know, I know. There is much I must accomplish. I feel the burden of it keenly.'

'I can be of some help regarding the cauldron you speak of. I have information,' said Calidus.

Veradis looked at the old counsellor. It was still hard to believe this man was one of the Ben-Elim, the sons of the mighty, angelic warriors of Elyon. He understood why Calidus maintained the secrecy of his identity, but he longed for the day when the ancient warrior would reveal himself. And he had *wings* . . .

Nathair brightened and sat straighter in his chair. 'Tell me.'

'I have gathered some knowledge of this cauldron. Many, many generations ago, before the Scourging, a star fell from the sky. The giant clans were different, then, less warlike. They forged things from this stone. You may have heard tales of the seven Treasures.'

'Aye, of course,' said Nathair, and Veradis nodded agreement.

'Well, it would seem there is some truth in those tales, is there not, Alcyon?'

'Aye,' said the giant. 'Before the clans came to be, there was but one clan. My ancient kin lived in the north-east, beyond Forn Forest. Seven Treasures are remembered amongst the loremasters, which were said to be forged from the starstone during that time: spear, axe, knife, torc, cup, necklace, cauldron . . .'

Veradis twisted in his chair, staring at Alcyon.

'Where? Where is it?' Nathair hissed.

'The Treasures were scattered,' Alcyon said, shrugging his huge shoulders. 'When the Sundering happened, when the one clan became many, there was a great exodus from the north. The Treasures were taken; wars were fought over them. Most were lost, or the knowledge of them was lost. So the tales say, at least.'

'I have received word that the cauldron is in Murias, a fortress of the Benothi giant clan,' Calidus said. 'I believe it is reliable.'

'Murias,' muttered Nathair. ' That is a long, long way to march a warband, even to sail one. We need clear passage through the realms between here and there.' He looked at a scroll on the table, held open with weights at each end, traced a line with his finger: 'Helveth, Carnutan, Isiltir, Ardan, Narvon, Cambren – all lie between here and Murias.'

'Carnutan, as you say, is dealt with,' Veradis said. 'And most of the others are those that have been promised aid. Surely we can use that.'

'Yes. Very good, Veradis. We will help these realms, do what we must to ensure our voice is heard by those in power.' Nathair frowned. 'I do not like relying on others' goodwill, though. As I said to my father, these alliances are fragile. An empire would be more practical, would it not?'

'Your will be done,' Lykos and Calidus said together, just above a whisper.

'Why not declare yourself now?' Veradis asked. He had heard Nathair mention *empire* before, but always felt uneasy, somehow. Now, though, after the campaign against Mandros, seeing the way the kings of the Banished Lands schemed, it was beginning to make more sense in his mind. 'Strike your banners, and see who stands with you.'

Nathair grinned. 'I thought you were the cautious one.'

Veradis snorted. 'Was.'

'Not yet,' Calidus said. 'Declaring your true identity will bring your enemies down upon you, I suspect, and travelling halfway across the Banished Lands, through countless other realms, will be like a lodestone to them. It is too dangerous. Best to wait, find this cauldron, this weapon, and return it to Tenebral. *Then* declare yourself.'

Nathair leaned back in his chair, tapping fingers on its arm. 'Good. I shall do as you advise. The way forward is becoming clearer to me. Two other things are in my mind.' He held one finger up.

'The Jehar swordsmasters, the ones that left Telassar so many years ago. Where are they?' He looked at Calidus.

'I do not know,' Calidus said, bowing his head. 'My sources, thus far, have found no word of them.'

'It is a matter of great importance to me, Calidus. I must know where they went, and why.'

'Aye. I will not fail you.'

'I know that, my friend.' He patted Calidus' shoulder. 'And the second matter.' Nathair held up another finger. 'Meical: my father's counsellor. He fled when my father died. I want him found.'

'Ah, now there I have some news,' Calidus said, grinning.

'Really?' Nathair raised an eyebrow.

'Only today, I have received information. Reliable information. Meical has been seen at Dun Carreg. In Ardan.'

'Dun Carreg. That is King Brenin's stronghold, is it not?'

'Aye.'

'Hmm,' Nathair muttered. 'That is very interesting. And it is a good deal closer to Murias than we are here.'

'What are you thinking, Nathair?' Veradis asked.

'Perhaps I should lead those that I send to aid Brenin, find out why my father's counsellor felt the need to visit him. And also to position myself within striking distance of Murias, with a warband about me.'

Suddenly the sound of horns blaring drifted through the unshuttered window. Nathair moved quickly to it, Veradis and the others following.

In the distance, on the edges of the plain, a dark shadow was growing, a cloud of dust above it, moving slowly closer. The faint rumble of hooves drifted up to them.

'What?' said Veradis.

'Come, to the walls,' said Nathair.

Soon they were climbing the battlement stairwell by the fortress' great gates. Veradis vaulted the steps, two at a time, breathing heavily by the time he reached the top. Warriors were gathered there, watching grimly to see who approached.

The host on the plain was closer now, not far beyond the lake village. The top of the stockaded wall of the settlement was now thick with people.

Sunlight glinted off spear-tips borne by the oncoming riders. A dust cloud hovered above them and the drumming of hooves rumbled thunderously. There were too many to count, but the host was at least a thousand strong. Veradis stared, straining his eyes, but could see no banner or markings that declared their identity.

Suddenly, as the host began to climb the gentle slope to the fortress, Veradis recognized them.

The Jehar had come.

'Veradis, Alcyon, with me,' Nathair commanded as he headed for the courtyard.

Nathair ordered the gates be opened and strode through with Veradis one side of him, Alcyon the other.

One man rode at the head of the Jehar, black hair tied back just as Veradis had seen him before. But this time he was dressed for war, in a black leather cuirass over a long coat of dark iron mail.

Sumur, Lord of the Jehar.

Veradis scanned the ranks behind him, saw both men and women amongst the host, all with their long, curved swords slung across their backs. Something struck him as different.

They have no shields, he suddenly realized.

Sumur raised a hand, reined in his mount, and the host behind him drew to a gradual halt, and silence descended.

Somewhere above a hawk screeched.

Gracefully Sumur slid from his saddle and stepped forward as the entire host dismounted.

'Nathair of Tenebral,' Sumur said as he approached, stopping a few paces before the King. 'I have come as I said I would, bringing the power of the Jehar with me.' He looked up at the battlements of Jerolin, packed tight with warriors, then back to Nathair.

In a loud voice he called out, 'Nathair, we pledge ourselves to you, the Seren Disglair. We, the Jehar, shall be your avenging hand.'

He dropped to one knee and bowed his head. With a great cry the entire host behind him did the same.

CHAPTER FIFTY-EIGHT

CORBAN

The Year 1141 of the Age of Exiles, Reaper's Moon

Corban ducked under the paddock rail and took a deep breath. The air was fresh, sharp, a chill to it that set his skin tingling, even though the sky above was blue and the sun bright. Summer was slipping away, autumn creeping in.

'Come on, Ban,' called Cywen.

She was standing in the meadow near the lone oak, Gar beside her. The stablemaster was holding the reins of his great piebald, Hammer, who had an extra saddle strapped to his flank. Shield was galloping around the meadow, turf spraying, showing off to his sire.

'Are you ready, lad?' Gar asked him.

'Aye.'

'Good.' Corban then unstrapped the spare saddle from Hammer and called his colt over, gently putting the saddle on Shield's back, then quickly hooking the bridle over his ears.

Shield stood calmly through the process, Corban having accustomed him to bearing the saddle. Today would be different, though. Today Corban would ride him.

'Up you get, then, Ban,' Gar said, tightening the girth.

Slowly he swung his leg over Shield's back, eased himself upright and took the reins from Cywen. He clicked his tongue.

'Walk on,' Gar said, pulling firmly at Shield's bridle. The colt resisted a moment, took a stiff step forwards, then another and another, until he was walking comfortably again.

After a while Corban got lost in the rhythm of it, the rise and fall, the constant movement of muscles beneath him. They were walking parallel to the giantsway now, a thin plume of smoke marking Brina's cottage.

Beside him Gar made a clicking sound and sped into a limping jog, moving Shield into a trot. 'You ready?' he asked Corban, glancing at him.

'Aye.'

Gar let go his grip of Shield, and Shield sped Corban away. Haltingly at first, but then with increasing confidence as they circled the paddock, to return to Gar.

'Do you hear that?' Gar said, his head cocked to one side.

'What . . .?' Then Corban did hear it: a distant rumbling. They both stared down the giantsway.

Slowly riders came into view, a wide column filling the road. Two men rode at the column's head, both large and broad, black haired and bearded.

One was Pendathran, his sword arm strapped in a bloodstained sling.

It was the warband returned from the Darkwood.

The man riding next to Ardan's battlechief was strikingly similar, but with no grey flecking his black beard – Dalgar, Pendathran's son. They both looked over as they drew near, Pendathran nodding sternly to Gar.

In the column that followed, single warriors led groups of riderless horses. *Many* riderless horses. Corban saw Halion and raised his hand to his swordsmaster. Halion smiled back, though he looked weary, pale, a raw scar on his cheek.

In silence they watched the rest of the warband pass by, heading for the winding road that led back to Dun Carreg.

The sun was dipping into the west, shadows lengthening in Dun Carreg, as Corban stepped out of his da's forge and headed for the stables. Storm fell into step behind him.

He was itching to hear news of Pendathran's warband, but little had been clear when he'd returned home yestereve, other than that far fewer warriors had returned than had ridden out. Making things worse, his da had kept him busy in the forge all day, much to his annoyance.

Cywen will know something, he thought. *Working in the stables, she hears all of the news first.*

He stretched, muscles aching after his day with hammer and

anvil. A sharp sea breeze cut through the lingering heat of the forge, and he was tugging his cloak tighter before the stables came into view.

Cywen was hovering by a water barrel, huddled in close conversation with Edana and Ronan.

Perfect, Corban thought. *Having a spy in the keep is most useful.*

'Oh, hello, Ban,' his sister said. He nodded to her and smiled at Edana and Ronan. The young warrior looked gaunt, black shadows under his eyes.

'Edana and Ronan were telling me about the Darkwood,' Cywen said quietly, looking over her shoulder for Gar. The stablemaster would not be impressed if he saw her standing around. 'Many died.'

'I saw the empty saddles. What happened?'

'We were outmanoeuvred,' Ronan said, his face bleak. 'For many nights we beat a path through that forest, our party split into three forces. It was a simple plan – we were all to push to the centre of the Darkwood, meet in the middle and catch Braith between us.'

He paused, reliving bad memories. 'Somehow Braith managed to swing around our flank. It would have been much worse if not for Marrock and Halion. They caught wind of it somehow, gave us a chance to pull shields and draw blades before the arrows started flying. Many died. More would have – we were pinned down – but that madman . . .' He snorted, shaking his head. 'That madman Conall *ran* at them. He jumped off his horse, lifted his shield and just *ran*, blind as my boots at a wall of trees and brigands, all trying to fill him full of arrows.' He laughed. 'That was all we needed. Pendathran went behind him, then Dalgar; it was like a dam breaking. Those brigands are courageous enough behind trees with a bow in their hands, but they were not so brave when it came to iron against iron.'

'Did they fight you, then?' asked Cywen. 'You know, hand to hand, I mean.'

'Oh, aye,' Ronan said, 'though some fought harder than others. Most of them are used to thieving from holds, or ambushing outnumbered warriors. There were still more of them than us, though, once we closed with them. At least, until Gethin and Evnis arrived, and Uthan, not long behind them.'

'Oh, they did play a part, then?' Corban said.

'Of a fashion,' Ronan grunted. 'Depends who you ask. Anyone

from Evnis' warband would tell you they won the battle.' He snorted. 'Ask me, I'll tell you they arrived when it was all but over. We would have fought longer, maybe lost a few more swords, but the outcome would have been the same.'

'What of Braith?' Corban asked, thinking of the man that had made an oath to him in this very fortress. And kept it.

'Braith? He was there. Plenty were looking to take *his* head. Pendathran got to him first.' The young warrior looked about, lowering his voice. 'Only by Elyon's grace he's still with us,' he muttered. 'That Braith can swing a blade.'

'What happened then?' said Edana. 'Not even Father has told me.'

'Braith sliced Pendathran's sword arm, was about to finish him, but those two brothers ran at him – Halion and Conall. Both went swinging at Braith like they were Asroth's Kadoshim.'

'Don't say that,' muttered Edana. She made the sign against evil.

'It's true,' Ronan shrugged. 'They did. If not for them we'd have brought Pendathran's corpse back.'

'Did they kill him? Braith, I mean,' pressed Corban.

'Nay. Some others fell in with Braith, held the brothers off. Halion told me after that one of them was the brigand we had here, the one they caught in the Baglun.'

Corban glanced at Cywen and swallowed. Somehow he felt relieved that Braith had survived.

'Anyway, that was when Gethin and Evnis arrived. The fight went out of most of the brigands, then and there. Braith got away, a few with him. But not many. We'll not be having trouble from them again, I'd wager. Not for a few years, at least – if ever.'

'Good,' Corban said with feeling.

'Were you hurt?' Cywen asked.

'Me? Not really. A few scratches. It was the first time I have killed a man. But I was not injured. More than I can say for many.'

Cywen reached out, tentatively, and brushed Ronan's arm with her fingertips. He took her hand, and squeezed it.

'So the Darkwood is clear, then,' said Corban, frowning at his sister.

'Aye. As clear as it will ever be.'

'Evnis was almost skipping,' Edana said disapprovingly.

'Why?' said Cywen.

'Because now there is nothing stopping his niece marrying Uthan. Poor Kyla.'

'What's wrong with Uthan?' asked Corban.

'Oh, it's not so much him. It's his father, Owain. Ugh.' She shivered. 'And it's given Evnis new vigour in trying to match me with Vonn.' She scowled again.

'When will they be handbound?' Cywen asked.

'Spring, I think,' Edana said. 'It is too close to winter, now.'

'So long as Braith does not fill the Darkwood again by spring,' said Corban.

Ronan shook his head. 'Winter is hard enough anywhere, but living rough in that forest . . . No. As I said, it would take years to restore the kind of numbers we slew. Their power is broken.'

Cold, stinging rain blew into Corban's face. He lowered his head, pulled his cloak tighter and trudged on, grumbling to himself. The Crow's Moon was not a good time to live by the Western Sea.

He had just finished helping Brina and was making his way home, images of hot bread and stew filling his mind. His pace quickened.

Brina had been different, of late – less harsh or abrupt, if not actually *pleasant*. And she had been giving him more interesting things to do: preparing poultices, mixing herbs and remedies, getting him to use the information that she had been bombarding him with over the last year.

Storm was padding in the grass, some fifty or so paces away, matching his speed. He glanced up, saw Havan getting closer, the fortress above obscured by rain and cloud.

The streets of the village were all but deserted, the only people around scurrying for their hearths as he and Storm passed through. He had just set his foot on the winding road that led to the fortress when a familiar voice called out behind him.

'Hello, Ban,' Bethan said as she reached him.

'Oh, hello,' he said, recognizing Dath's sister. 'Where are you off to?'

'Back up there. Going to see someone.' She nodded to the cloud-shrouded fortress above them. 'I've been helping in the smokehouse. Walk with me?'

Corban sniffed and wrinkled his nose. 'Been in the smokehouse too long, I think,' he said with a smile, pinching his nose. 'I'll walk with you – not too close though.'

She pulled a face at him.

'Who are you going to see?'

'I can't say,' she said, blushing red.

'Oh ho,' Corban said, 'that sounds interesting. Is someone court-ing you?'

'Perhaps,' she was smiling now. 'Won't be long, everyone will know. He has to talk to his da first, though.'

'Come on, Bethan, who is it? I won't tell.'

She just smiled.

They were about a third of the way up to the fortress, approach-ing a twist in the road. Suddenly Storm stopped, ears pricked forward. She was staring to their left, past a boulder, at a copse of dense, wind-beaten hawthorns. Corban strained, thought he heard voices though the wind and rain snatched them away. He stared at the copse, thought he saw movement within the trees.

Bethan heard it too and stepped off the path towards the hawthorns. Slowly they made their way closer, into the shelter of the copse, the sound of raised voices growing clearer as the trees shielded them from the full brunt of the weather.

Corban stopped behind a tree, holding a flat-palmed hand up to Storm. He peered into a small clearing, branches knotted overhead.

Three figures were standing there: Rafe and Crain, brandishing a practice sword – *his* practice sword – and Farrell. Rafe said some-thing, arms waving, then spat in Farrell's face.

The big lad lunged forwards, hands reaching for Rafe's throat, but Rafe jumped back. Farrell barrelled after him, swung a fist and caught Rafe a glancing blow across the cheek. Rafe staggered and Farrell grabbed him. Then Crain clubbed Farrell across the back with his wooden sword, sending the big lad tripping over a root, sprawling to the ground. Instantly, Rafe and Crain were kicking and beating him, the practice sword rising and falling.

Corban felt his fists clench, teeth grind, but something stopped his feet from moving. *Walk away*, a voice whispered in his head. *There's nothing you can do. They'll only hurt you again, shame you again.*

He glanced at Bethan, saw her mouth open in horror. She took a step forwards.

Corban grabbed her arm. She looked at him then, eyes full of compassion, of pity, and suddenly he felt his feet moving.

'Stay here,' he said, 'and hold Storm. Don't let her follow me.' He showed the wolven his flat palm again.

Then he was running forwards, threw himself shoulder-first into Crain's back, sending him flying into a tree. Crain's head made a loud *crack* against the trunk: he fell to the ground and did not move. There was a shocked silence as Rafe stared at him. Corban balled his fists and waded into Rafe, throwing punches, connecting with ribs and chin. Rafe swayed a moment, fell to one knee.

'You're going to pay now,' Rafe snarled, jumping up and swinging a wild hook at Corban's head.

Corban said nothing, well past talking. He ducked, stepped in close and sank a fist into Rafe's gut that doubled him over, sent a chopping right hook into his temple. Rafe dropped to the floor, rolled away, staggered back to his feet, shaking his head.

'You're the one that's going to pay,' Corban yelled, over a year's worth of pent-up rage boiling over in him. 'You're a *warrior*! Not to touch younglings. Tull will take your blade for this.'

'Not if he doesn't find out,' Rafe snarled, pulling his sword from its scabbard. Corban stepped back, wide-eyed. Rafe swung at Corban, but the strike was clumsy, Rafe still feeling the effects of Corban's blows. Corban jumped backwards. Rafe swung again, this time the tip of the blade leaving a red line on Corban's forearm. Suddenly pain exploded in his back and he was falling, leaves and damp earth filling his face. He rolled, saw Crain standing over him. Crain swung the practice sword at Corban, but somehow Corban caught hold of it, wrenched it out of Crain's hands.

Rafe put a boot on Corban's chest, pushed him flat and lifted his sword high.

I'm going to die, Corban thought, opening his mouth but nothing coming out.

Then a thunderbolt of fur and snapping teeth slammed into Rafe's chest.

'No! Storm,' Corban cried, levering himself to his feet with the practice sword still in his hand, pain pulsing in his back. Storm and

Rafe were rolling on the ground. Farrell was trying to rise, blood sheeting into his eyes from a gash on his head. Bethan ran into the clearing, eyes fixed on Storm.

'I tried to stop her . . .' she cried.

'Storm, *HERE*!' Corban shouted, but with no effect. 'Run, Beth, get help,' he yelled, pushing her towards the path. She looked back once and then was off.

Rafe screamed as Storm's claws raked his leg, then Storm's teeth fastened on his arm. He screamed again, higher in pitch, and Storm shook her head. There was a wet tearing sound as Rafe rolled free.

'No,' whispered Corban.

Storm stood before him, legs splayed, strips of flesh hanging from her jaws.

Rafe staggered upright. His arm was a mess of blood and fabric and flesh. Corban saw the glint of bone. Rafe sucked in a lungful of air and screamed.

Corban lurched forwards, grabbed Storm by the fur of her neck, shook her. 'With me,' he commanded, then turned and ran from the glade, branches and thorns scratching him, Storm loping beside him, panic pounding in his head like a drum.

He burst from the trees, rain and wind whipping at him, turning the blood staining Storm's jaws pink.

'What have you done?' he whispered. 'They'll surely kill you now.' He squeezed his eyes shut, breathed deep as Gar had taught him, then began to run again, down the hill, away from Dun Carreg.

Storm followed, Rafe's screams fading slowly behind them.

CHAPTER FIFTY-NINE

KASTELL

Kastell blew on his cupped hands, breath misting. He rubbed them together and tugged on his gloves.

'Mount up,' he heard Orgull call behind him.

Without a word, the small band of warriors swung into their saddles, Maquin kicking out the last embers of their fire. Kastell looked out over the river, wide and black in the grey of dawn, the merchant barge they were riding guard to being just a darker shadow on its waters. His face tingled as a snowflake drifted lazily onto his cheek. He glanced up, the thin, pale expanse of light high above him a distant reminder of the world beyond the forest.

Orgull set a horn to his lips, blew once, then they waited in silence. Their captain was bald and thick-necked, freakishly strong. His warrior braid was bound into a short beard.

Oars appeared on the barge and dipped into the water, the vessel beginning to move sluggishly downstream. With a jingle of harness Orgull led the warriors on the shore away, keeping pace with the barge, a thin layer of frozen snow crunching under horses' hooves. Maquin kicked his horse into a canter, catching up with Kastell.

'It's not all killing giants, drinking an' singing songs of glory round a hearth, eh?' he said, brushing frost from his grey-flecked beard.

'Huh,' agreed Kastell.

They were running guard to a merchant barge travelling down the Rhenus, heavily laden with salt and iron from the mines at Halstat. This was what the bulk of being a Gadrai warrior entailed, as the Rhenus was the main trade route between Helveth and Isiltir and for ten leagues or so it coiled its way into the south-western tip of

Forn Forest. Anything travelling on the river was highly vulnerable during those tree-shadowed leagues.

Kastell rode along the east bank of the Rhenus, the dangerous side, with a score of Gadrai warriors about him. Each man there had slain at least one giant, most of them more. Half a score more warriors were on the barge, in case any attempted raid got past the riverbank patrol.

In his four moons in the forest Kastell had witnessed two giant attacks, each one turning his guts to water.

Twelve warriors had died in those attacks, and Kastell had slain two more giants, adding two notches on his sword's scabbard to the one that marked the day he had slain his first. He glanced at Maquin, remembering that day. It seemed so long ago, now.

'I'd rather this than fight the Hunen any day,' he said to his friend.

'Right you are, lad,' Maquin grunted, eyeing the treeline to their right.

The other task that consumed most of a man's time in the Gadrai was clearing the east bank of the Rhenus. They were riding on a wide path, thirty or so paces between the riverbank and the treeline painstakingly cleared of any new vegetation or saplings taking root. It was a monumental job, and teams of warriors worked at it all year round. It was backbreaking work, but it was better to be attacked in the open space by giants than in the thick of the forest, and giants were not the only danger. Wolven prowled, though they had mostly learned to stay the other side of the Gadrai's boundaries. Also draigs, which went where they pleased; bats the size of Kastell's shield, which would suck the blood from a man, and great armies of ants like the one he had seen in Tenebral, that could strip a man of all flesh in a matter of heartbeats. He tried not to think of the many other, faceless, terrors.

Kastell felt a prickling sensation in his neck and turned to see Maquin staring at him.

'We've been here a while, now. You getting an itch in your toes yet? Or regret coming?'

'What?' stuttered Kastell. 'No. On both counts.' He smiled at his friend happily, a sensation that was becoming more frequent with each day he had been away from Mikil. 'My only regret is that I did not listen to you sooner. It was the right thing to do.'

Maquin grinned broadly.

'Besides, I like it here,' he added, looking at the river on one side, huge looming trees on the other.

The Gadrai – the warriors that patrolled the river's borders – had welcomed him, asking no questions of his past other than the details of his giantkilling. They felt just about as close as any kin he had ever known, at least since his mam and da had died. He *belonged* here, felt happy.

'Good,' grunted Maquin, nodding to himself. The old warrior reined his horse in, staring at the treeline. He cocked his head, listening.

'What is it?' Kastell whispered, scanning the shadows within the first trees. He saw nothing.

'Not sure,' Maquin grunted. 'Thought I heard something.' He shrugged and kicked his horse on.

A faint splash pulled Kastell's head round. Movement caught his eye, in the river. Something swirled in the murk, ripples spreading in a wide V. He squinted. Whatever it was, it was heading for the barge. Fast.

The other warriors had seen it. Orgull blew on his horn, figures on the barge staring out.

The thing in the water was big, Kastell realized as it pulled alongside the barge, almost matching its length. A warrior threw a spear, but it missed, swallowed by the river. Oars crunched and splintered as whatever it was beneath the surface ploughed into them. Shouts rang out, the barge slewing in the river's current. Then something reared out of the water, white scales glistening, higher than the barge's rail. It resembled a snake's head, but massive. It shot forwards, grabbed a man in its jaws, and dragged him screaming over the rail, his cries cut short as he disappeared beneath the surface.

'What was *that*?' Kastell hissed.

'A wyrm,' Maquin said, pulling his spear from its couch.

The waters shifted again, towards the rear of the boat, a grey-white snake surging out of the river, slamming onto the barge's deck. Its body bunched, seethed out of the water to coil onto the timber deck, then it slithered forwards. Kastell could see figures before it, yelling, brandishing weapons. His sword-brothers. One charged forwards, hacking at the menace with his sword. The snake's head darted out, lifted the man into the air, began to *swallow* him. Kastell felt his stomach lurch.

Then another beast was at the front, bursting up in a fountain of black water, making the barge list as it slithered onboard.

'Elyon help them,' Maquin whispered. At the head of their column Orgull was yelling something, then a cry went up behind them, from the trees. Kastell twisted to see giants lumber out of the shadows. Some hurled spears. A horse went down in a spray of blood, its rider tumbling into the river.

'At them,' Orgull bellowed, kicking his horse at the giants, his longsword sweeping from the scabbard on his back. Kastell dragged his horse in a half-circle, drew his sword and followed. He heard Maquin swearing.

He glanced down the line, saw other warriors following Orgull's lead. The giants came roaring out of the shadows, axes and hammers raised high. Kastell only had moments, but that was all he needed to see that they were outnumbered. This battle was lost already, his sword-brothers dead. It was just a matter of how they died, how many foes they took with them. A giant was charging straight at him, a male, dark moustache drooping, spittle flying from its mouth as it screamed a battlecry.

His horse slammed into the giant, Kastell at eye-level with it. Both of them staggered. Kastell swung his sword and felt it scrape along chainmail. The giant grabbed his horse's mane and yanked it, making the animal scream, then hefted a war-hammer. Kastell swung his sword again, but it only dented the giant's helm. His arm went numb from wrist to elbow from the blow. Then a spear was sprouting from the giant's throat, blood gushing dark. It tried to breathe, choked and sank to the ground. Maquin yelled something in his ear.

Kastell ignored him. He was now at the rear of the column, so with a grunt he spurred his horse into the heart of the battle. Somewhere ahead he heard Orgull's voice, saw him standing in his saddle, swinging his longsword in a great looping stroke. There was a jet of blood, a giant's head spinning through the air, then the big man was gone, obscured from view.

His horse slipped on something, a dead horse's entrails. He dragged on the reins, managed to keep them both upright. Before him a giant swung his hammer, smashing a man from his saddle, bones crunching as his foot caught in a stirrup. Kastell hacked at the giant, managed to find the spot on the neck between chainmail and helm. Blood spurted again, the giant turning, hitting out with a fist and catching Kastell's horse full in the mouth. It neighed and reared, hooves lashing out to send the giant crashing backwards.

Maquin spurred his horse, appearing in front of him to grab Kastell's reins. 'It is no use,' Maquin yelled over the din, 'there are too many. Best to warn Vandil and the others at Brikan.'

Maquin's words made sense, but Kastell had had enough of running. From the Hunen, from Jael . . .

Out of the crush before him a horse burst, big-boned and long-maned, carrying Orgull. 'Ride!' their captain shouted, digging his heels into his mount. Another warrior staggered from the ground and Orgull held out an arm, pulling him up into the saddle behind him as he sped past.

Maquin pulled on Kastell's reins again, turning his horse, and together they sped away from the ambush, thundering along the track beside the river. Kastell glanced back to see a handful of giants climbing into some kind of boat. They were pushing out towards the barge, where the two wyrms lay coiled. No one else moved on the deck. On the track behind, the battle was done, giants checking all the men were dead. Some of them started into a loping run, following them.

'Not again,' he muttered and leaned low to his horse's neck.

For a day and a night they kept moving, stopping only briefly. The giants kept coming, sometimes just a shadow behind, sometimes closer. Kastell counted at least five.

'They'll give up soon,' Alaric said in Kastell's ear, his breath making Kastell wince, 'we're getting too close to Brikan.'

'Hope so,' Kastell grunted. He was exhausted, and his legs and arse were aching worse than he'd imagined possible. Brikan was the Gadrai's main base in Forn Forest, a broken, abandoned Hunen fortress. Kastell had never liked it, but seeing it now would bring him more joy than even news of Jael's death.

'Still over a day's ride to Brikan,' Orgull said, cantering beside them, 'but I'm praying Vandil's got a patrol out this way.'

'Why'd they want that barge?' Maquin asked Orgull.

The bald captain shrugged. 'It was full of tin and iron. There's been plenty more like that on the river before, but I've never seen the Hunen attack in such force. Must've been forty or fifty of them.'

'Aye. And the wyrms.'

Orgull grimaced. 'Been trying not to think about that.'

They rode on in silence, Kastell fighting to keep his eyes focused on the track ahead. In the distance a draig roared, making the forest shake, but it was a long way off. Suddenly Kastell heard a pounding behind them. He twisted in his saddle, saw the giants. They were opening their stride, gaining.

'They know Brikan's close, they're running out of time,' Orgull shouted. 'Ride hard now and we'll lose them.' He blew on his horn, a ringing blast. Crows exploded from an ancient oak, squawking as they spiralled their way higher.

Kastell dug his heels into his horse. He could feel it trying for a burst of speed, but hardly anything happened. A shiver ran up its flank.

'Come on,' Maquin roared, keeping pace with him. Orgull was pulling away.

Then, suddenly, Kastell was flying through the air. He crashed to the ground and rolled in crusted snow, his shoulder exploding with pain. He staggered up, dragging his sword out of his scabbard.

His horse was trying to rise, whinnying in pain as a spear shaft poked from its flank. The giants were pounding towards them. Three of them, one female, Kastell realized, though only from its lack of moustache.

Maquin drove his horse across the track, between Kastell and the giants, and drew his sword. Further up the path Orgull bellowed again. Then the giants were upon them.

Maquin's horse went down in an explosion of blood and bone, an axe blade in its skull. What happened to Maquin, Kastell did not know. He ducked under a hammer blow, hacked at a wrist and felt his blade turn on hard leather. The giant kneed him in the chest and sent him tumbling through the air. He skidded to a stop a handspan from the river, now swordless, and willed himself to rise.

Orgull came galloping back down the track and left his sword stuck in the chest of the giant bearing down on Kastell. It collapsed onto him, pinning him to the ground, where blood gushed into his nose and mouth. Kastell choked and felt panic flutter in his chest. He couldn't breathe. He grunted, heaved, wriggled and managed to squirm out from under it, *her*, he realized. Then he climbed to his feet, spitting and retching.

Maquin and Orgull were standing together, two giants before them. Then the forest was filled with horn blasts, riders galloping down the track, and men were leaping out from the trees. One of them wielded two swords, moving in a blur. Vandil, Lord of the Gadrai. He slipped under the strike of a giant, struck twice in a heart-beat, the giant collapsing as his guts spilled onto his feet. The other giant lay still under the blows of Vandil's men.

As quick as that it was over.

'Where's the rest of your men?' Vandil asked.

Orgull grimaced.

'What happened?'

'Ambush. At least forty Hunen. The barge was attacked by wyrms.'

Men paused about him, taken aback by the mention of white serpents.

'Chief, this one's alive,' a warrior called, nudging one of the fallen giants with his boot.

'Bind him and bring him back to Brikan.'

Brikan was a squat grey tower ringed by a vine-choked, crumbling stone wall, a Hunen border post from a time when their kingdom spread north, south and east. It was on the far bank of the river, a wide stone bridge the only crossing within the boundaries of the forest.

The Gadrai were about four hundred swords strong, though at any given time fewer than half would be found at Brikan, the rest on patrol or escort duty.

Kastell rode alongside Maquin again, both on horses given up by their sword-brothers. Further ahead the giant was slung on a litter between two horses, its weight too great for a single horse to bear. As far as Kastell could tell, it was still unconscious.

Then they were over the bridge, Kastell nodding greeting to the bearskin-wrapped guards, and passed under the gate arch into a cobbled courtyard where men were gathering to stare. A giant had never been captured alive before. Vandil ordered for the unconscious captive to be bound to a training post in the courtyard.

'Wake him,' Vandil said, and a bucket of water was thrown into the giant's face. It groaned, a cut on its temple crusted black. Kastell stared in fascination – he had never had the opportunity to study a giant properly before. Its skin was pale and grey, almost translucent in places, with dark veins visible. Thick, heavy brows jutted over small, dark eyes, its nose and cheeks all sharp angles. A black moustache drooped around thin, bloodless lips. Its eyes slowly focused and looked about. Muscles suddenly tensed as it tried its bonds, the tattoo of a vine and thorns about one forearm rippling, and for a moment Kastell thought the chains would burst. Then the giant went limp, muttering something incomprehensible.

'What do you want with the barge?' Vandil asked. He was not an imposing figure, of average height, slim, with thinning hair and a chunk missing from the top of his right ear. Orgull towered over him, but Kastell had seen the Gadrai's leader in battle, seen him cut down two giants in the time it had taken him to draw his own sword. Never had he seen anyone move so fast.

'*Mise toil abair tusa faic,*' the giant mumbled.

'In our tongue,' Vandil said. 'I know you can speak it.'

The giant just glowered at him.

Vandil looked to the blacksmith that had fixed the giant's chain and took his hammer. 'I'll ask you once more,' he said to the giant. 'That barge was carrying tin and iron. What do you want with it?'

The giant scowled, gritted his teeth and spat.

Vandil swung the hammer, bones snapping in the giant's ankle. It threw its head back and howled, veins and tendons standing rigid on its neck.

Vandil raised the hammer again and the giant thrashed on the post, snarling curses.

'I'll have an answer,' Vandil said and swung the hammer again, this time onto the giant's knee. There was a sickening crunch.

Kastell winced and squeezed his eyes shut. As much as the giants were the enemy, this was difficult to watch.

The giant screamed until he was hoarse, finally just glowering at Vandil, breathing in deep, juddering breaths.

Vandil raised the hammer again.

'*Muid ga an iarann go cearta airm, ar an cogadh,*' the giant spat.

'In our tongue,' Vandil said, still holding the hammer high.

'We need the iron to forge weapons, for the war,' the giant said in the Common Tongue, though falteringly, his voice gravelly and pitched low.

'What *war*?'

'*An dia cogadh – the God-War.*'

CHAPTER SIXTY

CAMLIN

Camlin shuffled his feet, forest litter clumping under his boots. He was cold, cold to the bone. *No chance of that changing any time soon,* he thought sourly, looking up at the snowflakes filtering erratically through a latticework of leafless branches high above.

For over a moon now they had been tramping around the Dark-wood, Braith and the remnants of his crew. There had been more of them, after that day when they had finally stopped the cat-and-mouse game and faced the warband from Ardan: some had died of wounds or fever, others crept away in the night. He shrugged to himself, didn't blame them, in a way. That was not for him, though. He'd been here too long, the thought of walking away from the Darkwood, from Braith, an impossibility.

He heard something in the undergrowth beside the trail. Quickly he drew his sword and stabbed it into the soft earth at his feet, strung his bow, nocked an arrow and waited.

He heard it again and saw tendrils of ivy tremble slightly. He breathed in slow, and pulled the arrow back to his ear.

'Don't shoot, Cam, s'only me,' a familiar voice called. Braith stepped out from the undergrowth, arms raised, smiling faintly. 'Never have been able to sneak up on you, eh?'

'You should'na do that,' Camlin muttered, wiping his sword clean and resheathing it, 'I could've stuck you. Then who'd I have to blame for this mess we're in?'

Braith's smile grew broader, though Camlin noticed a new gaunt-ness to his features that he'd never seen before, no matter how spare the winter had been or how little sleep they had had.

'It's cold, right enough,' Braith said, wiping a snowflake from his nose. 'We'll head for the hills on the morrow, Cam, leave the trees behind for a while. One more night in the cold, and then it's warm beds, a roof and a fire. All of us will go – too few of us left to worry about going in shifts.'

'Ah,' exclaimed Camlin with pleasure. Every winter Braith's crew took it in turns to shelter in a village up in the high hills. The hills began half a day's walk from the Darkwood's north-west edge, the village being less than a day from there.

'Would've been welcome sooner,' Camlin said, not quite managing to keep a smile from his face at the thought.

'Couldn't risk it, Cam; you know that. Had to be sure we'd no unwanted guests.'

'Well, that's a certainty,' he muttered. 'Anyone following us'd either be froze to death by now, or bored to it, the time we've spent wandering these woods since . . .' He trailed off. None of them liked talking about *that* day.

'Aye,' Braith murmured, absently touching a raw scar across his forehead.

Camlin remembered seeing Braith earn that scar, seeing two warriors bearing down on his chief, backing him away from Pendathran, who had leaned pale-faced against a tree, blood pouring from a gash in his arm.

He remembered shouting, launching himself at the Dun Carreg enemy, heard others gathering behind him. He blinked and wiped his eyes, banishing the memory.

'Going to the hills. That'll be good, Braith,' he said, reaching out to squeeze Braith's shoulder.

'Go get some rest, Cam, warm your feet by the fire,' Braith said, smiling his famous smile. 'I'll take the next watch.'

Camlin turned and made his way down the trail to their camp, unstringing his bow as he went.

They set off before the sun came up, with an eagerness that had been missing for days. Even cold feet did not dampen Camlin's spirits.

Usually Camlin was one of the few that preferred to winter in the Darkwood, but even he would be glad to have a roof over his head and a bed. But more than that, he would feel safe.

The Darkwood had been his home for more years than he could

remember, and it had always felt safer than a fortress. Yet ever since returning from Dun Carreg he had felt anxious, as if someone was following him. He'd scolded himself enough times about it, cursing himself for a fool.

He'd told himself things would be different back in the Dark-wood, but he had not been able to shake a sense of doom, right up to that fateful day. They could have led Pendathran's warband a merry dance around the forest, or just disappeared. But Braith had been tired of running, and they had not sensed Gethin and his war-band sneaking up behind them.

They walked for hours through the forest, until Braith stepped cautiously forwards, his bow loosely nocked. Camlin and the others, about a score in all, moved out of the forest into open land and then down to a river's edge. Once there, they pulled at a mass of reeds and bracken blocking the path, revealing a dozen or so coracles neatly stacked against the riverbank.

They rooted around for paddles. Braith pushed the first boat, with two men in it, off into the water. The coracle moved with the current, then began to cut a line across the river as the two passengers began paddling.

'Next,' Braith said.

Before long the whole band were crossing the river, Camlin sitting behind Braith, paddling steadily for the north bank.

Soon they were across, the coracles stowed and they were heading for the foothills. The small party climbed, steadily, the land turning soon to steep-sided hills and wooded, stream-filled vales. Nestled in one vale, between two fast-flowing streams, was the village at last. Smoke rose in a ragged line from a roundhouse, a score of smaller sod-and-turf buildings nearby.

Waves of heat rolled out from the firepit, washing over Camlin, slowly seeping through the cold that had leached all warmth from his body. The usque he was drinking had helped speed the process, warming him from the gut outwards.

The rest of Braith's crew rimmed the firepit, drinking and eating with the somewhat uneasy villagers, the hunted look that had edged all of their faces over recent days slowly disappearing.

'What now, Braith?' Camlin said at last.

There was a silence. Camlin thought he should have kept his mouth shut, not asked the question, then Braith spoke.

'We'll winter here, get our strength and spirit back.'

Camlin took a deep breath, deciding to plough on. 'I mean, after that. What's next, Braith? Will things in the Darkwood ever be . . .?' he trailed off, not able to put his feelings into words.

'The same?' Braith said, staring at Camlin. He shrugged. 'All things change. But we will survive. That is what men such as us do. He fell silent awhile. 'More men will come to the Darkwood to join us,' he said eventually. 'They always have, eh? And then, who knows?' His face became severe, mouth tightening beneath his fair beard. 'Vengeance, Cam. That is what is in my heart, at least. All of us – we've one thing in common. The world's done us wrong: our kin, our lords, our *betters*. But a man can only do so much running, hiding. Time we gave some back, I'm thinking.' He suddenly smiled, the hard man of a moment ago gone, or veiled. 'Besides, for men such as us, we've no place left to go that's better, safer, than the Darkwood.'

Camlin nodded. Braith was right. The battle in the Darkwood had been an eye-opener, and no mistake, but there was still nowhere safer for men such as they.

He took another gulp from his jug of usque. Brenin had been a surprise, seeming almost good, fair. It was a shame more of Ardan's lords were not like their King. He spat onto the fire.

'You well, Cam?' asked Braith.

'Well? Aye, I suppose. As you say, I have survived.' He smiled humourlessly. 'I was thinking on Evnis,' he said slowly. 'You told me he would aid us, yet at the Baglun he betrayed us, had Goran slain and tried to kill me. And if he had not appeared with his brother's warband behind us in the Darkwood that day, things would have turned out different, Braith.'

'Aye, Cam, I know it.' The chieftain snorted.'That one's got it coming, for sure. No matter whose toes I step on.'

'What d'you mean, Braith? Whose toes?'

'Nothing.' Braith drank deep from his jug. 'Sometimes it can all get complicated, what we're doing, why we're doing it. Confusing . . .' He took another gulp. 'But vengeance is simple, eh? And Asroth knows, between us all we've got plenty to take revenge for. Vengeance, Cam. Vengeance shall drive us now.' He reached out and offered his arm to Camlin, who grasped it tight.

'Aye,' Camlin assented, holding Braith's gaze.

'What's your tale, Braith?' Camlin suddenly asked. 'What drove *you* to the Darkwood?'

He knew all the others' tales, but no one knew Braith's reasons. He had just appeared, and was well known for not wanting to discuss his own background.

Braith stared, then smiled. 'Now, that is complicated,' he said. 'Another time, Cam, I think. It's not a short tale, and I'm for my bed.' He suddenly turned serious. 'I'm up and leaving before the sun on the morrow. Be away two, maybe three days. You'll be chief while I'm gone, Cam.'

'Wha—? Going? Where?'

'Whisht, Cam, hold your breath now. No more questions. You'll know soon enough when I return. But you'll be chief till I'm back, Cam, you hear?'

'Aye, Braith. If that's what you want.'

'It is.'

Braith stood, smiled again and walked away into the shadows.

Camlin didn't think much of chiefhood. It might have been different if he'd been leading a raid, but nothing seemed to happen here. The first day after Braith had left things had been fine enough. Come the second day he started to feel restive, bored, and he had not been the only one. By the third day he was almost continually mediating between his edgy and increasingly unruly companions.

On the fourth day he rose with the sun and walked restlessly to the edge of the village. There a noise drew his attention, his hand reaching instinctively for his sword.

A line of men crested the hill: ten, twelve, more. He was about to turn and run for the roundhouse when he saw Braith with them. Steadily they filed down to the village, Braith at their fore, in deep conversation. There were a score of them, grim, hard-looking men bearing weapons. Camlin saw the glint of mail in one of the packs as the men splashed through the stream and strode past him.

Braith stopped. The man he was speaking to – dark haired, handsome apart from a scar beneath one eye – walked on towards the roundhouse.

'What goes?' Camlin said.

'Recruits,' Braith answered, eyes following the new arrivals.

'Recruits? I'd wager they're not woodsmen, Braith. What is this about?'

'It's complicated, remember. But for you and the other lads, you need recall only one word,' Camlin's chief said grimly.

'Vengeance.'

CHAPTER SIXTY-ONE

CORBAN

Corban ran over uneven, close-cropped grass until he reached the giantsway's embankment, and scaled it quickly, using the practice sword he was still clutching to lever himself up.

He stopped a moment, sucking in great ragged breaths, and checked over his shoulder to see if he was followed.

Rain was falling in great sheets, the fortress shrouded in cloud, but he thought he could make out the copse of trees where he had just fought with Rafe as a darker smudge on the hillside.

In his mind he could still hear Rafe screaming. He hoped Bethan was all right; he'd seen her running for Dun Carreg.

Dun Carreg. Word would be out soon, and they would not be long in coming for Storm.

She sat at his feet, calm, unreadable, pink spots of blood spattering her muzzle.

'Come,' he said. Setting his face to the west, towards the Baglun, he began running again, Storm loping comfortably at his heels.

His lungs were burning, feet throbbing when next he looked up, seeing the cairn at the top of the hill where Darol's stockade had been. He slowed but did not stop and carried on into the forest.

Eventually the road spilt into an open glade, its stone blocks giving way to earth and grass, the oathstone rising tall and dark in the glade's centre. He threw himself down at the slab's foot, back against it, chest heaving. Storm scratched at the earth, turned in a circle and lay at his feet. She nudged him with her muzzle and rubbed her head against him.

What am I going to do? he thought, staring at the wolven. He closed his eyes, and buried his face in the thick fur of her neck.

We must run away. For a while he imagined a life in the wild, just the two of them, maybe even leaving Ardan. Perhaps he could find Ventos the trader – he was his friend, he travelled the Banished Lands, and he would welcome the protection Storm would bring. But how would he find Ventos? And then the thought of never seeing his mam and da again, or Cywen, even Gar, struck him. It almost took his breath away.

He lay down on the wet grass and curled up against Storm, who sniffed his face and licked his cut arm. He wrapped an arm around her and closed his eyes, oblivious to the rain.

It was still raining when he woke shivering, though the fierceness had gone out of it. The sky was darkening, the clouds above the colour of cold iron.

Storm was sitting with her back pressed tight to him, looking out into the gloom of the giantsway.

With a sudden clarity he knew what he had to do. He could not run away with her; he could not survive in the wilds on his own, or abandon his family forever, and he could not take Storm back to Dun Carreg. They would kill her for sure.

'I must leave you here,' he said, his voice trembling. He leaned into her, stroked her, fingers tracing the dark marks on her torso, standing out stark against her white fur. At least in the Baglun she would have a chance, if she made her home in its depths, and food was plentiful. He took a deep, shaky breath, felt tears suddenly fill his eyes.

Slowly he stood, limbs stiff, using the practice sword he was still clutching to hoist himself upright. He took a few paces towards the glade's exit, then turned. The wolven was already standing, ready to follow.

'Hold,' he said, showing her the palm of his hand. He strode quickly from the glade. A last, backward glance showed her still standing there, ears pricked forward, copper eyes fixed on him, then he turned a bend in the road and was gone from view.

Moments later he heard the familiar thud of her paws as she ran to catch him.

'Please,' he said as she loped up to him. 'Don't make this harder than it already is.'

457

'No,' he said, louder. 'Hold.' He showed her his flat palm again, and obediently she stopped. This time he walked backwards, still facing her, palm out. After a hundred or so paces, when she was growing dim in his sight, just a pale blur on the road, she began to follow again.

'No!' He shouted this time, waved the practice sword at her. 'No!'

She paused, head cocked to one side, confused.

'No,' he shouted again and walked towards her, waving his arms, but she just stood there, watching him.

'Away,' he yelled, and she turned and walked a few paces, but as soon as he turned away she was following him again.

'They'll kill you!' he screamed now. He poked her with the practice sword, but she still did not move. 'Go away or they'll kill you!' he shouted again, tears in his eyes, and then he hit her with the practice sword.

She yelped, a whimper, crouched down, her ears back. Then he turned and ran.

He looked over his shoulder and she took a hesitant step after him, so he stopped, threw the sword at her, turned and ran again, tears clouding his vision.

At first all he could hear was the pounding of his heart, his own sobs. Then, somewhere behind, Storm howled. It rang long and melancholy through the forest, the sound cutting him like a blade, but he ran on, sobbing, stumbling, until he was clear of the forest, splashing through the ford.

As he passed Darol's hill a figure appeared on the road ahead, a rider, the dark shadow of a hound by the horse's legs. The figure dismounted as he approached.

'Ban? Is that you, son?' a familiar voice called out.

He threw himself into the open arms of his da and stood there long moments, Buddai sniffing him, Thannon just holding him, big hands stroking his wet hair.

'Where is she?' Thannon said after a while.

'Sh-she's gone,' he mumbled. In the distance another howl cut through the night, long and mournful.

'Come, lad,' Thannon said. 'I must take you to Brenin.' He

picked Corban up, set him gently on his great horse, climbed up behind him and together they began the ride back to Dun Carreg.

The feast-hall was more or less empty as Corban followed his da through it, the stripped carcass of a deer being taken from the burned-out firepit.

Thannon led him through a series of corridors, stopping outside a wide door, a warrior standing before it.

'You ready for this, Ban?' his da asked. Corban took a deep breath.

Brenin and Alona were the first people he saw, sitting in high-backed chairs. Tull and Pendathran stood behind them. Before them stood a small crowd: Cywen was there, tried to smile at him, his mam beside her, face strained and pale. He saw Bethan and felt a flush of relief at the sight of her.

Evnis was staring at him, along with Helfach and Crain. Quickly he looked away, fixing his eyes on the King and Queen.

A hush fell as he stepped into the room, the bulk of Thannon filling the doorway behind him. King Brenin frowned as he looked at Corban and ushered him forward.

'How, how fares Rafe?' Corban said quietly, head bowed.

'Brina tends him. She tells us he will live,' said Alona.

Corban blew out a long breath. 'Good,' he mumbled.

'No thanks to you,' a voice said behind him. Crain, he thought, though he did not turn to look.

'Silence,' Brenin said. 'All will have a chance to speak, but in your place. Otherwise I shall evict you all, call you back one at a time.' He stared over Corban's shoulder, eyes sweeping the small crowd.

'Corban,' he said. 'What has happened is grievous. Rafe is seriously injured, could have lost his life, on account of a creature that was in your care, your responsibility, as decreed by my wife in this very room. I would know the details of how this event came to be, before I pass my judgement, and for that purpose all here have been gathered. Now, tell me. What happened?'

So Corban began to talk, falteringly at first, but then more clearly, feeling almost detached from all that was happening. He had cried quietly all the way back to the fortress, trying not to let Thannon see, and now he felt numb, empty. He concentrated on keeping his thoughts fixed on the recounting of the tale, kept them from slipping towards Storm, alone in the Baglun.

When he finished, Brenin called forward Crain and heard a very different version of the story, of how Farrell had waylaid him and Rafe, then how Corban had set Storm on them. After Crain others were called to give testament: Bethan, Farrell, finally Helfach, who had been the first back to the copse with Bethan. Queen Alona interrupted them all a number of times, asking probing questions.

When all had finished there was a long silence, Brenin serious as he thought.

'There are two matters here,' the King said, breaking the silence. 'One is my judgement on Corban and this wolven.' He paused again, frowning. 'The truth, as I see it, is that this Storm acted much as any hound would have, though with direr consequences. Is that not so, Helfach?'

The huntsman shuffled his feet. 'I suppose so,' he muttered.

'If the animal was still here,' Brenin continued, 'it would have to be destroyed, for it has shown itself unsuited for life amongst us. But it is *not* here. The Baglun is a fitting place for a wolven, and, so long as it does not return here, I shall take no further action against it.'

'What?' blurted Helfach.

'Your son was part of something dishonourable, Helfach. He has brought shame on your family. Granted, he did not deserve such an injury. What has happened is a tragedy and you and your kin have my sympathy. Nevertheless, I see no fault in any that are gathered here.'

'Dishonourable? Only if you believe him,' Helfach said, pointing at Corban, 'and discount all that Crain has told you.'

'I do not believe Crain,' Brenin said coldly. 'Corban's tale is supported by two witnesses, Bethan and Farrell. That cut on Corban's arm was made by a blade, and Farrell bears the marks of many blows, more than one person could have given.'

Helfach snorted but said nothing more.

'My lord,' Evnis said. 'A question.'

Brenin waved a hand.

'Do I understand it that this wolven does not have your protection?'

'Protection? A wolven? Of course not,' Brenin said shortly.

'Then it would be of no matter to you if I chose to hunt it. As some recompense to Helfach, to Rafe?'

Brenin frowned but nodded. 'You may do as you see fit. What you choose to hunt in the Baglun is your affair, as long as it walks on four legs, not two.'

Evnis gave a curt nod.

Corban felt something twist inside, like a hand gripping his heart. *Hunt Storm.*

'The other matter is Rafe,' Brenin continued. 'He has drawn a blade on those who have not sat their Long Night, nor taken their warrior tests. All know that is forbidden, that the skills taught in the Rowan Field are for a purpose: to defend our people, those that cannot defend themselves – women, children, the old.' Brenin fell silent. 'Rafe's blade and spear are taken from him. I shall return them when, *if*, I see fit.'

'Aye,' muttered Helfach. 'My King,' he added.

'Good. Then let this be an end to it.' Brenin slapped the arm of his chair. 'Now be gone.'

The room emptied quickly. Brenin called Corban as he was about to leave.

'Yes, my King.'

'Do not stray too far from the fortress, for a while. And stay away from the Baglun. I would not hear of any hunting accident that had befallen you.'

'Yes,' Corban gulped.

'That is all, lad.'

'Th-thank-you,' Corban mumbled, then left the room.

His family were waiting in the corridor for him. Cywen took his hand, squeezing it. Then they walked in silence through the keep, out into the rain, all the way to his home.

Corban sat in his kitchen, let his mam make him a cup of broth. He drank some, though it stuck in his throat. After a while he begged tiredness and went to his room. He closed the door and threw himself on his cot, then the tears came again, his body shaking, wracked by great, muffled sobs as he thrust his face into his blankets. All he could hear was Storm's howl as he had run from her.

*

461

Badun appeared in the distance, a stark outline upon a hill, the smudge of the Darkwood filling the horizon behind it. Three moons had passed since the day Corban had left Storm in the Baglun, leaving only six nights until the Birth Moon. He still felt her loss, as if part of him was missing. He would still think he saw her in the corner of his eye, following him, but the pain that he had felt at first had dulled. It had taken some time. He had cried himself to sleep for over a ten-night, holding his tears inside until he had shut his bedroom door, been sure he was alone. He had resisted the urge to wander to the Baglun, knew that if he had seen her again then it all would have been for nothing, and it had not helped that some nights he had heard her howling, somewhere beyond the walls of Dun Carreg. Dath had told him that Storm had been seen beyond Havan in the dead of night, howling up at the fortress.

Evnis had ridden out every day, taking warriors from his hold, along with Helfach and their hounds, to hunt Storm. Every day they had returned empty-handed and as time passed they had ridden out less and less frequently, and had all but given up by Midwinter's Day.

Rafe had recovered, his arm deeply scarred, but healed. Corban had seen him rarely, had felt uncomfortable on those occasions, his mind always flashing back to that moment amongst the trees. Rafe had been beating Farrell, had tried to do the same to him, yet Corban felt mostly sadness.

He shifted in his saddle, absently patting Shield's neck. This was his horse's longest journey. Corban could feel the energy beneath him, Shield longing to gallop, but he had kept him steady, matching the pace of the great, grey-cloaked column he rode with, which stretched away before and behind.

Brenin and his court were travelling to Narvon, to witness the handbinding of Uthan ben Owain and Kyla ap Gethin. And more than that – to witness the binding of their two realms, or so Evnis kept saying to any that would listen.

Gar had advised against Corban riding Shield, had said he was still too fiery, but Corban had refused to go unless Shield carried him. After losing Storm it had just felt too much to be parted from Shield as well. Gar had eventually relented, though perhaps his mam's dark looks had played a part.

A horn blew somewhere ahead, Corban stretching to peer up the column. Marrock, who rode with Pendathran, blew the horn again, a long, clear note, and after a moment they heard an answer from Badun.

The town was much closer now, Corban able to make out figures lining the wooden walls. He saw the gates open, a line of riders issue out, Gethin with his daughter and an honour guard.

The two groups joined on the road, the column stopping for a while, then lurching into motion again. They followed the road past the huge stone circle, the great slabs rising above them; then they were past, following the giantsway under the first branches of the Darkwood.

As before, Corban rode in the company of Brina, as he was officially on the journey as Brina's apprentice, though he was still not wholly comfortable with that idea. In truth, though, most needed little excuse to join the small host. Even his mam and Thannon had come, riding somewhere behind him.

One night had already been spent in the Darkwood, now, and they were quickly approaching the second sunset. Thoughts of the Baglun Forest brought Storm instantly to the front of his mind.

He sighed.

'Do you feel safe here?' he asked Brina.

'Safe? Of course. Well, as safe as anywhere else, at least.' She glanced at him with one narrowed eye. 'Pendathran, though a clumsy, tactless oaf, has his uses. He is King Brenin's faithful hound, and when set on a task, particularly one that involves stabbing people, he proves himself remarkably efficient.' She looked around at the forest. 'This place is safe, or at least Pendathran judges it so, or he would not allow Brenin to ride through it.'

'*Safe, safe, safe, safe,*' muttered Craf, perched on the pommel of Brina's saddle.

'I've been thinking,' Corban said.

'Oh dear,' Brina sighed.

'About what you said before,' he lowered his voice, looked around. 'About *greed*. About Evnis and his brother, about their scheming . . .'

'And?'

'Could we not do something about it?'

Brina snorted. 'There is no point. Even if we did, and somehow managed to stop them, a score more like them would just spring up elsewhere. No,' she sighed, 'they are just a sad, depressing sign of the times, of our steady slip towards . . .'

'No,' Corban said. 'Truth and courage, my da taught me. Live by truth and courage and Elyon will see you through.'

'Really?' Brina said. 'I would have agreed with you once, boy, but I have seen too much courage go unrewarded, truth earn nothing but hatred and deceit. Oh, to be young again . . .'

Craf cawed and flapped his wings. '*Truth and courage*,' he squawked. Brina scowled at him.

'So you will do nothing, then?'

'What do you suggest?'

'I don't know.'

'*I don't know*,' she echoed, rolling her eyes. 'The sanctuary of youth. Let me tell you,' she waggled a finger at him, 'ignorance is *not* a desirable quality.'

'*Do nothing do nothing do nothing*,' Craf muttered, heaving his wings and lurching into the air, spiralling above them.

'See, Craf agrees with me,' Brina said, though she glared after the crow.

'I-I . . .' Corban stuttered. 'Better to try and fail, than not to try at all.'

There was a squelching sound and something splattered onto Corban's shoulder. He looked at the creamy-white slime, puzzled, eyes widening as he realized exactly what Craf had just done to him.

Brina barked a laugh. 'You see – that is what Craf thinks of your *truth and courage*.'

'I hate that crow,' he muttered.

'He's not all bad,' Brina said. 'There are some advantages, still, from acquaintance with an animal that has the gift.' She leaned closer and spoke quietly. 'Craf tells me things. Mostly about the weather, or snails, or frogs,' she shivered, pulling a sour face, 'but sometimes I hear something a little more interesting. For example, today he has told me that he has seen something.' She looked at him pointedly, then stared ahead. 'He has told me of a wolven that tracks us, just out of sight. A white wolven with dark stripes on its body.'

464

CHAPTER SIXTY-TWO

CORBAN

'How long?' Corban asked. 'Before we reach Uthandun?'

'We should see its walls before sunset.'

'Oh.'

Corban felt a pang of worry at the thought of their journey coming to an end. When Brina had told him of Storm following them he had felt both worried and excited. The worry had faded as they travelled through the forest with no sign or sound of Storm. Corban found it comforting knowing that she was close, whilst becoming more confident that she would keep her distance, not give her whereabouts away. What she would do when they reached their destination, though, was another matter entirely. He was starting to feel an anxiousness settle upon him again.

The long column crossed a bridge, Uthandun on a hill before them. Corban began to twist and turn in his saddle, constantly looking back at the forest.

'For goodness sake,' Brina hissed, 'try and be more discreet. Else you'll have Brenin's entire host looking over their shoulders.'

Corban grimaced and tried to sit straight.

'Craf,' Brina said. She leaned close to the bird and whispered something. With a croak and a noisy flapping the crow took off and swung back along their path, towards the trees of the Darkwood.

'There you are,' Brina said. 'Now stop fretting.'

'Thank you,' Corban said quietly.

Brina snorted.

*

Uthandun was a sparse, precise town, everything laid out in its place, high wooden walls neatly enclosing every building, every space, including its acres of paddocks.

Beyond the northern edge of the fortress, the hill it was built upon dipped gently towards a flat-bottomed dell, and it was in this dell that King Brenin and his company had to camp, as the walls did not have the room for them all. Brenin refused to leave his people and chose the dell over a chamber.

That night Corban sat with his family around a campfire – Gar and Brina as well. Craf fluttered around her, feeding noisily on strips of mutton she occasionally threw him. Unlike Dath, whose da had kept him at home, Farrell was there too. He had come to see Corban, the day after Storm had mauled Rafe. He found Corban in his garden, just sitting, lacking the will to do anything other.

'I . . . wanted to speak to you,' the lumbering blacksmith's apprentice had said. Corban just looked up at him, at his bruised face, his cuts cleaned and bandaged.

'Aye. Well?' Corban had said.

'I wanted to thank you,' he said. 'For what you did.'

Corban shrugged.

'It would have turned out bad. If you had not helped.'

Corban had not known what to say, so Farrell had just stood there a few moments, then turned and walked away.

Since then, though, he had seen quite a lot of Farrell – not so much to speak to, but just, around, hovering.

A figure loomed out of the darkness, wrapped tight in one of their company's grey cloaks.

'May I join you?' Heb the loremaster said, looking between Gwenith and Brina.

'Of course,' said Gwenith. 'Make space, everyone.'

'Pfah,' snorted Brina, but shuffled over to make more room at the fireside. 'Why are we so honoured?' she said. 'To choose our fireside over Brenin's?'

Heb scowled at her. 'As abrasive as your company may be, my dear lady,' he said, smiling falsely, 'it is more preferable by far to those seeking to *ingratiate* themselves with Brenin.'

'Oh?' prompted Brina. 'Uthan not to your liking?'

'I am not speaking of Uthan,' Heb grumbled. 'Oh, he is quite dull, but the poor boy can't help that, with a father like Owain. No, it is Gethin's *crowing* and Evnis' *fawning* that I object to. He thinks us all halfwits, blind to his clumsy attempts at manoeuvring Vonn as a candidate for Edana. Not that I even care much about that. Brenin can marry her off to whomever he wishes, though I am certain it will not be to any son of Evnis. I just resent being treated as a fool.'

'Perhaps you've come to the wrong fireside, then,' Brina said, causing a ripple of laughter.

'Being *called* a fool and being *treated* as a fool are two entirely different things, my dear,' Heb replied, smiling faintly. 'At least the conversation here may keep me awake.'

Corban grinned now. Brina and Heb were almost a match, he thought, in terms of wits and sharp tongues. It would be an entertaining evening.

Thannon leaned close to Corban and patted his son's knee with a big, calloused hand. 'Not long till your nameday, Ban,' he said quietly. Corban shivered with excitement.

'I've been thinking,' Thannon said. 'Once we get back, we should start work on your sword.'

Corban grinned. 'That would be fine,' he said. Finally, a real sword, hard iron instead of a wooden stick. 'Mighty fine.'

Thannon smiled back at him.

CHAPTER SIXTY-THREE

CYWEN

Cywen didn't like the stables at Uthandun: they felt too new. She was riding out today with Princess Edana and her parents. Most of their horses were stabled in meadows outside the fortress, but the royal mounts were kept within Uthandun's walls. She frowned to herself and shivered unaccountably. Something here didn't feel right. She wanted to go home.

Don't be such a bairn. She led her saddled horse out into the yard where Edana were already mounted.

And anyway, she had no reason to feel this way. Quite the opposite. Ronan had asked her to walk with him last night. He made her laugh and blush in equal measure. He had spoken of *them* as a couple, of asking her da for permission to court her. She felt a fluttering in her stomach, just at the thought of it, could still taste his lips. She shook her head and looked around shyly, as if people could guess her thoughts, just by looking at her. But no one was paying her any attention. Except Ronan, of course. They shared a smile.

They were going for a ride in the Darkwood today, King Brenin having said to King Owain that he would like to see something of the forest. Owain had immediately put a guide at their disposal.

Queen Alona was also coming with her husband, which meant Tull and a score more stern-faced warriors. She mounted quietly.

There was a clatter of hooves and Vonn rode into the yard. He dipped his head to Alona.

'King Brenin sends his apologies,' he said stiffly, 'but he and my father are unable to ride out today. They have been unavoidably detained.'

'Oh,' said Alona, then frowned. 'This place is so dull,' she said with a sigh. 'Well, as we are all here ready, we might as well go without them – wouldn't you say, Tull?'

'Whatever you wish, my lady.'

'Will you join us, Vonn?' she asked.

'I am afraid not,' the young man said. 'My father bid me return to him as soon as I have passed on this message.'

'Then I'd best not keep you,' Alona said.

'My lady.' He dipped his head and turned his horse.

'Why the long face, Vonn?' Edana asked as he passed them.

'Huh? Nothing.' He shrugged. 'Father . . .' he muttered, then shook his head. 'Nothing. Or nothing you would understand, anyway.'

Edana frowned.

Cywen scowled at Vonn, suddenly remembering that day in the paddock, when he had confronted Ban, when Shield had killed the hound. 'Perhaps you have broken his heart, Edana,' she said, 'now that he knows the two of you will never be handbound.' It was common knowledge that Evnis had been manoeuvring Vonn as a potential husband for Princess Edana. According to Edana, last night her father had made it clear to Evnis that this would never happen.

Vonn smiled humourlessly at her and leaned over in his saddle. 'Would you hear a secret?' he said quietly, not waiting for a reply. 'I am glad that we will not be bound. Glad. I love another.'

'Who?' the two girls said together.

Vonn grinned, suddenly looking handsome, and touched a finger to his nose. He kicked his horse on and left the yard.

Soon all were gathered for the ride, a score of grey-cloaked warriors about them. Tull headed the column, towering over Alona and the red-cloaked guide, a huntsman of Uthandun. Then they were on their way, through the hard-packed streets of Uthandun, out onto the green hill, and suddenly Cywen felt her spirits lift. She saw Corban standing by the bridge that spanned the river. There was only time to smile at him, then they had passed him by, cantering over the bridge and turning west along the river's bank before their guide veered under the trees of the Darkwood.

'Who do you think it is?' Edana said to Cywen as they trotted down a dappled path, the sun making shifting patterns on the ground as branches above swayed in the breeze.

'Who what is?' said Cywen.

'Vonn's mystery girl.'

'I did not think him the type to fall in love. He always seemed too arrogant.'

'There are always females *hovering* around him, though,' Edana said.

'Like flies,' muttered Cywen.

'Maybe he smells bad,' Edana said.

Cywen laughed.

'But I've never seen him look interested in any other women,' Edana continued.

'Thought he only had eyes for you?' Cywen said. 'Are you hurt?'

'Don't be stupid,' Edana said sharply. 'I just hate not knowing. We shall have to watch him a little closer, when we go home.'

'Watch who?' Ronan said as he cantered closer.

'Vonn.'

'Vonn. What for?'

'Because he has a secret,' Edana said mysteriously.

'Cywen,' Queen Alona called from the head of the column. 'Come. Ride with me.'

Cywen kicked her horse forward, Edana raising her eyebrows.

'I saw your brother, at the bridge,' Alona said.

'I did too.'

'How . . . how is he? Since that business with his wolven?'

'Well, sad, of course,' she said, not knowing how honest she should be. 'I hear him crying at night, in his chamber.' She shrugged. 'They had a bond.'

'It was a shame,' Alona said. 'But there was no other choice. After what that wolven did.'

'They deserved it,' Cywen snapped. 'Rafe drew his sword. I think they would have murdered Corban and Farrell, even Bethan – Storm saved them, did no different to what my da's hound would have done, yet *she's* punished, not Rafe or Crain. Ban went to help someone, and then *he's* punished. It's not fair,' she said, then blushed and closed her mouth. They were all thoughts she'd had countless times, but she had never intended to voice them to the Queen of Ardan.

Tull grunted beside them, something like approval in his eyes. Queen Alona frowned at him.

'And if it had been Corban that had had his arm mauled, or Farrell?' she said. 'Your judgement is subjective, Cywen. No, it was the only option. The wolven *should* have been destroyed.' Alona shrugged. 'Other than that, has Corban been different, in any other way?'

'No . . .' said Cywen. In truth Corban was changing in all kinds of ways. Ever since that man had left – Meical – he had seemed quieter, withdrawn. She had wanted to talk to him about that and tell him what she had overheard, but every time she tried, something stopped her, whether it be circumstance or just a feeling. And at other times he seemed like the old Ban, only more confident, more sure of himself – at least when he was teaching her and Dath their weapons. Without even realizing it, Corban had become their leader, the glue that held them all together.

'Not really,' she amended. 'He misses Storm.' She shrugged. 'And he sits his Long Night soon, takes his warrior trial. He is just growing, I suppose.'

Alona nodded slowly, thoughtfully. 'Tull, how does Corban fare in the Rowan Field?'

'Corban? He has done well, my lady. Very well. He could be a master with a blade, though . . .' he frowned, said no more.

'*Though* what?' Alona prompted.

'Nothing, really,' the warrior said. 'His style, that is all. It is different. Maybe because Halion is his master.' The big man shrugged. 'With a spear he is adequate: not the best, but not the worst. With a bow, well, let's just say that is not for him.'

'Thank you,' Alona said.

Tull was silent a moment, then spoke again. 'He has grit . . . courage. The deep kind. I've not seen it so clear in one so young before.' He nodded to himself and said no more.

They rode in silence a while, the thud of hooves, the creak and jingle of harness filling the forest.

'There is a glade ahead, my lady,' their guide said. 'A good place to rest the horses and stop for a drink.'

They spilt into the glade, the sunlight suddenly dazzling. Cywen was still at the head of their column, with Alona, Tull and their guide trotting into the centre of the clearing. The rest of them, Edana,

Ronan, the other warriors, spread to either side of the Queen, some dismounting.

Cywen looked up, blinking, and shielded her eyes from the sun's glare. Birdsong filled the glade, bees buzzing lazily around clumps of snowdrop and red campion.

Then the first arrow struck.

CHAPTER SIXTY-FOUR

CORBAN

Corban stood by the bridge, staring across the river at the Darkwood.

He missed Storm.

Two nights had passed at Uthandun and not knowing was finally becoming too much for him. Last night he had asked Brina if Craf had news of Storm. She had said only that the wolven was still here, prowling the fringes of the forest.

The drumming of hooves pulled his attention away from the forest, back up towards Uthandun. A group of riders were trotting down the hill, all in the grey cloaks of Ardan, apart from one red-cloaked figure at the front.

Queen Alona rode beside the red-cloak, a huntsman by the look of him, a bow and quiver strapped to his saddle. Tull towered beside them, a huge shield slung across his back. Behind them Corban saw Edana riding beside Cywen.

A score or so warriors of Ardan followed, Ronan first amongst them.

Alona's eyes hovered on Corban as they crossed the bridge. He smiled at his sister. Ronan nodded to him and then they were riding past, people crossing the bridge standing to one side to give the riders passage. Once on the far side they branched off the giantsway, then the red-cloaked rider took them into the forest.

Taking a deep breath, Corban shouldered a small sack and strode purposefully across the bridge towards the forest, not looking back. But soon something made him turn, and he paused to look back at the bridge, one figure catching his eye. He stayed where he was, the figure getting closer, walking with a distinctive limp.

'Why're you following me?' Corban said as Gar drew near.

473

The stablemaster blinked, cheeks reddening. 'What are you doing, wandering off into the Darkwood?' he said.

'I don't need following. I'm not a bairn,' Corban snapped.

'No, you're not. A bairn gets itself into less trouble than you,' Gar murmured.

'So. Why are you following me?' Corban repeated.

'Your mam asked me to. To make sure you stay safe.'

Corban grunted.

'What are you doing over here, then?'

Corban was silent a moment, considering his options; he could lie and return across the bridge. But he had made a decision, set his will to it, and he just could not bear to go back on it. He took a deep breath.

'I'm trying to find Storm,' he said.

'What? But she's in the Baglun.'

'No. She's here. Brina told me.'

Gar was silent, thinking it over. 'We should go back. Now,' he said eventually. He held up a hand to halt Corban's forming protest. 'I know you must miss her – I know I do. But, what is best for her? If you see her now, all you've done for her will be for nothing. They will kill her.'

'I, just, I've brought her food . . .' Corban muttered. His shoulders slumped, then he shook his head and straightened his back. 'No, Gar. She's followed me to another realm, almost a hundred leagues. I don't know what to do after, but I must see her.'

They stood there, branches and leaves rustling above, distant sounds from the fortress filtering across, blending with the river's steady murmur. Gar nodded. 'If your will is set . . .'

'It is.'

'All right, then.'

Corban blinked, his mouth open, ready to argue on. 'All right, then,' he echoed. 'Good.'

'So, where is she?'

Corban shrugged. 'Brina said the forest's edge.'

'It's a big forest, lad.'

'I thought it likely she'd be west, somewhere. Not too far from the fortress, if she's followed us here.'

'So, do you have a plan?'

'Aye,' Corban grinned. 'To walk far enough into the forest that I won't be heard at Uthandun, and start calling her.'

Gar snorted. 'That should work.'

So they set off into the trees, Corban going first, trying to follow a fox trail through the thick undergrowth. After a while they reached a stream, mushrooms growing in clumps along its bank.

'As good a place as any,' Corban said, feeling suddenly nervous. He cupped his hands to his mouth. 'Storm,' he shouted.

He repeated the call a half-dozen more times, then sat on a stump beside the stream and waited.

It was not long before Corban heard foliage rustle, off beyond the stream, and saw a flash of white. Then Storm was there, loping towards him. She jumped the stream and powered into him, both of them falling, rolling in the damp leaves and earth.

Corban was laughing, could not stop, though tears streaked his face. Storm was bashing him with her head, whining and rubbing her muzzle against him, her breath hot in his face.

'Whoa, girl,' Corban said, trying to sit up, pushing her off him. She bounced away, spun in a tight circle and jumped back on him. He slipped and fell again.

Eventually he managed to stand. Storm looked up at him. He glanced at Gar, saw the stablemaster actually smiling at him. His own jaw ached from grinning. Storm was thinner than he remembered, her fur dirty and mud stained. He reached for his sack, pulled out a leg of mutton he had secreted away from last night's meal and gave it to her. She instantly set to ripping strips of flesh from it.

Corban grinned at Gar, then dropped to his knees and buried his face in her fur.

They stayed like that a while, Storm eating hungrily, cracking bone between her powerful jaws to reach the marrow, Corban and Gar just watching her.

Suddenly Storm tensed, her head snapping up, looking over the stream. A sound filtered faintly through the forest: shouting? Screaming? the distant clash of iron.

'Come, Ban,' said Gar, splashing across the stream.

They struggled through thick vegetation at first, thorns snagging at their clothes, then they stumbled upon a wide track. In one direction they saw a lone rider, swaying in his saddle as he disappeared around a bend. Corban thought he wore a grey cloak. In the other direction, much closer now, was the noise that had drawn them. Beyond all mistake it was the sound of battle. Screams drifted up the track, iron clashing on iron.

'Off this track,' said Gar, slipping behind a tree. Corban followed, Storm beside him, her hackles raised. Slowly Gar picked his way through the forest, Corban and Storm behind him, moving parallel to the track.

The noise ahead stopped, the silence replacing it feeling heavy, oppressive. Still they made their way forwards, Corban trying to step lightly, every twig that snapped under his feet making him wince.

Then they stepped into an open glade, sunlight streaming down from above. Bodies littered the ground, men, horses, all still, blood soaking them, the grass. Crows exploded upwards as they entered the glade, squawking in protest. One stayed perched on a horse's flank, its beak dripping red. Flies buzzed in thick clouds.

Here and there, dotted amongst the fallen, were men in red cloaks, but most of the dead by far wore the grey of Ardan.

CHAPTER SIXTY-FIVE

VERADIS

'Finally,' said Veradis, reining in his mount and shading his eyes from the sun. He sat his horse at the head of a long, wide column of riders, Calidus and Alcyon either side of him.

'Impatient to shed more giant blood?' Calidus said, smiling thinly.

'No,' Veradis muttered, glancing at Alcyon. 'It is just good to reach a journey's end, that's all.' He frowned. 'Well, one part of the journey.'

The passes had opened early in the Agullas Mountains, Veradis leading a warband across the mountains into Helveth almost as soon as word of the early thaw reached him. He had been preparing all winter, after all, so he and his warband were more than ready. He was leading around five hundred men of Tenebral north, and half that number again of the Jehar rode with them. They were led by Akar, the first warrior he had met in the hidden vale. Veradis felt proud as he surveyed the column: his was a warband the likes of which had never been seen before.

Almost a whole moon they had been travelling, nearly two hundred leagues since Jerolin, and now the end was in sight: Halstat, where they were to join the kings of Helveth and Isiltir in their bid to break the strength of the Hunen giants, once and for all.

Helveth had proved to be a land of great lakes in the south, giving way to wood and vale as they travelled further north. Now they rode on a far-reaching plain, flat as far as the eye could see in all directions except north, where the Bairg Mountains loomed tall and jagged. Their destination, Halstat, was a mining town, grown rich on salt and iron from the mountains.

Veradis clicked his tongue, touched his horse's ribs with his heels and set off towards the distant town, the column of warriors lurching into motion behind him.

'We are not the first to arrive,' Alcyon said as they drew nearer. Before the town were scores of tents, two large groups clustered either side of a wide road that ran through the heart of the town. To the left of the road the banner of Isiltir snapped in a strong breeze, to the right the black and gold of Helveth.

'It would appear we are the last,' Calidus added.

'Our journey was the longest,' Veradis said, somewhat defensively. Though excited to be away from Jerolin at last, to be *actually doing* something, he also felt a pressure upon him. In Tarbesh, Nathair had commanded. The campaign in Isiltir Peritus had led. This time *he* was battlechief of this warband, his warriors' lives resting on *his* decisions. He felt the weight of that responsibility keenly. And Calidus' presence felt like some kind of watchdog, though he knew that was not Nathair's reason for sending the Vin Thalun. They would be fighting giants again, likely with Elementals amongst them, so the presence of Calidus and Alcyon would be most useful.

Horns began to blow from the town wall as they approached, and soon a small company was riding out to greet them.

'Have some wine, lad,' Braster said, holding a jug under Veradis' nose. 'You've ridden a long way. Sit down, sit down. Though be careful, those chairs are hard as old bones, and your arse must be sore enough already.'

Despite himself Veradis grinned as he took the jug from the red-haired King of Helveth.

He had just entered Braster's tent, summoned immediately to a war council. Beside the King of Helveth sat a face he recognized: Romar, whom he remembered clearly from Aquilus' council, and after. He smiled at the King of Isiltir. 'Well met,' he said.

Romar did not return the smile. 'Things have changed much for you, since last we spoke. I hear you are first-sword to your king now.'

'That is true, though there has been much grief as well as good.' He paused, a picture of Nathair sitting in a pool of his own blood flashing into his mind. 'But that is a subject for another time.' He smiled again. 'This is a time for greetings. Is your nephew Kastell well? Or are you still playing maid to his and Jael's squabbles?'

Romar looked away. Beside him sat another man who frowned at Veradis' words. The hilts of two crossed swords rose from behind his shoulders. Braster introduced him as Vandil, Lord of the Gadrai, a band of warriors that patrolled Isiltir's border with Forn Forest.

'You are well acquainted with the Hunen, then,' Veradis said.

'Aye. And they us.'

'Come, sit, let us get on with this,' Braster said, easing his barrel-chested bulk into a creaking chair.

Veradis looked over his shoulder, a shadow filling the tent's entrance. Calidus slipped into the tent, Alcyon ducking in behind him. There were gasps around the table, Vandil actually jumping to his feet, hands reaching for the hilts of his swords.

'Peace. They are with me,' Veradis said. 'Calidus is counsellor to my King. And this is Alcyon, his guard.'

Veradis took a place at the table, Calidus sitting next to him. Alcyon stood behind them.

'This is most unusual,' Vandil said, slowly sitting back down, eyes still fixed firmly upon Alcyon. 'May I remind you why we are all here, man of Tenebral.'

'To break the strength of the Hunen,' Veradis replied calmly.

'Aye. Giants.'

Calidus chuckled. 'The giants warred with each other for far longer than they have fought with our kind. You need have no concerns over Alcyon's presence here, or his loyalties.'

'He has fought beside me, and saved my life,' Veradis added. 'In service to Nathair he has slain giants – the Shekam of Tarbesh.'

'What is your clan?' Vandil said, eyes still fixed on the giant.

'The Kurgan,' Alcyon replied.

'My King sends greetings to you all,' Veradis said over the silence. 'He thanks you for your continuing support of the alliance begun by King Aquilus. He hopes you view my presence here as a sign of his commitment both to you and to the ideals of his father.'

'Of course, of course,' blustered Braster.

Romar looked away.

'How fares Nathair?' Braster asked.

'He is fully recovered now, though it took many moons. Mandros did great damage.'

'A pity he was not tried for the things he was accused of,' Romar murmured.

Veradis flushed, the words hitting a nerve. He regretted that he had had to slay Mandros, *hated* that he was now named *kingslayer*. *You had no choice*, whispered a voice in his mind. *And Romar was not there, who is he to judge?* 'He fought and lost, was tried by me,' Veradis said. 'And given more justice than he gave King Aquilus. Would you question that?'

'Yes, I would. A king should be tried by kings,' Romar said, meeting Veradis' gaze.

'In an ideal world,' Calidus said, 'it should be as you say. But in battle there are no guarantees. May I remind you that Mandros fled Tenebral. He attacked Peritus and Veradis, ambushed them whilst they forded a river—'

'Some might say he attacked a warband that had invaded his realm,' Romar interrupted.

'Mandros was guilty.' Veradis felt his temper stir. 'I stood outside the door when he . . . when he did the deed. I saw him flee. I saw Nathair with a knife in his side, saw Aquilus . . .' Suddenly he could hear Mandros' words from the forest glade, clear and sharp. *'Nathair killed Aquilus . . .'*

He rubbed his forehead and closed his eyes for a moment. *Don't listen to his lies*, the voice in his head murmured.

'Are you all right?' Calidus asked, touching Veradis' elbow.

'Aye.' He sat straighter. 'Mandros was a murderer, a liar, a coward.'

'Nevertheless,' Romar waved a hand, 'it does not change our ancient law, brought with us from the Summer Isle, that only a king can judge a king, and I am not the only one who is unhappy about what has happened. I have heard the same from Brenin, in Ardan.'

Braster slammed a fist on the table. 'That deed is done, Romar. It is past,' he growled. 'And to judge its merits is *not* why we have gathered here. There is a chance, here, to rid our borders of the Hunen. Would you destroy that?'

'We do not need . . .' Romar glanced at Veradis and Calidus, at Alcyon towering behind them.

'I say we do. And, besides, I gave my oath to Aquilus. That was not lightly given.'

The two kings stared at each other a few moments, then Romar looked away, and nodded.

'Good. Now, we are here to talk of how best to root out the Hunen.'

'But know this,' Romar said. 'When this is over, I will be demanding an inquiry into what happened in Carnutan – you do not take the life of a king lightly. My support of your alliance will be withheld until I am satisfied. *If* I am satisfied.'

Calidus frowned.

'What do we know of this enemy? Do you know their numbers?' Veradis asked, relieved to move away from the subject of Mandros. He had not liked Romar's questions, his accusations. Nathair's words came back to him. '*The powers are gathering – all will fight, either for the Bright Star or the Black Sun. The question is, who will fight for me, and who against me? Trust no one*.' Veradis eyed Romar suspiciously.

'No, for a certainty,' Braster said.

'Their numbers when they raid are increasing,' Vandil said. 'It used to be tens or twenties. Their last raid on Isiltir's border was forty or fifty strong. And they had wyrms.'

'Wyrms?' Veradis said. *First draigs, now wyrms . . .*

'Aye, wyrms. And they are preparing for something. For the God-War.'

Veradis felt Calidus shift beside him, stiffen. He looked at Vandil intently. 'You speak with great surety. How is that?'

'We took one prisoner in their last raid. He was put to the question, told us the raid was to steal iron. To forge weapons for the God-War.'

'Can I speak to this captive?' Calidus asked.

'No. He broke his chains, took his own life.' He shrugged.

'The success of our attack is essential, then,' Calidus said. 'They must be broken before they are fully prepared, before they march on *you*.'

'My sentiments exactly,' Braster growled.

'We know, or have heard rumour,' Vandil continued, 'that they dwell to the north-east of here, in a place called Haldis.'

'Our problem,' Braster said, 'is how to make them face us, fight us. It is unlikely they will just march out of Forn Forest to give battle. We have a great force massed here. We've considered just striking into the forest, but there is no guarantee they would face us, and, well, it's a big forest.'

'I can take you to them,' Alcyon suddenly uttered, his voice like stone grating over stone, making them all start.

'What . . .?' Romar said. 'Just march us straight to them? And what will make them stand and fight, stop them from disappearing into the forest?'

'The rumour you heard, of Haldis, is true. That is their dwelling place. I can take you there.'

'Would they not just hide from a force as big as ours?' Vandil asked, leaning forward in his chair.

'No. Haldis is not one of their fortresses, like Taur or Burna. It is their burial ground. It is holy to them, sacred. They would not suffer for you to set foot there – they would defend it. Every last one of them.'

A silence grew as they all stared at Alcyon. Then Braster banged the table again. 'Ha,' he shouted. 'You have useful friends, lad.' He beamed at Veradis. 'Unusual, but useful.'

The sun was warm on Veradis' face, the scent of pine sweet and heavy in the air as they rode along a wide track, twisting through the mountains.

Veradis' warband held the rearguard, the warriors of Helveth and Isiltir so many that he could not see the front of their long column, which, along with his own men, must number close to four thousand.

As usual, Calidus rode alongside Veradis, Alcyon striding along next to them.

'Alcyon, you are sure that you can lead us to Haldis?' Veradis asked the giant.

'Aye.'

'But, the Kurgan lived in the south and east, did they not? Have you ever been here before?'

'I have been here, though you are right, my clan dwelt far from these lands. I have seen Haldis. Even if I had not, the earth power would help me find it.'

'Ah.' Veradis said no more. He still felt uncomfortable whenever Alcyon's or Calidus' *abilities* were mentioned.

Still, those abilities had served him well before, and most likely would again. And Nathair had been adamant that Alcyon accompany him.

'*You will need him more than I,*' Nathair had said. '*There are no giants in Ardan.*'

He would have set sail by now, Veradis thought. When Veradis was leaving Jerolin, Lykos had said it was almost safe to brave the seas between Tenebral and Ardan, and that was over a moon ago. Nathair might already have arrived at Dun Carreg.

He felt a sliver of worry twist in his gut. He was glad, *honoured*, to be leading a warband in this campaign, but he always felt anxious when he was not guarding Nathair himself. Still, Rauca would be with him, and Sumur, the Jehar lord, with a few score of his warriors. They should be able to keep Nathair safe between them.

The sound of hooves drew his attention. Two riders were heading towards him – one an older man, grey streaking once black hair, the other much younger, a mop of unruly red hair escaping an iron helm. Veradis suddenly recognized them and smiled.

'Maquin, Kastell,' he called out. 'Well met.'

'We heard a rumour an ugly, broken-nosed bairn was leading the warband from Tenebral,' Maquin said. 'Kastell said it had to be you.'

Veradis grinned at them.

'So you've come to try your hand at giantkilling.' Maquin glanced at Alcyon.

'I heard you needed the help,' Veradis said, thinking of the draig tooth embedded in his sword hilt.

'Unusual company you keep, given our task,' Maquin murmured. 'Can he be trusted?'

Veradis sighed and explained again how Alcyon had fought beside him in Tarbesh against the Shekam. He realized he was becoming so used to the giant's company that it no longer struck him as strange. More than that, though, he was starting to feel defensive of Alcyon, to think of him as more than just a travelling companion. He was starting to think of him as a friend.

'So, how is life in Mikil? Have you both avoided any more hidings from your cousin, Jael?' he said, wanting to change the subject.

A brief look passed between Maquin and Kastell.

'We have moved on from Mikil,' Maquin said. 'We are part of the Gadrai, now.'

'Why?' frowned Veradis, remembering Romar's reaction in the tent, when he had spoken of Kastell.

'I fought, with Jael,' Kastell muttered. 'Things became serious. I thought it better to move on. Besides, the Gadrai are good to us. And it is every warrior's dream, to join them, in Isiltir, at least.'

Veradis looked at Kastell a little closer, saw he was leaner than he remembered, having lost the layer of fat he had possessed, his jaw firmer, his gut trimmer. But more than that, there was something new about him, a surety in how he sat his horse. He looked like a warrior, now, everywhere except his eyes. They seemed somehow sad, hesitant, still those of a youth rather than a man.

'I met your leader, Vandil,' Veradis said. 'So you live in Forn Forest now, protect Isiltir's borders from the forest's inhabitants.'

'Aye, just so,' Maquin said.

'But you are riding with Romar and Jael now? I have seen them both.'

'In a way, though we ride with the Gadrai, Romar is still our king,' Maquin said.

'Are things uncomfortable with Romar and Jael, then?'

'You could say that,' Kastell looked dour. 'With Jael, anyway. Romar would ride with anyone if they would help him get his special axe back.'

Calidus straightened in his saddle and rode closer to them. 'Axe?' he said.

'Aye. He calls it his axe, but it is a relic, from before the Scourging. A Treasure of the giants, if you believe the tales. Whatever it is, Romar wants it back. Pilgrims would travel from all over the Banished Lands to see it – it kept gold flowing into Isiltir like a river. Until the Hunen stole it.'

'And they definitely have it?' Calidus asked. 'How can you be sure?'

'I saw them take it,' Kastell said, wincing as if recalling a painful memory.

Calidus shared a look with Alcyon. 'They are preparing indeed,' he said to the giant.

'It is good,' Alcyon replied, 'they do our work for us. Now we will just take it back.'

Calidus grinned, nodded to Maquin and Kastell, twitched his reins and rode closer to the giant, whispering to him.

'You ride in unusual company, Veradis,' said Maquin.

'You are not the first to point that out,' Veradis said.

'Giants, and he . . .' the old warrior pointed at Calidus. 'He is no man of Tenebral, I'd wager. And then, there are rumours in our camp, of others with you: dour, black-clothed warriors with curved swords, *women* amongst them?'

'Aye,' Veradis said, smiling at their shock, remembering feeling it himself.

'Well? Who are they?' Kastell asked.

'They call themselves the Jehar. We found them in Tarbesh, while on a campaign to tackle another giant menace. You are right – they are unusual. But fierce. And loyal.'

'But why do they ride with you?' pressed Maquin.

'Forces are gathering,' Veradis said with a shrug, 'as King Aquilus predicted at his council. They have chosen to stand with Nathair.' He suddenly remembered Calidus at Telassar, wings spread, *unveiled*. He longed to tell his friends of it, but Calidus had sworn him to secrecy, for now. But he worried for Maquin and Kastell – good men potentially caught on the wrong side, if his suspicions about Romar were correct. 'Make sure you ride under the right banner, my friends.' He frowned. 'A king bent on greed – on going to war for gold – that I would be worried about. Especially at times like this. All will fight, Nathair says: it is just a question of *who for*. So just be sure who it is that you serve.'

'Well, I serve Kastell, and more often than not he just serves his belly,' Maquin said, slapping Kastell in the gut.

'What? All you do is steal my food,' Kastell complained, grinning.

They rode on together for a while, the three of them laughing and talking. As their path began to slope downward Maquin and Kastell cantered back to the head of the column. It was not much longer before Veradis saw his first glimpse of Forn in the distance: a huge wall of trees disappearing into the north, seemingly without end.

The sun was sinking, shadows of the trees stretching across the meadow when Veradis led his men out of the foothills. A base camp had been erected before the forest edge, from which to mount the assault, and the column passed wearily through the gates of its stockade.

'When we are close to Haldis we must spread out, attack from the front and both flanks,' Alcyon said to the gathered leaders at first light the following day. 'But until then we must travel in a column. Even then the going will be difficult.'

'Aye. That is as we planned,' Braster said.

'How many nights, until we reach Haldis?' Vandil asked.

'Five, maybe six,' Alcyon considered. 'I could walk it in two, but this many men,' he looked across the meadow, covered in the massing ranks of their warriors, and shrugged, 'we shall see.'

'Aye. But I do not want our warriors running out of food, having to turn back before we reach this place,' Romar said.

'Then tell your men to walk fast,' Alcyon grunted.

'Maybe we should take wains with our provisions. It will be slower going, but then we would not be ruled by time, and my men would be happier. It is the way we have always done such things.'

'No,' Alcyon said. 'Speed is vital. We must not give the Hunen a chance to gather their full strength. And the longer they have to prepare the more their Elementals will be able to lay traps for us. I shall take us as fast as you can manage.'

Romar scowled.

With much blowing of horns the warbands formed up, Vandil and the Gadrai at the head of the wide column, all grim, tough-looking warriors. Alcyon was with them, many glancing warily at him.

Veradis reached the front ranks of his warband. 'It is time,' he said and strapped his iron helm on, checked the straps of his shield slung across his back and the pack beneath it carrying his provisions. He felt a flutter of excitement in his belly, knowing they were on the brink of battle again as he stroked the tooth buried in his sword hilt.

Calidus was standing with the Jehar, waiting for him.

Horns blew and they lurched into motion, the forest looming dark and tall before them.

'All went well?' Calidus asked him.

'Aye. Romar grumbled, but Braster holds his leash, I think. Alcyon leads us.'

'Good. Romar troubles me,' Calidus said. 'His loyalties . . .'

'Aye, me too,' Veradis agreed.

Calidus looked wary, thinking. 'He is a thorn in our flesh, Veradis. He opposes Nathair, resents our presence here. And, like a thorn in the flesh, he will not just get better. He will work his way deeper, cause infection, division.'

'If he opposes the Seren Disglair,' Akar of the Jehar said, his clipped accent prominent, 'then perhaps his head should be separated from his shoulders.'

Veradis snorted and smiled at Akar, thinking it a joke, though the thought had some appeal. But Akar just stared back at him with eyes cold and unreadable. Veradis' smile faded.

Calidus chuckled. 'I shall reason with him,' the Vin Thalun said, 'before we consider anything more drastic. Besides, he has the Gadrai protecting him.'

Akar snorted contemptuously.

Veradis looked between Calidus and Akar, remembering Nathair's words concerning them. '*They have licence,*' Nathair had said, '*to do as they see fit in my service. You command my warband, Veradis, but I have given the Jehar to Calidus. You are a warrior, Veradis, not a politicker. Fight the Hunen for me, let Calidus worry about the alliance. You shall both do what you have to do.*'

Romar was trouble, of that he was growing more certain, but a *traitor*? Of that he was not yet convinced. And Maquin and Kastell rode with him. He frowned, worried. But Calidus was one of the Ben-Elim, a servant of *Elyon* – surely he would do what was right? As he stepped under the shadow of the trees, Veradis felt a sense of foreboding, taking his first steps into Forn Forest.

CHAPTER SIXTY-SIX

CYWEN

Cywen heard a whirring sound, a *thunk* like an axe splitting wet wood, and the guide tumbled from his saddle, a black-fletched arrow sprouting from his chest.

'Shields!' roared Tull, shrugging his from his back, then bellowed as an arrow sank into his leg, another piercing his horse's chest.

All was chaos. Cywen stared frantically around the glade. Warriors were shouting, crying out in pain, horses neighing, screaming as arrows tore into them from all directions. Half of the warriors had already fallen, either with arrows in their flesh or dragged down by their mounts. The rest were surging to Queen Alona, Cywen and Edana, trying to cover them with their shields, herding them back the way they had come.

There was another burst of arrows, more horses screaming. Then red-cloaked men were pouring from the trees all about, a line of them barring the track they had ridden in on, others blocking the exit at the far side of the glade, still more converging on the huddle of grey in the glade's centre.

Two of those still on horseback charged the exit. One fell immediately, his horse's legs slashed from under him, but the other crashed through, though he swayed in his saddle as his horse galloped away. Arrows skittered after him, Cywen not seeing if they found their mark or not.

The gap in the line closed up instantly.

'No use,' Tull shouted above the din, standing beside Alona's mount and holding his shield before her. 'Back this way,' he said, pulling the Queen's mount towards the edge of the glade, between the two exits.

A knot of their attackers suddenly crashed into them, some with spears. Tull roared, hacked at a shaft that pierced a gap in the shields and sank into the belly of Alona's mount. He grabbed Alona around the waist as the horse reared and fell backwards. Gently he set the Queen down, then threw himself at their attackers. In moments two had fallen, one's face smashed by Tull's iron-bossed shield, the other clutching at a gaping wound in his gut.

All of the horses were down now, Tull and a half-dozen others surrounding the women, backing away from their enemies. Cywen searched her protectors for Ronan, felt a surge of relief when she saw him holding a shield before Edana. She resisted the urge to reach out and touch him. Beyond Ronan there were grim-faced, snarling men all about them, circling the tight-pressed bodies of those trying to protect her. Men slammed into them. Iron clashed on iron and she heard the crack of bone, the *thwack* of iron cleaving flesh and men screaming, but still their small circle held. It moved back and left a handful of their attackers lying still on the churned grass.

'I want the women alive!' Cywen heard someone yell. Peering through the wall of her defenders, she saw at least a score of men around their few. Then the red-cloaked attackers were coming at them once more.

Again there was a short, furious clash, Tull in the middle of it, roaring a battle cry. Cywen remembered her knives suddenly, fumbled one from her belt and hurled it at a face in a red cloak – saw him fall backwards, clutching at his throat.

Then they were at the glade's edge, a wide tree at their back.

Tull and four other warriors in grey were still standing, one of them Ronan. Queen Alona, Edana and Cywen huddled behind them. She counted the knives at her belt. Three more.

Their attackers had fallen back, but had penned them in. They outnumbered the men of Ardan, but none was keen to be the first to charge. Others still hovered at the glade's exits, barring escape.

'We cannot turn and run,' Tull muttered, glancing over his shoulder into the forest. 'As soon as we were amongst the trees they'd be on our backs.' He paused briefly, thinking.

'Right, listen close, we've only a few moments while they catch their breath, gather their courage. This is the way it is going to be,' he said, fixing Alona with his gaze. 'Ronan, Ised, when I give the nod you are to lead the girls into the forest. Ised, you're the van; Ronan, rearguard.' Both warriors grunted.

'Me, Alwyn and Taren here, we're going to buy you some time.'

'No, Tull . . .' Alona blurted.

'It's the only way. They'll take you otherwise,' he said. 'And the rest of us'll still be dead.' He reached out and covered her hand with his. 'If you run, *live*, then our deaths will have worth.'

They looked at each other a moment, then Alona nodded.

'Good,' Tull said soberly. 'You might want to throw another of those knives tucked in your belt, girlie,' he said to Cywen. 'With me, lads.'

Then he was gone.

He charged forwards, no roaring battle cry this time, the enemy seeming almost inattentive. A rush had been the last thing they expected. Taren and Alwyn, both older warriors like Tull, followed the first-sword of Ardan. They ploughed into their attackers, swords and shields swinging, smashing men to the ground.

'Now, quickly,' Ronan hissed, tugging at Cywen's cloak.

She freed another knife from her belt and cast it at a man poised to hamstring Tull. The man howled, staggered backwards, trying to reach the blade lodged in his back.

Ronan grabbed her hand, squeezed it. 'Please, come,' he exhorted, one eye on Tull. She realized he was crying. She nodded and then they were dashing into the trees, branches whipping at their faces, following Edana's cloak into the twilight. Cywen looked over her shoulder once, heard Tull roar his defiance, caught a flash of red cloaks at the centre of the glade, then she could see no more.

CHAPTER SIXTY-SEVEN

CAMLIN

Camlin could not believe his eyes. The maniac with an arrow in his leg was *charging* them from across the glade.

He had been distracted, seeing amongst the female faces one he thought he recognized. He knew for sure when she threw a knife, knew her as one of the bairns that had been present at his escape from captivity, back at the fortress of Dun Carreg.

Then the keening of a blade slicing through air had registered, and he had seen that maniac charging at their line, other warriors following. Camlin stood at the end of the line they had formed around their almost-captives, saw the big man smash into the centre and Digased reel back, blood spurting from his throat. Then someone else, one of the new lads, collapsed, one side of his face ruined by a shield boss. There was confusion and shouting, the line he was part of pulling in to encircle the remaining Ardan warriors.

Camlin moved in cautiously, shield held high. He had learned quickly how dangerous this big man was, at least half a dozen of their crew having been slain by his hand alone. Then Braith was running from one of the glade's exits, sword in hand. The new lads' chief ran beside him, shouting something urgently, screaming it, with eyes wide, but Camlin could not hear him over the din of battle.

Then one of Ardan's grey-cloaks was down, still alive, though not for long. He clutched feebly at the grass, a red stain in the centre of his back. Then another grey-cloak fell, Cromhan's sword in his belly.

The big man roared, spun in a circle and threw his battered shield into a face. He swung his sword in great, two-handed sweeps until a space, a wide, blood-soaked ring formed around him. He grinned suddenly, face spattered with other men's blood. 'Who's next?' he roared, nostrils flaring.

Braith and his companions had reached them now, the man with him still yelling.

'. . . getting away!' the man shouted, pointing.

Camlin looked back and the women had disappeared. He saw a flash of movement amongst the trees, a pale face looking back at him, then it was gone.

'All scared of an old man,' the warrior at the centre of the glade panted. 'Best all run back to your mothers.'

One of the new lads stepped forward, a hard-faced, cold-eyed youth. He wore a coat of mail beneath his red cloak, looked like he knew what he was doing with a blade.

The Ardan warrior nodded to him.

They set at each other in a blinding flurry, the larger man moving shockingly fast. When they parted, his opponent had a gash in his thigh.

The big man attacked again, his blade sweeping high, then low. He pushed inside his adversary's guard, head-butted him right on the bridge of the nose. Red-cloak stumbled back, then his head was spinning through the air.

The big man smiled at the corpse, rested a hand on his leg and gulped in deep breaths. He was cut in a dozen places, a broken arrow sticking from a thigh, his sword notched, but he seemed undaunted. He straightened, held his arms out wide and turned slowly.

'Who's next?' he said again, spitting blood on the trampled grass.

Not likely, thought Camlin.

Then the big man's eyes fell on the new chief. Scar, they called him, after the white gash on one cheek.

'You,' the big man whispered, eyes widening.

'Tull,' Scar said, dipping his head as if to an old friend.

'So this is Rhin's doing.' He nodded to himself, taking note of the red cloaks. 'Didn't think Uthan and Owain had the stomach for this kind of work.' He snorted. 'Ready for your second lesson?'

Scar smiled, a thin, humourless thing. 'Much as I'd like to, I fear I will have to decline,' he said. 'You think me a fool? With your tactics? One last trick, eh? Every second counts, does it not, when an escape is underway?'

Tull shrugged, then launched himself at Scar.

'Braith,' Scar shouted, and the woodsman slipped his bow from his back, nocked an arrow and loosed it.

Tull grunted, the arrow sticking from his gut. He snarled, stumbled forwards, raising his sword.

The next arrow took him in the shoulder, spinning him round. He righted himself, took another step forwards, then sank to one knee.

Scar strode up and smashed his sword into Tull's, knocking the man's blade from his weakening grip. He stood over the kneeling man a moment, sword pointed at Tull's heart, then sank the blade almost to its hilt in his chest.

Tull coughed, blood filling his mouth, then Scar tugged his sword free.

'Here endeth the lesson,' Scar said, looking down at the dead man, then went to find Braith.

Camlin looked away. The man had had courage, and more to spare. He hadn't deserved those last arrows. *Life isn't fair, you fool, thought you'd learned that by now.*

Then the band of men slipped into the trees after their quarry, leaving their dead comrades in the silent glade.

CHAPTER SIXTY-EIGHT

EVNIS

Evnis looked out from the battlements of Uthandun and watched the last members of Queen Alona's party disappear into the forest. *Not long now.* He felt a spike of fear, knew he was risking everything, now, with the next play of the dice. But it still felt good. He stood there a long while, then headed back down through the streets, down a shadowed alley, then through a door into a deserted house.

He sucked in a deep breath, closed his eyes and sent his thoughts within himself. '*Athru mise, folaigh mise, cloca mise, talamh bri,*' he muttered. There was a tremor, as if the very earth and air rippled. He staggered slightly, then pulled out a brightly polished bronze mirror to check the results of his incantation. The face of another, younger, man stared back at him now, skin unlined, with full, fleshy lips. He almost laughed in amazement at his own glamour, then reached for the package he had left the night before. A few moments later he emerged from the house holding a thick-shafted spear, wearing an iron helm and a red cloak.

He smiled at the guards on the keep door, who grunted a greeting and let him pass unquestioned. Uthandun was full of red-cloaked warriors at the moment, a large honour guard having arrived with Owain from Dun Cadlas, so one more did not stand out.

He walked purposefully through the keep, mounting the stairs to Uthan's chambers until he faced the guard at his door. He continued smiling even as he rammed his spear-tip into the man's throat. Evnis caught him as he fell and lowered him gently, dragging the body into a shadowed alcove.

Uthan was a serious young man, he had discovered, old before his years and feeling the weight of leadership on his young shoulders.

He was often alone in his chambers, and so Evnis found him. He was looking out of his window as Evnis slipped in through the door.

'Is it time already?' Narvon's heir said when he heard the door open and close, still lost in thought.

When no one answered, Uthan looked round, but it was already too late. Evnis grabbed Uthan's hair, raking a knife across his throat in one brutal movement.

Evnis stood there a moment, shaking from the sudden violence of the moment. He wiped his knife on Uthan's shirt and gazed at the view recently admired by the Prince. A distant rider was moving erratically away from the Darkwood. *Braith has done his job well, if that is one of Alona's guards. Time to get out of here.*

He sheathed his knife, and exchanged the red cloak for another in his bag.

The new cloak was grey.

He gathered his energies, then began to sing, soft and quiet. The air rippled about him and he staggered. When he looked into his bronze mirror the face of Marrock stared back.

He walked calmly through the keep, exiting past the two red-cloaked guards.

'Can I help you, friend?' one of them said.

He shook his head, made sure they got a good look at him, then spun on his heel so that his grey cloak swirled out behind him, and left quickly.

He kept the glamour upon him until he was almost at the gates, then slipped into an alley to muster his power and reverse the transformation.

Vonn was waiting for his father, sitting a horse and holding the reins of another. His son was frowning at him, whether because he finally suspected something or because they had recently argued about the fisher girl again, he did not know. He would have to sit down with his son soon, bring him into the world that Evnis was walking. But not yet. He was not convinced that Vonn's youthful idealism had matured into something more practical, or where his ultimate allegiance would lie.

He spotted the distant rider, closer now, swaying unstably in his saddle – and he wore a grey cloak. *Definitely one of Alona's guards.*

'Ride to Pendathran in the camp. Tell him Queen Alona has been attacked in the forest, that he should muster some warriors and ride out fast but without drawing attention. I shall take the wounded rider to Brenin and organize our evacuation. Owain is about to strike.'

Vonn stared at him, looking uncertain, then galloped for help.

CHAPTER SIXTY-NINE

CORBAN

Corban walked through the glade of corpses. This was the band he had seen ride out – Queen Alona, Edana, *Cywen* flashed through his mind and he started frantically searching the glade, panic rising to choke him.

Gar was ahead of him, checking faces, kneeling, checking for signs of life. He stopped near the centre of the glade, beside a familiar body, an open space around it ringed with red-cloaked corpses.

Corban gasped as he reached Gar's side and saw the man on the ground.

Tull.

The warrior's lifeless eyes gazed past him, up at the blue sky above.

Storm nudged his hand.

'Cywen was with them,' Corban mumbled, 'and Queen Alona, Edana . . .' he felt his stomach heave and swallowed, trying not to be sick.

'Keep searching,' Gar said, moving amongst the dead.

Corban forced himself to look, battling the fear of what, of *who* he might find. Eventually he joined Gar by a great oak at the edge of the glade, Gar staring at a narrow, trampled track that led into the trees.

'They are not here,' Corban said.

'No,' Gar agreed.

'What happened here?' Corban whispered.

'Our Queen was ambushed. By King Owain's men – though that does not make sense,' Gar murmured. 'We are at their mercy at Uthandun.' He rubbed his stubbled chin. 'Anyway, Alona is not here.

She and some others escaped. Fled this way, I think. Or they were taken.'

'We must follow them, help them,' Corban said.

Gar looked at him, frowning. 'I will follow the trail, Ban, but you must go back. Brenin must be told and help must be sent.'

'What? No. Cywen is out there,' he said.

'No, Ban. It is too dangerous. And I will need help. There are too many of them for you or I.' He shrugged. 'You must go back.'

Corban glared at the stablemaster, who returned his gaze calmly. They stood there in silence long moments, then the sound of mounted warriors filtered into the glade, growing quickly louder.

Men poured into the clearing, two score at least, all in the grey of Ardan. Pendathran rode at their head.

Storm moved closer to Corban and leaned into his hip and leg, growling quietly.

Pendathran leaped from his horse and cried out when he saw Tull's corpse. He took a moment, then focused on Gar and Corban, taking in Storm's presence.

'Why are you here?' he said harshly. 'With that wolven too.' Behind him warriors were checking the fallen, spreading through the glade. Corban saw Marrock kneel beside Tull, and other warriors gathered around their fallen leader, Halion amongst them.

'We were in the forest, heard the sounds of battle,' Gar said.

'Where are Alona and Edana? What did you see?'

'What you see,' Gar said with a sweep of his hand. 'This is as we found it.'

'So where are they?' Pendathran demanded.

'I think they fled, this way.' Gar pointed into the trees. 'Fled, or were taken.'

Marrock joined them, stepped lightly into the trees and nodded to Pendathran. 'What would you have us do, Uncle?' the huntsman asked.

'We must split,' he said. 'If there is any hope of saving Alona we must grasp it. But this . . .' he glowered around the glade. 'This speaks of further mischief. If King Owain is moving against King Brenin, he will be in grave danger.'

He was suddenly all business. 'Marrock. Choose some men – ones that can move quickly, and will be up for a fight at the end of it. I will go back to Uthandun. If King Owain has not yet struck I am taking Brenin back to Ardan. Now.' He squeezed Marrock's shoulder. 'Look after yourself, and do all you can to get my sister back,' he said gruffly. 'If you are successful, make for the giantsway, but towards Ardan, *not* Narvon. We will try to meet you on the road. And Owain will pay dearly for this.'

Marrock wasted no time, calling out names. In moments a dozen men stood about him, Halion and Conall amongst them.

'I am coming with you,' Corban suddenly blurted.

'No,' Gar snapped.

Marrock shook his head.

'Cywen. My *sister* is with them. I am coming.' The thought of just running away was unbearable. He had to *do* something. Cywen was out there, scared.

'No, lad. You are not a warrior yet,' Marrock said, almost gently. 'It will be no place for you.'

'But . . .' he looked about, could think only of Cywen running through the forest. 'Wait – Storm can track them. She would lead us straight to Cywen. You'd not need to search for a trail, just follow her. It will speed your task.'

Marrock looked from Corban to the wolven and frowned.

'If there is a chance of finding Alona more quickly,' Pendathran said, preparing to leave, 'take it.'

Marrock nodded.

'But, boy,' Pendathran said, 'make sure that wolven does not bite any man of mine, or I'll string you up myself.'

'Aye,' Corban said.

'Farewell,' Pendathran shouted as he left the glade, his warriors following in a burst of noise and speed.

'Take this, Ban,' Gar said quietly, passing him a sword, taken from one of the dead.

Corban just stared at it, then clumsily strapped it on, adjusting the scabbard on its belt.

Gar shuffled amongst the fallen around Tull, took up another weapon and belted it around his own waist.

'You're not coming, cripple,' Conall said.

Gar glanced at him and said nothing, just continued strapping on the sword-belt. He loosened the blade in its scabbard.

'Cripple, I'm talking to you,' Conall said, louder, but Gar just walked over to stand beside Corban and Storm.

Conall strode over and grabbed Gar's shoulder roughly. 'You'll answer me when I speak to you – and you'll not be coming with us,' Conall repeated.

'I think I will,' said Gar.

'You'll slow us. Take the sword off and hobble back to Uthandun, with all the other women.' Conall was visibly furious.

'I'll go where the lad goes,' Gar said calmly and rolled his shoulders, his neck clicking.

'You'll slow us,' Conall repeated, stepping closer to Gar, almost nose to nose.

'No need to slow your pace for me,' Gar said. 'If I fall behind, I fall behind.'

'Leave it, Conall,' Marrock grunted. 'Gar's right, if he can't match our pace he'll just fall behind. There's no harm, no danger in that.'

Conall eyed Gar a moment longer, then nodded.

'Right, lad,' Marrock said. 'Let's see how good your wolven's nose is. Lead the way.'

Corban bent down to Storm. 'Cywen, Storm. Cywen. Seek.'

The wolven set off immediately, loping into the trees. Corban followed her, Marrock and a dozen warriors behind him, Gar leaving the glade last of all.

CHAPTER SEVENTY

CYWEN

Cywen blinked sweat from her eyes and staggered over a tree root. Ronan reached out and steadied her.

'Keep moving,' the young warrior said, glancing back over his shoulder. The forest behind them was empty, at least it *appeared* empty. They had been running for what seemed an eternity, Cywen losing all track of time, but she was sure the forest had grown darker, the shadows deeper, so it must be approaching sunset? *They would be safer once it was darker. Harder to track, surely?* She looked at Ronan, his red hair sweat soaked and plastered to his head, face gaunt with worry. She nodded and forced her legs to move, her lungs burning. Edana was only a little ahead, flitting amongst thick foliage, so she tried to increase her speed.

Her world shrank to the space in front of her, focusing on every step, avoiding every moss-covered boulder, concentrating on not losing her companions.

She could not believe what had happened. What was King Owain thinking? Was this a bid to conquer Ardan? And what about those still at Uthandun – King Brenin, her mam and da, Corban, Gar . . .

The idea of them dying, of her not seeing them again, hit her hard. She felt sick to her stomach and staggered. The figures she was following slowed, then stopped. Like Cywen, they were all too breathless for speech.

Ronan and the other warrior – Ised, she remembered – conferred in sharp whispers, Ised pointing into the forest.

'Do you . . . think . . . they . . . will . . . follow us?' Edana said, between gasps for breath.

Ronan bit back an answer.

'Of course,' Queen Alona said. 'Owain has crossed a line. He will not just give up, now. Darkness is our best hope – if we can keep ahead of them, reach the road . . .'

Birds squawked in the forest, back the way they had come.

'Better be moving,' Ronan said. 'Ised is a woodsman, best if he leads us. I'd only get us lost.' He smiled, weakly. 'I'll watch our backs.'

Ised set off, Alona and Edana close behind him. As Cywen gathered her breath and her will Ronan gripped her wrist. 'If it comes to a fight, stay close to me. I am oathsworn to Edana, but I . . .' He looked down. 'I would see no harm come to you. Stay close to me.'

She smiled, here, in the midst of the Darkwood, death breathing down their necks, and yet she felt such a rush of *joy*. She leaned forward and brushed her lips on his freckled cheek. 'I'll do that,' she whispered, then set off after the others.

They ploughed on, then there was movement at the edge of her vision, the sound of drumming feet.

'Run,' Ronan hissed, pushing her on.

Panic consumed her and she pounded into the forest – their pursuers were closing in. All of them sped up, though soon the sounds of pursuit grew even louder behind them. Cywen checked her belt for the the hilts of her last two knives.

'It is no good,' said Ronan, 'they will be on us in moments.'

Ised heard him and pulled up before a thick-trunked elm. 'We'll make a stand here,' he grunted, breathing heavily.

'Behind us,' Ronan said. He and Ised drew their swords and stood together, facing the shadows.

Cywen pulled a knife and glanced at Queen Alona and Edana.

Movement caught her eye, a figure, coming at them fast. She aimed and hurled her knife, hearing it *thunk* into wood. She whispered a curse and drew her last knife, then all was chaos. Warriors surged out of the darkness and targeted Ised and Ronan. A man screamed and fell at Ronan's feet, his lifeless head flopping close to Cywen. She stared at his dull eyes.

Ised grunted and dropped to one knee, then a blade chopped into his neck and he toppled sideways.

Edana screamed.

A red-cloaked warrior advanced on Ronan, others emerging from the gloom, all with swords drawn. Ten, twelve, more – Cywen counted. *We are dead.*

'Hold,' a voice shouted, and the man before Ronan paused, though he didn't lower his sword.

Two stepped forward, one younger, with a scar under his eye. Cywen gasped, recognizing them both. Rhin's champion that had duelled with Tull on Midwinter's Eve. Morcant. *What is he doing here?* And the other man was Braith – she would never forget his face after that night at Dun Carreg.

'We could use this one,' Braith said to Morcant. 'Better the message reach Brenin from one of his own warriors than one of ours.'

Morcant had a sword drawn, but held loosely. He paused.

A message. Please, Elyon, let them spare Ronan, let them send him to Brenin.

Morcant looked between Ronan and Braith, Ronan shifting his feet, a quiver in his sword arm.

Suddenly Morcant exploded into motion, faster than Cywen could follow. Iron grated on iron, Ronan twisting and shouting, then he was sinking, blood gushing from his throat. It took a moment to register in Cywen's mind, then she screamed and grabbed for him. She pressed a hand to his neck, trying to stem the flow, but blood poured through her fingers. *No, no, no, no, no!* she screamed inside, his weight pushing her to the ground, where she held his head in her lap. His eyes looked up into hers, blinked once and then became dull, sightless. She felt a confusion of rage and grief. Then she hurled herself at Morcant, stabbing with the knife she still clutched in one hand.

Morcant jumped back and swore as she stabbed him, the knife turning on his chainmail shirt. He clubbed her with the back of his hand and she fell to the ground, the metallic taste of blood in her mouth.

'Bind them,' Morcant said.

CHAPTER SEVENTY-ONE

CAMLIN

'We'll camp here,' Braith called, standing before a patch of open ground.

They had walked hard until sunset, Camlin behind the three women as they travelled through the forest. Their prisoners had made no trouble and kept mostly silent, walking with heads down, apart from the one Scar had clubbed. She had stared at Scar's back most of the time, her fury almost tangible.

Braith ordered the women to sit against a wide chestnut, where they were tied to the trunk and each other. Camlin looked around at the men making camp and failed to shake his dark mood. Out of the score of the old crew that had followed Braith out of the hills only eight remained, including him. The new lads had not fared much better, as only twelve of them moved around the fire and stream. Eight of their number lay dead in the grass back at the glade. He sat in the shadows beyond the fire's reach, his back to a tree, and began running a whetstone over his sword's edge. He had a bad feeling about this, a niggling sensation in his gut and a sense of dread to match. Braith had told them this was a ransom job. Kill the guards, grab the girls, wear the red cloaks of Narvon to throw anyone off their trail, then bleed a large pot of coin from King Brenin. That sounded good: plenty of coin poured onto a stiff dose of revenge. But things didn't feel right.

Braith had not given a straight answer on who the new lads were or where they came from, and as time had passed Braith had been dipping his head more and more to Scar, as if *he* were the crew's chief. And now, plain as day, Scar had known the big man, called him Tull. More than that, had some grudge with him. Then Queen Rhin had been mentioned. He had no axe to grind with *her* – Brenin and Owain were his problem – but taking orders from *any* king or queen sat ill with him.

He was starting to feel used, and he didn't like that one little bit.

And then there was the bairn. The one with the knives from Dun Carreg. She was tied to a tree, glaring holes into Scar.

He'd not be killing women or bairns – and Braith knew that.

Later, when he saw Braith slip into the trees, Camlin followed silently.

Camlin changed his approach now, holding his hands up. He didn't want an arrow in his chest.

Braith nodded a greeting but said nothing, and for a while they stood there in silence. Eventually Camlin spoke. 'What's going on?' he asked. 'I heard what the big man said, Braith, back in the glade. He knew Scar, and, that talk, about Rhin . . .' He ran a hand through his hair. 'Who *is* Scar? And why do you treat him like he's chief? You, who's not taken sauce from any man in all the years I've known you?'

Braith looked at him, his face expressionless.

'We've followed you a long time, Braith. *I've* followed you a long time. Think you owe me some truth here.'

'Aye, maybe so,' Braith conceded. 'Scar is Rhin's first-sword. His name's Morcant.'

Camlin folded his arms, waiting for the rest.

'You asked me back at the village what my story is, Cam.'

'Aye. I remember.'

'I am Rhin's man. I always have been. Well, as long as I can remember. King Owain killed my kin, my mam and da, over a border dispute. It was Rhin's people, in the village I took you to, that raised me. Rhin sent me here, with the task of becoming one of you.'

Camlin had wondered many things, but never this. 'Why?' he said, shocked now.

'To stir things up between Brenin and Owain. She wants their land, Cam, and she'll have it, too. Soon.'

'So this,' Camlin said, waving a hand back at the campsite. 'This is about more'n just coin and vengeance?'

'Aye. We're starting a war here. Soon enough Ardan and Narvon will be at each other's throats, and Queen Rhin will step in at the end of it, clean up the mess.'

After all these years of robbery, burning and murder Camlin felt he should have expected this, or at least not been surprised, but instead he felt foolish. And betrayed. Somehow he'd trusted Braith.

Somewhere in the forest a fox barked, like a bairn's scream.

'You could do all right out of this, Cam. You could join me. I'll be going back, soon. Back to Rhin. You've a good head on your shoulders, and at a time like this there's always need of those that can do our work.' He waited for Camlin's response.

'And if I don't . . .' Camlin said.

'Become chief here. For a while, at least. There should be easy pickings for a time, with both kings Brenin and Owain distracted. 'Course, once Rhin steps in, you'll have to find a new trade. She'll not have the likes of you roaming her land, takin' what you want, when you want.' He coughed, not quite a laugh. 'Times are changing, Cam. You move with them, or get moved *by* them. We've been through a lot together, you an' me. I'd be proud t'have you with me.' He reached out and squeezed Camlin's shoulder.

'Huh,' said Camlin, his mind racing, fighting the urge to shake Braith's hand off him. He didn't like this. The Darkwood life suited him. He had always had a chief, sure, but that was different to a king or queen pulling your strings. So that left staying in the Darkwood, becoming chief himself. He didn't fancy that much, either – and it wasn't exactly a long-term move, anyway, if what Braith was saying about Rhin was true. 'So, what's your plan, now, Braith?' he asked, struggling to keep his voice expressionless.

'The plan is to take the women across the river, to the village in the hills. From there deliver them to Rhin. Get paid.' He shrugged. 'After that, it's up to you.'

'So, why have you just not killed them? The women, I mean. Surely King Brenin's wife and daughter dead in the glade would have been the quickest route to sparking a war.'

'Rhin wants some leverage, some bargaining power, in case things don't go her way. Whether they're dead or not, Brenin'll think Owain's behind it, the red cloaks will make sure of that.'

'Good,' said Camlin vehemently. 'I'll not be part to the killing of women or bairns, Braith. I told you that back at Dun Carreg.'

'Aye, you did.'

'So, I'd not see any harm come to them.'

'Let me make this clear to you, Cam,' Braith said, an edge to his voice. 'We're part of something bigger here. Rhin's champion – I'm not scared to hold up a blade 'gainst any man, but I'd not rush it with him. I've seen him destroy men.' Braith stopped a moment, letting his words sink in. 'From what I know, there's no risk to any of them women, less they try t'run, or start screamin' their lungs out. But my point is this, Cam. Right now you're in no position to be giving out orders to anyone. Not yet. If you choose t'be chief, well an' good. But right now, it's Morcant that says what's what around here, and after him, it's me. Don't go forgetting that.'

Camlin frowned in the darkness.

They said no more, and a short while later Camlin walked back to the camp. On the way he unclasped his red cloak and let it fall to the ground.

At dawn, Camlin stirred, grey light filtering hazily down to the forest floor. Mist swirled up from the stream in thick coils and crept amongst the forms of sleeping men.

He looked past the fire to the tree where the women were bound and saw the girl from the watering pool staring straight back at him, so he walked over to the captives.

'I know you,' the girl said as he drew close. He did not answer, just offered his water skin.

'My hands,' she said, raising an eyebrow.

Of course. All of the captives' hands were bound tight, then bound again to each other and the trunk of the tree. He put the water skin to her lips. She pursed them a moment, eyes glaring at him. Looking closer he saw tear tracks streaked her grimy, bloodstained face.

'Drink, girl. You'll spite none but yourself.'

She glowered at him another moment, then opened her mouth and drank thirstily.

'I know you,' she said again when she had finished. 'You're not one of Owain or Uthan's men.'

'Best keep your observations to yourself,' he said, moving on to the next girl, awake now too.

He gave water to all of them, finishing before the eldest. Alona, Queen of Ardan.

'My thanks,' she said after sipping at the water.

He grunted, stayed squatting beside her.

'You must know, you will not get away with this,' she said quietly.'My husband, his anger will be great. But he would be grateful, generous to any that aided me . . . us,' she said, her eyes flickering across the girls either side of her.

'There's nothing I can do, other'n give a lady a drink of water,' he said.

'And for that kindness I thank you,' she smiled sadly.

'You,' a voice called out behind Camlin. 'Step away.'

Camlin stood and saw Morcant striding towards him, two of his lads behind with spears in their hands. Braith followed.

'What are you doing?' Morcant snapped as he reached them.

'Giving them a drink,' Camlin said, holding up the water skin.

'Why?' Morcant asked, eyes narrowing.

'Thought they might be thirsty.' Camlin shrugged. 'We've far to walk today.'

The rest of the crew were rising now. Camlin saw Cromhan wander closer, listening, Gochel setting off down the track to relieve whoever was on guard.

'Well, you've done your deed, now. Get on with you.'

Camlin looked at Morcant and felt a spike of anger. 'Last I remember,' he said, 'Braith was my chief.' He rubbed his chin. 'Think I'll be takin' my orders from him.' After Braith's revelations, and the fresh sting of his betrayal, this youngster strutting about and acting the lordling was becoming difficult to bear.

Morcant's hand twitched to his sword hilt.

'Go on with you, Cam,' said Braith, stepping close. They looked at each other, then Camlin nodded and walked away.

Morcant squatted before the women, staring at each in turn. 'We have a long walk ahead of us,' he said. 'Make no trouble and you shall have no cause to fear. Any mischief . . .'

So he's about threatening women and bairns, now, thought Camlin. He turned back to stand with Braith, arms folded. He knew he was being unwise: if Braith was wary of Morcant, any man should be, but he just didn't trust him. Unbidden the memory of his mam and Col came to mind, lying lifeless beside each other in their old yard. He looked around, trying to shift the thought and frowned. Gochel should be back by now.

'Rhin will never get away with this,' Alona said.

'She already has,' Morcant smirked. 'Now behave yourself, my *Queen*, none of your high and mighty talk, if you please. Remember you're my prisoner and you shall reach Cambren safely. You *and* your brat.' He smiled at Edana.

'Brave man, aren't you?' Cywen said. 'Taunting women. *Bound* women.'

Morcant looked down at Cywen. 'Who are you?'

'Untie me, then I do not think you would be so brave,' Cywen said furiously. Some of the men around the camp chuckled.

'I said, who are you? Whose blood?'

'My da is a smith at Dun Carreg. And he will kill you when he finds you.'

'Ah, now there lies his problem,' Morcant said, smiling again. 'I doubt that he shall *ever* find me. And you are of no use to me. In fact, you are a burden, an extra mouth to feed, another person to guard. And, on top of that, I find you irritating.' He looked at one of the warriors with him. 'Kill her,' he said.

There was a blur of movement as the man levelled his spear, then Camlin was suddenly moving too, drawing his sword. He chopped at the spear shaft, splintering it, and stepped in front of the girl.

'Leave her be,' he heard himself say.

Morcant smiled and drew his own sword.

CHAPTER SEVENTY-TWO

CORBAN

Branches whipped into Corban's face, stinging and leaving red lines across his cheek. He cursed under his breath and rubbed sweat out of his eyes.

He was ploughing desperately through the forest, Marrock beside him, Storm a dozen paces ahead with her muzzle low to the ground.

Corban was not sure how long they had been going – the trees blocked the sun – but the muscles in his legs were burning, his back was slick with sweat and his throat was dry. He sent a prayer to Elyon that they would find their quarry soon, but fear came on its heels. What would happen then? Battle? He gritted his teeth. *Cywen is out there. Fear will not rule me.*

Marrock glanced at him and smiled reassuringly. 'You're doing well, lad,' he muttered.

'Huh,' said Corban.

'How is it that your wolven is here?' Marrock asked.

'She followed us, me, from Dun Carreg,' Corban panted. 'I found out.' He wiped his face again. 'I could not leave her alone, here in the Darkwood . . .' he trailed off, not knowing how else to put it into words.

Marrock nodded. 'I thought it might happen,' he said. 'You're her pack. Makes sense she'd seek you out.'

'I just wanted to give her some food,' Corban said.

'She's survived long enough without you feeding her,' said Marrock. 'It's been, what, three moons now, since you left her in the Baglun?'

'Aye.'

'She's learned to hunt well enough, then, for she'd not be here if she hadn't eaten. Mind you,' he added, glancing at Corban, 'she's had a bit of help, there.'

'Help? What do you mean?'

'I saw your friends, giving her meat.'

'What? Who?'

'Farrell was one of them. The other, from the village, I think. A small lad.'

Dath. 'I didn't know,' Corban murmured.

'You have good friends about you,' Marrock said. 'Loyal.'

Corban looked back over his shoulder, at Gar, who brought up the rear of their column. 'I know it.'

'You can tell much about a man by the company he keeps, by his friends, *and* his enemies,' Marrock said.

Storm suddenly slowed ahead of them and crouched lower to the ground, ears flattening to her skull, tail flicking.

Marrock held a hand up and the column slowed. 'Stay back, lad,' he whispered. 'If there is battle, find Gar.'

Corban nodded but kept moving forwards, wanting to reach Storm. He felt a rumbling growl beginning to grow inside her as he laid a hand on her back.

Warriors moved past on either side of him, a sudden tension upon them all, then Gar was there, a reassuring presence at his shoulder.

Marrock was about a dozen paces ahead, hand on his sword hilt, eyes scanning the forest. He froze a moment, then ran forwards. The others gathered round him, Corban and Gar last of all.

The ground was trampled here, several bodies lying in the undergrowth, two in red cloaks, one in grey. Marrock knelt beside another, solitary grey-cloaked body, a gash across his throat.

Corban stared and felt his stomach lurch.

It was Ronan.

The warriors began searching the surrounding area. Nearby Conall bent, picked something up and showed a knife to Marrock.

'That's Cywen's,' Corban said.

'Are you sure, lad?' Halion asked him.

'It's hers, all right, one of her throwing knives.'

'Search the area,' Marrock ordered.

While the dozen men spread out, Corban knelt next to Ronan's body, remembered him laughing with them all, teasing Cywen, always guarding Edana. Tears blurred his vision. He saw Ronan's sword on the ground and picked it up, placed the hilt in the young warrior's hand and closed the stiffening fingers about it.

Gar's hand rested on Corban's shoulder. Corban rubbed his eyes and stood.

'They still live,' Marrock said as the warriors gathered about him. 'Of that I am certain. Though they were captured here, I think. The trail turns away from their previous course and heads east. We must press on.' He looked at Corban, who whispered to Storm, the wolven setting off again, nose to the ground.

They travelled fast, Storm setting a quick pace, a growing tension rising amongst them, knowing they were close.

Nevertheless, after what seemed an age to Corban, the forest began to grow dark and they had seen no further sign of their quarry. Marrock called a halt, Corban reaching for his water skin.

'It will be dark soon,' Marrock said to his gathered warriors. 'Those we follow will make camp and settle for the night, but we have a choice, gifted us by this wolven's nose. We either do as they do, make camp and continue at sun up, or we follow the wolven's nose through the night. I am for marching on,' he said, 'as long as we can move quietly, to close the gap between us and them.'

Heads nodded around him and he smiled grimly, his scar twisting his mouth.

'Good, then. Corban, lead us on.'

With that they set off into the deepening twilight, slower now, Storm loping ahead.

Corban stumbled, not for the first time, his boot catching in the vines that coated the ground. Marrock reached out and steadied him.

They had been walking a long time in darkness now, and Storm was a white streak about ten paces up ahead. Suddenly Storm stopped, Corban almost bumping into her before he realized. The line of warriors behind him rippled to a halt.

'What is it?' Marrock whispered.

Storm stood completely still, half-crouched, ears forward, looking fixedly into the darkness. Her lips twitched into a silent snarl, hackles standing as a crest between her shoulders.

'I think someone is there,' Corban said quietly. 'Up ahead.'

Marrock crept down the line, returning soon with Conall and Halion behind him. Without a word the two men slipped into the undergrowth to either side of the wolven and disappeared into the darkness.

Corban crouched beside Storm and strained to hear something, but for what seemed like the longest time all he heard was the beating of his own heart, the rustle of leaves and branches high above and the slow breathing of Marrock behind him. Then he *did* hear something else, or thought he did. A thud. He strained again, but there was no more.

Eventually a figure appeared up ahead, a deeper shadow in the darkness: Conall creeping towards them.

'That wolven's handy to have around,' he said quietly to Marrock.

'You found someone, then?'

'Aye. Man in a red cloak standing watch. Got a red smile to match his cloak now. Halion's hiding the body.'

Marrock called the other warriors up. 'Their camp cannot be far,' he said to them all. 'We have killed a guard.' Halion then crept out of the darkness to join them and nodded to Marrock. 'We shall wait here, until sunrise. It is not far off, now, and I do not want to stumble into their camp in the dark.'

With that they all settled into the undergrowth, Corban leaning against Storm, who pressed her muzzle into his hand.

'Good girl,' he whispered to her, tugging her ear.

Gar sat beside him. 'When the fighting starts, stay by me,' he said.

'Cywen is there,' Corban said.

'They will not be using wooden sticks, Corban. Come sunrise men are going to die. You stay by me.'

Corban did not answer, just sat there thinking of the bodies in the glade, of Tull, of Ronan in the forest. He shuddered, eyes drooping, and nestled his head against Storm's flank.

Corban woke with a start, as Gar gently shook his shoulder. Storm licked his face, her protruding canines pressing into his cheek.

There was a grey edge to the forest about him, a pale nimbus of light seeping through the canopy above.

'It is time to go,' Gar whispered and pointed at Marrock, who was gathered with the other warriors.

Corban rose stiffly and joined the hunters, feeling another burst of fear. He replayed Gar's words. *Men are going to die*. He swallowed, suddenly wishing he was anywhere else, then felt a rush of shame – Cywen was out there.

Conall returned, lifting a bloodied knife. 'Their next watch will not be seeing much,' he said to Marrock.

'We are splitting into two groups,' Marrock said to Corban. 'I will lead one, Halion shall lead the other. I am thinking that you should stay here and wait for us.'

'What? But Cywen is out there,' Corban blurted.

'We would not be here if not for him,' Halion said. 'He's earned more than being left behind like a bairn.'

'Aye, he has,' agreed Marrock reluctantly.

'And that wolven of his may help us yet,' Halion added.

Marrock assessed Corban a moment, then nodded. 'All right, then. You come with me, Corban.'

They set off immediately. 'Wait for my signal,' Marrock said in parting to Halion, who led his band to the left, Marrock heading to the right of the track they'd followed. Corban stayed near to the last warrior. Storm padded close to him, Gar immediately behind.

A new sound mingled with those they had become accustomed, growing louder. Running water. Soon they came to a wide dark stream and turned to follow its bank. Slowly, almost soundlessly, they crept along the stream's bank, through thick, spiky sedge and tall reeds. Something splashed into the water, a vole or rat startled by their presence, and for long moments they all froze, Corban holding his breath.

He was suddenly terrified, his palms sweating. *Men are going to die*. He sucked in a slow, shuddering breath, and whispered a prayer to Elyon.

Then they were moving again. Corban could see figures moving around the glow of a small fire, hear the chink of metal, and muted conversation as the camp started to wake. Instinctively he reached for the sword at his waist but Gar grabbed his wrist and shook his head.

Louder voices drifted across to them, from beyond the fire. After a moment of staring, searching the camp, Corban saw a group of red-cloaked men gathered before a wide tree, other figures sitting about the tree's trunk. He saw Alona, Edana beside her, then Cywen. He felt Storm tense beside him and wrapped a hand in her fur.

The light from above was growing now, details in the camp becoming clearer. Half a dozen men stood before the bound women, one of them talking to the women, it seemed. Then he heard Cywen's voice, sharp and clear. She was angry, furious, he could not mistake that tone. His heart lurched with joy.

Suddenly there was a flurry of movement, one of the red-cloaked men lifting his spear and lunging towards Cywen. Then another brought his sword across the spear, splintering the weapon, before stepping in front of the women. Was he defending them? And there was something familiar about the man.

Then another was drawing his sword.

He recognized them. Morcant, Rhin's champion, drawing his sword on Camlin, the brigand. But that made no sense.

'Be ready,' Marrock hissed. There was a loud shout from amongst the trees and Conall came hurtling out of the undergrowth, sword in one hand, knife in the other, and buried its blade up to the hilt in a red-cloaked warrior. Halion and his handful of men were close behind him, carving into the men in the camp.

Marrock cursed and launched himself over the stream's bank, his men following.

Then the world went mad.

Corban scrambled up the bank, stood staring, one hand on his sword's hilt, the other still gripping a tight fistful of Storm's fur. With a hiss Gar's sword left its scabbard, and he stood a pace before Corban.

Everywhere was a whirlwind of combat, men screaming, yelling battle cries, dying. The women were completely hidden from view, now, a seething mass of flesh and iron and leather and blood filling the space between Corban and the captives.

There were several red-cloaks on the ground, caught by the first rush of combat, but they were rallying quickly, fighting back with the ferocity of the cornered. There were still more red-cloaks than grey, or so it seemed to Corban as he tried to make sense of the chaos before him. As he watched he saw one of Marrock's men – he could not tell who – fall with a spear in his gut. Marrock smashed the spear-holder in the face with his sword's hilt, but then two red-cloaks were hacking at him and he was swept from view.

Corban tugged at his sword, felt its heavy, unfamiliar weight in his hand, and just stood there a moment, unsure what to do. He took a hesitant step towards the tumult.

'No,' Gar barked.

'But, Cywen . . .' Corban stopped, feeling he should do something, but part of him glad to just watch, his courage balancing on a knife's edge. He hesitated, then the decision was taken from him.

A cluster of bandits had seen him and Gar, came hurtling towards them, four at least, maybe five.

Gar took a few paces forwards, held his sword high in a two-handed grip, then they were on him. He deflected a spear-point aimed at his chest, knocked the tip into the ground, the man holding it grunting as Gar's sword opened his throat, then the stablemaster was ducking, chopping two-handed into the next man's ribs and in that moment Corban knew that everything he had seen of Gar in practice had been but a glimmer, the poorest reflection of what he was truly capable of. Watching him was almost beautiful.

Storm's muscles bunched and she flew away from Corban, leaping within a warrior's guard too fast for him to strike, her claws slashing at his torso even as her jaws ripped into his face.

Another warrior was trading blows with Gar, now, one who knew his trade, though he was still only just managing to keep himself alive, frantically blocking Gar's remorseless barrage of blows, each parried sweep turning effortlessly into another attack.

Then someone was past Gar and Storm, a warrior with sword held high, charging straight at Corban.

Corban took a step back and instinctively blocked an overhead blow, his arm numbing from the power of it. At the same time he stepped to the side and pivoted on his heel, the warrior hurtling past him. Too late, he thought to backswing, as the warrior turned, coming at him again. He blocked once, twice, three times, stepping back with each blow, feeling clumsy, panic flooding his mind, sparks flying from their grating swords. Storm snarled from somewhere behind him, the warrior's eyes leaving his to spot the wolven over his shoulder. In that moment Corban lunged forwards and felt his blade punch through boiled leather into the man's belly. Then he was yanking back, blood sluicing over his hand, his arm. The warrior was sinking to his knees, clutching at the gaping wound. Dimly Corban heard something, a scream, and realized it was his own voice, shouting some incoherent cry.

Storm was beside him again, snarling at the dead man, teeth dripping blood.

'Are you hurt?' a voice filtered through the fog, but all Corban could do was stare at the figure in the dirt before him. So still.

'Ban, are you hurt?' the voice said again, louder, more urgently. A hand grabbed his shoulder, turned him and he was looking at Gar, something fierce in the stablemaster's gaze.

'N-no . . .' he said, and shook his head.

'Good,' Gar grunted.

Corban stared past the stablemaster and saw the rest of their attackers dead, one's throat ripped out by Storm, three others cut down by Gar. Beyond them the battle still raged, though fewer men were standing. Corban could see glimpses of the women now, still bound to the tree, a small knot of warriors trading blows about them.

'Cywen,' Corban said and set off before Gar could respond, skirting the clumps of fighting men and moving quickly through the trees.

Halion and Conall fought before the bound women, bodies littering the ground about their feet. A man fought beside them – Camlin. The brigand chopped at a spear thrust, then, raising his sword, he slashed the rope binding the women to the tree. For a moment they sat there shocked, then they were on their feet.

Halion was trading blows with a tall, wide-shouldered warrior. Corban gasped as he suddenly saw who Halion was fighting.

Braith.

The woodsman took a step back, out of Halion's reach, glanced about the camp, then at his bleeding arm. He shouted something, the words lost in the din of battle.

Corban darted forwards, with Gar and Storm a pace behind, and slipped through to Cywen and Edana. The girls were wide eyed, staring at the carnage about them as Corban sawed at the bonds binding their hands. Cywen threw herself upon him, hugging him tight.

Shouting drew his attention back and he saw a handful of bandits running from the camp, Braith and Morcant amongst them. Marrock was nearby with Halion and Conall, as they clustered around the women.

Marrock held Alona and grinned at her. She smiled back, hugged him and kissed his cheek.

Of the twelve warriors of Ardan that Marrock had picked, only four were still breathing. Halion signalled to Conall and they moved to the edge of the camp, scanning the trees in the direction of the fugitives.

Corban suddenly realized Camlin was still there, looking confused. Marrock raised his sword.

'No!' Alona cried. 'This man saved us. They were going to kill Cywen. He protected her, protected *us*.'

Marrock frowned, sword still raised. 'Why?'

Camlin shrugged. 'Still asking myself that one,' he said. 'It just happened.'

'I am in his debt,' Alona said firmly.

'So, what do we do with him?' Marrock asked.

'They're coming back!' Halion shouted from amongst the trees. There was a whirring sound, Alona staggered and fell against a tree, an arrow sprouting from her back. Edana screamed.

'Out of here!' Marrock yelled. He grabbed Alona, put her over his shoulder and ran into the forest.

Edana and Cywen stumbled after them. Camlin stood for a moment, then followed Conall as he ran back towards his brother. Corban hesitated, staring back at the sounds of battle, and caught a glimpse of Halion amongst the trees. Then he followed the girls into the shadows, with Gar and Storm close behind.

CHAPTER SEVENTY-THREE

CORBAN

Figures flitted ahead of Corban, moving through the trees, and soon he was close behind Cywen. For a long time they just kept moving, the sounds of battle behind them long since faded into nothing. Marrock set their pace, carrying Alona and refusing to let anyone else take her from him. Eventually he staggered and almost dropped her and so they stopped, gasping for breath, Corban flopping to the ground beside Cywen. He reached out and squeezed her hand.

She looked at him, face dirty, eyes red-rimmed. 'I did not think I would see you again,' she said, smiling weakly.

'Storm led us to you,' he said, the wolven nudging Cywen with her muzzle.

'How is she here?' Cywen asked, tugging at one of Storm's ears.

'She followed us, from the Baglun. Are you hurt?'

'Me? No,' Cywen muttered, then her eyes filled, tears rolling down her cheek. 'Ronan . . .' she whispered.

'I know. We found him . . .' Corban said, but could find no more words.

'We must keep moving,' Marrock said, cradling Alona in his lap. She was white faced and unconscious, with hair plastered to her face. Edana sat beside her, stroking Alona's brow, face almost as pale as her mother's.

'You cannot carry her all the way to Ardan,' Gar said.

'I can and I will,' Marrock said.

'No. You will slow us. If we are being tracked we will outrun no one.'

Marrock glared at Gar but said nothing.

'Let us make a litter from our cloaks,' Gar said. 'Two can carry her easier than one, and she will be more comfortable.'

Marrock was silent a moment, then nodded curtly.

Quickly they made a rough litter. Marrock snapped the arrow in Alona's back and positioned her as well as he could, then they set off again. Corban led with Storm, with Marrock and Gar carrying Alona. They continued like this a long while. Gar was at the back of the small column again when he called out.

'Someone is coming, behind us.'

They picked up their pace, Corban feeling fear return in stomach-churning force.

'They are gaining,' Gar called out again. Marrock cursed, called a halt, and they turned to face their pursuers, lined protectively before Alona and the girls. Corban drew his sword and swallowed.

The sound of running feet grew louder, fast-moving figures glimpsed amongst the trees, then suddenly Conall was there, grinning between gasping breaths, Camlin behind him, Halion last of all. There had been two other warriors of Ardan still standing when Corban had run from the glade, but they were nowhere to be seen now.

'For . . . a bunch of . . . women, bairns and . . . cripples, you can . . . set a fair . . . pace,' Conall said, resting his hands on his knees. Despite himself, Corban grinned.

'Are you followed?' Marrock barked.

Halion shook his head. 'I think not. We fought long and hard. Two of our number fell. I only saw a few of our enemy that fled.' He grimaced. 'I don't think they'll be back again.'

'Good,' said Marrock, and slapped Halion's arm.

They rested a while, then, passing round water skins and strips of dried meat, Corban felt the fear of moments before melting away, exhaustion taking its place.

'Rhin shall pay for this,' Edana said, sitting and holding her mother's hand. The queen's breathing was ragged, blood at the corner of her mouth.

'What do you mean, *Rhin*?' Corban said. 'It is Owain that has done . . .' he trailed off, looking at Alona. 'I saw Morcant, Rhin's champion, back there.'

'That's right,' Edana said. 'Rhin is behind this. The red cloaks were to cast the blame on Owain. Why, I do not know, but it is Rhin's work.'

'She speaks true,' Camlin said. He had been silent until now, sipping slowly from a water skin, sitting apart from them.

'Why?' asked Marrock.

'She wants Narvon and Ardan,' the woodsman said. 'Thinks if Brenin and Owain try an' kill each other she'll have an easier time taking their torcs come the end of it.'

'So why have you joined us?' Marrock said, looking suspiciously at the woodsman.

Camlin shrugged. 'Wouldn't exactly put it like that.' He scratched his chin. 'Same as you, I've just found out Rhin was pulling the strings here. Somethin' I don't like 'bout that.' He paused. 'An' that Morcant, Rhin's champion – just couldn't stomach takin' orders from him.'

Conall chuckled.

'And that's why you changed sides?' Marrock pressed, still frowning.

'I'm not on any side,' the woodsman said. ''Cept my own. But, aye, that's why I did what I did. That an' her.' He pointed at Cywen. 'Morcant was going to kill her,' he said, holding Marrock's gaze. 'I don't take with killing women and bairns. And you've got a mouth on you, girl. Might be an idea t'think before you speak, in future.'

'As if she's never heard that before,' Corban said to Gar.

Alona moaned.

'We must get her back to Ardan. As soon as possible,' Halion said.

'Why not Uthandun?' Conall asked. 'It's nearer, and now we know it's not Owain that's betrayed us.'

'We don't know what happened when Pendathran went back there,' Marrock said. 'My uncle is not *diplomatic*. Owain may have new cause to bear us a grudge.'

'Uthandun would be unwise,' Camlin muttered.

'Why?' growled Marrock.

'Just something Braith said. Rhin had more'n one trick up her sleeve, I think.'

'So we must head for Ardan, then,' Gar said.

'That's a long walk,' Camlin said grimly. 'I'll take you, though. If you'll trust me.'

'How long will it take us?' Marrock asked.

'Depends. We could cut to the giantsway, then we'd make good time, but Owain may be watching it, or Rhin. If we march as the crow flies to Badun, carrying her all the way, maybe five, six nights.'

'That's too long,' Marrock said.

Camlin shrugged. 'Risk the road, cut it down to three nights.'

Just then Storm looked up, and whined. Corban saw movement in the branches above, then flapping heralded the arrival of an old, ragged crow. It landed on a branch just above Corban's head and began squawking.

'Craf . . .?' Corban whispered.

'Cor-ban,' the crow squawked. 'Cor-ban.'

'Asroth's teeth,' hissed Camlin, going pale. 'Did that mangy crow just speak?'

'Aye,' said Corban, suddenly grinning. 'It is Craf. Brina's crow.'

'Brina, Brina, Brina . . .' Craf stuttered and began hoping from one foot to the other.

'She must have sent him to find us.'

'Follow, follow, follow, follow . . .' the crow squawked, then flapped its wings and flew off, landing on another branch about thirty paces ahead of them. 'FOLLOW,' Craf screeched.

'He has Brina's patience,' Corban said.

Quickly the small band organized themselves and set off after Craf.

The rest of the day followed this pattern, following the crow as he flapped in front of them, stopping regularly on branches to let them catch up. Corban lost all track of time, direction and distance, but as dusk was beginning to settle about them Camlin announced that they had covered a lot of ground and that they were nearing the giantsway.

'That old crow's not stopping,' Marrock said, watching Craf disappear into the gloom. They carried on walking, Camlin taking the lead, and soon they stepped onto the road. There were glimpses of the sky above, dotted with the first stars of evening. Picking up their pace, they carried on in the darkness, but soon heard the sound of riders ahead. Quickly they moved off the road, then Edana was running, calling out to Brenin, at the front of the column, with Pendathran tall and wide beside him.

Corban and the rest stepped out of the trees, Marrock and Halion carrying Alona. A score of mounted warriors swept past them, forming a line in the road. Others circled them, jumping from horses and calling out. Corban suddenly felt weary to the bone and dizzy. Then Thannon was there, pulling him and Cywen into a tight embrace. There were tears on the blacksmith's cheeks when Corban looked up, tears in his own eyes and streaks on Cywen's face. Thannon pulled them close again, almost cracking bones, kissing them and ruffling their hair.

When they parted again Thannon grabbed Gar's arm in the warrior grip, pulled the stablemaster into an embrace and pounded his back.

Looking round, Corban saw Brina crouching beside Alona, Craf on the pommel of her saddle. Then warriors quickly lashed a stronger litter together and soon they were mounting up.

Their rescue party had brought horses, and soon they were heading down the giantsway to refuge.

Brina dropped back and rode alongside Corban and Cywen, smiling when she saw Storm loping along beside Shield.

'Will Alona be all right?' Corban asked.

Brina's smile vanished. 'It is bad,' the healer said, then she shrugged. 'Maybe. If we were back at my cottage I would have more hope. We shall see. But I am glad to see you still on your feet. You seem to be developing a distinct talent for being in the wrong place at the wrong time.'

Corban pulled a face and filled her in on events.

'Rhin, eh?' Brina mused when he'd finished. 'Well, there is more than one dice being rolled here, I think.'

'What do you mean?'

'When we left – in a rush, I can tell you – there was something afoot within Uthandun. Lots of horn blowing. And then we were chased. Pendathran led a band that fought them off, of course, but I suspect they will come again, when King Owain has been able to gather more warriors.'

'Craf helped us,' Corban said suddenly.

Brina smiled and scratched the crow's neck. 'He can be useful, occasionally.'

With that they settled into silence, and rode into the night.

Later, much later, Corban saw pinpricks up ahead – torches – they had caught up with the rest of Brenin's entourage. Gwenith wept when she saw Corban and Cywen and hugged then almost as tight as Thannon had.

Then a savage cry pierced the night. Corban looked down the column and saw Brina crouched by Alona's litter, King Brenin cradling his wife. Edana was holding her mother's hand again, lost in grief and sobbing.

Alona was dead.

The journey back to Ardan was very different from the one to Uthandun, a sense of dread and tension hovering over them all.

No more attacks from Owain came on the road and in just over a day's hard riding they left the Darkwood and saw the giants' circle of standing stones, with Badun's walls in the distance.

Brenin took council here. Gethin pressed for reconciliation with King Owain, still hoping Kyla and his son Uthan's handbinding could be salvaged. Brenin and Pendathran were more intent upon Queen Rhin, but agreed that Owain would be better as an ally than an enemy, so Brenin inked a scroll to Narvon's King, detailing Alona's death and Rhin's part in it, then a messenger was sent back down the giantsway, into the Darkwood.

'Begin mustering for war,' Brenin commanded Gethin in parting. 'Whether there is war or peace with Owain I will be marching on Rhin. Soon.' Then they left for Dun Carreg.

Spring had arrived with the Birth Moon and new life was evident everywhere, a stark contrast to the procession's black mood.

Corban was weary and sad when Dun Carreg came into view, high on its hill, with Havan nestled at its foot. The welcome cheers of the villagers quickly turned to mourning as news of Alona's death spread. Corban saw Dath in the crowd, nodded a grim greeting to him and noticed eyes following Storm.

Nothing had been said of the wolven's return; there were more important matters filling everyone's thoughts, but Corban expected some kind of reckoning now that they were back at Dun Carreg. Rafe and Helfach, at least, would not let the matter rest. Corban hoped Storm's part in the finding of the captives would be enough to allow her back to the fortress, though with Brenin's black mood nothing was certain.

I'll not give her up again, he thought. With a heavy heart he rode back inside the walls of Dun Carreg.

Corban ducked under the sweep of Gar's practice sword, pivoted on his heel and spun away, swinging a backslash at the same time. Gar effortlessly deflected it, pressing his attack. Corban parried one, two, three, four strikes, each one shivering up his arm, then he slipped on some hay and the tip of Gar's weapon was at his throat.

He wanted to say something, ask why Gar was pressing him so hard, but did not have the breath to form words. He wiped sweat from his eyes, walked to the water barrel and stuck his whole head in, spraying water as he pulled away.

He leaned against the barrel, watching Gar a moment. The stablemaster was putting their practice blades away in an old box beneath a pile of harness and tack. He had been different since their return from the Darkwood, less reserved, more driven, as if something had woken in him.

Corban blinked, thinking of the Darkwood. It was only two tennights ago that he had been crawling along the stream's bank. He looked at his hand, remembered the sensation of hot blood pouring over it, and shivered.

'Are you well?' Gar asked, coming over to the barrel and sipping from a ladle.

'Aye,' Corban muttered. 'Just remembering. The Darkwood.'

Gar nodded slowly. 'That's something a man never forgets – the first time he takes another's life in battle.'

'I still see his face,' Corban said. 'I can even smell him, sometimes.'

'Aye,' said Gar. 'The memory will fade, but never leave you – and it shouldn't. Not completely. It is no small thing, to take a life.' He sighed, 'You did well, Ban. I was proud of you.'

Corban blinked and flushed. He had never heard Gar talk like this.

The stablemaster gave Corban a long, measuring look. 'You are not the same lad that lost his practice sword at the Spring Fair.'

Corban could not meet Gar's gaze. 'I *feel* the same, in here,' he said, tapping his chest. 'I was scared, at the Darkwood. *Terrified*. It all happened so fast. I was not brave. He was trying to kill me, what else could I do?'

'What else could you do? Plenty. Let me tell you, every man in that camp felt the same fear you did. I certainly did. Both the brave man and the coward feel the same. The only difference between them is that the brave man *faces* his fear, does not run.' He stared at Corban with an intensity he had never shown before.

'You could have run, yet you did not. You could have stayed hidden by the stream, yet you did not. You *stood*, did what you had to do. That is all bravery is. I would ask no more of any man, or expect any more.' He almost smiled. 'You did well, Ban, very well. And, most importantly, you live to tell the tale.'

'I am glad about that part,' Corban said, wryly. 'Tell me, when we were by the stream I went to draw my sword, but you stopped me. Why?'

'Ah. A sword being drawn is the most familiar sound in all the world to any warrior. If any sound would have betrayed us, that would have been it.'

That made sense. Corban bid the stablemaster farewell, leaving to break his fast before going on to the Rowan Field. 'Your leg seemed much improved,' he called over his shoulder, 'when you were running leagues through the Darkwood, battling red-cloaks at the end of it.'

Gar stared at him a moment. 'It comes and goes,' the stable-master said, face as still as stone, then winked at him.

The Rowan Field was fuller than Corban had ever seen it before, war-riors arriving from all over Ardan. Word had gone out as soon as they had returned to Dun Carreg, of what had happened in Narvon, and it had not been long before warriors began to arrive, from ones and twos to bands of thirty or forty. Everyone knew that King Brenin was mus-tering for war, though much else was unclear. Once Dalgar arrived from Dun Maen, bringing with him the largest warband from beyond Dun Carreg and Badun, then the greater part of Ardan's strength would be gathered. Then, it was thought, they would ride to Cambren, avenge Alona's death on Rhin. There had been no news from Narvon yet, the messenger Brenin had sent still not returned. Rumours flew that Owain was dead, murdered by Rhin, that Uthan was dead, that

Rhin had invaded Narvon's borders. Corban shook his head. *Leave all of that for Brenin*, he thought, heading for a weapons rack.

Storm was padding beside him, many heads turning to watch her as they made their way through the Field. Nothing had been said of her return yet, but Brenin had other things on his mind. It would come, though. Corban had already heard whispers from Rafe and Helfach.

He reached the weapons rack, selected a battered practice sword and shield and looked about for Halion. He hefted the wooden sword. *Not long, now*, he thought to himself.

His nameday was just over a ten-night away. He felt nerves flutter in his stomach. His warrior trial. His Long Night. Thannon had had him working in the forge on his sword, first discussing the details: length, weight, hilt, then the harder work had begun, of smelting and forging, of hammering and cooling. It was almost finished now. Thannon had forbidden him from approaching the forge for the last two days, wanting to put the finishing touches to it himself. Thannon had set Corban at another project, as well. His da wanted a new weapon, and was fashioning a war-hammer, like the giant's one that hung in their kitchen, but smaller. That too was almost finished.

'Over here, lad,' Halion called, raising an arm so that Corban could see him. They walked through the crowds out into a part of the Field with space enough for them. Out of the corner of his eye Corban saw Dath, practising his bow, Tarben behind him, Marrock and Camlin to one side, watching. The woodsman had just stayed, seeming even to have fashioned a friendship of sorts with Marrock.

Storm flopped onto the ground with a sigh, her tail twitching, copper eyes watching Halion as he pointed his practice sword at Corban.

'Come, then,' Halion said, glancing at Storm. 'I'm glad she's learned the difference between practice and the real thing,' he said, then began taking Corban through his forms, duelling, like Gar, with a strength and intensity that had been absent before the Darkwood.

It was halfway to highsun when they switched to spear-work, Halion grunting approvingly at Corban's solid thrusts and blocks.

'Not long now,' Corban said to him as they stopped to rest.

'Until what?'

'My warrior trial, Long Night.'

'Aye,' Halion nodded. 'Do you feel ready?'

'I don't know,' Corban said. 'I think so. I *hope* so.' He pulled a sour face. 'What do you think?'

'I think you are ready. That is why I have requested your Long Night be brought forward.'

'What?' Corban was stunned. 'Why?'

Halion looked away, about the Field, at the countless warriors training. 'Because we will ride from here soon. I saw you in the Dark-wood, Corban. You made a difference.' He scratched his stubbly beard. 'And, I thought you would find it hard if you were left here, left behind. I don't know when we will ride out, but I feel it will be soon. Maybe before your nameday.' He looked at Corban search-ingly. 'The choice is yours, Corban, but Brenin has granted my request. You may take your warrior trial, sit your Long Night, early – if you would choose to.'

'When?'

'On the morrow.'

'*What?*'

Halion grinned. 'Less time to fret, then.' His smile faded. 'Riding to war is no jest, Corban. But I have trained you, seen you grow. It was the Darkwood that sealed it for me. The way I see it, you took your warrior trial then. You faced a man, a warrior, bested him in fair combat.' His smile flashed again. 'I have spoken to Gar, heard what you did. You are more ready than most who sit their Long Night, Corban. More than that, you deserve it and have earned it.' He shrugged. 'What difference is in a few days?'

Corban looked around the Field, warriors everywhere. How long he had dreamed of being one of them. And now the time had finally come.

'Well?' Halion said. 'What say you?'

'Aye,' Corban said firmly. 'Aye. And you have my thanks, Halion. You honour me.'

'Good,' Halion said, pleased. 'Then let us make sure that you are ready, eh.'

Suddenly horns blew, echoing around the Field. Corban saw a line of men file into the Field from the arch of rowans, Brenin at their head. Beside him marched Pendathran and Edana with Evnis and Heb behind, and half a score of Brenin's guard following.

Corban watched Edana. He had not seen her since their escape from the Darkwood, except at Alona's burial. The Queen's cairn had been raised on the hill beyond the fortress' walls, Brenin listing aloud the dead that had been left behind. Cywen had wept silently at Ronan's name.

Edana looked much the same as she had then, dark shadows under her eyes, face pale apart from red streaks where she had scratched her face in her grief looking like tears of blood running down her cheeks.

Brenin made his way to the stone court, warriors parting before him. 'Welcome, warriors of Ardan,' Brenin called. 'I have come here with news to tell. But first, an overdue task.'

Men were squashed shoulder to shoulder, listening to the King. Apart from Corban, who alone had a small ring about him where men made room for Storm – all had heard the tale of what she had done to Rafe. Corban nodded to Dath and Farrell as they squeezed into the space and stood either side of him.

'Tull, my first-sword, fell in service of me, defending my beloved wife, less than a moon ago.' There was a tremor in his voice. 'A better man, more loyal, more fierce, there has never been, and I fear we shall not see his like again.' He bowed his head, as silence filled the Field.

'Nevertheless,' Brenin said, looking about him again, 'it is not fitting for a king of Ardan to be without his first-sword. More so in times such as these.'

Murmurs rippled around the Field as men realized where Brenin was leading.

'One of you has risen high in my eyes, served me bravely, risked his life for my honour, proven himself in battle.'

Now silence fell again, seemed like a living thing, Corban feeling he could almost reach out and touch the tension that filled the Field.

'Halion, come forward.'

A pathway parted for the warrior, Halion stepping out before the King, looking awkward, amazed.

'Will you accept this charge?' Brenin asked. 'Become my champion, the defender of my flesh, my blood, my honour?'

Halion fell to one knee. He cried, 'I would, my King,' in a loud, clear voice.

'Then give me your sword.'

Halion stood, drew his blade and slammed it into the earth between two flagstones, where it stood quivering.

Brenin pulled a knife from his belt, with a quick stroke cut his palm and held his fist over the sword, blood dripping onto the hilt, the cross-guard, running down the blade. He beckoned to Edana, who stepped forward, took the knife and did the same, her blood mingling on the sword hilt with her father's. Then Brenin gave the knife to Halion. The warrior held it, looked from Brenin to Edana, then cut his own hand, and let his blood mix with theirs.

'Good. It is done,' Brenin said, as a roar went up through the Field. Corban punched the air with a fist, shouting as loud as any. He could not quite believe how Brenin had just honoured Halion, still thought of as an outlander by many. As Corban watched he saw Evnis move a few paces, and bend to whisper in Conall's ear.

'There is more,' Brenin called, holding his bloodstained hand up. Slowly the crowd quieted. Brenin turned to Heb, who passed him a small basket woven of willow branches. 'I sent a messenger to Owain, telling him of Rhin's treachery, of my wife's death. This is his response.' He dipped his hand into the basket and pulled out a severed head, holding it high for all to see.

'This is how Owain treats my messenger. Prepare yourselves for war,' Brenin shouted. 'Within the ten-night we will ride to battle, first with Narvon, then Cambren.'

There was more shouting, warriors yelling Brenin's name and battle cries. Over it all the sound of horns blowing, growing louder. At first Corban thought it was part of Brenin's call to war, but slowly those in the Field quietened. The horns still blew from the northern wall, not from Brenin's guards.

Slowly at first, then more quickly, men began making for the northern wall, Corban, Dath and Farrell amongst them. They climbed the wide steps and looked down into the bay.

A strange-looking ship was pulling into it, long and sleek, oars dipping in and out of the water like the legs of a many-limbed bug. From one of its masts a banner snapped in the wind, a white eagle on a black field.

CHAPTER SEVENTY-FOUR

KASTELL

Kastell grunted as he pulled himself up the half-buried trunk of a fallen elm, clambered down the other side and looked back at Maquin as the old warrior followed him.

Eight nights they had been trudging through this cursed forest, living in different shades of gloom. He should be used to it, having served with the Gadrai for so long now, but they had spent their lives around the river Rhenus, where the trees were thinner, the sky something that was at least seen most days. Here the chance of sunlight penetrating the thick canopy above them was less than slight. The trees were dense, the branches above interwoven like some ancient, untouched loom.

Maquin slipped on the trunk, steadied himself with his spear and swore quietly.

'Steady, greybeard,' Kastell said, and received a black look in return. Usually Maquin would have smiled, but eight nights in the embrace of Forn were taking their toll. Men were becoming edgier, especially as word had spread that they were finally nearing Haldis, burial site of the Hunen giants.

Behind Maquin the bald head of Orgull appeared, shining with sweat. 'Move on,' their captain growled. They were spread out in a loose line before the main body of their host, the Gadrai acting as both van and scouts in one.

Kastell stepped into the thick foliage, glanced ahead and saw the broad back of the giant that had been leading them, Alcyon. Vandil was beside him, unmistakable with the outline of his two swords crossed upon his back.

As unnatural as it felt, the giant's presence *had* been of great benefit to them. Not only was he leading them unerringly to their destination, but he had proved most valuable in beating off the Hunen attacks they had encountered so far.

All had been quiet until the third night into the forest, the only deaths being warriors on lone sentry duty, sucked dry as husks by the great bats of Forn. None of those casualties had come from amongst the Gadrai – they had lived in the forest too long and knew better than to close their eyes whilst standing guard – death's only warning could be a whisper of wings. Then the Gadrai had walked into a thick mist, dense and high. Alcyon had called a halt, waiting for his companion, Calidus, and together they had begun to *sing*.

Nothing had happened at first, but then a breeze had rippled through the forest, growing quickly in strength, until it raged through the trees. The mist melted before it, revealing a score of Hunen in the forest. The giants had flung their spears and retreated, realizing they were undone.

Since then there had been constant skirmishes up and down the long line of warbands, Alcyon and Calidus blunting the Elemental edges to the attacks and giving warning of giant ambushes. Nevertheless, many had died, and their pace had been slowed by the Hunen.

Today all evidence of the Hunen had disappeared. No ambushes, concealed pits, traps or mists, and by highsun Alcyon had announced that they were within a day's march of Haldis. 'They will not attack this day,' the giant had assured Vandil. 'They will spend their time readying the defences at Haldis.'

When a break was called, Kastell was happy to rest with others of the Gadrai, until he noticed Romar, presumably heading for council with Calidus, Alcyon and Vandil, and spotted Jael among the party. His uncle glanced back at him but Kastell scowled and looked away.

Romar had sent for him when the Gadrai had first arrived at Halstat. He had felt both excited and anxious stepping into Romar's tent, his uncle embracing him awkwardly.

'You've done well, I hear,' the big man had said, smiling.

'Me? Aye,' Kastell shrugged. 'I still live. In the Gadrai that is well enough.' A thought occurred. 'You have me watched?'

'Nothing like that. But I would be a poor uncle if I did not take interest in you.' Romar had ushered Kastell into a seat and poured him a cup of wine. 'I have heard from Vandil, that is all. You have survived giant raids, slain Hunen. You are growing into the man your father always said you would become.'

Kastell, swirled his wine, feeling uncomfortable. 'And how are you, Uncle,' he said, to change the subject. 'How go your plans?'

Romar now looked perturbed, 'Things have become complicated since you left. You have heard Tenebral's news?'

'Something, though I did not pay much attention.'

'Aquilus is dead,' Romar said. 'His son, Nathair, is now King.'

Kastell had suddenly thought of Veradis, the Prince's man who had stepped into the fight with Jael's cronies and stood up for him. 'How did Aquilus die?'

'Murdered in his own chamber. Mandros of Carnutan did the deed, 'tis said. Though he shall never be judged for the truth of it, now. He fled, but has since been slain by a force from Tenebral.' Romar took a long draught from his cup and poured some more. 'He was killed by your friend. Veradis.'

'Oh,' said Kastell, feeling suddenly more interested in this tale.

'Aye. He has risen far, your friend. He is now the first-sword of Tenebral. You will see him soon. He is to lead Tenebral's offering in this campaign.'

Kastell grinned. Veradis had been a friend to him when friends had been in short supply. Then he'd noticed Romar's face. 'Why so troubled?' he asked. 'Veradis is a good man.'

'Aye . . .' Romar shrugged, 'I thought so, too. But I feel uncomfortable; this shift in power sits badly with me. This has been ill handled, with Mandros not being judged. I am reconsidering the alliance with Tenebral.'

Kastell shrugged. Once the alliance had been of interest to him, when Romar had first spoken of it. But no more. He had a new family now, the Gadrai was all that mattered to him, and Tenebral seemed a long way away.

Romar then spoke his mind. 'Come back to me, Kastell,' he had said.

'What? I do not think that would be wise.'

'Times are turbulent,' Romar had said. 'I need people about me that I can trust. You are my kin, my brother's son.'

'You have Jael,' Kastell replied, trying to keep the bitterness from his voice.

'Aye,' Romar said. 'Jael. He is eager, for this campaign, for the alliance with Tenebral. Sometimes I think too eager . . .'

'What do you mean?'

Romar had waved a hand impatiently. 'Nothing,' he said. 'Jael aside, it would be good if you were with me. You are close to this Veradis, eh? That could be of benefit to me. I need someone close to Nathair's inner circle. Things are not as they were with Aquilus. This slaying of Mandros – I shall call for a trial into Mandros' death. Nathair must account for his actions, and something about this feels ill omened.'

'So you want me to spy for you,' Kastell had said.

Romar shrugged. 'In a way. We all have interests to protect, Kastell. For one, I want my axe back, and would reward handsomely any that help me.' He had then reached out and gripped Kastell's wrist. 'You have proved yourself with the Gadrai, but they are not your kin. We are blood. Come back to me.'

Kastell remembered Romar's look, almost pleading. It seemed so out of place; his uncle had always been so decisive, a leader of men.

He wanted to say yes, but memories of Jael flooded his mind. 'Jael said things. About my da,' he said instead.

Romar had frowned, but said nothing.

'He spoke of my da's *transgressions* . . .'

Romar was angry now but still he said nothing.

'But what did he mean?' Kastell pressed.

'I will not speak of it,' Romar said.

'Then I will not come back,' Kastell had snapped, suddenly furious. He had stood and stalked from the tent, his uncle glowering at him.

An argument up ahead distracted him from these thoughts, and he could just see Alcyon's bulk. Beside the giant someone was waving their arms, almost shouting, his gesticulations aimed at Calidus.

Kastell frowned and craned to see better.

The angry figure suddenly broke away, others following. It was Romar, his face flushed and his posture stiff with rage.

Calidus was watching Romar's departure, then turned to another figure to murmur an aside. Kastell squinted and saw that the man was Jael.

Sunset had come and gone, and there were small campfires flickering between trees as far as Kastell could see. He was sitting staring at the flames as great moths flapped around them, sending shadows dancing across his fellow warriors gathered about the fire.

A twig snapped in the darkness and a figure stepped into the firelight. Vandil nodded to them all and crouched down, Orgull offering him the wine skin. 'We're all set,' he said, wiping his mouth. 'Tomorrow's the last dawn the Hunen will ever see.'

'A big day for the Gadrai,' Maquin said.

'Aye,' said Vandil, looking into the flames. 'One I never thought to see.' He grinned, teeth flashing red in the firelight. 'A good time to be alive.'

'What is next?' Kastell asked, pausing the rhythm of his whetstone.

'Next?'

'After the Hunen.'

'Let's see if we live through the morrow, first,' Vandil shrugged. 'Have this conversation then, eh?'

'What about Drassil?' Suddenly all eyes were on Kastell.

'It probably doesn't exist. Men have tried to find it, searched for the treasure rumoured to be there. None ever came back. Shouldn't be filling your head with thoughts of that fool's gold,' Vandil warned. ''Specially when you'll need all your wits to keep your head from parting with your shoulders on the morrow.' He stood, took another draught of the wine and handed it to Orgull. 'Sharp swords 'n' clear heads, lads.'

'Aye,' the men around the fire assented as Vandil walked away, disappearing quickly into the gloom.

Soon after, Veradis found his way to their circle.

'Come, sit,' Maquin said. 'Share some wine with us.'

'No, I cannot,' said Veradis. 'I would speak with you both, though.'

Kastell sheathed his sword and pocketed the whetstone he'd been using to sharpen it. Veradis turned and led them into the darkness.

They followed into the shadows, where Veradis' features were silver-edged with moon-glow.

'Are you well?' Maquin asked.

'Me? Aye,' Veradis muttered, not meeting their gaze. He seemed uneasy, then finally looked at them. 'We are friends, you and I, are we not?'

'Aye,' Maquin said slowly. Kastell just nodded.

'That is rare,' Veradis murmured, almost to himself. 'Something of value.'

'What is troubling you?' Maquin said, softly but firmly.

'Your oath, first – that my words stay between us.'

'Aye,' they both said, Maquin frowning.

'Be careful who, or what, you trust, over the coming days,' Veradis said. 'Be on your guard, and not just from giants,' he added, almost a whisper.

'What do you mean?' Kastell asked.

Veradis looked at them both. 'Romar – he is making an enemy of Nathair. You would be wise to find a new lord.'

'Romar is my kin,' Kastell said. 'He took me in. Is there more that you are not saying, Veradis?'

'Just watch your backs,' Veradis said. 'That is all I can say, more than I should have,' then he turned and slipped into the night, before Kastell or Maquin managed to speak.

'What do you make of that?' Kastell said.

'I don't know,' Maquin murmured, 'but it sounds like trouble to me.'

CHAPTER SEVENTY-FIVE

CYWEN

Grass tickled Cywen's neck as she lay near the cliff's edge, looking down into the bay, watching the newly arrived ship. She was supposed to be helping Gar in the stables and knew she would get a tongue-lashing for her absence, but she didn't care.

Ever since the Darkwood, since she had held Ronan as he died, nothing felt important. The only thought that sparked a reaction was that of using her knives on Rhin's champion. She *hated* him, spent her time dreaming of revenge, then wept bitter, frustrated tears as the unlikelihood of that revenge consumed her.

Warriors were now disembarking from the ship, still flying its eagle banner. She was suddenly restless to be gone, running back to the fortress to join the growing crowd of those eager to greet the newcomers.

Then Storm was padding towards her, followed by Corban, with Dath and Farrell only just managing to keep up.

'Cywen, Cywen, you won't believe what's happened to me,' he said as he reached her, his words almost falling over themselves.

'What?' He seemed very excited about something, so she tried to appear interested.

'I am to take my warrior trial on the morrow – sit my Long Night.'

'*What?*' That did get her attention. 'Are you ready?' she said and saw his face drop, excitement melting into doubt.

'I don't know,' he said honestly.

'What I meant to say,' she interrupted, 'is do you *feel prepared*? Of course you are ready – we've the bruises to prove it, haven't we, Dath?' She nudged their friend.

'Oh aye,' he nodded enthusiastically.

Amongst the crowd now surrounding them, Cywen saw Gar. She tried to duck behind the bulk of Farrell, but too late, and a frown formed on Gar's brow as he limped over to them.

'Where have you been? You've been needed at the stables.'

She just looked at him and tried to think of something to say, but couldn't.

Gar's frown deepened. He opened his mouth – to say something unpleasant, no doubt – when the crowd about them suddenly grew louder. The new arrivals were entering the courtyard now, their horses' hooves clattering on stone. Cywen just stared, and promptly forgot about Gar.

A dozen or so warriors rode into the courtyard, looking fine in chainmail and black-polished leather, silver-edged eagles carved on their breastplates. But Cywen's eyes were drawn to the two who rode at their head. They both sat tall in their saddles, one dressed similarly to the other warriors, riding a spirited white stallion, two swords hanging from his belt. He was a young man with dark, curly hair framing a weathered, handsome face, bright blue eyes scanning the crowd. He smiled, at no one and everyone; Cywen felt suddenly as if he was looking at her alone.

She pulled her gaze away with an effort to look at the man riding beside him. She gasped as she saw his horse, a palomino of such quality as she had never seen before. It was lighter boned than the other horses, longer in the leg, almost dancing as it crossed the courtyard, a picture of grace and power. The man on its back was older, also dressed as a warrior, but this man was clearly not like the others. He had long, jet-black hair, bound with a strip of leather at the nape and a long, curved sword strapped across his back. There was something about him that reminded Cywen of Storm. He sat gracefully in his saddle, exuding a sense of strength and barely contained violence, a wildness about him.

She went to say something to Corban and noticed Gar disappearing into the crowd. Corban himself was pale faced, staring intensely at the curly-haired warrior.

'Corban,' she said and squeezed his arm. 'Corban, are you well?'

Her brother started but nodded, his colour returning a little. 'Aye, it's nothing,' he said.

Then King Brenin stepped out of the crowd with Pendathran, Halion behind them, looking uneasy in his new role.

'Well met, Nathair,' Brenin said, gripping the curly-haired man's arm as he leaned in the saddle. The noise of the crowd obscured the rest of what was said and soon after the party headed for the keep.

Much later Cywen was on her own in the hall after the feasting. Corban had been swept out by Thannon, eager to talk through the final details of the morrow. Edana slumped down in an adjacent chair, the outline of a warrior beyond her. Cywen expected to see Ronan for a moment, but it was Conall.

'Hallo,' Edana said, still gaunt from their recent experiences.

Cywen nodded. 'Haven't seen you, for a while,' she said.

'No.' Edana shook her head. 'Since my mam . . .' She looked away. 'Father worries for me. More so since the news of Uthan. He fears reprisals,' she sighed.

Word had reached Dun Carreg about a ten-night ago of Owain's son's death, rumour following the news like crows following blood. All that could be agreed upon was that Uthan was dead and that Owain held Brenin responsible.

'So Conall is your guard now?' Cywen said, wanting to break the growing silence.

'Yes.'

'How is your da?'

'Grieving. Angry. Very angry. The thought of revenge consumes him.'

'And you?'

'Me?' Edana said. 'I cannot believe my mam is gone . . .' She squeezed her eyes shut. 'I miss her. I want her back, wish that I had said things to her. And I want to be strong, for Da, but he doesn't seem to notice.'

'Have you spoken to your da? Told him how you feel?'

'No. He has been so inconstant – sometimes so sad, others, so *angry*. He scares me.'

'But he loves you, and if he knew how you felt he'd be sorry.'

Edana looked weary, then nodded. 'You're right. I will talk to him. But it would help if I had you near.'

Cywen sat there, wanted to say no, but Edana looked so pleading that she rose and followed the Princess through the keep.

Edana knocked at a familiar door and swept in, not waiting for a reply. King Brenin was sitting in his high-backed chair, discussing something with Evnis and Heb. Halion stood behind the King, hand on his sword hilt. Cywen's eyes flickered across the empty chair beside Brenin, where Alona had sat.

'Father, I . . .' Edana began, then halted, the stern faces of those in the room daunting her.

'What is it?' Brenin asked, looking annoyed at the interruption.

'I wanted to talk to you, Father. About . . .'

'Well, Edana?' Brenin said with a wave of his hand. 'Quickly now, I am busy.'

Then there was a knock at the door and three visitors from Tenebral were presented. Two had led the column, Nathair, Tenebral's King, and Sumur – a lord, Cywen had since discovered. The third was one of their honour guard, a young warrior with an easy smile, his raptor-like helm under one arm.

'Nathair, welcome,' said Brenin. 'Heb you know, and this is my counsellor, Evnis.'

'Well met,' the King of Tenebral said warmly, smiling at Evnis. 'My thanks for your hospitality – we are well fed, and rested now, so I thought to speak with you of why I have come.'

Cywen and Edana sidled to the back of the room, lest they be banished.

'As you have most likely heard, my father was murdered.'

'Aye. You have my sympathies,' Brenin said, inclining his head, 'Aquilus was a good man, a great man.'

'My thanks. His killer has since been brought to justice.'

'I have heard,' Brenin said, frowning. 'I would talk to you more about that, but now is not the time.'

Nathair continued, 'I have much to live up to, wearing my father's crown. And I am aware of his ambitions and his commitments. That is my first reason for coming here. I know that my father was committed to help you with your troubles – with lawless men on your borders. I have a small warband with me, still upon the ship. I would aid you in your endeavour and help you rid your borders of these outlaws. It would honour my father's wishes, and the alliance between us, which I hope you still hold to.'

'Ah,' Brenin said, humourlessly. 'I am afraid you are a little late to aid us in the struggle against the brigands of the Darkwood. We have dealt with them.'

'Oh.' Nathair looked downcast. 'That brings me shame,' he said. 'My father's other commitments, to Rahim, to Braster and Romar, have all been honoured.'

'No matter,' Brenin said. 'You have travelled far, and that speaks loudly of your commitment, and I did not tell Aquilus when my campaign would begin. You have undertaken much to come here. That I will not forget.'

'Is the matter resolved?' Nathair asked. 'Or can we provide other assistance, as recompense?'

'The brigands of the Darkwood are no more, though at great cost,' Brenin said. 'New and darker troubles have fallen upon my land of late. I find myself at war with my neighbour, Rhin. Even as we speak, I am mustering to ride against her.'

'What? How is this so?'

'You remember Queen Rhin?'

'Aye. A sharp tongue, a sharper mind,' Nathair said.

'It would appear Cambren is not enough for her appetites. She covets both Ardan and Narvon.'

'How could she hope to defeat you both? That does not strike me as wisdom.'

'Ah, she is cleverer than that, the old spider. There have been complications, with Owain. Rhin has brought about the death of my wife . . .' Brenin stopped and glanced at the torc on the empty chair beside him. 'And also the death of Uthan, Owain's boy. Somehow, she made it appear that Owain and I were the culprits, to set us at each other's throats. Thank Elyon, I have unmasked her plan, though Owain has not yet recognized it. He still holds me responsible for the death of his son. This is a conflict I will not ask you to join in, Nathair, though, in truth, I am certainly outnumbered.' His face reflected little, but his pain was clear.

'I am sorry for your loss,' Nathair said.

'She is sorely missed. And not only her.'

Just then the warrior with Nathair and Sumur took a half-step forward. 'My pardon,' he said, 'but I expected to see someone. A warrior I befriended, during Aquilus' council. Tull, your first-sword?'

'He was,' Brenin said. 'But he fell, defending my wife. Not that his sacrifice helped her, in the end.'

'That is a grievous loss,' the warrior said. 'I crossed blades with him on the weapons court. He taught me a few things.'

Halion chuckled.

'That was Tull,' Brenin said, the briefest of smiles crossing his face. 'My thanks for your words . . .?'

'Rauca,' the warrior said. 'My name is Rauca.'

'I will think on what part I may play in this,' Nathair said. 'There were few enough that stood by my father and his alliance. You honoured him, and I was yet hoping for Owain and Rhin's support.'

'There will be no peace between Rhin and I,' Brenin warned. 'Do not try and walk that path, Nathair. Things have gone too far. As for Owain – I would hope for peace with him, though if he stands between Rhin and me, he shall come to regret it.'

Nathair nodded thoughtfully.

Cywen thought his companion, Sumur, stiffened at Brenin's words. Here were people not used to instruction.

'As I said, I will think on the part I might play. I feel indebted to you, until my father's commitment is fulfilled.'

'As you will,' Brenin said with a wave of his hand.

'There was another reason for my journey,' Nathair said.

'Speak on.'

'I seek knowledge, information, on two accounts.'

'Aye. Well, I will help you, if I can,' said Brenin.

'The first is regarding giant lore, specifically the Benothi clan. This was a stronghold of theirs once, I believe. I am trying to unravel parts of the prophecy spoken of at my father's council.'

'Of course. Heb here is my loremaster, and Evnis too has no small store of knowledge regarding the previous residents of Dun Carreg.'

'Good,' Nathair said. 'My thanks.'

'And the second count?' said Brenin.

'Ah, yes. There were unusual circumstances around my father's death. One is that his longest, most trusted adviser just *disappeared*. He was seen leaving Jerolin just after my father died.'

Brenin's face registered some emotion, too fast for Cywen to read, then it was gone. 'That is unusual,' he murmured.

'My thoughts exactly. You know of whom I speak? Meical. Who read from the prophecy at the council.'

'Aye, I know of whom you speak.'

'Have you any news of him, of his whereabouts?'

A silence grew, and Brenin was the first to look away.

'He came here, briefly,' Brenin admitted, 'though I can tell you little more than that. He did not stay even a night. I know not why he came, nor where he went.' The King lifted his eyes, and this time did not look away.

Nathair was silent, expressionless. Until eventually he sighed. 'If you could enquire, of whom he spoke to while he was here, I would be most grateful.'

'Aye. Of course,' Brenin said.

Cywen's mind was racing. In her head she could see the man they were speaking of, sitting in her kitchen, like it was yesterday. And now a *king* had come searching for him. Was this linked to Ban as well? This Meical's visit certainly seemed to have been.

Nathair thanked Brenin, then took his leave, claiming tiredness from their journey.

A silence hung in the air long after the door had closed.

'What do you make of that?' Heb eventually said, his voice loud after the silence.

Brenin looked weary. 'Change,' he said, almost to himself.

'This alliance,' Evnis said, 'we would do well to court it.'

Brenin frowned. 'Once, maybe,' he said quietly, then, louder, 'I shall do as I deem right, Evnis.'

'Be careful, my King,' Evnis said. 'He was young, but there was a fire in him; and there *is* an alliance, realms joining together, with or without you. They could become a formidable strength. Something to keep close, or at least watch, I would say. Else one day they may be uniting to deal with troublesome Ardan.'

'Nathair is certainly ambitious,' Brenin said. 'But I do not trust him. Aquilus he is not.'

'This Sumur – what do we know of him?' Evnis pressed.

'The talkative one . . .' Heb said wryly.

Brenin shrugged. 'Only Nathair's introduction: that he is lord of some distant fortress, and now Nathair's personal guardian.'

'He knows how to use that sword on his back,' Halion interrupted.

'How do you know?' Evnis said, 'I didn't think he'd visited the weapons court.'

'He hasn't. There's just something about him. He's dangerous.'

Evnis looked sceptical.

Brenin was becoming impatient. 'Come, we have other priorities. But keep a watch on them. And, both of you,' he added, pointing a finger at Evnis and Heb, 'be careful what you tell him. What is it that he seeks about the Benothi? Report back to me. Every word.'

Suddenly Brenin noticed his daughter. 'Edana, I thought I told you I was busy. This is not the place for you now.'

'Yes, Father,' Edana said, eyes downcast. Cywen and Conall followed her to the door, Conall closing it fast behind them.

CHAPTER SEVENTY-SIX

CORBAN

Corban gulped back the last of a cup of his mam's mead, and smiled at Thannon, who winked at him as he stood to leave.

'Where are you going?' Thannon asked him.

'To see Dath.'

'Wait a moment,' his da said, shifting in his chair. 'It is a big day, the morrow, for you.'

'I know,' Corban said, 'which you've told me more than once today, already.'

Thannon shifted in his chair again. 'Please, sit with me a little longer.'

Corban sat back down.

'I remember the day you were born,' he smiled. 'I held you in one of my hands, you were so small. And now look at you . . .' He sniffed. 'I hope you know this already, but now's a good time for saying it. You are my greatest hope, my joy.' He reached out and gripped Corban's hand. 'No one could have made me prouder, Ban.' He tapped his chest. 'You make my heart swell.'

Corban swallowed, wanted to say something, but there was a lump in his throat that swallowing didn't move.

Thannon stood suddenly. 'Go see your friends. But not too late, mind – you'll need your strength for the morrow.' He grinned. 'Listen to me, I'm starting to sound like your mam.' He chuckled.

Corban smiled at him, then his da left the room, and Corban set off. The wide stone streets were mostly empty, dusk settling like a blanket upon the fortress. His da had never spoken to him like that before. He smiled, and felt a surge of love for the big man. But there was another face, amongst those childhood memories, in fact in almost every single one: always there, and a whole host of others, besides.

Gar.

In his own bluff way the stablemaster had been like a second father to him. Helping him, teaching him, rescuing him in the Baglun, *following* him into the Darkwood. Protecting him, with his own life, if need be. Without realizing it his course changed, and he found himself making for the stables.

He hadn't seen Gar since the arrival of the Tenebral party. One moment he was with them in the courtyard, then he had vanished. Corban remembered again how he'd felt when he saw the new-comers' leader – Nathair, Tenebral's King. Somehow this Nathair had seemed familiar, a memory tugging at the edges of his awareness. He had felt sick, suddenly, and thought he'd seen a dark shadow mar-ring Nathair's face. Just the memory of it chilled him.

He looked up and saw the stables before him, a light flickering high up in an unshuttered window – Gar's stable loft chamber. He'd lived there as long as Corban could remember, saying that if there was any trouble with the horses he needed to be nearby.

The stables were empty now, and Corban stepped through, the familiar smells of horse and hay greeting him. He climbed the hayloft stairway that also led to Gar's chamber. Storm followed him, silently as a wraith, as he made his way past stacks of tied hay. He paused before reaching Gar's half-open door.

Gar was sitting on his cot in the flickering torchlight, giving all his attention to a long, gently curved blade. The stablemaster worked oil into the blade with a cloth, then skilfully rasped a whetstone down its edge.

Corban stared. He didn't even know Gar possessed a sword, let alone one such as this. Then he heard footsteps coming up the stair-well, and without thinking, he slipped into the hayloft shadows with Storm.

A figure appeared and Corban's eyes widened to see his mam.

She rapped on Gar's door and strode through without waiting for a response.

'I got your message,' he heard his mam's voice, clear through the thin partition walls. 'What's wrong?'

Gar did not answer at first, and Corban heard only the *rasp* of his whetstone along the length of his blade. Suddenly even that stopped, the cot creaking as Gar stood.

'We must go. Leave Dun Carreg,' the stablemaster said.

'What?' his mam stuttered. 'That's not possible. Why?'

'You saw who arrived, this day?'

'Yes, but, it need change nothing.'

'You do not understand, Gwenith. The man with Nathair, I know him.'

'The man with . . . But how? Who is he?'

'His name is Sumur, and he is Jehar.'

'Gar, I do not understand. How can that be?'

'I do not know,' Gar said.

'Could you not speak to him, if you know him? Find out what this means? Maybe . . .'

'No,' Gar snapped. 'You remember what Meical said: speak to no one, not even if Aquilus' kin rides through Stonegate. I have not spent sixteen years *obeying* to stop now, when we are so close. And, besides, something is wrong. Very wrong.' Gar paused, the silence suddenly heavy. 'Sumur did not see me, of that I am sure. But for how long? We cannot stay here. *Corban* cannot stay here. We must leave, I am certain.'

'But where? This is too soon. We are not ready – *Ban* is not ready.'

Corban could hear Gar pacing. 'Plans rarely run to course, Gwenith. As to where: Drassil, of course. Where else?'

Moments dragged by. 'Very well. But not the morrow. He takes his warrior trial, sits his Long Night. Meical said he must do that, before . . .' her voice trailed off.

'Aye, all right then,' Gar agreed reluctantly. 'The morrow we prepare. The day after, we leave.'

Footsteps sounded as his mam left, Corban hugging Storm tight until they had long since faded from hearing.

Not until he heard the rasp of Gar's whetstone again did he dare move. He crept out from behind the hay-pile, holding his breath, then down the stairwell. Storm shadowed him into the darkness.

CHAPTER SEVENTY-SEVEN

VERADIS

Veradis shifted his coat of mail on his shoulders and looked up, seeing a pale blue sky through leafless branches. It was early, a thin film of mist clinging to the ground, the forest litter slick with dew.

He made his way through groups of quiet warriors towards Alcyon, ringed by the leaders of this small alliance. They had met the previous evening to discuss their battle plan, but Braster had insisted they also gathered at dawn to go over matters.

The red-bearded King nodded to Veradis. 'We all know what we are about this day, and we have only made it this far with the help of those with no obligation to be here.' He looked from Veradis to Alcyon and nodded curtly to them. 'Thanks are due.'

Romar looked away.

'That's it,' Braster growled. 'I'll see you all this night, drink to our victory with you. Until then: truth and courage, and may Elyon's hand be upon you.'

'Truth and courage,' Veradis repeated as the group split, heading for their various warbands, Veradis walking with Calidus and Alcyon. They were to form up behind the larger forces of Braster and Romar, the two kings commanding close to three thousand men between them. Veradis and his companions had a twofold task. First, to protect Alcyon and Calidus from any specific attacks. The giant and the Vin Thalun were the only means of counteracting the Hunen's Elementals.

Secondly, and only if the first task was deemed no longer necessary, Veradis was to lead his warband to the flank and do what damage he could, leaving the Jehar to protect Calidus and Alcyon. Calidus had pointed out that the Jehar were more than adequate protection, but Romar had been adamant that Veradis was to remain a rearguard force.

'Half a league and you will see Haldis, King's man,' Alcyon said, his teeth flashing fiercely.

'These giants,' Veradis said. 'There will be many of them – many Elementals?'

'Aye. But we will look after you, little warrior,' the giant said, a smile twitching at his moustache.

'That is not what I mean. How can only you and Calidus stand against so many Elementals?'

'You have seen him,' Alcyon said. 'You know what he is. We giants have lived long, yes, had a long time to learn our craft. But he is older, much older.' He shrugged. 'He is powerful.' Then the giant was gone, striding towards the black mass of the Jehar, his great broadsword slung over his back.

Veradis' warband was loosely gathered before him, a line of fifty men, ten rows deep. Bos grinned at him and moved so that he could take his place in the front rank. Somewhere ahead a horn blew once, and the host moved forwards, swarming around the thinning trees.

They reached the crest of a ridge and looked down on tilled and cultivated land, the signs of organized crop-growing looking strangely out of place in the forest. Then Veradis sucked in his breath as he saw Haldis for the first time.

A crumbling, vine-covered wall lay ahead, many sections fallen to ruins, leaving gaping holes in the wall like an old hag's teeth. Within there were huge cairns, hundreds of them, their stones thick with moss and yellow lichen. Then beyond this, a sheer cliff-face of dark granite rose up from the ground with a line of trees fringing its upper edge. Its entire face was covered in carvings: huge, snarling faces, warriors in combat, and all manner of creatures. Wolves, eagles, bears, draigs and snakes were represented, surrounded by swirling runes. At the escarpment's base was a great arched gateway, taller and wider than a dozen giants and black as night. Veradis shivered.

But there was no sign of the Hunen. No movement anywhere.

There was a strident horn blast from behind him. Alcyon, head, shoulders and chest above the tallest men about him, waved an arm, signalling to stop here, and the warband slowly came to a halt on the upper level of the slope.

The lower slope before them was a seething mass of movement of those ahead in the column, reminding Veradis of the ants he had seen in the forest near Jerolin. How long ago that seemed. The first ranks were splashing across a stream. Veradis made out the bulky shape of Braster, and before him the Gadrai. Then the first of the Gadrai approached the ruined wall, beginning to scramble across fallen stone.

A noise broke the tension he felt, as a high, pealing horn sounded from somewhere beyond them, an ethereal, haunting sound. Then something resembling smoke or mist poured from the black gateway in the rock face. Quickly this spread around the cairns, hugging the ground and flowing towards the crumbling wall and the warriors.

Many were within the wall now, and those in the front ranks stopped as they saw the mist approaching them. Silently the mist rolled across the still warriors, engulfing them and obscuring them from view, filling the entire area between the escarpment and the wall.

For long moments the whole dell was draped in an eerie silence. Then the screaming began.

Veradis took a step forward, and had to stop himself. Behind, he heard the deep voice of Alcyon rise up, blending with Calidus', growing louder, singing words he did not understand.

A breeze touched his face where there had been none, quickly growing in strength, gusts tugging at hair that poked from under his iron helm. The wind swirled about him now. It seemed to gather before his warband, snatching at leaves and ferns on the ground, then suddenly set off down the slope, howling, whipping up white-tipped foam on the stream before the wall as it rushed past and slammed like a physical thing into the wall and mist within.

The mist immediately skirting the wall just evaporated, but very soon the wind's effect lessened, as if it had run into a barrier. Alcyon and Calidus' voices rose in volume until the wind they had sent rushing into the dell made headway against the mist again, though slowly. The mist frayed, slowly dissolved, revealing their fellow warriors within the wall. They seemed somehow stopped in their tracks. Veradis strained to see and made out men's arms flailing, heard terror in the screaming, then realized what was happening.

Men were sinking into the ground, whole companies already

swallowed – marked only by iron helms, or a patch of hair, a shield, a grasping hand. The ground had turned to bog, a suffocating, sinking pit.

'Elyon help us,' Bos whispered.

Veradis forced his way back towards Alcyon and Calidus, men making way for him.

Alcyon and Calidus were standing with arms raised and voices intertwined, drenched in sweat, their muscles trembling.

'There is more than the mist,' Veradis yelled over the singing and the screaming from below. 'Look, the warriors are sinking into the very ground.'

Calidus' voice stuttered, faltered and he staggered forwards a step, Veradis steadying him.

'Closer,' the Vin Thalun croaked. 'We must get closer.'

Veradis nodded and returned to his warband, leading them forwards down the slope. A score of paces before the ground levelled he stopped, and heard Calidus' voice change in pitch, the alien words coming in a new rhythm.

Veradis' view of Haldis was restricted now, but he could still see a way beyond the wall, where the screaming was loudest. Men were still sinking, some flailing wildly and buried to their knees, hips and chests. Many were dead, mouths full of black earth, whereas others pushed against the sucking ground with shields, or were trying to dig themselves out with sword or spear.

Alcyon and Calidus' song rose in volume, the mist almost defeated now, lingering only as thin tendrils.

Something caught Veradis' eye – a movement near the stream, *in* it, the water swirling. Whatever it was, was coming closer, the wake of its passing flooding the banks behind it, thick sedge and reeds parting before it.

'Do you see that?' he said to Bos, pointing. Before the warrior could answer him something was emerging from the water, a silvery-grey head, rising on a thick, reptilian torso.

'Wyrm,' Veradis yelled.

It slithered onto the bank, great loops coiling out of the stream, and moved with alarming speed up the slope. Towards them.

It's coming for Calidus and Alcyon, Veradis realized. He shouted a command, his warband pulling in tight, forming a wall on the slope.

Behind him he heard the Jehar unsheathe their swords as one, a metallic clap of thunder.

'Don't like the look of that,' Bos muttered next to him.

Me neither, thought Veradis, though he kept silent.

The wyrm paused before their shield wall, body coiling beneath it before it reared up, arcing above the wall. It was huge, its head alone larger than a man, with great curved fangs longer than a sword. Shields shattered as it crashed into the wall, those before it crushed in an explosion of blood and bone.

The shield wall broke apart, men running in all directions. Veradis chased the beast, with Bos following, and Veradis slashed at the creature's body. His blade bit, though not deep, and something viscous and jelly-like oozed out from the cut. But his blow did nothing to slow the wyrm. It broke onto the slope beyond the shield wall now, a space of grass and fern before the loosely clustered Jehar. Behind them Calidus and Alcyon continued their song, as yet oblivious to the wyrm. This time the creature did not pause, just ploughed into the dark-clothed warriors. Instead of bracing to meet it they parted, allowed it into their midst, then swirled about it like black waters with their swords rising and falling.

The wyrm was at last wounded, black blood seeping from a thousand cuts. It roared in defiance and lashed out, catching a warrior in its jaws, blood spraying. But the swords continued to slash at it, and with a great shudder the beast crashed to the ground, spasmed and then was still. As things grew quieter about him, screams from Haldis below drifted back up to Veradis. The burial ground was still a bog, warriors suffocating in the dark earth, but as he looked back to Calidus and Alcyon he sensed a change in their song.

As Veradis watched, he felt a tremor pass under his feet, then saw a shift in the ground within the wall. It began to solidify, and men were able to resist their descent into the earth, while others were able to drag or dig themselves out with the last of their strength. Many were dead, caught in a permanent embrace under the crushing earth.

Calidus and Alcyon were both slumped on their knees as Veradis approached, gasping in huge, racking gulps of air.

'You've done it,' Veradis panted.

'For now,' Calidus wheezed, rolling onto his side.

Suddenly a roar erupted from behind the wall. Veradis turned, to see the mounds coming to *life*. He blinked, and saw giants leaping into focus. Whatever glamour had hidden them was stripped away and now they were rampaging amongst men who were not yet recovered from their encounter with the sinking ground. Their newest threat took the form of huge warriors wrapped in black leather and iron, wielding great double-bladed axes or crushing war-hammers.

Chaos erupted anew.

Hundreds had died in the suffocating earth, but there were still many of Braster and Romar's men left alive, though Veradis had never seen this number of giants gathered together. It was hard to make sense of the battlefield. Men were still confused by the mist and shifting earth, and the giants took full advantage, dealing out death with breathtaking ferocity. Everywhere Veradis looked he saw the pale-faced Hunen, laying about them with their axes and war-hammers, the warriors of the alliance struggling to reorganize themselves.

Alcyon was still on his knees, though his breathing was less laboured now.

'What shall we do?' Veradis asked the giant.

'Take your men down there,' Alcyon commanded, 'before the day is lost.'

'But . . . will you be safe?'

'Aye,' the giant grunted. He glanced at Calidus, still lying on his side. 'Their Elementals will not attack again, not with their own warriors in the thick of it.'

'Will they attack *you*? The wyrm . . .'

Alcyon shrugged. 'If they do, the Jehar are their match.' A smile flickered across the giant's face, more a grimace. 'We will be safe, King's man. Do not fear for us.'

Veradis considered a moment, then walked away.

'Make for the gateway in the cliff face,' Alcyon called after him, 'we shall meet you there.'

Then Veradis was taking his place next to Bos, jogging down the slope, splashing through the stream and skirting the wall to an entry point where it had crumbled to nothing. He led the men across a scattered pile of moss and lichen-covered rubble, then they were within the walls of Haldis.

Things were very different down here: the noise of battle ebbing and flowing from every direction, sometimes deafening, then eerily silent. The great mounds that filled the field obscured much of the view. Veradis lifted his shield and felt Bos' thud into his, the shield wall going up about him. He drew his short sword, and as one the warband of five hundred warriors began to make its way into the burial ground of the Hunen.

At first there was little resistance, then they came upon two score or so giants, savagely hacking at warriors still half-buried in the earth, frantically trying to free themselves. The first giants fell almost silently as the shield wall smashed into them, dozens of short stabbing swords snaking out. But a bellow from a dying Hunen alerted others. Suddenly blows were slamming into Veradis' shield and he almost buckled at the knees. Further off, more giants were gathering. Seeing the threat to their flank, they were pulling out of the main conflict and grouping to meet Veradis' shield wall. Even as he watched, they let out a great howl and began loping towards Veradis' warband, scores of them, axes and war-hammers held high.

Then giants crashed into the shield wall, hammering and beating against the wood and iron of their shields. The man to Veradis' right went down, a hammer blow breaking his arm and then his skull. Bos staggered beside him but held, others in the front row were dragged forwards by axes embedded in their shields, then hacked to pieces by the frenzied giants.

The line trembled, on the verge of breaking.

'Hold!' Veradis yelled, not knowing if anyone heard him, the din of battle almost deafening. He stabbed forwards, grunted as his shield arm numbed from the blows rained upon it, losing all sense of time, only the next moment, the next burning breath or lunge having any kind of meaning. Then, suddenly, the pressure on his shield was gone. He looked over its rim, saw that none of their attackers was still standing, though by the sound of it, battle still raged further away, amongst the mounds.

Bos was still there, blood sheeting one side of his face from a cut to his ear. The big man grinned at him, and Veradis felt himself smile in return as a measure of strength returned to his limbs.

Steadily the shield wall moved deeper and deeper into Haldis. Slowly and inexorably the Hunen were either cut down or pushed back, and the ground grew thick with the fallen. They came to a dense ring of warriors, bristling with sword and spear, being assaulted by a score of giants. The Hunen were dispatched quickly as the shield wall closed on them from behind. Braster was at the centre of the ring, pale faced and semi-conscious, wounded by a hammer blow that had crushed his shoulder. His battlechief Lothar stood over him. A litter was organized to take the wounded King back to the slope beyond the wall, then Veradis continued his journey through the mounds.

The sounds of battle grew again as they approached the cliff face and saw what seemed to be hundreds of the Hunen battling ferociously before the black gateway. Romar was amongst the Gadrai and Kastell was standing back to back with Maquin.

'Wall!' Veradis yelled, lifting his shield, locking it with those either side of him, and slowly, pace by pace, they forged their way into the battle. They kept pushing, shoving, grunting, stabbing, until they were almost at the black gateway where the last giants had been herded. Suddenly those left alive disengaged, turned and fled into the darkness behind them.

There was a moment's silence, then ragged cheers broke from the surviving warriors.

'Well met,' Veradis grinned, gripping Maquin's arm.

'I like your timing,' the old warrior said, grinning in return, then Kastell was there, smiling as well, though he grimaced at Veradis' face, splinters of wood still sticking from it where an axe had almost split his shield.

'With me,' called Romar, striding towards the arched doorway. He stepped through, took a burning torch from an iron sconce on the wall and walked into the darkness. Vandil followed, warriors flocking to him. Maquin sighed, nodded to Veradis and then followed his King.

'You coming?' Kastell asked Veradis as he followed the old warrior, a huge, bald-headed man that could have been Bos' father falling in beside him.

'Not yet,' Veradis said, 'I must wait here.'

'Scared of the dark?' Kastell grinned. He drew his sword and passed through the archway, what was left of the Gadrai about him. Within moments they were all swallowed by the darkness.

Veradis turned and scanned his warband. Many had fallen, and only about half of his original strength remained. He felt a sudden, fierce pride in them, knowing beyond any doubt that this battle would have been lost without them. They set up a defensive circle around the arch, but didn't wait long before Alcyon strode out from the cairns, his great broadsword red with blood, Calidus and the Jehar behind him.

'How goes it?' said the giant.

'Well, I think,' Veradis said. 'Most of this area is cleared, though it was hard fought. This place is a maze.'

'Romar?' Calidus asked, scanning the clearing.

'In there,' Veradis said, looking at the gaping doorway into the cliff side.

Calidus arched an eyebrow. 'Who with?'

'The remaining Gadrai – a hundred or so swords – maybe another hundred of Isiltir's warriors.' Veradis shrugged. 'The rest must be scattered amongst the mounds. If they still live.'

'All the rats gathered in the same trap . . .' Calidus muttered to himself.

'What?' Veradis asked.

'We must go, quickly,' Calidus said to Alcyon and Akar as he headed for the entrance. 'Romar will need our aid.'

'Do you need me?' Veradis called after the counsellor.

'You? No, Veradis, there is work to be done that you are not suited for. Guard this gateway, rest if you can. You have earned it.' With that the Vin Thalun disappeared into the darkness, Alcyon and the Jehar close behind.

Veradis thought of Maquin and Kastell, and his stomach lurched. He took a few paces towards the gateway, then stopped. *Leave the politicking to Calidus*, he remembered Nathair commanding. *You warned them*, said an internal voice. 'I did,' he muttered to himself and turned away from the cliff face.

Calidus is Ben-Elim, he thought. *He will do what is right.*

They were alive and had helped win the day. Yet somehow, despite his orders and his firm words to himself, he suddenly felt ashamed to be standing there waiting.

CHAPTER SEVENTY-EIGHT

CORBAN

Corban stepped out into the Rowan Field. The sun was still low in a cloudless sky as he gathered himself for what lay ahead.

'A good day for it,' Thannon rumbled beside him, and squeezed his shoulder.

'Aye,' Corban said, and felt a queasiness in his stomach.

Halion was leaning against a weapons rack and smiled, raising a hand when he saw Corban.

'I'll wait here,' Thannon said, 'watch Storm for you.'

Halion gripped Corban's forearm in the traditional manner. 'The Rowan Field welcomes you, Corban ben Thannon,' the warrior said formally.

'The Field honours me,' Corban gave the expected reply, and tried not to glance away from Halion as warriors began to fill the Field.

'I have something, for you.' Halion pulled a spear from the weapons rack. 'I think its weight should suit you.'

Corban took the spear in two hands, and held it horizontally. Its haft was carved from pale ash, with dark veins swirling through it and an iron butt capping its end as a balancing weight. The blade end was leaf-shaped, one long, sinuous curve from tip to hilt, unlike the wedge-shaped blades he was used to. Testing its weight, he lifted the spear to shoulder height, and found the balancing point almost immediately. It suddenly felt weightless.

Halion grunted approvingly.

'My thanks,' Corban said.

'It flies true. I thought it would serve you better than these battered things,' Halion said, glancing at the spears in the rack. 'It has served *me* well.'

'Is this a custom, where you are from?' Corban asked, frowning, suddenly realizing he had no gift in return.

'A custom? No, lad. I just have enjoyed teaching you. And this will be our last day. It is good to mark times such as this with a gift.'

Corban smiled. 'Again, my thanks.'

'Come, find a target, get used to it a little before we begin.'

Corban approved, as missing the target before countless warriors was not how he hoped to begin his warrior trial. They strode towards the straw targets and found an open space. Conall marched across the Field towards them before they could make further progress. He was scowling when he reached them, his usually handsome face flushed with anger. 'I had your message,' he said, 'or summons.'

'I just needed to see you, Con,' Halion said.

'What for? More orders?'

Halion frowned now. 'Aye, that's right.'

Conall folded his arms, and waited.

'You'll be guarding Edana as usual, but she's been given leave from the keep, so be vigilant.'

'I am a warrior, Hal, not a nursemaid.'

Halion sighed. 'It is a position of honour,' he said slowly, Corban thought perhaps not for the first time. 'And you need to rebuild Brenin's favour.'

'Favour. Honour,' Conall spluttered, 'to nursemaid a *child*. Why do you treat me so?'

'I am trying to *help* you, Con,' Halion said sharply.

'This is my last day of it,' Conall retorted as he turned away. 'Evnis has offered me a place in his hold. I shall stand under your shadow no longer.'

Halion made to speak, but Conall was gone before he could get the words out.

'Ach,' Halion spat, the anger on his face shifting into sadness. He looked at Corban. 'All my life, it seems, I've been trying to help him.'

'He's ungrateful,' Corban said impulsively.

'No, Ban, he just does not see it as help. Pride blinds him. Maybe it is I that have been wrong.' He shook his head. 'Anyway, you have other things more pressing than my brother's temper. Cast that spear, lad.'

So Corban did. His first throw was a little high, but he soon had the measure of Halion's gift and marvelled at the difference it made.

The Field was busy now, and he spotted many familiar faces, bar one. Then Gar too entered the Field, riding Shield, the stallion's brown and white coat glistening with sweat.

'Good, then,' Halion said. 'We can begin.'

The warrior measured out forty paces from a straw target and marked the spot with his boot-heel. 'Begin your spear trial, Corban ben Thannon,' he said loudly. Then, more quietly, 'Don't rush it because you have an audience. Wait till you find the place.'

Corban nodded, his mouth suddenly dry.

Setting his feet, he hefted the spear, lifted it to his shoulder and sighted the target. He concentrated on the sounds around him, focusing on the target as he'd been taught, the sounds fading until all that was left was his heartbeat, the weight of the spear and the target before him.

Then he threw.

The spear arced through the air, landing with a *thunk* about a handspan above the target's centre.

'One,' Halion called out.

Six more times Corban went through this process, allowing himself a smile towards Thannon and his other watchers only after his last throw. Next, Halion approached to present him with a practice sword.

'I'll test your forms first, Corban,' Halion said. 'No different from what we usually do.'

'Aye,' Corban said, feeling better, now, more at ease. He rolled his shoulders and swung the practice blade in some sweeping arcs to loosen the muscles in his back and arm.

Halion set his feet, raised his sword, and Corban attacked. He came at Halion with a high double-handed grip, methodically moving through the forms Halion had taught him, using footwork and sword angles to strike first at the quick-kill areas, throat, heart, groin, then the slow-kill points, then the places that would maim or disable but were not of themselves fatal. He tried to keep all Gar had taught him separate, but parts of the sword dance would creep into his attacks, usually making his movements more fluid. One strike would flow into another, reducing the response time of his foe.

This was not at all like the Darkwood, where death had hovered close, but where instinct had overcome his fear. Here he was enjoying himself. He felt himself smiling, a kind of fierce joy taking hold of him as he struck at Halion faster and faster, making the new first-sword of Ardan work hard. Halion moved with a grace all of his own, though, and although he was hard-pressed the warrior's guard was not broken.

There was a momentary lull as Corban realized he had passed through all of the forms. Halion stepped back a pace, raised his hand and grinned at Corban. 'That was well done,' he said, then marched over to a weapons rack, returning with a battered shield for Corban.

Corban saw that quite a crowd had gathered around him, faces recognizable as he glanced around: Evnis and Vonn, Helfach and Rafe. They were all staring, most with surprise on their faces, even Thannon and Dath. Corban frowned, not sure what had just happened. He caught Dath's eye then, and saw something in his friend's face – awe? Then he was slipping his left arm into the shield-straps and preparing for the second half of the sword trial.

This time Halion did the attacking, testing Corban's defensive skills, and Corban found himself more hard-pressed. Gar had never used a shield, so Halion had taught him all he knew here. Still, he did well, blocking the attacks, though many of them only just, and soon his left arm was numb as blow after blow shivered through it into flesh and bone. A few times he almost stepped into an attack of his own, the urge instinctive and close to overwhelming, wanting to use both sword and shield as a weapon; but he resisted, remembering this was a defensive test.

In time, Halion stepped back. 'We are done here,' the warrior declared.

Now Corban retrieved his spear and he saw Gar leading Shield out towards him.

This is it, he thought. The running mount, and then his warrior trial was finished, only the Long Night left before he passed fully into manhood. He felt his breath catch. He had become lost in the trial, in the moments of spear, sword, shield, strike and block, but now the enormity of it settled upon him again.

Focus, he told himself. Get this wrong and he could not say what would be worse: broken bones or the humiliation of it happening before the gathered strength of Ardan.

He rubbed the sweat from his palms, and gripped the spear more tightly. Gar was watching him keenly, waiting for his signal. At his nod, the stablemaster clicked his tongue, and set Shield into a gentle trot. Gar kept pace for a few strides, then the stallion broke into a canter and headed for Corban.

Corban hefted shield and spear and set his feet as the stallion approached, hooves sending tremors beneath Corban's feet. He began to move, then Shield drew level and Corban increased his pace, feeling the timing of the canter as his own blood and muscle pumped to match the horse's stride. Suddenly the rhythm was right and he angled in, reaching out with his shield-hand, grabbed a fist-ful of the stallion's mane, and used the horse's momentum to launch himself into the air.

There was a heartbeat that felt like an eternity as his feet left the ground. He was completely weightless, airborne, his body arcing up, legs scissoring, then, with a satisfying *thump* he landed in the saddle. Shield didn't even break stride.

He sat there a moment, feeling Shield's muscles bunch and expand beneath him, could hear only his own heartbeat pounding in his ears, then he was punching the air with shield and spear, the cold air whipping tears from his eyes. Distantly he heard noise, looked around to see people calling out to him, cheering, banging spears on shields. His eyes searched the crowd and found his da, who was grin-ning till he looked like his face would split. Corban raised a clenched fist to the blacksmith, and *whooped* with joy, then called to Storm.

The wolven bounded away from Thannon to run alongside Shield, matching the stallion's speed as Corban urged it into a gallop, turf spraying from its hooves. He held the reins easily, relaxing into Shield's rhythm. His eyes searched the crowd for Gar. The stable-master inclined his head.

Brenin marched onto the Field, accompanied by his retinue and the Tenebral guests. They stared as he galloped past, Storm loping beside him. Briefly he saw Nathair's eyes fix in surprise on the wolven, before their eyes met. The world seemed to contract sud-denly. The shadow was there again, a darkness that hovered about the King of Tenebral. Corban felt scared, suddenly, then he was past them and pulling on the reins to head back to Halion. He looked for Gar again but couldn't see him; he refused to dwell on the words he had heard yestereve which came unbidden to his mind.

He slipped from the saddle before Halion, glowing before his approving nod, then Thannon was beckoned forward, his bulk looming over both of them. He unwound a sword from a cloth wrapping, and offered it to his son. Corban sank to one knee to complete the ceremony.

'Corban ben Thannon,' Halion called. 'You came to the Field a bairn, you leave it as a warrior, as a man. Rise,' he said, his hand touching Corban's elbow, 'and take your sword.'

Corban stood, took his gift and gasped as he looked closer. The pommel was dark iron, carved into the head of a snarling wolven. His eyes flickered to his da's face, saw joy in the blacksmith's eyes as well as tears.

'Thank you,' he whispered, the blade hissing as he drew it from the leather scabbard. He held up the sword, sunlight turning it momentarily into a white flame, just like in the tales.

'Hold tight to your blade,' Halion said, 'and hold as tight to truth and courage. Now make your oath.'

'I pledge my arm, my mind, my soul, my strength in service of the two: King and Kin.' He drew his sword across his palm, dripping blood from a clenched fist onto the ground. 'I swear this by my heart, seal it with my blood,' Corban said.

Thannon grinned at him.

Cheers rang out from the crowd – a huge crowd now, all staring at him as if something *special* was happening – and then Thannon swept Corban into a bear-like embrace.

Cool shadow replaced bright sunshine as Corban rode under the arch of Stonegate, Storm an almost silent presence behind him.

The sun was dipping into the west, sending long shadows stretching out before him as Corban rode across Dun Carreg's bridge. When he reached the giantsway he set his back to the Baglun. He was riding to find a spot to sit his Long Night, and all the land between him and the Baglun felt too familiar. He wanted it to feel new, as everything else on this day of days had been.

He rode until the world about him was grey, shrinking before the red glow of the setting sun behind him. He finally reined Shield in before a dell, a boulder of dark granite offering some shelter from the sharp wind that rolled in from the coast. He dismounted, feeling the slap of the still-unfamiliar blade on his hip as he did so, and spent a long moment admiring his weapons. After tending to Shield it was a good while later before he was settled next to a small fire, looking up at the moon, which cast a pale glow across the land.

He felt exhausted, the excitement of the day finally waning and allowing him to consider Gar's ominous words. This talk of leaving Dun Carreg scared him. It was only at the thought of leaving it that he realized how much he loved this place and the people. His friends were here, and so was his heart. No. He was not leaving. No matter what his mam or Gar said, no matter what history Gar shared with Sumur. He was a warrior now, a man. He could do as he chose. His hand crept up to the braid that was now in his hair – his warrior braid, put there by his mam and Cywen that afternoon, bound with a thin strip of leather.

Halion had honoured him, requesting his warrior trial and Long Night be brought forward, but there was practicality in the decision, too. They were as good as at war with Rhin, and soon the warriors of Ardan would ride against Cambren. Every arm that could wield a sword would be needed.

He felt a fluttering of fear at that thought. *Riding to war*, but pushed it down. It would be better by far than *leaving*.

Instinctively he reached for the hilt of his sword and curled his fingertips around the hilt. It was a big sword, longer than was usual, with a hand-and-a-half grip. After much deliberation with his da he had decided upon this. Because of his training with Gar he favoured a two-handed blade, but that would rule out a shield, which he did not want to do. This way he almost had the reach of a two-handed sword, but – largely due to his uncounted toiling in his da's forge, as well as his training with Gar over the last two years – he had the strength to wield it like a shorter, lighter blade, and so could use it with a shield.

Soon his eyes began to droop. But the Long Night was to be spent in unsleeping vigil. He stirred himself with another memory of the day, an unwelcome one. Nathair. All over the fortress people were gossiping about the King of Tenebral. He was both handsome and pleasant, so was becoming increasingly popular. But there was something about him that nagged at Corban. And every time he saw him there was that shadow, a *presence* . . .

Seeing things that are not there is the first sign of madness, he chided himself, *at least that's what Brina has told me*. Still, that shadow . . .

He shivered.

Strange, unnerving sounds drifted on the night breeze. But Storm slept undisturbed. He blew into his cupped hands. It was cold, the sea breeze adding a bite to the already chilly air. He reached for a blanket from his pack.

I'll just sit for a while, he thought, *until the blanket chases the chill from my bones*.

With a start he woke, stiff all over. It was still dark, though there was a touch of grey in the sky, the stars fainter. His small fire had long since burned out, but he could see Storm and Shield, so dawn must be close. Deciding movement was better than staying still, he quickly collected his things together and began saddling Shield up. He felt guilty at dozing off on his Long Night and wondered if he should tell Halion.

Everything was done, Corban just slipping his spear into its leather couch on his saddle when Storm suddenly lifted her head, looked down the slope and growled.

Corban froze and followed the wolven's gaze.

A rider burst from the trees, splashed across the stream and galloped for the giantsway. He reined in when he saw Corban, turning his frothing mount in a tight circle.

'Have any others got through?' he said, his voice hoarse, almost a whisper.

'What do you mean?' Corban asked, hand gripping the hilt of his sword.

'Messengers from Badun,' the man grunted.

'No. No one.'

The man swore, spat on the ground and glanced over his shoulder. 'You must ride, they cannot be far behind,' the man urged. 'Badun has fallen.'

'What? But . . .' Corban said.

'Ride. There is no *time*,' the man snapped, then dug his heels into his horse, spurring it on.

Corban watched the rider disappear over the ridge, then noise from the valley bottom drew his attention.

Mounted figures emerged from the woodland, a dozen or so, warriors, by their couched spears. Corban frowned. There was something wrong about their movements, something furtive.

Then there was movement on the ridge of the far slope, perhaps a league away, maybe less. A dark line appeared on the giantsway: riders, a wide column, framed by a pale strip of light that preceded the coming sun. They were moving quickly towards him. Either side of the road more figures spilt over the ridge, moving like a dark stain across the land, spears and rippling banners silhouetted briefly against the lightening sky.

Corban just stared, watching. Then the rim of the sun appeared on the horizon and a host of spear-tips caught the first rays, sparking into light like a thousand candles. A war-host crawled across the slope towards him, a sea of red-cloaked warriors, the bull of Narvon snapping on countless banners.

Owain had come.

CHAPTER SEVENTY-NINE

CORBAN

Corban mounted Shield and guided the horse up the embankment to the giantsway. He looked once more at the host creeping towards him, his gaze flickering to the scouts picking their way down the slope towards the stream. As he watched, one of them signalled to the others, and pointed at him. His heart lurched as he kicked Shield into a gallop, voices rising behind him and the sound of hooves splashing through water.

He rode Shield hard, his heart pounding, and panic building.

Eventually Brina's cottage came into view, Dun Carreg a tall blur on the horizon in the still hazy light of dawn.

He reined Shield in, the horse blowing great gouts of breath in the cold morning air. Further ahead he saw a dust cloud marking the rider he had spoken to entering the village. He urged Shield towards Brina's cottage.

The healer was bent over her herb patch, tugging at a clump of hawkweed as Corban pounded up to her.

'Quick!' he cried. 'We must go.'

'What?' Brina snapped, scowling at the hawkweed that clearly did not want to leave the ground. 'Has one night alone in the dark unhinged your mind completely?'

'Owain's war-host, thousands coming,' Corban uttered breathlessly. 'A league or so back, but his scouts are not far behind me.'

Brina stared at him a moment, then shoved herself to her feet and bustled inside her cottage, calling to Craf.

'Hurry!' Corban yelled, and in moments Brina appeared in her doorway, a sack over her back, the crow flapping behind her, squawking a protest.

Surprising Corban with her agility, Brina pulled herself up behind him, wrapped her arms around his waist and then Shield was moving through the alder glade. Corban looked to the east and saw a line of riders strung across the road, moving quickly, more than the dozen scouts he had seen earlier.

He dug his heels into Shield's ribs, Craf a black smudge in the sky above him, and Storm running at his side. He cut across meadow to join the giantsway and set his face to Havan, bent low in the saddle, urging Shield on.

When he reached the village he shouted a warning as he rode through the streets to the roundhouse. But the rider had already spread the word and there were people everywhere, most of them making for the road that led up to the fortress. Corban made his way to Dath's home, jumped from his saddle and pounded on the door. Bethan pulled it open, a scowl on her face, but her words failed when she saw Corban's expression.

'What's wrong?' she said.

'Owain is attacking, you don't have long. Where's Dath?'

'Here, Ban,' his friend said, appearing behind his sister.

'We have to go.' Corban grabbed Bethan's shoulder, but she pulled back.

'Da . . .' she said.

'Where is he?'

'Back there,' Dath said, nodding into his home.

'Show me.'

Mordwyr was snoring in his cot, a jug of usque in his arms. It proved impossible to rouse him, until Brina pushed her way in and emptied a jug of cold water over his head. That and her scolding served to wake Mordwyr enough that he could stagger from their home, Corban leading him, and Dath balancing him from behind.

Corban told Brina and Bethan to take Shield and ride on ahead. He and Dath led the staggering fisherman through the village and joined a growing line of people making their way up the steep path to Dun Carreg. They paused a little way up, to look back over the village.

Smoke was rising from Brina's cottage, black, billowing clouds of it. Further away, at the edge of sight, Owain's host was a creeping smudge on the horizon. Closer, between the village and Brina's cottage, riders milled about on the giantsway, Owain's advance scouts. 'Come on,' Corban said, and turned towards Dun Carreg. When they were halfway up the steep slope, Mordwyr protesting all the way, there was a rumble of hooves ahead. Pendathran rode past them, with scores of warriors at his back. They continued down to the village and fanned out, protecting the villagers from Owain's advance scouts.

Then Gar was there, riding his great piebald stallion towards them.

'Is it true?' Gar said when he reached them. Corban just pointed at the land behind him, at the dark tide of warriors swarming across the meadows.

Gar stared a while as Corban eyed the packs tied to Hammer's side, the full water skins, a long object wrapped in leather strapped to the saddle. 'Going somewhere?' he asked.

'I was,' he said. 'Not now, though. Come, let's get you inside the fortress walls.'

With great difficulty, they hoisted Mordwyr into Gar's saddle, and made much quicker time up the slope. Corban's mam and Cywen met them in the courtyard, both dressed for a journey, he noted, in thick leathers and cloaks. Thannon stood beside them, scowling, his newly made war-hammer in his hands.

'Shield is at the stables – I've tended him,' Bethan said to Corban as she took Hammer's reins, guiding her da into the fortress. The rest of them made their way up the stone stairs to stand on the battlements.

The village was overrun now, the land about the base of the hill teeming with marauders, the dark mass beginning to swarm up the slope towards the fortress. The last of the villagers were crossing the bridge, Torin with them, driving a wain piled high with sacks and barrels, Pendathran and his few score warriors riding behind. When they were all across the bridge the iron-bound doors of Stonegate slammed shut, bars ramming home. Everywhere was the shocked murmur of voices. King Brenin emerged into the courtyard, with Halion and a clutch of other warriors about him, Heb and Evnis trailing. Behind them came the Tenebral visitors.

Brenin conferred with Pendathran a few moments, then climbed the stairwell. He positioned himself on the walkway above Stonegate, staring down at the bridge that spanned the chasm between Dun Carreg and the mainland.

In time the host's vanguard drew near, stopping two score paces before the bridge and spreading out in front of the fortress. Then Owain emerged from the mass of red-cloaked warriors.

'Cousin,' Owain called out, his voice ringing off the stone walls, his eyes scanning the battlements.

'Aye,' Brenin called back. 'I am here.'

'My son was more welcoming, when you visited my realm,' Owain said, gesturing to the barred gates.

'That is true,' Brenin called, 'but I was invited. You are not.'

Owain snorted. 'Let us dispense with this. You are trapped, no means of escape. Give yourself up, along with your daughter and Pendathran. Then you will save much needless bloodshed.'

'You are a fool, Owain. You are Rhin's tool in this, nothing more – her puppet.'

'Stop with your lies,' Owain roared and thumped his saddle. 'Marrock was *seen*, witnessed by many, leaving Uthan's chambers. *You* ordered my son's death. *You* killed him.' His rage looked set to dominate him for a moment, before he mastered himself, and glared up at Brenin. 'And in recompense I shall see you and your line wiped out.'

Brenin shook his head. 'You are blind. But even so, what can you hope to achieve? Look at these walls. Your threats are empty. You can bang on my gates until Midwinter's Day, and we shall hardly notice your presence.'

'Maybe,' Owain shouted up, 'if you had food enough. I am in no hurry to be leaving. Let us see how much your people love you when they are starving, when they are dying about you. Consider my terms,' he said. 'I shall return at the same time on the morrow.'

He began to turn his horse, then paused. 'Ah. I have something for you, to aid you in your deliberations.' One of his men untied a small sack from his saddle, and emptied its contents.

A head rolled across the flagstones. The face was distorted by a rictus of pain or fear, but it was still recognizable to all close by.

Gethin, Lord of Badun.

CHAPTER EIGHTY

CYWEN

Cywen muttered angrily to herself as she scraped Hammer's hooves clean, running her knife deftly around the rim, clumps of hard-packed straw and earth coming loose. The stables were empty of people. Almost everyone was out on the walls, just watching Owain's host, or training in the Rowan Field. That thought produced a fresh flow of expletives and she scraped more vigorously.

Two nights had passed since Owain had arrived, and Brenin had announced that anyone due to sit their Long Night before Midwinter's Day could take their warrior trial early, to join the fight against Owain. That meant just about everyone that she knew, including *Dath*.

Dath, whom she had sparred with almost every day – and *bested* every day. *And* that lump, Farrell, who was as slow as an auroch.

She grimaced, imagining them all together, playing at being warriors, at being men. Ronan's face came to mind, bright blood bubbling on his lips.

But it's no game, she thought.

None of them understood. Except Ban. He had been there too, had seen Ronan, and had even *fought*. She felt a sudden rush of pride, of love for her brother, as she remembered watching him take his warrior trial. She remembered the shock she felt as she'd seen his sword trial, seen how he'd set at Halion, with a growing sense of witnessing something special filling her. And she hadn't been the only one, going by the expressions of those about her.

The stable door opened and she blinked at the sudden burst of light flooding the darkness. And the figure silhouetted against the bright day was no less than Brenin. Evnis and his son were with him, along with Edana and Halion.

'I am looking for Gar,' Brenin said. 'Is he here?'

'No, my lord,' Cywen said. 'I thought he was out in the paddocks.'

'No, he is not,' Brenin said sharply.

'Then I am sorry, I do not know where he is,' Cywen said with a shrug. In truth Gar had been almost impossible to find for days, appearing only to issue a string of more commands, then disappearing again. He had been strange, ever since the day of Corban's warrior trial, as had her mam, both of them insisting she dress for a journey but not telling her where or why. Of course, that had all changed with Owain's siege, but still no explanation had been given, and Gar had become increasingly absent.

'Is it something that I may help you with?' Cywen asked.

'Perhaps,' Brenin said, preoccupied, clearly troubled to see Alona's favourite mare nearby. 'I need to know how many horses we have here – warrior mounts, not ponies.'

Cywen nodded. 'No more than two hundred, lord. Maybe fewer. I do not know the exact number, but thereabouts. I can find out for sure . . .'

'Only two hundred?' Brenin said quietly. 'That is not enough.' He shook his head, 'Yes, yes – find out.'

Only once since the siege had begun had there been any kind of prolonged battle. The day after Owain's arrival an assault had been made on the gates, warriors hauling felled trees capped with iron up the hill, attempting to batter the gates down. But they had been too thick, and the defenders above had let loose a constant barrage of rocks upon those wielding the battering ram. Scores had been crushed to death before Owain called his men back, with little more than scratches on the gates of the fortress to show for their efforts.

Dun Carreg seemed impregnable, but nevertheless there was a mounting tension spreading amongst those within the walls. With Gethin dead, and his warriors no doubt scattered, all hope rested on Dalgar and his warband from Dun Maen to break the siege.

Others entered the stables to join the royal group. It was Nathair with his usual companions, the black-clothed Sumur with his long curved sword on his back, and the eagle-guard, Rauca.

Cywen sidled over to Edana, who smiled at her, though her face looked strained.

'Got a new guard?' Cywen whispered, nodding towards Halion.

'Conall didn't like the job,' Edana said.

Cywen pulled a face. 'Why the horse count?'

'Father would have a force ready, for when Dalgar arrives. He will be outnumbered by Owain, and will need help.'

'Oh, I see.'

'I have been looking for you,' Nathair said amiably, a broad smile on his face.

'Have you?' Brenin murmured, his attention elsewhere, still rubbing the mare's muzzle.

'Yes,' Nathair said, the smile fading from his eyes. 'For some time, now.'

Brenin looked at him finally. 'Well, you appear to have found me. Forgive me if I have not been as available as you would have liked. These are unfortunate circumstances.'

Nathair made a dismissive gesture. 'I am in no danger, I am sure. Owain is bound by the Old Lore, as are we all.' The Old Lore was a set of customs that the Exiles had brought with them to the Banished Lands and included guest-rights: that a guest was safe at another's hearth and was due the right of protection by the hold's lord.

'Indeed,' said Brenin.

'I hoped to speak with Owain, make him aware of my presence here, and perhaps reason with him over this useless war.'

'Of course,' Brenin said. 'He returns to the walls each day. Speak with him then. Though I do not think you will change his mind.'

'Yes. Thank you,' Nathair said. 'I regret this situation you find yourself in, but I cannot remain here indefinitely. I must return to my ship – soon.'

'As you wish,' Brenin shrugged. 'I am sure that Owain would grant you safe passage. Is that what you wished to speak of with me?'

'In part,' Nathair said, 'and of Meical. I have spoken with your councillors on the other matter, regarding the Benothi. They were most helpful.' Nathair glanced at Evnis, who inclined his head.

'But I am still most keen to discover why Meical came here, where he may have been going. Anything.'

'Yes, yes,' Brenin said. 'Unfortunately, my time has been in much demand of late. I am sorry, but I have discovered nothing new. As I said before, I know not why Meical came here or where he went.'

Nathair frowned, not so easily put off.

'There must be something . . .' Nathair said. 'He must have ridden here – an impressive stallion, a huge grey. Was he stabled here?'

He was, Cywen thought, remembering the horse clearly.

'I don't work in the stables,' Brenin snapped.

Nathair frowned. 'But there must be someone, a stable boy.' He looked around, suddenly saw Cywen. 'You there, do you remember the horse I speak of? A dapple grey?'

All eyes suddenly focused on her. 'I . . . I remember him – the grey, I mean. He was beautiful.'

Nathair took a step towards her. 'Did *you* stable the stallion? Or speak with Meical, its rider?'

'No, I did not. That was Gar.'

'Gar?'

'The stablemaster.'

'I must speak with him. Where is he?'

Cywen shrugged. 'I don't know,' she said.

'I am sure he knows nothing,' Brenin interrupted. 'But I will see that he is questioned, inform you if there is any news of interest.'

Nathair turned back to Brenin. 'I would rather speak to him myself, particularly as your time is so stretched.'

'No,' said Brenin.

Nathair stood silent a moment. His eyes narrowed. 'I am accustomed to speaking to someone, if that is my inclination, my wish,' he said coldly.

'That may well be,' Brenin said, 'when you are in your own hall, your own kingdom. But I would remind you that you are a guest here, not king. And in *my* hall, *my* kingdom, I will do things as *I* please. And it does not please me to have others question my people. That is a task I reserve for myself, or those I deem appropriate.'

Sumur shifted, the barest movement of his feet, but suddenly there was a tension in his frame, the threat of violence in the air. 'That is discourteous,' he said softly in his guttural accent.

Nathair held a hand up to Sumur, as if to calm him. 'I have travelled a thousand leagues for this information,' he eventually said, something dangerous in his voice. 'I will not be hindered in this.'

Brenin returned his gaze impassively.

'Maybe you do not fully understand,' Nathair said. 'These are momentous times. Times of change. Times where choices must be made. A new order is coming. I shall remember those that help me, and those that hinder me, when my alliance is no longer in its infancy.'

'*Your* alliance? I thought it was Aquilus that birthed it?' Brenin said, raising an eyebrow. 'You are of a different cast, I think, from your father. And, yes, I understand very well the times we live in. I was at your father's council. I stood with him. Remember that.

'Allow me to give you some advice, as you are yet new to your throne. In future, try and have more care in how you choose to speak to a king, especially when he is in his own hall.'

'Mandros said something similar,' Nathair murmured.

Brenin scowled at Nathair. 'Mandros. Know this, Nathair: when my current troubles are resolved I will be calling for an inquiry into Mandros' death. Kingslaying is not lightly done, and I am unhappy with all that I have heard.' He at last left the stables, his party following. Evnis lingered a moment, a long glance passing between him and Nathair, then he too was gone.

Nathair turned back to Cywen. 'Tell this Gar that I would speak with him,' he said.

Cywen said nothing, and looked at her feet.

Suddenly horns sounded, an urgency in their tone. Nathair and his own companions left, the eagle-guard flashing a smile at Cywen as he went.

Crowds were making their way to Stonegate, where the horns were blowing loudest. Cywen darted ahead, ran up the stairwell and squeezed between warriors to peer over the battlements.

A warband was camped beyond the bridge, five or six hundred swords at least, which Owain deemed enough to contain any strike from within the fortress. The rest of the war-host was camped around the base of the hill, a black mass from this distance that spread throughout Havan and into the meadows round about.

In the distance, to the south, beyond Owain's host, there was movement on the horizon, a dark smudge moving slowly closer.

Dalgar.

She felt the tension, the hope rippling through those on the wall. Then she remembered Edana's words – Brenin wanted mounted warriors ready to give aid to Pendathran's son. She turned and bolted back to the stables, to find Gar organizing the chaos there as countless warriors prepared for battle. Pendathran was shouting a continuous barrage of insults at anyone he considered not moving at their fastest.

She dived in and helped saddle horses, tighten girths, strap spears to harness and a host of other things, until suddenly riders were thundering away towards Stonegate, a cloud of dust rising from their passing.

She did not pause for breath, but made her way straight back to the walls, squeezing through the crush until she had a view of the land below again.

Dalgar's warband was much closer now, close enough to make out tiny, individual riders, a wave of countless spear-points. Nevertheless, as they drew nearer Cywen was struck by how few they were compared to Owain's host. The King of Narvon must have emptied his realm to field such a gathering. Dalgar had maybe a quarter of what was arrayed against him. There were thousands within the fortress, evening the numbers, but they had to get across the bridge, which was only wide enough for ten or twelve mounted warriors abreast. And then there was the problem of the horses. Most mounts had been put out to pasture around Havan, as there wasn't enough room within Dun Carreg's walls.

Below, Dalgar and his warriors were now charging Owain's hastily drawn up lines. It was impossible to tell what was happening from such a distance, but Cywen could see the flanks of Owain's massed warriors curling around the smaller warband, like a huge fist closing.

Corban joined her, staring anxiously down at the battle far below. 'You're not joining those in the courtyard, then?' she said to Corban.

'What? No,' he said, shaking his head. 'Only proven warriors, on Pendathran's order.'

'You *are* proven,' she said defensively, but then felt relief overwhelm her annoyance. She would not like to see Corban in that.

Pendathran's voice sounded in the courtyard behind, shouting orders, and the gates creaked open, a flood of horsemen surging through them onto the bridge.

Owain's warriors were ready for them, a thicket of spears awaiting the horsemen.

There was a great crash as the riders ploughed into this wall of spears, wood splintering, horses screaming, flesh tearing and bodies flung into the air. The end of the bridge became a seething mass of horseflesh, blood and iron.

More of Owain's warriors were piling up behind the first rows of his spearmen. The bridge itself was crowded with Pendathran's men, and a bottleneck of the dead and dying formed between the two camps where the bridge met the land.

Cywen saw Pendathran on his great warhorse, plunging and rearing in the mass, the battlechief striking about him with his longsword. He hacked spear shafts in two, severed heads from necks and chopped grasping hands from arms as they reached out to pull him down. Slowly but surely the enemy line gave before him. He ploughed on, becoming the tip of an arrow shape as Ardan's warriors rallied behind him.

Then a spear sank into the chest of Pendathran's mount, its scream rising momentarily above the din of battle. It crashed into the ranks about it, red-cloaked warriors surging forwards, and Pendathran disappeared beneath like a man drowning.

A great roar went up from the warriors of Ardan as they tried to hack their way to their battlechief, but all was chaos, the bridge a boiling mass of limbs and leather and iron and blood.

Then Corban pointed – Pendathran was there again, his huge bulk the centre of a maelstrom as he laid about him with his sword. He retreated and sank into the line of his own warriors, and for a while the two forces fought on, men dying on either side, but neither gaining any advantage. Eventually, slowly, step by step, the men of Ardan were pushed backwards across the bridge, back into the shadow of Stonegate. Warriors from above flung rocks and spears at the men of Narvon as they came within range. A gap formed between the two sides as Pendathran and his surviving warriors retreated, and then with a slam the gates closed again.

Cywen ran to the other side of the wall, and looked down into the courtyard to see Pendathran sitting, pale-faced, his head in his hands.

The battle on the plain below still raged, the conflict seething closer to the fortress, as Dalgar desperately tried to cut his way to Dun Carreg.

But they were almost completely encircled, or so it appeared, and as Cywen watched, a shiver went through the battle, reminiscent of an animal in the moment before death. Almost immediately afterwards warriors began to break away from the main press of battle, moving back across the corpse-strewn meadows. At first a trickle of ones and twos, but quickly becoming a steady stream as Dalgar's warband was finally broken down and put to rout. Those fleeing were hounded by bands of mounted warriors. If any escaped Cywen could not tell.

In time a group of warriors rode up towards the fortress, about a score of them with Owain at their head. His eyes scanned the battlements as he reached the bridge, saw Pendathran up aloft and jeered. He reined in as he reached the carnage of the bridge battle, and warriors behind him pulled forward a horse with a body slumped across its back. Owain heaved it onto the ground and rode away.

Pendathran ordered the gates opened and made his way out across the bridge. Here he paused, but the massed warriors of Narvon made no move, no sound. He bent and lifted the abandoned corpse into his arms and carried the body of Dalgar, his son, back across the bridge.

CHAPTER EIGHTY-ONE

CORBAN

Corban leaned against the battlement wall skirting the Rowan Field, watching the sinking sun turning the sky to molten copper.

'A storm's coming,' Dath said beside him.

They had both taken their evening meal in the feast-hall, but the mood was dour in there after the previous day's events; Dalgar's defeat and death were still too fresh.

'So,' Corban said, to distract them both, 'we are both warriors now.'

'Aye,' said Dath, touching his warrior braid. 'For the most part,' he added. 'It doesn't feel complete, until I sit my Long Night.'

Or sleep through it, like I did through mine, Corban thought. 'Don't think Owain will let you ride past his war-host for that.'

'No,' Dath agreed. 'It is a good feeling, eh, passing the warrior trial?'

'It is that.'

In truth Dath had only just got through his trial: his spear-casting had been good, but his sword-work was hesitant, and how he had not ended up on his backside in the mud during his running mount Corban could not explain.

If bow-craft were part of the trials it would have been another matter. Marrock had already marked Dath as a future huntsman, he and Camlin having taken the youth on long forays into the Baglun. Even now Dath was leaning on an unstrung bow, gifted to him by Marrock and Camlin.

'What happens now, do you think?' Dath asked him.

'I don't know. Cywen's been talking to Edana, and it doesn't sound good. There was much hope resting on Dalgar . . .' Corban trailed off. 'Now that has failed . . .' he shrugged, thinking of Pendathran, of his pale, grief-stricken face as he had carried his son from the bridge.

'Owain will just sit outside the walls, wait for us to run out of food,' he continued, 'which, by all accounts, won't be too long. Too many mouths and no warning of Owain's coming.'

'There's enough warriors here to defeat Owain,' Dath growled, 'if only we could get past that bridge. They have us bottled in here like rats in an usque jug. If only there was another way out.'

Corban was silent, remembering the tunnels beneath the fortress. They could forage for food, lead surprise attacks on Owain. But what about the carcass they had found – the wyrm? What if there were more of them? He resolved to talk to Halion about this, suddenly feeling some hope.

'What about that king?' Dath said, jolting him from his thoughts.

'What king?'

'That Nathair, from Tenebral. I've heard he has a warband on his ship.'

Corban scoffed. 'If he has, it can't be many. Three score, four score swords? What could that do?'

'Huh,' Dath said. 'There's more'n just warriors on that ship.'

'Eh?'

Dath glanced down at the ship in the bay, lights winking into existence on it even as they looked.

'I was tending to Da's boat, on the beach,' Dath said. 'After I saw you riding out for your Long Night.' He pulled a face.

'And?' Corban prompted.

'And I heard *things*. Noises. From that ship, *strange* noises.'

'What do you mean? What like?'

'Like a beast. Like nothing I've ever heard before,' Dath went on. 'I've heard Storm growl before, and howl.' He glanced at the wolven, sitting on one of the giant steps on the stairwell. 'And that's enough to give me shivers. But this was worse – much worse.'

Corban chuckled. 'Dath, you're the one that told me Brina would steal my soul, remember? And the one that turned white when Craf squawked at you.'

Dath scowled. 'There's something on that ship,' he insisted. 'Something that's not human. That Nathair, he could use it to help us.'

'Even if there was a creature from the Otherworld sitting comfortably on *that* ship, why would Nathair choose to fight Owain? He is safe, covered by the Lore.'

Strong gusts of wind were sweeping in from the sea, now, swirling up the cliff face and fortress walls, bringing with it the taste of salt and rain. It was almost full-dark, but no stars or moon could be seen above; there were clouds scudding remorselessly towards the fortress, bloated and heavy.

'Best get off this wall,' Dath muttered, frowning at the sky as a fat raindrop landed on Corban's nose. 'It's going to be a bad one.'

'Aye, come on, then,' Corban said. Dath might have a fanciful imagination, but Corban trusted his friend's word completely when it came to weather. He picked up his shield and spear – he carried them everywhere since Owain's attack – and together they half-ran down the stairwell and across the empty Rowan Field, Storm with them.

The feast-hall was emptier than it had been, but still busy, and tucked away in the shadows were his mam and da, sitting with Farrell and his da, Anwarth.

Corban made his way over, Dath following.

'Hello, Ban, Dath,' Farrell said.

Corban nodded to the blacksmith's apprentice, and noticed the newly bound warrior braid in the big lad's hair too. *Look at us*, he thought, chuckling to himself, *all warriors now*.

Corban sat and listened idly to his friends for a while, Dath in the grip of some anecdote as his mind wandered. He leaned back in his chair and looked about the hall. His eyes fell on Evnis and Vonn, having a serious discussion, judging by the frown on Vonn's face. He had often wondered whether Vonn would fulfil his threat to him. So much had happened since that day in the paddocks, when Shield had killed Helfach's hound. Others came in for shelter, Tarben and Camlin, wrapped in dripping cloaks. They passed by Corban's table, both of the men nodding to him and Dath, and made their way to sit with a handful of warriors. *Strange*, Corban thought, *how one act can change so much*. Cywen had told him of how the woodsman had defended her, back in the Darkwood, *saved* her. 'Truth and courage,' he whispered to himself. His da was right. Truth and courage did matter, did make a difference.

Footsteps scuffed nearby and a shadow fell over him. Storm growled, a low rumble, and he looked up to see Rafe standing over him, his da behind one shoulder. More warriors from Evnis' hold were ranged behind them.

'I call you out, Corban ben Thannon,' Rafe said, loudly making the formal challenge for a duel.

The murmur of voices that had filled the hall wavered, a quiet spreading out from them in an ever-widening ripple. Halion frowned and said something to Edana. She moved closer to her father and whispered in his ear.

Corban looked up at Rafe and slowly stood, stepping away from his chair.

'Stand down, boy,' Thannon growled at Rafe.

'I am not a boy,' Rafe said. 'I am a man, and this is my right.'

Brenin had returned Rafe's sword to him, and had done it formally in the Rowan Field, the same day that Dath and Farrell had taken their warrior trials. Every arm that could wield a sword was needed now. So Brenin had said.

'On what grounds?' Corban said.

'On two counts,' Rafe replied loudly, looking about the room. 'The first is personal grievance. The second – breaking the word of your King.'

'What?' snapped Corban.

Rafe looked pointedly at Storm. 'That beast was banned from this fortress, forbidden from ever returning, on pain of death. I know it to be true, my da was there when our King spoke it, as were many other witnesses.' He smiled. 'Do you deny it?'

'Things have changed since then.'

'Do you deny it?' Rafe repeated, louder. 'Do you deny that our King spoke those words?'

'No,' Corban said, glaring at Rafe.

'Then let us proceed,' Rafe said. 'Let the Court of Swords judge our dispute.'

'Hold,' a voice rang out, all turning to see Pendathran standing. 'You cannot mean to allow this?' he said to Brenin, the King looking into his cup, swirling its dregs.

Slowly Brenin looked up, and focused with some difficulty on Corban and Rafe. 'What does it matter?' he muttered. 'Proceed.' He gave an uninterested wave. 'But only to first blood, not to the death. I have need of every warrior.' He chuckled to himself, little humour in its tone.

Rafe grinned and gripped his sword hilt, half-drawing it.

At this Storm snarled and leaped forwards, crouching between Corban and Rafe with teeth bared.

'Storm. *Hold*,' Corban cried.

'You see,' Rafe blurted, stumbling backwards. 'This beast is a danger. It should not be here.' He glanced at Brenin. 'You see, my King – your judgement was true.'

'Aye, perhaps,' Brenin muttered. 'Let your swords be the judge of it.'

Corban stared at the King, and felt his chest constrict, the implications of Brenin's words growing clearer. This had become far more serious than a grudge between childhood enemies. If he lost this the judgement would go against him. Storm could be put to death, and Rafe would surely insist upon it.

He tried to control his breathing and his suddenly racing heart.

Pendathran looked between Brenin and Corban. 'That lad, and his wolven,' he said, quiet but clear to all. 'They were of great help. In the Darkwood, in the rescue.'

'Rescue,' snorted Brenin. 'Aye, maybe they were, but Alona is still dead, is she not?'

'Aye, that is so,' Pendathran nodded slowly. 'But your daughter is not. She lives, still, in large part due to their aid.'

The two men glared at each other a moment, then Brenin lowered his gaze and took another sip from his cup. 'Dead. She is dead,' he said. 'Proceed.'

'What about the wolven?' Rafe said. 'Look what it did to me.' He pulled his linen sleeve up, revealing thick, silvery scars running almost from elbow to wrist.

'I shall take her out,' Corban said through gritted teeth.

'I'll do it, Ban,' his mam said.

'Take Storm and fetch Gar,' Thannon said quietly, looking at the warriors ranged behind Rafe. 'We may have need of him.'

Gwenith nodded and clicked her tongue at Storm. The wolven didn't move, stood twitching her tail at Rafe.

'Go,' Corban said, and reluctantly Storm followed Gwenith out of the feast-hall.

'Watch your step, Ban,' his da said to him, quietly. Corban did not hear. There was a battle raging inside him: anger, no, *fury* threatening to consume him, all Rafe's taunts and insults over the years merging into one injustice.

'I am surprised you have the stones to step in the ring,' Helfach said as Corban entered the makeshift circle they had prepared.

'Be silent,' Corban said, 'lest I send for my da, and have *him* silence you.'

Thannon grinned and patted the head of his war-hammer. Buddai growled.

'You . . .' Helfach spluttered and took a step towards Corban, fists bunching, Rafe and Crain moving with him.

Chairs scraped and suddenly Farrell and Dath were either side of Corban, Thannon towering behind them, and others converging from the hall's edges – Marrock and Camlin, Evnis and Conall.

'Enough!' Pendathran yelled.

Corban was staring into Helfach's eyes, almost nose to nose with the huntsman, feeling his heart pounding in his ears. The moment seemed balanced on a knife-edge.

Then the doors to the hall creaked open to reveal Nathair with Sumur, Rauca and others of his eagle-guard.

Corban stared at Nathair. The shadow about him was much clearer now. Corban shivered and almost thought he saw talons gripping the King, imagined red eyes smouldering in the shadow's depths. Something seemed to *whisper* in Nathair's ear. The King of Tenebral paused, looked at Corban and smiled, then Evnis called him to his table.

'I shall not spoil my son's moment,' Helfach hissed at Corban. He stepped out of the circle, Crain following him.

'Get this over with,' Pendathran growled, and Corban and Rafe moved properly into the circle. Rafe stood half a head taller than Corban, with long, quick limbs, though Corban was broader, and most likely stronger, he hoped.

Corban looked quickly towards the King's table and his eyes met

Halion's. His old swordsmaster put a finger to his temple and tapped it gently.

Think, Halion was telling him. *Anger is the enemy*, he repeated to himself, feeling his heartbeat begin to slow. *Remember, Storm is at stake here.*

He closed his eyes and took a deep breath, only opening them when he heard the rasp of Rafe drawing his sword, then gripped his own hilt and drew it slowly. He set his feet, raised his sword over his head, high, in a two-handed grip. Waited.

'Begin,' Pendathran said.

Corban burst into motion, striking at Rafe's head once, twice, three times in the blink of an eye. Rafe stumbled backwards, blocking Corban desperately.

Corban spun on his heel, was suddenly inside Rafe's guard and cracked his elbow into Rafe's cheek, sending him reeling back into a table. The huntsman's son lifted his blade as Corban ploughed forwards again, but he was off-balance, one hand trying to push himself off the tabletop, and Corban just slammed his sword into Rafe's, smashing it from his grip. Then Corban's blade was at Rafe's throat.

There was utter silence in the hall, only the crackle of flames from the firepit, and the ragged breaths of the combatants as Corban gazed into Rafe's eyes, saw fear, confusion and shame there. He flicked his wrist, ever so slightly and a thin line of red appeared on Rafe's neck.

'First blood,' Corban said and stepped back, sheathing his sword. Rafe remained frozen, breathing heavily, a trickle of blood running down his neck.

Corban glanced around, saw admiration in his friends' faces, satisfaction, and something else . . . *Everyone* was staring at him. He caught the eye of Nathair's guardian, Sumur, who was frowning, a question in his eyes. Then he was looking at the high table, Halion smiling with pride. Pendathran dipped his head.

'Is this matter at an end?' Corban said to Brenin, only now realizing that he felt breathless, that his chest was heaving. Suddenly, looking at the King, who still seemed – uninterested, somehow; he felt his earlier anger stirring again.

'Aye, the matter of your wolven is now decided,' Brenin slurred, his cup close at hand.

'It is a shame,' Corban said, the words gushing out before he could stop them, his anger making him reckless, 'that a father would think so little of his daughter's life. Storm and I deserved better than that.'

Brenin scowled, went to stand but staggered and sat down again. Corban's eyes widened, realizing how far the King was into his cups. He turned, and took his place beside his da and friends, feeling the flame of his anger still simmering within.

CHAPTER EIGHTY-TWO

KASTELL

Kastell shivered, the sweat of battle drying in this damp, suffocating tunnel.

He had caught up with Maquin, the two of them almost running to keep pace with the bobbing torchlight up ahead that marked Romar.

The sense of relief he had felt when Veradis arrived, turning the battle against the Hunen, was quickly evaporating. It had been replaced by a growing sense of foreboding.

They had been travelling along this tunnel for a while now, ever downward, leaving the light of day far behind. There were four or five score warriors ahead of them, Romar's honour guard, the rest mostly Gadrai. Orgull's bald head glistened in the torchlight, only a few strides in front of him, and at least that many warriors were behind, Jael amongst them.

The tunnel they were in was wide and high, its roof hidden in darkness. Torches lined the walls, giving off flickering pools of light, small stretches of near-solid darkness between each one.

Suddenly the warriors ahead were slowing and stopping. Kastell and Maquin carried on, moving closer to the front. At first Kastell thought they had reached a dead end, a wall blocking their way, but it was actually a huge barred doorway. On the ground before it glistened a heaped grey-white mound.

Then it moved.

The body pulsed, great looping coils rippling. A reptilian head rose, displaying huge fangs set in a wide, powerful jaw. The head snapped forwards, ripping the head from a warrior close to Romar. Men yelled, some moving to circle the beast, others stumbling away.

Then a great howling filled Kastell's ears, issuing from the side tunnels, and suddenly giants were pouring out of them, screaming their fury.

Then it was all iron striking iron, screams of pain and the rumbling bellowing of giants. Kastell had a momentary view of axes swirling, tracing arcs through the air in the torchlight, and of bodies slamming into each other. The wyrm was a writhing mass somewhere ahead, head darting, and men hacking at it. But the battle obscured his view. A man flew through the air and careered into him, knocking him to the ground.

An iron-shod boot crunched into the earth a handspan from his face and he scrambled up, seeing a warrior close by smashed to the ground by the giant who had almost trampled him. He swung his blade but he was off-balance and it glanced off the giant's leather cuirass. In return the Hunen swung his axe, but Kastell managed to turn it with his shield, sliced at the giant's exposed forearm but hit the iron-strengthened axe haft instead, the blow shivering up his arm. Kastell winced, and shrugged his shield off before the giant could pull him off his feet. He chopped two-handed with his sword at the giant's arm.

The giant roared, stumbled backwards into the seething mass of battle and disappeared, blood fountaining from its wrist.

Kastell sucked in a few ragged breaths, looking about. The ground was littered with the dead, the battle still raging and the wyrm wreaking havoc further up the tunnel. Behind him Maquin was trading blows with a giant, getting steadily pushed back. Kastell wiped sweat from his eyes and charged silently, swinging his sword, and together they dispatched the threat.

They moved forwards, fighting their way along the tunnel, until the wyrm lay before them, its tail twitching as it died. Giants were still all about. Orgull was fighting as he always did, his feet set wide, trading blow for blow with an axe-wielding giant. He was one of the very few that could, his size and bull-like strength making him almost a giant's equal. Vandil was virtually his opposite, the smaller, slighter man moving in a blur, his two swords in constant motion.

In the few moments that Kastell watched, the Gadrai's leader ducked a hammer swing and spun inside the giant's guard, his swords moving faster than Kastell could follow, then Vandil was spinning away. The giant looked confused, not yet realizing he was dead, as blood spread across his gut and groin.

Then Maquin took a blow to the side, and the old warrior grunted in pain. Before Kastell could check his friend, a Hunen with an axe was trying to take his head from his shoulders. The giant cracked the butt-end of its axe into his head. Kastell wobbled, staggered, his vision blurring – then something was between him and the Hunen and he heard the whistle of iron through air. The giant's snarl twisted into fear as a red gash opened across his throat. Kastell saw Vandil leaping away from him, a flash of teeth in a grin, then his lord was gone.

He looked to Maquin, and saw the Hunen that he had been fighting was now dead at his feet. There was a bemused look on his friend's face, his shield arm hanging limp at his side.

'Vandil . . .?' Kastell said, and Maquin nodded.

About them the battle seemed to lull, just for a few moments, and they leaned upon each other. Maquin's face was white, a sheen of sweat over it.

'Your arm? You are hurt,' Kastell said.

Maquin grinned weakly. 'Not dead yet,' he muttered.

They were about to step back into the battle when something happened, further back in the tunnel, a ripple running through all that fought, man and giant alike.

Kastell looked back.

Shapes appeared in the torchlight, dark figures swirling towards him, wielding long, curved swords in two-handed grips.

The Jehar, Veradis had called them.

They were systematically cutting through the Hunen, the giants falling before them. Kastell saw Alcyon, the giant, Calidus as well, fighting with surprising ferocity.

In short moments they reached him, and moved on to where Romar and the remnants of his honour guard battled.

And then, suddenly, it was over, the last giant falling to a dozen slashing swords.

Corpses were everywhere, the tunnel's floor hardly visible. It was difficult to count numbers, but Kastell figured no more than three score of the Gadrai still stood, if that. He shook his head – three hundred had come to Haldis. Romar was talking to Calidus, Alcyon beside them, the black-clad Jehar standing silently, utterly calm, as if they had not just fought a great battle. Kastell was discomfited to see women amongst their ranks. It jarred with all he had been taught, though if he was honest, the memory of how they scythed through the Hunen troubled him most. Women fighting more skilfully than *him*, than most here, was particularly disturbing.

Romar's voice rose, the King of Isiltir pushing past Calidus to approach the wide doors. He shouted an order and a dozen of his guard stepped forward and shouldered the bar free.

'You still live, then,' a voice whispered in his ear. Jael swept past him, a handful of warriors from Mikil with him.

Romar and his guard were pushing the doors open. They banged into the tunnel walls with a dull boom, then Vandil was calling the Gadrai forward, who settled about Romar protectively.

Calidus lifted a hand and led the Jehar after them.

CHAPTER EIGHTY-THREE

EVNIS

Evnis looked about the feast-hall, taking stock. Things were coming to a head. Tonight. And his rage stopped him thinking straight. A clear mind was what he needed, but Gethin's decapitated head refused to leave his thoughts. Owain would pay, not for killing his brother, but for robbing Evnis of his triumph, of Gethin witnessing his victory. Somehow it felt empty now, and that made him angry. He kept his rage within. *Focus, or your head will be rolling, too.*

His eyes fell on the boy with the wolven. Corban. Certainly there was something about the boy, arrogant as he was. He could not deny that it had been quite the duel, especially as he knew Helfach's boy was no idiot with a sword. And Rafe had a couple of years on Corban. A smile twitched his lips as he watched the lad, sitting with Thannon and a few others, laughing at something. They would not be laughing soon.

Nathair had asked him to arrange a meeting with Corban, said he wanted to meet the boy that had tamed a wolven. Evnis had snorted at that. Tame it was not.

His gaze rested on Nathair, reclining in his chair, observing. From the very first, when Tenebral's young King had approached him asking for information, he had known. Known that this man was special, had a role to play. And even if his own instincts had not served him so well, still he would have known. The voice had spoken, inside his head. It was not the first time he had heard it, guiding him over the years, but certainly it was the clearest. *Serve him.* Its command had been unmistakable.

He did not know how Rhin would feel, but she was not his master, whether she thought it or not. Asroth was.

So he had told Nathair about Meical seeing Brenin. That the two had definitely spoken privately, and at great length. Nathair had been grateful, and enraged. He did not shout, there was no outburst, but a coldness had possessed him then. This was not a man Evnis would cross lightly.

It is time, said the voice, a sibilant whisper in his head. He felt a stab of fear, knowing there was no returning from this next step. *Do it*, the voice snarled.

'With me,' he said, Conall and Glyn rising. He looked back once, from the doors. Brenin was still drinking, his head starting to loll. *Good*. He had been certain the valerian he'd arranged to be slipped into the King's mead would slow him, but waiting to witness it had been tense. It was a shame Pendathran had not drunk of it as well. *Can't have everything*.

He marched into the storm, heading for his hold. His last view of the feast-hall had been Vonn, glaring at him. He sighed. *Parenting was difficult*. They had argued about the fisher girl, Bethan, again. Vonn had told him that he loved the girl, wanted to be handbound to her. She was pretty enough, all right for Vonn to have some fun with, learn the ways of the world, but *handbound*? Vonn was destined for much better. Or better-born, at least. That had not gone down very well.

There would be time to smooth things over. After.

Soon they were back through the squall at the hold, Conall opening the door to his tower. He smiled humourlessly at the warrior. It had taken remarkably little to win Conall over. Pride was his weakness. Or one of them. Evnis had only to plant the seed, suggest that Halion was abandoning him for Brenin's favour, then water it with the King's very clear disrespect of Conall – a suggestion here, an observation there – and the beast had grown. When he had offered Conall a place in his hold the warrior had been tempted, almost eager, and only a small draw on the earth power had been needed to fan Conall's jealousy and paranoia.

Evnis headed straight for the basements. The tunnels had been boarded up for some time, after the encounter with the wyrm. But Evnis had known their value and had explored. That was how he had found the exit into the cave.

They waited by the tunnel entrance, and soon Evnis saw the

flicker of a torch, and heard the whisper of feet. Many feet. His messenger appeared, sent out alone before sundown. He was not alone now.

A dark file of warriors slipped past him, filling the basement. Forty, fifty, more – all wrapped in black, curved swords jutting over their shoulders. One of them stood before him, waiting.

See it through, he told himself. He stood and walked to the staircase. 'To Stonegate,' he said.

CHAPTER EIGHTY-FOUR

CYWEN

Cywen leaned against the wall and looked out into the darkness that surrounded the fortress. Rain lashed her, winds swirling and pulling. She didn't care; at least it meant she was alone, away from others that didn't understand.

She was standing on the battlements above Stonegate, the night hiding the warband below from view. In the courtyard warriors were huddled about a guttering fire, four score men or so trying to keep the chill at bay. Others, little more than shadows, stood by the gates.

Cywen sighed, a deep, mournful thing, and wiped moisture from her face.

'Chin firm, lass, it could be worse,' a voice said behind her. She started at a warrior standing close by, stepping out of the shadows.

It was Marrock. 'Least you're not still in the Darkwood,' he continued. 'And you're on the right side of this wall.' He looked out into the darkness.

She knew the truth of his words but could find nothing to say in response that didn't sound petulant, so she just nodded and turned away. He looked at her a moment, then walked on.

Absently she stroked the cold handle of a throwing knife, one of seven, strapped in a line along her belt. She was never without them now, not after realizing their worth in the Darkwood. Camlin, the woodsman, had returned one of them to her, saying it had ended up in his shield somehow.

Every day since her return she had practised with them, imagining Morcant was her target. Unlike Corban, or Brenin, she had no outlet for her vengeance, was not permitted to fight. It was unjust, and made her feel so *useless*, with a battle-host camped in Havan.

She glared over the walls, into the darkness and was about to turn away when she saw something. A movement, right on the very edge of her vision, where the darkness became complete. Leaning over the wall, she stared, strained, wiping rain from her eyes. Was that the drum of *feet*?

Then there were voices behind her, in the courtyard. She turned and glimpsed Marrock further along the wall, now looking in the same direction as she was.

A handful of warriors had strode into the courtyard and marched towards the fire, calling a loud greeting to warriors gathered there. She saw Evnis at their head, behind him a clutch of warriors from his hold, as well as Conall, Halion's brother. That one walked with a swagger, all confidence.

Maybe he felt her eyes on him, for he looked up at the walls, almost straight at her. He did not smile this time, though, as he was wont to do. She never made more of that than it was, having seen him behave the same with most women in the fortress, and no doubt all of Ardan beyond. This time he just stared at her, eyes narrowing, and began to walk up towards her.

Then Cywen spotted men, issuing from the street behind Evnis, spreading silently around the edges of the courtyard, clinging to the shadows beyond the firelight's reach.

Cywen opened her mouth to shout a warning, and heard Marrock's voice call out. Men about the fire looked to Marrock, then to the shadows, becoming aware of the creeping warriors.

Suddenly Evnis had a knife in his hand, and was shockingly plunging it into the chest of the nearest man. Then the shadows burst into life, warriors charging forwards with sharp iron in their hands.

All became chaos.

Many were cut down in that first rush, not even having time to draw their swords. Those that did manage to pull blades free of scabbards didn't do much better, the dark warriors carving through them with frightening ease. In moments almost two score men were dead about the fire as the warriors before the gate milled in shock, unsure whether to rush to their comrades' aid or stay and guard the gate.

Someone thought to sound a warning but the storm snatched the sound away as soon as it was made. It couldn't have carried much further than the courtyard. Men of Ardan stumbled from buildings around the open space, clutching swords and spears. Many of these fell quickly as they were still unprepared, thinking Owain had sent a sortie against the gates, but soon the courtyard was a seething hive of battle.

Marrock had gathered a handful of men about him from the wall, and was leading them down a stairwell, to aid those guarding the gate. The gate-guards were fighting with the desperation of the cornered, but the greater skill of the black-clad warriors was telling. If help did not come soon, the gates would be lost.

Cywen remembered her knives, and hurled one at the warriors attacking the gate-guards. A man fell backwards with her blade in his chest. She aimed another into the massed enemy and another fell. The next blade was for one of those blocking Marrock's way down the stairwell and the next saw another enemy on the stairwell collapsing. Then she snatched another blade from her belt and was cursing under her breath, scanning the crowd for a clear target.

She became aware of noise behind her and turned, to witness the beginning of the end.

Men were streaming across the bridge, weapons in hand, hundreds of them, and behind them more than she could count, their lines fading into the sheeting rain. Owain's host had somehow crept up to the fortress in the darkness, and waited for this moment.

She screamed, but no one paid any heed, either not hearing or too busy fighting for their lives. None except Marrock, who was being forced step by step back up the stairwell by a dozen black-clad warriors.

With horror Cywen realized the gate was lost. Even as she looked, the enemy were shouldering the great iron-bound bar from its seating. She sent a knife into them, but it didn't stop the bar from tumbling to the ground and the gates swinging open with a crash.

All in the courtyard seemed to pause for an eye-blink, staring at the gaping gateway. Then, with a huge roar, Owain's warriors poured through the open arch.

'Get to Brenin, along the wall – he must know,' Marrock shouted to her. Cywen stared, numbed by the shock of what she was seeing. Then Marrock was looking past her, shouting a warning.

She recognized Conall striding towards her, sword in hand, his face dark with menace.

Without thinking she hurled her knife at him. But he flicked his wrist, his sword sending the iron blade spinning away into the night. Cywen tripped as she tried to run.

'Get back, lass, out of my way,' she heard someone yell behind her, Marrock, trying to get at Conall.

She took a step but suddenly she did not *want* to get away, let others fight in her stead, again. She sprang at Conall, trying to avoid his sword hand. He was so surprised that his infamous speed failed him, just for a moment, and then she was inside his guard, kicking, punching, scratching, biting. Conall stumbled backwards, and tried to grab her, but she ducked and rammed her head into his belly. He *whoofed*, but one hand managed to grab her hair, hold her close. Instead of pulling away she pushed, with all of her strength and weight. Conall was already off-balance, so he staggered backwards, a heel slipping out over the wall's edge. He teetered there a moment, still gripping a handful of Cywen's hair, flailed an arm, then fell, dragging Cywen with him.

Together they hurtled towards the stone courtyard, towards a sea of warriors locked in combat. Cywen heard Marrock shout her name, somewhere behind and above, then, suddenly, all was darkness and she knew no more.

CHAPTER EIGHTY-FIVE

CAMLIN

Camlin gulped a last mouthful of mead from his cup, and shook his head when Tarben offered him more.

The feast-hall was quieter now, many having left for their own hearths and beds. There were still more than a few score, though, Camlin noted as he glanced around the room – mostly warriors, others in small clumps dotted elsewhere. The flames from the firepit were slowly sinking, sending flickering ripples of light and shade around the room. Camlin thought he could just make out that healer's crow, who led them out of the Darkwood, gripping a beam in the far corner. He could almost feel its strange beady eyes staring at him.

He glanced at Brina, sitting hunched in conversation with old Heb. As much as she scolded the loremaster at every opportunity, he could see there was an ease in their relationship. Torin and many from the village were also still here. And further away, in a dark corner, laughing, were Corban and his friends. They had been quick to support him, those two, when Corban had been threatened. Something about that scene had touched him. Friends that would guard your back in a fight were rare.

Something still lingered in the air after that Court of Swords, a tension, an excitement. There was certainly something about that Corban.

He chuckled to himself, looking at his own companions. He had gone from prisoner to warrior, most of those sitting with him now having served time as his guard. And even Marrock was one – he'd just left the hall to stand his watch on the wall – a good man, a good friend, a bitter enemy. *Friend.* He was still amazed by the turn his life had taken. Much as he preferred wood and sky to stone walls, he was glad he was here. It felt good, as if he were doing something right, instead of just what was right for *him*. Even though a good end to this siege was beginning to look more and more unlikely, he didn't care.

Suddenly the main doors banged open, rain and cold air sweeping in.

Evnis stood on the threshold, breathing heavily, his face glistening with sweat or rain. Shadowed figures hovered behind him.

'We are under attack,' he announced. 'Stonegate is breached.'

There was a moment of silence, then noise erupted. Some were shouting, questioning, as others leaped to their feet, benches scraping and falling over. Brenin just blinked owlishly and strained to focus on Evnis.

Camlin reached for his bowstring, wrapped in a leather pouch and began calmly stringing his bow.

Evnis rushed through the hall, towards Brenin, and shared a quick glance with Nathair, a handful of warriors and men from his hold behind him.

The sound of a horn blowing drifted in through the open doors, the wind swirling it around the hall.

Brenin stood, swayed and stepped out from behind his table. 'What do you mean?' he stuttered, a hush falling over the room as all waited to hear Evnis' words.

'Owain. Somehow the gates are open,' Evnis said, drawing close to Brenin. The King rubbed a hand over his eyes, and tried to stand straighter. Pendathran moved to steady him.

'Take Edana to her rooms,' Brenin said to Halion, and Halion managed to steer her a dozen paces towards the hall's back before she pulled indignantly out of his grip, and stopped to listen to Evnis.

Camlin realized that Nathair was somehow now standing beside Evnis. About a dozen of his guards, plus the dark-clothed warrior with the curved sword, were spread in a half-circle about Nathair and Evnis, mingling with others from the fortress and village. Camlin nudged Tarben's arm, not liking something about what he was seeing.

'How . . . how has this happened?' Brenin said, shock starting to sober him up.

A small group burst through the main doors. Camlin glanced

over to see Marrock, a handful of warriors at his back. His sword was in his hand and dark with blood. 'Evnis is a traitor,' Marrock roared, 'he has opened the gates to Owain.'

The sound of swords being drawn filled the hall. Camlin looked back to Brenin, and saw one of Nathair's eagle-guards standing with his sword-tip levelled at the King's chest. Slowly, so as not to draw attention, he reached down beside his chair for his quiver, and reached for a black-feathered arrow.

CHAPTER EIGHTY-SIX

CORBAN

Corban reached for his weapons, standing in the feast-hall beside his da, a scene of utter madness overtaking the room before him. Brenin was standing with a sword-point to his chest.

A terrible silence filled the room. Then Halion drew his sword, the familiar scraping rasp drawing all eyes to him as he began to walk towards Brenin, slowly, deliberately, his eyes fixed on the eagle-guard with a blade at Brenin's chest. Sumur padded forwards a few paces, and stood between Halion and Ardan's King. His hand was on his sword hilt, but he did not draw the blade on his back. Instead he raised a warning finger, as if scolding a wayward child.

'Hold, Halion,' Brenin snapped. 'Edana is your charge now. Look to her.'

Halion paused, conflicted, as he looked between King and daughter, then nodded.

Pendathran shuffled closer to Brenin, and received a warning glance from Sumur.

'What is it that you think you are doing, here?' Brenin levelled at Nathair, seeming suddenly more the man, the leader. He stood straighter, resolute.

'You have left me little choice,' Nathair said. 'Firstly, you lied to me.' The King of Tenebral stepped closer to Brenin, his stance threatening. 'I gave you every chance, every opportunity, but it seems that you have chosen your friends poorly. I know that you spoke to Meical. Where is he, now, eh? He ran when my father died, and is absent now . . .' He raised a questioning eyebrow. 'Secondly, you are going to lose. Owain has beaten you, though you refuse to see it yet. If I seek strong men for my alliance, then I would not look to you.

Outwitted by Rhin and Owain. Why would I choose to ally myself to the losing side?'

'Right and wrong stay the same,' Brenin maintained, unmoved.

'And thirdly,' Nathair continued, 'you question me about Mandros – dare to call me to account, demand an *inquiry*. I am King of Tenebral, High King of the Banished Lands. And more. I am Elyon's chosen, the Bright Star. You do not question *me*.'

'It appears I chose wisely,' Brenin said. 'Betrayal would seem to be in your nature.'

Sumur lunged forwards, and slapped Brenin across the face. 'You will not speak so to the Seren Disglair.'

Angry murmurs rippled through the hall, but no one moved, the eagle-guard's sword-point still pressed tight to Brenin's chest.

'What do you mean, *betrayal*?' Nathair hissed. 'What did Meical say to you?' With a struggle he mastered himself. 'As I told you before, my friends shall be rewarded, my enemies, punished. By hindering me, refusing me your aid, you chose to become my enemy. This,' he said, gesturing at the sword-point at Brenin's chest, 'is the consequence of your choice.'

'A fine logic,' Brenin snorted.

In the distance Corban could hear the sounds of battle, coming closer.

'Of course,' Nathair continued, 'I could not have achieved this without some assistance. Evnis, at least, is one that has exercised wisdom in his choice of friends.'

'Evnis,' said Brenin, the sting of this betrayal clear to all. 'Why?'

'Fain,' Evnis said, his voice shaking. 'You sealed her death sentence when you forbade my leaving the fortress. Because of your politicking.' He spat in Brenin's face.

The hall was silent, stunned as Brenin wiped the insult from his cheek. 'Fain . . . You hide your greed behind a cloak of revenge, Evnis. Power is what you seek, and will grasp it where you can. Elyon curse you both.'

Nathair intervened, bringing the focus back to him. 'I mean you no harm, Brenin, but you have stood in my way.' He shrugged. 'If your people remain calm, *sensible*, then there need be no bloodshed. More specifically, they need not witness *your* blood being shed. We shall just wait for Owain to arrive . . .' He listened to the growing sound of combat beyond the hall's open doors, '. . . which does not seem too far away. Then I shall hand you over to him and we can all be on our way.'

'You use words to cast a shroud over the truth,' Brenin said. 'Owain means for me and my line to be extinguished. You know that. Whether by your hand or by Owain's I shall die. But if my people fight, here, now, then at least my daughter, my *line*, has a chance of survival.'

Nathair held a hand up, but Brenin suddenly lunged forwards, swiping at the sword held at his chest and slicing his arm.

At the same moment there was a whirring sound, a wet *thunk* and the eagle-guard holding Brenin hostage collapsed, a black-fletched arrow sprouting from his throat.

A stunned pause settled on all in the room, then mayhem erupted.

Evnis leaped upon Brenin, reaching inside his cloak for something, the two of them staggering back into the table and crashing to the ground. Pendathran lunged towards Brenin, sword half-drawn, and collided with Nathair, then Sumur's sword was whipped from its scabbard. Pendathran fell with a crash onto the table, his throat jetting dark blood. Nathair's eagle-guards cut down Brenin's honour guard and formed a tighter protective half-circle about Nathair and Brenin. With a shout from Rauca the eagle-warriors raised their shields and linked them into a kind of wall as fighters rushed to Brenin's aid. Elsewhere, warriors from Evnis' hold set upon their neighbours in the hall.

There was another *whirr*, and a *thud* as an arrow found a gap between shields and another eagle-guard sank to the floor.

Corban scanned the room, and saw Camlin drawing another black-fletched arrow from his quiver. Men from Evnis' hold also spotted the woodsman and howled as they charged. But Corban was unsure where to join the melee. Brenin was fighting for his life, but Edana was also under attack, Halion was outnumbered, and his friends, Dath and Farrell, were also in danger. The hall was chaos, Evnis' warriors seemingly everywhere.

And then Thannon was howling, charging towards Brenin, who could be glimpsed still wrestling with Evnis at Nathair's feet. The blacksmith whirled his great hammer about his head, and began literally smashing a pathway to his King. Men from Evnis' hold were smashed to the ground, bones crushed by the hammer-wielder, with Buddai snapping and snarling by his side.

Without thinking, Corban followed him, his passage made easy as Thannon battered a path through, leaving a wake of the dead behind him. Corban held his shield high and jabbed with his spear at any that tried to come at his da from his unprotected side. Buddai guarded the other side and slowly, like the wedge shape of a spear-tip, they neared Brenin.

Suddenly a scream pierced the din of battle, high and shrill. Edana was screaming and staring through a gap in the crowd at her father, lying still on the ground. Evnis was astride him, his knife blooded.

Thannon bellowed and redoubled his efforts, sending his hammer crashing into the chest of a man trying to bar his way. Buddai leaped and clamped his jaws about another man's thigh, and the dog shook his head as Thannon swung his hammer. Corban shoved his shield forward and turned a blade aimed for Thannon's neck, then jabbed his spear out and felt it sink deep. He tried to pull back but the spear-point was stuck. Corban cursed, knew he should finish the wounded man but could not bring himself to, instead drawing his sword and ploughing on.

The three of them, father, son and hound, suddenly stepped into an open space, beyond it the half-circle of Nathair's eagle-guard with Nathair and Sumur standing calmly within. A dozen or so Dun Carreg corpses lay strewn before them – those that had tried to reach Brenin.

Everyone else was caught up in the conflict with Evnis' men. All Corban could make out in the chaos was that Halion still stood, with a handful of men rallied behind him now. Of Dath and Farrell he could see nothing.

Thannon strode towards the eagle-guards, one of their number stepping forward. It was Rauca, Corban realized, leader of Nathair's honour guard.

'Come no further, big man,' he said. 'No need to die fighting for a king already slain.'

'Alive or dead, you have my King in there,' Thannon challenged. 'I mean to take him from you.'

Rauca assessed Thannon, noting the great bloodstained war-hammer in the blacksmith's hands. He shrugged. 'We are no strangers to giants,' he said, then stepped back into line with his men. 'Wall,' he shouted, and the warriors' shields came together with a loud *crack*.

Thannon swung his hammer at a shield, but it held, the force of the blow dissipated by the supporting shields either side. Scowling, Thannon swung again, and Buddai leaped forwards, sinking teeth into a warrior's calf. There was a scream, the shield dropping slightly, and then Thannon's hammer crashed into the warrior's helm. He collapsed instantly and Thannon thrust into the gap in the line, but the ranks closed up too quickly, and a sword-point found Buddai. The brindle hound yelped and fell, and Thannon lunged forwards, battering at the shields to reach his hound. Corban gasped as a host of short swords suddenly jabbed forwards, seemingly from out of the shields themselves. His da grunted in shock as blades pierced him.

Corban opened his mouth, drew breath to scream, and reached out to pull his da clear. But something slammed into his side, sending him sprawling to the floor. He managed to keep his grip on sword and shield, and looked up to see Helfach and Rafe coming at him with blades drawn.

'No one to help you now, boy,' the huntsman snarled. Corban stood, looking desperately for his da, saw the big man stagger back from the row of shields and drop to one knee. Corban took a pace towards him, then Rafe was there, blocking his view. Panic-driven anger drove him to swing wildly at the huntsman's son, but his blade was parried easily. In his haze he almost forgot Helfach, remembering him as the huntsman slashed for his ribs. Corban caught the blow on his shield, blocked another from Rafe with his sword, and tried to draw both men in front of him. If he didn't focus he would be too dead to help his da.

Helfach and Rafe struck at him almost at the same time, one left, one right. Corban blocked Helfach's blow with his shield, parried Rafe's blade, and took a step back. They pressed forwards. Instead of stepping back, Corban smashed his shield into Helfach's face, punching at Rafe with his sword hilt. Helfach took an unsteady step backwards, but Rafe sidestepped Corban's blow, and hacked at Corban's side. Hoping Helfach was incapacitated, if only for a few moments, Corban spun around and blocked the sword swipe to his ribs. He stepped forwards with his shield lifted high, swept his sword underneath and felt it chop into flesh. Rafe screamed.

Corban saw terror in his enemy's eyes, then there was a white pain in Corban's shoulder and he was suddenly spinning and falling.

He looked up to see Helfach grinning wildly, blood dripping from a ruined nose, and from his sword-tip.

'This ends now, boy,' Helfach yelled and raised his sword, then Corban heard a deep-throated snarling growl and the huntsman was gone, tumbling away in a mass of fur and snapping teeth. Wolven and man rolled to a halt, Storm on top, jaws clamped around the huntsman's throat, his arms and legs battering futilely at her body. With a savage wrench of her neck, blood sprayed high. Helfach's feet twitched and then were still.

Corban staggered to his feet, pain radiating from his left shoulder where Helfach had stabbed him, and Rafe stumbled away back into the battle. But Corban only cared for his da, somehow back on his feet, though blood-drenched from many wounds.

Nathair stepped through the ranks of his guard, Rauca beside him, a deadly short stabbing sword in his hand.

As Corban watched, Thannon swung his hammer but the blow was slow and weak. Rauca ducked beneath it, and gave Buddai a sharp kick to the ribs. Then Nathair stepped in close and rammed his sword into Thannon's chest. They stood there a moment, then Thannon toppled backwards.

Corban screamed, a high wordless thing. He staggered forwards. Then a form swept past him – Gar, a curved sword strapped to his back. He was charging straight for Nathair and Rauca. The eagle-guard saw him and thrust Nathair back into the safety of the shield wall, then raised his sword to meet Gar. The stablemaster dropped beneath Rauca's weapon, rolled, came up behind him with his sword hissing fluidly into his hands, held high in his two-handed grip. Rauca turned as Gar was bringing his blade down, slashing the guardsman from shoulder to hip, shearing through leather, chain-mail, flesh and bone.

For a long, timeless moment the remaining eagle-guards just stared at Gar, as did Sumur and Nathair.

Sumur took a step forward. 'It cannot be,' he whispered.

A hand touched Corban's uninjured shoulder, his mam standing beside him with the spear he'd left in someone's ribs in her hand. He felt panic for a moment – she shouldn't be here – then together they ran to Thannon's side. Buddai had draped his body alongside his master's, and was pushing at Thannon's cheek with his muzzle. He whined as Corban and Gwenith crouched down.

Thannon's face was ashen, in stark contrast to his livid wounds. Corban squeezed his da's hand, and looked on helplessly. His mam lifted Thannon's head onto her lap.

'Hold on,' Corban whispered, grimacing at the uselessness of his words. Thannon tried to speak, but only a gargled whisper came out.

'Please,' Corban said, stroking his da's hand. The gap between each breath grew longer, more laboured. Thannon stared back, then he was gone.

Gwenith let out a great racking sob, and clutched her husband's hand. Corban felt lost and suddenly found it hard to breathe. He looked up to see Nathair watching, and felt a new depth of emotion, a rage, that he'd not experienced before. Nathair returned his gaze.

'I will kill you,' Corban said.

'Bring him to me,' Nathair demanded, pointing at Corban. His eagle-guards moved, the shield wall splitting.

'Get the boy out of here,' Gar snapped, stepping to face the remaining eagle-guards as they moved on him, circling him slowly, hesitantly.

'But where?' Gwenith said, still in shock.

'That way,' Gar nodded towards the back of the hall, where the feast-hall's survivors had gathered about Halion and Edana, fighting the last of Evnis' men.

Gwenith looked but couldn't move, couldn't stop the tears.

'Corban is all that matters,' Gar hissed. 'Move. Now.' He shuffled his feet to close off any approach to Corban and Gwenith.

Gwenith touched Thannon's face a moment, a goodbye, then she was standing and pulling Corban. He plucked his da's war-hammer from the smith's big hands. But Buddai refused to move.

Corban looked to Gar, not wanting to leave his father's body or the stablemaster.

'Go, Ban,' said Gar. 'I'll join you soon. Trust me.'

Corban grimaced, but ran with his mam and Storm, the hall

strewn with the dead. It was empty now save for Nathair and his eagle-guards circling Gar, and the continuing combat at the far end.

The clash of iron on iron erupted behind them and Corban stopped short, realizing he'd fallen for the stablemaster's ploy to make him leave. *Of course he lied, he's facing ten men.* But he looked back to see Gar fighting more like a shadow than a man – swirling and slipping amongst Nathair's eagle-guards. Blood sprayed as Gar's sword swung and slashed in an elaborate, deadly dance. Within moments men were staggering away from the conflict, or fallen, Gar in constant, fluid motion.

Then Gwenith demanded that he follow and they finally reached Halion. No more than a dozen fought with him, out of of the hundred or so that had filled the hall. Evnis' warriors had fared little better, though: less than a score of them now fighting to reach Edana and finish the conflict. Corban hefted his da's hammer and charged, Storm leaping ahead of him, hamstringing a warrior with one snap of her jaws.

Two fell before he reached them, knives jutting from backs, and he remembered who had taught Cywen to throw a knife. He grunted as he swung the hammer – which was in truth too heavy for him – and connected with a man's lower back instead of his head. That was enough, though. Corban felt bones shatter. He swung again, then his mam was beside him, stabbing a spear into someone's shoulder and Storm was snarling, ripping, tearing.

Evnis' warriors tried to turn and face this new threat, but in moments Halion and his fighters had dispatched the distracted, flanked warriors. Corban checked to find Camlin, Marrock and Tarben. He felt a surge of relief when he saw a pale-faced Dath and Farrell. Others were there too, amongst them Brina and Heb at the back, beside a weeping Edana.

Flames still flickered in the firepit, and death and destruction surrounded them on every side. In a shadowed corner beside a shattered table, the sounds of grief were clear in the lull. Corban squinted through the firepit's flames to see two men kneeling on the ground. One was Mordwyr, Dath's da. His face was distraught, but the sobbing came from the man next to him – Vonn, cradling Bethan's limp head in his lap.

The only other movement was at the high table, where Gar still fought, though of the ten eagle-guards only two still stood. Corban took a few paces towards Gar, a handful following, and spreading out about him. As he watched, Gar blocked an overhead strike, and sent his own blade slashing across his opponent's throat. Then, before that man had fallen, he was sidestepping, turning, and somehow reversing his sword grip to punch it into the stomach of the last guard rushing in behind him.

Gar stood still a moment, then slid his sword free, spun it and changed the grip yet again as his opponent's body sank to the ground. He finally turned to face Nathair and Sumur.

Sumur stepped forward, slow and graceful, still leaving his sword sheathed on his back. 'How is it that you are here, sword-brother?' he said.

Gar made no reply, except to shift his feet.

'You should answer, when I ask something of you,' Sumur continued. 'I am Lord of Telassar, Lord of the Jehar; lord of you, am I not?'

'Tukul is my lord,' said Gar.

Sumur shook his head. 'He was always misguided. Not equipped for this calling. Tell me, where is he? Here, in Dun Carreg? Ardan? Has he just abandoned you?'

'He would not do that,' Gar spat.

Sumur shrugged. 'Whatever you think, your task has failed. Come, sheathe your sword, join me. Look, the Seren Disglair stands before you.' Sumur gestured to Nathair, who stood tall, regal, and smiled warmly at Gar.

Gar assessed Nathair, contemptuously. 'That just cannot be,' he said and his eyes flickered, briefly, to Corban.

Sumur followed his gaze, and stared at Corban, his eyes taking in the wolven beside him. 'We have much to speak of, you and I,' he said. 'Come, sheathe your sword. Join me.'

'You were ever the honeyed talker,' Gar said. 'You may have fooled my father with your false tongue, become lord in his absence, but you never fooled me. Time enough for words when my spirit has crossed the bridge of swords. Until then I shall let my blade speak for me.' He flexed his wrist, his sword-tip spinning, tracing a circle in the air.

'So be it,' Sumur shrugged. 'When I am done with you I shall carve some answers from your boy and his wolven-cub.'

Faster than Corban could follow, Sumur suddenly had his blade in his hand. He heard rather than saw their first clash, iron ringing out as their swords sparked in a blurred flurry, their bodies spinning. The two men separated, neither breathing hard, and began circling, eyes measuring, assessing, probing. Sumur stopped suddenly, shifted his weight, then rushed in with his sword aloft. Gar spun from the curved blade as it slashed, was already striking at Sumur's waist, but the warrior was gliding out of range. Again they clashed, swords connecting this time, more strikes than Corban could count, then Gar was crouching low, slashing at Sumur's ankles, the warrior leaping and striking at Gar's head. The stablemaster swayed to one side, Sumur's blade missing him by a hairsbreadth. He twisted towards Sumur, chopped once, twice, then stepped gracefully away.

Sumur paused, glanced down. Two thin red lines had appeared upon him, one along his forearm, the other his chest. They were shallow cuts, of no consequence, but they showed who was the fastest, by the merest fraction.

Corban realized he was holding his breath, mesmerized by the intensity and skill of the contest he was watching. Nothing he had ever seen compared: the Court of Swords between Tull and Morcant appearing as clumsy children to this deadly, vicious offering. He glanced about, and saw all those with him equally absorbed in the life-and-death dance before them. For a moment, all thoughts of the battle still raging beyond the hall's doors was forgotten.

Clashing iron grabbed his attention again, the two men spinning and swirling like flames. For a moment Corban was unable to tell which was which.

Then one was retreating, backing towards a shape on the floor: his da's corpse, Corban realized. He uttered an involuntary groan as he recognized it, Buddai still maintaining his solitary guard. The warrior's foot grazed Thannon's arm and Buddai's jaws snapped out and bit into his boot. For a moment, less than a heartbeat, the flutter of an eyelid, that man was off-balance. His opponent's sword snaked out, and struck a deep gash on his shoulder, then the man was spinning away, out of range. He paused, to feel his injured shoulder and Corban gasped. It was Gar.

Suddenly Corban was terrified for Gar's life. His confidence, his *certainty* in Gar's ability drained away. Gar used a two-handed blade, used both hands, *needed* both arms, to wield it properly. This was a contest where the minutest change in balance would tip the scales, and both men knew it.

Gar scowled and rolled his shoulders, glancing fleetingly towards Corban. 'Go,' he mouthed silently, and Sumur smiled in anticipation.

Slowly Gar stepped away, in the direction of the hall's main doors, away from Corban, but before he had moved a handful of paces Sumur was lunging forwards.

There was another burst of sword strikes and parries, this time Gar steadily retreating, blocking, not even trying to strike back. Sweat glistened on his brow, as Sumur's attack became a blur, the warrior sensing the closeness of his victory.

Then men were pouring through the open doors, a fighting mob of both red and grey. They crashed into Gar and Sumur, sweeping them apart.

'Gar!' Gwenith screamed. 'Now. Come now.'

Corban added his voice to hers, though both Gar and Sumur had disappeared from view. Maybe Gar heard them, maybe he had made the decision regardless, but, as those about Corban were preparing to fight again, Gar appeared before them.

'We need to leave. Now,' he said. The stablemaster was exhausted and bleeding from his shoulder still, but there was something in his expression that brooked no argument.

Corban nodded. 'All of us,' he added, glancing at Halion and the others. Gar just shrugged.

Battle had consumed the hall again. Sumur, Nathair and Evnis were obscured from view by a tide of red-cloaks locked in combat with grey.

They were standing close to the rear of the hall, Halion and his small band of survivors curled protectively around Edana. So far, the renewed battle had not touched them.

'We must get Edana out of here,' Halion said, overhearing their words, looking at Gar curiously, as if seeing him for the first time.

'Aye,' Corban said. 'But how?'

'There is no path through that,' Halion pointed out, nodding at the battle in the hall, and looked back at the doorway leading into the keep.

'And no path beyond,' Marrock said. 'Most of the fortress between here and Stonegate is the same. And Owain holds the gate and bridge.'

All realized what that meant. There was only one known route in or out of Dun Carreg.

'I know a way,' Corban blurted, suddenly remembering the tunnels beneath the fortress.

'You are sure?' Halion asked.

'Aye. A secret way.'

'I say let us go and see,' said Marrock, 'not stand here debating its likelihood.'

Halion nodded and galvanized them into action. He gave orders to his remaining fighters, hurried over to the door at the back of the hall, and led the small party through.

Gwenith hesitated at the doorway, looking back at Thannon. Then her expression changed. 'Cywen.'

Corban tried to think of the last time he had seen his sister. Where was she?

'We must find Cywen,' his mam said.

Gar put a hand on her arm. 'We must get Ban to safety, and hope that we find Cywen along the way. If we don't, I will come back and find her, once Ban is safe. I promise you.'

'But . . .'

'She is brave, resourceful. If any can survive through this, it is her.' Gar held her gaze. 'We cannot risk Ban – the sacrifice has already been so great . . .'

Gwenith stared at him. 'You will come back for her?'

'On my oath, as soon as Ban is away from here.'

She nodded curtly.

Dath suddenly broke away, running back into the hall where his da knelt in mourning. Corban paused a moment, then followed, with Gar and Farrell close behind.

They caught up with Dath as he reached his da, still bent over the lifeless form of Bethan, cradled in Vonn's arms.

'Come, Da, quick,' Dath gasped. 'We must leave.'

Mordwyr looked up at him. Gently Dath slipped his arms around his da and tried to lift him. Corban went to help, passing his hammer to Farrell.

'Leave me here,' Mordwyr muttered as they hoisted him up, 'I have nothing left to live for.'

'Live for me, Da,' Dath pleaded, 'or if not, live to avenge Bethan.'

Vonn looked up at that and grimaced.

Mordwyr allowed Dath and Corban to steer him back to the doorway, Vonn following wordlessly. Halion and the others were waiting for them in the dark corridor beyond. Corban and Gar were last to step through the door, Storm squeezing past him. He looked back, into the hall.

'Da,' he whispered. Gar bowed his head.

Corban was about to turn away when a movement caught his eye. Nathair and Sumur were dragging Brenin's corpse to the side. The two men were staring straight at Corban. Corban was caught for a moment, staring back at Nathair. Gar jerked him back and slammed the door shut, dragging a long bench over to wedge against it. 'Time to mourn when we're off this rock,' he said.

Corban nodded, and together they ran down the hallway, Storm loping along behind.

CHAPTER EIGHTY-SEVEN

KASTELL

Kastell paced down a wide, spiralled pathway, the others near him in the dark, as it wound around a black open space. He took a few shuffling paces closer to the pathway's rim, looked over its edge and saw, far below, the glimmer of blue-tinged light.

The company walked in silence, the only sound the tramping of feet, the creak of leather. There was a heaviness in the air, a musty, old smell, which grew stronger as they walked deeper. Kastell began to feel anxious. Would there be more giants down here? Somehow the battle in the tunnel had felt final; there had been an extra ferocity to the Hunen, as if it were their last stand. But the Hunen were unpredictable. His thoughts returned to the battle amongst the mounds, the creeping mist and ground that had turned to bog. He shivered, recalling warriors sinking to a cold, suffocating death.

Then the ground levelled and he took in the sight ahead.

Warriors were spread before them, giants, kneeling in two great lines. Kastell quickly hefted his sword, then felt foolish.

They were dead. Long dead, the cadaverous warriors held upright by stiff coats of leather and chainmail, gripping axes or warhammers that were planted into the ground, the butt-end of shafts sunk into small holes dug into the stone. Tall posts with bowls of blue flame interspersed the twinned rows of dead warriors.

Slowly the party moved along the wide road, spreading out. Kastell saw something at the far end, marked by blue flame. He looked suspiciously at the Hunen on either side, half expecting this to be some new form of glamour. Perhaps the skeletal warriors would burst into life and attack them. His skin prickled, feeling as if they were staring at him; but there were only black, sightless holes in their papery faces where once their eyes had been. Wisps of braided hair and moustaches framed gaunt, angular skulls wrapped in taut skin, preserved for Kastell knew not how long.

As he drew closer to the cavernous room's end he saw Romar ahead. And Kastell finally saw what was placed there.

Upon a wide dais sat a stone chair, a throne, and seated in it was the body of a giant. He wore a coat of iron, made of small plates shaped like leaves, each individually stitched into the leather beneath it. Eerie blue flames flickered on the dull iron, the horsehair-plumed helmet upon its head and upon its greaved boots.

Bony hands gripped the long shaft of an axe, double bladed, with the metal looking different somehow from the iron everywhere else in the hall. It was dark, seeming to suck the torchlight into it rather than reflecting it like the other weapons in the chamber. What was more, Kastell had seen this axe before – in a hall in Mikil, guarded like treasure.

'My axe,' Romar breathed.

Alcyon and Calidus swept past Kastell with a score of the Jehar. He looked behind him, and more of the black-clad warriors were spreading about the hall amongst the remnants of the Gadrai and the men of Isiltir.

Alcyon and Calidus approached the dais. Calidus halted and Alcyon stepped up. He gripped the axe, then extracted it tenderly from the cadaver's skeletal grip. He lifted it before him, a look of awe and rapture upon his face.

'Hold,' a voice called out, harsh in the almost reverent silence. 'That is my axe.'

Alcyon stared at Isiltir's King, with his small, black eyes. 'It is Dagda's axe,' he said, his low voice almost whispering, though his words carried throughout the hall.

'Dagda? Who is, was he?'

'One of the seven forefathers, wielder of the starstone axe,' Alcyon breathed, as if reciting some ancient rote of law. 'This axe is one of the seven Treasures.'

'I know it,' Romar said. 'And it is mine. Give it to me.'

'This belongs to Nathair,' said Calidus. 'I claim it, as our only spoils in this, as our reward for aid given. You would not even have reached Haldis, let alone conquered it, without our intervention.'

'What?' Romar exclaimed. 'I think not. You have come here uninvited, joined yourself to our cause when you were not wanted, not needed, and now you seek to take for your own the greatest spoil of this war.' Romar stepped towards the axe, his challenge clear.

'I claim this axe as trophy for Nathair, King of Tenebral, our Bright Star, the Seren Disglair,' Calidus intoned. Kastell frowned, not understanding Calidus' last words, at the same time seeing their effect on the dark warriors about him, as they readied themselves, somehow.

'Nathair,' Romar stuttered. 'The *Seren* what? He is but a pup, a kingslayer, and he shall reap no gain from this, earn no coin from our spilt blood. Now,' he said, turning his gaze upon Alcyon, 'give that to me.'

'No,' Alcyon growled.

Romar placed a foot upon the dais, but Calidus stepped in front of him.

'Get out of my way,' Romar said, attempting to shoulder Calidus aside. But the thin man pulled the King round to face him.

Romar tugged against Calidus' grip. 'Let go of me,' he grunted, reaching for his sword hilt, his honour guard moving forwards.

Romar looked up just in time to see Alcyon swinging the axe, before it slammed it into his shoulder, cleaving the King from collarbone to ribcage.

There was a moment of absolute silence, then men were running at Calidus and Alcyon, the Jehar moving to protect them. Out of nowhere, battle was now raging all about Kastell, as fierce as when they had faced the Hunen above.

Kastell hefted his sword and shield, and moved instinctively to Maquin, covering his friend's wounded side as they stared, shocked by the ferocity of the fighting about them.

Even as Kastell watched he saw his Gadrai sword-brothers cut down, their opponents faster and more graceful than any swordsmen he had ever seen, all rivalling Vandil. Orgull battled nearby, slamming one of the Jehar to the ground by sheer brute strength, but another replaced him, easily trading blows with the bald warrior, halting his forward progress towards Romar's body.

Then a warrior was coming for him, a woman, Kastell realized, her sword held high. Kastell blocked her blow, but the woman used her momentum to sweep around him and swing her sword in a blow that would have hamstrung him if Maquin had not lunged forwards, turning her blade. She rounded on the wounded warrior, instantly seeing his weakness. Kastell blocked her lunge at Maquin, and then she was coming at him again, a flurry of strikes aimed at his head and throat. He fell with a crash onto his back, the Jehar's sword whistling where his throat had been. Instead of following instinct and rolling away, he rolled towards her, crashing into her legs. She fell and was almost on her feet when his shield smashed into her shoulder, knocking her back down, and Maquin's sword suddenly chopped into her neck. She jerked once and then was still.

Kastell lay there a moment, grateful, and slightly surprised still to be alive.

He hauled himself up to find battle still raging all about, broken down mostly into little knots of individuals now. Vandil was a blur, his two swords swirling and sparking against a Jehar's long, curved blade. He spun and struck, one of his swords burying itself in his antagonist's chest.

The blade stuck for a moment. Vandil tugged hard, and suddenly Alcyon was there. The giant struck. Vandil saw the blow coming and swung his free sword to turn the axe, but the blow had too much power behind it and smashed into his chest, sending him flying backwards in a spray of blood and bone. The Gadrai leader slid across the flagstoned floor, came to a halt with one arm twisted underneath him. He did not move.

'Come on,' Maquin shouted, and together Kastell and Maquin ran across the chamber to their fallen leader.

There was a crash behind them, and Kastell saw Maquin set upon by another Jehar. Then Orgull was there, the bald man ramming his blade's tip into Maquin's attacker's back. All three of them tumbled into one of the giant cadavers, disappearing in a cloud of bones.

He was about to leap after them when a figure stepped in front of him. Jael, sword in hand, and his cousin was smiling.

'Out of my way,' Kastell growled.

'We need to talk,' Jael said.

'*What?*' Kastell said, confused. *Talk? Here, now?* He pushed past Jael, then saw him move.

He managed to block Jael's lunge, just, but fell away with a deep gash in his arm.

'What are you doing?' he hissed, looking from his bleeding arm to his cousin.

'Claiming my throne,' Jael said, stabbing again at Kastell.

Their swords clashed, Jael pushing forwards. Kastell blocked a blow, lunged at Jael's chest, saw his sword turned as Jael spun inside his guard and cracked an elbow into his chin.

Kastell staggered back a step, tasted blood, then felt a blow to his gut, as though he'd been punched. He looked down to see a sword buried deep in his stomach.

Suddenly his legs were weak, and he felt unbearably tired. Cold.

Jael ripped the sword free, laughing. 'I owed you that,' he said.

Kastell tried to answer, but his voice wouldn't work. He felt himself falling, vision blurred, then he felt cold earth on his cheek. The last thing he saw was Jael's boots.

CHAPTER EIGHTY-EIGHT

CORBAN

The corridors were dark and silent, the faint noise of battle only occasionally filtering through open doorways. Corban and Gar soon caught up with the rest of the company, numbering around a score now. In near silence they ran, twisting and turning until Halion finally led them into a room.

It was Brenin's chamber, Corban realized, dominated by a huge, carved bed. Halion marched out onto a balcony and began helping people climb over and drop the short distance to the empty street below. Marrock and Camlin automatically went first, scouting out the street and then signalling for others to follow.

Corban was at the back of the party, and helped his mam climb over the balcony. Gar, Farrell and Halion were all that were left.

Suddenly a thought struck him. 'Storm will not jump,' he said. 'Not over the balcony's ledge, into something she cannot see.'

'Step back,' Farrell grunted. He yelled, 'Move away!' to those below and swung Thannon's hammer, smashing a large portion of the balcony's rail down into the street.

Farrell grinned and shrugged sheepishly.

Quickly the last of them climbed down, Corban having to urge Storm to follow.

'Good,' said Halion, organizing the small group. 'Now, as quick as we can to the pool.'

They were a ragged, unsteady mass as they headed off, Marrock leading, Corban and Storm bringing up the rear, with Gar one side of him and Farrell the other. Camlin came last of all, constantly glancing behind.

Every now and then they would hear the clash of arms, but nothing came near enough to see. They were in the rear quarter of the fortress, most of the fighting still raging between Stonegate and the keep.

Corban saw a black flicker behind and above as he glanced over his shoulder, the orange glow of flames from burning buildings illuminating the sky above the fortress. He saw it again, and heard the flap of wings, then saw Craf swoop low over Brina ahead. Somehow he felt relieved that the mangy old crow at least was still with them. So many had died.

He winced as he ran, his shield rubbing on his wounded shoulder. But he could still move his arm and lift it, which was a blessing, though not without pain. Then with no warning, warriors were pouring into their path from a side street – a score, maybe more, all in the red of Narvon. They had not seen Corban's small band, until Marrock ploughed into them. Then Halion and the warriors with him carved a path straight through the middle of the surprised enemy, Farrell roaring and swinging Thannon's hammer as if he had been born to it. Storm leaped snarling onto a terror-stricken man, her jaws clamping around his throat and face, claws slashing at his belly. Camlin ran silently into the skirmish, sword snaking out left and right.

With a flash of pain Corban drew his own blade, and with Gar guarding Corban's wounded side, they joined the fray. Within moments it was over, the last man of Narvon standing pounced on by Storm, who made short work of him.

Halion did a quick head count, and found only one of their number had fallen. However, others had been wounded. Dath's face was covered with blood, and Tarben was limping, but nothing seemed fatal. As they regrouped, more shouting could be heard nearby.

'We must move,' Halion said quietly, 'we made quite a noise just now. Others may have heard.'

They set off again, but heard the dead from their recent skirmish being discovered, then they were being tracked in earnest.

Corban had been running for a while, just focusing on the flagstones when something made him look up. He saw Brina and Heb drop back. At first he thought it was because they were struggling to keep pace, but as he reached them he realized that was not the case.

They didn't even seem to be breathing hard, then the two of them stopped and turned to face the darkness behind them.

Corban approached Brina and Heb and opened his mouth to hurry them along, then saw that they were muttering to themselves. No, *chanting* or singing, in hushed tones. He glanced at Gar and looked back down the street as the sound of pursuing footsteps grew louder. Again he went to hurry them, then stopped in alarm.

Mist was rising from the ground, like steam, but thicker. It broiled outwards, filling the street.

Brina swayed, and Heb reached out a hand to steady her. The two looked at each other, nodded and set off after their quickly vanishing warriors. The sound of flapping wings drifted down from above.

'I don't like that,' Farrell muttered, eyes fixed on the mist that was still expanding at an alarming rate before their eyes, boiling along the street towards them.

'Me neither,' Corban said and as one they turned and ran, chasing after Heb and Brina.

'What happened? Back there?' Corban whispered to Brina as they all paused to catch their breath. 'What did you *do*?'

'Surely not more questions now.' Brina rolled her eyes and turned away from him. 'Another time.'

'Corban,' a voice called out, Halion. 'Come, show us this tunnel, then.'

Corban led the company past the pool, and down the steps to the cave that led to the well. He paused just inside as he realized he had no flint to light the torches.

After a brief conversation with Halion, Marrock and Camlin lit torches for the party from the iron sconces set in the walls, fumbling hastily at flints from their belt pouches.

Quietly, like a mourning procession, they filed down into the cave, hope and doubt visible on their faces.

Corban quickly knelt, lay flat, and edged out over the well's rim, his mam crouching to hold his legs. His hand scrabbled around a moment, then he found the hollow with its cold handle within and turned it. There was a *hiss* and *click* behind him, then a collective gasp rippled through the company as the door became visible to all.

Corban rolled back to his feet, and couldn't help but grin at the gawping faces. He marched over to the stone door and pulled it wide, its hinges grating.

'Hold,' Halion said. 'Who else knows of this?'

Corban shrugged, and winced at the sharp pain in his shoulder. 'None that I know of.' *Except Cywen.*

'My father knows of it. Maybe one or two in his hold,' a voice said from amongst them, Vonn stepping forward. 'At least, so far as I know.'

'How can we believe *him*?' another voice called out: Dath, glaring at Evnis' son.

Vonn looked at him belligerently. 'True, my father has turned traitor. But I have not. I swore an oath to Brenin, to Ardan. I will not forsake it as easily as my father has . . .' he paused, his voice almost breaking. 'And I have lost someone, this night. Someone dear to me.' He looked about, defiant. 'From this night on my allegiance does *not* lie with my father.'

Halion stared at him a long moment, then nodded. 'Come with us. But know this: you will be watched, and if you prove us false you will die.'

Vonn nodded his agreement, and then they began filing through the stone doorway, Corban watched his mam pass, then she paused.

'Cywen,' she whispered. 'I cannot leave her. I must go back.'

'I shall return for her, once you and Ban are away from here,' Gar said. 'Think, Gwenith. You cannot go back.' His eyes flickered to Corban, then back to Gwenith. She stood there, shaking as the first tears came.

'I must,' she whispered.

'You will not find her,' a voice said, the last of those coming through the open doorway. It was Marrock. 'I saw her . . .'

'Where?' interrupted Gwenith. 'When?'

'I saw her *fall*,' Marrock said, each word slow, deliberate. 'From the walls above Stonegate.'

'What?' said Gwenith. 'I don't understand?'

'She was fighting, with Conall.' Marrock looked at Halion, who turned at the mention of his brother.

'Conall, you say?' he said roughly.

'Aye. He was part of Evnis' treachery, at the gates,' Marrock spat.

'Cywen was throwing *knives* at those warriors, the ones like Sumur. Conall tried to stop her. They both fell.' He shook his head.

Gwenith gave a racking sob, and turned into the tunnel's darkness, Gar following. Marrock looked at Corban. 'Many of us will grieve after this night.'

Corban couldn't speak; suddenly he felt sick and bone-weary.

'Come, we must be away,' said Halion, wrestling with his own grief, and Corban pushed the stone door shut.

The journey through the tunnels passed in a daze for Corban, haunted by memories of Cywen, almost as if she were walking beside him.

Eventually they spilt out into the wide circular room that Corban had visited. The carcass of the snake was still there, though far more decomposed than the last time Corban had seen it. Great strips of skin were hanging loose, vertebrae gleaming beneath. And it stank.

The group paused to stare at it.

'How much longer?' Halion asked Corban.

'It is hard to measure time in here,' Corban said, 'but we are about halfway to the end, I think.'

'Huh,' Halion grunted. 'And then what? Where does this tunnel lead?'

'To a cave that opens onto the beach.'

Halion looked about in wonder. 'How has no one ever found this before?'

'The entrance was concealed with a glamour. I only found it by accident.'

'Lead on.'

So Corban did.

For a long while they marched through the high-roofed tunnels, darkness always before and behind them. No one spoke, at first, all lost in the horror of the night's events, and also in the sheer astonishment that they were walking through tunnels far beneath their homes – tunnels that had been hidden here for untold generations. But slowly the silence lifted, people beginning to murmur amongst themselves.

Corban remained at the front, Storm padding beside him, leading them deeper, ever downwards into the depths of the rocky outcrop. He suddenly realized that someone had been walking next to him for some time. It was his mam. Silently she reached out and held his hand. They walked like that a long while, trudging ever deeper into the depths of the hill.

Eventually their path began to level out and soon they found themselves in the cavern that Corban remembered, wide and high, with sea rolling and swelling sluggishly through the straight-sided channel.

Corban stopped and looked down at the dark waters as Halion came to stand at his shoulder.

'The path to the cave is over there,' Corban said, pointing. 'It looks like a rock wall, but it's a glamour – left by the giants, I suppose.'

Brina and Heb hurried over to where Corban pointed, Brina thrusting her hand into the rock face. It disappeared, right up to her elbow, and she chuckled.

'Excellent,' Heb said. 'Here all these years, and we never knew.'

'We are close to the beach,' Halion said. 'We need to be clear on what happens next once we are out of here. We are not safe yet.'

While they were discussing options, Corban heard something, in the water.

'Did you hear that?' he muttered, prodding Gar.

'I did,' said Gar, squinting into the gloom.

A shape reared from the water, a solid mass in the darkness, just beyond their torchlight. Then it exploded towards them: a wyrm, grey-white scales dripping wet, fangs bared. It was bigger than the carcass in the cavern – much bigger – and lunged straight at Corban. He tried to dodge, but the beast was moving too fast. Then Storm barrelled into its neck, claws ripping into the creature's flesh. Her momentum knocked the wyrm off-balance as her weight dragged it down. Storm's own prodigious fangs sank deep into the wyrm and it let out a hideous noise, and spasmed on the ground. Its muscles rippled furiously, and Storm was sent hurtling through the air. She crashed into a wall, whimpered, and sagged to the ground.

'No!' Corban screamed. He would not lose another this night. He drew his sword and charged for the wyrm.

Everyone about him seemed released from a spell by his movement, most following him to attack. The wyrm reared above them, confused by so many attackers and blows. It dispatched one fighter with a vicious bite to his neck. Then Farrell surged forwards, swinging Thannon's hammer into the beast's head. There was a sickening *crunch*; the wyrm flopped bonelessly to the ground and lay still.

Tarben stepped forward and drove his sword into its eye. 'You can never be too sure,' he said to those staring at him.

Corban rushed over to Storm. She rose unsteadily, and whimpered when Brina examined her shoulder, but apart from that she seemed uninjured.

'She'll live,' Brina pronounced and Corban breathed a sigh of relief.

They tended their wounds, then gathered before the glamoured wall. Halion stepped through first, leading Edana by the hand. She had said nothing since the feast-hall, and walked forwards passively now, with eyes downcast. Corban blinked as both of them disappeared into the rock. Then more were moving forwards, Marrock, Camlin and others, until he was one of only a few that remained.

'Come along,' Heb called out to him. Only Gar and his mam were left with him now, and Storm. Gar motioned for him to go first. He closed his eyes instinctively as he stepped into the rock, and almost staggered when he met no resistance, or almost no resistance. There was a building pressure, all about him, in his ears, his skin tingling, then he was through, the small company gathered on a narrow rock shelf before him.

He heard Storm whine, looked down, saw she hadn't come with him. For a moment he just stood there, unsure, then stepped back through.

Storm was standing before the rock wall, ears flat to her head. She saw him and turned in a circle, whining.

'She refused to go through,' Heb said. 'I tried to give her some assistance, but she gave me a look that left me in no doubt that she did not want my help.'

Corban spent a while trying to coax her through, Gar and Gwenith pushing her from behind, but with no success.

'Come – on,' Corban muttered, trying to pull her through. 'You're – embarrassing me. Even Craf didn't make this fuss.'

Eventually, on Gar's suggestion, Gwenith tore a strip of cloth from her bag, and Corban tied it around Storm's eyes, stuffing more in the wolven's ears.

'Works with horses,' Gar said with a shrug.

Then they tried again.

This time was more successful, and when Storm's head and forequarters passed through the glamour Corban removed her blindfold. She saw the path in front of her and suddenly bounded across. Heb came last of all.

They were in a high cave, clinging to a narrow, slippery shelf of rock that skirted the slow-churning swell of sea water. It foamed white where it battered upon jagged, crusted rocks. The sound of surf beating against the shore filled the cave, echoing about them.

Hesitantly the small company moved off, Marrock and Camlin slipping ahead to scout. The path twisted and turned, the cave growing wider as they moved along it. Soon Camlin returned, hissing for them to douse their torches. When they turned another twist in the path Corban saw moonlight pouring through the cave's mouth and gleaming on the lapping water.

Slowly they crept out of the cave's entrance, and saw Havan's beach not far away beyond a short expanse of shallow water. The storm had broken, thin rags of cloud scudding across the moon.

All seemed quiet, although the dark clumps that were fisher-boats beached on the shore could have hidden many watchers. Out in the bay Corban could just make out the dark bulk of Nathair's ship, rising and falling gently on the swell of waves.

Halion called them all together, and soon they had a rough plan and were crossing the water towards the beach, trying not to splash. The tide was ebbing, the water cold enough to snatch Corban's breath. Then they were picking their way over the beach, Dath and Mordwyr taking the lead, until they came to their own fisher-boat, leaning on its keel in the shingle.

With great effort the entire party, near enough a score of them, pushed the small boat down the beach towards the water's edge. Corban's heart thundered with every crunch of shingle beneath feet or the boat's sliding keel. He almost cheered when he felt waves lap across his feet, then felt the boat shift as it was gripped and tugged by the sea's gentle sway.

Dath and Mordwyr clambered aboard, the rest of them pushing the boat out further, then they all ran for the wooden quay a little further along the beach. Boots thudded on wood as they hurried along its length and waited for Dath and Mordwyr to bring their skiff around. Corban saw the sails unfurl and ripple as the wind caressed them, then suddenly they filled out, waves foaming white about the prow as it cut a curving line across to them.

Of all of the moments Corban had experienced this night, right now he felt the most scared, as they waited almost defenceless at the end of the wooden quay. He glanced up at Dun Carreg, now a hulking shadow in the first grey of dawn, and saw an orange glow as the fortress burned still within its great stone walls.

Suddenly Mordwyr's fisher-boat loomed close, and he threw a coil of rope across. Halion caught it and others helped pull the boat in tight, then people were clambering aboard. Soon they were pushing away, most of them finding somewhere to slump exhausted on the boat's deck, though it was a tight squeeze in a three-man craft.

To reach the open sea they had to pass by Nathair's black ship, as it clogged the mouth of the bay. There were lanterns lit, but again no sign of people. As they reached the closest point, when the black hull was no more than a score of paces away, Corban heard a snuffling or growling and remembered teasing Dath about so-called noises on this ship. Had it only been last night?

Storm snarled, her ears flat to her head. Then, suddenly, a *roar* erupted from somewhere deep within the ship's belly, all on the fisher-boat staring wide-eyed as they slipped past the larger vessel. Corban gazed back the whole time they were exiting the bay, expecting something to happen, but there were no further alarms. And then, suddenly, they were out in the open water just as the first rim of the sun clawed its way over the edge of the world. Corban felt his eyes roll, his eyelids suddenly heavy.

'Here,' a voice said beside him. 'You should have this back.' Farrell was offering him his da's war-hammer, still caked in dried blood.

'Keep it,' Corban said. 'It is too heavy for me. And you looked like it was made for you.'

Farrell looked at the hammer, clearly tempted. 'No,' he said, shaking his head. 'It is your da's. It would not be right for me to have it.'

Corban lifted his arm, winced as pain lanced out from his shoulder blade. He pushed the hammer back towards Farrell. 'I mean it. I could not wield it as it was meant to be wielded. Please, I would be glad if you kept it.'

'Truly?'

'Aye. Only use it to avenge my da. That is all I ask.'

Farrell considered, then managed a smile. 'I am honoured,' he said.

'Aye. You are,' Corban mumbled.

'So,' a voice called out from further up the boat. 'Where is this fisher-boat taking us?'

All were suddenly listening, heads swivelling to look at Halion and Marrock, sitting together in the prow of the boat, Edana between them. Marrock shrugged, and looked at Halion.

'In truth, my only thought has been to get away, from there,' Halion said, nodding towards the fortress. 'Which we have done.' He dipped his head to Corban, then looked at Edana. The Princess was sitting with knees drawn up to her chest, tear tracks clear on her dirty face. She gave no sign as to whether she was listening or not.

'My oath, and Brenin's last charge to me, was to protect Edana,' Halion said. 'But how may I best do that? Dun Carreg is overrun, Ardan's other fortresses fallen.' He looked weary. 'Narvon is obviously out of the question, as is Cambren. Where else is left?'

It sounded to Corban that Halion was voicing an internal logic that had already been minutely examined, and he remembered Gar telling him that Halion was a strategist. But Marrock must have taken it as a question, as he spoke up.

'We could make for Dun Crin, the old giant ruins,' the warrior said, others near him nodding.

'I know of it,' Halion said. 'A ruin in the heart of a great marsh, to the far west of Ardan.'

Marrock nodded a confirmation. 'A good place to lie low. If word were to spread of Edana's presence there, maybe more would rally to her, and give us a chance to strike back.'

'Strike back, aye,' Halion muttered, thinking. 'That would be my first inclination also. But that would not be putting Edana's safety first. If word of her presence did get out it wouldn't only reach friendly ears. Owain would hear of it.' He shrugged. 'Edana needs her kingdom back, no doubt, and I mean to help her, or die in the trying. But we must decide how best to achieve that aim.'

He looked at the small party in the boat. 'If what we discovered in the Darkwood is true, then Rhin will soon strike at Owain. When her forces are in motion, when Owain has more to consider than securing Ardan – *that* would be the time for Edana to rally a warband about her. But until then she must be hidden.'

'I shall take Edana to my father,' he said finally. 'He is her kin, though more distant than those we have been speaking of.'

'Who?' said Marrock. 'Who is your father?'

Halion looked at him, his face unreadable. 'I am the bastard-born son of Eremon ben Parloth, the King of Domhain,' he said, then turned away, resuming his staring out to sea.

Muttering rippled through the company, but no one objected to Halion's decision. And Corban felt many things suddenly made sense about his old weaponsmaster. He shuffled to the back of the skiff and his mam came and stood beside him. She wrapped an arm around his waist, and together they looked back at Dun Carreg.

The first rays of the sun were gleaming on its stone walls, and here and there dark plumes of smoke rose up into the pale blue sky.

My da is in there, and Cywen. He swallowed, a lump in his throat, and tears came at last. He gripped the fisher-boat's rail to stop his hands from shaking.

'Ban, there are things we must talk about. Things I must tell you,' his mam whispered beside him. He looked down at her, and she seemed older somehow, more careworn at this moment.

'Aye, mam,' he said, a tremor in his voice. 'But not now. Soon, but not now.'

'All right,' she nodded, seeming relieved. 'Soon.'

And so they stood there, arms linked about each other, watching Dun Carreg shrink into nothing. Corban knew, beyond all measure of doubt, that from this moment things would never be the same again. His life had just changed irrevocably and forever.

Acknowledgements

There have been many helping hands along the way. Firstly I must say a thank-you to Paul Isted, whose thumbs-up was just the encouragement I needed at a pivotal moment.

I would also like to thank those that took the time to read my doorstep of a manuscript, when I am sure they all had much better things to be doing. Edward Gwynne, Mark Brett, Dave Dean, Irene Gwynne, Mike Howell, Alex Harrison, Mandy Jeffrey, Pete Kemp-Tucker, and my good wife Caroline, without whom I would never have put pen to paper in the first place.

Thanks are due to John Jarrold, my agent extraordinaire, for his belief and guidance – a true gent and a scholar, if ever I met one – and also to Julie Crisp and Bella Pagan, my editors at Tor. Their polishing skills are immense.

Thanks also to my mate Andy Campbell for some cracking photos, affectionately referred to as The Blackadder Sessions.

Oh, and a note to my oldest friend Sadak. Are you going to read this now?

extras

orbit

meet the author

JOHN GWYNNE studied and lectured at Brighton University. He's been in a rock 'n' roll band, playing the double bass, traveled the USA, and lived in Canada for a time. He is married with four children and lives in Eastbourne, running a small family business rejuvenating vintage furniture. *Malice* is his debut novel.

introducing

If you enjoyed
MALICE,
look out for

A DANCE OF CLOAKS

by David Dalglish

The Underworld rules the city of Veldaren. Thieves,
smugglers, assassins... they fear only one man.

Thren Felhorn is the greatest assassin of his time. All the thieves'
guilds of the city are under his unflinching control. If he has his way,
death will soon spill out from the shadows and into the streets.

Aaron is Thren's son, trained to be heir to his father's criminal
empire. He's cold, ruthless—everything an assassin should be.
But when Aaron risks his life to protect a priest's daughter
from his own guild, he glimpses a world beyond piston,
daggers, and the iron rule of his father.

Assassin or protector; every choice has its consequences.

PROLOGUE

For the past two weeks the simple building had been his safe house,
but now Thren Felhorn distrusted its protection as he limped
through the door. He clutched his right arm to his body, fighting

635

to halt its trembling. Blood ran from his shoulder to his elbow, the arm cut by a poisoned blade.

"Damn you, Leon," he said as he staggered across the wood floor, through a sparsely decorated room, and up to a wall made of plaster and oak. Even with his blurred vision he located the slight groove with his fingers. He pressed down, detaching an iron lock on the other side of the wall. A small door swung inward.

The master of the Spider Guild collapsed in a chair and removed his gray hood and cloak. He sat in a much larger room painted silver and decorated with pictures of mountains and fields. Removing his shirt, he gritted his teeth while pulling it over his wounded arm. The toxin had been meant to paralyze him, not kill him, but the fact was little comfort. Most likely Leon Connington had wanted him alive so he could sit in his padded chair and watch his "gentle touchers" bleed Thren drop by drop. The fat man's treacherous words from their meeting ignited a fire in his gut that refused to die.

"We will not cower to rats that live off our shit," Leon had said while brushing his thin mustache. "Do you really think you stand a chance against the wealth of the Trifect? We could buy your soul from the gods."

Such arrogance. Such pride. Thren had fought down his initial impulse to bury a short sword in the fat man's throat upon hearing such mockery. For centuries the three families of the Trifect, the Conningtons, the Keenans, and the Gemcrofts, had ruled in the shadows. Over that time they'd certainly bought enough priests and kings to believe that the gods wouldn't be beyond the reach of their gilded fingers either.

It had been a mistake to deny his original impulse, Thren knew. Leon should have bled out then and there, his guards be damned. They'd met inside Leon's extravagant mansion, another mistake. Thren vowed to correct his carelessness in the coming months. For three years he'd done his best to stop the war from erupting, but it appeared everyone in the city of Veldaren desired chaos.

If the city wants blood, it can have it, Thren thought. *But it won't be mine.*

"Is that you, Father?" he heard his elder son ask from an adjacent room.

"It is," Thren said, holding his anger in check. "But if it were not, what would you do, having given away your presence?"

His son Randith entered from the other room. He looked much like his father, having the same sharp features, thin nose, and grim smile. His hair was brown like his mother's, and that alone endeared him to Thren. They both wore the gray trousers of their guild, and from Randith's shoulders hung a gray cloak similar to Thren's. A long rapier hung from one side of Randith's belt, a dagger from the other. His blue eyes met his father's.

"I'd kill you," Randith said, a cocky grin pulling up the left side of his face. "As if I need surprise to do it."

"Shut the damn door," Thren said, ignoring the bravado. "Where's our mage? Connington's men cut me with a toxin, and its effect is...troublesome."

Troublesome hardly described it, but Thren wouldn't let his son know that. His flight from the mansion was a blur in his memory. The toxin had numbed his arm and made his entire side sting with pain. His neck muscles had fired off at random, and one of his knees kept locking up during his run. Like a cripple he'd fled through the alleyways of Veldaren, but the moon was waning and the streets empty, so none had seen his pathetic stumbling.

"Not here," Randith said as he leaned toward his father's exposed shoulder and examined the cut.

"Then go find him," Thren said. "How did events go at the Gemcroft mansion?"

"Maynard Gemcroft's men fired arrows from their windows as we approached," Randith said. He turned his back to his father and opened a few cupboards until he found a small black bottle. He popped the cork, but when he moved to pour the liquid on his father's cut, Thren yanked the bottle out of his hand. Dripping the brown liquid across the cut, he let out a hiss through clenched teeth. It burned like fire, but already he felt the tingle of the toxin beginning to fade. When finished, he accepted some strips of cloth from his son and tied them tight around the wound.

"Where is Aaron?" Thren asked when the pain subsided. "If you won't fetch the mage, at least he will."

"Lurking as always," Randith said. "Reading too. I tell him mercenaries may soon storm in with orders to eradicate all thief guilds, and he looks at me like I'm a lowly fishmonger mumbling about the weather."

Thren held in a grimace.

"You're too impatient with him," he said. "Aaron understands more than you think."

"He's soft, and a coward. This life will never suit him."

Thren reached out with his good hand, grabbed Randith by the front of his shirt, and yanked him close so they might stare face-to-face.

"Listen well," he said. "Aaron is my son, as are you. Whatever contempt you have, you swallow it down. Even the wealthiest king is still dirt in my eyes compared to my own flesh and blood, and I expect the same respect from you."

He shoved Randith away, then called out farther into the hideout.

"Aaron! Your family needs you, now come in here."

A short child of eight stepped into the room, clutching a worn book to his chest. His features were soft and curved, and he would no doubt grow up to be a comely man. He had his father's hair, though, a soft blond that curled around his ears and hung low to his deep blue eyes. He fell to one knee and bowed his head without saying a word, all while still holding the book.

"Do you know where Cregon is?" Thren asked, referring to the mage in their employ. Aaron nodded. "Good. Where?"

Aaron said nothing. Thren, tired and wounded, had no time for his younger son's nonsense. While other children grew up babbling nonstop, a good day for Aaron involved nine words, and rarely would they be used in one sentence.

"Tell me where he is, or you'll taste blood on your tongue," Randith said, sensing his father's exasperation.

"He went away," Aaron said, his voice barely above a whisper. "He's a fool."

"A fool or not, he's my fool, and damn good at keeping us alive," Thren said. "Go bring him here. If he argues, slash your finger across your neck. He'll understand."

Aaron bowed and did as he was told.

"I wonder if he's practicing for a vow of silence," Randith said as he watched his brother leave without any hurry.

"Did he lock the outer door?" Thren asked.

"Shut and latched," Randith said after checking.

"Then he's smarter than you."

Randith smirked.

"If you say so. But right now, I think we have bigger concerns. The Gemcrofts firing at my men, Leon setting up a trap...this means war, doesn't it?"

Thren swallowed hard, then nodded.

"The Trifect have turned their backs on peace. They want blood, our blood, and unless we act fast they are going to get it."

"Perhaps if we offer even more in bribes?" Randith suggested.

Thren shook his head.

"They've tired of the game. We rob them until they are red with rage, then pay bribes with their own wealth. You've seen how much they've invested in mercenaries over the past few months. Their minds are set. They want us exterminated."

"That's ludicrous," Randith insisted. "You've united nearly every guild in the city. Between our assassins, our spies, our thugs... what makes them think they can withstand all-out war?"

Thren frowned as Randith's fingers drummed the hilt of his rapier.

"Give me a few of our best men," his son said. "When Leon Connington bleeds out in his giant bed, the rest will learn that accepting our bribes is far better than accepting our mercy."

"You are still a young man," Thren said. "You are not ready for what Leon has prepared."

"I am seventeen," Randith said. "A man grown, and I have more kills to my name than years."

"And I've more than you've drawn breaths," Thren said, a hard edge entering his voice. "But even I will not return to that mansion. They are *eager* for this, can't you see that? Entire guilds will be wiped out in days. Those who survive will inherit this city, and I will not have my heir run off and die in the opening hours."

Thren placed one of his short swords on the table with his uninjured hand. Holding it there, he met Randith's gaze, challenging him, looking to see just what sort of man his son truly was.

"I'll leave the mansion be, as you suggest," Randith said. "But I will not cower and hide. You are right, Father. These are the opening hours. Our actions here will decide the course of months of fighting. Let the merchants and nobles hide. *We* rule the night."

He pulled his gray cloak over his head and turned to the hidden door. Thren watched him go, his hands shaking, but not from the toxin.

"Be wary," Thren said, careful to keep his face a mask. "Everything you do has consequences."

If Randith sensed the threat, he didn't let it show.

"I'll go get Senke," said Randith. "He'll watch over you until Aaron returns with the mage."

Then he was gone.

introducing

If you enjoyed
MALICE,
look out for

VENGEANCE

by Ian Irvine

*Ten years ago, two children witnessed a murder that still
haunts them as adults.*

*Tali watched as two masked figures killed her mother, and now
she has sworn revenge. Even though she is a slave. Even though she
is powerless. Even though she is nothing in the eyes of those
who live aboveground, she will find her mother's killers
and bring them to justice.*

*Rix, heir to Hightspall's greatest fortune, is tormented by the fear
that he's linked to the murder, and by a sickening nightmare
that he's doomed to repeat it.*

*When a chance meeting brings Tali and Rix together, the secrets of an
entire kingdom are uncovered and a villain out of legend returns to
throw the land into chaos. Tali and Rix must learn to trust each
other and find a way to save the realm—and themselves.*

CHAPTER ONE

"Matriarch Ady, can I check the Solaces for you?" said Wil, staring at the locked basalt door behind her. "Can I, please?"

Ady frowned at the quivering, cross-eyed youth, then laid her scribing tool beside the partly engraved sheet of spelter and flexed her aching fingers. "The Solaces are for the matriarchs' eyes only. Go and polish the clangours."

Wil, who was neither handsome nor clever, knew that Ady only kept him around because he worked hard. And because, years ago, he had revealed a gift for *shillilar*, morrow-sight. Having been robbed of their past, the matriarchs used even their weakest tools to protect Cython's future.

Though Wil was so lowly that he might never earn a tattoo, he desperately wanted to be special, to matter. But he had another reason for wanting to look at the Solaces, one he dared not mention to anyone. A later *shillilar* had told him that there was something wrong, something the matriarchs weren't telling them. Perhaps— heretical thought—something they didn't know.

"You can see your face in the clangours," he said, inflating his hollow chest. "I've also fed the fireflies and cleaned out the effluxor sump. Please can I check the Solaces?"

Ady studied her swollen knuckles, but did not reply.

"Why are the secret books called Solaces, anyway?" said Wil.

"Because they comfort us in our bitter exile."

"I heard they order the matriarchs about like naughty children."

Ady slapped him, though not as hard as he deserved. "How dare you question the Solaces, idiot youth?"

Being used to blows, Wil merely rubbed his pockmarked cheek. "If you'd just let me peek..."

"We only check for new pages once a month."

"But it's been a month, look, *look*." A shiny globule of quick-silver, freshly fallen from the coiled condenser of the wall clock, was rolling down its inclined planes towards today's brazen bucket. "Today's the ninth. You always check the Solaces on the ninth."

"I dare say I'll get around to it."

"How can you bear to wait?" he said, jumping up and down.

"At my age, the only thing that excites me is soaking my aching feet. Besides, it's three years since the last new page appeared."

"The next page could come today. It might be there already."

Though Wil's eyes made reading a struggle, he loved books with a passion that shook his bones. The mere shapes of the letters sent him into ecstasies, but, ah! What stories the letters made. He had no words to express how he felt about the stories.

Wil did not own any book,, not even the meanest little volume, and he longed to, desperately. Books were truth. Their stories were the world. And the Solaces were perfect books—the very soul of Cython, the matriarchs said. He ached to read one so badly that his whole body trembled and the breath clotted in his throat.

"I don't think any more pages are coming, lad." Ady pressed her fingertips against the blue triangle tattooed on her brow. "I doubt the thirteenth book will ever be finished."

"Then it can't hurt if I look, can it?" he cried, sensing victory.

"I—I suppose not."

Ady rose painfully, selected three chymical phials from a rack and shook them. In the first, watery fluid took on a subtle jade glow. The contents of the second thickened and bubbled like black porridge and the third crystallised to a network of needles that radiated pinpricks of sulphur-yellow light.

A spiral on the basalt door was dotted with phial-sized holes. Ady inserted the light keys into the day's pattern and waited for it to recognise the colours. The lock sighed; the door opened into the Chamber of the Solaces.

"Touch nothing," she said to the gaping youth, and returned to her engraving.

Unlike every other part of Cython, this chamber was uncarved, unpainted stone. It was a small, cubic room, unfurnished save for a white quartzite table with a closed book on its far end and, on the wall to Wil's right, a four-shelf bookcase etched out of solid rock. The third and fourth shelves were empty.

Tears formed as he gazed upon the mysterious books he had only ever glimpsed through the doorway. After much practice he could now read a page or two of a storybook before the pain in his eyes became blinding, but only the secret books could take him where he wanted to go—to a world and a life not walled-in in every direction.

"Who is the Scribe, Ady?"

Wil worshipped the unknown Scribe for the elegance of his calligraphy and his mastery of book making, but most of all for the stories he had given Cython. They were the purest truth of all.

He often asked that question but Ady never answered. Maybe she didn't know, and it worried him, becauseWil feared the Scribe was in danger. If I could save him, he thought, I'd be the greatest hero of all.

He smiled at that. Wil knew he was utterly insignificant.

The top shelf contained five ancient Solaces, all with worn brown covers, and each bore the main title, *The Songs of Survival*. These books, vital though they had once been, were of least interest to Wil, since the last had been completed one thousand, three hundred and seventy-seven years ago. Their stories had ended long before. It was the future that called to him, the unfinished stories.

On the second shelf stood the thick volumes entitled *The Lore of Prosperity*. There were nine of these and the last five formed a set called Industry. *On Delven* had covers of pale mica with topazes embedded down the spine, *On Metallix* was written in white-hot letters on sheets of beaten silver. Wil could not tell what *On Smything*, *On Spagyric* or *On Catalyz* were made from, for his eyes were aching now, his sight blurring.

He covered his eyes for a moment. Nine books. Why were there *nine* books on the second shelf? The ninth, unfinished book, *On Catalyz*, should lie on the table, open at the last new page.

His heart bruised itself on his breastbone as he counted them again. Five books, plus nine. Could *On Catalyz* be finished? If it was, this was amazing news, and he would be the one to tell it. He would be really special then. Yes, the last book on the shelf definitely said, *On Catalyz*.

Then what was the book on the table?

A *new* book?

The first new book in three hundred and twelve years?

Magery was anathema to his people and Wil had never asked how the pages came to write themselves, nor how each new book could appear in a locked room in Cython, deep underground. Since magery had been forbidden to all save their long-lost kings, the self-writing pages were proof of instruction from a higher power. The Solaces were Cython's comfort in their agonising exile, the only evidence that they still mattered.

We are not alone.

The cover of the new book was the dark, scaly grey of freshly cast iron. It was a thin volume, no more than thirty sheet-iron pages. He could not read the crimson, deeply etched title from this angle, though it was too long to be *The Lore of Prosperity*.

Wil choked and had to bend double, panting. Not just a new book, but the first of the *third shelf*, and no one else in Cython had seen it. His eyes were flooding, his heart pounding, his mouth full of saliva.

He swallowed painfully. Even from here, the book had a peculiar smell, oily-sweet then bitter underneath, yet strangely appealing. He took a deep sniff. The inside of his nose burnt, his head spun and he felt an instant's bliss, then tendrils webbed across his inner eye. He shook his head, they disappeared and he sniffed again, wanting that bliss to take him away from his life of drudgery. But he wanted the iron book more. What story did it tell? Could it be the Scribe's own?

He turned to call Ady, then hesitated. She would shoo him off and the three matriarchs would closet themselves with the new book for weeks. Afterwards they would meet with the leaders of the four levels of Cython, the master chymister, the heads of the other guilds and the overseer of the Pale slaves. Then the new book would be locked away and Wil would go back to scraping muck out of the effluxors for the rest of his life.

But his second *shillilar* had said the Scribe was in danger; Wil had to read his story. He glanced through the doorway. Ady's old head was bent over her engraving but she would soon remember and order him back to work.

Shaking all over, Wil took a step towards the marble table, and the ache in his eyes came howling back. He closed his worst eye, the left, and when the throbbing eased he took another step. For the only time in his life, he did feel special. He slid a foot forwards, then another. Each movement sent a spear through his temples but he would have endured a lifetime of pain for one page of the story.

Finally he was standing over the book. From straight on, the etched writing was thickly crimson and ebbed in and out of focus. He sounded out the letters of the title.

The Consolation of Vengeance.

"Vengeance?" Wil breathed. But whose?